EMPTY CRADLE

The Return of Holly Aniram

by Emmy Jackson

Designed by Tara Keezer

ISBN: 978-1-986-42584-1

foreword

If you're still reading this: thank you so much for taking this journey with me. Writing can be a lot like being in an empty room, speaking at length into a microphone that may or may not be plugged into a loudspeaker somewhere. Even though the things I'm trying to say run up and down the scale from whimsical to profound, to know that just one person out there's listening is incredibly rewarding.

A lot of people helped along the way, too: patient and merciless beta readers, Marc, Poe, Beckie and Darrin who made the cover happen; Tara, who did the interior and exterior layout of all the Empty Cradle books. The Lost Toys Wasteland tribe, who probably weren't aware they were living in Ivy's world for a while. Aesthetic Perfection, I:Scintilla and other bands who provided inspiration and vital writing soundtracks.

There are more stories in this world, of course, as I get around to telling them. Some of them will end up at *www.emmyjackson.com*. There are also other surprises hiding there too. The rig driven by Shiloh's Benzer buddy Spiker is real, and it lives at my house. It's one of four Empty Cradle-themed vehicle projects making the neighbors wonder what's wrong with me.

If you're into post-apocalyptic vehicles, there's also *www.willitwasteland.com*, which is a catalog of real-world "wasteland" vehicles running around out there. Ivy says it's good to be able to recognize another traveler's rig on sight, after all.

chapter 1

Sixty-four days before Princess Aiyana's trimester celebration

Unlike many falconids, Nefelibata preferred flying in cities to open air. The large cities were best, whether it was the skeletons of pre-Fall urban areas or a living metropolis like Strip City. She liked the chaotic wind patterns created by the tall buildings, and took great delight in coasting up and down them, skimming the sides of the glass and steel behemoths.

Strip City's variegated buildings made it a lovely airspace for dawdling. The cool wind in her feathers was pleasant, and the vibrant city jangling below her was a welcome change from the quiet desert she was used to in her home nesting grounds near Old Santa Fe. In fact, it seemed that she was rarely on her home grounds lately, flying one Long Loop after another to carry and collect news.

She didn't mind that, either. Nefelibata enjoyed being in new places, and enjoyed meeting new people. The professors, for instance. She'd initially sought them out from pure curiosity, after the words of the enigmatic Teller, Severina. On her last Long Loop to Geowa and the ruins of New York City, the Teller had drawn on a slab of brick for Nefelibata, a rough pencil sketch of a man she identified as Professor Elden Ono, from a big university in Sino-India. "It all starts with him," she'd said. "It starts in Strip City, with him." Severina had scrawled a date, as well. It was rare for her to give an exact day.

Severina had given Nefelibata many interesting strings over the years, but she hadn't managed to weave them into anything coherent thus far. It felt like she was getting close, though, and the Santa Fe Council agreed, and continued sending her out to gather news. There was, as the felids were fond of saying, a bad storm coming. Nefelibata had hitched rides with caravans where she could instead of flying all the way across the continent, the better to reach Strip City in time. By asking the right questions to the right people, she had found Professor Elden Ono, and conspired to meet him.

The professor was an affable academic, the head of a group of students and professors from a university in Singapore, with a pleasant face, stringy gray hair and a penchant for scruffy pre-Fall cardigans of a stubbornly outdated style. Nefelibata always delighted in talking to mariners and foreigners about the world beyond North America. She dressed in human clothes and made friends with one of the graduate students with the group, an intensely flirty red-haired boy named Gurrit. Seizing the opportunity, she settled in and dated him for a week, which enabled her to have dinner with the group and meet Professor Ono face to face. She met the rest of his staff, too: four senior professors and five eager graduate students, including Gurrit. The group was accompanied by a cohort of collar-wearing servants as well, as was common among middle- and upper-class Inchins.

She didn't let them know she was a shifter, of course. Nice as they were (with the exception of Professor Rehsil), they were still Inchins, and their views on shifters were dismissive and prejudiced at best, homicidal at worst. Gurrit romanced her happily. As far as he was concerned, she was an attractive and fine-boned North American girl whose face was unmarked by the infertility-inducing sickness that most human women went through. The group welcomed her as well, as they were undertaking an immersive study in North American culture. Gurrit explained that Strip City offered a unique blending of cultures, as well as being the only safe and civilized outpost on the North American continent. Nefelibata disagreed, but didn't debate the point.

Now, on the day that Severina had given her, she intended to watch Professor Ono carefully, for some hint as to what he might be starting, or what might start with him. She tore herself away from surfing the air currents to dive into the city, gliding over building tops until she reached the second- and third-level apartment that the university group had rented out as a temporary office. Nefelibata had gone there with Gurrit, and knew that Professor Ono and his servant stayed in the loft above the offices.

She stayed high and then dove quickly, wings folded, the better to reduce the chance that people would notice an enormous eagle landing on the building's roof. It was a practiced maneuver that every hatchling learned early, coming in fast. It was useful for hunting as well as for not causing a stir. Falconids were small of stature as humans, but their bird-form was much larger than any other raptor. Nefelibata's wingspan was thirteen feet fully extended, and a sudden landing could panic livestock and humans alike.

The roof was warm between the solar panels, which she was careful not to walk on. Strip City was alone among the walled cities in having working solar power, courtesy of Sino-Indian investors. The apartment had a skylight, so she walked over to it and looked in. She was rewarded with a view of Professor Ono's bedroom, where he and his servant shared a bed. He was in the bed now, but he wouldn't be going anywhere for some time. Nefelibata's hopes sank suddenly; Professor Ono was obviously dead, his face gray and the bedclothes tucked around him as though he was sleeping.

Judging by the state of the room, he hadn't been discovered yet. She hesitated, then shifted and looked for the skylight's latch. She had a peach-sized pouch with a garment folded up inside in case she had to cleave to human modesty, but didn't unfold it just now. She might need to shift back and fly away quickly. She opened the skylight wide and slipped in, dropping to the floor next to the bed.

The apartment was silent. Now that she was in human form, she could smell a heavy miasma that mingled spilled food, shit and blood. Ono wasn't bleeding, though. She knew the smell of death well enough. She'd flown through the charnel-house aftermath of battles between Sam Ward's army and unsuspecting small villages plenty of times the past few years. It still upset her. War was for warriors, not professors. The loss of knowledge was the most tragic of all, she thought.

A spiral staircase led down to a great room that had been converted into academic office space. Nefelibata squatted to look downstairs. She heard nothing moving, but waited to be certain.

The apartment was empty, and she descended. She saw Professor Hatton first. The youngest of the academics lay flat on his back between the front door and kitchenette. He had been shot in the chest, a massive and messy exit wound painting the wall behind him. Nefelibata sighed sadly. Professor Hatton had been quite enthusiastic, an expert on 20th century history, and she'd liked his youthful demeanor.

There was a second body in a splattered mess of blood in the kitchen, and as she came down she could see a pair of small legs sprawled in the bathroom. She rushed there first, thinking instinctively that it might be a falconid, but it was just a small human. She recognized the short, dark-skinned woman as Yinka, Hatton's servant. Someone had bashed Yinka's brains out against the side of the toilet, and judging by the condition of the small bathroom, there had been quite a fight.

The body in the kitchen was Professor Rehsil, Ono's department co-chair. Like Yinka, he'd been brutally beaten, and thrown through the kitchen table as well. Nefelibata saw that the floor was covered in broken glass and dishes so she didn't go close, mindful of her bare feet. The professor was only recognizable by his hair; his face had been savaged until it was nothing but meat.

Stomach churning, Nefelibata looked around the apartment for other bodies, and found none. Before she could conduct a more thorough search, perhaps to figure out why this had happened or who had done it, she heard voices in the hallway, approaching the door. She raced quickly up the steps, hopped onto the dresser, grabbed the edge of the skylight and pulled herself up and through. Just before the glass clicked back into place she heard the apartment's front door open.

The building was just high enough that she was able to jump off and find a thermal to climb. The glass muffled the sound of screams as Nefelibata flew away.

chapter 2

Four days before Princess Aiyana's trimester celebration

After Mahnaz, the rat-faced chancellor, was solidly asleep, Shiloh eased out of the bed. She donned the awful scratchy jumpsuit the sailors had given her to replace her sarong and padded quietly into the hall. The massive *Excelsis* thrummed lightly, her engines sounding far away yet present in faint vibrations through the walls and floor. It was a reminder that this gargantuan object, this floating building, this oceangoing prison, was still just a vehicle taking them all...somewhere.

Not knowing where they were going was just a part of what had Shiloh restless. She'd gotten only glimpses of her surroundings, and felt better when she knew where all of the hallways and doorways went. She expected plenty of them would be off-limits to her, based on the faintly condescending-yet-polite attitude of the crew whose space they were very much in. She remembered feeling the same way about the guests at the circus though, and behaved with the proper mixture of respect and deference. She wasn't above making eyes at a few of them either, not that she'd risk upsetting Chancellor Mahnaz by indulging in a dalliance with a sailor. There was too much at stake.

And speaking of that...she needed to get back to the solitary cells. Shiloh wandered, unchallenged by sailors or soldiers, through open bulkheads and down staircases. What Zhuan had said about the ship not needing much security most of the time seemed to be true, and the main passageways were all open. Shiloh found her way back to the uppermost level of the prison deck, to one of the two solitary-cell halls. The floor grates creaked softly under her feet, and the lights in the plastic-walled cells were dimmed. The first three were still empty; the cell where Swan had been earlier was also empty now. In the fifth, the ursid sat, his back against the wall. He wasn't asleep; he was staring right back at her, knees up, massive hands on them. He had heavy features, an angry brow line, and was bald except for a topknot. "So," he said.

She raised her chin, determined to not be afraid of him. It didn't matter if his hands were as big as her head, or if he could go bear any moment. He was behind a thick plastic wall, she had nothing to fear...except what he might say. Shiloh took a deep breath. "What you said before, about me," she said.

"Is true."

"Yes, but did you mean—"

"Meant exactly what I said." He tilted his head. "You don't talk like a felid. Guess you couldn't, if you wanted to pass."

"Are you going to...tell them?"

He stared at her for a long moment. "Why would I care what they know?" he replied finally. "Your name?"

"Shiloh Gallamore. What's yours?"

"I am Shamshoun."

Shiloh looked up and down the small corridor. The nighttime lighting was faintly red, and blue reflected from both ends of the hall, glowing from the security monitors by the doors. "I shouldn't stay long."

"No, you shouldn't. Sleepless walker."

"I'm not the only one who isn't sleeping," she said, a little defensively.

Without getting up, he stretched out his arms; his hands touched the opposite walls of his cell well before his elbows were fully extended. "You have liberty to walk. Why are you not sleeping, Shiloh Gallamore?"

"Why do you think? My friends hate me now, because I'm in bed with the chancellor. I sleep next to a man who will kill me if he finds out what I am. And if I hadn't jumped into bed with him, I might already be dead. And I don't know what to do next, other than keep fucking him and hope he doesn't look too closely. Which—I know—is suicidal."

"You plan to shift in your sleep?"

"Of course not," she sniffed. "But I'm still afraid. Because I'm not stupid. And you scared the shit out of me earlier."

Shamshoun gave her a curled upper lip that might have been a smile and nodded. "Good."

"Good?"

"Be afraid. Your kind don't last long here. Not so good in cages, you cats."

"They're not 'my kind,'" she muttered.

Shamshoun took no notice. "If the men in white don't cut them up, they get themselves shot. Go mad and bash their heads against the walls till they're dead. Claw out their own eyes."

She swallowed, though her mouth was dry. His casual description of felids gone mad hurt her heart, as much as she disliked them. "How did you know? About me?"

"Heard your drum, felt your rhythm. Same way I knew to wake up when you came to visit."

Shiloh said nothing; Shamshoun seemed to be not all there, but something about his manner was comforting. "I like your voice," she said.

"So did my children," he replied, and the way he said it she didn't have to ask where they were. The dread in her chest stirred again, like a cold finger pressed against her heart.

"I'm sorry."

His eyes went hard, like shiny stones. "Silenced drums," Shamshoun said. "Their song is finished. I'll join them soon enough."

"How long have you been here?"

"I don't care. Spin me a story."

"What?"

"I've been too long in this little box, Shiloh Gallamore. Too far from the earth and her song. Tell me what I've missed. Your kind are good at spinning stories."

There was a faint undercurrent of pleading hidden deep in Shamshoun's gruff command, and Shiloh let his 'your kind' comment slide because of that. "What do you want to hear? I don't know many fairy tales," she said, even as she said it realizing this wasn't true. She'd heard and memorized plenty of them from the circus' storyteller.

"Tell me where you were, before you came here. You and the others, the angry one."

"Swan?"

"Your hateful friend, with the white hair. She's gone below now. Fought with the guards. They don't always bring them back. But she's human. Why are they collecting humans, Shiloh Gallamore? Tell me why these people are special. Tell me what you've seen. And you'll come back tomorrow. If you don't, maybe they'll find out they have a felid in their prison after all."

She glared at him. Was this a trap? Would they have planted a shifter to talk to her and get her to tell him their secrets? That made no sense; from what she'd heard, if they knew the truth they'd realize that Ivy and the others weren't the criminals they had been mistaken for.

Of course, if they knew the truth, they'd also kill her outright.

"You don't have to threaten me," she said.

"So don't be threatened, little sister." Shiloh bit her lip, debating, and put her hand to the clear plastic wall that separated them. Shamshoun leaned forward and reflected the gesture back at her, touching his large fingers to the spots where hers were. He said nothing.

She decided to trust him.

chapter 3

Five days before Princess Aiyana's trimester celebration

Shiloh's story

The seasons were starting to slide a little bit, from high summer into late summer. We were a ways north of Strip City but the terrain was the same; sweltering plateaus then a ridge of mountains that dropped suddenly down to cooler temperatures and the great big ocean, spread out like the end of the world.

Swan didn't care for the view, and she bitched and grumped while Ivy picked her way down. She was glaring at the ocean like it had done something nasty in her hair. At the moment this meant that she was looking over the top of the rig's windshield, because the trail down was steep. She had to put her hands on the roll bar to brace herself. Our little rig bounced on the twisty trail and tossed us around like mad in the back. "Sorry," Ivy said as the Vovo—that's her rig's name—took a big bounce and Kroni lost his grip and slid all the way across the back into me. He's big but he moves like an acrobat, so I got a face full of dreadlocks, but it didn't hurt.

"Don't fling your damn passengers out, Travelmaster," Swan said. Nobody but Swan called Ivy that.

"We're fine," I said. Our gear was strapped down well enough that it didn't slide, so Kroni and I were the only loose objects, other than pillows. I had a good grip on a grab rail. "It's a beautiful view," I said.

"It is," Kroni agreed.

"I think I might go for a swim. Will we be here long enough for that?" I asked.

"A swim? Miss Kitty, if you go in that water I will roll you in the sand until the stink is off afterward."

"Don't call me Miss Kitty. Why are you in such a bad mood all of a sudden?"

She looked back at me, her white hair whipping around. I glared right back. "Doesn't feel right, that's all," she said. "Travelmaster, are you sure this is where we're supposed to be?" she asked Ivy.

"It is," Ivy said. She always sounds calmer when she's driving, even if we're going down a rocky sandy slope, weaving between craggy boulders, and it's obviously hard work for her. "This, this, this is the right place." She took a hand off of the wheel and swiped it through her short dark hair, brushing away dust and sand. I was sitting on the passenger side of the car so I could see the scar that looked like a badly drawn line from the corner of her eye to her ear, standing out against the dirt. I could see one of the dots she drew on her cheeks, also. It had something to do with finding her sister, and while she'd been traveling with Gallamore's circus it earned her the nickname "Dots." She never answered to that one either.

"Well it doesn't feel right. Kroni, tell her it doesn't feel right." He just made a noise in the back of his head like he was neither agreeing nor disagreeing with Swan, which wasn't really what she wanted, so she huffed again. "You're sure this person knows about your sister?"

"Met her in person, he says," Ivy said.

"And it's not a trick? You go asking everyone about her all the time, surely someone's going to figure they can lure you into an ambush like that."

"Why, why would they, Swan? What do we, we, we have that's worth taking?" I couldn't see exactly what Swan did, but I guessed she had reached over and poked Ivy's belly lightly, indicating her womb. "That's not how that's done," Ivy said, dismissing the possibility.

"Well, no, the man don't use a finger, he takes his—"

"I *know* how babies are made, Swan, you know what I meant. This isn't a trap, and the man I met is not baiting us."

"How do you know?"

"I just do. This is right. And if it's not, I'll let you kill anybody you want to. So please calm down."

Swan sat back, then reached both hands up and tapped them on the top of the windshield. The city tattoos on her shoulders curled and furled with the flexing of the muscle under her skin. "We come a really long way on the say-so of a mariner," she said. Ivy didn't answer her.

I could smell the ocean now, a huge, thick salt smell. We were at the bottom of the slope, and the remnants of a road crossed our path, jagged chunks of rock that Ivy stopped rather than driving across. Past it, sand took over, a flat expanse that ran about two hundred yards to the ocean and was broken only by a couple of large fluff-grass topped hills that looked like islands. There was a long-broken pre-Fall building some distance to the north of us, but no other vehicles in sight. Ivy looked through the windshield for a long moment, then shut the Vovo's engine off. "We should walk from here," she said. "If we get stuck on that sand I'll never get out."

The sound of the water pressed in. I'd heard it before, in Savannah, but it was different here, bigger and more energetic somehow. It brought a pleasant breeze, too. I closed my eyes for a moment and let it tickle my face. Ivy got out of the car and looked around with her hand on the metal of her rig. *Touching dirt,* she called that first moment of stepping out. Kroni didn't say anything, but he climbed over the side and out, shifted into his deer form, and started strolling toward the building. He looked like he was daring the world to try something.

I stood up and stretched. Every time I thought I was going to be miserable traveling in the back of Ivy's open rig instead of in a comfortable trailer like I used to, I was wrong. In Astoria I had picked up some pillows for my corner of the rig, and traveling back there was verging on pleasant. I had a parasol for sunny days, and a nice afghan for chilly ones. Come fall, Ivy was talking about trying to find a rig with a roof though, so we wouldn't be limited to traveling in warm places.

The sand was warm, and it felt good on my toes. Ivy was standing by the front of the Vovo now, leaning on the front bumper and looking at the water. I stopped next to her. I forget how tall she is because she tends to be invisible, but she's half a foot taller than me, three inches taller than Swan. She was looking at the ocean, but her eyes were far away. "What now?" I asked. "Wait?"

She nodded.

"Do I have time to swim?"

"No," Swan said. "We're going to spar."

I wanted to roll my eyes and groan, but I didn't give her the satisfaction. Ever since Swan had decided over a drunken campfire that I needed to be more useful when ugliness invariably arose and that I needed to learn how to fight, she seemed determined to prove to me that I was going to be useless at it. At first she sobered up and wasn't going to. That got me stubborn about it, and I spent a day badgering her until she could act like it was my idea and not hers, and then she started teaching me. Sort of. Swan wasn't really *teaching* me that much, or at least it didn't feel like it. Her method of "sparring" seemed to consist mostly of beating on me until she got bored with it and it wasn't funny anymore. How long this took varied according to her mood.

Frankly, I had survived worse teachers, and I do like learning new things, even unpleasant ones, so I didn't complain. I think this annoyed her even more; she wanted me to whine about not wanting to, and I never did.

Even though I really wanted to go for a swim, I stepped away from Ivy and out onto the sand. At least the landings would be relatively soft if she threw me. I decided that I wasn't going to let her throw me today. How I planned to accomplish this, I had no idea. Swan hadn't taught me how to hit or kick her yet, and when I tried she either swatted it away or laughed at me. She insisted this was how she had learned.

Maybe I'm a faster learner than she is. I thought of how not to get thrown. I thought of partner acrobatics, and all the ways in which I've learned to complement the other person's balance. Reversing that was a surprisingly easy adjustment. My weight's carried lower than hers. I just had to keep her from picking me up.

She strolled casually after me, and I stopped and waited for her. "C'mon," she said, cocking her head at me. I took a step in her direction, not sure of what I'd do exactly, and she did it for me, slapping me high on the temple and then across the belly. That was her concession to the fact that we weren't actually trying to kill each other—open hands instead of closed fists. I retreated, ducking my head to protect my face, hands up, and she said, "No, no, no." I remembered that she'd told me never to duck my head, and remembered why when she gave me a hard slap right on the top of my head that drove me to my knees.

I hit the ground and rolled to one side, avoiding a kick that flung sand past me. I rolled again, since it put me where she couldn't hit me.

"Remember while you're rolling around, you gotta know where I am, Shiloh."

That part was easy—I knew where she was, she was behind—ah, *shit.* Swan put her arm around me from behind, across my chest, then kicked my feet out from under me and I hit the ground on my back.

The sand wasn't as soft as I hoped it would be. Swan knelt on my chest, pinning my arms, and started planting little slaps all around my face and shoulders. I flailed, but she had my upper body pinned. Arching my back did no good, so I reached upward with my legs, trying to lever her off, wagging my head back and forth to try and protect my face. "Whoo, you're strong, girl," she said, and I realized that I was lifting her up a little bit. My feet were behind her head. "You want to get out of this? Try to get your feet under my arms." Swan didn't lean back or try to help me, but she did stop smacking my face. That was enough for me to focus, scissor my legs and hook both of my feet right under her arms. "How's it you're so bendy? Now slide up so your knees are at my shoulders and straighten—OUHHHHH!"

I did as she said. When I uncoiled she went down easily, and it knocked the breath out of her, she slammed into the sand so hard. I hadn't meant to, was just doing what she told. The motion brought me up so now I was sitting up between her legs, with her arms trapped under my knees. I scooted quickly forward and sat on her chest, to see if it was as easy to hold her down as she had me. Swan coughed, trying to recover, and I resisted the urge to smack her while she was trapped.

"Fuck me, remind me never to wrestle with acrobats," she gasped. "Okay, now get your fat butt off of me."

"What, you can't get up?" I asked. "You should try to get your feet under my arms." I was pretty sure she couldn't. Maybe she'd told me to do it because she didn't think I could either. That would've explained why she was so surprised.

Her voice got higher and quieter at the same time, the way it does when she's getting ticked off. "Shiloh, if you don't get your ass up off of me, I will stick my boot in it."

"So you're really stuck?"

"Of course not. But we aren't rolling around on the ground, we're teaching you how to fight. We keep on thrashing around like this, you're like to start taking your clothes off."

"I think if more people were fucking instead of fighting the world would be a better place."

Swan rolled her eyes. "Folks who can't fight always say that."

"And fighters who don't think it's true just never fucked the right person."

"You offering?"

I thought about it a moment. There had been a cute fender boy going east at the last overnight stop we'd made, but nobody since then. From the way Ivy was talking we were likely to spend the next couple of nights out in the dirt, and it was a lot easier to sleep if I was curled up next to someone. That was one way that my new...family, I guess—was different from the circus, too; I hadn't fucked any of them.

Not for a lack of interest. I thought all of them were beautiful, in their own ways, but Swan mostly liked boys. She'd been with a couple of girls, or said she had, but it wasn't really her thing. She liked to tease about it though. Kroni only had eyes for Swan, not that she was aware of it. At least not consciously. Even though she fucked around all the time, he never did, and I got the feeling she'd make noise about it if he did. Lucky for her he wasn't interested. And Ivy wasn't interested in anybody at all. She had let me curl up with her a few times, when I really really needed a warm body, but when I touched her tit she moved my hand and said, "Please don't," and I behaved myself so I wouldn't get kicked out of her warm spot.

It was better that way, I realized. I couldn't say how, but it felt better that I hadn't fucked any of my friends. So I smiled down at Swan, and played her game. "Not today. I want to be sure you could handle it."

Swan laughed, then rolled her hips to one side, trying to buck me off. It didn't work. I'm shorter than she is, but we weigh about the same. If anything I weigh a bit more than she does. I really did want to see how long I could keep her down, even though the longer she was down the madder she was going to get. "Okay, seriously, Shiloh, you're getting a bloody face when I get up if you don't let me up right now."

"Why are you being so unpleasant today?" I asked her, shifting my weight to keep her arms pinned.

She kicked her legs but still couldn't move. "Your fuzzy gash is pretty unpleasant and you're shoving it in my face. How would you feel?"

"I mean before that. You've been crabby all morning. Why don't you want to be here?"

She sighed explosively. "What does it *matter*?"

"Well, I'd help if I could."

"I appreciate the concern." The tone in her voice said she did anything but.

"Do you? What's wrong?"

Swan pushed up again, getting her heels underneath her and bridging up as hard as she could. She still couldn't lift her shoulders off the ground with me sitting there, though. I was beginning to enjoy this, and understood why she lorded getting the upper hand with me so often. She let out a little growl of frustration and flopped back down. "I don't like the water, okay?"

"The water?"

"Yes. I almost drowned when I was just a little thing and I really, really, *really* don't like water, if there's more than a washbasin full of it. And now we're parked right next to a whole world made of water. There ain't anything I can do about it 'cept be bitchy, so that's what I'm doing."

I felt a little badly for teasing her. "See, that wasn't so hard. Using words is better." I got up off of her, and took a couple extra steps out of arm's reach, just in case. "I'm sorry that happened to you."

"Yeah, well, don't be. Just don't go telling everyone."

"I don't gossip," I said.

Her face was still marked with angry creases, but she gave me a little nod. "Yeah, I guess you never did, at Gallamore's." After that her eyes went past me, toward the water. I turned, expecting her to be staring at the waves, but there were people there, three of them walking up the beach.

There were two men and a woman. The taller man was dressed in fancy reds and blacks, with an extravagant hat and striped, blousy pants tucked into knee-high boots. Up top, a close-fitting shirt was accented by strappy arm bracers and a cowl, and a wide-brimmed hat kept the sun off of his face. He was armed with a pistol and a sword, and had a hip pouch like Ivy's, too. His bright clothes looked like one of the costumes designed for the circus' traveling show, except they were well-made enough that they were clearly his everyday wear. He was bigger and darker-skinned than Kroni, with broad shoulders and a beard that was as elaborate as his outfit, as though someone had put a crab on his face, traced it, and then trimmed his beard to match. He was smiling, and I got a good vibe from him.

The shorter man was also wearing a sun hat, and relatively nondescript clothes that didn't fit him all that well. He was pale-skinned, sunburned in fact, and what I could see of his hair was white and curly. He had a potato nose and a lumpy face with cheeks that wanted to smile, though right now he looked nervous, like he would rather be anyplace else.

The woman had incredibly long hair tied back in a braid that went down past her hips. She wore a blue outfit with white details that looked like a cross between pajamas and a uniform, big boots that didn't match it, and there was a big arty silver collar around her neck. The shape of her face was familiar, and as Ivy started forward and there was an almost palpable jolt of emotion that passed between them, I realized she looked just like Ivy, only a lot cleaner.

Swan had forgotten all about being annoyed. "Huh," she said, with a quirky little smile on her face. "Looks like we found Holly."

"Or she found us," I said.

Ivy took a couple of steps, then a few more, and then she was running. Holly—as she got closer I could definitely tell this woman was Ivy's twin—did the same. They both ran, their feet kicking up sand, and when the distance between them shrank from a hundred and fifty feet to five they both stopped. Holly said something, but they were too far away for me to hear what. Then she reached out and touched Ivy's face, and Ivy did the same thing back to her. There was a crazed moment where I thought they were going to melt together into one person. They didn't, of course, but they did embrace and kind of sink down to their knees in the sand, both of them crying what I hoped were happy tears.

The two men continued to approach us, skirting Ivy and Holly at a respectful distance. It wasn't necessary; in that moment it was obvious that a scrunge match could have broken out all around them and they wouldn't have noticed. Their world had shrunk to the two of them for now.

"Now how the hell did Pinkie end up with Ivy's sister in tow?" Swan muttered. She yelled, "Is that Marcus goddamn McEvoy I see? What are you doing back out of the city, Pinkie? And where'd you find another Aniram?"

The smaller man sighed like he'd been asking himself the same thing. "They seem to find me," he said.

"Well, this one's been looking for t'other one for a long time. You done good."

Some of Marcus' nervousness seemed to fade. "That makes me quite happy to hear. Allow me to introduce my companion. Captain Murrough Hardson, this is Swan Dallara, and, ah, I don't believe we've met," he said, looking at me.

"Shiloh Gallamore," I said.

"Yes," he said, finally letting that smile free. I liked him. He seemed harmless. The captain, on the other hand...well, I liked him too, but for different reasons. And he wasn't one of my traveling companions. Maybe, just maybe, I wouldn't be spending the night alone after all. "Captain Hardson commands the *88 Fists*, a privateer marine craft that travels the globe. Swan and Shiloh are Ivy's traveling companions. And there is usually another...?" Marcus asked, his voice trailing off.

"Kroni's around," Swan said. Marcus looked relieved and I realized he was worried that Kroni might have died. Not a ridiculous concern, given the way things are out in the dirt.

"That's good to hear. I look forward to chatting with him. And the rest of you, of course." He shook himself, as though trying to find his equilibrium. "Forgive me, it's been a bit...of a whirlwind. My life has changed a great deal, in light of some discoveries about my circumstances. And I admit there was some trepidation about coming along to this meeting."

"Why, 'cuz you thought the Travelmaster was gonna kill you?"

"Ah, something like that, yes," he said, blushing.

Swan caught the confused look on my face and explained, "Last we parted ways, before we started with Gallamore's, Pinkie here was traveling with us. But he wasn't honest about where he was from, and that ticked Ivy off something fierce, especially because she found out not five minutes after a dear friend of ours got hisself killed. She was in a killing mood and that got directed at Pinkie. Not that she would have done it." She winked at me and added, "I don't think, anyway. Ancient history now, I'm pretty sure your name's good with her again," Swan said, nodding toward Ivy and Holly, who were now sitting on the ground forehead to forehead, eyes closed. There was something a little mystical about the way they were melting together.

"I do enjoy doing good deeds," Hardson said, looking at the twins. Then he looked back at me, caught me looking at him.

"Captain Hardson brought us here," Marcus said. "Holly and I have been sailing with him for the better part of two months, now."

"I had hopes of convincing her to stay aboard."

"As your li'l wife?" Swan asked. Her tone was challenging, but not nasty.

"That was the thought at the time. She was quite resistant."

"Well, congratulations!" Swan laughed. "Now you've got two of them!"

Hardson rolled his eyes. "I don't think so. This is where we part ways, once appropriate reunions have been made."

Marcus looked surprised. "You're putting us off?"

"Not you. You're welcome to sail with us, professor. But after her demonstration the other night, I'm inclined to agree with Holly that there's no place for her aboard *88 Fists*. A shame, but true."

"What happened?" Swan asked with a grin. "She bite your goosh tube?"

I expected Hardson to be angry, but he laughed. "Oh, gracious no, nothing like that! I haven't taken her into my bed. It's more complicated than that. But some things have happened that I can't forget." He looked at me again, and there was something there, a spark of interest. I mirrored it, and saw that he'd gotten the message.

"I know what that's like," Swan said. "Which reminds me..." I didn't realize she was talking to or about me until she spun and punched me in the face. My nose and lips seemed to disappear in a red-hot explosion of numb pain, and the impact rang in my skull, blurring out whatever words of surprise Hardson and Marcus yelled. I barely even saw it coming, and was on the ground on my knees before I had figured out what happened. There was a tingle at the base of my spine as I hit the sand. The surprise and hurt had been so great I'd almost shifted into cat-form, involuntarily. I wouldn't have been more embarrassed if I'd shit myself.

I was angry, even angrier when I took my hand away from my face and saw blood on my fingers. Hadn't she seen that I was *flirting?* I came up off the ground and went after her, hearing some nonsensical swear words coming out of my mouth as I did so. She was waiting for me, caught me by one arm and the shoulder as I reached her and threw me up and over her hip. I still twisted and smacked her in the eye as I went over, though, and when I hit the ground I kicked up as hard as I could and caught her in the stomach. Swan huffed like she'd have had a compliment if I hadn't knocked the air out of her, and then she dropped down on me and hit me in the face again, with a fist instead of an open hand. I covered my head with my arms, and Swan opened her hands to smack my ribs and chest instead. Trapped under her attack, I couldn't help myself, and squealed in fear, kicking uselessly at the dirt. It was too much violence, enough to burn through my anger, I didn't want to fight any more; my face hurt too much.

Hardson yelled again, and then there were several other voices, raising up from all around us, and a gunshot that froze the entire scene.

I uncovered my face and saw...soldiers. There were at least twenty of them, some clad in dark blue and black, some with the patchwork uniforms and red armbands of Sam Ward's Army, and they had guns trained on everyone—on Ivy and Holly, on Hardson and Swan, on me. Farther up the hill I saw that they had Kroni too, on his knees and trussed up with his hands behind his back.

One of the soldiers grabbed Swan roughly and pulled her away from me. "Get off of her!" he yelled, and threw Swan to the ground. She called him a cunt-licker and started to get up, and got stomped on her tailbone for the trouble. That shut her up, sort of.

Another of the soldiers slung his weapon over his shoulder and knelt next to me. He offered me a white cloth for me to press to my bleeding nose and lip. "You're okay," he told me. He had an accent. "You're safe now."

The obvious smart thing to say was, "Thank you," so I did.

chapter 4

*One hundred and twenty-seven days before
Princess Aiyana's trimester celebration*

Shamshoun threw himself out the window.

He'd been betrayed, that much was obvious when four armed men, presumably Sino-Indian commandos, burst through the door. Two had slickguns, the other two carried whiplike shifter snares. He registered the threat, realized that it meant someone somewhere had turned this meeting into a trap, and then he stopped thinking. It was no longer time to think— it was time to escape.

The quickest way to do that was through the window, six feet to his right. The little gray-walled office was sparsely furnished, just a single rolling table and two rolling chairs, a paragon of impermanence. As Shamshoun moved, he shoved the table toward the door, to slow the attacking commandos down and spoil their aim. The nearer of the two chairs he snatched up and thrust in front of him as he hurled his two hundred and sixty-pound bulk at the glass.

There was an explosion of shards and sunlight and noise, and he was outside, in the hot dry air three stories above Strip City. Behind him one of the slickguns went off, a coughing explosion heralding a load of hyper-slippery goo that thankfully went over Shamshoun's head. Even a graze and he'd be covered in clingy, frictionless slime that would make it impossible to fight, run or even stand. The nonlethal weapons meant they wanted him alive, but that might be worse than death.

Shamshoun fell.

His jump had taken him out and away from the building, over the sidewalk, curious pedestrians looking up at the sound of shattering glass. He could see that he was coming down over the street, already descending past the zenith of his leap, and that he was going to land on a car, a yellow and blue car, one of the taxis that prowled Strip City's streets day and night. Shamshoun fell, and knew he'd stand less chance of hurting himself if he was in his bear form, so he shifted. His clothes came apart as he did so. There were no seams up to the task of conforming to the almost instantaneous change in his shape. He was already facing down, and it was an instinctive motion to get his paws under him. The taxi's roof buckled under the impact, spraying shattered glass in all directions. The chair went even farther, crashing into traffic a lane over. Shamshoun was already moving, scrambling forward down the car's hood, stunned muscles throbbing but responding. He had to keep moving, to get out of range of the slickguns.

He moved, feeling the remains of his clothes shredding, the last few seams bursting and the cloth sliding off of his fur. Strip City wasn't exactly unfriendly to shifters, but with the number of Sino-Indian tourists it wasn't welcoming either. Shamshoun had dressed in human clothes to blend in, and now they were destroyed. A concern for later.

He charged away from the car he'd landed on, returning to the sidewalk. Better to mow down pedestrians, no matter how rude it was, than to be killed by a car. Thankfully, a bear at full gallop was not a sight that inspired many humans to stand their ground. Behind him, the slickguns coughed again from the windows and noisy splattering sounds told him they'd fallen short. They were effective stopping weapons, but only at short range.

Shamshoun stopped and stood on his hind legs, trying to catch the rhythm of the commandos, of their weapons and armor. The first four had not followed him out the window but there might be more on the street. They would have a truck of some kind—*there* it was, bursting out of a side street ahead of him, a slate gray armored throb of scent and noise with a more threatening quality than the traffic around. As it turned in his direction, scattering taxi and pedicab traffic, he saw a familiar face in the passenger seat: Vitter.

Shamshoun dropped back to all fours with a grunt of agitation. *Not Vitter, not here*—but it was not time to think, it was time to run. The road was on his left, and traffic wasn't slowing much for the excitement. Other drivers veered around the stopped taxi, making it difficult for the commandos' truck to reach him. To his right, a small storefront, a sweet shop with curious faces pressed to the glass.

Their curiosity turned to agitation and concern when Shamshoun hooked a paw in the handle to open the door and thrust his bulky body inside. There was an immediate stampede toward the back. There was another exit there, then. Good. He paid the patrons no mind, casting his head left to right to get the layout of the place. The greater threat lay outside. Shamshoun stepped to one side of the door, away from the window. The commandos would assume he'd fled through the shop, so he waited. The scent of sugary frosting and pastry was enticing, seeming to call to him, but he ignored it, shut his nostrils to the siren song of sweets.

Shamshoun waited.

The door was narrow, and they could only come through one at a time. First through was a man in street clothing with a shifter snare at the ready. His eyes were on the back of the shop so he didn't see Shamshoun until it was too late, a massive paw already coming down to knock the snare out of his hands, breaking one or both arms before the hateful weapon could be deployed. Shamshoun battered the man to the floor. His opponent curled into a defensive fetal ball, protecting himself and clearing the next commando's field of fire at the same time. He had seen them do this before, though. He dug his snout into the man's belly, forcing it into the tangle of arms and legs. Shamshoun couldn't bite, but he could push and lift easily with a heave of his neck. The curled-up body came off of the floor in time to catch the gel round from the slickgun the next commando fired. Covered in zero-friction slime, the man fell and slid back out the door in the direction he had been pushed, leaving a trail of gel on the floor and sidewalk that would make the entryway treacherous.

Shamshoun bellowed at them, so they'd see that he wasn't afraid. He had escaped them in Sino-India, where their numbers were greater, their supply lines stronger, and they were willing to kill him. Here, they weren't, not even with Vitter leading them. The commandos didn't even carry sidearms. In the Brother Nations they could kill shifters with impunity, but the laws of Sino-India didn't extend to North America.

A third commando threw the door open and leapt over the slick spot, barely making it. Shamshoun bellowed and raked claws across his face and chest as he landed, sending him to the floor screaming.

They wouldn't be deterred for long. He turned and fled for the back door, scattering chairs and tables before him. The space hadn't been furnished with bears in mind, but then human spaces rarely were. At least the doors had push bars instead of knobs. Shamshoun passed by the kitchen, smelling at least two people hiding in there, then down the rear hallway to the back door. He went out without slowing, eager to get through it before the commandos inevitably blocked both doors and boxed him in.

Shamshoun staggered sideways and roared, assaulted by a jolt of pain.

Something had bitten his shoulder, fiery pain stabbing deep into his body, a sting like the largest wasp imaginable. He whirled to find the source of the agony. He'd been shot. It wasn't one of the commandos, but a fat tourist wearing turquoise, who'd been among the sweet shop's patrons. He carried a heavy-looking satchel, a gambling souvenir. A little pistol wavered in his hand, not a gunpowder weapon but some sort of stun device. It was painful, but clearly designed to incapacitate a human—not a large bear. Shamshoun slapped the fat, capacitor-equipped dart out of his shoulder and then turned on the man. The pain in his shoulder disappeared under a wave of adrenaline as he launched himself at the fat man, clubbing him to the ground. The people to either side of the man screamed, fleeing again. Shamshoun's attack ripped the gun from the man's hands and peeled the jacket from his back. He was too enraged to be careful, and bones snapped, flesh tore. He battered the man some more, feeling the panic rippling outward through the small, rapidly dispersing crowd. He used it to his advantage, whirling, roaring and baring his teeth. This was not city behavior, and possibly foolish in Strip City, but Shamshoun was not thinking, he was escaping.

He was angry. He hadn't come into this city, which reminded him far too much of the place he'd fled from, to fight. He just wanted his family back. If they wanted him to fight for that, though, he would. He'd tear the whole city down.

Shamshoun took a breath. He was falling into the song of the pain and anger. It was time to start thinking again, while he had half a moment. Everyone was running away from him, and the commandos hadn't caught up yet. In fact the fleeing crowd was making it harder for them to reach him. It was time to escape, not to fight. Not to die. Fighting in Strip City would get him dead.

He took the opening. He fled down an alley, running in the same direction as some of the people who were running from him. He ignored them, passing several, intent on putting blocks between himself and the commandos. Using the alleys to cover distance, rather than forcing his way up the sidewalk and making the chaos worse, moved him beyond the no doubt rapidly spreading reports of an ursid gone insane attacking people.

Shamshoun slowed to a walk, seeing that he was now alone, and shifted. Only the slip-waist of his pants had survived the fight, leaving him with a long, shredded loincloth. His shoes had split and fallen off long ago. There was a spreading bruise and a small burn on his shoulder from the stun-pistol as well. No lasting damage done. Time to keep moving. He was attracting stares, but not as many as he would have were he near the casinos, where there were more tourists, more Sino-Indians. He was closer to Old Town, where Strip City's locals lived, and the people here were more used to seeing shifters from time to time. That said, ursids in cities were rare. He wouldn't be able to hide long.

Shamshoun headed for the market, moving fast. Farther removed from the straight-edged, electric world of Sino-India, the market offered varied sounds and smells, and tighter buildings with more corners to hide in, and hopefully more sympathetic people. If the commandos tracked him here, they'd be the ones who would stick out.

He had to get out of the city. A pedicab slowed nearby, and he climbed aboard, directing the rider to take him to the market. He was surprised the man picked him up, since he was clearly carrying no money, so perhaps he looked somewhat terrifying yet in need. Shamshoun closed his eyes and let the rhythm of the city carry him, the hateful sterile hiss of the electric cars, the chirp and squeal of the slot machines that seemed to be audible no matter where one went. He didn't like the sounds, so far removed from the cool green heartbeat of the forest, but by becoming one with it he was better able to disappear, to flow with the pulse of Strip City, as alien as it was. Shamshoun moved faster this way, faster than the commandos could hope to force their way through. Moving this way, he'd be out of the city before they knew which direction he'd gone.

chapter 5

One hundred and twenty-six days before Princess
Aiyana's trimester celebration

>> Safety concerns continue for attendees of the Deshmu family-sponsored 15th annual Brother Nations Inter-Disciplinary Conference, held for the first time in North America. With plans for a special series of seminars on the social and economic state of the fallen superpower on the schedule, organizers thought it appropriate to host the conference in Strip City. This has drawn criticism from many, voicing concerns that the pleasure-seekers' North American outpost lacks the security for such an event.

It could be the first of a wave of events on the North American continent, however. Though the former United States and Canada have been dark since the Colony Conflict, no fewer than six events are scheduled in Strip City this year, including a concert by pop star Shaii. "Strip City has established itself," "King" Pravit Deshmu said, "and I think it's time that the rest of the Brother Nations acknowledged this."

—Owl News Syndicate

Holly struggled to keep her face neutral, so her amusement wouldn't show. It wasn't hard at first, with the fat-tired truck bouncing beneath them and just enough wind to kick up dust into their faces. The other passengers, including Elden, were focused on the driver's shouted narrative. Their tour guide, who called himself Bazell, was explaining what had happened to the cities of San Francisco and Oakland after the Colony Conflict, pointing out former landmarks. Referring to the world-changing event as the "Colony Conflict" was a dead giveaway that he wasn't really a scav. North Americans called it "the Fall," Holly knew, and most were unaware of the EPRC attack or why the nation-destroying event had even happened over a century ago. Bazell's audience of twelve was rapt, but all Holly wanted to do was laugh at him.

Oh, he dressed the part, more or less, except that his boots were a bit too well-made. But there was something missing, something she couldn't quite put her finger on. Maybe it was the fact that his ridiculously tall-tired rig had an electric-motor assist for its gasoline engine, something that was more or less unheard of outside of Strip City. Maybe it was his long, pointed beard with bird's bones woven into the muttonchops, or his too-clean face, or his artfully distressed green leather jacket and belt, which made her think of a lizard. And he was too well-fed. Or maybe it was just the way he'd casually tossed away a perfectly good plastic cup before the "wasteland adventure tour" began, dumping the rest of his water and pitching the cup into a trash can. Holly knew there wasn't a scav alive who'd toss a treasure like that so casually.

She found the tour ridiculous as a result, and spent some of it imagining that as a bored and boring teenager, one day Bazell had seen a real scavenger for the first time, somewhere in Strip City. Holly saw young Bazell immediately taken by the rough appearance, the hardscrabble subsistence lifestyle, and emulating it. The more his peers laughed at him, she imagined, the more proudly he wore it. And he eventually emigrated to Strip City for good, and pretended to be one. He wasn't quite dedicated enough to really give up city life and go out in the dirt, but part of him wished he was, and he played the part of knowledgeable scav with an intensity that bordered on desperation.

In any case, Bazell was very much not a real scavenger. Holly could tell even though she hadn't been out in the dirt since she was a child. This "adventure tour" was just Bazell's idea of what he thought Sino-Indian tourists imagined a scav's life looked like.

The bumpy, rutted trail overlooked the largely abandoned remains of San Francisco, but they didn't enter the city and turned back into the hills instead. Holly waited until Elden was looking her way, and flashed a brief, privately amused smile at him, while taking care to show that she wasn't looking at the rocky outcrop that Bazell was identifying as a "known biter's nest."

"What is it?" Elden asked. A gust of wind cut across the back of the open truck, threatening to take his hat off, and he clamped it down with one hand. The hat was a souvenir, a floppy sun hat in a "native" style that no North Americans actually wore outside of movies.

Rather than saying anything aloud, which might have embarrassed their tour guide, Holly cut her eyes in his direction, shook her head slightly, and let her smile deepen. When Elden nodded in understanding, she let her face go neutral again. No sense in ruining the illusion for everyone else. Elden's colleagues from the university wouldn't have any more idea than he did, but she'd let her benefactor explain to them later. They all looked out of place here, barely outside the confines of Strip City. So did she. But that was okay. They weren't that far outside the wall.

Bazell brought the rig to a halt, and unsnapped his holster. "Now, sometimes if we stop here for a spell, we can get a look at a biter or two. They don't pop their heads up much during the day, but let's take a walk and see if we get lucky, eh? Everyone okay with that?" he asked. The challenging tone in his voice dared anyone to say they were too afraid to risk it. Holly glanced at Elden, then at the other passengers. Professor Aidanab was a severe-looking man in his mid-forties who seemed more like a lacrosse player gone to seed than a professor of modern history. Professor Dineen had brought his plump, disinterested wife and two of his students, Rei and Gurrit. Dineen was actually a science professor, but his research frequently focused on North America and the hyper-natural energy flowing to and from the continent since the Colony Conflict. Both he and his wife were pinch-faced and disapproving, as well as ill-dressed for a ride in an open truck. Holly guessed they'd probably throw their clothes away upon returning to the hotel, rather than risk taking imagined bugs back to Singapore.

There were five others in addition to the university group. All of them were young, in their early twenties and also from Sino-India judging by their clothes and attitude. They reminded Holly of the students, and might well have been students on holiday; the timing was right for it. There were three boys and two girls, and both of the girls had Cradle's masks, carefully concealed under makeup. Holly had heard them whispering and knew they'd noticed that she was fertile, and they also hadn't failed to notice her collar. She was the only domestic on the tour, and she imagined that there'd be some tongues wagging privately as to why Elden would pay to take his expensive Myawi domestic on vacation, let alone a tour.

No matter, though, that wasn't their business. Holly stood with the others as they began to clumsily disembark. The rig seemed to have been designed to make ingress and egress as difficult as possible, forcing passengers to either walk awkwardly between the front seats, fumble over the gearshift, and climb over the sides (a six-foot drop to the ground), or to use a little chain ladder at the very back. Holly held back, letting the rest out and then making her way nimbly down the chain ladder. "A real scav rig would be easy to get in and out of," she said to herself.

They were in winding, hilly terrain, with century-old grapevines growing wild and tangled into high thickets. Bazell was pointing to the "biter's den," high up on the ridge, about a hundred meters away. Holly scanned the area, thinking of that initial moment of touching dirt with her mother and sister when she was a child and feeling the mingled thrill of excitement and trepidation that had always accompanied it. She remembered it even now, what...seventeen years later? It had been so long since they had died. She stepped up onto a rocky outcrop on the other side of the rig, shading her eyes against the late-spring sun.

While their guide went through his well-rehearsed patter, Holly toyed with the idea of all of them being thrust into the wilds for real. This truck, lost in the dirt! Gurrit and one of the other young men looked strong enough, and Aidanab as well. The rest would have to toughen up; Dineen and his wife would almost certainly be quickly consumed by North America if they didn't get to a place with electricity and running water. Holly imagined she herself would be, too, if she weren't fertile—though the idea of the threats she'd be susceptible to was chilling.

"What are you looking at?" Elden asked her. He seemed to have lost interest in Bazell as well, trusting her impressions of her home country.

"He's taking us on a closed loop that he can control—he might even have actors pretending to be biters. Those 'nomads' we saw weren't real, they were carrying far too much cargo on their truck. But I don't think we'll be that far from a real road, either. I was trying to see if I could find it. There's not enough other—there it is," she nodded, pointing to a barely-visible break in the vines a short distance off.

"I don't see it."

"Come closer to me." Elden stepped close, and she leaned into him. "Look where I'm looking," she said, and pointed. "See?" Elden nodded, and Holly smiled.

"Such a small road?"

"There's not much up this way," she said. "Probably leads to a single farm somewhere. No reason for many travelers to come, so the road wouldn't be much more than a footpath."

"Let's go look," Elden said. "I'd love to see it."

Holly didn't think that her clothes were going to be much good for exploring in the dense overgrowth, but nodded anyway. She glanced at Bazell's group; they were still looking at the fake biter's nest. Elden was already pushing through the grapevines toward the scav trail, so she followed him.

Her shoes were little more than sandals with closed toes, more suitable for the carpeted floors of their hotel and the clean, tiled streets of Strip City than to the uneven, rough ground. Elden hadn't bought her heavy boots like his, and they wouldn't have looked right with her outfit anyway. She held her arms out to keep her balance, and followed. He moved inefficiently. Elden was a professor, an academic, not used to quite so much physical activity, but he wasn't afraid to get his clothes dirty. That was one of the things she liked about him. Holly could hear him breathing hard before they'd gone far, but he was determined. The grapevines snatched at their clothes and scratched exposed skin as they pushed forward.

The warm air was dry, and she inhaled happily. Outside of Strip City, it smelled so much cleaner. The air at home in Singapore wasn't nearly as polluted as some cities, like Mumbai or Hong Kong, but there was a definite scent of artifice, of man-made things, that wasn't immediately evident until she could note its absence. Outside Strip City, the world swallowed up the evidence of human habitation quickly, scents and all. Holly wondered how long it had been since she'd been this far from a Mandina's Megastore or a sidewalk. The ground under her thin shoes triggered a fresh bit of nostalgia; she hadn't had her first pair of shoes until she and her sister Ivy were seven.

"My feet have gotten tender," she said, mostly chiding herself. Elden gave a little chuckle that suggested that he'd heard her, and she expected he'd ask her to elaborate later. She knew he'd chosen her partly because of her background, and he asked her about her life before Sino-India constantly even though after almost twenty years away it often felt like she didn't have much to contribute.

There were grapes on the vines, little clusters of black globes. Elden picked a few.

"They'll be sour," Holly said, remembering long-ago experiences with wild grapes. Elden popped one into his mouth anyway, then made a face as he chewed it.

"You are absolutely correct." He offered her one, and she took it. It took a small effort to keep the frown off of her face, at the taste. At least they weren't rotten.

They reached the road, which was bigger than Holly had expected. It was like looking into a tunnel, two narrow dirt tracks framed by wild grapevines on either side. "Amazing," Elden whispered.

"It is, isn't it?"

He handed her the grapes, which she pocketed, and knelt, running his fingers through the dirt as though he was trying to plant a seed. Elden kept digging, scooping dirt out of the hole he was making. When he was about wrist-deep, he said. "Heh. As I suspected. The original pavement is beneath. This was a larger road before the Colony Conflict, I'd imagine. Most of the scavenger trails began life as paved roads." He stood, shaking dust off of his hand.

Holly looked up and down the trail, listening to the quiet countryside. It wouldn't do much good to remind Elden of the potential danger. She'd seen him in discovery mode before, and knew (thankfully not from experience) that it would be almost impossible to get him out of a burning house if he was absorbing new information. Hopefully, though, nothing would—

"Hsst," Holly said.

"I beg your pardon?"

"I heard something." She listened, and it came again, a rustling in the underbrush not fifteen feet from them. "There's—"

She had no need to finish. Something exploded out of the grapevines just ahead of them. It was a man, thick and powerfully built, bald except for a topknot, wild-eyed and naked except for a rough scrap of clothing tied around his waist that wasn't long enough to cover his genitals. His skin was pale and covered in streaks of dirt as well as scratches from running through the grapevines.

Holly wasn't trained as a bodyguard, but instinctively put herself between Elden and the man anyway. As she stepped forward, he shifted, turning into a bear. The change was so sudden and it had been so long since she'd seen a shifter that Holly took a step backward as soon as she moved forward, tripping over her own feet and sitting in a humiliating sprawl in front of Elden. He dropped down behind her.

The ursid roared at them. Holly regained her composure as quickly as she could, managing to keep her scream in (unlike Elden), but she didn't know what to do. If the bear-shifter attacked, she'd throw herself in front of it to protect her benefactor, certainly, but doubted her probably extremely painful death would do more than slow the beast down.

"Wait!" she said, holding her hands out in front of her. Elden clutched at her shoulders, hard enough to hurt, but the ursid didn't move toward them. "We're going," she said. "It's okay, we're going." She'd been a child the last time she'd seen a shifter, and it had been a canid; they were practically people. Ursids were a different matter entirely. She hoped it spoke human words. Not all of them did. Most rarely encountered humans.

The ursid inhaled and exhaled deeply, twice, then shifted back to human form. He remained crouched down on all fours in front of them, the scraps of his loincloth snapped off in the transformation. His eyes remained wild, showing whites all the way around. He made a noise in the back of his throat, a keening sound that rose until it became a shout, much higher-pitched than she'd have expected from a man of his size. Holly flinched backward again, her heels digging at the ground. She had to get to her feet without looking threatening.

She started to move, and then the ursid's eyes went past them, to the break in the grapevines that they'd come through. Bazell leapt into the road, brandishing his gun and screaming, "Get down! Get back!"

Holly wasn't sure which of them he was yelling at, but Elden threw himself to the ground. The ursid shifted immediately. His body seemed to rotate around his rear legs and he melted back into the grapevines. Leaves shuddered in a retreating susuruss.

"Are you hurt? Are you hurt?" Bazell screamed at them shrilly. He kept the gun pointed down the road, but the barrel shook. He was breathing even harder than Elden had been.

"We're fine," Holly said. She considered adding that she didn't think the ursid would have harmed them, the way it had hesitated, but Bazell did not seem like he'd be mollified by that.

"Why did you two wander off? You could have been *killed!* Damn fool tourists!"

Elden shook himself. "But we were not," he said. He stood up straight, as though he were in front of a class, seeming to ignore Bazell's height. Professor Ono could be a very different man than Elden Ono. "Shall we return to the truck now?"

"What did you do? Why did you go into its territory?"

"It ran into us," Elden said calmly. Bazell didn't seem to hear. Holly wondered if he was reconsidering his desire to be a scav, and if that was making him angry.

"An ursid! Balls of a *snake*, an ursid! We could all be dead."

"Yes," Elden said, "I'm sure your insurance rates would have sprouted wings."

Bazell glared at him for a moment, clearly wanting to say something else, then uncocked his gun angrily before holstering it. He turned around and headed back toward the rig.

chapter 6

One hundred and twenty-six days before Princess
Aiyana's trimester celebration

Nothing says you've arrived quite like a well-trained, high-end domestic, and many of today's top stars are happy to show off their fine taste and their willingness to help the less fortunate with their trusted and faithful Myawi girls. Always on the outskirts but never out of the spotlight, the girls from the top domestic school have a knack for knowing just what their benefactors want, and for looking great while providing it. Check out our shots of some of the hottest stars' Myawi girls here!

—Owl News Syndicate

On their return to Strip City, their tour guide exhibited a blend of humility and thinly veiled hostility that Holly found fascinating. Bazell didn't address the two of them directly after the incident with the ursid, partly because every time he looked like he was going to, Elden gave him the professorial look again and shut him down without a word. Instead, he regaled the rest of his audience with tales of scavs and unwary travelers mauled and consumed whole by ursids, of children stolen from their families by canids, of falconids diving screaming out of the sky to tear the eyes out of their enemies' heads. Some of the horror stories were the same ones Holly had heard in Singapore, with only the geography changed.

Holly and Elden sat at the back of the tour rig and discussed their excitement with Professor Aidanab. "The man has no idea what he's talking about," Elden said. "I am fairly certain that all of the attractions we saw were staged. And the way he reacted to seeing that ursid was not the response of a seasoned veteran of North America's wilds. He was positively hysterical!"

"It's possible he was just worried for your safety," Dineen interjected. Before he could elaborate, his wife tugged sharply at his shoulder and whispered something in his ear, and the two of them fell into a heated discussion. His students looked uncomfortable.

"It might be worth incorporating some of that into our talk," Aidanab suggested. The Brother Nations Inter-Disciplinary Conference was drawing academics from all over Sino-India, especially as this was the first time it had actually taken place in North America. The Singapore University had sent Elden and the other professors to be a part of a battery of presentations about North America, past and present, and among them was a folklore roundtable that Elden and Aidanab were moderating. Holly listened to their discussion, knowing she'd probably need to add to Elden's notes. "I think that Mr. Bazell is giving us some of the best examples of local myths and legends as we speak."

"Very much so," Elden agreed. "Let's get together with Doctor Rehsil as soon as we get back, and discuss it with him." He turned to Holly. "We're going to spend an hour or two meeting. I'll have a list for you once we're done, so why don't you take that time to yourself, and then we'll have dinner."

She nodded, her eyes on the horizon, watching the landscape curl slowly past. She didn't generally care to be left to her own devices. Elden always thought he was being generous, but she disliked the unstructured time. Especially with no chores to fill it. It was easier to find things to do at home.

After they returned, she went through their room quickly, straightening some things that the hotel staff had missed. With that out of the way, Holly freshened up and considered her shoes, which were in quite a sorry state after the afternoon's adventures. She still had an hour and a half. That would be plenty of time to replace them. In fact, the idea of her wearing a pair of real North American shoes might even appeal to Elden, proud as he was of impressing his friends with her heritage. He had left her a credit tab, so she locked the room up and took an elevator to street level.

Strip City was noisy and garish, in a perpetually-festive way that was a marked contrast to Singapore. It was nothing like the wilds of North America either, of course, but the city maintained a mien of constant party that was infectious. The casinos' open fronts beckoned, the sound of slot machines and other games of chance ringing into the street and blending with music from half a dozen different directions. Strip City lacked the computer cafes and three-dimensional public ads that were more common in Beijing or Singapore, but that seemed to be fitting with the throwback nature of the place.

Holly moved comfortably with the crowds, people-watching and letting the world swirl around her. She was already thinking forward to the evening; once she found shoes she could return to the room and make sure Elden's dinner reservations were confirmed, and then she'd need to freshen up.

And after dinner, of course...Holly couldn't help but cast a thought toward what came after that, thanks to the many threads of sex woven into the tapestry of Strip City's streets. In addition to its notorious red-light district, the city seemed to thrive on the promise of sex, thousands of women wearing makeup to hide their Cradle masks. Not that any of the tourists were under any delusion that the prostitutes were fertile. Holly imagined that many of them assumed her makeup covered a Cradle's mask as well, and in fact she applied it a bit more thickly than necessary so they'd think just that. Her collar protected her from theft at home, but overseas, with the trackless wastes of North America so close at hand, there was no telling what could happen.

Lost in thought, Holly nevertheless made her way along the street until she reached one of the glossy, chrome-floored shopping centers. Everything was so *garish* here, even while selling some of the same things she could buy at home. She skimmed the souvenir shops and clothing stores, eyes peeled for some rugged-looking boots, but found only a mockery of them, mass-produced shoes with deceptively thin soles that were made to look like some designer in Hong Kong or Guangzhou imagined the shoes of North American dirt-dwellers would look. She'd have to get away from the larger shops if she was going to find the real thing.

The more she thought about it, the more fixated she became on finding authentic shoes. They wouldn't be much use at home, but it would definitely amuse Elden.

For that, though, she was going to need help. Fortunately she hadn't gone far or wasted much time. Returning to the hotel, Holly went to the concierge's desk. She had already frequented it many times during their stay so far, and many of the staff knew her by name. It was a reflex; Holly tended to introduce herself to the hotel workers the same way she would other domestics, and they seemed to look upon her more fondly than they did other guests because she didn't talk down to them.

The concierge was helping another customer, but Holly recognized the security guard who stood nearby, just about to step away on business. Actually, it was Doniphan Barro, who wasn't just a security guard but the head of security, come to think of it. His eyes lit up briefly in recognition when he saw her. He had razor-stubborn hair dusting his cheeks and chin, and a brow could have been swiped from a movie star. For some reason he struck Holly as the sort of man who was secretly a sculptor.

"Good afternoon, Holly!" he said, letting his poker face slip to give her a smile.

"Hello, Mr. Barro. I hope you are well?"

"Just fine, just a fine day at the Mirage. The animals are behaving themselves," he added with a chuckle.

"That's good to hear." Men's responses to meeting a Myawi always fascinated Holly. Barro's neutral expression returned almost immediately. She guessed that it was because he was used to dealing with call girls. The best way to cultivate his attention was to flirt less, not more. "Would you be able to help me with a little errand?" she asked.

"If I can't, I'll find the person who can. What do you need?"

"Some authentic boots. The shops all have shoes imported from home, and I was hoping to find something North American. Something tough."

"You mean like a pair of Reds or Ducks, from back east. They sell those in Old Town. Cheaper than those Sino shoes, too."

"Which is ironic, since they're so much better made."

"Kinda clunky, if you ask me. What do you need 'em for? They're not going to go with your beautiful clothes. Shit, you're going to take an adventure tour, aren't you?"

Holly smiled and let him assume.

"Yeah, you'll definitely need better shoes, if you take a good tour. Your boss want to see the wild stuff?"

"He certainly does," she said. "And he's my benefactor, not my boss."

Barro's frown made his eyes all but vanish. "So that works how? He adopted you?"

"From the Myawi school, in a way, yes. Something like that." She had tried to explain domestics to Barro once before, but it had been lost on him. Seeing his face darken further, she defused it by adding, "It's the best school; hundreds of girls are turned away every month. And prospective benefactors as well. They're very selective about matching us to ensure compatibility."

"Okay," he said, nodding. "Which tour are you taking?"

"We were thinking of Bazell's. Do you know him?"

"Aw, that guy's half a brain short of being a shithead," Barro scoffed. "He's a fancy stuck up pretender. Come talk to me tomorrow, I'll get you a seat on Akair's tour. He's the real deal."

"I'll tell the professor," Holly said. "I'm not sure we'll have time, though. The convention starts tomorrow. But first, the shoes?"

"Oh! Right, shit, sorry. You're going to want to visit the merchants in Old Town. They're the ones who trade with the scavs." That they called a part of Strip City "Old Town" was a curious affectation, considering the entire city had been built from the salvaged parts of what had once been Las Vegas, barely thirty years ago. Barro shouldered his way to the concierge's desk, looked through a drawer, then handed her a card with text in English, Chinese and Hindi. "This is a good shop, in a pretty safe neighborhood."

"Thank you," Holly said. She slipped the card into a small wrist pocket inside her oversized sleeve.

On impulse, she rushed back upstairs to see if Nielle or Lakshmi wanted to come along. It would waste a bit of time if they had to get ready, but for some reason Holly didn't feel like roaming the city alone.

Lakshmi was busy; Professor Dineen's wife already had her washing the clothes she'd worn on the tour. Nielle wasn't, and told her to come up. Unlike Yuying or Shmi, whom Holly had known for years, Nielle was a Lotus Flower girl she and the others had met on the ship on the way to Strip City; her benefactor was Aldo Vitter, a government official of uncertain rank who'd been dispatched to attend some of the meetings and seminars that Elden was presenting. Holly hadn't seen Mr. Vitter, but she had gotten to spend plenty of time with Nielle, who had been given a great deal more free time. She got the sense that Vitter had brought Nielle more because he was expected to, than out of any actual need.

Nielle was in the suite she'd been sharing with Vitter, and when she opened the door at Holly's knock, she did so with a lazy smile. The odor of burning cannabis wafted out of the room. "Hullo, Holly," she said. "Smoke?" Nielle had blue contact lenses and long, straight hair in the Lotus Flower style, which was similar enough to Myawi that the school had been accused of intentional mimicry. Her skin was so pale it looked like it was stretched thin over her face.

"No, thank you." Holly didn't like marijuana, didn't like the way it slowed her body down. She also tried to avoid drugs because Elden didn't approve, though electrostim bumps were another matter entirely; on busy weeks she was doing them daily. "I've got an hour or so to go shopping, and I'm going to the Old Town to look for some boots. Would you like to come along?"

"Of course!" Nielle said, her smile broadening. It took her just four minutes to get ready, and they went back downstairs. Because she was away from her benefactor, she had dressed somewhat shabbily, though her collar still marked her as a domestic. Holly tried not to judge her—Lotus Flower girls were different from Myawi, after all—but she couldn't imagine going out with such a disheveled look. Even if Elden wasn't with her, she was still representing her school. She didn't even own anything so scruffy as the little airy kangaroo tunic Nielle was wearing, something perhaps a bit too summery for the weather. In the end it didn't matter, of course. Holly enjoyed spending time with her new friend.

Almost as soon as they came out of the elevators, Barro had a pedicab waiting for them. This wasn't the first time Nielle had been on her own in Strip City, and she relaxed in the pedicab after Holly handed the card to the driver. "What kind of boots are you looking for?"

"Something...North American," Holly said.

"Missing home?" Nielle asked, her voice like a wink.

"No, of course not. But we took an adventure tour this morning, and my shoes are completely torn up. And since I'm here, it seemed like a good time to get something that I can't get in Singapore."

"It's okay, I know you really want some boots like the ones you had when you were a little girl. When did you leave North America?"

"When I was eight," Holly said. "I was too young for boots then. I never had my own pair."

Nielle looked at her with a teasing smile, but didn't make a joke. "Why not?"

"Children don't get boots till they're done growing. Too much trouble to make or trade for new ones every month. I had a pair of tire sandals, or I went barefoot." Holly noticed that their driver hadn't spoken. That was odd; usually the pedicab drivers were quite talkative. Their driver hunched over the pedals, sweat slicking his bare back as he fought with the electric cars whirring past them in the main travel lane.

"Tire sandals? Made from old tires?"

Holly nodded.

"Quaint." Nielle rubbed her cheek thoughtfully, as if scratching her Cradle's mask. "Well, we shouldn't have any trouble finding shoes for you. Might be a bit blocky to go with your outfit, though."

"That's okay, Professor Ono will like it. He likes anything to do with North America."

"Lucky for you. Mr. Vitter really hates this place. To hear him talk, he wishes every time he comes here could be his last." As they rolled away from the flashy casinos and hotels and into the more run-down section of the city where the North American dwellers were more plentiful, Nielle said, "This part of Strip City always makes me feel very far from home. Not so much for you I suppose though, eh?"

Holly suspected there was a jab in there, but ignored it. "I haven't lived here for a long time," she said. "I barely remember what it was like." The sounds and scents of the old-town market didn't inspire any sense of nostalgia in her.

"The shop that the concierge told you about is coming up," Nielle said, pointing. "After we go there, I'd like to stop at another place as well, if you don't mind."

"Of course not."

"The old town is so exciting, isn't it?"

"It certainly smells exciting," Holly said. Judging by the stink, there was at least one open-air toilet nearby. Strip City insulated its tourists from this part of town for a reason.

"They allow shifters in this part of town too, so be careful."

"Why? Afraid you'll have to tell Professor Ono that I've been gobbled up by a man-eating canid?"

"That would be an awkward conversation. Perhaps I could just get one of these market girls to wear your clothes. He'd never notice the difference. You Myawi girls are all so *plain*," she joked. When Holly didn't reply or show any response, she added, "And so hard to tease, too."

The shoe trader was all Holly could have hoped for and more. With her allowance from Elden she was able to buy a pair of nice Wing boots that still smelled of the oil that had been rubbed into the red-brown leather, as well as a pair of more delicate-looking replacements for her destroyed flats. Everything was less expensive than she had anticipated, so Holly also got two pairs of nice knee-high socks, hand-knitted from soft cotton yarn. On impulse, she bought a pair of tire-sandals for Lakshmi as well.

Nielle watched Holly pack her little shoulder-bag with amusement. "Your benefactor must really like you, turning you loose with an allowance like that," she said.

"I do my best to be exceptional," Holly replied, slipping her arms into the straps of her parcel so it could hang unobtrusively on her back and slipping her hair free from the straps with an unconscious arm flourish. She intended it as a joke but judging from Nielle's reaction it came out more earnestly than she intended.

"I bet you do. Now it's my turn."

Nielle led the way to another little shop several streets over, much smaller and dimly lit. The sign over the door said, *Makkhana: Imports*. The place reeked of a dozen different flavors of incense and the walls were covered in baskets, tapestries and an assortment of pre-Fall decorations. Some of the decoration was in a northern Indian style that Holly recognized. Nielle greeted the proprietor familiarly, hugging the young, paunchy man. He had a similar face and skin tone to Nielle. She was noticeably taller than he was, which didn't affect the apparent family resemblance at all. Holly wondered if he was Makkhana, but Nielle didn't introduce them.

"We'll be just a moment," she told Holly. "Try the hanging chairs, they're just marvelous." She and the shopkeeper went to the back of the store and disappeared through a curtain.

Holly had seen hanging chairs before, though not exactly like these fragile-looking constructs of wood and cloth. She took Nielle's suggestion and sat in one, letting the chair take her weight. With her feet off of the floor, she could feel the weight of her new boots, gravity tugging her feet and ankles toward the floor. The chair swung lightly, reminding her of a gently swaying tree branch.

They hadn't told her what she should do if a customer came in. Holly looked around the shop from her perch, trying to identify all of the wares. If someone did enter the store, perhaps she'd be able to offer to help them.

Oh, well. She'd worry about that if it happened. It would be just as easy to tell someone that it wasn't her shop, after all.

Holly wondered what the purpose of Nielle's visit was. Perhaps the man behind the counter was a distant relation whom she'd tracked down. Her stern benefactor wouldn't approve of her taking time to visit family— few did—but Nielle had managed to steal a few minutes nonetheless. The idea of a clandestine reunion made Holly smile.

After a few minutes she stood and began to walk the shop slowly. Holly was careful not to disturb anything, but was fascinated by the unusual assortment of wares on display. Upon closer inspection, the Indian tapestries looked new, but were hung alongside genuine antique pre-Conflict blankets from North America. The baskets stacked next to the hanging drapes were, upon closer inspection, full of neatly folded clothes. She found leather satchels, which were also filled with clothes, hats and other items. Apparently the shopkeeper stored his overstock in them. Toward the front of the shop, a glass display case contained knives, cheap jewelry, jangly coin belts and a small collection of pipes and puzzle boxes.

There was a pretty trunk at the very front of the shop, also. It was sitting askew, as though it had recently arrived. It was old, but Holly had never seen one like it: almost three feet tall and five feet long, made of wood with copper cladding around the edges and corners. At a glance, it appeared pre-Conflict, but as she looked closer the dark-stained wood seemed to be new, and the framing screws were also fresh. The clasp was an intricate iron and wood piece that looked older than the rest of the trunk. When Holly touched it, it opened easily and silently. The lid popped ajar as if on a spring, or if the trunk was perhaps overstuffed. She smelled jasmine, and thought she heard a light electronic chirp as well. What was in the trunk?

Holly started to lift the lid, and suddenly Nielle was at her elbow. "Careful what you wish for," she said, "you just might get it."

"What's that—" Holly jumped, dropping the trunk's lid. It closed and latched itself. "Fuaa, you startled me."

"All done, twitchy girl," Nielle laughed. There was nothing in her hands, but the large center pocket of her kangaroo tunic was weighed down with a package of some kind. "See something you need to take home?"

"No," she said, covering up the rush of startled adrenaline with a smile. "This is an unusual trunk. Is it new, or restored?"

"New," Nielle said. "I believe there's a little craft shop somewhere south of Mumbai that's making replicas of pre-Fall artifacts, then shipping them here. Looks the same, but much sturdier. And cleaner."

Holly nodded. "I've never seen such a thing." She looked at it a while longer, as if expecting the trunk to do something. It didn't.

"Shall we?"

"Yes, we should get back. Elden will be finished with his meeting shortly."

"By all means. Can't let the benefactors down, now can we?"

They found another pedicab to take them back to the hotel. Holly was quiet on the way back. Nielle was friendly enough, but her habit of not taking her responsibilities seriously grew tiresome. Holly was used to dealing with girls from lesser schools, whose training wasn't as good as hers, but Nielle's attitude seemed to dismiss the very idea of taking pride in being a domestic. Beneath the friendly teasing, Holly felt like the Lotus Flower girl actually did think less of her for being focused on doing the best job she could for Elden. The moment of insecurity passed as she turned her thoughts toward dinner.

chapter 7

Five days before Princess Aiyana's trimester celebration

After the lightning-fast capture on the beach, the soldiers and Sam Wards whisked Shiloh and Marcus away from the others. A speedy, tube-framed four-seat buggy with a Sam Ward flag bounced across the sand, and one of the uniformed soldiers motioned them aboard, then jumped in with them. They were a study in contrast; the Sam Ward's scruffy, durable handmade clothes looked like castoffs compared to the slate gray tactical gear with integrated body armor that the foreigners wore.

The newcomer pulled his helmet off, revealing mahogany-colored skin and incongruous sandy blond hair. "Holliday," he said, introducing himself to Shiloh and Marcus. He didn't acknowledge the Sam Ward soldier. "We're very glad that we found you safe, Professor McEvoy. Who is the other prisoner?"

"Anna Vienna," Shiloh said, before Marcus could answer. She had been thinking quickly during the short ride. They had seen Swan beating her up, and assumed she wasn't with them. "I was a performer with Gallamore's Traveling Extravaganza when it was attacked. The circus was destroyed. They...took me with them." It occurred to her belatedly that Anna was first to mind because Holliday's accent was similar.

"That's terrible," he said. He took a silver pouch from his vest, squeezed it and tore it open. It contained a small folded towlette, which he handed to her. Shiloh was pleasantly surprised to discover that it was not only moist, but warm. Wiping the crud off of her face felt heavenly. "How long have they been holding you?"

"I'm...I'm not sure. It's been at least two months. Most of the time they won't even tell me where we are."

"Why were they beating you?"

"I tried to run away," Shiloh said. She sounded and looked nothing like Anna Vienna, of course, but Holliday had no way of knowing that. In fact none of them did, unless by chance there was someone who'd actually seen the Extravaganza perform. She hoped that was as unlikely.

The buggy sped up the beach. Shiloh saw a pair of small boats with several men guarding them, and there was a much larger ship off-shore. It was a boxy thing, like a building sitting on the water. "We'll take you to the *Excelsis*," Holliday explained. "You'll be safe there."

"What sort of ship is the *Excelsis*?" Marcus asked.

Holliday looked at him with a grin. "Officially, Professor? No kind of ship. It doesn't exist." He didn't elaborate, and though Marcus asked a few more questions of both Holliday and the Sam Ward driving the buggy, he got no answers from the military men. Holliday motioned one of the other soldiers into the boat, then helped them aboard and climbed in himself.

Shiloh's head swam, as if she'd been hyperventilating. She was deathly afraid they'd just shoot Ivy, Swan and Kroni (and Ivy's sister), yet proud of herself for thinking quickly of a way to escape the same fate, at least for now. And it was hard not to enjoy the bouncing of the small boat as it leapt across the waves toward *Excelsis*, salt spray cool and fresh-smelling on her skin.

It took about five minutes to reach the larger ship, and then they were winched up onto the deck. Shiloh had never been on a ship before, though she'd seen the massive luxury liners at Strip City's docks, and the floating city *Everlasting* from a distance. *Excelsis* wasn't as large as *Everlasting*, but it was a sizeable thing, and the deck was easily big enough for two scrunge fields if it weren't for the large building that took up most of the center. Shiloh saw equipment, bristling antennas and many markings on the walls, but none of it made much sense to her.

There were sailors there to help them aboard, wearing uniforms similar to but less elaborate than the one Holliday wore. They had no body armor or weapons; she quickly deduced that they were just sailors, teamsters in the greater scheme of things. There were two other men as well, dressed in smooth-chested gray civilian clothes. The larger man looked like he'd been opened up and packed with extra muscle (much to the dismay of his shirt), and he had buzz-cut hair, walnut wood-colored skin and flinty, disinterested eyes that bounced over Shiloh like she was a piece of furniture. His sleeve was open on one bicep, showing an elaborate, bright green tattoo that stood out against his skin.

The smaller of the two men stepped up, officious and barrel-chested, with shaggy black hair and thick glasses. He had short legs and a small stature in spite of his big chest, so he looked like someone had dropped a fat body onto someone else's legs, and his clothes had been tailored to fit his awkward shape. "What's the meaning of this, Holliday? What's the shore team up to?"

"All is clear, Chancellor," he said, sounding bored. "Vitter captured the Myawi, and her contacts from the look of it. And we've rescued their hostages."

"Hostages?" the chancellor said, his eyes bouncing right over Marcus to Shiloh. "Why, that's terrible. Those animals. But you're safe now." He stepped forward. He had a nasal voice that immediately began to get on her nerves. "To think that you were captured by such people. We were aboard an unarmed diplomatic vessel when they attacked us yesterday. A terrible battle. They killed nearly everyone aboard, you know. You're very lucky."

Shiloh let him take her hand, and touched her collarbone with the other. She took a little breath, met the chancellor's eyes, opened her mouth as if she was going to speak and then closed it again. She rounded her shoulders, making herself seem smaller. It was a fairly weak effort, all things considered, but she still hooked him in that instant.

"Who is she?" the chancellor asked.

"Anna Vienna," Holliday said. "A kidnapped circus performer. Let's get them into quarters. Vitter's bringing the prisoners up shortly and we're pulling anchor."

"Anna. Miss Vienna," the chancellor said. "I am Enjay Mahnaz, chancellor and aide to the Deshmu family. This is my bodyguard, Dorim," he added, gesturing to the big man with the green tattoo. "You're in good hands." He punctuated this with a squeeze of her hand, and she returned it.

She and Marcus were led through a nearby door, and into the *Excelsis*. The sunlight and warmth of the day seemed to disappear instantly, and the metal walls closed in around them. The air smelled close and antiseptic, like a hospital. Holliday led them through another door to a conference room, windowless, relatively featureless except for a long table and a dozen chairs. "You'll be safe here," Holliday said. "I don't anticipate any problems, but it's best if you wait here until the prisoners are secure. The captain will be down to meet you once we're underway."

Shiloh breathed a quiet sigh of relief. They were bringing her friends to the ship, or some of them at least. All was not lost. Mahnaz came with them and pulled up a chair as well.

"I'm sure you're very confused," he said, pushing his glasses up his nose. "It's very fortunate that we found you."

"We're quite grateful," Marcus said. "But it's true, I'm still confused. Can you tell us more about this ship?"

"Of course." Shiloh could tell Mahnaz liked having things to explain. "The *Excelsis* is loosely referred to as a research and interment vessel. It's the only one of its kind. Owing to the difficulties and dangers inherent in imprisoning shifters, the government created the *Excelsis* as a place where they could be held, where they wouldn't be a threat to the general populace. This also affords opportunities for research and study. The shifters here are secured, so there's no danger to us even though there are a large number on board."

"How many?" Marcus asked.

"Over two hundred, I believe. The captain says their capacity is five hundred seventy-five."

"And how did it come to be here?"

Mahnaz smiled. "The *Excelsis* was the closest ship available to respond, after we were attacked. We departed Strip City a day behind Princess Nipa's ship and escort—for that, I thank goodness it was just us. I'm sure the pirates were targeting the princess. We fought them off, but the ship wasn't seaworthy after the battle. Because of my position, and the upcoming trimester celebration, of course, the military security offices took great interest in the attack, and it turns out that the pirates were acting under the directive of a group of wanted terrorists with known ties to the Ivory Sisters." He leaned forward with a severe nod, as though Shiloh was supposed to know who that was.

Were Holly and Ivy the "ivory sisters?" She hadn't heard either of them mention such a thing, and Ivy hadn't ever had any contact other than trade with mariners, as far as she knew. Marcus was listening, and she did the same. Maybe it would be clear after a while.

"You're linked to the Deshmu family," Marcus said. "Do you think the attack was targeting you, then?"

"Oh, almost certainly. Vitter and Zhuan, the security men, think that the terrorists are trying to make a statement on the eve of the trimester celebration. Fortunately, I always travel with Dorim, who has a keen ear for trouble."

"Yes, of course," Marcus said.

"As it is, I may barely make it on time. Hopefully the weather is on our side."

"I imagine this ship is much slower than yours was."

"Very much," Mahnaz said somewhat sourly. "But it could be worse. I could be at the bottom of the ocean. And I've had a fascinating, up-close look at this ship as well. Very educational."

"Oh, I'm envious. Even under the circumstances, I'm sorry I missed it."

"I'm sure arranging another tour won't be a problem, once things have settled down. Are the two of you at all hungry?"

Shiloh met Mahnaz' eyes and nodded. "I am. Or at least some water?"

He bounced gracelessly out of his chair, ready to be the hero. "Let me see if I can get you anything. I'll be back in a moment."

When he was gone, Marcus turned quickly to her. "That was quick thinking," he said in a low voice. "Why did Swan attack you?"

"We were sparring," Shiloh said. "She's teaching me to fight and she was in a bad mood, so she cheated."

"I have experienced that mood myself," he said ruefully. "I traveled with Ivy and Swan and Kroni, many months ago." Shiloh nodded. She'd already decided to trust Marcus, so it didn't matter much if he had history with them. "Anna?" he asked.

"From the circus," Shiloh said. "She died. But I don't want them to know my name, in case they can look it up."

"Why not?"

"I'm..." Dammit, even now she didn't like the way it sounded when she said it, like an admission of some kind of sin. "I'm a felid."

Marcus' eyes widened. "Oh. Oh, my. That's bad. That's very very bad."

"Gee, thanks."

"No, I don't mean it like that—"

"I know what you mean. And I know."

"It's much worse than that, though. Sino-India..."

"I know. Kroni told us."

"He's been?"

"He's from there. He escaped."

Marcus looked genuinely upset. "And now it sounds as though we're headed back. If they find out, they'll kill you."

"I know, but thanks for saying it out loud, it's really great to hear," she said sourly.

"I'm sorry. It's just that I'm in a strange position. They seem to have gotten the idea that I was Holly's hostage. I don't know why they think that." He wrung his hands. "I don't know what to do."

"Figure out where they are, and get them out. Simple."

"Who? Oh, the others...I don't see how we're going to accomplish that, my dear," Marcus said. "I'm afraid I'm quite useless. I'm an academic—an historian! We can't—" He was interrupted as the door opened and Mahnaz came in carrying some small boxes and water bottles.

"I got some things from the galley. We're between meals, Anna, so it's just some water, rice cakes and candy. There will be more later." Shiloh opened one of the bottles of water and tore eagerly into the rice cakes and gummy candy. "I'm so sorry for your ordeal," he said to both of them, but mostly to Shiloh.

"Thankfully, it's over," Marcus said. He was a terrible actor, but Mahnaz didn't seem to notice.

"It is indeed. They're bringing the prisoners on board now." Shiloh listened, but didn't hear anything. She wasn't sure what she expected to hear. "Once they're secured, the captain wants to talk with you, and I'll see if he can arrange a tour of the facility. I believe the captain is not used to having civilians aboard," he added with a rueful grin. "That said, the accommodations are much nicer than I anticipated. So, tell me about your research, Professor," Mahnaz said, sitting down at the table with his arms folded. "I read quite a bit about you in the news, after you were kidnapped. Quite an inspiring story, actually, leaving everything you knew behind to come back to Earth. Has it been a difficult transition?"

"Tremendously," Marcus said, sounding as though he was launching into a story he'd told many times already and wasn't in the mood to tell. "I had assumed that it wouldn't be that terrible—after all, people are people, no matter where you go—but in fact, everything changed. Customs are different, the environment is different, the very air is different. I feel like I'm still encountering new things every day, and I've been here for almost two years."

"And what's the biggest change that you've experienced?"

"Things are much bigger planetside. Not in terms of actual, physical size necessarily, but the *world* is bigger. The horizons are farther away. The sky itself is farther away. The weather is more extreme. I think that this has an interesting effect on the human psyche as well. With a bigger world, a bigger sky, we are quickly reminded of just how insignificant we are. Even growing up in orbit, with the interstellar infinite stretching out on all sides, doesn't seem to have the same effect. I have written almost two thousand pages of material, since I arrived. And I don't feel nearly finished with it, there's just so much. It would take a small army of men like me to truly capture this!" he laughed. Shiloh couldn't tell if Marcus was over-animating his story in an effort to seem more casual than he was, or if he was honestly more interested in talking academia than in finding out the particulars of their situation. That was just as well, though; it gave her the opportunity to shut up and listen, and thus made it less likely that she'd betray herself by asking the wrong question at the wrong time. Marcus' comments about where he was from made no sense whatsoever, but Shiloh couldn't figure out what sort of euphemism it might be, or perhaps it was some self-referential joke from a book he'd written that Mahnaz had heard of.

Marcus started nattering to Mahnaz about North America and some of the things he'd seen there, and he had a good storytelling voice. Shiloh put her chin on her hand and closed her eyes. Given time he'd put her to sleep, just like Tom, the circus' storyteller always did. There was an undercurrent of terror that kept her from dozing off completely, though. The *Excelsis* was a bad place; Shiloh could feel that.

With her eyes closed, she just listened for a while. Not to Marcus and Mahnaz, whose voices blended into a patter that was easy to tune out, but to the ship itself. It seemed to be made of other sounds, hums and throbs and mechanical noises, as though it were alive around them. It wasn't the same comforting mechanical tremble as Ivy's rig though; this was more substantial. She felt like a fly on a cow, holding herself very still in hopes of not being swatted off.

Shiloh opened her eyes when the door opened again, admitting two men. One wore a suit similar to Mahnaz only dark red, and the second was in a much more elaborate version of the sailors' uniforms. The red-suited man had white hair and a curiously small face with black eyes. "I am Zhuan," the man said without preamble and without asking their names, "and this is Yang, the captain of this ship." Yang nodded very slightly in acknowledgement of his name. The look on his face made it clear that all of them (possibly including Zhuan) were barely-welcome guests aboard the *Excelsis*. He had intelligent eyes and a face so bland that it seemed like it would disappear entirely if he took off the uniform. "You will be safe aboard the *Excelsis*."

"Zhuan is Mr. Vitter's supervisor," Mahnaz explained quickly.

The officious man in question gave Mahnaz a brief glance. "We will talk later, about your experience with these people." He looked directly at Shiloh. "You were kidnapped from Gallamore's circus?"

"Yes," she said.

"We are bound for Singapore and unable to return you to Strip City at this time." He had a clipped, efficient manner, as if annoyed at the amount of time the conversation was taking. "When we reach Singapore, arrangements can be made for your safe return home."

"Thank you."

"You seem nervous."

"Of course I am," she said, thinking fast. "It's not as though they're far away from me."

Zhuan glanced at Captain Yang, who sniffed and shrugged. "I see. Come," he said, opening the door and motioning for Shiloh and Marcus to follow. They did, Mahnaz trailing behind, and Zhuan led them back out onto the deck, up a staircase and back in again. This hallway was quieter, the throb of the engines less pronounced but there was a different sort of sound in the air, one she couldn't quite place, a high-pitched whine.

They were in a hallway with doors at each end. The walls were thick, clear plastic from floor to ceiling, and Shiloh realized that they were cells, eight of them, running the length of the hall. The floors were metal grates, just rough enough to remind Shiloh that she was barefoot.

"This is the isolation ward, where individual prisoners are separated from the general population," Captain Yang said. His voice was deep yet tight, as though he spoke only with great reluctance. At the corner of her vision, Mahnaz nodded eagerly. "As you can see, the doors are unbreakable and bulletproof, and they are locked electronically, with a mechanical failsafe should something happen to the power. I think you're quite safe."

Only two of the eight cells were occupied. Next to her, Marcus said, "Ah." Shiloh followed his gaze and saw Swan in a cell. Judging by the state of her clothes and face she'd inflicted some wounds on her captors, a favor that had been returned. When she saw Shiloh, she was off the molded bench in an instant, rushing across the cell and slapping a hand against the clear plastic, inches from Shiloh's face. "Hey." Shiloh flinched even though she was six feet from the wall. The thick plastic was vented and didn't muffle the sounds from within. When she reacted, Swan smacked the barrier again. "*Hey!* You listen to me, little Miss Fluffy. This ain't over, you hear?" Her face still hurt where Swan had punched her, and the bruise there didn't feel like it was finished growing. Shiloh touched her face and stepped back, not sure if Swan was genuinely angry or just pretending, if she'd understood why Shiloh had let them think she was a prisoner. "I'm going to get out of here, and I'm going to kill you. Kill. You. I'm going to find out how your mother died, and I'm going to kill you the same way. You hear me?"

Shiloh decided that Swan probably wasn't acting. Mahnaz stepped in between her and the wall, blocking Swan's view of her, and gave Swan a stern look, which she laughed at.

"I wouldn't hide behind that one," she said. "Unless you want to watch him die first."

"You will return to your bench," Captain Yang said, "or be punished."

Swan stood at the wall a moment longer, meeting Shiloh's eyes over Mahnaz' shoulder. There was nothing friendly there. She then shrugged, turned around and returned to the rear of her cell.

"You see?" Zhuan said. "I will take you to see the general population cells as well. You are quite safe aboard this ship."

At the far end of the hall was a second prisoner, whom Shiloh didn't recognize. A huge man in a loincloth, he had stood at the back wall of his cell and ambled forward when the group approached.

"Ursid," Zhuan said. "He is being held for political crimes, so they have removed him from the general population."

"I heard about this one," Mahnaz said. "The terrorist who killed Porto Grosvenor. They recaptured him in Davao, yes?"

"That is correct."

The ursid looked at Shiloh with interest, then tilted his chin up as if scenting the air. "Well, that's interesting," he said, his voice a rumble that seemed to shake the plastic walls of his cell. He moved forward. He was at least six and a half feet tall, and seemed nearly as wide. "Aren't *you* a tasty-smelling little thing."

Shiloh realized that he could probably smell that she was a shifter. If he said as much, they'd throw her in a cell next to him. "I can't be here," she said, panic melting the edges of her voice even before she decided that it was okay to let that show.

"Don't listen to him," Zhuan said. "He is just trying to frighten you."

"Please, no, I can't do this." Shiloh backed away, even though doing so took her toward Swan's cell. She was trapped in the middle of the hallway between the two. "I don't want to see the other cells," she babbled. "I don't want to see."

"It's okay, I'll take her to my cabin," Mahnaz said. He put his arms around her; Shiloh stiffened for an instant, then decided to go with it and let him enfold her protectively.

"I'd like to see the rest, if that's acceptable," Marcus said.

"Of course. Chancellor, if you will see to Miss Vienna, the professor and I will continue."

Captain Yang grunted, dismissing the entire melodrama, and left.

Mahnaz took her back down the hall, positioning himself so he was between her and Swan as they passed that cell. Shiloh closed her eyes and kept them that way, felt herself spirited out the door and away from Swan's verbal abuse, away from whatever the ursid might be about to say. "There's no need to be frightened," Mahnaz was saying. His comforting hand on her shoulders had drifted down to the small of her back. "You're perfectly safe aboard this ship. They won't be getting out."

"I just want to be somewhere quiet," she said, following him up a stairway and to the passenger cabins. Once there, he sat on the bed next to her while she lay down and buried her face in a pillow. Mahnaz rubbed her back endlessly, unwilling or unable to keep his hands off of her body. He might think it strange if she tried to fuck him immediately, so she made no overtures in that direction, but she also didn't twitch or protest when he let his hands drift far down the small of her back, testing the curve of her rump. He'd suggest that she stay in his cabin tonight, if she was still upset, and she'd agree, and when he inevitably tried to fuck her, she'd let him. This infatuation could be useful.

chapter 8

*One hundred and twenty-six days before Princess
Aiyana's trimester celebration*

Shamshoun lay on a rocky outcropping more than twenty miles from Strip City, listening to the world and rolling thoughts around in his mind. The ambush meant that somehow they had learned of his intention to smuggle Pepper and the cubs out of the Brother Nations. His initial escape to North America had been hasty, driven by necessity, and the seven months since he'd arrived he'd thought of nothing but getting them here so they could be with him, in safety.

That moment seemed farther away, as he let the world reel past him. He could almost feel the rush of Strip City even though it was just a glow on the horizon, and behind it, feeding it, the similar but louder hiss of Sino-India. Shamshoun's mate and children were in danger, just as he'd been when the commandos burst through the door of the false meeting. Either his trust had been misplaced, or Vitter had found those who helped him and made them his own. Or killed them. Which was the truth didn't matter—either way it meant that Pepper and the cubs were likely to be walking into the jaws of death, or worse.

These things Shamshoun felt in the world-rhythm. He fought despair, and tried to listen closer. There were always other voices in the cacophony. The pedicab driver who'd taken him to the Old Town for free. The fat man who'd shot him and been mauled for his trouble. The tourists he had surprised in the grapevines, fleeing the city. The nomads who had cooked the skinny javelina he'd caught and shared in exchange for a trip farther away from Strip City.

His thought went back to the tourists. Shamshoun pondered, listening to his heartbeat, tapping his fingers against the stone in time with it, eyes open to the dark evening sky but not focused. He looked past the fear for Pepper. He couldn't help them if he succumbed to panic.

Presently it came to him. The female tourist with the silver collar, the domestic. It was her scent; he'd caught it later in the day. After slipping out of Vitter's grasp, he'd fled through Old Town and taken refuge with Makkhana, the Ivory Sister who'd helped him escape Sino-India the first time. Makkhana had hidden Shamshoun in his shop, and when he had come out, after dark, the air had just a hint of the domestic's scent. She'd been in the shop while he'd been hiding there.

Strip City was not a small place, yet they had crossed beats in the rhythm twice in the same day. Shamshoun listened to the world, feeling for the beats that linked them. Her reaction when he had burst out of the vines in front of them had been that of someone unafraid of shifters, not a typical Sino-Indian response. She hadn't been raised to fear them. So she was North American, serving as a domestic over there. Unusual. And she hadn't immediately attacked or threatened him, just made peaceful gestures and words. She was not Vitter's, though not known to Shamshoun as one of Makkhana's Ivory Sisters girls either. Would she have let him know if she was? The benefactor might not be sympathetic. Very few were, considering the Ivory Sisters' stance on domestics.

The night seemed to deepen as Shamshoun probed the mystery, moving his fingers in slow circles on the ground. His gaze remained focused on the sky, but the stars became dimmer, swallowed up by the blackness.

There was a whispering rustle, a sound in the night. Shamshoun lay still, thinking it might be coyotes or an errant skunk, but both of those creatures would have been warned off by his scent. After a moment he heard footsteps, the soft tread of human feet ascending his rock. He inhaled and caught the scent of a falconid, female. And she carried food.

"Hello," she called. "My name is Nefelibata, and I come as a friend." She stopped a respectful distance away. "I welcome you to the northwestern territory. I've brought you food. I know you had trouble in Strip City today."

He said nothing, and did not move to indicate that he'd heard her other than to stop moving his fingers.

"There was a man named Vitter. He is the one responsible."

Shamshoun rolled slowly over and sat up, his legs crossed. He looked out over the edge of the rock, deliberately keeping his back to Nefelibata.

"May I sit with you?" she asked. "I would...like to play my song with yours for a while."

She was familiar with ursid customs. It had never occurred to him to wonder if they were the same in North America, but it seemed that this was the case. He patted the ground next to him, and introduced himself.

"Thank you, Shamshoun. You honor me." She placed a small cloth with smoked meat, potatoes and a large helping of berries between them. "I came from the southwest territory to find you with some urgency. And difficulty. Flying at night is...unpleasant," she added a bit ruefully. "But I thought that we should talk."

"Vitter. He is here for me."

"He is not. It's serendipity, on his part. He was here already, but not searching for you. When his network uncovered you, he was conveniently close by."

Shamshoun grunted.

"He has traveled a great deal these past few months. To Little Rock. Bigmouth. Savannah. He tried to find the felid stronghold, and he will try to find Severina the Teller, the oracle of Geowa."

Shamshoun did not know any of those places, and shrugged, waiting for Nefelibata to explain why this should have any interest for him.

"He means to bring them here."

"Who?"

"Men from Sino-India. He means to bring the Brother Nations to North America, and if he does it will mean death for your kind and mine. You know this."

"It is a large place," he said. "Plenty of room to avoid them."

"I don't think this will be possible if he has his way, Shamshoun. He failed to find the felids, and Severina went into hiding. She knew he was coming. But he's made contact with Sam Ward's army."

Shamshoun shook his head. "I have been in Strip City only a short while, friend. I don't understand the significance, and I do not much care. I need to go to help my family."

"We can help you."

"You want something in return."

"Yes." Nefelibata hesitated thoughtfully. "I would like for you to travel with me to speak with Moll. She is the great bear of the northwest. She will not meet with me, and I need your assistance in convincing her of the threat that Vitter and the Brother Nations pose."

He huffed. "You mean to raise an army against them?"

"I mean only to make others aware of the threat. One you are familiar with. One you have fought against."

"I did not mean to," he said tersely. "I did not seek a fight." Shamshoun clenched his fists briefly.

"I can help you," she said. "Come with me."

"No. I must go to Pepper."

"Where is your family?"

"They are to travel from Taipei."

"If you come with me, Shamshoun, I can send people I trust to help them. Please. Your assistance is needed, and this matter is of utmost importance."

He took a deep breath. "I have trusted too many people already," he said. Agitation put a warning tone in his voice.

Nefelibata didn't flinch. "I understand," she said. "I am willing to help you get back to the Brother Nations, if you would consider assisting me upon your return? Based on what I know of the situation, I am concerned that you won't reach your family in time, but I understand that you must go. I will get you to Astoria, and get you passage on a quick ship back. I do this expecting nothing in exchange, but I hope that you might be willing to meet with Moll, upon your return?"

Shamshoun met her expectant gaze. The falconid was honest about what she wanted, and seemed to be hiding nothing. "Yes," he said, thinking of Pepper with something like hope. The world had found a way for him. He would make it in time.

chapter 9

*One hundred and twenty-six days before Princess
Aiyana's trimester celebration*

>> Our contacts on the floating city *Everlasting* report that Samuel Hudson Ward, leader of the provisional Restored North American State, is dead. Ward's campaign to bring order to the lawless region and further the reconstruction of the fallen world power met a sudden end when its leader was killed by a sniper during fighting at the Walled City of Detroit.

Ward's sizeable military force is reported to be in disarray, with no clear successor emerging. Though viewed favorably early in his campaign, recent skirmishes in Indianapolis and St. Louis reportedly turned public opinion against Ward, and made the maintenance of supply lines difficult.

The idealistic American people have always resisted attempts to reunite, since…

—Owl News Syndicate

>> More trouble from the notoriously difficult waters between Zeeland and Australia has been reported, as the cruise ship *da Vinci* was attacked and plundered this week. The liner, operated by YSM Cruise Lines, was en route to Adelaide when it encountered pirates in the Coral Sea. After looting the ship and passengers of valuables and supplies, the attackers left, and the ship was able to reach Brisbane. YSM reports only minor injuries among the ship's 638 passengers and crew.

As tensions between Zeeland and the Brother Nations increase and economic sanctions continue, operators of pleasure craft have been warned that pirate activity in the region is increasing. The Rainbow Snakes, Australia and Zeeland's guerrilla army, have taken to plundering defenseless cargo and cruise ships for funds and much-needed supplies as a result of the successful Sino-Indian blockade.

—Brother Nations Free Wire

>> In rural areas of India, China and Korea, it is not uncommon to encounter shifters. The transient population of canids and cervids has long been a problem for citizens outside of the large cities. In addition to squatting on private land and ignoring environmental and social rules, these unnatural nomads spread crime and disease. Learn about what the government and law enforcement are doing to combat this menace—and how you can protect yourself—in our seven-part series, "Robbery, Rape and Rabies," starting this week at…

—Yǔyīn of the Brother Nations

"You look pensive," Elden said. Holly had been listening to his recollection of the day, and keeping an ear on the goings-on of the restaurant around them. It was a quiet, private place, intimately lit with candles and a three-piece band (a sitar, saxophone and tabla). The music was soft enough that she could hear the familiar noises of the kitchen and wait-staff moving about, and amused herself by trying to figure out what they were up to. A soft clash of pans here, a dropped piece of flatware scooped up from the carpet there.

Holly smiled. Unlike many benefactors, Elden didn't seem to mind if she showed an emotion other than "cheerful." In fact, over the years she had learned that he liked having his little glimpses into what she was thinking. He enjoyed the intimacy of knowing her that way, and so she often let her trained Myawi mien relax a bit when they were in private. "I was planning our day tomorrow," she said. "You'll have to get to the conference center by eight, and you will have talks until eleven, then two more in the afternoon. I'll make sure you get lunch. I'm working at the registration desk for part of the morning."

He nodded. "And?"

They played this game sometimes as well. "And?"

Elden tented his fingers with a pleased smile. "And that's not all that's on your mind. You're nervous about something."

"Well, our encounter with the ursid this afternoon was quite a thing."

"It was," he agreed. She could tell that he was still a bit shaken from it, but hiding it. "But it's past. There's something closer to home, isn't there?"

Now she could let him have his nugget of insight, a peek into her thoughts. "I'm worried about dinner," she said with a sigh.

"Dinner?"

"Yes."

"But why?" He tilted his head quizzically.

"Because it might not be good."

"This is one of the finest restaurants in Strip City, and they specialize in classic North American beefalo," Elden said. Holly knew this, of course; she'd already looked it up on her portable. "I'm sure there won't be any problems."

"But there might be. And there won't be anything I can do about it." Holly met Elden's eyes, then shrugged with a wry smile. "So I'm worried. I don't like being unable to know if it will be okay or not until after it's too late to fix."

His smile slowly melted into laughter. "Oh, Holly. Always needing to be in control!" She joined him. "You do realize that the point of going to a restaurant is to let others do the work for you, right?"

Holly pursed her lips and frowned slightly, as though she were pondering the concept. "That's just not my idea of fun," she joked. "Leaving things to chance is stressful." There was a grain of truth to that, even though they were being jovial. The Myawi school had taught that control was everything—control of the situation, of the room, of the circumstances, of the conversation and of course herself. She might not be aggressively in charge or leading, but it was good to be in control, to some degree. It made things look effortless.

"Well, I want you to enjoy yourself."

"I am," she replied.

"We did have quite the adventure this afternoon, as you said."

"Very true. You did say you were hoping for something more authentic than the false tour?"

"So I did. Be careful what you wish for, eh?"

Holly kept the frown off of her face. "Odd—that is the second time I've heard that phrase today."

"Is it, now? Do you think that was a feral ursid?"

"I don't know much about shifters other than what I've read."

"Didn't you tell me once you knew one as a child?"

"We did. A canid, named Arty. He traveled with our caravan for a while. I don't remember him much, though, he seemed just like everyone else. I remember he shifted for us once. It was a bit frightening, a bit fascinating."

"And he was urbanized," Elden said. "This ursid was almost certainly feral, yet so close to a city! I wonder if perhaps the destruction following the attempted civil war has affected their habitat and food sources."

"The cities that were damaged the worst in the fighting with Sam Ward are all much farther east," Holly said. "Days' and days' travel."

"Still, something must have driven him away from his forest."

Holly nodded in agreement.

"I am surprised, however, that his penis wasn't larger. Did you think it was somewhat average?"

"I haven't seen many ursid penises," Holly said.

"Well, what did you think of that one?"

"I suppose I'd have to wash it before I decided," she deadpanned with a practiced enigmatic look, making Elden laugh. Their first course arrived, putting a temporary end to the conversation.

The appetizer was an intriguing construct of small beef ribs, nori, spiced mayonnaise and flash fried cabbage, served on rice. It was nicely presented, Holly decided, and a worthy start to the meal.

"Courtesy of the university," Elden said. "Enjoy. Assuming it crosses your high threshold, of course."

"It does," she said with a smile.

"Fantastic."

They enjoyed the meal, and afterward Elden continued telling her about the meeting he'd had with Hatton and Rehsil, and their plans for their talk. Holly listened with one ear—once he'd had a couple glasses of wine Elden tended to repeat conversations they'd had already, as he was doing now—and let her mind drift a bit; the better to process Strip City's sensory overload. They'd been menaced by a bear-shifter in the morning, and she'd gone shopping that afternoon. She hadn't really stopped to think about any of it.

"We'll need to have a dinner on the trip back," Elden said, drawing Holly's attention back to the present. "I'd like to hear everyone's feelings about the convention." This wasn't just posturing—as co-chair of the North American Studies Department, Elden was responsible for making sure these events served the university's needs in the end. An informal setting was preferable to a series of tedious and time-consuming meetings to convey it all. That said, Elden rarely passed up a chance to show Holly off either, and dinner parties were his favorite method.

Holly nodded. "How many?"

"Everyone who's come with us. No need for entertainment, we'll make this more of an 'I survived the wilderness' party," he added with a surprisingly youthful smile.

"A 'you're not rid of us yet, Singapore' party?"

"Exactly!" he laughed. "One last gathering to celebrate our safe return."

"I'll organize it. Did you decide on buying that armoire?" Elden had spotted a fantastic pre-Colony Conflict piece being used as a rolling cabinet to display baked goods. He'd been entertaining the idea of bringing it home and having it restored. Holly wasn't averse to the idea; it would make a nice addition to Elden's collection of functional antiques.

"I think that I will, if a suitable price can be agreed upon."

"You should offer to buy a more suitable display for them," Holly suggested. "That might get you a better deal than a straight purchase."

He nodded. "You may be right. I'm fascinated by the regularity with which they'd rather trade than sell here. Thank you, Holly."

By the time dinner was finished and the conversation tapered off, Holly had a rough idea of what needed to be done on the long boat ride home, three days hence. Of course she'd thrown hundreds of parties for Elden in the eight years he'd been her benefactor, so she'd had plenty of practice. Plans for shopping and working with the ship's crew to present the meal appropriately were almost second nature, and she tackled them subconsciously as she went about her evening routine when they returned to the hotel.

One of the few things Holly didn't like about traveling with Elden was that it was harder to be transparent. Once he was asleep, usually after sex, she liked to tend to some matters privately. It was a good time for cumbersome tasks like brushing her hair out, or getting a head start on the next day's chores, but with the two of them in the same room it was much harder to manage this without disturbing him. In hotels, he liked to wrap his arms around her from behind and stroke the side of her breast with his thumb, and she could tell he'd fallen asleep when the thumb stopped moving. Once he dozed off, Holly was stuck in bed with him.

At home she had her own room and her music box to help her sleep. Holly lay awake for about an hour, waiting for her mind to shut off, and even that felt strange, to go to sleep so soon after he had.

She thought about the shop Nielle had taken her to, and about Bazell's "adventure tour," and about the convention which was about to begin, and all of the random administrative tasks that would fall on her shoulders.

Much to her surprise, she was looking forward to going home to Singapore when it was all done. North America had been interesting, and even fun occasionally, but it wasn't her proper place.

chapter 10

*One hundred twenty-five days before Princess
Aiyana's trimester celebration*

>> Government limitations on the use of hyper-natural energy (HNE) by corporations are being challenged once again, as the Reprieve Group is petitioning to allow its use in the ongoing cleanup of the Yongbyon site. Yongbyon has been abandoned for over a century thanks to extensive radioactive leakage and contamination from the multiple nuclear facilities that were destroyed during the Colony Conflict. Cleanup of the site has been exacerbated by economic factors, but the Reprieve Group says that Yongbyon is long overdue for rehabilitation and rebuilding. At issue is the danger of, as Husang Jarama put it, "replacing one perversion of nature with another."

—Versamel Boom Newsmag

>> A village near Baokang, Hubei province, was the site of what local officials are calling an unprovoked and horrific massacre by shapeshifters. Over two hundred people are believed to have been killed in the attack, which took place in the dead of night. Victims were stabbed, clawed and bitten to death, with women and children dismembered in the streets. Several villagers are also reported missing, though these reports have yet to be confirmed pending an investigation.

"It happened too quickly for us to fight back," said Yang Shangben, a survivor of the attack who lost his wife and two small daughters in the assault. "They came out of the darkness and caught us in our beds."

Government officials have ignored repeated concerns about the reports of shifters living in the woods in the area. Locals have reported food, pets and livestock stolen at various times, and there are many voices raised to ask the obvious question: why wasn't something done sooner?

—Yŭyīn of the Brother Nations

Elden insisted that she wear her new Wing boots to the convention, in spite of their clashing with her Myawi garb. Shmi and Yuying were amused, and claimed sarcastically that she looked quite stylish. Sitting at the registration table, the boots weren't visible, but Holly felt proud of them anyway. Holly saw Nielle, though only from a distance as the girl followed in Vitter's wake, carrying his briefcase or writing down notes as he dictated to her.

There were three domestics and one office secretary at the registration desk, so the uncollared woman was in charge. Her name was Omy. She was from the Beijing University, a career administrative assistant with an eyeglass computer monitor and a tiny throat mike. She seemed to be having constant phone conversations, even as she snipped unnecessary orders at Holly, Yuying and Shmi. Omy didn't seem to be able to tell them apart, even though they looked nothing alike. Lakshmi was a full head shorter than either Holly or Yuying, and her slight frame belied the fact that she had borne two children for the Dineens before ORDS took that option away. The family raised them as their own, since Mrs. Dineen had been infertile since she was fourteen. Shmi hovered cheerfully; she had always been fascinated by Holly because of her North American heritage. They made quite a pair: at five foot seven, Holly was eight inches taller than her friend, and Yuying had cheerfully pointed out once that although Lakshmi was several shades darker, their skin shared the same golden undertone. Shmi joked that they were like sisters and had taken to wearing her hair in the extra-long Myawi style. Holly helped her style it every few days, lest it degenerate into a hopeless mass of unruly waves. Furthermore, their clothes were different as well. Yuying's sleeveless one-piece pantsuit was extravagantly patterned, and its thin material was designed to accentuate every jiggle of her backside. It wasn't particularly appropriate, but she didn't have much choice in the matter. Holly's standard Myawi outfit was considerably more restrained in spite of a dramatic neckline, with silver trim setting off the deep wine colored fabric whose clingy bits were much better managed. Shmi was dressed in a dress that copied the Myawi style in cheaper material, though it was a curious shade of beige that Myawi wouldn't have ever used and didn't complement her skin tone at all.

Holly was aware, without judgment, that she was much better-dressed than either of her friends. This wasn't unusual.

The convention was well-attended, and a steady flow of arrivals kept them busy for the morning. Sour-faced Omy was prone to annoying the visiting professors with her bullheaded manner. Holly found herself politely intervening more than once, and rather uncharitably envisioned Omy living alone in a cheerless Beijing apartment with only a cockatiel to keep her company, and that the bird was the only creature that truly loved her. She kept this nastiness to herself. To her credit, Omy soon figured out that Holly had a knack for knowing the right thing to say, and would step aside to take important calls.

"I don't know who she's talking to," Shmi grumped. "It's not like she can get calls from home on that thing."

"Perhaps she's coordinating with her department," Holly suggested. "I don't think the BU people are allowed to bring domestics—she's the only assistant most of them have. The rest are grad students."

"Well, turning that many professors loose without handlers is just irresponsible," Shmi deadpanned. Holly laughed, and turned the smile into a pleasant greeting for the next person in her line.

The morning went quickly, and as the conference got into full swing, things slowed down so they could talk without being irresponsible. Yuying wasn't much of a conversationalist, and spent her spare time on her little portable playing games. The event was actually considerably less hectic than Holly's usual day, with Elden focused on his panels. As a result, she'd overprepared somewhat, leaving time for gossip.

"Hanging in there?" she asked Shmi. "You look tired."

"Long night in the hotel room," her friend said. "The professor and the missus are fighting again."

"Oh, no."

"Eh, what else is new? Only difference right now is that they don't have work or women's clubs to hide from each other in, and the kids aren't around to keep things civil."

"Is it bad?" Holly glanced to see if Omy was within earshot, but the secretary had moved off toward the restrooms. Shmi would probably have answered anyway; the girl had no shame when it came to talking about her benefactor family, even when she ought to have exercised some restraint.

"About the same as usual. I don't think he realizes how much she dislikes him. Or that she knows how much sexytime he's spending with me."

"How would she not know? It's not as though you aren't in the same house."

"Oh, he brings me into the bed when she's there sometimes," Shmi rolled her eyes. "But he'll also meet me during the day while I'm running errands, or when she's out shopping."

Holly was surprised. "Doesn't he have classes to teach?"

"He seems to fit it all in." She wiggled her eyebrows at the dirty pun, then shook her head. "In any case, it's not as though I'm going to hide it from her when she asks. He hasn't even thought to tell me to cover for him. Not even when she's fighting with him. It'll get worse before it gets better."

"I'm sorry you have to deal with that."

"I'll be all right. Nobody's directing anything at me this time. Not like last summer."

"Did you end up filing a report when she slapped you?"

Shmi shrugged. "Nah. Axtellia's wouldn't do anything anyway, not till she did real damage. And it hasn't happened since. She knows it's not my fault. So is your mister going to breed you out, or what?"

Holly gave Shmi a frown. "That's an awful question!"

Her friend showed no remorse. "Gotta do something, if he's not going to."

"It's rude to presume, Shmi."

"Oh, shush't. You've been with your mister for how long? Going on eight years? And you haven't caught yet?" Shmi scoffed. "You can't tell me he's not throwing ghosts."

Holly started to reply, but the clocks chimed the hour. Right on schedule, doors to conference rooms began opening as the assembled academics began moving to the next events on their schedule. They coalesced into clumps of two and three, a few solitary bodies moving more quickly among the crowd, many of them paging through portables or books. Holly saw Elden coming her way with two unfamiliar men. By their look she guessed that they were fellow professors.

"Holly," he said with a smile, approaching the table. Elden's companions wore similarly impressed expressions upon seeing that she was a Myawi girl. "Have you got my notes for the next seminar, dear?"

"Of course, Professor," she replied with a smile, making quick nods to both of the other professors. Elden only called her "dear" when he was showing her off. She reached to the neat stack of his papers next to her without looking, found the appropriate sheaf with her fingertips, and handed it to him with another little nod. She'd expected this, and even tied each set of notes with a small ribbon. Presentation was everything, after all. The other two academics murmured in appreciation.

"Thank you," he said. He turned his hand as he took the papers, and Holly took the cue and deposited an affectionate little kiss on his knuckles.

"You must tell me how you managed to afford a little Myawi goddess on a professor's salary," one of his companions said.

Elden smiled. "Shrewd and creative investing, of course."

When they were gone, Shmi said, "Well, then. That was educational."

"He likes to show me off."

"I would, too! You Myawis are crazy," she said, smiling. She added in a lower voice, "I think I'd bite the mister's hand if he tried that on me."

"It's not so bad. I don't mind. It makes him happy." She didn't add that she liked feeling exceptional. It seemed like a conceited thing to say.

"Well, you're a better person than me, then. Anyway, on account of all the fighting, the professor said I could have free time this evening. Are you free?"

"I'm not sure," Holly said.

"Well, let me know if you are. I'm going over to the Old Town, by the docks. That's where you got me those sandals, isn't it? Nielle and me were there last night, and we met some mariners. There's a fellow I want to introduce you to. He's never seen a Myawi before, and didn't believe me about you guys."

She tilted her head at Shmi. "Believe *what?*"

"That...just, everything. Anyway, you have to come meet him. I promised. You'll like him, he's very elegant, for a mariner. His name's Hardson."

"I doubt I'll have time for that, Shmi. I do have quite a few duties, you know."

Shmi rolled her eyes. "Ask for the night off," she whined.

"Another time."

"Oh, the next time we're in Strip City? You're no fun."

"That is my curse," Holly said, and Shmi giggled.

chapter 11

*One hundred and twenty-two days before Princess
Aiyana's trimester celebration*

>> Minister of Foreign Affairs Shen Zhuan called again for the enactment of laws
limiting or prohibiting the export of vehicle tires and other maintenance components to North America. Though the land poses no military threat, many are
concerned that supplying the nomads who roam the interior of the continent will
lead to industrialization on a much larger scale, which could lead to other issues.
"The treatment of women in North America is barbaric," Zhuan told reporters. "The
Christian religion dictates that women are little more than property, and it's clear
to me that by providing transportation and equipment to these people we're just
encouraging the spread of that bad attitude."

Opponents of the law observe that only the small number of legal cargo carriers currently traveling to and from North America will be affected by the legislation. Black-market goods will continue to flow across the ocean, with even less
government control over what is being exported. "Free trade will make it more
difficult for North American warlords to secure a supply line for restricted goods,"
said David Caleb, a representative of the Bright Spirit Corporation. "An open market is actually easier to regulate, because nobody has anything to hide, and we are
better able to track who is buying what."

—Owl News Syndicate

>> Will the economy be destabilized if we take a greater role in North America's
recovery? That is the question that's being asked by many experts as the Brother
Nations' stars meet behind closed doors to contemplate the establishment of a
satellite government in North America. For thirty-six years, Strip City has been an
unofficial center of Sino-Indian activity on the wild continent, but the resort city has
operated entirely outside of government support and has no embassy or established government. "Of course the ruling families of Strip City want to see things
remain the same," said Minister of Foreign Affairs Shen Zhuan. "Right now they are

free to operate outside the law and without repercussions. For all of the casinos and entertainment, it's important to remember that Strip City is nevertheless an anarchy." Zhuan is proposing the establishment of a second city, farther inland, with direct connections to Beijing and Singapore. The proposition has been hotly contested as a waste of time and resources.

This has raised issues about communication as well as economics. The infrastructure of North America's mainland remains in a shambles, and the continent is largely beyond the reach of long-distance electronic data transfer. Will direct radio and written communications be enough to link a colonial government to home?

The potential benefits to the people of North America are obvious...

–Tinzee's Tea Room

Conference over, the university group returned to Singapore on the same ship that had brought them to Strip City two weeks before. The *Mermaid's Parasol* was a relatively compact hydrofoil with space for about seventy passengers and several small berths, one of which Elden and Holly had booked. It was considerably less opulent than the floating hotels that ferried many of the gambling tourists to Strip City, but the *Mermaid's Parasol* was also much faster, shaving a full day and a half from the trip.

Docked next to the ocean liners, the *Mermaid's Parasol* looked like a whippet among St. Bernards, a tiny, svelte thing possibly unsuited to the rigors that the larger boats would shrug off. Holly liked that it seemed to have been designed to be underestimated. It had a sharply pointed prow and a bulbous, rounded rear section housing the staterooms, and this gave it an awkward look. Once on the open ocean, though, it rose up on its foils and skimmed the surface of the water gracefully.

The smaller boat also left the dock with less fanfare. Where the cruise ships set sail with crowds, fireworks and music, the *Mermaid's Parasol* just slipped her moorings and glided out to sea, as casually as if she were going a few miles down the coast rather than starting a seven-thousand mile voyage.

Elden boarded and went right to bed, saying he felt a bit under the weather. Holly had figured out easily that he got a touch seasick and didn't want to admit it, even to her. She confirmed quickly that he still wanted to host his wrap-up dinner tomorrow, and then she made sure he was comfortable and let him be.

She couldn't check to see if the other domestics she knew were busy, but guessed that Shmi would be busy in her benefactors' cabin, considering Professor Dineen's wife's protests that their domestic had enjoyed the trip more than she had. Yuying had been fighting a nasty cold for the last day of the convention and would very likely not be involved either, and Professor Hatton's girl Yinka was almost as businesslike as a Myawi, so if she was idle she'd be napping or finding some busywork. Holly went to the forward deck, which was equipped with a glass promenade from which she could watch the water race under them. The promenade was popular: the *Mermaid's Parasol* was up to speed, there was a real risk of being blown off the exposed upper decks. Hidden vents channeled some outside air in, creating an artificial breeze as the boat rushed out to sea, leaving North America behind.

Nielle approached her shortly after they departed. "Hi there," she said, joining Holly by the windows. "In that much of a hurry to get home?"

"Looking forward to it," she agreed. "Though I was actually thinking about how much more pleasant this trip across the ocean has been, compared to the last time."

"The last time? Would that have been when you first left North America?"

Holly nodded.

"Tell me about it."

There was a teasing lilt to Nielle's voice whenever she spoke to Holly. She'd gotten used to it, so that made its sudden absence even more noticeable. It was like Nielle was speaking to Holly as an equal for the first time. Because Nielle seemed honest, Holly told her the story. "My family was traveling down the coast from Astoria, just past Coosbay I think. It's about a day north of Strip City."

"I've heard of it."

"Pirates attacked Coosbay, just a single boat, but they had guns big enough to put holes in buildings. Our caravan fled, and when the pirates overran the village they came after us. They used the ship's guns to destroy the road, and hit our home as well. My sister died, and they took my mother and I with them. There were ten or fifteen other women from the town. They were taking women, like they used to do..." she shrugged. She didn't really want to tell Nielle her life's story, but it was too late to politely decline. "In any case, we spent six days in the belly of a pirate ship. There was a storm. The ship rolled so much we thought it would sink. It was terrifying. It smelled. Urine and vomit and sweat. It smelled like fear. And it was dark. One of the women they grabbed was fertile, and the pirates...kept her. After the ship docked in Sino-India they handed us over to some men and she wasn't with us any more."

Nielle nodded. "What happened after that?"

"Are you okay? You look ill."

"Getting used to the boat. Listening to you talk helps, you have a wonderful voice. Tell me more. It's a terrible memory, I know, but I'd like to hear more." Nielle's eyes remained fixed on Holly.

"It's not all that terrible. It was frightening at the time, but it ended well. I was selected for the Myawi school, and my mother by YYI. She got a job in a factory town near Semangat Terang."

"Did she?"

Holly nodded. A sea bird of some kind traced the waves ahead of the boat for a moment, then angled away from them, disappearing from view. "In those days the pirate trade for women was dying, and they hadn't yet passed the last few laws that made it illegal for schools to take women who'd been kidnapped or forced. So my mother was offered a job—they couldn't very well put us back where they found us, after all. And she's been in Semangat Terang ever since. She has an apartment there."

"And you've got a good benefactor, and the top domestic school to train you," Nielle said. "Sounds like it did all work out." The sardonic tone was creeping back into her voice.

Holly ignored it. "It did."

"I'm sorry to hear about your sister. Was she older or younger?"

"Four minutes younger, my mother said."

"Oh! A twin sister!"

Holly nodded with a small, emotionless smile. "What about you?"

"There's just one of me," Nielle replied. "My family gave me away." A couple other passengers ventured onto the promenade to look out the windows; they sat in a pair of leather recliners and didn't acknowledge Nielle or Holly. "That's not strictly true—they did get a stipend from Lotus Flower, but they don't like to call it *selling*, you know. I'm from Kanpur, and my father was blessed with two fertile daughters and three with ORDS. There were lean years and not enough food to go around, so off the three of us went. Find a better life with Lotus Flower," she said, mocking the school's advertising jingle.

"Are you not happy?"

"I am happy, but...dissatisfied," Nielle said. "Life isn't without its perks, though. Do you want a tiny cake? The Poussinis gave me a pair of little cakes baked in cans, the North American way, as a gift for Mr. Vitter. He had to stay in Strip City, so I'm taking some of his extra luggage back with me and the cakes will be stale by the time we get home. No point in letting them go to waste. We could share them before dinner."

Holly considered. Cake sounded like fun, but she wasn't sure that eating another man's gift was entirely ethical. Nielle sounded like she'd done it plenty of times, though. Elden would be in the room reading or watching television, assuming he was awake at all, and was unlikely to be in the mood for dinner, a massage or anything else tonight. "If I'm free," she said finally.

Nielle smiled. "Great! Meet me before dinner. Mr. Vitter's cabin is number 4. I've got to go."

Holly wondered what pressing business Nielle could have with her benefactor still in North America, but didn't pry.

chapter 12

Shamshoun made his way north to Astoria, where Nefelibata had promised him there'd be a ship waiting. The falconid was truthful, and in short
order he was on his way back across the sea. He imagined that he could
feel the earth dropping away as the water consumed the world, leaving him
with too much time to think.

His descent from reclusive but friendly craftsman to hunted terrorist
had been swift. He could have described it in a few sweeping arm movements and steps if he were telling his story through dance—the quiet life
in his remote cabin, the fight with a rabid canid in the market in town,
the snap of the poor unfortunate's neck and the awful feeling of inevita-
bility as the doctor told him that a blood test was required to receive the
vaccine. When the results came he had fled, of course, but it hadn't been
long before the folk were beating the bushes for the ursid who'd been living in their midst. And when they had found him, he'd only been defending himself, of course, but that wasn't how the survivors told it. He'd had
no way of knowing that one of the men, a cadet, was from an important
family, several times removed, but still enough to turn a simple fight into
an accusation of assassination. Shamshoun had escaped with his life, but
apparently the boy had been better-connected than it seemed, because Vitter had taken an interest in him, regardless of his lack of complicity in the
entire matter.

The train derailment was another story entirely. Shamshoun had meant
for that to happen. Sometimes he imagined playing the song for people: the
discovery of the cars full of shifters bound for an unknown prison from
which they wouldn't return, the rhythmic pounding of his hammer against
the track, the thunderous crash as forest and upended train met at speed

and the gasps of the survivors as they fought their way out of the broken prisons.

But of course Vitter had found him, drawing upon threads Shamshoun hadn't even realized he'd left. There was no going back at that point; there was only flight, a careful and measured departure, and he'd thought that it had gone smoothly until Vitter appeared in Strip City.

Now, uncertainty. He had to get back, and quickly. Astoria was the only other major city on the coast, and it was unlikely that boats at the smaller towns would be traveling straight to Sino-India—there would be more coastal trawlers, carrying goods up and down the coast. Shamshoun traveled directly to Astoria. He was able to track and kill an elk outside of town, used some of the meat to trade for rides along the way to speed his progress, and made it there in two days. The falconids had gotten him passage on a smallish boat carrying crates and crates of the pre-Fall goods that Sino-Indians seemed to have a never-ending appetite for. The ship was a new Sino-Indian design and relatively quick, able to cross the ocean in just five days.

He decided that it would be better to stay out of sight, and he spent as much of the trip as possible in his cabin, his thoughts on Pepper and the cubs. Shamshoun wasn't travelling to make friends.

They tried anyway, of course. He took his meals with the crew, and there was incessant talk of Princess Aiyana Deshmu, and her recently-announced trimester celebration. Shamshoun had heard of her; the Deshmu family was not actually royalty, but in the public eye it may as well have been. When the eldest daughter Aiyana had married Haichen Qui, scion of one of the wealthiest families in China as well as a popular singer, it seemed to be one of the few things that all of Sino-India agreed was a wonderful thing. The family was influential in politics and media by dint of wealth and charisma, but held no elected office; they had been referred to as royalty for years, as a simple honorific, and that extended easily to the children. Glamorous and beautiful, the celebrity power couple was rarely out of the tabloids, and nearly universally adored. Shamshoun didn't take much interest. Both of the Deshmu daughters were still fertile, a very lucky sign. The younger, wild little Nipa, was unwed at seventeen and the Deshmus were notably breaking tradition by not arranging marriages for both of their daughters, though this had worked out well for the powerful family thus far.

The upcoming celebration of Aiyana's pregnancy, which was entering its third trimester without complications, was going to be a lavish, twenty-four hour media event with literally hundreds of entertainers and luminaries coming together in Singapore to perform and offer their good wishes.

As with so many things in Sino-India, it was an amusing distraction, nothing more. There was a pile of month-old electronic gossip magazines on board, and Shamshoun read most of them out of boredom. He enjoyed observing the activities and goings-on of Sino-Indian stars and politicians, though he took it less seriously than some. It was a pleasing distraction as he quietly waited out the ocean crossing. He didn't like being so far from solid earth for so long.

After five days, the slow-moving boat was finally within sight of land. Shamshoun emerged from his cabin to smell the air and listen to the beat of the world, closing his eyes and savoring the green scent as it fought its way through the odors of salt and drowning.

But something wasn't right. He squinted over the distance as the ship passed within half a mile of shore, easing ever closer to the jagged line of buildings etching the horizon. The world seemed to tremble in warning, and Shamshoun listened.

That was it. They would know he was coming. Of course they would. He had gotten away from Vitter momentarily in Strip City, but the man had almost certainly picked up his trail again. Shamshoun became certain that more soldiers were waiting for him on shore. He couldn't smell them on the wind, couldn't see them of course, but something in the rhythm suggested that it was so.

He gauged the distance to shore. It would be a long swim, but he could do it. Shamshoun glanced back and forth to see if any of the sailors were watching, ascertained he was more or less alone, and jumped overboard, shifting as soon as he hit the water.

chapter 13

One hundred and twenty-two days before Princess
Aiyana's trimester celebration

>> Review of "Spiderwebs:" Argyle has created a stylish world, and one that neatly mirrors the fears of many people in its depiction of its young and old protagonists working together against the threat from the oceans. The spiderweb-like tendrils of the "Joyous Ones" are visible in nearly every scene, turning the atmosphere claustrophobic in spite of the bright colors and optimism of society. Our heroes face not only the immediate threat posed by the fish people, but also the ongoing judgment from above. Argyle has long been outspoken about the quiet threat posed by the space colonies, and though this film is less heavy-handed than some, the director's standpoint remains clear.

–Tinzee's Tea Room

Holly checked on Elden, who was asleep with a book on his chest, as she'd figured he would be, then went to Vitter's berth. Nielle welcomed her in and indicated that she should sit. The *Mermaid's Parasol's* staterooms were tiny, with barely space for a pair of beds and a side table, and a layout that suggested they were lucky to be getting that much. Nielle had nevertheless given it a festive look, dimming the light and arranging the cakes on the small table just so. Both were frosted into smooth discs about six inches across, one brilliant sky blue with a white flower on top, the other white with a blue flower. From the shape, they'd been cooked in a salvaged pre-Fall metal container; common enough in North America but considered quaint in Sino-India. They were on matching plastic plates.

"Oh. I didn't realize this was a date," Holly joked.

Nielle laughed. "If it is, does that mean I get a kiss?"

Holly gave her best 'I-won't-tell' look, and Nielle laughed again. It was easy and safe to joke, and if it turned out that Nielle was serious, Holly knew Elden wouldn't mind if she kissed another domestic. Sex might require her to ask first, but Holly didn't care one way or the other, so whatever Elden wanted was fine. She'd never had another domestic request her in bed before, though she'd certainly heard of it happening, mostly without benefactors' knowledge. Precedent or not, it didn't hurt to consider all of the possibilities. Holly was fairly certain Nielle was kidding. She could almost always read Elden's friends; other domestics' motives could be difficult but she was rarely wrong.

Nielle interrupted her thoughts, sitting across from her. "Have you ever been on a date?" she asked. "Not one your benefactor has sent you on, I mean. Well, I'm presuming—does he loan you?"

"Sometimes," Holly said.

"I thought so. Most Myawi benefactors like to show off." She looked Holly in the eye. "Does that bother you?"

"Being lent, or your assumption?"

"Either one."

"No."

"Oh, good. I get so sick of playing falsewife for Vitter all the time. When I get around housegirls sometimes I just can't resist the luxury of being *rude*." She laughed again. "I don't mean any offense. Anyway, I went to the Lotus Flower school when I was seventeen, so I'd been on a few dates by then. You went to Myawi much younger, than that, yes?"

"I was eight."

"As I thought. So you've never been on a date."

Holly shrugged. "Only as a gift from Elden to someone. Are you trying to make me uncomfortable, Nielle?"

"No, I'm not. I'm sorry."

"It's okay. You weren't succeeding."

Their eyes met, and they both laughed. "Oh, you're too much! I've met Myawis before, and you all have that trained, engaging manner, but you're charming for real, aren't you?"

"Madam Allterra called it *precocious,*" Holly offered.

"Well don't give it up. I want you to enjoy yourself, since this is your first date. And I'm only teasing about that, of course. Your mister has you off pleasing people enough, you won't have to worry about it from me. Unless you really want to, of course."

Again Holly's mind touched briefly on the idea of having sex with Nielle. The thought was a like a cobweb, barely there and then gone in an instant, insubstantial and too light to have any weight. "I'm happy to please

Elden," she said.

"What about yourself? No—don't answer that. I know what they taught you to say, and I hate hearing it. Let's have a date." She clapped her hands lightly with genuine pleasure. "Which cake do you prefer, the blue or the white?"

"Blue, I think." Holly smiled.

"Blue it is! Pardon my utensils, they're all I could filch from the galley. Can you believe that one of the crew asked if I'd be cooking for them on the voyage?" She blew a raspberry and cut Holly a piece of cake with a flimsy plastic knife. "I told him—politely—that he should ask my benefactor. That should fix him."

"Perhaps he was mistaken. Professor Ono is having a group dinner for the faculty tomorrow evening," Holly said. "The university-staff domestics will be taking over the galley for that."

"Of course you will. What're you having? I should have you save me something." The blue-frosted cake was white on the inside, and when Nielle cut herself a piece of the other it turned out to be white-frosted and blue on the inside. "Hmm. I don't know if that blue is authentic to North America."

"It could be," Holly said. "They don't have food coloring but if it's got blueberries in it, that will turn the pastry blue."

"Good point." Nielle took a bite. "You're right! It's blueberry. So. You're living in Singapore, correct? Do you have any friends?"

"Of course. Some of them are here—I believe you've met Lakshmi and Yuying. All of the other University department heads have housegirls, so I end up working alongside them frequently. If there's one thing these men love more than academia, it's throwing parties and inviting each other. Why do you ask?"

"Mr. Vitter may be moving to Singapore soon, to do some work with the university, and I'm hoping there will be familiar faces." Nielle coughed into her hand lightly, held up a finger to excuse herself, then coughed more deeply. "Oh my! Pardon me. So you'll show me around, of course?"

"Absolutely. Especially since we've shared this special night."

Nielle laughed, which started her coughing again.

"You've already met Lakshmi. I'll introduce you to Yuying once she's feeling better. You'll get along, I think. Are you okay?"

"Fine," Nielle said between coughs. "What school is she from?"

Before Holly could answer, Nielle let out a furious, strangled cough that doubled her over and turned her face red.

"Oh, uh," she choked. "Can't breathe." Nielle's throat had swollen alarmingly, and hectic blotches of red were appearing on her neck and near her collarbone.

"You're turning red," Holly said, forcing calm into her voice to mask her own rising panic. "I think you might be allergic. Look at me, Nielle." Nielle tried to respond, but only coughed weakly, clutching at her throat. The elegant silver weave pattern of her Lotus Flower collar was disappearing under swelling flesh. He eyes rolled in panic. *"Nielle!"* Holly said, more sharply. She took Nielle's hands, which clutched at hers. "Where's your key? Where does Mr. Vitter keep your key?" Domestics' collars were form fitted and locked to prevent theft. In case of medical emergency, though, the benefactors carried a key that would unlock the complicated clasp.

"Ack," Nielle choked and fell out of her chair.

Holly moaned as she realized Vitter might have the key with him, or in his luggage, and they were already two hundred miles from the coast. "Nielle!" she called again. The woman's face had gone an alarming shade of purple. She clutched frantically at her throat, trying in vain to dig her fingers down to the collar and pull the unyielding metal away.

Holly ran to the door, throwing it open. "Help!" she shouted, racing into the passenger cabin up front and toward the medical bay beyond. The *Mermaid's Parasol* was large enough to have a doctor on staff, thankfully. "Help, please!" Heads in the rows of seats, two wide chairs per side, turned to look at her.

A crew member was at her side immediately. "What's trouble?" he asked.

"She's suffocating," Holly replied, forcing herself to stay calm. "We need a Lotus Flower master key, to get her collar off."

"Domestic?"

"Yes, sir. Cabin 4."

The sailor keyed his radio and relayed the situation in Hindi.

Holly started moving toward the stateroom. The man followed, as did a couple of curious passengers.

"We don't carry master keys," he said. "What's happening?"

Holly didn't need to explain as they had already reached the room. Nielle was thrashing now, kicking at the wall and bed in desperation. She had knocked the table over and clawed at her neck until it bled. "I think it's an allergic reaction. She just ate cake."

"Shit," the sailor said, stepping forward and fighting a bit to get past the kicking legs, easing Nielle's hands away from her neck. It had swollen so much she looked like a bullfrog. The skin was stretched taut and the color of an eggplant. Her jaw worked as though she was gasping for breath, but she made no noise.

Holly heard footsteps behind her, urgent, and stepped to the side so she wasn't blocking the doorway. The ship's doctor fought his way through the other onlookers, asking the sailor a question in Hindi. Neither paid any attention to Holly. They blocked her view of Nielle, thankfully, and the doctor spoke in low tones. Her kicking slowed somewhat, partly because the sailor was holding her down. Holly had to listen to catch what was said; her Hindi was fluent but they were speaking rapidly. "No, we don't have master keys," the doctor snapped at the sailor. "Hardly have domestics on board, the keys cost too much. Is this the one traveling alone?" Nielle's heels drummed on the floor. "Knife. Miru, give me your knife, we're going to have to trach her."

Miru, the sailor, pulled a knife from his belt and handed it to the doctor. A thrill of alarm went through the deepening crowd of passengers at the door. Holly could feel them pressing against her back.

"Is there anything I can do?" Holly called from the doorway.

"I have all I need," he replied without looking up. From a form-fitting bag slung over his shoulder, he began pulling out gauze, bandages, sterile wipes and a short length of clear plastic tubing.

The assembled crowd let out a collective sigh as the doctor cut into Nielle's throat below the collar. Holly saw a flash of fresh blood, and then the doctor's hands covered it up, working quickly.

The noise seemed to annoy him. "I need these people out of here, Miru," he said. The sailor rose immediately, coming toward the door with his hands out in an unmistakable "show's over" gesture. Holly let herself be ushered out with the rest. If they needed her, they knew where she was.

Some of the other passengers took a bit more convincing, and as she left she could hear a rumor of food poisoning beginning to swirl.

Elden was awake when she let herself back into the cabin. Holly immediately put on a pleasant face, smoothing the concern and shock away. "Did I miss dinner?" he asked.

"Not yet."

"Damn."

She smiled, burying her confusion and concern for Nielle deeper. "I'll bring you a meal, when they serve."

"Thank you. Something about ocean travel makes me terribly antisocial. I just can't abide the thought of having to mingle with the other tourists. I'm sure they're perfectly pleasant people, and it's a terrible thing to say, but I find the stories of their Strip City experiences to be universally and uniquely depressing. Once you've fetched dinner, why don't we play chess?"

Elden had taught her to play, and once he'd discovered that she had an aptitude for it and was not shy about handing him defeats almost as often as victories, it had become a weekly thing for them. "Of course. There may be some delay in dinner, though. There was an incident. Nielle, Mr. Vitter's domestic, has fallen ill. Very badly." Holly refrained from speculation, though a part of her was certain that Nielle was dead. Guessing only led to rumors.

Elden's brows came together. "Oh, no! What's happened?"

"We were having a snack together and she began choking. It was food she brought with her, not the ship's food, but some of the other passengers are concerned that it was food poisoning."

"That poor girl. And such trouble for Mr. Vitter. He'll be coming to Singapore, you know."

"I heard, actually."

He put his book down and reached down for his slippers. "I'll need to go and see how she's doing, then. Keep an eye on her for him." Holly nodded and followed.

The stateroom door was closed, the clutch of passengers gone, so they went to the infirmary. The doctor was there, and a still figure lay on the table, covered by a sheet. There was an unpleasant scent in the air, burned around the edges by disinfectant until it was just a *dead* smell. Holly recognized Nielle's shoes, and felt as though someone had kicked her in the stomach. Only half an hour ago they'd been laughing together, pretending to flirt.

Elden introduced himself. "I'm a colleague of Mr. Vitter's," he added. "I'd like to offer assistance, if there's anything I can do. What happened?"

"She had an allergic reaction to something she ate," the doctor replied, speaking English because Elden had addressed him so. "We don't have facilities to do an autopsy, or transport the body, so we'll have to bury her at sea. I've taken samples of the cake she was eating and some blood, but my preliminary accident report is that she had an allergic reaction and choked to death. You reported that she was wheezing and unable to breathe. I attempted a tracheotomy, but was unable to clear her airway."

"She was coughing, not wheezing," Holly corrected.

"I'm sure you were mistaken. Allergic reactions constrict the airway and cause wheezing." The doctor seemed genuinely upset beneath his clinical demeanor, and she had to make a conscious effort to resist frowning. The emergency had rattled him; she supposed that he was the sort of man who preferred easily-solved puzzles and relatively minor transit issues. He genuinely wanted to help, but was neither used to nor happy with challenges, and content to stick with his own narrative.

"I'm sure you did everything you could," Elden said.

Holly touched her own collar, unconsciously. Elden carried her key with him, she knew, though she'd never seen it. An image of Nielle's purple face flickered through her mind. The doctor hadn't said anything about her neck swelling up and the collar strangling her, but that was what had happened. But it couldn't happen to her. Nielle wasn't the first domestic to die after her collar couldn't be removed during an emergency, but they were always freak accidents, and Elden was prepared for such an emergency. She'd be fine.

"If you could sign this form," the doctor said, handing Elden an electronic clipboard. "In her benefactor's stead."

"Of course." While Elden busied himself with reading the paperwork, Holly looked around the infirmary, finally meeting the doctor's eyes. He looked at her with sadness, and his eyes went to her collar—larger and more elaborate than Nielle's Lotus Flower collar—before he turned away. Holly told herself again that it wouldn't happen to her. It was a danger, to be sure, but they had thought ahead, addressed it.

As they returned to the room, Elden said, "Such a shame."

"Will her family know?" Holly's imagination served up an image of Nielle sinking slowly into the depths of the Pacific, hair drifting delicately around her face in slow motion, sunlight glinting on the collar's bright facets as she sank.

"I'm sure the Lotus Flower school—that's where she was from, right?—will tell her family. Does that upset you?"

"It's an upsetting situation."

"That it is. Why don't we get in touch with Mr. Vitter once we're home, and let him know what happened. I'm sure the travel company will report to him, of course, and his insurance, but I think he'd appreciate something more than just a sterile document. I can't imagine what I'd do if something happened to you."

"I suppose I shall make sure nothing does, then," she replied, eliciting a chuckle.

chapter 14

One hundred and twenty-one days before Princess Aiyana's trimester celebration

>> A ship carrying the survivors of an expedition to South America was rescued off the coast of Peru this week. The *Livewire* left Singapore six weeks ago with a crew of forty-two, bound for the Peruvian rainforest on an ironwood-harvesting mission. The ship was reported overdue on the fourteenth, and its discovery with eight survivors aboard came as "no surprise" to seasoned mariners who are familiar with the dangers facing expeditions to the formid-controlled South American continent.

The price of lignum vitae ironwood, which is used for a number of medical and artistic purposes and comes only from the rare lignum vitae tree, encourages several hundred mariners annually to send ships to South America in search of the material. Though dangerous, the work is very lucrative. Julius Harvester, captain of the Vergissmeinnicht, has made multiple trips to South America, some more successful than others. He says, "You make landfall on the continent, you should be prepared to lose half of the people what goes ashore, maybe more…"

—Owl News Syndicate

Sometime in the small hours of the night Nielle's body was dumped overboard with whatever ceremony the sailors saw fit to give her. Even Holly missed the short funeral, and she rarely slept more than four hours a night. She was surprised, and quite dismayed. She had thought she would fold a paper boat for Nielle and send it with her; she doubted the girl was much for tradition, but Holly felt better making some gesture. Her feelings about it were confused and she wanted to do something and put it out of her mind. The secretive disposal of the body left her feeling unsettled, as though the business would be forever left unfinished.

The captain and crew urged the other passengers to relax and not let the incident spoil the voyage; death at sea was a peculiar thing, but not unheard of. The doctor reassured everyone that the food was safe, and that Nielle had died due to an allergic reaction, not bad food.

Nevertheless, it cast a pall. Holly could tell it was on the minds of the other passengers; the boat was too small for anyone to avoid the hallway where the staterooms were, and the door to Vitter's cabin remained closed.

Elden decided that they'd have their dinner regardless. "Tragedy shouldn't deter us, after all, and should serve to help underscore the unpredictable nature of life in North America. The arrangements to use the large room have been made, correct?"

The ship had a communal dining room and a smaller room designed for meetings. Holly had gotten the impression from talking to the crew that it was reserved primarily for staff meetings, but they had agreed to let the university group use it for dinner, and she nodded. "I made sure the room was properly set up and our food separated from the ship's. I brought several North American dishes to make."

"Excellent! You've worked so hard this week, Holly. A bit of rest would do you well, I think."

"Yes, perhaps after the party—"

"No, no, I want you to rest. I know you and Nielle were friends. I'll let Aidanab handle the rest. His girl Yinka can do a fine job."

Holly sighed, swallowing a bitter lump of disappointment. "She will," she agreed.

Yinka was from the Waveform school, a smaller domestic house in Mandalay, and she was odd. Dark-skinned and round-faced, Yinka had emigrated to the Brother Nations from Tanzania and the talk was that being a domestic was about all that she was suited for. She had a brusque mien, a fantastic eye for detail and a tendency toward obsessiveness. Holly suspected she had some form of autism.

Holly had planned and supplied for a seafood medley, with a lobster and tomato bisque to start and steamed lobster, pan-seared scallops and boiled oysters in a buttered, real-cream roux as the main course. She was loath to turn her carefully selected menu over to someone else for preparation, but if it had to be anyone...well, at least she didn't have to stand aside while Shmi destroyed it, and burned the cake besides.

Efficient little Yinka didn't let Holly's discomfort deter her in the least from throwing a proper party as she saw it, even going so far as to rearrange the dining room upon her arrival. "This is the way I prefer it," Yinka said matter-of-factly. "This way will make it easier for everyone." She was not one for idle chatter, and Holly respected her wishes with a smile and secretly clenched teeth.

Of course the party came together well, and chances were most of the blended faculty and graduate students in attendance (many still bleary from the conference's hectic schedule) were unaware that Holly wasn't in charge. This made the humiliation of being forced out of control only slightly easier to take.

Lakshmi helped to keep her mind off of it, peppering her with a generous helping of gossip between courses, as the domestics had a chance to convene in the *Mermaid's Parasol's* galley. Rather than using the ship's staff, Yinka dictated that the five housegirls traveling with the university group would act as wait-staff for the entire party. Again, the fact that it was the same decision Holly herself would have made was more of an annoyance than a relief. For what seemed like the hundredth time in an hour, she put on a neutral, pleasant face and let Yinka call the shots.

"Wait," Lakshmi caught her as she was carrying two bowls of bisque out, following Yuying and a girl named Maire who'd traveled with one of the graduate students, "you're going to the right side of the table. Rehsil's there. Is that okay?"

"It's fine," she said, wishing that the disagreement between Elden and Dr. Rehsil over the way the latter had treated her hadn't been so public. "He hasn't been grabby. And Elden says that if he touches me I've permission to make him stop."

"What's the matter?" Maire asked.

"Holly and Dr. Rehsil."

"I forgot about that," Yinka said, overhearing. "Holly, you and Yuying can trade if you want. Rehsil has the bisque without onions, don't mix up the bowls."

"It's fine," Holly repeated. "And the bisque is getting cold."

"I remember now," Maire said. "Professor Ono sued Dr. Rehsil, didn't he?"

"Wasn't a suit. But it was about Holly. Ono loaned her to him, and he *tortured* her. Broke two of her fingers, tied her up with ropes." Lakshmi lowered her voice to a whisper. "There was a dog..."

"There wasn't a dog," Holly said.

"Still, Rehsil's a pig." Yuying had a shovel-shaped face with a broad jaw and a long nose, and as a result she had an excellent glower.

"That's an insult to pigs," Maire muttered. "You know he's under investigation, right? After his last housegirl died, they barred him from benefactoring any more."

"Tince *died?*"

"Shmi, I thought you knew all the news. She did. About four months ago."

"I thought he sent her back to Axtellia's?"

"He did," Maire said sourly, "but only because she was in a coma. Fell in the shower, he says." she added.

"Of course she did. That's why they're investigating." There was a murmur of assent.

"They investigate if you lose more than three domestics in five years," Yinka said. "It's law. The soup needs to go." She snapped her fingers.

"That won't stop the goat," Shmi said. "They always find ways to get another one." Yuying and Maire went out and Yinka turned to the stove; Lakshmi touched Holly's shoulder, urging her to wait a moment. She took four steps to the sink and stuck two fingers down her throat, gagging audibly. She turned around with her hand cupped. "Which one is Dr. Rehsil's?"

"This one—oh you can't—*Shmi!*" Holly gasped as Lakshmi dumped the contents of her hand into the bowl, then swirled her fingers around in it to mix it in. Holly looked up to see if Yinka had noticed, but it had gone unnoticed. She almost reflexively dumped the soup down the sink, but then she'd have to get another bowl, assuming Yinka had even made enough extra for Rehsil to have a second helping.

"There. Nice and special for him." She grinned, and while Holly hesitated she nudged her through the door, past the point of no return. "Don't let it get cold."

The relative quiet of the kitchen was replaced by a hubbub of conversation as she passed through the swinging door. Yinka had sat guests down both sides so there was room for all twenty-four of the university's group. Holly had soup for Rehsil and the student who had accompanied him, and she made her way easily down the side.

Holly relaxed into her usual serving pace, but was anything but calm. Regardless of how she felt about Rehsil, she couldn't serve him a bowl of soup with *vomit* in it! That wasn't the Myawi way. But it was too late to turn around and return to the kitchen either; that would be awkward. And there was a good chance the Dineens would let Rehsil flog Shmi if they found out what she'd done. Holly briefly considered pretending to stumble and spilling the soup, but such public clumsiness was, if anything, even less acceptable than just serving it. She moved down the long table to where Dr. Rehsil sat, heart racing with each step. It felt like everyone in the room was staring at her. And then she was standing at his chair. No other ideas had occurred to her; she had no choice but to offer the proper bowl to him. Rehsil was one of those people whose ugly personality was perfectly masked by his face. He had flawless tawny skin with a warm hazel undertone, a strong jaw and a neatly trimmed black mustache that perfectly split the difference between action-star bushy and teen-heartthrob wispy. He was athletic, had a full head of black hair and looked ten years younger than Elden, though the men were both in their early fifties. Rehsil was Elden's counterpart in the North American Studies department; together the two of them were tasked with keeping the university's output current in that arena with regular papers and presentations.

The bowls and saucers of lobster bisque glided to the table right where they belonged, but before she could move on and escape back to the kitchen, she felt Rehsil's thick-fingered hand on her wrist. "It's very nice to see you, Holly," he said. "You look marvelous, after your trip to the homeland."

"Thank you," she replied, moving her arm out from under his.

The hand transferred itself to her waist. "Has it made you wish you could return?"

From the head of the table, Elden noticed the two of them talking. Holly caught his eye, saw him clearing his throat to intervene, and gave him the barest of headshakes, letting him know he didn't need to speak up for her. No need to cause a scene.

Elden caught the look, nodded and returned to his conversation with Professor Hatton, though she could tell he was still watching. Dr. Rehsil's hand dropped to her hip and tightened. "If you were mine, I wouldn't risk taking you so far from home," he hissed.

She thought of cutting remarks in two languages but defaulted to politeness. "I'd feel quite safe, I'm sure," she said. Putting herself two steps ahead in the conversation, she could see how he might take that as a compliment, and took steps to extricate herself without encouraging him. "I'm sorry to hear about Tince. I hadn't had a chance to say."

He squeezed her again, and Holly turned gently against his wrist, her motion forcing the hand off in a natural, nonaggressive way. His smile turned stern. "She was nothing," he said, his tone making it clear that he didn't believe she was sincere. Holly struggled not to react—it was the only sincere thing she'd said to him so far. "I'll get another as soon as my name is cleared. And it will be. Perhaps I'll buy one of your Myawi sisters."

"Good luck," she said. They both knew he couldn't afford a Myawi and almost certainly wouldn't pass the background check. Elden wouldn't get angry if she was rude to Dr. Rehsil, so she walked away without excusing herself.

This had the regrettable effect of making him call after her, and when Rehsil snapped, "Hey!" she stiffened a bit but kept going as if she hadn't realized he was addressing her. Either he'd make the other guests think she was being rude, or they wouldn't notice. Those who knew about the unpleasantness he'd subjected her to might whisper about it to their seat-mates, but the timbre of the room didn't change much; most of them didn't even notice.

And he had a fouled bowl of lobster bisque, that she'd given to him. The thought put a cold lump in her gut, even though she'd gotten away with it.

Holly went through the swinging door into the kitchen, escaping the spotlight, and stepped immediately to the side, putting her back to the refrigerator door. The metal surface hummed under her fingertips. The galley of the *Mermaid's Parasol* seemed suddenly unfamiliar, even though she'd been in and out of it all day. What was she doing here? For a moment Holly couldn't remember why she'd come through the door, or what was on the other side of it, or what she was meant to do next. Her collar seemed to squeeze her neck and she took a single deep breath, trying to center herself. Lakshmi came through the door a moment later and touched Holly's hand as she went past. The flyby reassurance was unnecessary, but appreciated.

There wasn't time to waste being upset, though; there was a party going on, after all, and even if she wasn't in charge, it *was* her responsibility. Holly jumped right back into the fray; the first course had been served, and Yinka needed them to go on to preparing the roux. Maire was younger and Yuying had been ill, so Yinka had them in the kitchen getting the seafood ready and washing the dishes, respectively. Holly joined them; it was a convenient chance to make sure they were working well.

Lakshmi was back in a moment. "All set. What's next, Yinka?" Yinka quickly put her to work searing scallops.

"Hey, Yuying," Shmi said, "tell them about the professor's sketchbook."

Yuying was up to her elbows in washwater, and she blushed and giggled. She was a bit loopy, thanks to a massive dose of antibiotics she'd taken.

"No, seriously. It's the funniest thing, you have to hear." Holly smiled at the gossip and shook her head. The others rarely prompted her for embarrassing details about Elden; she wouldn't let that aspect of her Myawi training slip even for friends. But Yuying was a Lotus Flower, so there was nothing holding her back.

"What sketchbook?" Maire asked.

"The professor has a sketchbook. He draws in it every day," she said. "There are hundreds of pictures. And all of them are pictures of himself, doing the same thing..." She trailed off and giggled again.

"What's he doing?"

"He's punching animals. In the face." The housegirls broke up into giggles, kept just quiet enough that they wouldn't carry out into the dining room; even Holly smiled. "I'm not kidding. All sorts of animals. Dogs and cats. Horses, turtles, giraffes, badgers. An elephant. Any animal you can name. My favorite is the pangolin."

"Penguin?" Yinka asked.

"Pangolin. It's a—"

"I know what a pangolin is."

Yuying ducked her head. "Sorry. But he has a penguin too. Several different species in fact."

"Why does he draw that?"

"I don't know. I just saw the sketchbook when he left it open, then went back and looked at them all later. I don't think he knows I've seen it."

"Professor Aidanab's a strange one," Maire said.

"He's not so bad," Yuying said.

"Not a bad kind of strange. No stranger than any of the other profs, certainly."

"Time to refill drinks," Yinka announced, snapping them all to attention. Holly nodded and left the younger girls to the dishes and tea prep.

The rest of the evening was thankfully uneventful, and probably would have been even if Yinka hadn't made a point of keeping Holly away from Rehsil for the rest of the night. It was a fancy bit of social engineering that was smoothly handled; Holly was impressed.

chapter 15

*One hundred and seventeen days before Princess
Aiyana's trimester celebration*

>> Soressonhaus announced today the upcoming auction of an impressive collection of antique furniture, housewares and other goods. The pre-Colony Conflict goods are part of a recent discovery in the ruins of London, brought back by the *Wan Niguel. Wan Niguel* was dispatched to the Atlantic Ocean and North Sea last year for purposes of geological analysis as well as humanitarian aid to the scattered tribes still living on the British Isles. After making landfall, the crew traded medical supplies for directions to a large cache of antiques that survived the unrest that brought Europe to its knees a century ago, following the Colony Conflict. Most experts agree that the most significant sales will be the two lots of antique Rolex and Patek Philippe wristwatches, a pair of Guarneri violins, and a well-preserved Nissan Skyline automobile…

                                                          —Owl News Syndicate

>> Oh yeah, right around the time of the Colony Conflict, things were pretty dire. The UN was screaming for limitations on HNE research before someone conjured up another super-storm like the one that pretty much erased Miami and the Florida Keys, not to mention the shifter issue. India had just fought a very short, surprise war in which it crushed Pakistan, and China was making noises about calling bullshit and stepping in. With something like ninety percent of women sterile from ORDS and the few fertile ones getting caught in the crossfire half the time, the last thing the world needed was a massive war. Never mind all the little ones—I remember reading that there were no fewer than sixty-seven active conflicts going on that year, and that's just governments shooting at governments. But, of course, nobody was willing to be the one to step forward and say so. At least, nobody who stayed alive for long.

    Then the Colony Conflict, the Fall of North America and Europe, the EPRC bombardment, whatever you want to call it, happened. It was a bad day for 'sorry,' that's for sure. India, China, South Africa and Australia all petitioned the colonies—while the bombardment was going on, mind you, so on the other side of the world, cities were crumbling around unsuspecting civilians—for mercy and amnesty. And it was granted, with some significant terms. Nuclear arsenals and missiles capable of leaving the atmosphere had to be disassembled, or the colonies would disassemble them with the EPRC and all treaties would be void. Satellites would continue to exist only at the colonies' agreement, on a case-by-case basis. North America and Europe are blackout zones, as well as no-fly zones. No air travel across the Pacific, though flights over Africa are allowed.

Hey, at least it put a stop to all of the fighting. Well, almost all of it.

But we're talking about China and India here. Two nations each thrust into bed with a hated enemy, with strict instructions not to fight. The colonies did not hesitate to imply that they would intervene should war break out between China and India, and they were not specific as to whose side they'd take.

So, the two decided to kiss and make up, and the Brother Nations was born. Sort of. A staggering influx of refugees from Western Europe helped to blur nationalistic issues and keep things from blowing up—as well as giving people convenient scapegoats. The vast increase in intermarriage forced upon everyone by ORDS helped too. You can only hate your neighbor so much when you have to marry his daughter to keep your family line alive, right?

Fast forward a hundred years or so of change. Socially, China and India get along just fine. Politically, the story is one of infighting behind closed doors, constant maneuvering, and often thinly veiled hostility. Smaller, disadvantaged nations on the subcontinent were divvied up between the two through alliances and absorption, and exist now primarily as states or de facto colonies within the greater Sino-Indian republic. If you follow politics closely, you'll no doubt notice that Korea, Malaysia, Taiwan and the rest almost always take a partisan line when there's a disagreement between China and India. It's fractious, but it's stable, and nobody wants to upset that.

China and India do realize that they're in a good position. Allied, they're the last superpower on the planet in terms of technology, wealth, quality of living and military might. Australia and South Africa got stroppy during negotiations after the Colony Conflict, and had to dismantle their air forces. While Sino-India's honor-bound to refrain from exploiting this advantage and conquering them, it's aware that it could if it wanted to. The colonies seem to be okay with letting Sino-India intervene in smaller conflicts, since that tends to result in less chaos, not more. That's why there was no protest when they intervened in Oman and the Gulf, when the nonsense broke out over there between the folks who were left after that nuclear exchange before the Colony Conflict. And it worked—things are actually quiet over there, and Egypt and Kenya have taken steps toward opening trade.

Now, Sino-India has been told to stay out of North America, at least on a large scale, but the fact that Strip City was allowed and that smaller expeditions are okay suggests that the colonies want only to avoid a major invasion. Three of the Five Families of Strip City are Beijing-based, you know, and that country has sent emissaries to other parts of the continent as well, so there's clearly a desire to get North America in China's pocket before making it an equal partner in the Brother Nations. This is a development that India would almost certainly protest vehemently. The long-term economic advantages would be huge, especially in the event of a falling out between China and India. In fact, if the balance was upset to that extreme, it might even provoke one...

—Excerpt from Marcus McEvoy's interview with sailor Razor Witt

Holly was grateful when the *Mermaid's Parasol* arrived at the dock in Singapore.

Elden had gotten on the phone as soon as they'd come within range, so the car was waiting for them at the dock. "I've spoken to Vitter," Elden told her, "and he asked me to collect his luggage, rather than entrusting it to the dock crew. See it to the car. I've got to go directly to campus. I'll see you at home this evening."

Holly nodded. Elden was nothing if not predictable; she'd expected he would go straight to his office, which gave her a chance to do a once-over of the house, tending to whatever dust had collected in the two weeks they'd been gone, and to have dinner ready for him. There would be a large pile of mail, both physical and electronic, for her to go through as well.

But first, there was additional luggage to be dealt with. Vitter and Nielle had been traveling light, it seemed; the crew of the *Mermaid's Parasol* handed over a single small, wheeled Lancelot-brand suitcase, a garment bag and an open-topped plastic bag with odds and ends that she recognized as Nielle's toiletries and other sundries that would have been unpacked in the stateroom. The crewman who handed the items over had her sign a form, and seemed embarrassed about it. Holly thanked him politely before adding the suitcase to the cart with her own bags.

Elden's car was a Daimler g-50 City, several years old and painted a particularly garish shade of red. The little car was limited on cargo space, so Holly filled the trunk and then piled the rest of the luggage into the child-sized back seat. She climbed back into the front, tapped the auto-drive and return-home switches, then sat back as the steering wheel retracted to give her more space. The car's electric motor hummed and it quickly joined traffic.

They lived northeast of the blocks of skyscrapers that defined the heart of Singapore, in one of the housing towers adjacent to campus, so she had at least a thirty-minute ride in this traffic. She tapped the news icon on the screen. A confident-sounding male voice read the latest headlines, working his way through political, entertainment, weather and economic news. When one of the synopses sounded interesting, Holly tapped the appropriate icon on the screen to hear the whole story.

While she caught up on the news, she checked the bag with Nielle's sundries, trying to determine if any of it was simply trash that Vitter might not want returned. It was unlikely that he'd have much use for hair curlers or Nielle's toothpaste, after all. Then again, he might want such things for his next domestic, if he got another. Best just to return everything. There was such a thing as helping too much.

At the bottom of the bag was a paper-wrapped package about the size of half a loaf of bread. The paper was elegantly sealed with wax and a ribbon, which caught Holly's eye, and as she was about to set it aside she saw that the seal bore the stylized elephant's head logo used by the Ivory Sisters.

She chuffed in surprise. The Ivory Sisters was a cadre of activists who focused on the rights of domestics, led by a pair of women named Phoebe and Jae, whose real identities weren't known. The group campaigned against domestic school recruiting drives, protested for additional rights for infertile women, and Holly had even heard that they would kidnap housegirls, remove their collars, and turn them loose far from home, encouraging them to start new lives. The Ivory Sisters weaponized their sense of humor; their protests were frequently harmless but poignant pranks, such as the time they had dressed over fifty women as Rising Sun girls and had them fall all over each other trying to wait on Prime Minister Riyat as he attempted to walk from his office to his car.

It was most intriguing that Nielle had this package—and not surprising, considering the girl's cavalier attitude toward being a domestic. Was it the package she'd collected at the little store in Old Town? Holly thought that it might be. Whether Vitter knew what Nielle was up to was another question entirely. Some benefactors, Elden included, disagreed with the Sisters' methods but did agree that they had worthwhile things to say. Elden might not object if she asked permission to work with them. Holly didn't care to do that, but the idea of a Sino-India without the Ivory Sisters seemed like a sad thing, and she certainly didn't want to be responsible for making it thus. Best to be careful about who she showed it to, apart from Elden. She put the package in her own bag, so she could think about what to do with it later.

The rest of Nielle's effects were more easily sorted, and she was done long before she got home. Thinking she'd probably be travel-weary later, Holly closed her eyes and napped for a few minutes, waking immediately when she felt the car turn down the familiar drop into the parking garage. Their tower was a modest one. It was quiet, populated largely by other academics. The four-building complex was concealed behind large, carefully tended hedges that formed ten-foot living walls around the outdoor exercise areas. Elden had joked that it must remind her of the walled cities in North America, but she had politely corrected him.

The car cruised silently into the underground garage, parked on the inductive charger in Elden's spot and shut down to await the next errand. Holly unloaded the bags onto a cart, took the elevator to the twenty-third floor, and staged everything in the mudroom.

Elden's home was decorated in approximation of a pre-Fall North American style, with many real antiques mixed in among the reproductions. It was larger than Elden needed; Holly speculated that he might have bought it hoping one day to fill the three extra bedrooms with a wife and children, or possibly with children from her. As it was, the space was taken up by books and antiques.

A quick walk-through of the large kitchen, great room and fancy sitting room, pantry, dining room, all four bedrooms and Elden's office confirmed that all was well, and Holly had the house squared away, the mail delivery resumed, their bags unpacked and a menu planned for dinner in less than forty minutes. She anticipated Elden would be home by seven. Thankfully it was Tuesday and her usual tasks for the day were light—after helping Elden with his evening research and sex, she'd be able to get herself to sleep perhaps earlier than usual. If the long trip began to get to her, she'd bump with her electrostim and get through it that way.

Within minutes of her having the house back online, Lakshmi called. Holly barely had time to get the video display to warm up before Lakshmi started talking. "Wasn't that *fun*? I can't believe we went to North America! You must be headed to the shops. You need to go to the shops, right? So do I, we shall go together. We can talk on the way there!"

It could be hard to get a word in edgewise with Lakshmi when she was wound up. Holly was used to it. The Dineens lived four floors down, so she spent a lot of time with the little Axtellia girl.

"That sounds like a good plan. When are you free?"

"Now. The kids are off to school, and the lady of the house—" Lakshmi glanced over her shoulder and her voice dropped to a whisper, "—is passed out drunk. The mister and missy had a long fight last night. Haven't spoken since we disembarked."

"Oh no! What about?"

"Think Professor Dineen wants another housegirl now. Missy says one is enough."

Holly sighed. She wasn't in the mood for gossip; she wanted to get back to her routine. She considered the tasks she had left for the day. She could run to the shops now. It hadn't been her original plan, but she was willing to improvise for the chance to spend some time with Lakshmi. In spite of traveling together, they'd hardly seen each other. "Let's talk in the car," she said. "Coming up or should I come down?"

Holly barely had time to get out her electrostim crown, bump, and then put it away before Lakshmi appeared at the door, her hair not quite brushed enough, cheerfully flushed from running up the steps. Her plain Axtellia collar glinted with anodized bronze at her neck, and in her haste she'd tied her belt wrong.

Holly fixed Shmi's clothes with a grin. "You didn't need to rush, silly. I wouldn't go without you. Do you want me to braid your hair?"

"Nah." Lakshmi threw her arms around Holly in a big leaping hug, and they shared a long embrace.

"It's so good to see you, too," Holly said in Hindi.

"I'm sorry we didn't have any time together on the trip back," Lakshmi replied in kind as they walked to the elevator.

"Agreed." Holly had entered her destination from the house terminal, so the car was ready for them in the parking garage, air conditioning already whirring. It was a rare sunny day, but hot and humid, and the car had warmed up considerably since she'd parked it an hour ago even though it was indoors. Once Holly typed her access code, the little Daimler chimed a welcome message and set off dutifully.

"I want to hear all about what happened!" Lakshmi said, switching back to English. "You were there when Nielle died!"

Holly nodded, feeling the sting of loss again. "She had an allergic reaction, the ship's doctor said. I think her collar strangled her. There was no key." She almost told Shmi about the doctor correcting her, but found she couldn't bring herself to potentially spread a rumor.

Where Elden hadn't understood, Lakshmi did instantly. "That poor girl. What about her benefactor?"

"I haven't met him. I will, I'm sure. Apparently Mr. Vitter has an interest in North American studies as well. And now I'm thinking about Nielle again, and I'd rather not. Tell me something fun." Shmi played with the radio feed, eschewing the politics in favor of entertainment headlines.

"Well...the new Vengopal movie is coming out this week. You have free time on Saturday afternoons, right? We could go."

"Is that the one set in South America?"

"With the bug-shifters, yes!"

"It sounds silly."

"But it's based on truth! There really are bug-shifters there. They're termites, I think. They took over the whole continent."

"They're called formids. I've read about them," Holly said. The car glided into the downtown shopping district, and the sheds and awnings of the farmer's market slid into view.

"Oh, this is *so* much faster than the bus," Lakshmi said. "I wish Professor Dineen would give me access to the car."

The auto-drive chimed, letting Holly know they were at their destination. She tapped the touchscreen and the car pulled up to a loading zone at the curb. Once they were out, Holly took the remote and sent the car off to find a parking spot.

"So, the movie?" Lakshmi asked. "It'll be fun, promise."

Holly laughed. "That's what you said about the last one!"

"Yeah, but...okay, I'm sorry about that. But really, Shairpie trying to pretend she's a loving mother looking for her lost baby when she's been sterile since she was thirteen? You can't have had high expectations for that. She only got that role because she's the director's half-sister. At least you know this one's mindless going in. You can't possibly be disappointed by Rahul Muzzin and Noah Bosel fighting giant termites."

"I'll give it a try," Holly said. Vengopal's films were entertaining escapism, if nothing else. "Oh, I've missed this," she said as they entered the open-air market. "Good vegetables don't exist in Strip City."

"The professor made you cook? Isn't that what hotels are supposed to do?"

Holly indulged a humble smile. "Force of habit. Besides, the hotel's chaat was terrible. I made Professor Ono's snacks and lunchboxes myself."

Shmi shook her head. "I have no words," she said. "Did you see the construction for the trimester celebration? They're completely rebuilding the old stadium."

"I read about it."

"Are you going to go?"

She shrugged. "Elden hasn't talked about it."

"The university has invites. Faculty are fighting over them. You should work your magic and get invites for yourself and Professor Ono."

"That'll depend on what he wants to do."

"Oh, you're *sure* to be able to go! How could they not send you? You're the only Myawi at the school."

The market was a wide space between buildings in an otherwise industrial area, walled in by skyscrapers on three sides and a low-rise slash of warehouses that flowed toward the ocean like a river of solar panel-tiled roofs on the fourth. The market was cross-shaped and covered by umbrella-like awnings offering equal protection from rain or sun. Large solar-powered fans kept the air moving, helping to bring the heat down to a comfortable level. Of course it was moderately thronged, as usual, and Holly and Lakshmi began shopping with practiced ease. They stopped while Shmi looked through a selection of curries and spices, and Holly made a point of not looking over her friend's shoulder. Most domestics had recipes they'd learned from the school's archives or made up themselves, and it was impolite to seem as though one was trying to steal them. Besides, Holly had left Myawi with far more culinary skills than Axtellia's taught.

"Keep an eye out for college boys," Shmi said when she finished. "It's that season again, it seems." It was not an uncommon entertainment for young college men to assault domestics. Gangs of them would attack housegirls, sometimes raping them, and then steal their collars. The police would intervene if the boys were caught in the act, but wealthy parents usually ensured that consequences, if any, were minimal. It was a game to them; many young toughs were even unaware that domestics were actually protected by the laws. "A girl got stolen just last week at the market down by the docks. Axtellia girl." Lakshmi paid for her spices and tucked them into a sleeve pocket.

"Did you know her?"

"No. Less said the better though, it's bad luck. Tell me what you remember most about the wasteland. I still haven't forgiven you for taking that trip."

She thought about it a moment. "The carcasses of cars and trucks," Holly said. "When we took the adventure tour—which was ridiculously fake, by the way, you missed nothing—we passed a few when we were on the real scav road. If a vehicle breaks, the scavs will strip it of everything useful. Eventually all that's left is the shell that's too heavy to drag away, and then it becomes part of the landscape. I saw some covered in grapevines. It's haunting, but beautiful."

"You should write a poem," Shmi said. She stayed close to Holly, as the taller woman had an easier time breaking a path through the crowd.

"I'll leave that to Ephilia," Holly said with a smile.

"Oh, but you'd be fantastic! Especially with your accent."

"Perhaps. But it's not my style."

"If you say so." Their second stop was a vegetable stall, followed by another and then a bread shop. Holly made her own bread, but liked to buy her flour from a particular seller. She used her halting Mandarin with him, knowing that it tended to get her better service. Shmi followed suit, filling her own bag. As they left the baker's, she looked past Holly's shoulder and said, "Where to next? Also, don't turn fast, but we've got stalkers. Four boys, about six stalls down."

Holly smiled, picking up on Lakshmi's subtlety. The occasional threat of violence was a fact of life for unaccompanied domestics. From a distance they would appear to be sharing a moment, not discussing potential danger. She took note of the boys out of the corner of her eye and got back to business. "I need to get a pineapple," she said, nodding toward a vendor across the center aisle. "I didn't like the ones up at the front." They crossed, keeping an eye on the boys who were following. Holly paused a moment and looked directly at them. They were definitely college students, wearing the familiar uniforms of first-years. The one whose eye she caught started back for a moment as if surprised to see her face full on, then realized he was looking back at her and averted his gaze. Sometimes it was enough if they knew they were being watched.

Today, no such luck. Holly and Lakshmi made several more stops, picking up meat, fresh eggs and more vegetables (as well as Holly's pineapple) and the four young men continued to follow, becoming more brazen.

"They're finding their stones," Lakshmi said nervously. "We'd better ask for help."

There was no guarantee that a shopkeeper would call a policeman for them. Bystanders often failed to get involved in incidents involving attacks on domestics, for fear of awkwardly offending a person who was within his right to treat his domestic as he saw fit. The police would generally take them seriously, but that could lead to further embarrassment when they had to call Elden to pick her up.

Holly said, "We have the car. Let's just go home. I still need cheese. I'll have to go out again." She took out the car's remote and triggered the pickup signal.

"Where will the car meet us?"

"At whatever loading zone is closest. We can keep walking."

"Yes, do that." Lakshmi's voice shook. "If they get close to us, get behind me. I have a Spitting Cobra." She took a small packet out of her bag and palmed it.

"Shmi! Put that thing away!" The Spitting Cobra was a lime-green triangular bulb about the size of a plum pit, with long wings on either side so it couldn't be accidentally swallowed. It was designed to be held in the mouth, where a bite would break the seal and enable the user to spit a jet of aerosolized sulfuric acid from a tube protruding from her lips. Spitting Cobras were illegal, owing to the inability to keep a cloud of acid from injuring innocent bystanders or property. Since domestics' benefactors could be held liable for injury and damage they caused, even to attackers, it was doubly ridiculous for Shmi to be carrying one. "Where did you get that?"

"Makes it safer to go out at night," she replied.

"Put it *away*. There's a breeze. You'll burn your own face off." Shmi stowed the Spitting Cobra as they moved into the hot air outside the market's fans. They were soon on a nearly deserted sidewalk, dramatically isolated compared to the bustle behind them. Holly quickly saw that a spate of afternoon deliveries had arrived, leaving the nearest curbside loading zones choked with trucks and other commercial vehicles. The car wouldn't be able to meet them here. They kept moving rather than stop outside the doors, Holly keeping the car's remote in her hand. She didn't turn, but heard the doors open again when they'd gone half a block, followed by at least four sets of footsteps and the sounds of the boys' laughter.

Elden's little tomato-colored Daimler passed them, then pulled obediently into a clear space at the curb a few cars ahead of them, popping its doors open. The pace of the footsteps behind them increased immediately as the boys figured it out. Lakshmi grabbed Holly's elbow. "No time for dignity, *run!*" They raced for the car.

Holly got there first, threw her purchases inside—*oh dear, the eggs*—and then pushed Lakshmi ahead of her and into the car as a hand grabbed her elbow. Holly turned with it, rotating her arm out of the boy's grip and taking a step to the side so he came off-balance. The step also took her away from the car, and in that moment another of the college boys got between her and the open door, grabbing for Shmi.

Holly evaded another clutching hand, then lunged over the boy, slapping the emergency button on the dash. In the event of a mugging, the autodrive had a quick-escape algorithm that immediately fled if the coast was clear, as well as signalling the police. The Daimler's electric motor spooled up instantly and it accelerated. Someone outside the car grabbed Holly's ankles and she was dragged back out the open door. The car raced up the block with Shmi and one of the college boys inside, the door closing automatically as soon as it was unobstructed.

Holly struggled against the hands on her ankles, kicking out but keeping her eyes on Elden's car as it disappeared around the corner. She had the nonsensical thought that if she could break free, she could run after it and catch up. It was a ridiculous notion. A second pair of hands clamped down on her arms, then a clean-smelling hand was slapped over her mouth. "Got you!" one of them yelled.

Holly had been trained in abduction and assault situations. The Myawi school taught its girls to evade or avoid, in that order. Evade capture, avoid injury. There were too many attackers and they already had her, so her aikido training wasn't going to help her evade. Holly went to avoiding, crossing her forearms over her face and pulling her knees to her chest, making herself as small as possible. She dared not lash out. They had her now; the best option was to not let them hurt her too badly.

Holly was lifted and, when she remained in her protective ball, pushed to the ground. She was on a concrete floor, powdered with fine dust that smelled of neglect. Hands pried at her arms and knees, trying to spread her apart, and she resisted. She was struck, kicked, but they couldn't reach anything vital, and Holly shrugged off the painful blows to her shins and shoulders. Someone lashed at her with a switch of some kind, and she held her position against the burning impacts that shredded her sleeves.

"Over here! Bring her over here!" a deep, burly-sounding voice yelled, and she was lifted again, strong hands on her ankles and around her wrists. Holly was carried through a doorway, the sounds changing as she was hauled indoors. They tried to stretch her out again, but she focused on her core, kept the muscles tight, and they still couldn't pry her knees down.

Seams tore as they pulled at her clothes. One of them said, "Just let her go," and the others did. Holly tumbled onto her side. Someone kicked her in the tailbone. That nerve-shattering impact almost uncoiled her, but she held. Something soft hit the ground next to her, a bag of some sort, and then a dull thunk of plastic, something sloshing faintly.

"Going to take your face, whore," a voice full of ugly amusement said in her ear. Holly identified the sloshing. They had a jug of either acid or kerosene. This was worse than the usual thrill-assault.

"Leave her be. Here, here, use the shim." The bag was unzipped.

"What kind of collar is that?"

"Myawi," said the one close to her head, who'd been holding her arms. "We got a *Myawi!*"

The third boy had a reedy, young-sounding voice. "She's going to be fun."

"Don't be stupid, we're not raping her. Dewzy said not to. Get the trophy," the deep-voiced one said.

Metal clashed softly, someone lifted her braid and then Holly felt something cold slip around the edge of her collar at the back of her neck, forcing its way between the warm, comfortable metal and her skin. It felt like having a cuticle pushed back, uncomfortable and intrusive, and she struggled to stay in her ball.

"Got it," a third voice behind her said. A hum went through her collar, and she felt it vibrating against her skin. "Okay, take it off."

The soap-scented hands were in her face again, worming their way down the side of her neck. She rolled her head and tucked her chin, trying to keep them away. She failed; a moment later, the fingers were hooked through the double-orbit loop around Holly's throat. The boy gave a massive yank, jerking Holly violently forward. It felt like he had nearly torn her head off, and the surprise of it made her drop her hands to catch herself as she tumbled forward, legs flailing to keep herself stable.

The hand yanked a second time, and Holly came briefly to her knees before falling.

"Iya, iya, it's still locked!"

"Then unlock it, idiot!"

"I did! The keymaster didn't work."

"Figure it out while I get her clothes off then," the would-be rapist said.

The words made Holly realize that no one was holding her, and kicked her out of her shock and confusion at whatever they were doing to her collar. She had to run, and she did, exploding up off of the floor and taking the college boys by surprise. The object that had been stuffed under her collar snagged briefly on something that fell to the floor behind her. One of the boys cursed and made a grab for her long braid, but missed.

She ran through the doorway and saw that they had carried her into a warehouse, into one of the offices. The building was empty, the floor littered with discarded trash and dust. Holly made for the outside door, the one she assumed she had been bundled through. She dared not hesitate, with the boys at her heels.

Rotten luck stopped her. She reached the door a few steps ahead of them, just out of grabbing reach, slammed into it—and stopped cold. The door opened inward, not outward. That moment was all it took for the college boys to catch up. It didn't even occur to her to yell. If she'd called out, someone might have heard outside, but a voice from her childhood rose in her head automatically, intoning, "A Myawi never screams."

So she didn't. She pulled away from the hand on her shoulder, rolled her wrist deftly out of another's grip. The third boy grabbed her hair, wrapping the thick braid around his hand and pulling her head back. She was dragged back into the warehouse. Sudden inspiration drove Holly to throw herself backward, toward him, and then turn and drop to the floor so she was facing him on her hands and knees. He didn't let go and she crawled rapidly forward, flinging herself between his legs. This moved her out of reach of the other two and simultaneously pulled him into an awkward position when he didn't let go of her hair. He ended up doubled over with his arm between his legs. Holly stood up before he could regain his balance and he turned a somersault, landing flat on his back.

There was no time to savor the unintentional comedy. Holly ran for the door again. This time she was tackled, hit hard by a full-body blow. She was airborne for a moment before landing prone on the floor with a body on top of her. The impact crushed the air out of her with a harsh bark. The other two immediately piled on, making it harder to breathe and impossible to get up and run again. Holly threw her hip to the side and rolled onto her back, trying to ball up again. A bright bolt of pain blew through her chest, and she curled halfway up but her body refused to go any farther. Someone grabbed her hair, lifted, then slammed the back of her head into the floor. Consciousness swam, but Holly held on to it, continuing to try and cover her face and belly.

Her left hand was pulled out to the side, and the full weight of one of the college boys bore down on it. Another lay across her legs. The pain in her chest increased, and she couldn't get a full breath. Her face was covered in dust, so she kept her eyes tightly shut.

"Hit the keymaster again," growled the deep-voiced one, who held her arm now. "Go get it." The third boy ran off to the offices, came back sliding on the dusty floor. Holly's head was pulled to the side and her collar buzzed again. It remained unyielding when it was yanked.

"It's still not working."

"Give me that thing. Take her arms." They switched positions, and the boy across her legs tightened his grip. When Holly struggled, one of them kneed her in the ribs. This time the pain was a flash of white heat that erased everything for a few moments.

When she came back, Reedy Voice was yammering with excitement. "She's fertile. I'm going to put my baby in her. Don't mess her face up. I'll get my father to buy her for me."

Deep Voice laughed. "You're a fool. She gets a baby you're not going to know whose it is."

"I'll know. I'm going first."

"I told you, Dewzy said we're not doing that."

"He's not gonna know."

Whatever device they were using on her collar buzzed again, and the deep-voiced boy growled in frustration. Holly crossed her ankles and pressed her knees together, desperately fighting against Reedy Voice, who was trying to pry them open to get her pants off. Deep Voice made no effort to stop him. He clawed her shoes off, tossing them away. Holly wished she had worn the boots she'd bought in North America; they would have provided their own resistance.

"Quit making her fight. I'm going to ping Dewzy, and see if he knows how to open a Myawi collar."

"This is gonna be so good."

"I didn't think anyone around here could afford a Myawi."

"Some of the profs make good money."

"Yeah, but not *that* good."

Reedy Voice laughed. "She looks just like Hizari's Myawi. There were pictures of her at the last festival online."

"They all look alike," Deep Voice said. "They all have the same hair and style."

"Yeah but this one ain't had ORDS." Her collar buzzed again, and again. The fourth boy pulled on it. "Still locked."

"I *know*."

The door to the street crashed suddenly open. Holly heard it strike its stops and bounce back. She opened her eyes and turned her head, blowing to get the dust out of her eyes. All she could see was a powerful, broad-shouldered silhouette, backlit by the outdoors.

"Release her," the man said, his voice a calm but thunderous boom. He spoke again in Mandarin, and Holly caught enough to tell that he'd repeated the command.

"Mind your own business," Deep Voice shouted back. "This is my domestic."

The interloper had not stopped moving forward since he'd come through the door, and the boys seemed to realize all at once that he was already within ten feet of them. Two of them jumped up. It was too late. "You're a liar," the man said. His arm pistoned forward, almost too quickly to see, and crushed the first boy's face with a gloved fist. Holly saw his cheekbones cave in. The college boy went to the floor without a sound. Reedy Voice let go of Holly and started backing away.

Up close, she could see that the man wasn't that much larger than the college boys. He was an inch or two taller than her, and his powerful build appeared more so because of the armored coat and shoulder pads he wore. His face, in her blurry vision, consisted of mirrored sunglasses, a bushy mustache and a beret. She did instantly see the Myawi crest on his shoulder pad and the purple sigils tattooed on each bicep, each glowing with an arcane internal light. It was the first time Holly had seen an HNE-enhanced person, other than in movies.

In the moment that it took her to recognize this, the man had closed the distance. The next few seconds passed in a very clear swirl of actions and reactions. Holly didn't move, at once fascinated and startled by the speed with which it all unfolded, shocked by the casual shift into bloody violence. She wasn't sure if he reached Deep Voice or Reedy Voice first, but he seized the boy by the neck and lifted him with no apparent effort. He hit the boy in the stomach, twice, then pivoted and slammed him into the floor, scattering the bag and jug.

As the last college boy started to flee, the armored man casually removed a collapsible baton from his belt, extended it with a snap of his wrist, then threw it at the boy's legs. It struck him in the knees, taking him down easily.

"Fucking filth," Reedy Voice, who'd just been slammed into the floor, gasped. "How *dare* you?" Holly was astounded that he had the cheek to spit insults. The big man looked down at him impassively, then stomped on the plastic jug that had fallen next to him. The impact blew the cap off and the bottle collapsed, unleashing a massive gout of clear liquid onto the boy's face, neck and chest. He began howling in agony immediately as the acid went to work on his flesh.

Holly's savior strolled to where Deep Voice had fallen. The terrified student rolled over and crabbed backward, but before he got far the man stomped his crotch with a heavy boot, then kicked him brutally in the face.

Holly felt detached from the moment. She felt no malice from the man, and stayed on the floor where she was as he casually retrieved his baton and returned to her. She shifted position subtly, so she looked comfortable, and hid her now-bare feet. It was habit.

Instead of beckoning her to stand, the man crouched in front of her with a creak of leather. "I am Kalida, Holly," he said, "and you are safe, little goddess. You can stand."

The sigils on Kalida's arms weren't static; they seemed to swirl slightly. Was she in shock? The uncanny motion on his skin was mesmerizing. She could just barely see Reedy Voice writhing in her peripheral vision. His screams tapered off, either because he'd passed out or because he was dead. She suppressed the urge to go check on him—at the very least, she couldn't go near him with her feet bare and acid all over the floor.

Kalida didn't offer a hand, and let her stand up on her own. It wasn't easy. Daggers of pain pierced her side under her left arm. Holly let the pain bleed over her, forced herself not to react, forced herself to rise normally. When she was standing, he reached around behind her neck and pulled out the metal clip that had been stuck into her collar.

"Your collar triggered an emergency signal," Kalida explained. "I am a Singapore Protector."

She nodded. She'd heard whispers in the past, about Myawi's Protectors, but the school kept their existence hidden. Their role was to intervene in situations like this one, but they stayed so far out of the orbit of the girls themselves that it hadn't even occurred to her that rescue might be on the way in a situation like this one. As she thought of it, her brain racing as the shock caught up to her, she realized it made perfect sense: if she had known, she might have been much less aggressive about risking injury to defend herself.

Kalida had collected the college boys' backpack, and stuffed the wires of some electronic device back into it before slinging it over his own shoulder. Deep Voice coughed and tried to move, and Kalida paused long enough to stand on his neck until he stopped.

"Thank you for coming for me," Holly said.

He grunted in acknowledgement. "I will take you for medical assistance. My car is outside."

"Oh, that won't be necessary. I've got—"

"Not a suggestion. Your benefactor has been notified. Come with me, Holly." He steered her toward the door with a gentle but firm hand. The knuckles of his gloves were thickened and rigid, filled with some sort of armor as well.

Holly didn't argue, hoping the checkup wouldn't take long as she still had to prepare Elden's dinner, not to mention getting herself cleaned up. Another fierce pulse of pain shot through her side and she had to struggle to stay upright. She was hurt worse than she'd thought, and already thinking of ways to subtly conceal the injury from Elden while she healed. "My friend Lakshmi, she was in the car. Is she safe?"

Kalida nodded. "The police caught the code and stopped it. The girl was not hurt. The attacker fled," he added with a hint of disdain in his voice.

Outside, there was a nondescript gray car at the curb, and Kalida opened the back door for her. The car was a Bright Spirit Tiger, the same model that the Singapore police used, but unmarked. Inside, the smooth plastic seats used by the police had been replaced by soft leather and deep carpet. It looked and felt like a luxury car. Holly eased into the seat with a sigh of relief, favoring her right side.

The door was closed gently behind her, and Kalida climbed into the front, his leather jacket creaking. "Take this," he said, passing a small geltab and a single-serving bottle of water back to her. "It will help you to calm down."

Holly felt quite calm, but Kalida didn't seem to be offering the medicine as an option. She swallowed the pill, immediately realizing that she was going to be quite calm indeed. The drug gave her a warm feeling from head to toes, pushing the pain from her ribs away, and she let herself drift on a mellow wave. The city seemed to move around the car, and she was aware of it without paying too much attention. It felt good to sit still, so she leaned her head against the window and took a moment to just let things slip past.

The Myawi school had an office located outside the city. The school itself was in Hong Kong and all training was done there, but the office and the park surrounding it had been designed as a miniature version of the elegant Myawi campus. The building resembled a temple flanked by two wings. The side buildings were sculpted with a firm but delicate style that made them look like wind-carved sand, and the intricate contours seemed to change from one day to the next.

Holly was familiar with the place; she and other Myawis living in Singapore came for medical exams and supplemental training regularly. Kalida drove past the main entrance, however, entering via a second gate that was so subtle it was almost hidden.

The secondary drive led to the back of the buildings, a more business-like area. There were other Tigers like Kalida's parked there, and two vans as well. Holly was familiar enough with servants' entrances to recognize where they were. She'd never been this way; when she came in for her appointments she entered through the same stunning atrium that prospective benefactors did. Today she was using the door that the people who served as domestics to the domestics used. The muzzy thought made her smile.

Kalida pulled up to the door. This time he got out and came around to help her, and she was rather enjoying the feeling of being seen to, so she let him guide her through the door. Her feet seemed to barely touch the ground, and Holly guessed that if he let her go, she'd fall over. There was a disconnect between her head and body; she could feel that her side hurt, and her scalp where her hair had been pulled, and her arms and shins where she'd been hit with the switch (and was bleeding), but these were abstract facts and not directly related to any discomfort she was actually feeling. She could tell that if she allowed herself to notice that it hurt, it would.

So she didn't.

The bump she'd taken before shopping was still affecting her, so she was alert in spite of being disconnected from her body. Kalida led her through glass doors and into a small anteroom with several monitors on the wall, and from there into a narrow, carpeted hallway with pictures on the walls and doors off either side. There was another atrium at the far end, and he eased her into a chair there. Had she cared to, she could have felt a great deal of pain from her side as she sat, and had she chosen this she would have successfully hidden it from him. "Wait here, Holly. I will return momentarily." He left her there and went through a door. When he came out, he was no longer carrying the backpack he had liberated from the college boys. Two more Protectors came with him. Both were larger than Kalida and similarly built. Their fierce demeanor evaporated as they looked Holly over, greeting her as "little goddess" and taking note of her injuries without touching her. She was reminded of men looking at a scraped automobile.

"You leave any of 'em alive?" the taller of the two asked. This one also had purple HNE sigils on his arms; the third didn't.

"Yes, Anshul."

"Shame. Little shits from that school have been attacking domestics outside the market for months. I was hoping they wouldn't get one of ours."

Kalida merely nodded. He took a step toward Holly, but the shorter one stepped slightly in front of him, continuing the conversation as if she wasn't there.

"You said they were carrying acid, though? I'd report that to Rajesh."

"I plan to."

Anshul rolled his eyes. "Rajesh won't do anything about it, Wian. And it's not going to matter anyway. They escalated to acid, and Protector Kalida killed at least one of them. They won't go near another Myawi again."

"Two." Kalida said, his voice uninflected. "I killed two."

"Active threats," Wian said. "Good work."

"I want to know where they got the keymaster from. That's equipment for professionals, not college slobs."

"Professionals would know better than to attempt Myawi," Kalida said.

"Right, so where'd they get it?"

"I will find out," he said, stepping to the side and forcing Anshul to let him pass.

Anshul turned and glanced at Holly. "Good work, good rescue," he told Kalida. "And you as well," he said, bowing slightly to address her. "You conducted yourself well, brave girl." Holly intended to tell him thank you, but the words seemed to fade out before reaching her lips.

"She's pacified," Kalida said. He held out a hand to Holly, and she rose.

"No disrespect taken," Anshul said, bowing again. This time Wian bowed as well.

Kalida nodded to Wian. "Go refill my kit." He steered Holly away, continuing down the hall. They went through another set of doors, and were in a hall Holly recognized; they had entered the Myawi doctor's office from the rear. The décor was more elegant in the public areas, with walls painted the dark blue and silver Myawi colors and backlit chrome inlays.

The examining rooms were equally luxurious, since very occasionally a benefactor would accompany his Myawi girl to her checkup. The floors and walls featured ornate tile work, and the chairs and examining tables had handsomely carved fascias masking their utilitarian nature. It was designed to subtly complement the Myawi look, and all of the school's public spaces made the girls look even more otherworldly. Now that she was back on familiar territory, Holly seated herself on the table and waited. Kalida nodded to her, murmured a farewell, and left.

After a few minutes, the doctor came in. She saw Dr. Olai regularly, and liked her. Seeing her today was especially poignant, because of her history. Olai had been a Myawi girl in Chennai when, over a decade previous, she had been a victim of an acid attack. The chemical burn had mangled the left side of her face and ruined her décolletage, and her benefactor had immediately retired her. Some girls became teachers at this point, training new girls, but Olai studied medicine and was hired on to treat her fellow Myawi graduates instead.

Holly liked Dr. Olai. The years and multiple surgeries had smoothed much of the damage, but scar tissue was still clearly visible on her neck and left forearm. The body work had fixed the skin of her face, leaving her with a significant droop under her artificial eye and a one-sided quirk of her lips as souvenirs of the attack.

Dr. Olai was concerned and upset. Holly didn't know if she'd been told about the acid or not. Either way, now that they were alone Holly could be honest about what hurt and what didn't.

"It's okay to cry, little goddess," the doctor said. Holly didn't feel the need, and merely nodded politely. As soon as Dr. Olai got her undressed and flat on the table she looked at the painful spot beneath Holly's arm and hissed in sympathy. "Aiyaa, that will have to be knitted," she said, making some notes on her pad. As she did, a row of the mosaic tiles in the wall slid aside, the small door masked by the edges of the tiling, and a pale blue structure emerged from the wall with a soft hiss of electrohydraulics. The bone-kntting machine looked like a pair of massive metal mantid arms, tendoned with wiring.

In her slightly drugged state, the bone-knitting machine was a fascinating experience. Holly was familiar with the computer-controlled device, which operated at a nearly microscopic level and wove chains of polymers that repaired damaged and torn tissue and bone, encouraging new growth in their place. When Dr. Rehsil had broken her fingers, they'd knitted them, and the digits were achy but usable by the end of the day.

This injury required a larger knitter, of course, and Holly lay on the table while Dr. Olai swung the machine into position. The doctor asked questions, keeping her alert in case of concussion, and Holly answered them, forgetting queries and responses almost immediately. Dr. Olai did ask about the same Vengopal movie she and Shmi had been talking about, but that was the only nugget of conversation that stayed with her.

After a local anesthetic, she dozed through the test, scans, and programming, then woke up briefly when the machine went to work. It didn't hurt; the sensation was one of two points of pressure alternating as the slender needles operated beneath her skin. Extractors drained the blood from burst vessels from the surrounding flesh as well, minimizing bruising. It wasn't an unpleasant feeling; the machine had a rumble not unlike a feline purr and gave the sensation of being kneaded somewhat aggressively by a mechanical cat. The rhythm lulled Holly back into dozing. As she floated at the edge of consciousness, she prepared a dinner menu.

chapter 16

Shiloh fell asleep for a couple of hours after her evening tumble with Mahnaz, until his snoring inevitably woke her up. She didn't mind; it was a good excuse to slip quietly out of bed and leave. Dorim, who appeared to be Mahnaz' bodyguard, had been shunted off to a separate cabin, so she didn't need to avoid him.

The *Excelsis* was operating with a skeleton crew. Half of her sailors— the more combat-experienced ones, from the sound of it—were on the *88 Fists*, keeping that ship "pacified." As a result, Shiloh didn't encounter anyone as she moved through the ship, avoiding the bridge. She'd memorized the route to the solitary cells easily enough, and at this time of night there was only one thing to do, really.

Swan was gone, but there were two prisoners on Shamshoun's hall again; the second was Captain Hardson. He was sitting against the wall, dozing, and didn't stir when she passed his cell. Shamshoun was sitting against the back wall of his own cell, which seemed to be his default position.

"Back again," he said.

"You don't give me much choice," she said sourly.

"All your choices are your own, Shiloh Gallamore," he replied.

"Hey, be careful. My *name*."

Shamshoun made a face that wasn't quite a smile and definitely wasn't an apology. "Of course."

"Well, if you want more stories, I'm here."

"So you are. Take me away from this little plastic grave. I would like to hear more about North America."

She had guessed by his accent that he'd never been there, at least not for long. She'd thought about a couple of stories she could tell him. Though it irritated her that he was blackmailing her, Shiloh could understand his desire for some kind of distraction. She'd given herself a goal of making Shamshoun smile, at least once. "There's a lot to tell," she said, sliding down to sit in front of Shamshoun's cell. It felt strange and unfriendly to look down on him and talk. "I traveled all over, with the circus and after. I've been to all of the walled cities."

Shamshoun didn't move, but his eyes went from her face to over her shoulder. As she thought to glance and see what he might be looking at, Hardson cleared his throat. "We've got a visitor, it would seem," he said. He'd moved to the front of his cell. "It's nice to see you again, lovely little one."

Shiloh smiled up at him. "You too."

"I sense subterfuge of a sort."

"I had to," Shiloh said.

He raised an eyebrow. "Understood. Yourself and Mr. McEvoy both. I'm glad to see both of you taking as much advantage as you safely can."

Shamshoun chuffed sarcastically.

"Laugh if you want, my taciturn friend. She's as much a prisoner as we are. More so, if they find out where her sympathies lie."

"You know so much?" the ursid said.

"I know quite a bit. Your secrets are safe with me, of course. We are all on the same side. Yes, yes, I know, men in adjoining cells are apt to say such things without regard to circumstances, but in this case I believe it to be the truth. I have crossed paths with the Sisters enough times."

"Sisters?" Shiloh asked.

"The Ivory Sisters."

"I don't know who they are."

"Well, this must be very interesting for you then," he said with a wink. "Shall I regale you with tales of Phoebe and Jae, the shadowiest shadowy heads of the table? Phoebe's rumored to be an escaped domestic, or possibly the human child of a falconid, nobody's sure and of course no one has ever seen them. And that's just the part that people agree upon. You know how tongues wag at sea."

She pursed her lips in a little pout, aware that he was making a dirty joke. "Til today I've never been on a ship."

"Then I am sorry mine couldn't be your first," he said, making a motion as if he was doffing his hat and putting it to his chest. "I would be honored to welcome you into my home, and would make you most comfortable.

This craft...she's not a welcoming place."

Shamshoun chuffed humorlessly.

Shiloh glanced at him, then back at Hardson. "I've noticed."

"Ironic. She used to be a pleasure craft. A veritable floating hotel, in fact. It's a shame, what they've done to her."

"A floating hotel?"

Hardson nodded. "I don't know what her name was previously, but she dates to before the Colony Conflict, which you'd call the Fall, I believe. You wouldn't know it from the retrofitting, of course," he added, knocking on the thick plastic wall of the cell with a contemplative knuckle, "but such is the price of progress."

"I think I hate the ocean," Shiloh said.

Hardson feigned shock. "But my dear, you've only seen the ugly side of her worst tenants! Surely, you'd give her a second chance."

"Should we live so long."

"I have every intention of doing just that. And seeing you at large gives me a renewed surge of optimism." Shamshoun chuffed again. "Scoff if you desire, my very large and ill-tempered friend. I intend to put my trust in my heart, and await my moment."

The ursid waved a hand dismissively. "I know this tune already. And sing quietly. Many wrong ears here."

"I'm not concerned. I've said nothing they don't already know."

"Then be quiet so she can tell me stories of North America."

Hardson laughed. "My apologies. I did not mean to intrude."

chapter 17

Forty-seven days before Princess Aiyana's trimester celebration

Shiloh's story

After I decided to leave the circus and leave Strip City with Ivy, I cleaned out my room at the Laddin and joined Ivy, Swan and Kroni. It was a scary moment for me, that leaving for the last time. A bunch of the performers came to see me off, Kinzelle and Maisie and Domino and even Cadge, the ones who'd survived that awful spring, and it felt like they were genuinely sad that I was leaving. But at the same time, Gallamore's wasn't home any more, so I didn't change my mind.

I was nervous because I had no idea what use I was going to be. I was grateful to Ivy for saying I could travel with her, but I'm a performer and that's about all I know how to do. All the things that I'd seen to be useful out in the dirt were things that Ivy and Swan and Kroni could do without me, and I usually got in the way in fact.

It turned out that Swan at least had already thought of that. Almost as soon as I met up with them, Swan told me to go with Ivy to talk to Izzy Burdan, head of the Burdan family. The way it was explained to me, Mr. Burdan knew where Ivy's sister was, and also owed a debt to the Poussinis, because one of his security guards shot a Gallamore driver less than a week before the traveling show was supposed to leave town. The Poussinis own Gallamore's, so Ivy took over the driving slot for the Burdans in exchange for whatever Izzy knew about her sister. She ended up being my driver, which was how we met and why I was now here. Swan said, "Go with her. You know how to talk to these fucks," meaning the Burdans and the other Strip City stars. "She doesn't."

That was pretty much true from what I'd seen. Scavs are honest with each other, to a fault I suppose, and Ivy is too polite to call someone out

110

when they're lying to her. It's like she can't even fathom why someone would do that. This makes it easy for men like Izzy Burdan to fuck with her. Which, of course, he had; he didn't know anything about her sister at all. I could tell by the way that he sat in his huge desk chair looking down at us (the whole desk was on a raised platform). He was annoyed to even have to deal with her again. His body language said he didn't have anything to give her, and had probably expected her not to come back to Strip City at all. There wasn't much I could even do at that point, other than hoping she didn't try to smash his head in. Thankfully, she didn't.

"I'm afraid we don't keep those sorts of records on guests," he told her when she asked about her sister. "It's not customary to record the names of domestics, you see. It seems to be a fair bet that's what she is." He said this like he was being helpful, but we both already knew that Ivy's sister was probably a domestic. "I did some checking, and it looks like the best person on staff to talk to about this would have been Doniphan Barro, our former head of security. He had the most interaction with our convention visitors from the Brother Nations. Unfortunately, as you know, Mr. Barro was killed in the altercation that arose from our...misunderstanding. As far as I know he didn't keep any files."

Ivy blinked, like she was trying to figure out what to say. Kroni had told her on the way back that there was a good chance Mr. Burdan had been lying about knowing where her sister was, but she still looked like a fish trying to breathe air as she faced the reality of it. She'd gone all the way across the continent just about, nearly gotten killed several times with the circus, and then had to nursemaid the tattered remnants back to Strip City after the disaster, and it was all for nothing.

"Is there anything you can do at all?" I asked. It was weak, but better than nothing. I couldn't flirt with Mr Burdan because it wouldn't work; I had a reputation in Strip City and if he wanted me (or I him) it would've already happened.

Anyway, he was prepared for that. "I made arrangements with the Poussinis to make certain you're paid the wages that Gallamore owes you both, of course," he said. That was a garbage promise, seeing as how Mr. Gallamore had already told me this earlier in the day, and Mr. Burdan had nothing to do with making it happen. "I've also arranged for you to keep the vehicle you were driving."

That made Ivy's cheeks darken. "That, that, that that's *my* rig," she said.

"You were driving it, of course, but legally it still belongs to Gallamore's Travelling Extravaganza, my dear."

"No, that's wrong. March traded it to me. They were going to leave it behind after its heart got cacked, and he said I could have it."

"Do you have paperwork to that effect? A transfer of ownership?"

Ivy made the drowning-fish face again. Scavs didn't keep ownership papers on their rigs, after all. There were just few enough of them that they all knew whose rig was whose, and disputes rarely happened. I figured it was another garbage bonus. Mr. Gallamore owed the lives of all of the performers and teamsters who'd made it back to Ivy, and would have let her keep the Vovo if she asked. I could tell she didn't know this though. I figured she was torn between being angry that anyone would consider taking the rig away from her, and glad that Mr. Burdan had supposedly made sure nobody would.

Before she could decide how to respond, he said, "Don't worry, it's taken care of. We'll also get you outfitted, of course. Will you be headed back east?" Mr. Burdan didn't want us in Strip City, that was for certain.

Ivy exhaled through her nose, which she does when she's annoyed. "I don't know. There's no cargo going east, since Sam Ward. Big caravans take it all."

"Let me offer you this: I'm told that a group of travelers from the Brother Nations left on a trip into the dirt two days ago. I think they're headed for the Mississippi River, actually. Deep into the continent. I suspect you could catch them, and I can ask around to get more information on where exactly they were going. In the meantime, you can also re-outfit your buggy and supplies courtesy of the Burdan family. The Sino-Indians were travelling with at least one domestic, and perhaps she may know how to contact your sister."

"You really want us gone, don't you?" I said.

He smiled a wolf's smile at me. "I am doing what I can to help."

There wasn't anything to do but take what he was willing to offer, though. Ivy was impressed with the supplies the Burdans provided; I couldn't help but think it was less expensive than it would have been to outfit her for real, with a better rig. On the other hand, it was probably more expensive than it would have been to just kill her, so that was something.

When we got back to the Old Town, where Swan and Kroni were staying with the rig, I filled them in on how it had gone. Ivy didn't want to talk about it. "Do we know much about them?" Swan asked.

"Not really."

"It's rude to follow people."

"Well, I, I, I found out too late to meet them. They're two days ahead of us, so we'll have to catch up." That was essentially the entire discussion. Traveling the world with Ivy means that we generally go where she wants to go, and there's no arguing about it.

Crossing the desert and mountains as a single vehicle's a really dicey prospect, because there are so many little gangs of raiders out there, perched on scraps of territory, one after the other. Kroni suggested going the long way around, up the coast to Astoria and then through the northern badlands. Ivy said they were their own special kind of hell—the kind where it's hard to find food or fuel, but she did seem to think that was preferable to going hard through a dozen packs of pirate bands.

Then Swan met a trio of Benzers, the evening before we were headed out of town. Benzers are strange folks; they tend to keep to themselves, and only interact with people who can help them with their rigs in one way or another. This means that mostly they talk to other Benzers, unless they're looking for trade. For some reason they were interested in the Vovo, though, and after I dropped several hints Ivy finally figured out that it was a good idea to actually talk to them in more than monosyllables. They ended up talking about vehicles for the rest of the afternoon. In the morning we breakfasted with them, around their little camp outside Strip City.

The hills are pretty. They're covered in overgrown grapevines, and it's pleasantly cool at night. I wandered a short distance away from the campfire to look at the sky, but heard coyotes so I returned before they could get bold.

The Benzers parked their cars around the campsite, nose-in, as if the vehicles were a part of the group as well, and the more we talked to them the more that seemed like it was the case. They let us join their circle, though, and Ivy parked the Vovo the same way. With them parked together like that, I noticed that all of the Benzers' rigs had the same sort of grill, an upright chromey thing with a ring-shaped ornament on top, like a target. The Vovo had an upright chromey grille too, but no ornament, and it was shaped differently. That wasn't strange—most scavs' rigs didn't look much alike other than having four wheels. What was interesting was seeing three that were similar, at least in the shape of their body panels and lights.

Walter was the oldest, with age-weathered, gold-toned skin and silver hair, and his car was the shiniest too, a silver four-door that looked just like a picture of a pre-Fall car. He didn't have any gear racks or anything on it, and he was even a little persnickety about letting Ivy look inside of it, but he did. Loosa's was the biggest, a taller rig with big tires and space enough for her to sleep in back if she wanted to. Hers looked more like the rigs we usually saw out in the dirt, more cargo-capable vehicles. Loosa had close-set, suspicious eyes and a cap of tightly curled hair that was thinning. She had a little dog that traveled with her, and she carried parts and stuff for the other two in addition to her own supplies. Spiker's car was the only one that wasn't silver; it was a faded green four-door with a rusty hood and a lot of dents. He had big tires on it as well as gear strapped to the roof, and it ran on slurry instead of corngas like the other two. He was self-conscious about his car not looking quite as good as the others did, but I liked the way it looked. There was something lived-in yet loved about it that made it feel more like the Vovo. Spiker was the youngest, too. From listening to him talk to Ivy it sounded like he had found his rig and only recently gotten it running with Loosa and Walter's help.

He was also the cutest. He had perpetual blond scruff on his face, and a pair of wings tattooed on the back of his neck. The tips wrapped around toward his ears. I was actually feeling a bit down that I wasn't going to get to jump him, when Ivy came right out and asked Walter if we could travel with them. Benzers usually don't caravan. They used to cross paths with the circus from time to time but would never follow us.

Walter gave Ivy a long look, though. "You know Middlegate?" he asked her.

She shook her head.

"Safe fuel stop, not quite halfway to Salt Lake. Not a lot of folks know it. We'll be rolling fast. Keep up, if you want."

Ivy nodded to him, but when he turned away I saw her smile. She told me and Swan and Kroni to be ready to fly so we were packed up, and after breakfast was cleaned up and the Benzers pulled out, we pulled out with them.

As we got farther from Strip City, the roads twisted up into mountains for an hour or two, everything surrounded by trees and the road bending back on itself over and over and sometimes washed out by rockslides. After that, it stretched out and flattened out, and that was when things got interesting.

I think the Benzers were trying to leave us behind. Loosa was leading the way, and then when the road straightened out, Walter suddenly shot past us like we were standing still. His rig positively *roared,* and then it was gone, past us and past Loosa and streaking for the horizon like it was being chased by demons, or like it was demon itself. Ivy actually made a little noise, and Swan yelled, "Sweet banana!"

Just after that, Loosa sped up too; her big rig started pulling away from us. Even though it had been a couple of months since the Gallamore's caravan had broken up, I was still really used to traveling in a very organized pack, so all of the cars speeding up and breaking formation was nervous-making at first. Spiker sped past us too, and gave me a wink as he went by. That made me glad; I'd been making eyes at him all through breakfast, even though I hadn't had a chance to talk to him.

I saw that little smile on Ivy's face again, and she moved her hands and feet to talk to the Vovo. It listened to her, and soon the Benzers weren't getting farther ahead of us any more. The road kept mostly straight, but wound up and down hills, and every time we came over a hill or around a gentle bend, we were a bit closer to Spiker. Eventually Ivy passed him again, and settled in behind Loosa's rig. Walter was farther ahead, but we tucked into a nice dusty train with Loosa ahead and Spiker behind. Ivy pulled a little to the side and next to Loosa, so she was partly out of the bigger rig's dust. That was a relief. The Vovo only has a slice of canvas for a roof over the front seats and no side windows, so it's only good for keeping the rain out and the sun off your head. I was a little envious of the Benzer's roofs and windows, to be honest. Swan had taken to putting her helmet on to keep the dust out of her face, and Kroni just didn't seem to care that much.

Ivy...I had never seen her so happy. She usually got more talkative while she was driving, but today there was no conversation. It was too windy anyway, plus the noise of Loosa's rig and the Vovo yowling would've made it even harder. I know driving's hard work, so I took out one of the oranges we'd traded for before leaving Strip City and peeled it for Ivy. She accepted the slices gratefully.

The next set of big hills, we pulled ahead of Loosa. Swan gave the Benzer a little wave as we went past, and I saw her laugh.

Kroni was watching the hills around us and the road behind, as usual. He suddenly slapped the side of the car to get Ivy's attention, and pointed at the horizon to our right, to the south, where there was a dust trail visible. It was too far out to see the rig that was making it, but it definitely seemed to be headed our way.

Swan flipped her helmet's visor open. "Ugliness on the way," she said.

Desert pirates are scary. We never had to deal with them when traveling with Gallamore's but our trip back to Strip City after the disaster, when it was just six rigs, was a bad time. One of the surviving clowns died during that trip, shot by an arrow, and it was a miracle we didn't lose any rigs. My heart started to pound as Swan and Kroni geared up to defend us.

Slowly, the dust trails moved closer. There were a dozen of them, churning along, and then another side slap and a stern "Ware" from Kroni told us that there were more coming from the north as well. I'm useless in these things; to give me a gun is just a waste of ammunition. The best I can do is squish down in the seat and stay out of the way. Fortunately, Swan and Kroni prefer that to my attempting to help. Even Ivy would rather shoot over my head than give me the gun. I hate feeling useless, but the three of them still seem to like having me along and don't get angry when I can't help out with the shooting.

But then something kind of wonderful and impossible happened. The horde that was approaching from the south got close enough that we could see them for a while, and then they began to drop back. First the larger rigs, and then the buggies, and then the bikes, which got close enough to take a few long-distance shots at us but that was it. I think we were going too fast for them to keep up, in the end. Once the side road they were on intersected ours, they began to drop back quickly.

Ahead of us, Walter dodged some sort of trap in the road. Ivy had been paying close attention to his driving, and ducked around the pit in the pavement as well. I looked to the rear, and the other two swerved past it easily. The pirates from the north kept pace with us, but there were only two of them and they weren't close enough to shoot.

"I've never gone this fast for this long," Ivy said. She sounded impressed, and delighted. "This is a good rig."

More miles and more big hills and long stretches passed, and then as we came around a tight-ish bend, Walter suddenly pulled off of the road toward a large metal tube half-buried in the ground. There were chunks of similar material scattered around; it looked like someone had dropped a huge ceramic toy on the ground, let it shatter, then poured dirt over it until it was half-buried. Walter's car veered off into the dust and slid to a stop, and he jumped out with a big gun in his hands. Ivy did the same, pulling in next to him at an angle, similar to the way we used to with Gallamore's. Loosa and Spiker did the same, and we formed a little square.

Swan and Kroni were over the side of the car in an instant. All three of the Benzers took up positions too. I stuck my fingers in my ears; gunfire is amazingly loud, especially up close. The two rigs following us never had a chance, really. The minute they crested that hill, Kroni and Walter fired at the same time. Swan and Loosa opened up an instant later, and I could actually see the bullets making holes in the two rigs. I hate fighting, but when it's happening it's impossible not to watch. The trucks chasing us dodged and weaved, maybe not entirely intentionally, and they came to a stop about twenty yards from us. As they did, men jumped out and every one of them got shot down before getting a chance to fight back. Just that quickly, eight men went down.

It got really quiet. Our engines were silent, and the two rigs chasing us were grumbling quietly, but there were no other sounds. The three Benzers moved forward like synchronized dancers, guns at the ready, and Kroni and Swan joined them. Ivy looked at me, her eyes asking if I was okay, and I nodded. She doesn't do a lot of rushing about, because of her knee, but I've seen her fighting people up close and she's just as fierce as Swan (though she doesn't enjoy it as much).

With our pursuers confirmed dead, Walter shut off their rigs. Swan and Loosa came back, each of them carrying two rifles. "New toys," Swan said. "Fancy ones, too."

Loosa whistled. "Where d'you think Sam Wards got fancy weapons and rigs like that, anyway?" That took me by surprise. I hadn't seen them up-close enough to realize they were Sam Wards. If anything, that was even scarier than desert pirates.

"Must've had 'em when the army went toes-up?"

She shook her head. "This stuff's too new. Everything's too new."

Ivy perked up. "The rigs are new?"

She nodded. "Looks like. New like Inchin stuff, but I never heard of rigs coming from there. Only small things."

"They have Inchin cars in Strip City," Ivy said.

"Like those?"

I looked at the rigs that had been chasing us. They were blockier-looking than the usual scav truck, all flat angles. They seemed to have more lights and less windows, and they were all painted dark dull gray. I hadn't ever seen a rig like that in Strip City, and Ivy agreed.

We would have talked about it some more, but then Walter came back from the site of the firefight, gave Swan a friendly punch on the shoulder, and nodded at Ivy. "Nice drive," he said. "You'll want to top up on oil if you have any. Fast burn like that, most rigs will drink a bunch of it, leave you running hot."

She nodded. "How far to Middlegate?"

His face broke into a huge smile, for the first time since we'd met him. It made him look like an unusually wrinkled and straggle-haired boy. "We're there," he said, and raised his arms over his head, clapping briskly in a short rhythmic pattern.

All around us, the ground made scratching noises, and doors started to open up. Straight out of the ground, doors flipped open, seven, eight, nine of them. They were camouflaged with sand and rocks, so we hadn't seen them before. If we had stayed on the road we'd have sped right past them.

"Holy shit," Swan laughed. Ivy was smiling too.

"You want to take one of the shiny ones?" Walter asked her.

She looked at the bigger trucks, and I could see her considering it. I kind of hoped she would, since it would mean more space inside, but she frowned and said, "No thank you." The Benzers nodded and seemed to approve.

The people coming out of the ground were perfectly normal-looking dwellers, if anything a bit cleaner than most. They obviously knew Walter, and Loosa seemed to have some friends among them too.

And that was Middlegate. It was a little town of about six families and a fuel depot. They got by trading fuel and other desert scavenge to travelers and Benzers, and there was a big caravan that came through and traded them food and gas for the wrecked and abandoned rigs they found. After the Benzers and Ivy spent some time taking parts off of the Sam Ward trucks, they traded them for all the fuel we could carry. I helped her hand-pump it into our tank and only splashed a little bit on myself this time, which was an improvement over the first time I tried it.

And that night, I humped Spiker. It was a good day all the way through.

chapter 18

Ninety-six days before Princess Aiyana's trimester celebration

>> There's panic in the city of Shanghai this week as reports continue to come in of a shapeshifter at large in the city. Officials first became aware of the creature Tuesday, when HNE detectors at a civic center were triggered. Eyewitness reports suggest that it is either a canid or ursid, and citizens are urged to stay alert, keep indoors at night and avoid letting children play unattended.

"We think it came in on a ship from North America," said police chief Banjou Angling. "There have been no injuries, and a team of specialists from the Office of Foreign Affairs is tracking the beast within the city." He went on to remind residents of the dangers of confronting or attacking shapeshifters, and advised calm.

–Heart of Singapore News

>> The popular series, *St. George, Dragon Hunter,* has been green-lighted for a fourth season this fall. The show, which follows the exploits of self-styled dragon hunter "Saint" George McForster as he roams the globe chasing down escaped HNE-created cryptids, has been a great success for its production company, Waring Industries, and for McForster as well. Styled as a documentary, part of the show's appeal remains the unanswered question of whether *St. George, Dragon Hunter* is truly clever fiction, or if McForster and his crew are actually hunting dragons, jiangshi and sprites in their travels. The show's fourth season is rumored to take McForster and his team into the Andes Mountains, to hunt…

–Tinzee's Tea Room

>> The role of hypernatural energy (HNE) in the development of shapeshifters is well-documented. Before the efforts of the world's HNE laboratories became obsessed with experiments in the name of curing ORDS, however, there was a veritable free-for-all of creative scientific expression, for lack of a better term. North America especially is littered with the remnants of imaginative experiments, chi-

meras and hybrid flora and fauna created as HNE-attuned individuals and scientists alike turned nature on its ear in the pursuit of their particular (and often peculiar) worldviews. When it was discovered that the effects of HNE were akin to what was once known as magic, the field attracted a great many would-be wizards...

–Versamel Boom Newsmag

On Wednesday nights, Holly and Elden played chess. It was a diversion that she looked forward to, an extension of the private time they shared where he encouraged her to be herself.

In the month since the attack, she had enjoyed the pastime as a chance to sit for a couple of hours. The bone-knitting had fixed the damage, but the fatigue and dull aches had a habit of recurring without warning. Dr. Olai had told her this was common with knitting jobs on serious injuries and nothing to worry about as long as it didn't go on for more than eight weeks. Elden had read the injury report but didn't ask about her discomfort. He was more interested in their new armoire, which arrived from Strip City two weeks after they got home.

Today he sent word that he'd be running late, and she had his dinner ready for him as soon as he walked in. He was positively ebullient, and it was obvious to her that it was something more than the chicken tortellini soup that had him so bouncy. She had changed into her green and white outfit, which was his favorite, and he didn't even notice.

He didn't like to be pressed with questions the moment he walked in the door, so she waited with an expectant eyebrow cocked. Elden knew she could tell he was positively bursting with news, and he kept her in suspense for a few minutes.

After a while it became a game of its own. Once he was settled in, Elden sat and ate in satisfied silence, waiting for her to ask. Holly continued to wait, not saying anything. She was perfectly willing and capable of sitting there for an hour if she needed to. He'd never lasted more than twenty minutes, though.

This time Elden caved in four minutes. "Exciting news for the department," he said.

"Yes?"

"Oh, absolutely. We've got a professor coming, from Luna."

Holly let her surprise show. The massive space colonies orbiting the planet were something she rarely thought about—most people didn't—because travel between planetside and space had been aggressively suspended over a century ago, as one of the precursors to the Colony Conflict. Upon realizing that the ORDS epidemic was only happening on earth, the colonies had effectively quarantined the planet, and backed it up by destroying all of the ports capable of sending shuttles into space. "How did he *get* here?"

"One-way trip. The official story is that it was specially arranged between the Lunar University and our administration," Elden said proudly. "His shuttle crash-landed in North America almost two years ago. He was thought to be dead, but he's been wandering the continent, chronicling their culture and recording oral histories the entire time!"

"That's...amazing."

"Isn't it? It's a one of a kind opportunity, Holly."

"You said 'official' story. Is there a real story?"

Elden chuckled. "There is. He was involved in a minor scandal—an affair with a student. Rather than be fired and de-tenured, he accepted this assignment. I get the feeling that the student's parents were well-connected enough that his, ah, survival wasn't expected. And I am certain that he wasn't informed of this beforehand."

"You mean they crashed his shuttle on purpose."

"I couldn't say for certain. But I hear whispers that he was on a trajectory for the Gulf of Mexico instead of the Sea of Japan, and that's an awful long way from any kind of useful assistance. And the fact that he struck land instead of water? He's a very lucky man." Holly nodded. "In any case, he'll be at the disposal of our department, passing on his research, and we're going to help him publish as well. Of course I'll be petitioning for a place in the department for him, too. It's not as though he can go home."

"So he came here knowing he'd never be able to return?"

"He did."

"Interesting."

"This is so exciting! This man, Marcus McEvoy, has done what hasn't been done for years. He's explored the interior of North America, met the people, seen the cities. Just the fact that he's alive is exceptional!"

"It's not so terrible as all that," Holly said.

"And yet fully supplied military expeditions have failed to return. And so many independent researchers...we haven't been able to get funding for a North American exploration for twenty-five years, large or small. Nothing that attempts to go farther inland than the coastal cities."

Holly nodded, pondering. "Maybe Mr. McEvoy has some insight into the culture, since the colonies were responsible for the current state of

North America in the first place."

Elden laughed. "That could be. I don't imagine he identified himself as a colonist. I can't see that being well-received. Even though he's not a military man, I suppose most people there must blame all colonists for the destruction."

"Most people don't know the colonies exist." She had told Elden that before; he always seemed to forget it. "I had never heard of them until I entered the Myawi school. I think it's more likely no one would have believed he was from outer space."

"That's right, you have told me that. Why do you think it isn't taught?"

"I think they honestly don't know. Some time between the Colony Conflict and now, people just...forgot. With all of the destruction, I'm sure there was more interest in surviving than in history lessons. And now..." she shrugged. "It's true they're visible, but if you don't know to look for them, the colonies are just bright stars."

Elden nodded in agreement. Holly saw that he was finished eating and took his plate. "He should be arriving in a few days. As will Mr. Vitter."

"Dinner?" Asking was a formality; she could practically tell Elden what he wanted without prompting.

"Yes, indeed. A smaller, more intimate event I think. We can host it here rather than at the department. I believe Vitter planned to talk to Mr. McEvoy as well, and this will be a good opportunity. Invite Hatton, Rehsil and Aidanab. And Mr. Vitter of course. We'll all be working together on his project."

"So Vitter's coming to the university with a *project*," Holly said.

"Oh yes. Much different from the usual. Secret, in fact. Vitter's government ties have a very strong interest in North America. Ministry of Foreign Affairs, that sort of thing. You'll have to forgive me if I'm much more secretive than usual."

"I'll keep that in mind."

Elden's excitement left him distracted, a fact that he conceded after Holly beat him two games in a row. He was rougher than usual in bed later; she chalked that up to exuberance rather than vindictiveness. She'd endured far worse, and after Elden fell asleep she crept out of bed to clean up, check to see if he'd left any bruises, and stretch. Her side didn't hurt at all; that was an improvement.

While she was up, Holly did a quick tour of the house, straightening as she went, and tended to a few of the e-letters that Elden needed her to take care of. He didn't have a secretary of his own at the school, and occasionally sent her half-written mails to finish, edit and send. Some had to be translated into Hindi, for communication with other parts of Sino-India.

Holly looked out the window with a sigh, resting her fingers on top of the computer's translucent monitor frame. Singapore's lights drowned out even the bright stars that were the space colonies, but she looked up at the sky anyway, trying to imagine what it would be like to voluntarily leave one's home permanently, in search of knowledge. As far as she knew, communication with the colonies was restricted to high government and military offices, so it was likely that Marcus McEvoy couldn't even send or receive messages from his friends and family.

They'd have to become his new family at the university. He'd find a place with the department and settle in Singapore.

Oh, but she was getting ahead of herself. Holly smiled at the daydream. She hadn't even met the man yet. It was too soon to speculate as to where he'd fit in. She imagined him to be a restless, intrepid sort, always focused on the next new thing and impatient with the trappings of society or the slow, steady pace of academia.

Beneath her fingers, the computer chimed a message. It was Lakshmi, asking if she was still awake. Holly smiled and toggled a chat, quickly brushing her hair out of her face with her fingers as the video came up.

"Hi, Holly! Benefactor asleep?"

"Of course he is," she said. "Going there myself soon enough."

"No, not yet! You've got to come with me to the Crystal Turtle!"

The Crystal Turtle was a little dance hall that catered to domestics that was located in the basement of a larger bar. "Oh, Shmi, that's such a silly place."

"How would you know, you've never been?"

Holly laughed. "You've never been either, as far as your mister knows! You always sneak out to go dancing. You're going to get in trouble someday." Her computer chimed another message—this time it was Yuying, sending her move in a word-puzzle game they played back and forth all day. Late evenings were an active time for domestics, as they grabbed a few minutes to socialize before bed.

Lakshmi rolled her eyes. "They're not going to do anything. I get all of my chores done. You should come with me."

"What if the club gets raided again?" The Crystal Turtle had been shut down twice thanks to allegations that the Ivory Sisters had dealings there.

"Oh, stop it. Come with. You Myawi girls never have any *fun*."

Holly bit her lip, pretending to consider it. Slipping out while Elden slept was unthinkable, partly because he might wake and need her, and mostly because she preferred to use any extra hours shaved from her own sleep schedule to get a head-start on tomorrow. "Not this time, Shmi," she said, smiling gently. She started taking her hair down to brush it out before bed, and that made her intent clear.

"Okay, okay. I had to try." Lakshmi smiled. She was grinning and putting on flashy earrings. "One day I'll corrupt you. You'll be the first Myawi at the Crystal Turtle," she added with a touch of personal pride.

"That will be quite a day," Holly said. She sent a move in response to Yuying's and another of her ongoing games chimed less than a minute later. They could keep her up all night if she let them. "You have fun, and be careful. I've got to go." She signed off.

Checking the time, she saw that she had three hours to sleep before she'd have to be up to make Elden's breakfast. Perfect. Holly went to her own room, where she slept two or three nights a week. Some benefactors gave their girls rooms that were little more than garrets, but Holly's room was as big as one of Elden's guest rooms, and he'd let her decorate it quite nicely with a canopy bed and furniture that matched the rest of the house. He didn't make her entertain in her bed if he loaned her to a friend. This was her space.

She lay on her back atop the covers, fully dressed, and turned on her music box. She'd had the little device since the beginning of her Myawi training, and the melancholy tune it played always acted as a signal for her brain that it was time to sleep. Holly was usually fast asleep before the ninety-second melody ended and the music box shut itself off.

chapter 19

Ninety days before Princess Aiyana's trimester celebration

>> Davao police assisted military units in the capture of an ursid near Davao today. The creature had reportedly stowed away on the *Telluride*, a private cargo vessel sailing between Shanghai and Brisbane. Experts say the ursid may have been disoriented and boarded the ship accidentally. After arriving in Davao, the ursid leapt over the side of the boat and swam for shore, leading authorities on a fifteen hour chase and hunt before it was tranquilized and transferred to a secure facility late last night.

It is believed that this ursid is the same creature that recently terrorized Shanghai and evaded capture for a week.

—Owl News Syndicate

>> So many of our political minds continue to think of North America in terms of the United States of America. But this model is outdated by almost a century. It is much more like the Brother Nations on a smaller scale, with cities instead of nations. If it were up to me, I would forge alliances just as Beijing and Mumbai did. Dallas, Little Rock and Bigmouth would be powerful allies. Nawlins' HNE power is said to rival India's. I would expect the most resistance from the great matriarchies in Detroit, Astoria and Savannah. Once the largest cities have become allies or been dissolved, the smaller cities and threats like the felid "Stronghold" and falconid nesting grounds can be easily addressed. Of course, convincing men like Chancellor Shay of this course's strategic wisdom continues to prove difficult.

—Do You Believe This Shit? by Rosso Patek

Just before dinner, a storm blew up, a late-afternoon drenching that soaked the city and then settled in to stay for the evening. The steady downpour didn't deter any of the guests from coming, to Holly's relief, and the evening proceeded with a constant background chatter of rain against the windows.

She served the oxtail consommé with a homemade crostino float first, then followed it up with the North America-reminiscent rabbit served three ways. She'd made rabbit ravioli with rosemary and goat cheese, and managed to pull off some particularly difficult rabbit-sausage Scotch eggs using quail eggs. For the third part, she'd braised the rabbit in port with mushrooms and shallots. She'd managed to find fresh parsnips, wax beans and carrots to go with, and was quite pleased with the results.

While she served, she made the guests' acquaintance as well. Marcus McEvoy looked nothing like Holly expected. He was younger than he looked at first, thanks to curly, colorless hair, but at the same time older and less athletic than his adventures suggested. In fact, though he was plump, Marcus looked very much the worse for wear after his trip from Strip City. His clothes were a patchwork, mismatched in a charming, academic way. He carried himself similarly, awkward at times but composed and comfortable when the conversation turned to his various areas of expertise.

He reminded Holly a bit of Elden, in fact. Marcus was less self-assured, of course, being utterly unfamiliar with the customs, culture or weather of Singapore (the poor man appeared to be melting in the heat and humidity), but at heart Holly could tell that he and Elden would be kindred spirits. It was easy to envision him as a restless academic who'd taken the chance to go on a grand adventure, but now that he'd done it he found himself not quite belonging in his old life any more. Nor was he truly adventuresome.

The other dinner guests, brought in to provide a private welcome to Marcus upon his arrival, exhibited varying degrees of compatibility. He got along well with Hatton, who was a junior professor in the department and generally agreeable. Marcus fell almost instinctively into the role of higher-tenured professor with him. Aidanab was interested in Marcus' less academic pursuits and more in how he'd survived in the wilderness, and Dr. Rehsil vacillated between deferential and almost comically impolite. He greeted Marcus warmly, and listened raptly to the stories Marcus shared, but Holly had also seen the emails he'd sent through the department two days before Marcus' arrival demanding credentials and expressing skepticism that Marcus was actually the visitor from the Lunar University that he claimed to be. More than once he made a comment that seemed intended to trick Marcus into revealing himself as an impostor.

Vitter was harder to read. His military and government ties showed in his reserved manner and aloof, calculated responses. He was thickset and his tailored suit appeared to hide a body that was more athletic than his age might suggest. Holly could also tell that being nice didn't come naturally to him; he seemed to be doing mental gymnastics just to remain cordial. He regarded Marcus, and the rest of the academics, as one might look at chess pieces, considering the location and usefulness of each. He was paying attention to the domestics as well. Though he didn't go out of his way to speak to her or Yuying, she could tell he was as aware of them as he was the professors, which was unusual. When she took a moment to tell him, "I'm terribly sorry about Nielle," he paused for a moment with a quizzical tilt to his head before looking at her.

"She was a good girl," Vitter replied with a lingering look at Holly's face.

She met his eyes for just a moment, then nodded and bowed. She still hadn't decided what to do with the Ivory Sisters package that had been in Nielle's effects, and had fostered an idle hope that some conversation with Vitter would give her an idea of how to proceed. For now, she could tell only that talking directly to him about it might not be a good idea. Unfortunately by now it had been long enough that mentioning it to Elden would also be awkward. She considered the ways she might try to return it to the Ivory Sisters anonymously. Shmi would be better suited to such machinations, and might know someone.

Setting that aside for the moment, she listened to them talk. Elden preferred his dinners informal, so once they were done serving she and Yuying sat at the table with their benefactors, like spouses.

"So what was the trip planetside like?" Vitter asked. "I believe you're the first to make the descent—and survive—in almost a hundred and sixty years."

"Terrifying!" Marcus said cheerfully. "Much of it was freefall, you understand, and I was strapped into the pod quite securely. There was nothing for me to do but ride along, as the craft was fully automated." He talked as though he had written a speech for himself. "The descent seemed to go on forever. I didn't even realize that my pod had gone off-course, you know, until I landed in such a remote area. Even then, I assumed the first people I saw were from Shanghai, and spoke Mandarin to them. It was a touch embarrassing, I must admit."

"You've written quite a lot of material—well over two thousand pages, I believe the document was. How did you collect all of that?"

Marcus smiled. "Just an ordinary notepad," he said. "I picked up an expedition-grade power tablet before I left. Overbuilt for what it's needed for, I'm sure. But shockproof, waterproof, and easily written on with a stylus. The battery has a twelve-hour charge and recharges in about an hour, of course. I found that on cloudy days, atmospheric interference would extend that time to about three. And I had a spare battery. I must admit, when I realized I wasn't in Sino-India I took to carrying extra paper and fragments of books I'd found to conceal the unit, lest some gleaner decide to take it from me." He chuckled. "I needn't have worried, of course. I don't think I encountered anyone who even knew what it was, or noticed that it was anything other than a paper notebook. Electronic devices are almost unheard of there. I made the notepad my most prized possession. More than once, circumstances caused me to lose what supplies and souvenirs I had gathered, but I made sure to defend the notepad as if my life depended on it."

"How long did it take you to figure out where you were?"

"The first scavs I met were quite friendly, and were happy to help me get my bearings and a ride to the city of Norleans, in exchange for the remains of the pod." He gave a self-deprecating laugh. "I learned later that, in North America's barter system, these scavs got the better end of the bargain by far."

"What would they do with it? It was just an unpowered descent pod, wasn't it?"

"Even if it had an engine, they wouldn't be able to fly it," Vitter said. "Not with the EPRC."

Marcus glanced at Holly. He'd been sneaking looks at her all evening, and on his arrival had favored her with a lingering stare. She was fascinated because his look had more naked curiosity than lust. He looked at her as though he'd never seen a woman before, but that was a ridiculous notion. Still, it seemed that he couldn't keep his eyes off of her, whenever he thought she wasn't looking. In that same moment she caught Vitter also looking at her. It was a piercing look, searching patiently, and she was struck by the crazy idea that he *knew* she had the Ivory Sisters package.

Vitter's gaze shifted as Marcus addressed his comment. "No, no, you misunderstand. The scavs tear things down. As the name suggests, they make their living by finding pre-Fall items and trading them as raw materials. They were keen to disassemble the pod, and trade the metal, wiring and other components. I imagine the pieces of it have long since been turned into other things by now. The process is quite fascinating—remarkably like watching the consumption of an animal's corpse."

"So, the people of North America are like maggots," Rehsil sniffed. He seemed equally malicious and offended.

"I would think that to be a gross misrepresentation. My analogy was a poor one."

Elden cut in. "Not as poor as you might think. Absent the revulsion that we feel about the process, scavenger animals do perform a vital service to any ecosystem. I say it is no different for the social ecosystems of North America. The scavengers are needed, to continue the decomposition of the old society and let the new flourish. What do you think, Holly?"

Rehsil bristled when Elden invited her to the conversation. Holly took a bit of guilty pleasure in the fact, even though she felt as though she didn't really know all that much more about North America than he did. Elden liked to present her as a representative of the culture of her birth, though, and she had learned to speak with some authority on the subject. Her childhood experiences informed her somewhat, and she found the often sketchy reports on life in the wild continent to be very easy to understand and interpret. Besides, her talking gave the rest of them a chance to politely eat. "All of the travelers are helpful to the walled cities," she said. "And vice versa. The scavs bring goods from other cities as well as scraps, and the nomads trade in knowledge and cultural exchange. This is vital, because so few city dwellers go out into the dirt. And of course the cities and towns offer food, safety and doctors. Implying that one is superior to the other is a bias because we're used to the cities, I think. In North America, though, one couldn't exist without the other."

"Precisely!" Marcus said. "This exchange is usually facilitated by a unified government, but in the absence of such in North America, a symbiotic relationship has developed all on its own."

"So there is really no centralized government?" Vitter asked. That seemed like an odd question—certainly that was something he should have known. Holly kept the surprise off of her face, and wondered if Vitter was feigning ignorance to see what Marcus knew. She could feel the intrigue happening, even though she couldn't quite determine what Vitter was after.

"Not a unified one. The walled cities are the closest thing, and they have very localized influence. Apart from the loosest cooperations, they are too far apart to form any kind of a strong governmental body. It's such a large place, with so few people, the distances involved make it difficult. Especially without reliable telegraph or radio communication. Most people in North America, apart from the scavengers, just aren't that interested in the world beyond perhaps a fifty-mile radius of their home or farm."

"Interesting," Vitter said. "I would be interested in discussing your experiences, Professor McEvoy—"

"Marcus, please."

"—yes. I was given to understand that Sam Ward and his followers were representatives of a unified North American government, or were attempting to establish one. As I believe I mentioned to you previously, the curious and total failure of all diplomatic missions to North America, for the better part of the last century, to even return home in a recognizable form let alone establish any formal trade or political connection, is quite a mystery."

"Perhaps your diplomats were taking the wrong approach? I know that customs can vary quite widely from place to place. In one city, a smile and a nod are considered a greeting, and in another they can be seen as a challenge to a duel."

"As you say," Vitter said. "But let me give you an example. Beyond the walled cities, the only organized groups seem to be headed by shifters. Both the falcon and felid shifters have quite extensive kingdoms, it would seem. I recently organized an attempt to open trade with the felid nation, and things seemed quite promising. And then they abruptly broke off contact. I was unable to reestablish negotiations."

"Perhaps they found out how shifters are treated in the Brother Nations," Hatton said with a touch of bitterness in his voice.

Vitter frowned at him, as did Rehsil. "The felids are not *in* the Brother Nations, and thus not subject to our laws. And I made it quite clear to their king that we would freely sign a non-aggression pact and an agreement of understanding between us."

"They do have a reputation for being exceptionally mercurial," Elden said, nodding. Marcus opened his mouth to say something, but Elden talked over him. "And considering the felids' history, they have plenty of reason to mistrust treaties. They started as a race of lab animals, did they not? I suppose it's lucky they didn't change their minds mid-stride in response to some perceived slight and kill you on the spot."

"I suppose that's true. Yet you were able to meet with common folk and heads of state alike, quite safely, Dr. McEvoy. Why do you think that is?" The other professors had fallen back, giving Marcus and Vitter the floor.

Marcus gave another self-deprecating laugh, a default response from him. "'Heads of state' is a bit misleading, to be fair. I'd hardly apply the term to the matriarch of a small village, for instance. Norleans and Dallas are much larger, of course, and I did meet their respective leaders, but it's not as though there's a prime minister or chancellor."

"As you say. But I think it's clear why I need the expertise of you—

and this university's department—to further the interests of the Brother Nations in this arena."

"Does your supervisor feel the same way?" Hatton interjected to the tune of a lightly annoyed look from Vitter. "I believe I saw a quote from him yesterday indicating that he favored a more direct approach."

Holly met Yuying's eyes across the table, and both of them rose as one to clear the dishes and start serving the third course. Holly took the dishes from her side of the table and stayed in the kitchen to start poaching the artisan cheeses and pears she'd selected earlier in brandy, cinnamon and clove. From the kitchen she couldn't hear the conversation turn, but when she returned to serve it seemed that the subject hadn't changed much other than to get slightly more contentious.

"You say there have been no successful settlements by the Brother Nations," Hatton said. "What about Strip City?"

Vitter sniffed. "A resort run by rogue business interests with a thin veneer of legitimacy. From a political standpoint, it's an expensive vanity project, and the men who footed the bill are content to be gangsters. They have no interest in opening up the continent, or in the good of the nation."

"That's always the problem when politicians and businessmen clash, isn't it?" Hatton replied. "Even though their expansionist leanings aren't all that different in spirit."

"So," Vitter said, returning to Marcus, "you crash-landed, found your way to Norleans, and then what?"

"Well, I had no way of contacting anyone in Sino-India or at the university to let them know what had befallen me, of course. With no radio or means to communicate, I thought it best to turn to my primary arena of interest—North America. It was quite an unexpected opportunity! I had hoped to learn what I could from the university here in Singapore, but never imagined that I might actually go to North America and study the land from within. In truth, it was beyond anything I could have anticipated, and so I chose to make the most of it. I approached the Loyola-Tulane university in Norleans, but they did not believe that I came from the colonies and threatened psychiatric evaluation. This was my first encounter with the curious fact that most North Americans are completely unaware of the colonies' existence, even so-called institutions of higher learning. As you may know, mental evaluation in Norleans tends to involve massive amounts of HNE, so I felt it prudent to make my exit hastily."

"Evidence suggests that there is a working HNE lab at Loyola-Tulane."

"There are several in Norleans!" Marcus replied. "It is something of an obsession there. They have large and small facilities. The one at the university has been operating since the Fall. The city's wall is HNE-powered, in fact."

"Amazing," Elden said.

"It is certainly a thing to see. A deep, dense forest that seems to spring out of nowhere, containing flora and fauna quite fantastical. And somewhat sentient as well, I am told. One must travel through it to leave the city by land in any direction, and woe unto those who threaten or displease the city masters."

This seemed to wake Aidanab up. "They've continued to develop hypernatural animals? Have their experiments with HNE on humans gone as far as China's augmentation programs? Have they created new shifter breeds?"

"None of the above, from what I saw," Marcus said. "I thought that military applications of HNE-enhanced men and creatures had stopped in the Brother Nations as well, though, due to poor results?"

"There is a port as well, though," said Vitter, returning them to the subject at hand. "Why didn't you just sail to Singapore from there? At least one of the floating cities stops there regularly."

Marcus laughed. "Well, naturally I wanted to see more of North America. I met a shifter, a felid, and traveled with him to Savannah, and from there north."

"What of the danger?"

He gave one of his shrugs. "I suppose it never occurred to me that I might be in danger."

"Holly has told me of Savannah," Elden said. All eyes turned to her for a moment, and she gave a brief smile of acknowledgement but didn't take the stage from Marcus.

Rehsil tented his fingers. "And the people of North America? One would assume that a man of your knowledge would quickly rise to power—or find himself burned at the stake—in such a place, but this didn't happen. You made friends, I'm sure. I can't imagine you'd have survived if you didn't."

"Perhaps not," Marcus said, his voice far away for a moment. "Survival can be such a tenuous thing. I was also struck by a sense of profound displacement, as you can imagine. I have experienced things that my great-grandfather never did—the sun on my face without filtered glass. The open sky. Breezes. Dirt." He glanced at Holly and smiled, and she returned it. "I felt like such a visceral, natural thing, as though I'd never had the experience of truly feeling the human animal inside of me. I confess I rather enjoyed getting dirty and sunburned." Marcus laughed, and Elden and Vitter joined him.

"Do you wish you'd stayed?" Aidanab asked.

"With all due respect to the fine people of North America—absolutely not! It was an entertaining—and occasionally dangerous—experience, but I find that I am quite enamored of air conditioning and running water, both of which are in short supply there. It is also rather easier to get shot at."

"Indeed," Vitter said.

Holly rose silently to clear the third course, and Yuying followed her lead. They ushered the group into Elden's sitting room and served tea while he showed off some of the antiques he'd collected.

Vitter left not long after the meal finished, but the others lingered, making the most of the social time. Holly stayed out of their way, though she followed some of the conversation from the dining room as she and Yuying cleaned up; a rambling debate she'd heard before, about whether North America could be successfully made into a Sino-Indian colony or ally, the historical reasons why it would or wouldn't work, and about what that might mean for both respective populations. It was one of the few times that Elden and Rehsil seemed to be able to have a civilized discussion that didn't quickly turn personal and contentious.

"I would urge a great deal of caution," Rehsil said. "When China and India were inundated with hordes of European refugees after the Fall, the changes to our culture were tremendous. I think that we, as a people, are lucky that the societies were able to integrate relatively bloodlessly. But the tensions still exist—witness the recent riots in Singapore and Mumbai."

"I'd hardly call a few dozen student activists being shot with teargas and slickguns a 'riot,'" Elden interjected.

"Be that as it may, with the wrong influences, or too much upheaval, the balance could crumble quickly."

"And what do you see happening in that case?" Marcus asked.

"At worst? Open warfare. This nation has no fewer than a hundred distinct ethnic and social groups, many of whom do not speak the same language or worship the same gods. The Brother Nations may stand as a beacon against the chaos that has swallowed the rest of the planet, but that is not guaranteed to always be the case. And even the strongest brotherly bonds are not immune to conflict."

"Which also serves as an argument for expansion," Elden pointed out. "Giving those potentially contentious groups more space to live in, where they aren't forced to interact—"

"Or compete for resources," Hatton added.

"—could have a mutual calming effect on any unrest."

"Years of armies traveling the world with the intent of conquest would suggest that you're incorrect in that assumption," Rehsil said.

Holly stood in the kitchen doorway, listening, and caught Marcus looking at her again. He looked away quickly. She found that a bit charming; so many men had no problem staring openly.

Marcus cleared his throat. "If I may? It's a common misconception that North America's a wasteland full of bandit-king warlords keeping harems of women as baby machines. The truth is, and has been for a long time, that such a social system just doesn't work in the long run. I have written about this at length, in my editorial appendices. Immediately after the Colony Conflict, it's true that many such bands of marauders sprang up in North America, some of them quite large. But at the same time this was happening, communities were also rebuilding themselves. The Conflict caused a great loss of life and damage to the infrastructure, but the land itself was intact, unlike with a nuclear bombing or chemical warfare. Once the dust settled, those who knew how didn't have trouble securing the bare necessities of life, and from there improving it. It was quickly established, especially in the northern part of the country, that a stable agricultural town had a much better chance of surviving the winter than a roving band of raiders—all they had to do was wall themselves and their assets away and wait out the siege.

"In many cases these towns went a step further, actually recruiting guards from the very bands that were attacking them. 'Join us and we will feed, clothe and house you,' I imagine the pitch went. 'We'll tend your wounds and give you clean water.' A persuasive argument indeed, for the records show that it was successful much more often than it went badly for the village. The first walled cities began to grow in places where anarchy and lawlessness were eradicated, as you can imagine. The goal of the average man is, after all, to find peace and safety, rather than endless conflict."

Holly noticed that the other professors had responded almost instinctively to Marcus' tone of speaking. He was giving a lecture, no longer just talking, and so they didn't interrupt and gave him their full attention. Even Rehsil had shut his mouth to listen. She imagined that they were behaving the way they wished their students would. For his part, Marcus was more animated than he had been earlier in the evening, and as he hadn't been drinking enough wine to be tipsy, he was clearly feeling passionate about his words.

"As for the women," Marcus continued, "the scenario most people imagine is equally unsustainable, in the long run. Women held captive as fertile baby machines and infertile sex slaves. Hah! How long do you imagine that you could keep half of the population—or more!—forcibly enslaved, regardless of how many weapons you had? It's a teenage boy's fantasy grown into a false assumption of policy, is what it is. Such a scenario assumes a level of passive acquiescence on the part of not only the fertile women, but all of the women in the society that's just nonexistent if they all start out as slaves. This is especially true when you consider the rather headstrong and individualistic tendencies of North Americans. It works for a short time, but eventually—in two generations, or less—it breaks down, and the order falls apart.

"Little Rock is the example for sustaining such a system: it requires the buy-in of the female population—that is, the women *themselves* have to support and believe the system. In Little Rock as well as a few similar enclaves in North America, this is accomplished with religious beliefs rather than coercion or violence. Though some could say they amount to the same. And it still only tends to remain stable on a small scale. In Little Rock, I learned that dissension among women is fairly common, and those who show signs of nonconformity to the belief system are forced to bear children if they are fertile, and simply exiled if not. In extreme cases they are executed. 'Exile' may be a harsh term; there is a complicated process of excommunication that gives the victim the impression of having been 'free to go' all along, if she does not agree with the system. Of course, there is the specter of eternal damnation looming as well. And this is a hard thing to thrust upon a girl who's in her early teens, you can imagine. But Little Rock has proved very adept at preemptively removing or silencing potential dissidents from its midst, well before the system can be threatened. That said, the city's poor reputation among travelers has affected trade dramatically. Trading bands with female members won't go there if they can avoid it, which limits the incoming goods. When I was there, the city was in a poorly-disguised state of poverty, and it remains to be seen how long the center will hold."

"An excellent analysis," Rehsil said. "We must speak on this further."

"I'm sure Mr. Vltter will be disappointed that he left early," Aidanab said with a little laugh.

"I imagine he knows all of this already," Elden replied.

Holly wasn't surprised when, at the end of the evening, Elden offered her to Marcus. Her benefactor had noticed the traveling professor's interest as well, of course. Marcus didn't drive, so Elden sent the car to ferry them to his university-sponsored lodgings. He was excited by the self-driving Daimler, and made Holly show him all of its features, from the onboard email and video to the coolbox and heated seats. The rain had stopped, but he wanted to see the windshield wipers work anyway. He was excited by everything he saw, it seemed.

"And it will drive itself home?" he asked after the car dropped them off, watching it go. They were just off of campus, in a quaint little block of recently-built apartments designed to look like old American brownstones.

"Yes, and in the morning Elden will send it to pick me up. It is quite convenient." Marcus fumbled with the lock, which used an old-fashioned metal key, and Holly waited patiently, gauging how tipsy he was. He wasn't impaired, she decided, just unfamiliar with the procedure.

The apartment was sparse, barely furnished—it wasn't as though Marcus would have had any furniture. "I did have some luggage when I arrived," he said, "books and things, but North America has a way of...taking things away from you, let's say. Some things I traded, others were lost in a fire."

"I'm sorry to hear. Would you like help in replacing them? I'm sure over the next few months, as you're working with Elden, we can find many new things to decorate with. And books. You'll need a library, of course." She figured it was fair to assume he'd be settling in Singapore, as he'd talked at length about doing just that at dinner.

"Well, I appreciate the offer. Can I get you something? I'm afraid there's not much..."

"That's *my* job," Holly said lightly. "Would you like something? If there's something you need that you haven't got, I can go out to get it."

"At this hour?"

"I have my ways," she said with a smile.

"I'm sure you do. Professor Ono did say that you were one of the highest-trained housegirls? Myawi school, yes? I saw an article about your school in my reading materials, on the trip over from Strip City. Professor Ono says you're as special as you are beautiful."

"I'm glad I make him happy, Professor McEvoy."

"You don't need to be so formal with me. Professor Ono says he enjoys your company because you're willing to talk freely with him. I would imagine that many of you don't. Indentured servitude can be a ticklish social position. But you should feel free to talk with me as you would like. As an historian, I would dearly love to hear your thoughts, unfettered by decorum."

"Are you trying to get me into trouble?" she teased.

Marcus laughed. "Of course not! I don't want to hear any secrets you shouldn't be telling me. I am just asking to hear what you're thinking. Honestly."

"Honestly?"

"Yes. Please, sit."

She'd have felt better getting him a drink, but sat. She'd been challenged by Elden's friends before, and it usually turned out that her being frank was not what they were looking for.

He practically clapped his hands with pleasure as he joined her on the cheap sofa. "Now. Tell me what's on your mind. What do you think of, when you've been sent off with a virtual stranger like this?"

"How to serve them, of course."

"Serve?"

"The same sorts of things I do for Professor Ono."

"So, you'd clean my house?"

"Of course, if you wanted me to."

"Do you often find yourself doing the housework of the men Professor Ono loans you to?"

"Quite frequently," she said with a smile, thinking of the filth she'd scrubbed out of many a bathtub.

"And cooking?"

"Yes."

"And...sexual services?"

"Yes," she said again. He seemed to think she'd be reluctant to answer that. If he expected an emotional response, he'd be disappointed. And as she considered it, something clicked. "There's nothing wrong with providing sex for Professor Ono's friends if he sends me home with them," she said. "But I do wonder why you brought me home with you. You aren't interested in women, are you?"

Marcus reddened, confirming her suspicions. "I don't know why you'd think—" he stammered.

"I can tell," she said mildly. And now she had control of the conversation again. "Don't worry, if you prefer that nobody knows, it's not my place to share."

Clearly still ill at ease, Marcus tried to settle himself. "Well," he said, running a hand through his curly white hair. "Well."

"I doubt anyone would be upset, though. Is it a taboo in the colonies?"

"It can be."

"Fear not; I am a bottomless cavern of secrets," she said. "Let's let it be what it is, and not worry about it. So since you don't have any interest in sex, and don't need your apartment cleaned, why did you accept Professor Ono's offer?"

"It...seemed like the polite thing to do."

Holly angled her head. "A man loans you a housegirl who cost more than his house, and you accept just to be polite?"

Marcus gasped. "More than his house?"

"By about half again its value," she amended. "We're not supposed to know that, but I do."

"Is that common?"

"Very uncommon. I suppose he was quite taken with me."

"I can see why."

"Can you?"

"Of course! Just because I didn't want to have you over for...carnal reasons doesn't mean I can't see that you're articulate, witty and charming. Quite an interesting contrast to...well. Yes, I suppose there was another reason I wanted the chance to talk with you in private. I wasn't sure if it was appropriate to say at the dinner table, but during my North American travels, you see, I met your sister."

Holly stiffened from her spine to her toes. "What do you mean?"

"Your twin sister Ivy. Ivy Aniram. That's your family name, isn't it? I met her. Traveled with her for a time, in fact."

A tremble found its way into her hands, and she stilled it by clenching her fingers. "You must be mistaken," she said, meeting Marcus' eyes. "I did have a twin sister, but she died when we were children."

"I assure you she is alive and well!" Marcus said cheerfully. "And she's looking for you. She said your mother used to make you wear a dot on your cheek, and she wore one on the opposite side, so the adults could tell you apart. When I met Ivy, she wore them on both cheeks, so you would know her."

A sob tried to escape Holly's throat. She locked the sound away, kept her face neutral. She was a porcelain doll.

"She seems to be quite well respected among the travelers and scavs. Quite a few people know Ivy Aniram."

Holly smiled privately. "I haven't heard that name for a long time, except in my mother's letters—oh, rabbit of the moon, our *mother!* You have to let her know, Professor McEvoy. That is, I would appreciate it if you could get word to her."

"Please, call me Marcus. I would be happy to deliver the good news to your mother. Ruth is her name, correct?"

Holly wondered if this could be an elaborate joke. Her heart pounded madly in her chest and she was on the verge of truly losing her composure. Could this have been staged for a television show? But she'd never heard of one targeting domestics, and if there were, surely Elden wouldn't allow such a cruel joke as to tell her that Ivy was alive. She decided to believe Marcus. If it was a joke, she'd take the humiliation in stride. "Yes. She lives in Semangat Terang, it's a factory town near Tumpat."

"Yes, I suppose it would be awkward for you to travel there, with your duties to Professor Ono. I would be happy to go."

"Thank you. I write her letters every month, but I think she should know as soon as possible, and from your words directly. And you'll be able to answer any of her questions better than I."

"Have you ever visited her?"

"No. It's only about an hour via the express train, but the workers in the factory-towns are extremely busy, and she's a supervisor, which means she'd hardly have the time. They don't get much vacation time. She has been pooling it, though. She had a chance to visit last year, but there was a storm in the mountains. Maybe this fall though." It was perhaps indecorous, but Holly changed the direction of the conversation without regard for what Marcus might want to discuss. "How was Ivy? Was she well? Where is she?"

He didn't seem to mind being quizzed. "She's a scavenger, with her own vehicle, so I couldn't say where she is now. I met her just north of Nashville. She's healthy and seems content enough. She is obsessed with finding you, of course. Shortly before we met, she was injured in an attack, and left with a limp and a rather characterful scar on her temple. I'm sorry," he said, breaking off suddenly, "does that upset you?"

Holly got control of her face. "Of course it does. You say she had recovered, though. How long ago was this?"

"I last saw her shortly before coming here. She got me safely across the wasteland to Strip City, in fact. So ironic to meet you less than two months later."

"Do you know what exactly happened to her leg?"

"A torn ligament of some kind, perhaps her ACL. Obviously the doctors in Detroit lacked the facilities to easily repair it, and they would be unlikely to waste the resources on a scav anyway—I am sorry."

"It's okay. I remember how it was."

"She was doing well in spite of her injury. She fabricated herself a brace so she could walk, and was no longer traveling alone when last I saw her."

Holly ignored the knot in her stomach. She and Ivy had missed each other by a matter of weeks, or less, if Marcus was correct about when he'd been there. Not that the odds of a chance encounter were high in the chaos of Strip City, but the thought was like a twisted knife. "And you say she's looking for me?"

"It was her obsession. She said she dreamt about you. That was what led her to Strip City: a particularly vivid dream of you, in what I believe she thought was one of the hotels there."

"I *was* there," Holly said. Habit kept her voice neutral, but she felt as though a storm had blown up inside of her head. Her mind was a thundercloud.

As if mirroring her mood, there was a sudden cloudburst outside, a crash of thunder followed by rain tumbling down as though a faucet had been opened. Marcus jumped, and Holly smiled.

"Forgive me," he said. "I find weather very difficult to get used to, though endlessly fascinating."

"What are the colonies like? Climate-wise, that is?" She wanted to talk about something else now. If they went on about Ivy, it felt like her mind might spin itself into uselessness. Holly wanted to tell Marcus to leave for her mother's now, to get him on the road. Possibilities went off in her head life fireworks. Her sister was *alive*.

"There's a range," Marcus said. "The temperatures vary somewhat in different areas of the frame, and Control regulates gradual changes in the ambient temperature. It's very subtle, but the changes simulate seasons in a way that's been found to have a positive effect on the population. There aren't extreme changes, of course, but public areas will be around ten degrees in the winter and are taken up into the twenties for the summer months. But of course there's not much of what you'd call 'weather.' It doesn't rain, and the only wind comes from air movers."

"So you've never seen snow."

"I have, actually! From a distance, to be sure. It was visible in the mountains when we crossed the wasteland. I was unable to see it up close, however. Some day, perhaps. There is a device that makes snow, on the starward end of the frame, that is used to show schoolchildren what it is like. But I'm sure it's not the same as wild snow."

Holly laughed. "I hope I'm there the first time. I'd love to see your reaction."

"That exciting, is it?"

"Maybe. It's just such an interesting opportunity, to be there to watch someone experience so many things for the first time, as an adult. It must be frightening sometimes, being so far from everything you know."

"I've adjusted," Marcus said, shrugging. He looked at her for a moment. "You're distracted."

"Of course I am. After what you've just told me, why wouldn't I be?"

"Yes, I suppose that's quite true. I am sorry if I upset you."

Holly laughed again, amused by the sudden realization that Marcus had said what she usually said. "It's perfectly all right, Marcus. It's wonderful news, just a bit overwhelming."

"Well, I will do my best to get word to your mother as soon as possible. They have given me leave to travel as I will."

"Did Ivy tell you about her?"

"Some. But I'd love to hear your side of the story. After you and your mother fell out of the truck, Ivy said that everyone thought you were dead."

"She didn't fall," Holly said. "She jumped. We hit a bump, and I lost my grip and fell over the side. My mother yelled at Ivy to stay and then jumped out after me. I landed on the ground and she got to me. And then we were surrounded by men—the pirates who had attacked our caravan."

"Where was this?"

"Not far south of Astoria, on the coast. We were on our way back to Astoria, in fact. My mother was born there, and we were traveling back to visit friends of hers she hadn't seen since before we were born. Pirates sometimes come ashore and attack travelers."

"What did they do?"

"Took us with them. We heard them shooting, and destroying the rest of the caravan as they took us, and saw the burning vehicles."

"Did they kidnap you to be their servants, or to bear children?"

"My mother was infertile, and I was just a girl, so they took us to Sino-India to sell to a domestic school. That practice isn't legal any more, hasn't been for about ten years." She recounted the rest of the story to him, remembering telling Nielle about it a few months before. "I spent most of the time grieving for Ivy. I had never been apart from her, my entire life, until that day."

"You were eight, according to Ivy. Is that correct?"

"Yes," she said with a smile.

"That must have been terrible."

"It was."

"It's certainly a much happier ending than one might have expected, considering the way it began." Holly nodded in agreement. "Can you tell me more about your Myawi school training?" he asked with barely a hesitation. It seemed that once he got started he couldn't ask his questions fast enough.

"What do you want to know?" Holly asked. She'd be keeping her clothes on, but suspected it was going to be a very long night nevertheless.

chapter 20

Shiloh's story

We ended up staying in Middlegate for a few days. We stuck around partly because the Benzers didn't seem to be in any hurry to leave. I think Walter might have been fucking one of the dwellers. I'm not judging him though— I did, too. Swan acted like she was going to find a playmate herself, but she never did.

Another reason for not leaving was that Middlegate was just kind of nice. They lived in holes in the ground, but that's a misleading way to describe them. Really, they had dug big, elaborate pits, and then put on roofs and buried them. When they invited us into their homes, they had multiple rooms, with wicker and wood floors and real walls, a lot of it salvaged pre-Fall stuff that was cozy. And it was cool; the desert above was hot, but they had clever air tubes that let breezes through without letting too much warmth out at night. They used old pre-Fall bottles to make grids that let in light but weren't obvious from ground level. Even if you knew they were there, it was easy to miss Middlegate when all of the doors were shut. Most of the big caravans apparently didn't know they were there, and sped past all the time.

And they had a bread oven. Oh, the bread! They had built a stone enclosure big enough to park a rig inside into the side of one of the hills, and used it to bake bread. Dozens of loaves at once; they traded the bread to their chosen travelers, too. It was wonderful stuff; I ate a lot of it. They were so far off the beaten path that my performances earned us quite a bit of bread, food and fuel. They'd never seen Gallamore's of course, so I did my new routine and the one from last year's show, and I was able to do Cadge's and Anna's and some of the acrobats' performances as well. I even managed Algo's juggling, though I was never as good as he was. Not that it mattered, of course, since he was dead. The first time I did his routine, it made me cry afterward.

Ivy and Walter also did a lot of mechanical repairs in trade when they weren't working on the Vovo and the other Benzers' rigs.

So the story behind Middlegate and its underground houses is a neat one. The Fall happened suddenly, brought the buildings and bridges and planes down without warning—but not all of them. Like Detroit, and Savannah, and some other places, a few planes managed to stay aloft as well, for a while. One of them was piloted by Captain Sandy Collins, who was flying about two hundred passengers bound for Salt Lake City when the rest of the planes in North America came down. He tried to land in Salt Lake City, but the airport there was a smoking ruin. So he kept going, even though he didn't have enough fuel to get very far. When he couldn't go any farther, he did his best to land the plane with no electrics or assistance on the only road beneath them. It mostly worked; the big jet skidded off of the road and hit a building, but all of the passengers survived.

The building they hit was hundreds of years old. It was a little restaurant, and it was actually the only building in Middlegate, even before the Fall. It was a tiny town, just the one building—the only one for hundreds of miles in fact—and Captain Collins put his plane right through it. Luckily, the folks living nearby thought it was funny more than anything else. It was pretty clear that help wasn't coming any time soon, so some of the plane's passengers set off walking to get help. The rest, including Captain Collins, stayed in Middlegate. Since there wasn't much to build houses with, they started digging their underground homes, sometimes using parts of the plane to help themselves along. They fixed up the building that the plane hit, a little, but it collapsed during a snowstorm about thirty years later and didn't get rebuilt.

And that's how the little town got there. Middlegate has about forty-five people living there, and they say that's three times as big as it was a hundred years ago. It's a close-knit community, and self-sustaining enough that they didn't need to do much trade other than with the Benzers and one or two of the caravan groups that pass through. It was strange to me to think that if we hadn't been rolling with the Benzers, they wouldn't have opened their doors and we'd have driven right past (and never gotten to sample their wonderful bread).

As it was, we spent our few days there, and Ivy and Kroni talked a lot about whether we should continue east, or turn around and go back to Astoria. It wasn't really an argument, I didn't think. Ivy wanted to go to Astoria, but it wasn't the right direction and she couldn't pretend it was. Especially since we'd already gone to the trouble of crossing the most dangerous part of the wasteland. From Salt Lake on east, it's almost all empty land, farms and cities that Sam Ward burned out. The desert pirates don't come that far east of the mountains. Ivy says it's because then they have to deal with ranchers and farmers, and they'd rather wait in the desert like spiders.

More so than when traveling with the circus, I found that rest time was important. With Gallamore's, all I had to do was practice. With just the four of us, there were always little things to do: the Vovo needed things fixed, clothes needed mending, guns needed to be cleaned and reloaded and so on. Ivy liked to go through her little tool bags and make sure everything was there. She also kept things wrapped a certain way; she had little pouches with doodads that were tied together ready to be traded, and other little pouches that she had counted roundrocks or rems into so she didn't have to count them in front of people, she could just hand the pouches off. All these little chores took time, and if they got put off too long, like they had a few times when weather and encounters with bad folks made necessary, things got chaotic.

If there's one thing that makes Ivy cranky, it's chaos. She deals with it well enough in the heat of the moment, sure, but if it goes on for too long she starts to get snappish and obsessive. She'll even yell at Swan at times like that.

At night, we stayed above ground with our rigs, while the Middlegate dwellers went back underground—those that didn't stay near the fire to chat. Walter had suggested to Ivy that she pull a part off of the Vovo and clean it, so she was doing that. Whatever the part was, it stank of corngas, and the stuff she was using to clean it smelled even worse. She didn't seem to mind. Kroni sat with her, using the same stuff to clean one of his big guns.

I didn't have anything to do, so I was lying in Ivy's hammock and looking at the sky. It's really easy to forget, but doing nothing is nice, too.

"So you're not sure if we should be driving east now?" Ivy was asking Kroni.

"I am not sure of anything," he said. "I know that Mr. Gallamore and Mr. Burdan told us that the Sino-Indian group was traveling with a domestic. But it is also true that there are many people traveling with domestics in Strip City."

"So, so, so you said," Ivy replied. "But Mr. Burdan also said he thought she might actually know my sister."

"I know. And it is also to Mr. Burdan's advantage to have you out of

Strip City. You made him look bad."

"He made himself look bad. You think he lied just to get rid of us?"

Kroni shook his head. "I do not know. And this is a strange situation. We appear to be following one group of Inchins, who were in turn followed by another."

"Could have been the second group was part of the same caravan," Ivy said. "Carrying supplies?"

"Maybe."

Ivy worked in silence for a moment, finishing what she was doing. She stopped, put the engine part down, and wiped her cheek. Her hand left a dusty smear of brown. "You weren't too happy about the idea of going to Astoria to find a way to get to Sino-India, either."

"I was not. If nothing else, this path is certainly safer than that one."

"I can't help thinking that if she's still across the ocean, we're going farther away from her."

He nodded. "That may be true. Though you know as well as I do that sometimes the way forward is a sidestep."

She nodded. "Don't have to like it though."

I knew we were leaving soon, and it was a longish ride across barren territory. I was a bit worried. I felt like I was going to get anxious soon. One of the things my body likes to do to remind me that I'm not the same as the people around me is that I don't get monthlies the same way Ivy does and Swan used to. The best way to say it is that I go into heat, just like a fucking cat or a dog, and if I can't find playmates for those days, it's awful. I get edgy without cuddling at the best of times, and I have trouble sleeping if I don't fuck, but for those few days every month or so, it's so much louder than usual, loud enough to make me nervous. It's like my body screams, convinced that if I don't get sex every hour, I'm just going to die, and never get any again. When I traveled with the circus, there was almost always a convenient playmate that I could keep around for a couple of days and pretty near fuck to death. Traveling with Ivy and the others, that wasn't an option. I can keep it to myself within reason, but I still didn't want to be out in the middle of nowhere when it happened. What was I going to do, beg Ivy to stop so I could pounce on the first farmboy I saw?

When I think about it, I'm pretty sure that's how my mother died. She was in heat, and she went to a small village and fucked all of the men, every last one of them, and the women got together and killed her. It was hard to keep that thought out of my head at that time of the month—unless I was fucking. How ironic is that?

chapter 21

Eighty-nine days before Princess Aiyana's trimester celebration

>> What do you think, readers? Should the Société de Conservation de la Culture Française (SCCF) be allowed to move the remains of the Eiffel Tower from Paris to Colombo? The debate continues, as the group of investors based in Singapore and Colombo is said to be moving forward with the elaborate (and extremely costly) plan to rescue and rebuild the famous landmark. The SCCF has purchased a site to be designated as a French historical district in Colombo, where many refugees from Western European nations settled after the Colony Conflict.

The gesture has been lauded by expat nationalists, of course, but there is reported to be a strong opposition from the few remaining residents of the long-ruined city. Believe it or not, a small number of people refused to vacate the city after it was destroyed in the Colony Conflict, and have been living there ever since! Officials estimate that between four and ten thousand Parisians still make their homes in what's left of the city, just barely keeping it from succumbing to nature, and naturally they consider themselves the heirs to France's long and storied history. For over a hundred years they have defended the partially-collapsed Eiffel Tower from the ravages of scrap metal salvagers and weather, and it looks like they're prepared to hold out against the SCCF as well...

–Tinzee's Tea Room

Holly wasn't sure what to expect, but nonetheless felt relieved when Elden expressed intrigue and excitement at the news of Ivy. "Phenomenal!" he said when she told him about it over breakfast. Holly had returned from Marcus' apartment when the car came for her at five-thirty, prepared Elden's breakfast and the materials he needed to take to school that day, and they had time to chat over breakfast.

The news about Ivy distracted Elden so much that he didn't ask about the sex, which was convenient as Holly didn't want to have to blatantly skirt the issue of Marcus' homosexuality. Elden would want to know why they hadn't had sex, if he asked, and then it would stick out in his mind no matter what convenient deflection she offered. Better if it didn't come up at all.

"Does he know how to find her?" Elden asked.

"No. But I...may I request a favor?"

"By all means."

"I'd..." she trailed off. It felt strange to make a personal request of Elden, even if he'd given her permission to. She gathered herself, annoyed with herself for stammering. "I'd like to search. If she was in Strip City recently, someone will surely know how to find her. She's been looking for me, according to Professor McEvoy."

"And if you find her?"

"I would like to bring her back to Singapore with us, of course. I don't know what she could do, but perhaps you could talk with the people you know in immigration." Holly lost her voice again. A pleading tone wanted to worm its way into her voice, so she cut herself off.

Elden held up a hand, shaking it in the negative. "I wouldn't thrust her upon the mercy of the state. She could come live with us. I think after you've been so long apart, that's only right, don't you?"

Her heart surged. "Live with us here?"

"Would you want that?"

"Absolutely, Elden. Thank you. Thank you so much." She felt like she was glowing.

He smiled. "It's my pleasure, after all that you've done for me. We'll go to North America. I'll take some time off. The semester is almost over anyway."

"Elden!"

"What?"

"You're not usually this...reckless."

"Well, I'm in a reckless mood. It's not every day that there's a chance to reunite a family," he said with a grin.

"Elden..."

He held up a hand. "No words. You've more than earned this. I'm sure you know that even though I'm your benefactor, I think of you as a friend. More than."

She wasn't sure how to respond to that, so she just nodded.

After Elden left for campus, Holly struggled to focus. She wanted to call Marcus, to ask when he planned to go to Semangat Terang, to ask him more about Ivy, but of course that wouldn't be proper. Rude, even. Regardless, Marcus had neither phone nor email yet, so calling him wasn't an option. This didn't stop her from thinking about Ivy all morning. It was shameful, that Holly hadn't consciously thought of her twin in so long. She looked up news from Strip City, playing the ridiculous odds that there would somehow be an item that was obviously related to Ivy. The biggest stories were increased pirate activity near Hawaii, ground being broken for a new hotel partially funded by the Deshmus, and an opinion piece about a security guard who'd shot a young boy to death and subsequently been reassigned to a casino in Mumbai with no criminal charges filed.

It was as interesting as news from Strip City generally got, but it wasn't satisfying at all. Then again, it wasn't as though they'd be getting news from anywhere else in North America, where Ivy might be.

Holly tumbled back through her own memories instead, to foraging for asparagus and berries with her sister, the two of them always trying to collect more than their mother could. To skipping stones on the banks of any river or pond that they could find. To the awful spring when they'd both had whooping cough and their mother got the Cradle at the same time. To tree-climbing contests and weaving flowers into belts and crowns.

It felt like something that had happened to someone else.

Once she finished her morning house chores, Holly sent Lakshmi a note giving her the basics of what Marcus had told her. The response was an immediate video chat, which Holly didn't answer; the only thing that lay in that course of action were a thousand questions, most of which she couldn't or wouldn't answer, and then Shmi would sulk about it. Possibly for days.

She tried to get back to work, still beset by childhood memories. At one she did her daily exercises, then returned to her room to change back to presentable clothes. When she did, something caught her eye as she pushed the closet door shut, and she paused. It wasn't just being distracted about Ivy, there was something more. Holly took a mental inventory of what she was seeing and figured it out in a moment: the Ivory Sisters box was gone. She'd stowed it under a box of extra rain gear, and now that box was at the bottom of the stack.

With a frown, she squatted and looked quickly through the closet, but there weren't many places for it to hide and she knew she hadn't misplaced it as she'd had no reason at all to move it. It was gone.

Well. That was certainly unnerving. Elden was unlikely to have taken it, as he didn't go in her room, and certainly didn't root about in her closet. Holly thought about the evening before, and through all the semi-chaotic activity of the party she was reasonably sure that nobody had gone into her room. Vitter was the first man she thought of, naturally, but as she thought her way back through the evening she couldn't think of a time when he'd have had any reason to go near her room. Elden's guest bathroom was in the front hall, and for Vitter to randomly detour into their private areas would have attracted interest.

As she thought about it, she remembered that Vitter definitely hadn't been carrying anything when he had left, nor did he have any obvious pockets large enough to contain Nielle's package. So...one of the other professors? That made even less sense.

She gave a little sigh. Well, if someone asked her why she had it, she could certainly counter by asking why they'd been in her private space. And the truth was simple enough. She had nothing to hide, and her motives were no more sinister than not wanting to cloud Nielle's reputation after her death.

Thinking about Nielle took her right back to Strip City, and back into her own memories. Of the time she'd torn the hem of her dress and Ivy had ripped hers as well so they matched. Of playing on a big, bare mound that turned out to be a massive fire ant hill while their mother fished. Of huddling together in their rig's bulletproof hardbox when there was danger. About fresh cherry pies baked on bricks.

There might be cherries at the market, come to think of it, and Elden might like a cherry pie. There was not a time when Elden didn't love cherry pie—in fact, it was one of his favorite North American treats. Contemplating dinner brought Holly back into the moment. She focused on dinner, on the pie, but Ivy wouldn't go far from her thoughts. She tended to some other minor tasks: a lamp that wasn't working, an adjustment to the climate control to help it keep up with the steadily increasing humidity, the cleaning she'd put off in the morning. There was an hour left before she needed to start dinner, and would normally have taken the time to change linens, but today a head-clearing nap seemed like a better plan.

Some days nothing went right. This was one of those; she slept for almost two hours.

"Rabbit of the—" Holly swore, throwing herself out of bed with considerably less grace than was decorous. Elden would be home in half an hour and she hadn't even *started* dinner, let alone the pie she intended to bake.

Holly gathered herself as quickly as she could, checking the computer as she went into the kitchen, and saw that Lakshmi had called twice. As usual, the girl seemed to be looking for the best way to escape responsibility, and finding out the rest of Holly's story made the perfect excuse for shirking her duties. In spite of her desire to get out of work, Lakshmi wasn't very efficient—a flaw that Axtellia domestic training apparently failed to correct.

Today Holly was in no position to criticize. With an eye on the clock, she hastily pulled together Elden's meal, creating a reasonable facsimile of a North American-style roast while simultaneously assembling a canned-peach pie, since she hadn't gotten cherries. She risked scorching the greens that she was flash-frying in order to sneak in time for a table setting. When the computer chimed to alert her that Elden's car was three minutes away, she was just about ready.

She'd salvaged the day, but only just. Holly definitely had to get Ivy out of her head. It would work out as it would, and there was nothing she could do right now. She had to keep telling herself that.

As soon as dinner was finished, the sleepiness pressed in again. She did an electrostim bump before Elden went to bed to give her the energy to finish the evening's chores, and it had the added benefit of speeding her brain up enough that she finally put Ivy out of her mind for a while. When she finally tumbled into bed, her music box put her right to sleep, and she found herself dreaming almost immediately, with no recollection of dozing off.

She was at the wheel of a large, battered car of some sort. It had no windows, and the back was open but there was a roof over her head. She was in the middle of a driving thunderstorm that hammered on the roof like a drum. It wasn't the warm rain of Singapore, but a cold, sharp-edged downpour. The car she was in seemed to be all bare metal surfaces and hard edges, the seat unyielding but comfortable, the steering wheel warm under her hands. The rain was coming down so hard she could barely see much beyond the car's hood at first, and there was a louder roar ahead of her, the sound of a roaring river almost drowned out by the rain.

She was cold. She'd gotten wet in the rain, and her fingers and feet were cold, her clothes soaked to the skin. Her knee throbbed with agony and her hands were filthy. The rain wasn't falling on her head but it was coming in the open roof behind her, wetting her shoulders, leaking down her back.

She was driving the car. More accurately, she was in control of the car, which was at the top of a muddy slope. A rope ran from the front of it to another vehicle farther down the hill, and she had her foot on the throttle, keeping it carefully modulated so the wheels wouldn't spin as she drove slowly backward. She was pulling the other vehicle away from the water, away from danger. Holly squinted out into the storm, keeping her eyes on the rope, which vibrated with tension.

Off to the sides of the truck, Holly could see people standing, watching the proceedings. Though the truck was doing all of the real work, she was at the wheel and might as well have had her own hands on the rope. She could feel their interest, and their need. They were counting on her to bring the stranded vehicle up. She could see now as her eyes adjusted to the curtain of rain that it was in danger of being swallowed by the raging flood,. Holly wasn't sure what to do but keep her foot carefully on the pedals, so she did. In some corner of her mind she realized that she didn't know how to drive this car, but it was happening and she didn't question it.

Thunder struck.

Suddenly there was a thump, a crack, the sound of a rope parting and cutting through the air, audible above the rain. As the sound echoed away, she looked at the rope attaching her car to the stricken one. It was unbroken, but her direction was reversing. The truck she was trying to rescue was pulling her now, downhill. She was sliding forward, tied to the stricken vehicle, and she felt her car slide forward into its own tracks in the mud. Within a heartbeat it had accelerated beyond control. The other vehicle hit the water and was swallowed by the maelstrom, and Holly thought she saw people swept out of it and into the wild river. Waves surged, and it disappeared.

Now the downward pull took on a new urgency. The river was pulling her in. Holly pushed the brake pedal harder, to no avail. Her car was on mud and it was going downhill faster and faster. She didn't know how to stop it. The people were counting on her and she didn't know what to do, she didn't even know how to drive—

Holly woke up with a gasp, kicking at her blankets. Her heart raced. She recalled times when she'd dreamt about North America before, but never this vividly. This had been—it took only a moment for her to figure out that she'd been dreaming that she was Ivy. The hurting knee, the scavenger's clothes—all of that had come from Marcus' description. It didn't feel like a dream that was a chaotic mélange of things she'd heard, though. She had felt like she was *there*.

Had she dreamt about—*as*—Ivy before?

chapter 22

*Eighty-seven days before Princess Aiyana's trimester
celebration*

>> Disarmament talks between Luna Colony and Beijing ended recently, with no forward motion reached on an agreement to widen the colonies' global restrictions on flight and long-range nuclear weapons. The web of EPRC satellites will continue to enforce a no-fly zone over North America and Europe, and Luna's defense minister Eric Delongchamp says that the colonies will also continue to target suspected long-range missile installations without warning. Two such facilities were destroyed last year, resulting in eighty-six deaths. Officials from the Brother Nations insist that the attacks targeted simple munitions manufacturing facilities that were not capable of building orbital craft and have criticized the colonies' decision...

—Yŭyīn of the Brother Nations

>> Violinist Hope Shankar continues her tour of the Brother Nations with a performance this Wednesday at the Gubala Opera Hall in Singapore. Shankar's enthusiastic appearance alongside Oskar Deshmu at last year's Classic Festival skyrocketed her to fame, and she has been playing sold-out shows since...

—Shairpie Shrivastva's Den

Holly had never taken much notice of the days' passing before, other than to keep track of each day's routine. With Ivy on her mind, however, the days suddenly seemed to simultaneously drag and speed past. Marcus left on a tour of Sino-India that she assumed would take him at some point to Semangat Terang, and though Holly knew it was ridiculous to expect word from him, every day without news tumbled into insignificance. She felt as though she was wasting time, and even though she knew she shouldn't be, she thought frequently of Ivy as well.

During her cognitive therapy session she shared some of these thoughts with Dr. Olai, who expressed concern.

"Has my benefactor complained that I am thinking of Ivy too much?" Holly knew it was unlikely that he had; she hadn't even mentioned Ivy to him for a month.

"He has not. Elden seems quite content with your performance. Yet, you must stay focused, Holly."

"I know."

"If your sister is alive, she will be a very different person than the child you knew. She will not have had your advantages, and will have had a very different life than yours. Many people in North America have a negative opinion of domestics." Dr. Olai shifted in her chair, deftly spinning her pen in her fingers. "It's possible that your sister might share this prejudice, or even be jealous of the privileges that you have received as a result of your training. As tragic as this would be, it is best to prepare yourself for the possibility that she may not recognize you for the exceptional person that you are."

"I will keep my thoughts under control."

"Good girl," Dr. Olai said. After the biweekly interview, Holly went for a short physical examination. She often had the thought that she was like a car going to the shop for maintenance. She found the comparison mildly amusing, and said as much, but Dr. Olai grew grave again. "That comparison really concerns me. Let's talk about what might be making you feel this way. Do you really feel like some sort of...appliance?"

"Not exactly."

"Service does not equal servitude, Holly. Myawi is what you are, not a task that is thrust upon you. Elden chose you to be a part of his life, and you know how vital you are in every aspect of his life. Does he make you feel unappreciated?"

"Of course not." Holly was immediately sorry that she had mentioned it, and felt slightly ashamed. Yet as Dr. Olai continued to talk, Holly's thoughts kept straying to the day of the college boys' attack. There was a spot of agitation that had fluttered around the edges of her thoughts ever since: she had been willing to accept any abuse that was visited upon her, because that was what her training dictated to protect Elden from a possible lawsuit should she injure one of her attackers by defending herself.

But...what about her? The Protectors had come for her, true. She couldn't be ungrateful for that. Myawi had taken care of her. Still, there was something discomfiting about relinquishing that responsibility to someone else.

The train of thought went nowhere, curled around itself and collapsed into incoherence. She made a mental effort to push the uncomfortable feelings to the back of her mind, and returned her focus to the doctor's words.

Holly rode her bicycle to the therapy appointments, because the ride helped to clear her head afterward. Today was especially refreshing; it was raining lightly, and the air was pleasantly cool, the sidewalks empty. She got home early, which made dealing with the roast duck she had planned for dinner that much easier. Holly busied herself making pasta by hand.

When she finally got around to checking the computer, there were several confusing messages from Lakshmi and Yuying referencing travel plans, suggesting that they could coordinate. She puzzled these over until Elden got home. She could tell immediately from his cagey manner that he held the answer to the cryptic messages.

Tonight, at least, he didn't try to keep her in suspense. "We're going to Strip City," he said. "As soon as the semester ends." That was in two weeks. "Research and sabbatical of sorts. At least, that's the official story."

"Official story?"

Elden's smile deepened. "I've been talking with Vitter, and he's agreed that his project would be greatly helped by having Singapore University staff in Strip City for a time. So the extended trip will have financial assistance from the government. We'll be able to bring half the department! I've already spoken to Rehsil, Hatton and Dineen about it."

Holly gave Elden a surprised smile. "So soon after the conference, too. That's impressive."

"It is! We'll need to rent an office of some sort. I'm hoping to bring at least two of the TAs along as well, summer internship. Let's plan for two months." She'd never made arrangements to rent a building before, let alone one overseas, but his confident assumption that she'd figure it out was gratifying. Elden grinned at her effusively, thoroughly pleased with himself. "Professor McEvoy will be touring the country for another four weeks, I'm told, but perhaps we can convince him to join us as well when he returns."

"This is shaping up to be quite an exciting summer. Is there any sort of office in particular you'd like me to look for?" she asked.

"Something outside of the tourist areas, I think. We should try to do some interviews with native-born Americans, as Professor McEvoy did, and I think that staying away from the casinos will facilitate that." Elden touched a finger to his lips, thinking. "That will help us to search for your sister as well."

"I'll see what I can find in Old Town." Holly's heart raced. They were really going to look for Ivy.

"You're looking at me like I've just performed a miracle," Elden said.

"Perhaps you have."

He waved it off. "I am doing what anyone would do for a friend. To be reunited with one who's been lost for so long. I don't think that anyone would shy away from bringing that kind of goodness into the world."

She rose to tend to the dishes. "Still. It means the world to me."

"I am hoping it goes well. How would you feel about sharing a home with your sister?" Elden asked.

Holly couldn't help but beam. "I think it would be wonderful. I couldn't be happier."

"And how would you feel about sharing me with her?"

"That would be quite nice," she said reflexively. A heartbeat later she realized what Elden was suggesting and turned away so he wouldn't see her cheeks flush in shock. Surely he—no, of *course* he'd think that, he was a man. "Of course, she hasn't had the same training that I have, you know," she added as a gentle way to redirect the conversation away from the response in her heart which was, horrifyingly, to slap him in the back of the head as hard as she could and snarl that she was *not* having sex with her sister, thank you very much. She'd have to find a way to keep that from becoming an expectation of Elden's, or get herself right with the idea that it would happen.

She didn't want that. It was an unusual feeling; normally she was happy to do anything that would please Elden. There was a moment of honest concern that he'd press the issue, but he let it drop, turning the conversation to more trivial matters. "One thing is for sure; I like the weather in Strip City better."

"It is milder," she said.

"What were the summers like when you were a child?"

"It depended on where we were," Holly said absently. Elden was done eating, so she took his plate and set it on the ledge where she could ferry it into the kitchen later. "I think I liked it best when we were in the mountains. It was cooler, and there were no insects."

"What about your sister? Did she feel the same?"

"Yes."

Elden smiled. "Remarkable." After dinner, he got on the computer, preoccupied with beginning to make travel plans of his own (and passing word of his departmental coup to other colleagues of course). Holly cleaned up, began a preliminary search for rental properties in Strip City, and then went out on the balcony for a moment, listening to the city humming below. She looked to the sky, but a heavy curtain of clouds blocked any view she might have had of the stars. The smell of fresh rain weighted the heavy, warm air, but this high up it also carried city-stink, and she retreated gratefully into the air conditioning.

To silence the tumult of uncomfortable thoughts, she threw herself into late-evening chores, though there weren't many. Elden worked late and wasn't interested in sex, so Holly consulted some online brokers and, in a short time, found a few suitable rental properties in Strip City, and forwarded those to Elden. She responded to Yuying and Lakshmi's earlier messages, and worked out some quick travel arrangements as well while she waited for her benefactor to finally turn in (she never slept before he did, in case he needed her).

As soon as Elden turned off his lights, Holly put on her music box and lay down. North America was at the front of her mind, and Ivy of course. She was going back. Strange that the idea of ever going to North America again hadn't crossed her mind while she was there, or on the trip back. She just wasn't in the habit of giving much thought to anything beyond the immediate future. Holly could plan the next two days down to the minute, but she didn't put much thought into what came after that, and this realization had the tremble of an important epiphany. Before she could do much with it, she fell asleep.

chapter 23

Seventy-nine days before Princess Aiyana's trimester celebration

>> The deadly formid shifters, whose colonies were responsible for forcing human civilization off of the South American continent, have been quiet for years. Could that change?

Originally bred as factory workers, the formids quickly bred out of control and turned on their masters in Brazil. It happened with shocking swiftness. Barely five months passed between the day of Walter Guerro's famous last voicemail to his business partner—"There's a queen, Harry! Blow it all up! Blow it up now! Don't wait for us!—" to the final evacuations and the destruction of the Panama Canal to stop the formids' advance north into Central America. Hundreds of thousands of refugees flooded coastal cities in Australia, China and Africa, and hundreds of thousands more died at the hands of the unstoppable formid army. Things have been quiet ever since, barring the occasional attack on a lithium or ironwood expedition into South America's interior, but could that change? Luiz Derosa, a behavioral biologist whose grandparents were among those evacuated from Lima, warns that it might. "Should the formids decide to seize a boat, they would have no problem reverse engineering the design of anything on board, or even the ship itself. In less than twelve months we could see a formid army sailing into the Brother Nations, colonizing the smaller islands before mounting an assault on the mainland." Derosa met with Minister of Foreign Affairs Shen Zhuan to discuss strategies for dealing with such a possibility. He added that the colonies have already turned down Zhuan's request for EPRC support, as well as denying permits for the construction of nuclear cruise missiles to strike at the heart of the formid nation...

—Do You Believe This Shit? by Rosso Patek

>> There are calls for new safety measures after another contestant was grievously injured during filming of the gladiatorial-combat show, *Hero*. The show pits armored fighters against one another to settle legal disputes, and has proven

to be extremely popular in its two seasons. Host Helmut Chen says, "Our show strips away the nonsense and red tape that the average man must go through, and returns him to the visceral core of what it means to be human in this complicated world. By becoming a *Hero*, a man has the opportunity to solve his problems simply and without shame." Chen went on to say that the show will not add any safety measures, because the threat of injury is part of the program's appeal.

There have been complaints of *Hero*-inspired vigilantism in some districts...

–Diāo Girl

Of course the office they rented in Strip City was much shabbier than the carefully staged photos provided by the realtor. Holly had seen minor flaws in the place and pointed them out, but Elden, ever the academic, was seduced by the attached living quarters, or maybe just by the fancy spiral staircase via which they were accessed. "This way we can centralize office functions, but we'll always be nearby," he said.

In person, the minor flaws turned out to be major ones. Small cracks in the paint were actually gaping holes in the walls. What looked like dust was actually the beginnings of a mold colony. The carpet would have to be removed entirely. The sink spat rusty orange water. And the fancy spiral staircase had three loose steps. Holly might have been able to get away with saying, "I told you so," but she didn't try.

Upon their arrival she set about turning the loft space into a passable replica of the university's office space. A top-down cleaning took her the better part of two days, during which Elden held staff meetings at the hotel suite that Rehsil had rented. Holly took advantage of the rest of the group's just-arrived excitement to get the necessary work taken care of. She was bumping with the electro every eight hours to keep herself going almost twenty-four hours a day, but it was worth it. By the time the professors and their chosen students were ready to finally begin working, Holly had the office space cleaned top to bottom. She'd had stairs repaired and the carpet removed and hauled away, revealing a wood floor that she polished. She cajoled their landlord into hiring a local handyman to paint some of the damaged trim and fix the pipes, and then used about half of the money Elden had allotted her for office supplies to purchase desks, bookshelves, filing cabinets and chairs for the office space. She had enough left over to get a pair of nice replica pre-Colony Conflict sofas and a low table made from what appeared to be a truck's hood, and used them to create a sitting area away from the desks, for a more informal space.

With all of that work done, the place had its advantages. The businesses on either side were rarely occupied, belonging to a debt collector and a shabby therapist's office. The storefront below them was completely empty, and the walls were solid cement blocks all around. As a result, it was quiet, and the somewhat worse-for-wear exterior of the building seemed to be more in keeping with the group's research than a fancy glass office would have been. Hatton and his student Gurrit laughed and said the group was wrapping itself in the skins of true North Americans.

Upstairs, the living area was larger than they needed, so Holly only furnished part of it, acquiring a bed and a nightstand with a small desk for Elden to work at and yet another bookshelf. She decorated the space with curtains, creating a smaller virtual bedroom so they'd have more private space. Elden would no doubt fill the space she left open over time with pre-Colony Conflict antiques he found while roaming the city, or if they ventured beyond it...

Would they leave the city, if that was what it took to find Ivy? The thought gave Holly pause. Not because she was concerned about leaving the city, of course, but because she wondered if Elden's determination stretched that far. It wasn't hard to think about the many, many expeditions that had gone east of Strip City and never returned.

And in contrast to them, there was Marcus. His success might bolster Elden's desire to explore more of the continent.

Holly shook her head. That could be weeks away. She found herself stuck on trying to think of what she'd be making for dinner, since she had yet to find a reliable market other than the chaotic, sometimes unreliable merchants' market. How could she ponder things that far ahead?

And yet, they nibbled at her. Keeping her thoughts in the moment was getting to be a difficult task. She needed a bump, and went to the bathroom to get the electronic crown out from its carrying case.

Once that was done she set to the task of setting up Elden's office, making sure he had contact information for the rest of the staff, who were scattered about in about a half-mile radius in various Old Town apartments and hotels.

Of course in the excitement of taking most of the department overseas for an extended research study, it hadn't occurred to any of the professors that they weren't taking any of the secretaries, or any of the office infrastructure that the university provided. Holly chose to take up the slack rather than remind Elden of this beforehand, so she was prepared with lists of responsibilities for herself and the other domestics, and even a few of the graduate students. Yuying and Shmi accepted theirs with rolled eyes and mock-complaints about Myawis being demons from hell. Her fellow domestics were ultimately good-natured about it, though, for which Holly was grateful.

Elden and the other professors responded predictably, by hardly noticing at all. They were accustomed to things being done for them, before they asked, and keeping up this status quo was not cause for praise or celebration. Holly didn't mind, and prided herself on keeping the satellite office running smoothly. If anything, this was easier than working with the secretaries at the university, who had a tendency to be protective of their turf when it came to the domestics.

Elden instructed her to her organize biweekly staff meetings, the better to keep some semblance of academic habit, and after just a week things were running smoothly enough that she was able to let things move on their own.

This morning, while Holly and Yinka set breakfast out, Hatton showed Elden, Aidanab, Rehsil and Dineen his latest souvenir. The young professor had gone completely native, outfitting himself like he imagined a scavenger would dress. Holly thought he looked like Bazell, the fake scav tour guide, but kept it to herself. It was entirely possible, she mused, that he was *trying* to look like Bazell. He'd gotten a gun from somewhere, a ridiculously huge pistol, and was showing it off to the others. The weapon was garishly deadly, and its chromed barrel was almost as long as her forearm.

"Pre-Colony Conflict," Hatton was saying. "Five-shot, fifty caliber. It's been rebuilt at least once, because the grip isn't original, but that just meant I got a better price on it. You can't find guns like this in Singapore for less than the price of a small car," he said.

"May I?" Rehsil asked. Hatton gave the gun a fancy twirl and handed it to the doctor.

"Careful," he said with a grin. "They say you shouldn't point it at anything you don't want to destroy."

"Very nice," Rehsil said with a nod, and passed it to Aidanab. The gruff older professor handled the gun with a bit more respect than the other two had, snapped the cylinder out and looked down the barrel, his lips pursed in appraisal.

"The vendor sold me a custom holster as well. What do you think?" Rehsil handed the gun back, and Hatton holstered it. "Like this, facing forward, you see? Easier for me to draw across my body."

"It's riding too high," Aidanab said. "I can show you later. You should take me to the shop where you got it, also."

Holly passed Shmi on her way back into the small kitchen. "Idiot,"

Shmi muttered.

"Do *not* call my benefactor an idiot," Yinka hissed. All of them were practiced at speaking low enough to keep their conversations private, and the professors and grad students didn't hear them in spite of the lack of a partition between the kitchen and the living area that served as meeting space and office.

"Sorry. I don't like guns, especially when they're treated like toys."

"I'm sure Professor Hatton knows what he's doing," Holly said, partly to mollify Yinka who was still bristling. Yuying was also adept at playing peacemaker, and patted her shoulder. Holly figured it was a good time to change the subject. "I got some bad news," she told them. "Do you remember Mr. Barro, from the hotel we stayed at for the convention? Apparently he died."

"The one who was sweet on you?" Yuying asked, her eyes wide in surprise.

"Which ones *aren't* sweet on her?" Shmi laughed. "Myawis are specially trained to make men fall in love with them everywhere they go."

"Don't be crass," Holly said. "He was very nice."

"What happened?"

"I'm not sure. There was some sort of problem at the hotel, burglars or something, and he was shot."

"That's awful," Yuying said.

"That's life in North America, it sounds like," Shmi said.

"I know, but it's strange to hear of it happening up close, to someone you've met. Usually when you go to a shop and the clerk isn't there any more, it's because she changed jobs, not that she's dead."

"Funny old world, isn't it?" The four of them didn't speak for a moment, sharing a private moment of silence for Mr. Barro while the professors launched into their meeting.

Shmi broke it first. "Well, I have some good news. My friends who were here when we were at the conference are back in Strip City also."

"The pirates?" Yuying said, amused.

"Yes! Holly, you *have* to come meet them this time."

"Why me?"

"They're nice," Yuying said. "Really interesting folks. I think the girl's name was Razor, that I talked to."

"I promised them I'd introduce them to a Myawi," Shmi said. "They've never seen one before, except on TV."

In spite of years of training, Holly almost rolled her eyes. "I'll think about it," she said.

chapter 24

Shiloh's story

A day or so east of Salt Lake we stopped at a collection of pre-Fall buildings and tents that even Ivy didn't know the name of. She had it marked on her map, said it didn't really have a name. Swan said it should be called "Horrible Little Shithole" and Kroni agreed with her.

There were a couple of merchants trading fuel and supplies but the town didn't appear to have any permanent residents, just cadres of fenders and a few scavs, whoever was passing through and needed to stop, and maybe a few people who were stranded until they found rides out.

"I can't trust places without nomads," Ivy said as we bedded down for the night. "If travelers won't take their families to a place, that's never a good sign." She was right, too; there wasn't a single nomad rig anywhere in Horrible Little Shithole.

The campfire was lively enough, though. Because I was still winding down from my anxious-time—we met *nobody* for those three days, so the less said about that the better, I was nigh-intolerable—I was hypersocial. I met a whirl of people throughout the evening. I spun hoops for a while, which made me a bunch of new friends. Ivy stayed with the rig; Swan found herself a boytoy and disappeared.

As the evening wore on and the levels in the bottles dropped, the boasts and travel stories got wilder, the dares got more outlandish and I had my selection of playmates. I ended up going with a fellow named Egg. He was from Winnipeg, had short black hair and dancing eyes and had been talking all night about snow and drilling holes in the ice to get fish in the winter. He described the cold so well I wanted to shiver, and since I was the cutest thing 'round the fire—it's not bragging if it's true—it wasn't hard to get him to come with me. He even had a tent that blocked out a lot of the sound. While he was taking off my shirt he told me it was because it had extra padding to keep the cold out.

Unfortunately it was still a tent, so twenty minutes later I had the unique experience of hearing it ripped open, followed by Egg being pulled off of me and tossed aside like a rag doll. There was a rush of cool night air, chilling my sweaty skin, and I bounced to my knees. I probably shouted in outrage, too.

There were three men standing in the ruins of the tent. The second-biggest one, who'd just thrown Egg off of me, said, "Trying to rut with humans. You're disgusting."

I recognized him by his accent, even in the dark. Called himself Yanwu. He'd been around the fire with two of his friends, all three of them Inchins who had come across the desert from Strip City, and before that, from across the ocean. Yanwu was a big fellow, about Kroni's size, with a face that looked like it had been stepped on before it was finished forming, and purple tattoos covering his arms and chest.

The shredded tent collapsed, and the glow from the big campfire hit all three of them. On Yanwu's right was Blizzard, who was almost twice his size. Blizzard was older than Yanwu. He had more hair than his body knew what to do with, and it was mostly white against his brown skin. The fuzz covered his chest, arms, and back, and he had a beard and a mane of it around his head, too. All that was visible of his face were dark eyes staring out of that explosion of white hair and a potato nose.

The third one was Kaluku. Fish-eyed and whip-thin compared to the other two, he gave the impression that he hung around to pick over whatever Blizzard and Yanwu left behind. He wore two pistols and a belt of mismatched bullets, and his hands fidgeted on them constantly.

I was more annoyed than afraid. Egg stood up, covered in dirt, and started to step back in between me and the Inchins. Blizzard said, "Lie down and wait," grabbed him by the neck and just kind of...fell on him, crushing him to the ground.

"You're disgusting," Yanwu said again.

"I didn't ask your opinion," I told him. "Fuck off."

"Shifter demon filth. It makes me sick to see your kind with pure humans."

"What does it matter to you? Jealous?" It was uncommon for people to know I was a shifter without being told, but it happened sometimes.

His expression didn't change; a thick jet of black spit shot from between his lips and landed on the blanket at my feet. "I don't fuck shifters," he said. "I kill them."

And then I got scared. I hadn't chatted him or the other Inchins up earlier, when they'd been watching me perform, because they felt wrong, and now this...well, it wasn't doing anything to change that impression.

When I perform for people, I get a good feeling. Everyone's happy, enjoying my show, and I'm happy to entertain them. I take their good energy and feed it back to them, amplified. But sometimes, there are people in the crowd who don't give any energy. Whether they're not having fun, or there's something else going on, they're like voids. Yanwu was one of those. He just stared at me with his blank eyes, moving slowly forward. I wanted to back up, but some instinct told me that if I ran, he'd chase me, and I wouldn't get far. Standing naked in front of people doesn't bother me, but under his gaze I felt extremely, unpleasantly vulnerable.

Egg struggled vainly against Blizzard, but couldn't even get a hand free. Blizzard rumbled with amusement, and farted on him.

Yanwu was still moving forward, and I didn't want him close enough to grab me. He wouldn't really kill me, would he? They were just trying to scare me. I tried really hard to believe that. "Don't touch me," I said. He towered over me. I was within his arm's reach now.

His eyes were like glass beads. "Abomination," he said, and reached for my neck.

I couldn't move. I knew I should move, but I couldn't. This was ridiculous, I'd just been fooling around with Egg and now this, from crazy men who didn't even know me?

His fingers reached my neck, four on one side, thumb on the other. They were warm and hard, like hot stones. They were about to squeeze, I knew, and then I heard Kroni say, "Shift and run."

When he wants to, he has a ringmaster's voice. It makes your body obey first and think about it second. He had used it during fights before, and he was using it now. I did just as he said, taking a step backward and shifting, and it made perfect sense—I could outrun any human in cat form. Stupid that it didn't occur to me. Kroni said something to me once about having to accept that form as a part of myself, but I wasn't in the mood to hear that when he told me so I didn't give it much thought.

The night air instantly became brighter and I ran. Darkness descended as I ran away from the campfire, but I could see just fine, and I was easily out of reach in just a couple of bounds. I turned back, and saw Kroni grappling with Yanwu, fist to fist. They seemed evenly matched until Kroni ducked his head and shifted. Yanwu tried to keep his grip but got a faceful of antlers. He shifted again and threw a flying kick into Yanwu, knocking him back.

Kroni was still outnumbered, though. Kaluku moved away and to the side, drawing one of his guns. Kroni saw him, and was turning to face him when Blizzard lunged and fell on him, same as he had on Egg. Kroni shifted as he went down but Blizzard was like an avalanche of hairy flesh. Kroni was driven to the ground, two legs sticking out uselessly.

I turned around and started back to the scene, toward Kaluku. I wasn't going to let him shoot Kroni. I was fast, but before I got there, two other fenders had already grabbed him. There was a swarm of people coming from the campfire, drawn by the scuffle. Kroni and Blizzard were separated, and more arms kept Yanwu from jumping back into the fight. The shouting quickly became deafening. Still concealed by the dark, I pulled up short, then turned again to go get Ivy. She was usually the first to respond when Swan got into trouble, so it seemed natural that she should know what was going on now.

When I returned with Ivy (after shifting back and putting on a skirt and jacket, since it was still kind of cool), the three Inchins were standing together inside a ring of fenders, and Kroni and Egg were on the other side. Torches had been brought close, lighting the circle, and Egg had put on a pair of pants. There were two women standing in the middle of the fray; Swan and an older woman who was built like a beefalo.

"There," Kroni said, seeing me and Ivy, and the crowd parted to let us through. I glanced at Ivy; she looked grim.

When I came into the light, Yanwu started shouting in another language, and Blizzard shouted back at him. The fenders around them started hollering as well, yelling at them to shut up.

"This about you?" Swan asked me, leaning in so I could hear her. Her voice was uncharacteristically quiet, but hard-edged. She wasn't accusing me of anything, and sounded genuinely concerned. With the tangled remnants of Egg's tent and my clothes in it nearby, it was pretty obvious that I was involved, even if for some reason I wanted to deny it. I just nodded. When I got close enough, she reached out and stroked the side of my face with surprising gentleness. "You okay?"

"Kroni saved me," I told her, and she smiled.

The raised voices began to turn into a new scuffle, people shoving and jostling back and forth. Someone put fingers to their lips and whistled until the shouting stopped, voices melting down into a low mumble. "What's the story, then?" the big woman asked me, loud enough to be heard by everyone else. "Tell it to me short."

I heard my voice like it was coming from someone else. Whoever she was, she had a quaver, part fear and part anger. "I was in the middle of a good time with Egg, when those three ripped the tent open and pulled him off of me," I said, indicating the Inchins. Kaluku yelled and called me a liar, and someone smacked the back of his head and told him to shut up.

"Why'd they do that?"

"The big one—Yanwu—said he was going to kill me." I hesitated. The words, *because I'm a shifter* didn't want to come out of my throat.

There was no need, though; what I'd said seemed to be good enough. "He put his hands on you after that?"

I looked at Yanwu. "Yes, he did. He grabbed my neck."

The woman turned to him. "Open your mouth, and use it to tell me why you tried to snap this girl's neck. No speeches."

Yanwu didn't look at her. He met my eyes, and put more black spit on the ground between us. "Demons deserve death." Then he looked around the circle at everyone. "Those who protect them as well."

"Scale it," Ivy said.

"With pleasure," Swan replied. I hadn't noticed she was carrying her scattergun, but she had it in her hands in the blink of an eye and aimed it at Yanwu's face. The other fenders behind and around the Inchins stepped away.

"You don't have to kill him. Just shoot his cock off or something—"

The roar of her shotgun interrupted me, and Yanwu dropped to his knees, then to the ground, his face gone. Kaluku hit the ground next to him, writhing and yelling in pain; he'd been hit by some of the shot as well. Blizzard winced like he was hit also, but didn't go down.

I looked at Swan, wondering if she'd even heard me. She shrugged, and I knew she had. "No point in having a crazy fucksmear like that running around looking for you," she said. "Plus he ruined my night, makin' me put my tits away to come out here and sober up. 'Sides that, it teaches the other two a big useful lesson about how adults behave. Doesn't it, boys? Or would you rather lie down right next to him?"

"They come from out on the sea," someone said. "They don't know any better."

"Looks like they're going to learn fast," the big woman said. She stepped up and touched Swan's gun, pushing the barrel gently down. "I don't think you're welcome here tonight," she said to Blizzard and Kaluku.

"We...we're traveling with Mill Flentroy," Kaluku said from the ground, holding his bleeding arm.

A man at the edge of the crowd, presumably Mill, spoke without unfolding his arms. "I don't vouch for crazies," he said in a flat voice, then turned around and walked away from the ring. A few other people broke away from the group to follow him. I kind of hoped they were offering Mill their services to fill the sudden vacancies in his group.

"As I said, fellows: *walk.*"

Kaluku started to say something, looked across the crowd at me, and then his huge companion pulled him up.

"Don't look at her like that," Swan said. "And don't be sullen and spiteful about being in a mess you created." She nodded toward the edge of Horrible Little Shithole.

Blizzard stared for a long moment, then turned around and started walking. The circle had already parted for him. Kaluku followed.

Soon I was standing between Swan, Ivy and Kroni. I felt...encircled, which was like being wrapped up in a concealing blanket. It was nice. Egg came over to us, standing a little bit shy of Kroni. He had my clothes, which he'd salvaged from what was left of his tent, rolled up in a little ball.

"You okay?" I asked him. He didn't look much the worse for wear, just embarrassed at being taken down the way he had.

"I'm good. So, you uh, want to...?" he angled his head back toward his wrecked tent.

Swan actually laughed. I gave him a little kiss on the cheek and said, "No, thanks." I kind of wanted to, but the desire to curl up in my corner of the Vovo was stronger, even if I had to be alone for the night.

chapter 25

Sixty-six days before Princess Aiyana's trimester celebration

>> Tonight we take you inside the incredible car collections of Pravit and Ramzi Deshmu! The popular "king" of the Brother Nations' favorite family and his younger brother have long been fans of the automobile, and they've each got a collection of immaculately restored vehicles, from the gas-burning behemoths of pre-Colony Conflict America to the five new Rolls-Royce Specters he had specially customized for each member of the royal family. King Deshmu's tastes range far and wide, and his cars have come from every corner of the planet. Most of them are used on a regular basis as well! Join us as we go…Inside the King's Stable!

—Shairpie Shrivastva's Den

Marcus arrived early in the afternoon, appearing at the door with a secretive smile. The other professors were out doing interviews; Holly had stayed at the apartment because the locals tended to stare, making her a distraction. "I told Professor Ono and Doctor Rehsil that I wouldn't be coming into town for another three hours," he said. "I thought you'd want to have some time alone to talk first," he added with a conspiratorial wink. He had new clothes, surprisingly stylish, that clashed with his awkward face and mien.

Holly smiled and let him in. "I appreciate it," she said. "Can I get you something to drink?"

"Yes, please. I find that I can't get used to how dry the air is here, even so close to the ocean."

"Not that close," Holly said. Strip City was almost twenty miles from the coast. "But I understand what you're saying. Would you prefer water or tea? I remember you don't care for the soda."

"Water is fine, thank you. I made it to Semangat Terang, you know."

She felt a grin spread across her face.

"It was a very enlightening experience. I could tell you all about the manufacturing complex there, quite a history, but I'm sure that you are interested in other things."

"You talked to my mother?"

"Ruth played a very big role in the history of the complex. It seems that your family is quite good at—"

"Marcus, *please*," Holly said. "You already have my interest, you don't need to tease me."

"Yes, of course. Forgive me," he said with a smile. "Won't you sit? I'd like to think you don't need to be so formal with me."

"Formal is what I do," she said, and sat. To make Marcus more comfortable, she plucked a few grapes from the bunch in the bowl on the table and nibbled on them. Her fingers didn't want to sit still.

"That's much nicer. One thing I've enjoyed about talking to people, planetside, is that I'm not the professor any longer. I quite prefer a more informal approach, talking to people as equals rather than students or ranked professors. So!" he said, clapping his hands and consulting his tablet, where he'd clearly prepared a report, "your mother, Ruth, formerly Ruth Aniram, was trained by YYI as an industrial domestic. A factory worker. She went to work at the automobile and battery factories in Semangat Terang sixteen years ago. The training lasts about a year, and so it was easy to figure out where to start. And, as I said, they remembered her.

"It would appear that she didn't take well to being separated from you. Ruth was quickly identified as a discipline risk. She fought with her supervisors, and attempted to leave the facility on numerous occasions. The Semangat Terang factory has a small city appended to it, with a section for the industrial domestics and another for the regular workers. I was fascinated to learn that the indentured workers and the voluntary ones work side-by-side, with no regard for collars or status, even though their quarters are segregated. But I digress. Where was I?" Marcus took out his little notepad and looked quickly at it. "Ah, yes. In her fifth month of service, after a request to be allowed to see you was denied, Ruth threatened a shift supervisor with a crowbar and walked off of the factory floor. She hijacked a truck and got five miles off of campus before police stopped her. She was sentenced to some time in an isolation unit—this is a practice that has been stopped, by the way, I'll get to that in a moment—and then when she returned to work, she apparently sabotaged one of the machines on the factory floor. There was no damage, but it did stop production for several hours. She was reprimanded and returned to isolation. Two weeks later, upon her release, she did it again, and this time she actually caused an explosion that injured sixteen people and put the plant out of commission for a week. During that week she escaped from isolation, hospitalizing two security guards in the process, and hijacked another vehicle. This time she was caught after the car's battery ran out forty miles from Semangat Terang."

"She was coming to find me?"

"Presumably, though she had no idea where you were. I don't think that she was told which school you had been accepted to, so she couldn't have had a specific destination in mind."

Holly struggled to come to terms with this new information. Nothing in her mother's letters ever suggested the level of unhappiness that the actions that Marcus was describing would indicate. And the violence? Her mom was always protective of she and Ivy...but this level of destruction? Of *revolt?*

Wait, it wasn't unthinkable. Ruth had jumped out of a moving truck to save her—that was why they were in the Brother Nations in the first place. Holly imagined that she hadn't hesitated. Ruth had been a city guard in Astoria, and she was a child of the revolution that had rocked that city fifty years before, when the women had taken over from the men. She hadn't seen her mother fight, but she'd *heard* it, huddled with Ivy in their house-rig's armored safe-box when their caravan was attacked by a group of raiders.

A wave of shock rolled over her. But the letters! Her mother always seemed so supportive of her training, so happy for her...why would she have felt it was necessary to come and *save* her? Why wouldn't she have told her she was coming? Holly felt suddenly dizzy and ill, and forced herself to take a deep breath and regain her composure. Marcus seemed not to notice, and continued with his narrative.

"This is where it gets interesting. After she was taken back, she was punished physically. There are no official records, but I was able to learn through hearsay that they beat her so badly she couldn't walk, and was in the infirmary for almost three months. The rumor is that her tongue was cut out as well. I know, it's barbaric, but they're just rumors, there are no official documents. Bear with me, there is an uplifting ending to this story. After recovering, Ruth went back to work yet again, with extra supervision. She was a model worker for a week—and then I am told that she somehow got onto the factory floor one night. In one evening, she nearly destroyed the entire complex. She set fires, she destroyed vehicles, she turned machines on without their safety limiters in place. She even threw acid into the raw materials storage. All manner of sabotage. It was as though the year she'd spent at Semangat Terang, she'd been doing nothing but figuring out how to do as much damage as possible. She barricaded herself inside, and it took four hours for military snipers to bring her down, according to the news reports I read."

Holly gasped. Had she misheard…?

Marcus didn't notice. He was caught up in his lecture-energy. "The case was a turning point in the legislation of domestics. This incident didn't receive widespread media attention, but behind the scenes it had farther-reaching effects than any activism. Because of your mother's dedication to finding you, because of her refusal to accept being separated from you, there are now laws against domestic schools separating mothers from their children. And furthermore, most schools will no longer accept refugees who were taken by force. Your mother may have single-handedly cut the legs out from under what was, just over a decade ago, a burgeoning industry in the kidnapping of women and children from all around the world."

"But…you're saying she's dead?"

"Yes, she is, I'm afraid."

Holly couldn't feel her fingers. She moved them, but they were still in another plane. "I don't understand. She wrote me letters. Sent pictures. She was a supervisor in Semangat Terang."

"Yes, I wondered about that as well." Marcus looked slightly uncomfortable. "I did look into this, and it seems that—and I could not substantiate this—that some domestic schools, when children were separated from a parent, would, ah, fabricate letters from the family. To make them feel more comfortable in the new environment. This is usually done for a few years, until the training is complete, and then it's no longer needed. I don't know why you received them for so long."

Holly was looking at her hands, which were twisting a piece of grape stem over and over, winding it until the fibers split apart. Her mind whirled, threatening to spin completely out of control. *Control. Control the moment, control the room.*

"It really is something to be quite proud of, you know."

She didn't say anything for a full forty seconds, though she could feel the silence growing awkward. "Well. I'm quite glad you think so."

He shivered slightly, as though the temperature in the room had suddenly dropped. "I beg your pardon?"

"You wanted me to speak to you as equals? Like we were just chatting, not domestic to benefactor?" Holly pushed her chair back and stood up, looking down at him. "Well, then listen to this: you are a horrible, horrible person."

"Holly—"

"Shut up. You kept me waiting for almost a month, then strolled in happy as a clam and with a smile, told me my mother is dead."

"But it happened so long ago—"

"Not for me it didn't," she said, lowering her voice so she didn't shout. "Up until five minutes ago, I thought she was alive and proud of me. Is that your idea of an uplifting ending to your presentation?"

Marcus cleared his throat and stood up as well. He still looked uncomfortable. His eyes darted around the kitchen, not meeting hers. "I suppose I may have been a bit thoughtless. It was very exciting to uncover her story, you must understand. I met some fascinating people, some who even knew her. Perhaps you could correspond with them too. I brought information, so that you could—"

"So it didn't even occur to you that I might not share your excitement? Marcus, you left everyone you know behind you, you *know* what it's like to lose people. To lose your family."

"Well, this is hardly the same thing..." he said. "I had time to consider... and, as far as you knew, she was living a rather meaningless life—now you know she's something of a hero—"

She moved like lightning, grabbed him by the collar hard enough to pop stitches, and shoved him backward. Marcus tripped over his own feet and fell. *"Meaningless?"*

"I-I only meant from a historical perspective!" he cried. "Of course Ruth was important to you, I'm not belittling that. I only meant to say—"

"If you were on my space station I'd throw you off too," Holly muttered, turning away from him. She immediately regretted the nasty comment, but didn't apologize. What was the matter with her? She'd just *attacked* Marcus. She flexed her hands, trying to slow her breathing.

"I am sorry for your loss. Truly."

"May I be alone for a while, please?" she asked.

"Of course," Marcus said, sounding grateful.

She was so lost in thought that she didn't even notice him leaving, but in a moment she was alone in the apartment.

It crept in slowly, unstoppable. Her mother was dead. Had been, for years. But she'd been writing. She'd been happy and supportive, and proud of her. No: she'd been dead the whole time.

No. Holly didn't want to think about it.

Had died less than a year after they had been kidnapped.

Please, no, I don't want to think about this.

Had died before she'd even graduated from the Myawi school. Long before.

No, that couldn't be true. She'd written to say that she was proud. She'd enjoyed the pictures—

Had been dead for eight years by then.

No, please.

Had died thinking she'd lost both of her children. Failed them.

Holly bit her thumb, trying to distract herself.

Had died alone and in pain and thinking she'd lost her children.

And then Holly had forgotten all about her sister. Assumed she was dead and left her behind. How had she forgotten? How had she taken the letters as proof that her mother was out there? And she'd *forgotten* Ivy...

She was making a sound, and became aware of it as a noise outside of herself. It was going to get louder. *A Myawi never screams. A Myawi never screams. A Myawi never screams.* Holly bolted for the bathroom. The rolling chair was in her path, and she flung it aside, sending it into the sitting area where it knocked over the end table. There was no time to run water, so she knelt and thrust her head into the toilet, as far as it would go, her face completely submerged, and then she screamed. It was huge, taking the air out of her lungs, a scream that came up from the soles of her feet. She collapsed like a deflating balloon, pouring everything out in bubbles and muffled burbling in the toilet. Holly surfaced long enough to fill her lungs, water streaming from her hair and face, and then did it again. She gripped the cool sides of the toilet so hard her knuckles cracked.

At the end of the second scream, she sobbed, a massive involuntary hiccup that filled her lungs with toilet water. Holly fell backward, coughing, choking. She fell over on her side and left a trail of water behind her, and now she made noise. She heard herself cough, sob, retch and gag. Without warning, she vomited. Her entire body was betraying her, would rather rip itself to pieces than remain a part of the miserable, pathetic thing that called itself Holly and strutted about with Myawi self-importance. She didn't blame it.

She opened her eyes and saw the cabinet, and had the urge to punch it, to break the door, or break her hand, or both. Holly didn't do that; she sat up and kicked it instead. Her heavy Wing boot smashed the wood into several pieces, ripping one of the hinges out and sending it sailing past her head.

It didn't make her feel better. She contemplated destroying the entire apartment, but didn't move. Toilet water dripped from her hair and soaked her pants. If she stood, she'd see herself in the mirror, and she wasn't ready for that. A fist through the mirror, a shard of glass for her throat. Worthless *cunt*.

Except she wasn't. Far from it. She'd cost more than Elden's house, hadn't she?

It wasn't her fault, and yet it was. Holly had believed in Myawi, had believed that she'd accomplished something by becoming a domestic, had made herself—had *let* them make her—into a shining example of the lie they sold. And she'd believed it all, had thought it really did make her special. But no. Her mother was dead, her sister was gone, and she was a glamorous, glorified slave. And she'd have to clean up the mess she'd just made too, both of the bathroom and of herself.

What time was it? 4:30. Rabbit's mortar, Elden would be home soon. She packed her thoughts away, pushing them out with a dinner plan, with evening plans, with all the dozens of plates she needed to keep spinning in order to make life look effortless. Holly got up and brushed her hair back into place with her fingers. Her eyes avoided the mirror.

Time passed in a blur of non-thought, and at the end of it she realized that she had cleaned up the bathroom, concealed the broken door, tidied the apartment and prepared Elden's dinner while in her fugue. He was smiling across the table, thanking her for yet another meal well done. "You are the best part of coming home at the end of the day," he said. "Though I would say that this wine is a close second," he added with a chuckle.

She replied with a smile she did her best to feel. "Productive day?"

"Yes, quite," he said. He went on for a few minutes about the minutia of his meeting with the graduate students, but Holly didn't follow it. Normally she would have, paying attention to what he was doing and asking questions. Tonight she all but ignored him, a dim reflexive part of her brain paying enough attention to parrot words back at him and make him think she was interested but not retaining any of it. Finally, Elden asked, "Is there any word from Professor McEvoy? He was supposed to arrive today," and that roused Holly from her reverie.

"There wasn't," she lied. She lied! Had she really just *lied* directly to her benefactor? Not a lie of omission, or a half-truth to save his feelings, but an outright *lie!* And it had been astonishingly easy.

"Well, the transportation situation here can be unpredictable."

"He also has acquaintances in Strip City. Perhaps he had other business to attend to first." As she said that, she spared a moment to wonder where Marcus had gone. He hadn't said anything about lodging.

"That's also true. I'm sure we'll hear from him soon enough. I think he'll be quite interested in what we've gathered so far."

She nodded in response, then let the silence stretch out for a moment as she considered her next words. "Elden, may I ask a question?"

"Of course."

She realized she couldn't look at him while asking, and stood suddenly, clearing her plate and busying herself at the kitchen sink. "When—if we find Ivy, my mother should know. I know that I won't have time, but do you think it's possible that Ivy could go to see her?"

"Semangat Terang has quite a restrictive visitation policy," Elden said without hesitating. "But you should write to her, and I'm sure they'll make an allowance for her to visit. The corporate slave-drivers can't be that insensitive, can they?"

But they would, she knew. Whatever letter she sent, there would be an unexpected and unhappy response telling her that unfortunately, Ruth just wasn't able to take the time away to see her children. But she'd send her warmest regards, and hope that maybe next quarter, next holiday, next season, there would be a chance. It had always been that way, hadn't it? Her mother—they'd even stripped her surname from her—had been dead before Elden had even met Holly, that bright and sunny day in the Myawi visitor center's courtyard.

"I'm glad she's always been there for me," Holly said, keeping her eyes on the dishes, on the immaculately clean counter, on the pleasantly tiled backsplash that she'd picked out to complement the floor tile. "I don't know what I'd do without her."

"I'm sure she's not going anywhere," Elden said. "She'll be there for you for many years to come." She looked into Elden's eyes then, to see if she could detect any hint of remorse in them as he casually perpetuated the lie that he had been feeding her for years. He *had* to have known...the deception had been going on since he'd become her benefactor. There was no guilt there. He changed the subject without missing a beat, "Would you pour some more wine, please?"

Holly turned her attention to the bottle and used the task as a opportunity to collect herself, concentrating with an effort to keep her hand from shaking as she poured. Her thoughts were swirling, but she focused and steadied her hands. She took a deep breath, and arranged her face into a smile. "It's Wednesday. Would you like to play chess, once I've cleaned up?"

"Of course," Elden said. "And while we play, let's discuss traveling the coast. It seems unlikely that your sister would be in Strip City, so I think that we should plan to travel north, to Astoria. We should be able to book passage on a coastal ship."

"Are you sure that's wise?" she asked. "That's North American wilderness."

"True, but we've got two advantages that the official expeditions have not: you, and Professor McEvoy."

"Once he arrives. If he's willing to go."

"My, aren't you cynical this evening?"

Holly paused, dish in hand. At the mention of Marcus, her mind had wandered back to her outburst at him earlier. Though her expression stayed neutral, she felt a nudge of anxiety. She was fairly sure that Marcus would keep the incident to himself, but if he decided to tell Elden what happened, there would be questions. Upset or not, she shouldn't have acted out like that. She pushed the thought aside, and answered with a wan smile in an attempt to pacify Elden. "I'm sorry. Passing mood," she said. "I'll set up the board."

"No, I can do it. You finish."

She was merciless but distracted, doing well with her openings but ultimately losing each of three games. It was as though she couldn't separate the game from the things she'd learned, and Elden's every move seemed to be designed to cut her off from her past somehow. There had to be some way that she could play to make him understand what was going on in her head, to communicate that she now knew he'd been lying to her for most of their life together. That as much as he cared for her, the Ivory Sisters were right, she was ultimately property in his eyes. Did being indispensable and perfect in every way change this fact? He couldn't live without her, and yet he'd set everything up to make her think it was the other way around. Holly couldn't stop herself from trying to make the chess game illustrate this fact, with predictable results. She wanted so badly to win, and instead she lost quickly, and repeatedly. "I seem to be off of my stride," she said wryly, conceding her third straight checkmate.

He gave her a gentle smile, gathering the pieces to put the board away. "Well, you've had a busy week. I'm sure that for every thing I know you've done, there are five more things it didn't even occur to me that you were up to, keeping things running smoothly. And I'm sure your sister is on your mind." He gave her a sidelong glance. "I know I've thought about her. I can't wait to meet her." Did his eyes wander down her body as he said that? Holly felt a flare of something unfamiliar, like indignation. There was something in the look she really disliked. She kept it inside, and Elden smiled at her. "Let's call it a night."

This was a practiced routine as well. Elden never seemed to get bored of watching her undress. Of course he wouldn't; she'd spent years honing her manner of doing so to his exact preferences, both spoken and unspoken.

And for the first time in recent memory, she didn't want to.

No, that wasn't true. There had been times when she hadn't wanted to, it was just that it didn't *matter* what she wanted. Elden took care of her and what he wanted was what she wanted and that was the way it was. All it took was that feedback of pleasure, the knowledge that she was giving him what he wanted, and she could be happy too.

This time, she was conscious of trying. He was there, beneath her, enjoying her hands and mouth on him, and she reached for the reflected pleasure, to take it into herself along with him. But it wasn't there. Holly looked down at Elden and saw her benefactor enraptured with pleasure, eyes and mouth half open, hair spilling across his face and sticking to his sweat in ugly spikes, but there wasn't anything there for her. He was getting what he wanted, true, but he'd tricked her and outmaneuvered her to get it. He and a legion of teachers and mistresses at the Myawi school had tricked her into thinking that she *wanted* to give this to him, had stolen her away from her life and made her forget that the decision was hers to make, not to adapt to.

Elden's hands, which had once felt comforting and pleasant suddenly felt too warm and wet, leaving trails of imaginary filth everywhere he touched her. She panicked, felt a sensation like she was trying to flee her own body, tried to find a comfortable place in her head. There wasn't one; her fulfillment came from him, always him. She bent down over him, close enough to kiss, desperate to find some connection, but Elden was lost in passion, thrusting upward with his hips and pulling her chest down to his. She felt trapped in his embrace as he whispered in her ear, "I love you, Holly."

Had he said it to her before? Surely he had, but she couldn't remember when. There was a numb, distant roar in her head, a dissociative sort of outrage. How *dare* he say those words? Her jaw clenched, and she thought, *You don't even know what that means.* Barely thinking about what she was doing, she pulled him up and wrapped her hair very suddenly around his neck. She brought her right foot up to pin it to the bed, her hips still locked with his, held his arms down with her hands, and straightened her elbows, pushing away from him. The hair pulled tight around his throat. Holly arched her back, pulling as far away from him as she could.

At first he didn't respond, but then she saw his eyes open as he tried to speak and couldn't, then realized he couldn't breathe either. She pulled tighter, even though his air was already cut off, choking off the blood flow as well. Elden was unused to violence, and didn't seem to be certain how to react. His hands clenched and he pushed up against her, but she had leverage. It seemed to go on forever, and the longer it went on, the more confused he seemed to get. He struggled, but she held him down. It was easy. She'd never noticed before, not consciously, but she was as strong as he was.

His face turned scarlet, then purple. He had opened his mouth, and his jaw worked as though he was talking, but with his windpipe squeezed shut no sound emerged apart from a soft cackling. It reminded Holly of faraway laughter. She was keenly aware that if she didn't stop he was going to die, but suddenly that didn't seem like such a bad thing.

Elden's flailing got weaker. He kicked his legs and bucked his hips, but she held on and pitching her up and down only tightened her hair further around his distressed neck. She felt him spasm inside her—he'd come! She made a noise of revulsion, and struggled to keep the bile in her throat from rising. She felt violated, humiliated, and instinctively pulled away from him, which only tightened the makeshift noose further. Something cracked audibly inside of Elden's throat. His body stiffened once more, then went limp beneath her. Holly froze. Her leg was cramped and painful, but she couldn't seem to move.

She continued to hold on, her arms rigid. If she leaned forward and looked down into his face, she'd see that Elden wasn't in there any more. Holly's leg cramped, but she waited, counting slowly in her head as if she were brushing her hair. She decided she'd hold him for as long as she customarily brushed her hair for him. She counted slowly, patiently, to five hundred.

The loudest sound in the room was her breathing. When she finally let go, unwinding her hair from his neck, she expected him to gasp and start coughing, but he didn't move. Elden had gone rubbery and slack. His face was swollen and discolored, making his familiar features look ruined and pathetic. Holly pulled the blanket up over his head, then lay atop the covers next to him and stared at the ceiling, listening to the city hum and shush outside the window.

chapter 26

Sixty-four days before Princess Aiyana's trimester celebration

>> Tragic news from North America as Strip City-based entertainment conglomerate Gallamore reported today that its North American traveling circus has been lost in the second month of its spring and summer tour. The show's seven-month tour of the interior of the troubled continent was the only one of its kind. Details are extremely limited, but rumors suggest that the company was attacked about a week ago by one or more factions in the ongoing civil war in North America. It is not known if any of the show's one hundred and six staff, including forty-seven musicians and performers from the Brother Nations, have survived.

Founded eight years ago, the traveling circus was hailed as an important step in uniting the fractured tribes peopling the former world power as it toured the interior of the North American continent. Critics were quick to point out the dangers of taking a well-equipped traveling circus into the lawless, impoverished wastelands of North America, where bandits are desperate for food, fuel and supplies. Perhaps predictably, Gallamore's show has been plagued by trouble in each season…

—Silverado North American News Feed

A fusillade of impatient, angry knocks at the door downstairs roused Holly. She didn't wake so much as melt into consciousness; the noise was like a train bouncing across an uneven spot in the tracks, the sound of the real world clicking back into place. The day's light was strong, and she heard the moderate bustle of Strip City outside: cars, people, sounds of life. It was midmorning at least. She'd slept well past her usual four-thirty wakeup time, but for some reason that didn't make her anxious. She stretched her legs one at a time, flexing her feet and toes.

Another series of rapid-fire knocks assaulted the door. She turned to Elden, and saw the lifeless lump lying beneath the sheet. The memory of the events of the previous night returned all at once, and hit her like a bucket of freezing water. The weekly staff meeting! She looked at the clock; it was almost nine. How had she slept for almost *ten hours?* That was more appalling, in the moment, than the fact that she'd killed Elden. Even with the body in bed next to her, this whole situation didn't seem entirely real. What *was* real was the knocking at the door.

She was in motion without thought, as light on her toes as possible so that whoever was at the door couldn't hear her thumping around upstairs. Emergency primping was part of her training, almost second nature, and she didn't have to think about it. Her hands swiped her hair into a quick tailed bun as she stepped into her shoes. Her blue and orange outfit was the quickest. She'd worn it the day before yesterday, but the zip-and-belt closure was fastest. She smoothed her clothes and padded quickly down the stairs, another round of banging at the door setting her nerves on fire. No time to swipe on makeup, brush her teeth or check the mirror to be sure her silver collar wasn't smudged. Fortunately she'd cleaned up before chess the night before, so the living room, kitchen and public areas were presentable.

Less than a minute had elapsed from the time that the sound had awakened her. There was no telling how long the knocking had gone on before that, though. She had trained herself to be a light sleeper so it probably hadn't been long, but then she'd never slept for *ten hours* before, either. She paused before the door. A deep breath, a proper Myawi smile on her face, and then she opened it, hurtling headfirst into her fate.

It was Rehsil. Of course it was Rehsil. Holly smiled at him, which of course did nothing to improve his attitude. His eyes skipped over her, past her to the breakfast nook, and he saw that the table wasn't set. He also saw that Elden wasn't there, and his face seemed to curl in on itself slightly, becoming the menacing sneer that he reserved for women when no men were looking. "Moon rabbit's balls, you bitch. Keeping me waiting on the porch like that. What's the matter with you?"

"I'm terribly sorry, Dr. Rehsil," she replied, turning away and bowing slightly to invite him in, careful not to make eye contact. "We've gotten an extremely late start."

He scowled at her and pushed past, headed for the kitchen. "The professor wanted a little morning quickie, eh?" Rehsil chuckled. "He must have given it to you good—the coffee's not even on, is it?"

"I'll have it ready in just a moment."

Dr. Rehsil threw himself angrily into a chair across from the window and looked out at the street. She moved past him, graceful and casual, purposefully unobtrusive. Holly's hands moved on autopilot, her mind turning on other things. Coffee, grinder, filter, brewing. Cut fruit was already in the refrigerator—when had she prepared that?—and she put it on the table. The coffee pot had a three-minute cycle, so she excused herself to run quickly upstairs under pretense of checking on Elden.

She checked her face in the mirror, swished mouthwash, touched up her makeup, and grabbed her electrostim rig from under the counter. The rush of adrenaline was fading, turning to panic, and she needed something more. There was no time for a slow burn so she powered it on, slid the crown over her temples and turned it all the way up, letting the electricity flow through her skull for a full thirty seconds. There was a bit of a jolt at first because she had it up so high, and then the familiar virtual fingers sank into the pulp of her brain, massaging the lobes and folds and making everything so much clearer. For a few seconds the world seemed to run at double-speed, but then it snapped back to normal. Holly felt faster, though she knew she wasn't. The virtual feeling made the situation seem a bit more manageable, at least for the immediate future, the next few minutes.

The clarity was welcome. She tucked the crown back under the sink, out of sight, and checked herself once more in the mirror. She'd tell Rehsil and the others that Elden was feeling ill, which would get them through the meeting quickly enough, and that should buy her a few hours alone in the apartment afterward to think about what to do next. How long could she put the others off? She could run their "office" without Elden for days if she had to. The body would have to go. That was a problem for after she'd made it through the meeting though.

She skipped quickly back downstairs just as the coffee finished, and served Dr. Rehsil before he could get up and do it himself, which would no doubt put him in an even more terrible humor.

"You're just begging to be hit, aren't you? That's the problem," he said. "Professor Ono doesn't beat you enough." She said nothing, placing his cup in front of him. She had seen his preference for cream enough times, but he tasted it and poured it on the floor. "This is disgusting," he said. "Make me another, and don't rush this time." As she turned to refill the cup, he reached out and grabbed her leg, sliding his hand up her thigh and squeezing. He had hard, cold hands, as though he were made of stone. She remembered him putting them on her the night she'd spent with him; she remembered that they didn't even warm up when he slapped her repeatedly. His fingers were like little mouths on her skin, tasting her.

Holly freed herself with a gentle turn of her hips and returned to the refrigerator to put out juice.

Rehsil bent down to take notes out of his bag, grumbling. "I don't care if you're a Myawi, Holly," He said. "You think because you've been trained as a rich man's toy that you're better than other housegirls? He paid too much for you. You're a stupid slut just like all the others, and—"

Rather than waiting to hear what else he had to say, Holly hit him across the back of the head with the orange juice carafe. She was aware of both having considered doing it and of being simultaneously appalled and unsurprised that she already had, all at once. It was a heavy, handsome glass pitcher, and it burst into extravagant fragments on impact, leaving her with the handle in her hand and orange juice on her shoes. Rehsil was drenched in citrus and rocked forward with the blow, his face striking the table.

She expected him to go down and stay, but he came right back up. Rehsil shouted in rage and spun out of the chair. He didn't wait for her to stammer out a false apology; he hit her in the face, screaming in Hindi. His breath smelled like meat.

The punch was a starburst of impact that emptied her mind of thoughts. She dropped the pitcher's handle. Holly's belly struck the counter; for a moment she wasn't certain where she was, or how she'd gotten turned around. The disorientation got worse with a second explosion of hurt as he punched her in the ear. She thought of Tince, the Axtellia girl that Rehsil had beaten into a six-day coma from which she never awoke. He'd do the same to her.

Whatever veil of civility that existed between them was gone, and he was hitting her exceptionally hard, in the head again, in the shoulders, low in the back. He kicked her in the leg and she growled in the back of her throat, a shout that never reached open air. *A Myawi never screams.*

The closest thing to her on the counter was the can of coffee, so she grabbed it and flung it in his direction. Rehsil took an instinctive step back. Holly steeled herself for him to come at her again. She knew he would. He looked like he hadn't decided if he was going to hit her or grab her, but he came. When he did, she was ready, and seized his wrist in an aikido hold. She stepped into him, took his balance and performed a perfect wrist reversal. She'd been taught and practiced the maneuver endlessly in self-defense classes at Myawi, and Rehsil flipped violently onto the table in spite of outweighing her by fifty or sixty pounds. It was easier than she expected. She had never thrown an actual assailant before, and it surprised her so much so that she let him go as he hit the table, his legs sweeping the breakfast tray and dishes to the floor. The table broke under his body, a floor-shaking crash that made her glad there were no downstairs neighbors.

Rehsil was panting like a bull, nowhere near done fighting, malice pouring off of him like steam. She had to hurt him while she still had the advantage, so she threw herself on his back, both knees down, all of her weight. The impact drove him onto the ruins of the table and knocked his wind out. He snarled, trying to get up, and she reached forward, snatching his mug from the wreckage on the floor. Holly hit him in the back of the head with it, her hand wrapped over the top of it, base down. The impact jarred her wrist, all the way up her arm, and she heard him gasp in pain. She hit him again, and again. Rehsil started to try and push himself up, and she kept hitting him in the head so he'd stay down.

Holly thought again of the night Elden had loaned her to Rehsil. He had burned her with hot incense, laughing, and broken two of her fingers to see if he could make her scream. She hadn't. Elden had sued him for damages afterward, but the covered medical bills didn't erase Rehsil's laughter.

The mug went loose and fell apart in her fingers. Without hesitation, she grabbed another one, and resumed pistoning blows into the back of Rehsil's head. She kept hitting him, and she didn't want to stop. The second mug broke more spectacularly, shattering against the back of his head. The third mug encountered much less resistance. Holly stopped when she saw brain matter. Her right hand was gloved in gore, and a sunburst of blood patterned the floor around Rehsil.

She dropped the mug and pushed herself up off of him. He did not get up. Dr. Rehsil would never be getting up again. Holly's head spun for a moment, and she took a breath to center herself. Her face was tight and hot where he'd hit her, painful and numb at the same time. There was blood coming out of her mouth, and she put her hand up to catch it, three fingers full. The punch to the face had split her lip.

And then there was another knock at the door. She'd left it unlocked, and Professor Hatton and Yinka walked in.

Adrenaline and the electrostim had her brain in overdrive. Holly limped toward them. Hatton and Yinka were frozen in place, their smiles frozen and cracked, aghast no doubt at the state of the apartment and the state of her face. Yinka came forward, asking, "Holly, what's happened?" and Holly shoved her out of the way, barely hearing her words. She moved without thinking, and plucked Hatton's ridiculous revolver from its dangling holster with her left hand, pushed it into his chest and pulled the trigger.

Her hand was jolted as if a horse had kicked it, and the explosion was so loud it seemed to go on longer than it actually did, echoing around the room and obliterating everything else. Her ears were instantly ringing. The back of Professor Hatton's jacket exploded outward with a spray of blood and gore that splattered the door and ceiling behind him. He never had a chance to react. She imagined there was a confused, disbelieving look on his face, but she didn't see it as he crumpled to the floor.

Holly bent and placed the gun carefully on the floor, flexing her fingers, then turned to face Yinka.

From the state of Yinka's face, she was screaming, but the tinnitus shriek in her ears made it impossible to be certain. Yinka started yelling things, gesturing toward the kitchen, probably asking what had happened. The state of the place was answer enough, she imagined. When the girl said her name, it was clearer, though the voice was barely a murmur beneath the noise in her ears. "Holly." Yinka fluttered her hands and started to cry. "Holly."

"We're free, Yinka," she said. "We can just go."

She shook her head, and started speaking again.

"I can't hear you," she said, struggling to focus on the murmuring.

"We can't just go!" Yinka was shouting. "No we can't. You have killed my benefactor! You have to turn yourself in. They'll execute you. Holly, you're so wonderful and you're a Myawi, why would you *do* this? You have to turn yourself in. They have to execute you now! What will Professor Ono do without you?"

"Not very much," she said without thinking. The blood in her mouth was annoying her, and she spat it out indecorously. "I killed him first. Yinka—" Holly realized the girl was going to bolt, and stepped forward as Yinka made for the front door. She blocked the smaller girl's path and tried to grab her. Yinka dodged away, losing her hairbow to Holly's grasping fingers. She changed course and ran for the bathroom. Holly reached the door a step behind her and got her hand on the doorknob as it slammed, but the latch clicked before she could turn it.

She hit the door with an open palm. "Yinka! Listen to me!"

"Muh wah muh yuh muh wah!" she heard through the door, parsing it a moment later: *You have to turn yourself in.*

"I don't, Yinka."

"It's the law!"

"We're in North America, Yinka. We can just walk away. Take our collars off." Holly had no idea if this was true. She'd heard of the Ivory Sisters removing collars, but had no idea how. Maybe if she could find her key in Elden's things.

It didn't matter; Yinka wasn't convinced, and if she left, she was going straight to the authorities. "No, we can't. You have to turn yourself in." Her voice was watery with tears. "And if you won't then I will, and you've killed my benefactor, so I'll have to go back to the school, and start over. It's not fair, Holly, how could you do this?"

"I'm sorry," she said, her voice almost a whisper.

"You have to turn yourself in and tell them what happened!"

"I know." She stared at the door, barely listening to her own voice. The responses were automatic, whatever it would take to get Yinka to stop yelling. Holly went to the front door, and locked it. Professor Dineen never came to the morning meetings, preferring to show up around lunchtime, but it wouldn't do to have one of the grad students walk in. Holly had actually liked Professor Hatton, and the students were nice. She didn't want to have to hurt them. She was aware, somewhere in the back of her mind, that she didn't want to do what she was about to do, either.

"How could you do this, Holly?" Yinka's rant continued. "It's so foolish."

"I know," she said again. Then she kicked the bathroom door, right next to the doorknob. The impact rattled it in its frame, and Yinka wailed, begging her to stop. Holly kicked the door again, and it burst open, taking pieces of the jamb with it. She charged into the room. Yinka tried to run past, but Holly caught her by the neck and flung her back into the bathroom. Tiny fingers scratched at her face; Holly pushed the hands and surprisingly sharp nails away and wrestled Yinka to the floor. She squeezed the girl's neck to get her to stop screaming. "Just be quiet!" she shouted over Yinka's screams. "Just be quiet and I'll tie you up, I won't hurt you!" She wanted to try and get Yinka to understand that they weren't enemies, that they were both victims, but she didn't have enough breath to make the words.

Yinka wasn't going to be quiet, though. Not after being pushed to the floor, not after being hit. *Just hold her down,* Holly thought. They struggled, a flailing confusion of fingers and forearms. Yinka made up for the size disadvantage with desperate fierceness; she went for Holly's eyes, and scratched her cheek and neck. *Just hold her down.* She got a fistful of Holly's hair and yanked, wailing at Holly to stop. Holly stayed on her, silent and determined, and got slapped in the eye. *Just hold her down.* She let go of Yinka's throat, leaned back to protect her face, then grabbed the girl's hair at the crown of her head, seizing the little bun there, and slammed the back of Yinka's head into the side of the toilet.

The screaming abated. As with Rehsil, Holly found that she couldn't stop once she'd started, and she banged Yinka's head against the hard porcelain until the caterwauling and flailing arms and legs ceased. *Just hold her down,* she thought, even while realizing that was not what she was doing at all. The toilet was spattered with blood, and the back of Yinka's skull was caved in, shattered. Her eyes were open, staring in dull surprise but seeing nothing.

The apartment became very still and quiet, as though the city outside had somehow disappeared from existence. Holly released Yinka's head, and it stuck to the blood-encrusted base of the toilet. She flexed her fingers and stood up, backing out of the bathroom. She was suddenly exhausted, barely able to move. If the police had broken the door down in that instant, she'd have just stared at them. She certainly wasn't in any condition to receive guests.

She climbed the spiral staircase slowly, mindlessly, discovering new hurts in her arms and legs the whole way, and went to the master bathroom. Locking that door behind her as well, she took a deep breath and started to run a bath.

She undressed slowly, easing out of the torn and bloody clothes, undoing her hair the rest of the way. The room filled with steam, but she left the vent fan off. Her swollen lip throbbed painfully, and her fingers all felt sprained, the knuckles threatening to swell up too. She felt hot lines all over her face and neck where Yinka had clawed at her. Holly got into the tub and let the water rise around her, discovering a scraped knee that she hadn't been aware of.

She stopped the water when it reached her armpits, closing her eyes. It was hot, hotter than she usually ran it, but it felt good. *Ready?* she thought, decided a moment later that she was, and dropped her arms into the water. The cuts on her fingers and arms lit up like fire, pain racing up and down her limbs, letting her know each and every little place that her skin had been torn. Holly breathed through it, flexing her fingers in the water, her blood and Rehsil's and Yinka's streaming away, fading into a light tint in the water. The heat was heavenly. As the hurt faded, Holly closed her eyes and gave herself over to the water. She immersed herself to the chin and let her hair float around her, listening to all of the sounds the apartment wasn't making, then tilted her head back and enjoyed the glorious rush as the water reached her scalp.

I didn't, she thought.
You did.
I didn't mean to. I had to.
You didn't.
I couldn't have.
You could.
I'M SORRY. I'M SO SORRY.
Are you? Would you be comfortable in this bath if you were sorry?
Shut up. Shut up. Shut up.

She soaked for a long time, forcing her thoughts to stop, drowning them in scalding water. Afterward she rose, dried herself off, dried and brushed her hair, dressed in fresh clothes, then lay down on the bed again, on top of the covers. Elden's body was a cool hump, and she kept her shoulders slightly hunched so she didn't touch it.

She dozed, and for the second time was awakened by knocking at the door. The world always kept moving. There was no waiting for whatever thoughts she wanted to have. She imagined herself made of steel, and the thoughts fell away. Less startled this time, Holly rose and went to answer it, this time moving as quietly as she could and looking through the peephole first. Seeing that it was Marcus, she quickly opened the door and grabbed his sleeve, pulling him inside. She closed and locked the door behind him.

Marcus' eyes widened as he realized the state of the apartment and what he was looking at. "Hol—" he started.

His voice was already too loud, driven to shrillness by shock, so she slapped a hand over his mouth and squeezed lightly. "Shut up," she said quietly. "I know. Just shut up." She took her hand away.

"Did you do this?"

"Yes."

"Gracious, the...is that Doctor Rehsil?"

"Not any more. Don't miss him, he's not worth it. Of all of them, not him."

"And where...is Professor Ono?" he asked reluctantly.

"Upstairs," she said without looking at him. Holly's voice sounded to her like it was coming from outside of herself. Marcus headed for the staircase and started up. "I wouldn't," she said. He did anyway; she heard him reach the top of the steps, cross the room to the bed, and then a sobbing gasp as Marcus discovered Elden's body in the bed. She went to one of the chairs in the sitting area, where she could see the door but not Rehsil's body in the kitchen, and dropped into it.

He descended the steps slowly. "What...Holly, what have you done?"

"I think the answer to that question is somewhat obvious," she said, inspecting one of her bruised knuckles. "The question you should be asking is, what am I going to do next?" He got a stricken look on his face, and his eyes gauged the distance to the door. She huffed a humorless laugh without smiling. "I'm not going to do that," she said. "Sit down."

"Holly, I—"

"*Sit.*"

Marcus sat, perching on the edge of the chair opposite her.

"This is a death sentence for me," she said. "I have earned a bullet in my brain."

"What happened?"

Holly shrugged slightly. "I don't know exactly. I was thinking about the fact that he lied about my mother, and about my entire life, and..." she shrugged again. "It doesn't matter. I can't take it back. Domestics who murder their benefactors don't have much of a future."

"Holly, this must be...that is, I can't imagine what you're going through."

"Don't try. I don't care. Where's my sister?"

He opened his mouth, then closed it. "I, ah...I have no idea."

"You're going to help me find her."

"I'm not sure how I can—"

"I'm not asking."

Marcus started to say something else, and Holly looked past him, a meaningful glance at Hatton's body on the floor. He followed her gaze, then swallowed heavily. He looked a bit ill. "Okay. I'll do what I can."

"Thank you."

Yet another series of rapid-fire knocks on the door made both of them jump. Holly recovered first, took a deep breath, and crossed the room quickly to look through the peephole. Lakshmi stood outside, carrying a small box of what appeared to be vegetables and wine. "Rabbit's mortar," Holly whispered.

Lakshmi knocked again. "Why are you standing there?" she called through the door. "Let me in, this box is heavy and I don't have a lot of time."

"Can you come back later, Shmi?"

"Are you cracked?" She kicked the door. "Hurry up, the market took forever and the mister and missus are probably five minutes behind me! You're getting an apology-basket for them missing the morning meeting, so you'd better let me in."

Holly opened the door and pulled Shmi inside, closing and locking the door behind her as she had with Marcus.

She was talking the moment she came through the door. "What's that smell? Do you believe this? Missus wants a cheese tray with her afternoon tea, they're coming here to talk with Professor Ono and she wants to tag along, sends me to the market to prepare it so it's ready when they get here, I know she's just trying to find reasons to yell at me and *what the what the what fuck shit fuck fuck Holly why is Professor Hatton on the floor he's bleeding is he dead? Is he dead?*" Shmi dropped the box; the bottles of wine clanked noisily against each other but didn't break. "Is that Doctor Reh—did he, your face, I'm really, I don't know what..." She started to hyperventilate.

Holly took her firmly by the shoulders and turned her away from the carnage. "I'm in a lot of trouble, Shmi."

She flailed, throwing Holly's arms off. "You?"

"Yes."

"You? This?"

"Yes. Yinka and my benefactor too."

Shmi's voice rose to a shrill screech. "*Holly, you killed Yinka?*"

Holly took Shmi's shoulders again, gently, in case she tried to bolt. "I can explain. I promise. You say Professor Dineen is coming?"

She nodded, eyes huge, trying to slow her breathing by counting under her breath. "Are you going to kill him too?" Shmi's eyes suddenly focused, and her expression became speculative. "Will you kill the missus?"

Marcus stepped forward. "Holly, no."

She gave him an annoyed look and released Shmi. "Of course not. But there's no time to clean this up."

"What if we just lock the door and refuse to let them in?"

Shmi rolled her eyes. "Who *are* you? Have you met the mister?"

"She's right, we have to go. Shmi—"

She pulled herself up to her full, diminutive height. "I'm not explaining this mess. I'm coming with you."

"I don't know where we're going."

"Back to my place, of course. The mister and missus will be here, and then they'll have screaming horrorfits about this—I hope she vomits—and then they'll be busy with the police. Time for you to hide a while, and they won't think to look for you there."

"They might, if you're missing," Holly said.

"Truth." Shmi handed her the keys to the Dineen's apartment. "Go there and wait for me then. I'll go back downstairs to the market for some more stuff, then come in a couple minutes before they arrive and scream a lot, and then I'll come home while they're busy crying and making reports and hopefully vomiting and getting it in her hair."

It was the best plan they had for the moment. Holly nodded quickly, her mind racing to figure out what she could pack in two minutes.

"I think that I should stay here as well," Marcus said.

"No, you shouldn't," Holly replied. "I'm going to pack a bag, I'll be right down. Don't let him leave," she told Shmi. The tiny woman gave her a nod, then looked sternly at Marcus.

She wanted to smile at the little tableau, but it never reached her lips; her mind was already racing away, trying to think of what she needed to take with her. There was barely any time to consider where she might be going or what might be coming next, so she moved automatically, slipping her feet sockless into her Wing boots, sweeping her toiletries, makeup, music box and electro kit quickly into a satchel. Holly took Elden's computer, the portable file box he kept his research in, and grabbed his wallet as well. There was something else...but she didn't have time to think of it. Given a few more minutes she could probably have packed for multiple contingencies, but if she was still here when Professor Dineen and his wife arrived, things were going to go very badly. Holly didn't think she'd have any problem killing Dineen or his wife, but there was no telling how Marcus or Shmi would react if she did. And she didn't want to have to kill all of them. She might, if she had to. She could, if she had to. But she didn't want to. Was that enough to exclude her from being a monster? She pushed the thoughts down.

Back downstairs, Marcus and Shmi hadn't moved. He looked a bit less nervous. "Okay, we're going. Use the back door, the fire escape, at the other end of the hall," Holly told Marcus. On her way to the door, she detoured long enough to scoop up Hatton's gun, which she'd kicked under the couch. It barely fit in the bag.

Lakshmi handed her an orange and a small wedge of cheese from the basket she'd brought. "Be careful," she said softly, stepping out the door with them to wait outside. She had collected her box of groceries, and turned toward the stairs to the front of the building. "I'll see you soon."

"You too," Holly said. She felt the urgency of the moment weighing on her. She steered Marcus out the proper door, and they quickly put distance between themselves and the apartment. The moment she was on the street, every face seemed familiar, and she was convinced they were moments from running into one of the grad students, or someone who'd seen her shopping, or that the alarm would go up behind them, news racing out over the wires and web that a Myawi had murdered a bunch of people and was on the loose.

But this was Strip City, she reminded herself. There was no wire, and hardly any web. She just had to get off the street before someone who knew her face saw her here, and then they could disappear. Once out of the city, into the interior of North America, it was unlikely she'd be caught.

When they reached the Dineens' apartment, let themselves in with Shmi's key, and got off of the street, Holly explained this to Marcus. He shook his head. "I don't think it will work," he said. "You can't exactly walk out of the city. There are no settlements, no other cities within walking distance. The desert...there's not really a way to walk across that. You'll have to find a ride."

"Makkhana," she said.

"Pardon?"

"Makkhana. There's a shop, called Makkhana. I think they have a connection to the Ivory Sisters."

"The...ah, yes, the domestic-liberation front. I suppose it makes perfect sense they'd have an outpost here. The last stop on their underground railroad, perhaps. Do you know someone there? Have you been in contact with them?"

Holly shook her head. "No, never." She thought of Nielle. "But I knew someone who did. Maybe. We'll go there, once Shmi gets back."

"You should eat."

"I'm fine."

"Your hands are shaking. And you're clutching your parcels as though they were your only link to sanity."

"Really, I'm fine." She made a conscious effort to sit still and relax her joints, one at a time. It worked.

"I don't understand, Holly. Whatever else he was, Professor Ono was good to you, wasn't he? You seemed to be friends, partners even. And I was told you've been with him for many years."

"Elden lied about my mother," she said, not looking at him. Her voice buzzed strangely in her ears. "He was the one who told me she was alive."

"And you killed him for that?"

"I don't know what I did," she said. "All I know is that I didn't punch the cabinet because it's not myself I want to hurt."

Marcus frowned. "I don't...I don't understand what that means."

"I didn't think you would. You can't talk to me about this. You can't understand and I don't owe you an explanation," she replied, and had nothing else to say until Shmi returned, less than twenty minutes later.

"Worked better than I thought," she said with a mischievous grin. "Don't know how long it's been since I screamed that much. The police asked the missus to make me leave if I wasn't going to calm down, so she did. I'm to prepare a late dinner for them as soon as they get back. Think I might just shit in a pot full of milk and leave it on the stove for them."

Holly managed a wan half-smile. "I don't think there's time for that."

"So we need to get out of here, but you have to tell me what happened and why you killed Yinka. Where are we going?"

"Marcus is going to help me find Ivy."

He shook his head nervously. "I really don't see what help I'm going to be."

"I didn't expect that you would," she said snappishly, surprised at the tone coming out of her mouth. Part of her wanted to break his head open and leave him here in the Dineen's apartment, but she needed him. He was her only tenuous link to Ivy.

Shmi took less time than Holly had to pack—"I'm getting new clothes," she said, "not taking any of this trash with me," and Holly marveled a bit at how quickly and easily she'd shrugged off the role of domestic. It had never been who Shmi was, Holly supposed. Not so, herself.

So what was she now?

She pushed the question aside, opting instead to find an enclosed pedicab on its way to the Old Town shops, where she remembered Makkhana's mysterious store to be. Holly sat between Marcus and Shmi, mindful that whether they knew her or not, many people would still remember seeing a Myawi on the streets. Perhaps she should take Shmi's lead and replace her clothes. Somehow, the notion of wearing clothes that didn't identify her as Myawi was frightening. She wanted to voice this, but couldn't think of the words, so she said nothing. She was thinking of too many things as it was. The bump had worn off. The world seemed to have sped up and tossed her halfway off, and she was being dragged along.

The shop was where she remembered it, and it was deserted as it had been before. There was a different man at the counter, balding and thinner and younger than Nielle's friend. Holly asked if Makkhana was in.

"He isn't," he said politely, glancing from Holly to Shmi, then at Marcus. "I'm Mungaphali. Can I help you with something?"

Shmi stepped forward. "I'm exhausted. Wouldn't it be great to retire young?"

His grin didn't change, but Holly thought it took on a decidedly guarded air. "Life places many burdens on us that can be hard to relinquish."

"I'm ready," Shmi replied immediately. "We both are."

Holly glanced at Marcus, who looked as confused as she was, but both of them remained silent. Mungaphali said, "I see," and stood, motioning for them to follow. He led them to the back of the shop. Hidden by the curtains that draped the walls there was a door, and he closed it silently. As he did so, a red light came on, revealing that they were in a very short hallway with doors at either end. With the four of them in there, it was as crowded as an elevator. "Please wait here," he said, and continued through the second door, which he closed behind him.

"Shmi?" Holly asked.

"You said they were Ivory Sisters."

"I did. Was that a code of some kind?"

Shmi nodded.

"How did you know it?"

"It's what you tell them if you want to...you know...retire. Girls talk about it all the time."

"I've never heard it."

"Well not with *Myawis*," Shmi said, embarrassed. "You guys are...you know."

Holly nodded in understanding, masking a twitch of hurt feelings.

"You shouldn't have killed Yinka, you know."

Holly nodded again. She wasn't sure how to respond. There wasn't time to fall at Shmi's feet begging forgiveness, and she wasn't sure if Shmi even wanted that.

The door that Mungaphali had entered opened, and he smiled at them. "May I have the gun?" he asked Holly. "It will be returned to you, of course." She took it out of her bag and handed it over carefully. As its weight left her hand she wondered how she'd carried it for so long without noticing. "Thank you. If you will," he gestured for them to follow. The next room was a typical back office: a desk and file cabinets in cluttered disarray, and a battered green door beyond them that led to a staircase to the basement.

Once downstairs, they were wrapped in a comfortable invisible curl of incense, and the tapestries and art on the walls gave the cellar a warm, inviting feeling. The floors were comfortably carpeted, the furniture low and surrounded by pillows for sitting, and the fabric-draped ceiling brought the space down in a way that was comforting rather than claustrophobic. Makkhana was seated at the table with a portable computer station in front of him, shoved in among candles, drinking glasses, an incense burner and a plate of dried fruit. When unmoving he appeared to be a part of the room; his dark olive skin and bushy beard and sideburns conspired to make him look like an unusually realistic sculpture of a man. He looked up at the three and smiled pleasantly. He pushed back from the desk, revealing a belly like an uncooked loaf of bread. Mungaphali bowed and returned upstairs. Holly dimly heard the door at the top of the steps latch behind him.

"I remember you," Makkhana said to Holly. "Nielle's friend. I was sorry to hear."

She angled her head quizzically. This wasn't the man Nielle had met, either.

He smiled. "Apologies. I saw you, but you did not see me." He indicated a pane on the computer screen, showing a video feed from the store.

"I was there," Holly replied. "When she died."

"Doubly sorry. Why would you return?"

"I need the help of the Sisters," she said, doing her best to mask her uncertainty.

Makkhana arched an eyebrow enigmatically. "You seem quite composed," he said. "Practically perfect in every way."

Shmi started to speak, but Holly spoke first. "I've killed my benefactor, and three other people," she said. "I suspect the news will be talking of it shortly."

This seemed to take Makkhana by surprise. "I see," he said, tapping the table next to his computer. "Please, sit. I'm sure this story has a long version and a short version."

Holly knelt on a pillow. Marcus and Shmi followed suit. "Which would you prefer?"

"The short, please. I do have work to do. Why did you kill these people?"

She realized she wasn't sure what the answer to that question was. "I... don't know. My benefactor lied about my mother, and I had that in my head, and I wanted to kill him and I did."

"And the others?"

Holly was aware that Shmi and Marcus were looking at her intently. "It got out of hand."

"I can only imagine. The tighter a spring is wound, the more powerful it is when it uncoils. Are things back under control now?"

Control. He was talking to her like a Myawi representative, she realized. Trying to calm her down, perhaps. "I don't know, Mr. Makkhana," she said. The honorific was automatic, and she grimaced slightly to hear it.

Makkhana noticed this as well. He kept his eyes on her, but tapped briefly at the computer with one hand, passing his hand across the screen to change feeds as he asked Shmi and Marcus to summarize their involvement as well, cautioning them not to give him their names. The computer chimed just as Marcus was beginning to elaborate on his connection to the university, and Makkhana held up a hand as he read the news on the screen. After a moment, he sat back with a satisfied sigh. "I am going to assume that you are Holly."

"Aniram," she said. "Holly Aniram."

"It's nice to meet you, Holly Aniram. I have news for you, good and bad in equal measure. The good is that we are going to help you without hesitation. We will need to get those collars off of you, and get you beyond the reach of some very, very determined people. The bad is that I cannot take your collar off."

At the thought of having her collar removed, Holly's heart raced. She realized that the very notion of it frightened her, even after all of this, and hated herself for it. Makkhana's immediate assertion that he couldn't remove it came almost as a relief. "Why not?" she asked.

"Myawi collars require a unique key, available only from the school itself, or your benefactor. We've never been able to break the encoding."

She remembered the college boys who'd attacked her and failed to get her collar as a trophy, and nodded. "But Shmi?"

"Oh, that's easy," Makkhana said. He pushed himself to his feet and crossed the room to a handsome trunk made to look like an antique. Holly recognized it as the one she'd seen when she'd first come to the shop with Nielle. Makkahna opened it with an unconscious flourish and removed a device that looked like a hammered-flat skeleton key from one of the small drawers in the lid. It had a battery pack crudely riveted to one end. "Fortunately for you, my dear, Axtellia collars are much easier to confuse," he said to Lakshmi. "May I?" When she nodded, he lifted her hair out of the way, passed the key over the back of Shmi's collar, and the little metal circle popped open with a click and a chirping sound.

She handed it to him gratefully, rubbing her neck. "Thank you."

"What is your full name?"

"Lakshmi Terada."

"It's nice to meet you, Lakshmi Terada."

Marcus was smiling. "Is that a common ritual for the women who've been freed?" he asked. "To give them their full names again?"

Makkhana smiled. "It's just mine. But I like to think that it's a good one."

"It is surprisingly moving. How many domestics have you freed?"

"Ah, that's a question for later, my well-schooled friend," he said. "We've got other business to attend to."

"Do we?"

Holly felt Makkhana's attention switch from Marcus back to her. "We do indeed. Holly, I've a favor to ask of you."

"Forgive me if I ask what it is first."

"I'd expect nothing less. I ask because we've never had a Myawi in your position before. I wonder if you'd consent to an interview."

"Interview?" Marcus and Holly said at the same time.

"A what?" Shmi said.

Makkhana smiled. "An interview. On video. I'd like for you to talk about your life. How you became Myawi, what the schooling was like, how the experience was for you."

She frowned. "Why?"

"Education. The people that I work with—"

"The Ivory Sisters?" Marcus asked.

"One way of putting it, yes. We are opposed to the continued use of domestics, of course. It is not always a popular viewpoint, and we believe that by telling people your story, more will understand our mission. We have done this many times before, and I can show you the videos if you have not seen them."

"I've seen a couple," Shmi said, perking up with excitement. "There was that girl Lyn, and another one named Pharii, right?"

Holly angled her head, considering.

"You are wondering about the benefit to you?"

"I wasn't, but I am now."

Makkhana smiled. "It would be purely to aid our cause. We will help you whether you agree to be interviewed or not."

"Help?"

"Passage out of the city, to Astoria. From there you will be easily beyond the reach of anyone who'd come for you. If you'll give us a few days, I think we can find a solution for your collar. I assume that you don't want to wear it for the rest of your life."

Holly touched the metal at her throat. "I don't mind it for now," she said absently.

"You're not one of them any more," Shmi said.

"I know. I should have thought to look for Elden's key. We won't be able to get back into the apartment now."

"I could try," Shmi offered.

"How? What will you tell Professor Dineen when he asks where your collar is?"

"I'll sneak in," she said.

"Not past the police," Holly said firmly. "And I don't know what the key looks like. It could be anywhere."

"They keep you ignorant of that on purpose," Makkhana said. "Myawi keys can be built into a number of devices, and the domestics themselves can't be allowed to know which one their benefactor has chosen."

"But why? It's not as though we would remove it."

"Not even now?"

Holly touched her collar again, the familiar satiny feel of the metal on her fingertips oddly comforting. "I think...that I will do your interview," she said.

He beamed and clapped his hands once, a happy gesture. "Excellent! I shall prepare you places to sleep. You are free to leave, but I think it is safer if you stay out of sight. Especially you, Holly. You are extremely visible."

"I suppose I'll have to get new clothes," she said wryly.

"Till you get that collar off it's not gonna make any difference," Shmi said.

chapter 27

Holly's music box put her to sleep as usual. If she'd been worried that committing multiple murders and destroying her life would affect her sleep, she was pleasantly mistaken. She slept without dreaming, and woke just before four to the irregular sounds of Shmi breathing on the other cot and the street noises that leaked in through the small basement window. There was no reason to get up, so she lay with her eyes open in the half-light. She catalogued aches and pains from the day before. Her restless fingers folded and refolded the edge of the blanket. Part of her mind was convinced that she should be getting up to make Elden's breakfast, to straighten the kitchen, to set his notes for the day out and prepare—

"You should throw yourself off of a building," she whispered to herself. She didn't mean it, but the shame at having freed herself from being a domestic and yet still feeling compelled to perform the duties was like a physical thing sitting on her chest. A cascade of unpleasant feelings rushed in like static, so many she couldn't even identify them all. All she wanted was to find Ivy, but did she *deserve* to? What would Ivy say, seeing her ruined sister, her twin who'd forgotten about her until a clumsy historian had accidentally reminded her?

Holly didn't have to listen to her own thoughts, though. She rose silently, easing out of the cot and taking her electro kit out of her bag. She plugged it in, gave her brain a gentle bump, and clarity returned. Her mind seemed to race out of the fog of bad feelings and self-recrimination. The tingle in her fingers was a phantom sensation, but it was familiar and that was pleasant. She was moving now, she wasn't feeling or thinking. All motion, no feeling. Much better. Much more efficient. There were a lot of things to be done.

Without thinking, she retrieved her toiletry kit from her bag, and did her makeup. Her cheek hurt where Rehsil had punched her, and it had swollen slightly. Her nose hadn't broken, thankfully, but it had bruised as well. There was little denying that she had been in a fight. Makeup covered it well enough for a cursory glance, though someone who knew her would be able to tell that her face was out of proportion.

With that tended to, she left the room. Makkhana was awake, or perhaps he too hadn't slept. The air was cinnamon-colored with incense, and he sat in front of the computer, fingers chattering away nonstop. "Good morning, early riser," he said. "Just sending correspondence home. Morning and afternoon line up strangely for us, as you know."

Holly nodded.

"Care to begin our conversation, while the others sleep in?"

"Of course," she said.

"Wonderful. I have the camera set up already." He motioned to a nondescript chair that had been draped in fabric, with blank blue curtain hanging behind. Makkhana touched a switch and the area lit up gently. The backdrop effectively masked the size and particulars of Makkhana's little apartment, so there wouldn't be any way for a viewer to tell where it had been filmed.

"So," he said as Holly got comfortable, "why don't we begin with your name?"

"My full name?"

"Of course. It's only fitting that you get used to it again."

"My name is Holly Aniram," she said.

"Feels good, doesn't it?"

"It feels strange," she replied. He was a skilled interviewer, and they fell quickly into a comfortable routine. Makkhana asked a series of practiced questions, and then urged Holly to talk about her life, both before and after she and her mother had been taken to Sino-India. He didn't do much to drive the conversation, instead letting her decide what she was going to talk about. She told him about her early days at the Myawi school, about the rigorous training routines and social development. About the friends she'd made. About the pride of finally earning her collar, of being chosen by Elden.

"The Myawi school has strict appearance guidelines," he said. Holly had been talking for over an hour, and realized for the first time that Marcus was sitting behind Makkhana, almost invisible in the dark. "Was that strange to you, to be chosen because of the way you look?"

"Not at all," she replied. "We were aware of it. The school was quite open with us on the matter. It was to reinforce the idea that, in spirit, we are all sisters."

"It seems like there was a great deal of indoctrination—"

"It wasn't indoctrination. We aren't fanatics."

"Forgive me. Let's say...an emphasis, then, on what it meant to be Myawi."

Holly nodded. "It is an important lesson. If you know you are special, you will carry yourself like you're special. Even if you are not the center of attention, people will know that you're in the room, even if you're not making a sound."

"And were you trained to achieve that regal bearing?"

"Of course!" She smiled and shared her memories. "At one point it involved carrying a full cup of tea on top of my head, as I walked across a flexible balance beam. And it had to be done quickly, because the exercise was timed." In the wings, Marcus chuckled. Holly let that flow into a series of humorous anecdotes. She had many, and she told him the ones she reserved for parties as well as the ones that weren't supposed to leave the school. After that she talked about her life with Elden. She described her weekly schedule for Makkhana, and then described a typical day.

"It sounds like you were his secretary as much as his domestic."

"That's not uncommon," she replied. "If we can find a way to do everything, or better yet, to make it appear that we're not doing everything even when we are, then that's the goal. He certainly paid enough for the privilege."

"Do you know what Elden paid to become your benefactor? What he paid for you?"

Holly winced internally as Makkhana dropped the syntax that pretended being a domestic wasn't a form of slavery. "I do," she said. "I know that I was substantially more expensive than his house. Which, I might add, was not exactly a hovel."

"And where did you live?"

"Clementi," she said, "close to the university." Holly talked about her life and her relationships with other domestics, and with Elden's fellow faculty members. This led naturally to a description of what had happened that awful night with Rehsil, and then of some of the other unpleasant encounters with colleagues and students of Elden's she'd been loaned to. "Wait...he had you servicing his students?"

"Not frequently. But occasionally he would build a good relationship with one of them, and I was offered. Only after the student was no longer in his class, of course."

"But you had sex with them."

Holly barely kept her eye-roll in check, but allowed herself a slightly condescending smirk. "If you could call it that. Between their inexperience and excitement, many times I found myself doing most of the work just so they wouldn't embarrass themselves in front of their friends, who were often watching. Or waiting for their turn." She heard Marcus make another sound, this one less amused. "I was treated well, for the most part. And I will admit that I enjoyed cleaning their houses. They were more grateful for that than the sex, sometimes." Holly realized she was feeling a rising measure of agitation, as she thought about all of the things she did to please Elden, without thought for herself. She tamped it down, keeping it out of her voice.

If Makkhana was shocked by anything she'd told him, he didn't let it show. "But you were never given a choice in the matter."

"No. You have to understand, though, that I was happy to do what was asked of me, no matter what it was. I trusted Elden. If someone was not nice to me and I let Elden know, he wouldn't let that person borrow me again. He wouldn't willingly send me to someone who'd hurt me."

"Like with Dr. Rehsil."

"Precisely. No one else was as bad as him."

"To jump forward a bit; he is one of the men you killed, isn't he?"

Holly nodded, noticing Makkhana's incense again. It was a calming blend of smells, though she couldn't place them. "But that wasn't why. I wasn't trying to...avenge what he'd done to me."

"What were you doing?"

"I don't know. It never occurred to me to *want* to have a choice." The words fell out, and she frowned.

Makkhana seemed to sense her stiffening up, and changed the subject. "What about incidents outside the home? How were you treated by the general public? Was there ever abuse from strangers?"

"Rarely," she said, but gave Makkhana an appraising look. "There are crimes against domestics, but I was only ever attacked once." Something about his nod suggested that he already knew about the college boys' attack. Holly described the incident and her injuries for the video, including the appearance of Kalida, the HNE-enhanced Protector.

From there they talked about Holly's travels with Elden, and about some of the things she'd seen. She told him about learning of her mother's history from Marcus, but didn't mention that Elden had loaned her to him or that they'd spent a platonic night together. Finally, Makkhana asked her about the murders, so she could tell her side. She was surprised to find it easy to talk about, using the same matter-of-fact tone with which she discussed her sexual encounters. In fact the entire interview felt like an unburdening, and when it was over he asked her if she had any other thoughts, or anything she wanted to say to whoever saw the video.

And she didn't. There was nothing left to say. The lingering thrill of the electrostim was still there, but Holly didn't feel the least bit chattery. She wanted to sit absolutely still, to become a statue and disappear.

Which was quite impossible, with everyone else in the room watching her, of course. When Makkhana turned the light off, she saw that Mungaphali and Shmi were there also. "You never told me about all that stuff happening after you shoved me into the car," she said to Holly.

"I suppose I didn't," she replied.

"I knew they beat you up a little, but not that you needed bone work..."

Holly just shook her head slightly. "It was nothing."

"You saved me, you know. Maybe saved my life."

She repeated the gesture.

Shmi saw Holly's thousand-yard stare, tried to follow her gaze briefly, then squatted down and touched her hand. "Are you okay?"

"Just tired. And I could use some sun. I think we should go for a walk. Like market day. I feel like I should be shopping right now."

"That's just your old life talking."

"There's nothing wrong with listening to it," she said. "Makkhana, Shmi and I would like to go for a walk."

"I don't know if that's wise."

"I wasn't asking," she said. "We'll be discreet. I will buy some of the clothes you've got upstairs, to hide...mine." The only item of clothing she really wanted to call hers was her Wing boots. And maybe the collar, which in spite of everything it represented felt like it was a part of her. "Marcus will pay for them."

"Excuse me?" He caught her eye. "Oh, yes, I suppose I shall."

"Won't be necessary," Mungaphali said. "Consider it trade for the interview." Holly nodded, accepting the terms.

"I should hear back from Huasheng this afternoon about your collar," Makkhana said. "And transport will be arranged tomorrow. They'll be looking for you by then. Possibly for all three of you."

"Oh, dear," Marcus mumbled. "Will...will we be safe here?"

"I'm sure you will. The story hasn't gone wide yet, it's still just a murder-incident in Old Town. Once they know who it was, and what school Holly was from, I expect the skies to light up."

Holly nodded in agreement. "Then I'd best go for my walk sooner rather than later," she said.

Makkhana seemed like he was about to say something else, but didn't. Mungaphali brought local clothes for Holly and Shmi, including sun bonnets and scarves. The summer sun was bright enough that their wearing protection would make sense, as well as obscuring their faces. Marcus showed no interest in joining them, having fallen deep into conversation with Makkhana, and Holly didn't invite him. She tucked her new cotton scarf into the top of her collar, where it tickled her neck but draped over the bright silver to make it less noticeable, and they departed.

"Where are we going?" Shmi asked.

"To the docks, to talk to *your* friends, and find a ship to take us to Astoria."

"Isn't Makkhana going to do that?"

"So he says. I haven't decided if I'll accept yet. I don't know why he wants to help me, what he wants in return."

"The interview? The Ivory Sisters don't ask for anything in return for the domestics they help."

"That just means they're taking what they want without asking," Holly said. Lakshmi looked up at her with a worried expression and let the subject drop. They walked until they were near the edge of Old Town. As pedicabs began to flit, looking for passengers going toward the casinos in the center of Strip City, Holly hailed one, and asked to be taken to the Laddin.

"I thought your friend there died?" Shmi asked.

"He did. From there we'll catch a motor cab to the docks. Unless you'd like to take us that far?" she asked their driver with a smile in her voice.

Their driver considered the fifteen-mile ride for a moment. "To be honest, not really, miss."

"I appreciate your honesty," she replied.

chapter 28

Sixty-three days before Princess Aiyana's trimester celebration

Holly looked for the name of the bar as they entered, but it didn't seem to have one in spite of having an entrance directly on Dealey, the main road near the Strip City docks. The sign on the front window depicted a cat laying half in and half out of a sunbeam.

"I hope they're still here," Shmi said. "It's just like a movie, isn't it?"

The bar looked like a small, pre-Colony Conflict building that a truck had backed into. The side walls actually leaned, as if the whole structure was in the process of falling over, and the décor was dark wood and red glass with a polished Victorian look. It was also tilted where necessary to heighten the impression of a building on the verge of collapse. Given the time of day, it wasn't terribly busy, but as Holly scanned the place a man rose from the bar and made a beeline for them. He certainly looked the part of a pirate, with an elaborate burgundy and gold coat festooned with epaulets, piping and all manner of gingerbread that made the fact that he was not a small man even more notable. A matching hat was a mishmash of several styles, and sported two large feathers. He had dark brown skin, amused eyes, and a masterful, gray-dusted beard that reached his chest and had been sculpted into elaborate curls and whorls on his cheeks.

"Captain Hardson!" Shmi said with a happy smile, but the man didn't acknowledge her.

Instead, he turned to ease past them, his barrel chest just brushing her shoulder as he spoke sotto voce, "Pardon me, my lovely. Join us in the corner, won't you?" He kept going past them, to a large corner table at the back of the restaurant.

Shmi turned and followed the captain, so Holly did as well. The other patrons looked like mariners, mostly, a mix of extravagantly-dressed men like Hardson and men in the coveralls of Sino-Indian corporate cargo ships. She imagined there were a few people who were playing at being sailors as well.

Hardson and his crew were in a C-shaped booth overhung by the sloped-in wall, away from the bar. There were four people at the table, and as the two women approached Hardson nudged two of them to give up their seats, one at either end of the booth. Holly sat and ran her hand over the red velvet cushion with a private smile. Looking back through the little bar, nobody appeared to have followed her path, and there were no eyes on her. She kept the bonnet and headscarf on nevertheless.

Once they were seated, Hardson took Shmi's hand and gave it a gentle kiss. "Lovely Lakshmi. So pleased to see you again," he said.

"Things have changed," she said.

"So I gathered. You look very...free," he added with an exaggerated gesture, a hand flourish that indicated his neck.

"I do. And I am. And I finally brought my friend to meet you. This is Holly. You wouldn't *believe* what it took to get her out of the house." The burst of incredibly black humor almost made Holly laugh out loud.

"I thought that might have been you," Hardson said. His voice was warm, even a touch flirtatious, but held a heavy measure of cunning. She imagined him having been the sort of child who always had the biggest, fanciest lollipop, but only ate it when others were watching. She wanted to dislike him, but her heart was resisting feeling anything at all.

"Thought what might be me?" Holly asked.

"The domestic, thought to be Myawi, who's responsible for six murders in Old Town. Breaking news, that is. The *Fists* was scheduled to sail today, but since I knew that the lovely Lakshmi was back in Strip City, I thought we'd dawdle a bit, just in case it turned out to be related to you. There aren't many of your kind this side of the ocean, you know. I was quite excited about meeting you, and plunged into fathomless despair for days when I was unable, upon our previous crossing of paths. Ask Razor; I was inconsolable."

"And why did you delay your departure this time?"

"Why, to offer you my assistance, of course. You and lovely Lakshmi weren't available to sail on my ship before, but now...you might be. Assuming my speculation proves to be true."

"Your speculation," she repeated, a touch of amusement leaking into her voice though she didn't smile.

"I have been known to be given to flights of imagination," he replied with a grin. "And I know the lives of big-city domestics are fabulously glamorous. There was a show about that, wasn't there?"

Shmi smiled. "You mean *Cake and Mortar?* That's such a stupid show, being a domestic is nothing like that! It has been an interesting day, though."

"I imagine," Hardson said. He spoke to Shmi but winked at Holly, and she had to admit that he managed to make the gesture charming. "And you are a vision," he said, addressing her directly. "Positively otherworldly. I can see why they call Myawi girls 'little goddesses.'"

She wasn't in the mood to be reminded, and angled her head slightly to acknowledge the compliment.

"I have daydreamed of having a Myawi of my own. But then, what man hasn't?" He shook his head sadly. "Far beyond my means, I'm afraid. I do quite well, naturally, as captain of my own ship, but nowhere near Myawi money. Unless of course I were to take my crew's share. Minnijean, would you mind giving up your shares for a few months, so I can get a Myawi girl?"

One of the sailors at the table, a middle-aged woman with smiling cheeks and her graying hair tied back in a tight ponytail, laughed. "I'll get you a picture of one and something slippery for your hand instead, how's that? Don't annoy the girl." Shmi laughed too, but it sounded to Holly like she was having trouble staying on the leading edge of the witty banter.

The captain angled his head at Holly. "I apologize if I'm being overly forward. Am I?"

"Not if you routinely attempt to woo every woman you meet," Holly said, "and seduce her into sailing aboard your ship."

"Clearly you've given this some consideration."

"Not really. But I might have some interest in the latter."

"Well, don't let me bully you into agreeing to anything you *aren't* interested in," he said with a theatric beard-stroke.

Holly made an extreme effort, and found her smile. It felt hollow, but Hardson returned it, and Shmi seemed to relax a bit as well. "I think I can keep my virtue intact. What remains of it."

"Where are my manners? Lakshmi my dear, when last we spoke, it was as coherent as a drunken scrunge match, but this is a civilized luncheon, is it not? I must introduce my companions! Compatriots, sailors, friends and lifemates—I present to you eighty-three percent of the senior crew of the *88 Fists*."

Holly made no effort to keep the appraising look off of her face as she scanned Hardson's companions. Charming as he was, she wasn't in the mood to play social games and hiding this fact was already making her weary. She wondered what it would take for her to feel safe enough to be friendly in return.

"The bearded terror standing next to me is Dilly, short for Dillygaff Henderson. He runs the *Fists'* farm. Don't let his smell put you off, he's actually gentle as a big-eyed cow when the situation calls for it." Dilly didn't smell, but he had lumbered to his feet when Holly and Shmi approached, and murmured a hello, avoiding eye contact. He was about six and a half feet tall, extravagantly bearded and built like an unusually muscular landmass. His huge, swarthy arms were sleeved with blurry tattoos whose faded colors made Holly guess that they were Japanese-style, but the images had been lost to the sun. He seemed confident and comfortable in his skin right up until the moment that he met her eyes, and then he swallowed nervously. "Next to him is Razor Witt, chief combat officer." Razor was the opposite of Dilly, slender and a few inches shorter than Holly, with delicate features, close-cropped black hair and dark gray paramilitary clothing that she recognized as being secondhand and Sino-Indian. Razor had narrow features and intelligent eyes, and grinned sardonically when referred to as an officer. "XO Fry down there is a North American like you, as noble a warrior as they come." Fry was a tall woman, over six feet tall and powerfully built. She had gray eyes, short hair and a Cradle's mask, and she had outlined the rosacea-like scarring on her cheeks with black tattoos, filling in orange highlights to create a pattern that resembled flame. She seemed indifferent to Holly and Shmi. Holly noticed that she was also the only member of the group with an obvious sidearm. Fry looked tired more than anything else, as though the flames on her face were a symbol of something she no longer felt. She seemed less at ease than the rest. "And Minnijean is our chief supply officer—though in reality she's our mother bear, in charge of keeping us civilized. Which can be a challenge," he added with a laugh. Minnijean raised a hand to Holly. She seemed like she'd be more at home in a bread-scented kitchen rather than a mariner's bar. Still, she had a similar hardness to all the others and it wasn't hard for Holly to imagine her killing a man, messily, to protect her own and feeling no remorse.

"You talk about them like they're family," Holly said.

"They are. Life aboard the *Fists* is a very fine life. We don't have to steal crew members, because she'll become your home."

"Do you take passengers?" Shmi asked.

"Only when they're willing and available," he said salaciously. This made Shmi giggle. "Forgive me, I couldn't resist. Yes, we do."

"What percentage of them find themselves so enthralled that they can't bring themselves to leave?" Holly asked. This elicited a chuckle from Razor.

Hardson smiled like a merchant humoring a difficult customer. Holly was struck again by his ability to do this without being condescending or insulting. So much of her time had been spent around awkward, blunt academics that his happy chatter was both refreshing and disorienting. "I know you've got tremendous problems, exquisite girl," he said, suddenly serious. "And I admire that you're prepared to pretend that you don't. But I do understand the trouble you're in, I think, and I'm willing to help."

"In exchange for?"

"Shrewd as any scav," he said.

"I was told it's dangerous to accept rides from strange men," she said with another coy yet humorless smile. "Especially when the ocean is involved."

"I suppose that depends on where you're going."

"Astoria," she said. A moment later she realized that if the police questioned him, he might tell them where she'd gone, whether she traveled on the *88 Fists* or not. She was on a short timetable. But no matter, she'd already said it.

"We're sailing south," Dilly said. "Looks like you're—"

Hardson elbowed him lightly in the ribs. "We're on quite a flexible schedule," he said. "Our lives are grand adventures, and we go where the winds take us."

"No, we don't—" Dilly began.

This time Razor interrupted him. "Don't trump your captain's ace, Dilly."

Holly observed the interplay with mild amusement. "If you can take us to Astoria, then I'll consider it."

"No farther? There's a wide, wonderful world to see beyond the coasts."

"No farther." Holly stood. "Perhaps some time you'll tell me how it is you have a farm aboard a ship."

Hardson made a face of disappointment. "Not staying for a drink?"

Shmi followed Holly's lead. "Not today, boys," she said with a smile. With a polite bow, Holly left, and heard Shmi fall in behind her. This time she spotted the name of the place: the Half Cold Cat. Strange enough to stick in her head easily. Clever. "So," Shmi asked as they left the Half Cold Cat, squinting as they entered the sun again, "do we wait to see what Makkhana offers us?"

"I'll hear him out. I haven't made a decision yet." She looked out at the docks, considering the ocean beyond and trying to think of what needed to be done next. She knew her collar had to come off, but pushed the thought aside. Getting the key would be difficult now that the apartment was a crime scene, and she still didn't like thinking about not having it any more. An alternative would come to her if she waited.

That left getting out of the city, which could be more difficult than it seemed. Momentarily overwhelmed by the paths before her (and beginning to think that she ought not to have skipped breakfast) Holly lost track of her surroundings until Shmi tugged at her sleeve lightly. She glanced at her friend then followed her nod up the sidewalk, where a man in a broad-shouldered jacket was coming toward them. Heavy gloves and boots, knee pads, utility belt—it was a Myawi Protector. It wasn't Kalida, but he was familiar. She'd seen him at the Myawi school, after the attack. His expression became amused when he saw the recognition dawn in Holly's eyes.

If they ran back to the Half Cold Cat, would Hardson and his crew protect them? Would they even be enough? She remembered how casually the Protector Kalida had beaten the college boys. But surely a group of mariners would be more of a challenge? That wasn't a sure thing, if he was HNE-enhanced. He'd be stronger, possibly faster. "Back," she said to Shmi, turning to run.

Holly took a single step and then everything went wrong. Her legs and arms went completely rigid, rendering her as stiff as a board. She pitched forward, unable to catch herself, and actually fell onto Shmi, spilling the two of them to the ground. The pain hit a moment later, and the ululating cry that Holly could hear was herself. They fell in a tangle on the sidewalk. Shmi scrambled free, and tried to help Holly up, but it was no use. The pain went on and on, and Holly couldn't unclench her muscles, unlock her hips or knees or flexed feet, couldn't bend her arms or stop making that awful chattering scream long enough to tell Shmi to just run, get away.

And then they were surrounded by uniformed men, and the Protector, and a man Holly recognized: Vitter. He looked down at her, his face impassive though he could clearly tell she was in pain, and said simply, "Get them in the car."

Holly was lifted. The pain stopped, and her arms and legs went limp, though it was several seconds before it occurred to her that she could move them again and when she did they weren't very responsive. She tried to speak but only a single sobbing sigh came out.

The men who'd lifted her wore military uniforms, though not like any

Holly had seen before. She and Shmi were bundled into a boxy armored vehicle that had pulled up to the curb and shoved into seats that lined the sides of it. Rigid harnesses were pulled down over them, locking into place with a sharp clack. Holly reached up and put her hands on the bars over each of her shoulders, but they were as firm as if they were a part of the truck's frame.

Vitter reached out and tapped Holly's collar with a smile. "Now, where did you think you were going? And what have you done with Professor McEvoy?" His face went hard. "I sincerely hope, for your sake, that he's still alive."

The truck accelerated hard, but the windows were small and high in the sides so Holly couldn't tell where they were going. She saw that the Protector had boarded as well, and when he removed his helmet, revealing small pale blue eyes, curly hair, bronze skin and a square, flat face she remembered him. Anshul, his name was; he'd been at the school when she'd been taken there after the college boys' attack. The memory caused her anger to rise; suddenly she was thinking about acid attacks and the college boys and furious at everyone around her, with the senseless desire to struggle out of the restraints and go for Anshul's eyes even though she knew she couldn't fight these people. She forced her face into stillness, easing into her Myawi mask. The bland, neutral expression didn't feel like it fit her any more.

Vitter saw her glance. "Anshul is working with us," he said. "Your school was all too happy to put him at my disposal. They're keen to learn what went wrong with your training. Honestly, your lobster soup is delicious, but I'm not sure it's worth five murders," he added.

"Four," Holly corrected him, realizing belatedly that Hardson had said there were *six* dead. So the news was still garbled, apparently.

He arched an eyebrow. "Indeed," he said, and offered nothing else for the rest of the drive. Holly assumed they were headed back into Strip City, and she was correct. Presently the sounds of traffic swelled around them, and when they stopped and one of the soldiers opened the back door, letting light flood in, Holly saw a familiar street. They were back at the apartment.

"Put her scarf up," Anshul said. Hands pulled Holly's bonnet back into place.

"Good thought. Won't do to have the media see her." Vitter went to the door and looked out. His motions were efficient, military, and clashed with the indifferently fitted suit he wore. "Okay, let's get them inside. Quick-quick."

They were hustled into the house. Holly didn't resist; Shmi struggled briefly but there was a man at each of her shoulders and they simply picked her up and carried her. In seconds they were back in the upstairs apartment. Holly couldn't tell if the faint odor of blood was real or if it was just her imagination. She hadn't noticed it previously. None of the damage had been cleaned up, but the bodies were gone and small lines had been drawn the floor. Holly knew from crime shows that they marked the spots where scanning cameras had been placed to digitize the scene, creating a three-dimensional model of every minute detail.

Holly and Shmi were put into chairs in the meeting area, in front of the fireplace. They weren't restrained, but they were outnumbered and unarmed. Vitter pulled one of the chairs from the kitchen and sat on it, oblique to Holly but well within her field of vision. "So, Holly," he said conversationally, "what in all the planes of existence have you gotten yourself into?"

"That's what I said," Shmi interrupted.

"Shh," Vitter snapped at her. "I need to know a few things, and then Anshul will take you home. I believe there are some people at Myawi who would like very much to talk to you. Tell me what I want to know and I can make sure your incarceration and execution are humane. You know what often happens to domestics when they're awaiting that time, don't you?" He met her eyes, but she didn't respond. She wouldn't let him see how rapidly her heart was pounding. "So. I need to know what you've done with Professor McEvoy, of course. I need to know what you've done with Professor Ono's research and his computer. I need to know who sent you to collect these things and eliminate the university team. And I need to know who the falconid who was seen leaving afterward was reporting to. That's all." The last was said with a touch of sarcasm.

Holly's fear was colored with genuine confusion. Who'd *sent* her? Vitter was clearly terribly mistaken, and it was on the tip of her tongue to tell him so when he nodded to Anshul and the agonizing, limb-extending pain came back. Her back arched, her arms and legs flexing out of her control and she fell right over the arm of the chair, landing on her side on the floor. Shmi called her name, then screamed it, but Holly couldn't respond. She could hear herself making that chattering scream again, and tried to fight through the pain. *A Myawi never screams,* she thought wildly, *a Myawi never screams.* She was being electrocuted, that was what was happening. It went on and on, and she tried to send her mind away from it, succeeding partially. She couldn't stop crying out and she could feel that she was drooling as well. She couldn't move. Anshul. He was doing it, the Protector had a control of some kind in his hand and he was pointing it at her. Was it her collar? Was he making her collar do this?

And then it was over again, and her body went limp on the floor. Holly sobbed and struggled to move her arms so she could wipe her mouth. The pain kept going, in an exquisite rush.

"Holly!" Shmi cried again.

"I'm okay," she gasped.

"I had the feeling you were about to lie to me," Vitter said. There was pleasure in his voice, but he wasn't smiling. "Shall we try again? Where is Professor McEvoy, or his body at least?"

"I don't understand," Holly said. "Please."

Vitter shook his head in disappointment. "I thought they were supposed to be smarter than this," he said over his shoulder to Anshul, who chuckled and hit the button again. This time she was ready for it. Holly managed to stay silent as her back arched in agony, her muscles locked rigid. It was pain, that was all, and they'd taught her how to take herself through it, away from it. She'd done the same when Rehsil had broken her fingers at his dining room table. *A Myawi never screams.* But this...this wouldn't stop. The shock of the pain was passing, and she was getting angry. It was an exhausting, all-consuming anger. Maybe it was Anshul's smile that was somehow full of hate at the same time. *Shut up,* she thought. *Shut up. Shut up.*

"Stop it! *Stop it!*" Shmi shouted.

When it ended this time, she collapsed with a sigh. If she'd had more time, more clarity, she could have spun a convincing story for Vitter, perhaps. Or perhaps not. The man was smart, even if he was drawing connections where they didn't exist.

He leaned forward in the chair, as casually as if he were at a dinner party asking for a refill of his drink. "You did take Professor Ono's research, didn't you?"

"Yes," Holly said without thinking. It was as though her body was betraying her brain, anything to avoid that burning pain again. Her shoulders and calves felt horribly cramped, as though she'd just run a mile carrying a dinner table on her back. "I did, I did."

"Good. Now we're getting somewhere. Have you delivered it to the Sisters yet?"

"No," she said, shaking her head. "No."

"Outstanding. Good girl. Now you'll take us to where it is, of course."

"No," Holly said again.

"No?" Vitter turned to Anshul, who extended his arm theatrically and pressed the trigger device again.

Nothing happened. The Protector pressed it again, to no avail.

"Well?" Vitter asked.

"Battery's run down," he said.

"That's a shame."

Anshul and one of the soldiers stepped forward. Before they could seize Holly, Shmi jumped to her feet. Holly saw her put a small green tube in her mouth. The object turned out to be her Spitting Cobra. With a snarl, she bit down, blew and sprayed Anshul and the other two soldiers with a massive cloud of acid. Vitter was on the other side of her, but dove for cover nonetheless. All three of the others went to their knees with cries of pain and alarm. Shmi snatched the trigger that Anshul had been using out of his hand and shoved it into Holly's then pulled her to her feet. "Run run run!" she cried, teeth clenched around the weapon in her mouth. Holly barely heard her over one of the soldiers' shrieks that he was blind.

Holly stumbled up. Shmi spat out the empty Spitting Cobra and they dodged past the incapacitated soldier. The second soldier staggered for the kitchen sink. Anshul was better off than the other two. He had dodged part of the spray, but the left side of his face was flaring violently red, the flesh starting to look boiled. He caught Lakshmi by the back of the neck just as she pushed Holly forward, almost into the door, and she yanked it open and was outside before she realized Shmi wasn't following.

Anshul lifted the tiny woman off of her feet. "My name is Lakshmi and my benefactor is Professor Qasim Dineen of the Singapore University!" she shouted. "Please contact him with any matter regarding my behavior or—" The Protector's fist, with its weighted glove, hit Shmi in the mouth hard enough to knock out two of her teeth. She stopped like she'd been switched off, head lolling back in a semiconscious daze.

"You're not Myawi," he said. His voice was full of rage, and the burn on the side of his face was beginning to bleed. "I don't give a shit whose you are."

Holly stopped in the outside hallway, and Vitter met her eye. This time he did smile.

Then he crossed the room, closed the door, and locked Holly out in the hall. She ran forward, too late, and banged her fist against it. On the other side of the door, there was a scuffle, a sound of Shmi crying out weakly, and then she let out a terrifying watery squall. It was cut off abruptly, then came back.

"Shmi!" Holly cried, hitting the door again, trying to hear what was going on. She should run, but she couldn't leave Shmi behind. Her friend screamed and coughed, then plunged into silence again—they were drowning her, Holly realized with cold horror. They were to the right of the door, they were in the bathroom and they were drowning Lakshmi in the toilet.

As soon as she knew what she was hearing, she could see it in her head, the awful reality of two large men holding the tiny woman down. Holly heard Shmi surface and cry out before going silent again, and her feet scratching at the floor. And she couldn't help. Shmi was going to die.

Holly rushed forward and hit the door in rage, then kicked it hard enough to dent the metal. The door didn't yield. She could throw herself against it until they finally opened it, and Shmi would still be dead and then they'd kill her too, and it would be no less than she deserved. Holly let the hopelessness wash over her, and tried to succumb to it, but she stood up and ran anyway.

Holly bolted down the hallway and out the front door, taking only a moment to pull her scarf back up over her hair. Not that it mattered if she was recognized at this point. There was a Myawi Protector here, and Vitter and the police were here, she was no closer to freedom than if she'd been in Singapore. So she ran, and cried for Shmi. She was aware of people on the sidewalks exclaiming as she went past, not recognizing her but curious about the running, weeping woman, but nobody stopped her. In Singapore she'd have attracted a police officer, at the very least, but Strip City's Old Town wasn't so civic-minded.

When the accusatory voice in her head snapped that this was all her fault, Holly ignored it, forced it to the back of her mind with all the rest of her feelings. The tears, however, wouldn't stop.

After what seemed like a lifetime of running, of looking over her shoulder expecting one of the soldiers to be right behind her, of knowing she should stop because she was drawing attention to herself but unable to do so, Holly burst back into Makkhana's shop, lungs burning and tears running down her face. Makkhana was at the register today, selling incense to a customer who looked at her curiously.

Makkhana was on his feet in an instant. "Thank you for coming by," he said to the customer, then to Holly, "What happened?"

"Shmi," she gasped. Words were impossible. It felt as though the moment she recovered enough breath to speak, she was going to break down crying again. It was already happening, in fact.

Makkhana quickly but gently led her into the back, toward the steps to the basement. "Was she caught?"

Holly nodded. "Drowned," she whispered. Mungaphali and Marcus were in the basement, and she saw them converging with concern. She stopped and tried to seize control of herself, taking a deep breath, focusing on her center. "Vitter found us," she said. "They killed her. I got away." She didn't tell them that he'd asked for Marcus.

"What's that in your hand, Holly?"

She looked down, realized she was still clutching the device Lakshmi had tossed to her. "The Protector had it." That was important. She couldn't stop the tears leaking from her eyes, but her voice was getting stronger. Holly pushed the despair and horror and rage farther away. She had to focus. "Vitter had a Myawi Protector with him. He had this. It...electrocuted me, somehow. If the battery hadn't died I wouldn't have gotten away."

"A Protector? *Here?*" Makkhana said. "So quickly. How is that possible? May I?" She handed the little device to him, and he looked at it with great interest, frowning.

"Careful," Marcus said, leaning in closer to see as well. "You don't want to injure anyone."

"It's only dangerous to her," Makkhana said. "And I suspect it won't do a thing right now." He pressed one of the buttons; a blue light lit up on the top of it, but nothing else happened. "It's not the device's battery that's died; it's your collar."

Holly touched her throat. "I don't understand."

"Your collar has a number of functions. If someone attempts to remove it, or if you're stolen, it notifies Myawi of your location. Your benefactor or Myawi can use this feature to track you as well. It monitors your vitals—heart rate, blood pressure and statistics, your sleep, the usual things. And, it can serve as a shock collar."

"What?" Marcus gasped. "But...why?"

"That's how they caught you, isn't it?" Makkhana asked Holly, paying little attention to Marcus.

She nodded. "I didn't understand. There was so much pain. I couldn't move." She told them a shortened version of the afternoon's events, leaving out the trip to see Hardson. She watched the confused look on Marcus' face change to honest distress, and that made her like him a bit better.

"I doubt the collar was designed with sustained use in mind. They've run the battery down. Which means we haven't got much time."

"Time?"

"Until it recharges. The battery's inductive. It charges through your skin. It should take eight to ten hours to get back up to full strength. Once that happens, they'll be able to track you again."

"How do you know this?"

"I have friends who acquired an early blueprint of a Myawi collar, with the standard features. No coding information, unfortunately. And this isn't a key, just a controller."

Marcus handed Holly a handkerchief, and she wiped her face gratefully, avoiding the bruises from her fight with Rehsil. "You have a lot of friends. And why didn't you warn me about this before?"

"Because only the Protectors have the signal-trackers, or the shock remotes. I had no idea there was a *Protector* in Strip City. I don't even know why they'd have one here. Something strange about all of this."

"He was from Singapore. I saw him before, after the college boys' attack. Rabbit of the moon, my life has become a violent place the past few months."

"Interesting."

"So they will be able to follow me anywhere I go?"

Makkhana shook his head. "Not exactly. Within Sino-India, yes— it can use the wireless towers and global positioning. I suppose with the Myawi school's cooperation they could hit you with a bullet from a sniper drone if they wanted to. Here, the satellites are only accessible to the colonies. I imagine they were able to track you from the ground, by RF proximity. Much less precision, and it wouldn't work at all if they were more than, say, ten miles from you."

Holly took that in for a moment. "So I've got to get out of the city."

"I would advise that with some haste, yes. I have no doubt Vitter is looking for me as well. We'll be disappearing as soon as you go. If you hadn't come to me the way you had, I would have assumed you worked for him. Even now I'm not certain."

"Why not?"

His tone was matter-of-fact. "Because of what happened to Nielle."

"But...that was an accident."

"Oh, an 'allergic reaction,' was it? She was carrying words and paper for me. She was poisoned."

"The cake? It was intended for her benefactor—"

"Stop being naïve, Holly. Anyone who was tracking Vitter's movements knew he wasn't getting on that boat three days before it sailed. I suspect Vitter sent that 'gift' himself."

"Were you?"

"Was I what?"

"Tracking his movements."

"As best I could. He doesn't make it easy. Now gather your things, you must be on your way—" As he spoke, there was a loud thump from upstairs. Makkhana took a deep, tremulous breath. "That will be someone kicking our door down. You were followed." Mungaphali moved immediately for the steps, and rushed up. The door closed and latched behind him.

"I'm so sorry," Holly said, suddenly seeing that Vitter had let her escape on purpose. "I didn't think—"

"It's okay, you couldn't be expected to. This way. Grab your bag." Makkhana moved calmly to his computer, where he tapped quickly at the keyboard, then removed a piece of the unit and pocketed it. He handed the Myawi Protector's control device to Holly. "You may need this."

She took it, then quickly collected the things she'd brought with her. Lakshmi's little bag was still by the bed where she'd spent her last night; Holly grabbed it as well. She was carrying four bags now, awkwardly. As she exited the room, Marcus took one. Upstairs, boots tromped wildly about, objects falling.

Makkhana looked disapprovingly at her. "You're somewhat burdened."

Holly thought of what Vitter had said about Marcus' research. "Some of it is for you," she said.

He raised an eyebrow. "Is it, now? This way, then. Quickly, quickly." A hidden door led to a second set of stairs leading down, and he ushered them into a narrow, dirt-walled tunnel. "There are no lights," Makkhana said, "but the floor is smooth. Run straight forward. You will see the light from the second door before you run into it, I promise." With that, he closed the door behind them, sealing off the light from the basement. There were two clacks as the door closed, and Holly guessed that the second was the door's disguise falling back into place.

"What about Mungaphali?"

"If that is Vitter, he is probably dead, or will be soon."

"*What?*" Marcus cried. "You're a peaceful organization! Why would Vitter kill—?"

"Not now. Quickly," Makkhana said again, urging them forward. The sounds from behind were muffled, and she imagined that his body almost blocked the tunnel. Holly began walking through the dark, her eyes wide but absolutely unable to see. She could feel Marcus behind her, his hand on her shoulder, and she moved faster, pushing forward into the blackness. There was an awful feeling of not knowing where she was coming from or going to; it felt like she was falling horizontally. Holly felt her heart rate increase dramatically, felt herself start to hyperventilate, and pushed it back. *Not now.*

"What's at the other end?" she asked, not slackening her pace.

"Door. Stairs," he replied. "An apartment. Another block."

"And what then?"

"We'll need to keep moving. I have a safe place. I can upload."

"When my collar recharges, I'm a danger to you again," she said. "We're not going with you." Were there sounds in the tunnel behind them, the door being forced open? Or was that their own footsteps echoing back at them? How far had they gone?

"Holly?" Marcus said. His hand on her shoulder faltered slightly, then got firmer as Makkhana pushed him to keep him from slowing.

"Are you sure? We can protect you."

"I don't *want* you to."

He paused. "I don't understand, Holly."

She didn't answer. She thought of the people who were now dead after trying to help her: Lakshmi, Mungaphali...it was enough to firm her resolve. Ahead, she saw light, the outline of a door. She slowed her pace, hand questing forward for a doorknob. She found it, twisted, blinded herself momentarily with daylight. This door opened into a room with considerably more light than the one they'd left, waist-high windows looking out onto a scruffy alley. Holly saw the tires of a car through the partly-drawn blinds; they were in a half-basement. Marcus and Makkhana followed her, and as Makkhana closed the door she saw that there was no knob on this side.

She looked around the room. Mats on the floors, mirrors on one wall, a low table at the far end with some books on it and a large, closed cabinet. The walls were unadorned. "This looks like a yoga room," she said. "Yours?"

"A friend's," Makkhana replied. "It won't take them long to assume there's a back door, even if they can't find it, and widen their search."

Holly nodded. "Then this is where we part ways." She handed him Elden's computer and file box. "Do whatever you want with this."

"You are a rare specimen indeed, Holly Aniram."

"Don't say nice things about me," she snapped. She wasn't sure why the compliment annoyed her so much, but she was conscious that her anger was misdirected. She put on her Myawi-face again. "I'm sorry, Makkhana. Thank you for helping me. I'm sorry about Mungaphali. Marcus, come with me."

"Where are we going?"

The three of them ascended to street level. Holly deliberately paid no attention to Makkhana once they were outside; she didn't even want to see which direction he went in. She reached into her bag and her fingers touched Hatton's gun. "To get a car."

"I was under the impression that domestics were not taught to drive."

"We aren't," she said. Traffic was sparse, but after walking out to a busier street there were more vehicles to choose from. She stood on the corner, shading her eyes with one hand, looking for a car like Elden's little Daimler. Most vehicles had autodrive, but Elden's was the only one she'd ever learned how to use.

Unfortunately, she didn't see any vehicles bearing the familiar roof and hood design. She did, however, see something better: a garishly rough-looking green truck on tall tires with an open bed and two rows of seats in the back. It was Bazell, rumbling along in his currently empty adventure tour rig. It was a stroke of luck, and she decided not to question it. The light at the corner turned red, and traffic slowed to a stop. The adventure tour rig was barely a lane away, and Holly walked briskly toward it and drew Hatton's gun.

She stepped up onto the fender, climbing into the passenger seat. Bazell looked her way sharply, saying, "Adventure tours start from the—" and then he saw the gun and his eyes went wide.

"Take me to the docks, please," she said with her best smile. She could feel something wrong with the look on her face. Holly supposed she looked more psychotic than friendly, especially with the weapon.

"You're that...that's a..."

"Be quiet, Bazell," she said. "Does this thing have an autodrive? Don't speak, just nod."

He nodded yes, his lower lip trembling.

"Holly!" Marcus yelled, rushing toward the rig.

She ignored him and looked down the long barrel at Bazell. "Set the Half Cold Cat as a destination, and then get out, or I will kill you," she said.

Bazell's mouth worked and his eyes were on her throat. She wondered if he was shocked by the gun, starstruck by her Myawi collar, recognizing her from before or confused by some combination of the three. "I—" He was boggle-eyed and completely soft. His uselessness annoyed her so much it made her physically angry. This idiot had thought he'd protect them from an *ursid?*

She heard Marcus approaching from the left, so she kept her eyes on

Bazell's face, held her arm out to her right and squeezed the trigger. It was a miracle she managed to hold on to the gun; the recoil flung her arm up and over her head, wrenching her shoulder. Out of the corner of her eye, she saw one of the traffic lights explode in a jolly spray of sparks and plastic as the massive bullet obliterated it. A pedestrian screamed and then there was the unmistakable heavy pounding sound of two cars colliding. She aimed the gun back at Bazell. "Right now, please," she said, hoping she wouldn't have to shoot it again because she wasn't sure she'd be able to keep her grip on it a second time.

Marcus had climbed into the back of the rig. "Holly, don't do this. Don't kill anybody else."

"Shut up."

Gasping like a fish, Bazell reached down, tapped quickly at a touch screen hidden low on the dash and framed to look like a piece of junk. He had to input the name twice because his hands were shaking.

"Go," she said when he finished. He did, and she got into the driver's seat. She gave Marcus a sharp look, and he clambered up into the front passenger seat. Holly tapped the destination button—thankfully Bazell had done as she asked rather than sending the truck to the nearest police station—changed the route preference to 'urgent,' and breathed a short sigh of relief as the fake scav rig leapt into traffic. The autodrive wouldn't exceed the speed limit, but it would find the quickest route and communicate with the street grid to avoid traffic or other delays.

She was fairly certain that the gun only had three bullets left, assuming it had been fully loaded when Hatton was carrying it, and she had no idea how to reload it. It could come in handy, though. That was a flashback to her childhood: everything could have value to the right person. Never discard something useless without first checking to see if it could trade for something useful.

"Where are we going?" Marcus asked. He recoiled slightly, and Holly realized that she was looking at him with an appraising gaze, perhaps wondering what she could trade *him* for.

"A pirate offered me transportation to Astoria," she said. "I am going to accept his offer, because I have no other choice." The breeze blowing over the low windshield fussed with her bonnet, and she tied it tighter.

"Do you think it's wise?"

"Wisdom is not an option for me at the moment, Marcus."

"I'm sorry."

"For what?"

"For all the things that have happened to you. For the position you find yourself in."

She sighed, looking away from him. "Don't feel sorry for me."

"Why not?"

"Because then I'll have to decide if you truly are, or if you're pretending to be empathetic because you're afraid I'm going to kill you. And I don't feel like thinking about it."

The subject thus extinguished, they both watched Strip City roll past at a satisfying pace as Bazell's rig found the quickest route out of town. Holly slouched in the seat, then reclined it as far as it would go, putting her farther out of sight of casual observers. She looked up at the sky, which was relentlessly blue and cheerful. When the bulky truck cleared the inner city and joined the faster freeway loop leading out to the coast, its tires murmuring loudly on the pavement, she allowed herself to relax a little bit.

Of course, that was when the pursuit materialized.

"I think there is a truck following us," Marcus said. Holly raised the seat back up and looked out the rear. Sure enough, a burly dark blue truck, not dissimilar from the one that she and Shmi had been stuffed into earlier in the day, was some distance back. Unlimited by the autodrive, it appeared to be gaining on them. Marcus followed her gaze. "Do you think they'll catch us?" he asked.

"Probably."

"I am beginning to despair every time I get into a vehicle in North America," he said. "It never seems to go well."

"You'll have to tell me the story some day."

"Stories, plural. If we survive this, I'll be happy to."

"We'll survive," she said. Turning to face the front again, she considered the car's steering wheel, and the pedals.

Then she turned off the autodrive and put her foot on the accelerator. The truck surged forward wildly, then flashed an admonishment on the dash and braked as she nearly ran into the car in front of her. Bazell had anti-collision systems as well. She wasn't sure if she was disappointed at the lack of verisimilitude or grateful that it was based on a modern vehicle that would be easier to drive than a real scav rig. The steering wheel resisted her efforts to change lanes, but eventually did so, and she sped past the car she'd almost rammed, catching a frown from the driver as she went past.

The wind roared over the windshield, making her eyes water. Marcus belted himself in and looked nervous. The long, straight road crested a hill and the ocean seemed to spread out in front of them, the horizon becoming water and clouds. A thick knot of civilization began almost as soon as they were over the hill and stood between them and the water, the gently tended vegetation turning quickly to buildings and side streets as the freeway became something smaller. This part of Strip City was much more businesslike, devoted to the port and the goods that came in there, as well as the needs of the mariners who, like the scavs who came to Strip City from the south and east, rarely entered the city proper.

There were more cars as well. Holly threw the wheel left and right to dodge the vehicles that seemed to appear in her path. There was an art to making it turn smoothly, and she didn't have it. The truck groaned and shuddered as its automatic stability control systems worked madly to keep from rolling over. With each swerve it got more and more out of shape, making it harder to avoid the next obstacle.

When it was too much, Holly gave up on the street and swerved onto the sidewalk, grazing a trash can and a lamp post. A door opened suddenly on the right, inches away. Holly couldn't see what manner of vehicle pulled out in front of her, but it was laden with boxes and not heavy enough to stop Bazell's careening truck; there was a shattering of plastic, a screech of scratched metal and a sudden storm of tumbling boxes. Holly jinked instinctively away from whatever she'd hit, belatedly, then overcorrected and scraped the side of the truck along the building bordering the sidewalk. She swerved away from that and back out into the street, sideswiping another car.

Things were happening faster than she could process them. There suddenly seemed to be cars everywhere, moving in every direction. The dashboard lit up with lights and shrieking buzzers, and Holly wasn't sure of what was happening. She lifted her foot off of the gas to hit the brake, and suddenly there were several loud, earthshaking thuds as the truck reared back, leaving its occupants staring at the sky for a moment before it returned to earth with a teeth-jarring crash

Silence. Shouts. A hiss of liquid dripping onto hot metal. Holly shook hair out of her eyes and looked quickly around. She'd run the truck into a gap between two other vehicles that was too narrow for them to fit through. Bazell's rig had climbed up on the cars, and the impact had carried all three cars forward, into an intersection. At least two other vehicles had piled into the resulting mess. Her chest and wrists hurt from striking the steering wheel, but Holly was reasonably certain that she was ambulatory. Strange; it seemed like she should've been hurt worse. The door on her side was wedged shut by another car. It wasn't as though she was trapped, of course; there was no roof.

"Marcus? Are you hurt?" She heard him try his door, which creaked open slightly before jamming. "We have to go." People were rushing to help the occupants of the other cars, but as they were in the middle of the tangled wreck no one had reached them yet. Holly unbelted herself and slid down from the driver's seat, dragging her bags after her. They had to climb over the other cars, and once on solid ground she could feel that she was lightheaded, jazzed with shock and adrenaline. Marcus was a bit wide-eyed as well, but at least he was compliant. She tried to remember which way the bar was. "Let's go," she said. "Keep moving."

In the chaos of the moment, no one noticed them leaving, and they were quickly around the corner and headed against the flow of onlookers pressing in to see what all the crashing was about. Holly guessed that the truck that had been following her would be catching up at any moment.

"Wait," she said.

"What's wrong?"

"Vitter. Caught us outside the bar. He'll know we're going there. We need a pedicab." Another block, and they found one. Holly hailed it and climbed aboard. The driver glanced oddly at them, covered as they were in dust and possibly bits of broken glass. "Can you take us to the docks, please? The *88 Fists*." She breathed a sigh of relief when their driver nodded with a cheerful smile and started pedaling.

When they reached the ship, Holly paid their driver (she was going to run out of cash quickly, but hopefully that wouldn't matter soon) and they approached the ship. It was larger than she expected, a converted pre-Colony Conflict ship that was dressed up with colorful tapestries and decorations on the upper part of the hull, but still very well-worn. From their angle down on the dock Holly couldn't see much of the deck, but there was a small floatplane—that looked nearly as old as the ship itself—perched at the rear of the plane, with a crane that she presumed was used to lift it down into the water. The docks were loud, full of the sounds of machinery and shouting, but as they drew close they could hear the flutter of the *88 Fists'* flags, and something about the noise was comforting.

Almost as comforting as the ocean beyond the boat.

Like most of the other old ships, the *Fists'* hull was patched with repairs on top of repairs. Rather than letting the fresh metal rust, however, the newer panels had been painted with bright colors. The dazzle was disarming; the *88 Fists* looked proud to be old.

There was a young man slouched at the gangplank leafing through a book. He was bald, wearing bright green pants and no shirt, and so skinny that his hands and feet looked too big. "May I see Captain Hardson?" Holly asked. He took one look at her and sat up straight. "My name is Holly Aniram."

"Yes. Uhm, yes, miss. Right away." He jumped out of his chair and ran up the gangplank. Holly assumed he was going to bring Hardson back, but she started up the plank to board the ship anyway. She didn't want to stand on the docks, which were beginning to make her feel somewhat exposed. Vitter wouldn't be far behind, and she didn't know how long the wreck she'd caused would hold him up, or if it would be an effective distraction. She was thankful that the drones common around Singapore were nonexistent in North America, otherwise he'd have had little trouble spotting her on the streets no matter where she went.

They reached the deck. Hardson met them within moments. "It's good to see you again so soon, my dear," he said, bowing.

"I would like to accept your offer of transport to Astoria," she said. "For myself, and Marcus."

"Marcus McEvoy, captain," he said, introducing himself with a hearty handshake. "And yours is a wonderful ship."

He nodded in response. "And where is the lovely Lakshmi?"

The cheerful anticipation in Hardson's voice hit her square in the heart, and her chest and throat tightened. Vitter could show up at any moment, so she forced control into her voice and spoke tersely. "The police killed her. They drowned her in a toilet and made me listen."

Hardson's face went immediately stony. "I see. Yet you are here, now."

"You'd rather I stayed and let them kill me, too? They underestimated my desire to get away from them."

"So it would seem. I suppose we should get you out of sight then. This way." She followed him gratefully; every second spent outside she felt less safe. If Vitter and his soldiers suddenly rushed onto the docks, would Hardson give her up? Would he accept a bounty for her, if there was one? Would he fight if they tried to take her by force? Holly couldn't keep herself from wondering, and the stress of that uncertainty, on top of everything else, was too much.

Hardson showed them to a little cabin. The windowless berth was sparsely decorated, but there was a bunk bed and a small desk without a chair, both firmly attached to the wall. The chipped paint on all of the furniture suggested that it had been exiled to this room from other parts of the ship. A small stack of framed art and some desultory pillows thrown into one corner furthered this impression.

"Your castle," Hardson said. "Our guest quarters are somewhat minimalist, but you'll find them clean and, most of all, safe," he said.

"Thank you," Holly said. "How long is the trip to Astoria?"

"Usually takes about three days. We have a couple of stops along the coast. People to see, you know. We'll break port in the morning." He saw that she was about to protest and forestalled her. "I know, the powers that be are hot on your heels at the moment. But if we set sail immediately, they'll have plenty of excuse to suspect that you're the reason. We've already scheduled to sail tomorrow, which won't draw any attention."

Holly nodded. "And what if they come on board all the ships to look for me?"

His smile held more than a hint of mischievous malice. "Oh, the enforcers of Strip City know much, much better than that. Now, if you'll excuse me."

Hardson departed, and Holly sat on the bed with a sigh. Marcus cleared his throat lightly, setting his bag on the desk, and she realized that she'd all but forgotten he was there. He had a unique ability to blend quietly into the background.

"It has been a long day," she said softly.

"I can only imagine."

"I think that I would like to take a nap."

"There's nothing stopping you, you know."

"But there is. I'm not supposed to be napping at this hour. It's almost six-thirty. I should have made Elden's dinner an hour ago, and be straightening up while he meets with the grad students. Who, I imagine, are quite at loose ends now. Except maybe Gurrit, he's got a local girlfriend. Professor Dineen is not very good at delegating responsibility, and they've all lost their advisors. I suppose this sabbatical will be cut short," she added with a humorless laugh. "I think it's safe to say that I am the worst Myawi in the history of the school."

"Do you still consider yourself a Myawi girl?"

She touched her collar. "This says I still am."

"Well. I don't know that it's my place to say so, but I think it's possible that, as you are, ah, forging new ground, let's say, in your experience as a domestic, that you can worry less about what is appropriate for a particular hour." Her response was a weary smile and a nod. "And, if it helps, I would certainly give you permission to take a nap, as there are no dinner dishes to clear, and any meetings, as you say, have been cancelled."

She laughed. "Believe it or not, Marcus, that actually does help." Holly didn't add that she resented him for it, because the reflexive relief just reminded her of what she'd been for so many years.

She slipped her bag off of her shoulder onto the bare mattress next to her, and took out her music box. "I should be asleep in about two minutes. You can turn it off then, if it bothers you." She lay down on her back with her knees up, crossed her arms on her chest, and switched the music on. Holly surprised herself by dropping off immediately.

chapter 29

She awoke with a slight start, realizing instinctively she'd been sleeping for at least six hours. It would be close to midnight—a glance around the dark room told her that there wasn't a clock handy, but she was reasonably certain of the time—so she wasn't due to do any work for Elden soon but...

...Oh. Right.

Holly relaxed, partially. There weren't any pressing duties, but there was a strong sense of something important. Where was she? They were on the *88 Fists*, soon to depart Strip City for Astoria. They were safe for the moment, she and Marcus, because Hardson would...

Her collar.

That was it, that was it. "Marcus," Holly whispered. She could hear him breathing heavily on the other side of the room, from the floor. "Marcus," she called more loudly, and he snuffled awake.

"Holly," he said, sounding like a sleepy hound.

"I need you to deactivate the collar again," she said. When she sat up, her neck and shoulders gave a fierce twinge, reminding her that they'd been in an auto accident a few hours ago. "It's been almost eight hours."

"Beg your pardon?"

"My collar," she said, more urgently. "Makkhana said the battery would recharge in about eight hours. If it recharges, they'll be able to find us immediately. It needs to be drained again, until we're at sea."

Marcus was rousing himself, comprehension dawning. "Yes, yes, of course you're right." She heard him push himself to his feet with a grumble, and then the lights came on, revealing their badly-furnished little "guest berth." She squinted. "Oh. Sorry."

"It's okay. Were you...sleeping on the floor?"

"I don't like the upper bunk. I fell out of one as a child," he admitted with a little smile.

"I'll take it later, then."

"So. How do we discharge the collar?"

"You'll have to shock me."

Marcus' eyes went wide. "I beg your pardon?"

"You heard me." She dug in her bag for the controller Shmi had stolen from the Protector. *She gave her life to get this,* Holly thought suddenly, and felt her jaw clench. "One of the buttons on this should set it off." She handed it to Marcus.

"What...what do you want me to do?"

"Don't be obtuse. We need to burn the battery down, before the tracker is reactivated."

"Yes, but Holly, there's got to be another way."

"There's no time to think of one, Marcus. I can't do it myself, I'll drop the controller. It won't hurt me."

"You're sure?" He looked dubious.

"Absolutely. Do you think the Myawi school would give my benefactor a tool that would...damage his investment?"

Marcus sighed. "I suppose not," he said, and started pressing buttons. The first two did nothing; the third sent a familiar jolt through her. She had opened her mouth to say something, and her jaw slammed shut with an audible crack as she barked in pain and spasmed, slipping sideways on the bed. It stopped immediately. "I'm so sorry!" Marcus cried. "What did I do wrong?"

"It's fine," she gasped. "That's the right one. Do it again."

"You said it wouldn't hurt! That looked incredibly painful."

"Of course it hurts, Marcus. I meant that it wouldn't damage me permanently."

"We can't do this."

She met his eyes. "We have to, and there's no time to argue about it. Push the button."

"I can't. I won't."

"Yes, you will."

He looked away, and she reached out and grabbed his forearm. "Marcus. Don't make me go ask someone else to do this. I want to be able to trust you." She moved on the bed and lay down, so she wouldn't fall, then looked at him again.

"I'm sorry," he whispered, and pressed the button. This time the pain went on, but she didn't scream, didn't make a sound other than a hissing inhalation through her clenched teeth. She was aware of her hands clutching the bed hard enough to drive her fingers into the mattress, of her back arching and hyperextending, and out of the corner of her eye she could see Marcus' pained expression. He looked like a child forced to hold down a pet during surgery, and she wanted to slap him for that. *This isn't about you, Marcus!* she thought. She rode the waves of pain, feeling tears sprout from her eyes. She could do this. She wasn't screaming, just gasping, even though it was going on and on. How much power did that *fucking* battery have?

And then it was over. The pain was gone as soon as it started, leaving only a collection of aches from over-clenched muscles. Her shoulders now felt as though she'd wrenched her arms out of their sockets, or tried to.

"Did that do it?" he asked.

She tried to speak, found that she couldn't for a moment. "Yes," she said finally. "Yes, I think it did." She didn't want to, but said, "Try the button again."

"Are you sure?"

"*Marcus.* Do as I say."

"Okay, okay." He pressed it again, and nothing happened. "If there's a battery in there, it's definitely discharged."

"Good," she said, nodding and sitting up. "That should keep it off until we've sailed away from Strip City. Have you been in here the entire time?"

"After you fell asleep I explored the ship. Captain Hardson asked me to stay below deck until we're at sea, but I was able to meet some of the crew. Minnijean, who runs the kitchen, I'm sure you'll meet her. There's Razor—did you know that he has a pet duck?—and Anami, the chief security officer. If we want to help out with shipboard tasks we're to discuss that with Embrosia the personnel officer, who's quite pleasant. I also met some of the engineers. Vadim, Bob...well, actually there seem to be several Bobs. I confess I think they are joking with me. That said, I was also able to see the mess area and below-deck public areas. Quite a cozy ship, it is. I would enjoy being able to see pictures of what she looked like before the war, when she was first commissioned."

She nodded, rubbing her neck.

"You're sure you're okay?"

"Yes, Marcus, I'm just tired. I'm sure I look haggard, I haven't brushed my hair or seen a mirror all day."

"You look quite beautiful, actually."

"Please don't say that. I don't want to hear it right now."

"I'm sorry. Does it upset you because of...the things Professor Ono made you do? With other men?"

"I don't know why it upsets me. I just don't want to hear it."

"Captain Hardson spoke very highly of you. Both your beauty, and your personality. Though I got the sense he doesn't know you all that well."

"He doesn't."

Marcus tilted his head. "Does anyone?"

She stared at him for a long moment, not sure what the answer to that was.

There was a knock at the door, and Hardson opened it a moment later. "Professor McEvoy, hypnotic Holly. Everyone is decent? Good. I just stopped by to let you know we'll be departing at first light. Nothing to fear. My humblest apologies if I interrupted something," he added with a wink and a grin.

Holly realized that her hair and clothes were in disarray, and that she'd been gasping and shaking the bed. "You didn't hear what you think you heard," she said.

"Why, I heard nothing at all, heavenly Holly! And my ears are *very* good. I'm sure if there was something to hear, I would have noticed."

The more she responded, the more he was going to tease her, so she said nothing. Holly stayed where she was, and didn't give him the satisfaction of trying to straighten her hair or clothes. "Is there anything you need from us?"

"I suppose we can discuss trade for travel later. I thought I would give you the opportunity to do so before we cast off, just so you did not feel as though I deliberately put you in a poor negotiating position."

She shook her head. "I do not mind discussing it after we are at sea."

"Professor Butterfly?" Hardson asked, grinning at Marcus.

"It's McEvoy, actually. I suppose I will defer to Holly's request. Though, I will say that I am happy to pay my way with stories and tales of North America and the history of the world. I know that these voyages can get long and tedious."

"Indeed they can. I shall leave you two. In the morning, Minnijean will come and let you know when you are free to roam the ship, after we're safely away." Hardson bowed and closed the door.

"That was strange," Marcus said. "Why would he think my name was Butterfly?"

"He doesn't." Holly resisted the urge to make a face of irritation. "He was calling you a butterfly."

He frowned. "But why?"

"Because he thought you were sticking your tongue in my flower."

"In your...I...oh. *Oh!*" Marcus blushed, his face and ears going crimson. "He must have heard the sound, when you—"

"Yes."

"Oh, this is terribly embarrassing."

"I'm not embarrassed. It's a logical assumption. He probably thinks I asked you to accompany me, so no one would suspect I was the runaway."

"We should explain—"

"I don't really care," Holly shrugged. "It's the middle of the night and I want to get some sleep." She climbed out of the bed and up to the top bunk, so Marcus wouldn't have to continue sleeping on the floor. "We'll talk more tomorrow."

"Good night, Holly."

chapter 30

Thirty-seven days before Princess Aiyana's trimester celebration

Shiloh's story

"I'm amazed they got this far," Swan said when we found what was left of the Inchin group. When they turned south after St. Louis, Ivy followed them. We were about two days behind them at that point according to the vine, so she put the Vovo on a little barge that took us a hundred miles or so down the river, saving us a few hours of travel over land.

Finding their wrecked truck was a surprise. We were starting to get close to Little Rock, and the terrain was getting more hilly, the roads narrower and more deeply wooded. It was hot too, and the air was so humid everything seemed to be wilted. With the road curling over itself the way it did, we didn't see the mess until we came around a corner and were looking right at it. Ivy hit the brakes and said, "Ah," in a little voice. "That was them."

Swan nodded. Ivy shut the Vovo down, and Swan pushed herself up and out the window to get a better look. It looked like their truck had run into a large bank on one side of the road and flipped over. There was a drop on the opposite side, and the rig had gone down in it and flattened the roof. The wreck wasn't smoking, and there were leaves on the upturned rig, so it had been here for a little bit.

There was some gear scattered around, and there were two bodies. It creeped me out. Something about the idea of being thrown out of a crashing vehicle really bothers me. I've never figured out why.

"You sure that was them?" Swan asked. Kroni was already out of the rig, shifting to sniff the air.

"Yes," she said. "That's Nellie Whit's old rig, and he traded it to the Inchins back in St. Loo. And, and it looks like some of that gear came from Strip City. The, the, the green boxes," she said, pointing at a couple of dented metal cases that were open and empty. They had some sort of yellow stenciling on the side.

"Well, that's disappointing. Think it was an honest crash, or a spider?"

"Neither. Little Rock."

"We've gotta be fifty miles out from the Rock, Travelmaster."

"Seventy. Vine says they've been sending out parties farther and farther," Ivy said. "And there's a trench in the road that ran that rig into the bank. Wouldn't be surprised if the driver was still in the truck and shot."

"Well, in that case I hope your sis wasn't with them."

Ivy shook her head. "She wasn't. The girl with the collar they were talking about is there," she said, pointing to one of the bodies.

"Is that good news or bad?" I asked. "Bad for her, obviously, but..."

"I suppose it's both," Ivy replied. She made no move to climb out of the driver's seat. "Are we alone here, Kroni?" she asked. He grunted an affirmative. She nodded to him and touched dirt. I could see her putting on a pragmatic face, pushing away any concerns she might have had about the people to focus on what we might be able to scavenge from the wreck.

"Stay in the rig, Miss Kitty," Swan said. "We're inside the Rock's hunting grounds."

"I run faster than you," I replied, and jumped down as well. Swan snorted, and all three of us moved down into the ditch where the Inchins' rig had crashed. It looked like whoever had attacked them had taken the weapons and food, but left a lot of other gear behind. Ivy didn't spend much time looking at it; she crawled carefully inside the wreck, a little clumsy because of her knee brace, and began pushing out anything that looked like it might be useful. With Kroni standing watch, it was on me and Swan to ferry everything back to the Vovo. We'd done this plenty of times; picking through it all was a task for later, when Ivy knew we were safe.

"Anybody in there?" Swan asked.

"Driver," Ivy said. "Face shot."

"Shit. They keep this up, nobody at all's gonna go near that goddamn city. They're already starving."

Ivy pushed another green box out, followed by a small crate with several cast-iron pans in it. "Tell them, not me."

"Nah, fuck 'em, they can starve. Looks like the girl died in the crash, and someone shot t'other one in the back," she was saying as I carried the big green box up to the Vovo.

Kroni shifted. "There were two more. Taken to the Rock," he said.

"Stealin' women?"

He shook his head. "Both male."

"How, how long ago?" Ivy asked.

"Yesterday."

"Ha, we almost caught up to 'em. What next, Travelmaster? We gonna go rescue them?"

Ivy actually laughed. She doesn't do it very often, it's really short, like a cross between a bark and a snort. "Let's head a little farther east, to Nashville to resupply, and then north to Detroit." I understood; with her fertile and me looking like a fertile human, we weren't going anywhere near Little Rock. We'd never come out again.

I looked at the woman who'd died, and that little shiver went through me again. She was on her back, one arm folded across her belly, her eyes closed as if she were sleeping, but her hips were turned completely sideways to her body in a bad way, feet pointing almost up toward her shoulders, and there was a bit of blood around her mouth, which ants had already discovered. She had a pale Cradle's mask and short, straight black hair framing her narrow face. The silver collar around her neck had a stylized flower etched into each side. There was a similar flower on the hem of her shirt as well. The leaves around her neck were disturbed, like somebody had tried to take the collar off but couldn't work the clasp.

I could see what had happened in my mind's eye, saw her tumbling flailing through the air, helpless to stop, hoping she could at least roll with the impact, then hitting the hard ground square on her shoulders, folding violently in half, the snap of her back breaking...agh.

"Looks like she got flung out when the rig went over," Swan said, looking over my shoulder.

"Yeah," I said. I was looking at the girl's feet; she had these tiny slipper-like shoes on, utterly useless out in the dirt. The soles of them were shredded. She didn't belong out here, and I wondered who'd have brought her this far.

"Hey," Swan said, nudging me, and I realized I'd been staring. "Time to roll."

I heard myself say, "Yeah," again. I was very glad to be heading back the direction we came.

chapter 31

Out of habit, Holly awoke just after dawn. Even without a window, she could tell it was dawn; her internal clock murmured that it was time to get up and make Elden's breakfast. She envisioned herself throwing a Myawi who looked like her overboard, and lay in bed trying to go back to sleep. The irony that *all* Myawi looked more or less like her kept her awake.

An uncertain amount of time later, the structure of the *88 Fists* vibrated, seeming to come to life. A pulsing throb, almost too low to hear, worked its way through the ship, rose to a crescendo like the purr of a herculean cat, then settled down. On the deck, distantly, a whistle blew, barely audible down in their cabin. Holly imagined that the floor twitched softly, thought she could feel the bed pitch slightly as the ship moved away from the dock. It pitched again some time later, though, so she wasn't sure exactly what she felt, or if it was her imagination.

There was a light tap on the door. Marcus snuffled in his sleep; Holly hopped down and opened it. It was the cheerful older woman Hardson had introduced at the bar as Minnijean. She smiled broadly. "Welcome aboard."

"Thank you."

"Just stopped by to let you both know we're away from port."

"How far?" Holly asked.

"We've been underway for a good hour now. I'd say we're at least thirty miles from the city."

Surprised that they'd been on the move so long, Holly nodded and returned the smile, surprised to find that hers was genuine. "May we—" she glanced back and Marcus, who hadn't stirred. "May I, that is, come up on deck?"

Minnijean gave her an apple-cheeked smile. "Of course, my dove.

You'll want to eat something as well, I'd imagine. Unless the sea doesn't agree with you."

"No I don't get sick." Holly followed Minnijean out of the cabin and down the narrow hallway to the stairs leading up.

In the daylight and away from port, the *88 Fists* seemed much friendlier, if such a thing was possible. There was no land anywhere in sight, the horizon a band of flat blue on all sides. Unlike Holly's last ocean crossing, this ship wasn't in a hurry, so she could lean on the railing and look at the ocean without the wind tearing at her. Holly took a deep breath, smelling the unfamiliar scent of the ocean and feeling as blank as the horizon.

She heard flags flapping, and looked up to see laundry strung on lines across the upper decks. Many of the flat panels had been painted with murals, weatherbeaten drawings overlaid by newer work until the entire ship was a crazy-canvas of art that matched the tapestry-covered inner halls. Holly scanned the deck, and saw a large garden with retractable covers spread out over several flat surfaces, answering her question about farms aboard the ship. There were children tending to it. The sight made her smile.

"That's a look I like to see," Hardson said. His voice came from above, and it took her a moment to realize this. He was standing at the railing a deck above her, hands behind his back, the very picture of a confident captain. She'd been looking at the ship itself and looked right past him. "Oh, dear. I'm sorry if I startled you. Worst thing in the world, to see a woman's smile vanish at the sound of your voice."

"I was...thinking about something else," she said.

"You seem more relaxed, now that we're underway."

"Well, don't worry, I'm still plenty stressed. Once we get to Astoria I'll feel better. How long is the trip, again?"

"Yes, the trip north. There are some things to...negotiate, regarding that."

Holly glanced around, saw no crew within earshot. "Yes, we were going to discuss it today."

"For you, heavenly Holly, I have good news and bad news."

She folded her arms.

"The good news is that your passage will be free of charge. You and Marcus are guests of the *88 Fists*."

"And the bad?"

"We are not going north."

"Hardson..."

"I apologize deeply and truthfully, Holly, but the matter is out of my hands. Mama Lola has decided that we need to sail south."

She kept her face as neutral as she could, clenching her teeth, then relaxed and filtered the agitation out of her voice. "What do you mean?"

"We have business in Zeeland. And that is where we are bound."

"I don't suppose it would help to offer money."

Hardson shook his head sadly. "I really am sorry. But perhaps in time, you'll come to see the *Fists* as home."

"To be honest, this reduces the chances of that. Who is Mama Lola, and why are you blaming my abduction on her?"

"I respect the woman far too much to make a scapegoat of her, Holly. This is her ship."

"I thought you were the captain."

"I am." He laughed self-deprecatingly. "It's complicated."

She considered for a moment, looking up at him. It was getting hard to keep the fury off of her face. "I am losing interest in talking to you."

"That's fair," he said. "Let me know if there's anything I can to do make your room more comfortable. Do you want to bunk with the professor, or would you like your own space?"

"Does it matter?"

"It does. Even if you'll only be with us a few weeks, you're just as valuable as if you were one of my crew. And as such..." Hardson brought his hands around in front of him. Holly saw that he had her electrostim kit, tiara and music box, and as she realized this he cocked his arm back and threw both as hard as he could, over the side of the ship. She didn't even hear the splash, though she saw it.

This time the shock reached her face before she could smooth it out. Her voice followed. "Why did you do that? Hardson—that was *mine*! I *need* that!"

"No, you don't," he said. "I don't allow drugs or stim crowns on my ship."

She tried to speak, and nothing came out for a moment, so great was the unexpected shock of loss. She thought, nonsensically, of Shmi, and wanted to start crying. "But why my music box?" Her words were horrible, her tone pleading; some half-buried Myawi part of her was suitably appalled.

He looked confused. "Music box?"

"The other thing you were holding. That was my music box!"

Hardson frowned, considered, then nodded. "Oh. I do apologize, I thought that was a part of the kit's battery pack. Was it sentimental?"

Holly sighed, reeling in her emotions and feeling them burn as she did. She rubbed her temple with one hand. "Does it matter?"

"It does. I'm sure it doesn't seem that way now because of your dependency, but I mean no malice."

"I'm not *dependent* on the bump. If you had asked, I would have turned it over to you. And I won't be able to sleep without my music box. You've done me quite a favor."

"You have my sincerest apologies. I'll get you another at the first opportunity."

"You *can't*. It's a Myawi music box and they don't *sell* them."

He tried for a wry grin, his elaborate beard curling around his face. "We're not off to a good start, are we?"

"I definitely don't want to talk to you any more right now."

"I understand." Hardson sounded genuinely apologetic, but she thought cynically that he had shown a knack for putting on the right face.

"Don't understand. And don't come in my room again unless invited. If I have something you'd like me to discard, you can ask me and I'll do it."

He bowed. "As you desire."

Holly didn't have a door to slam dramatically, so she turned her back on him and stared at the water. She hadn't realized how much those little things meant to her until they were gone. And now they weren't going to Astoria, ostensibly on the orders of someone who was Hardson's superior even though he was the captain.

Worse, she was finding it hard to care. She'd wanted to get away from Strip City, but Astoria had been an arbitrary destination. Beyond that, she had a vague desire to find Ivy, and a rather disturbing desire to return to Singapore and...set it on fire. Elden's house, the office, the university, the market. All of it.

Right now she could set Hardson on fire, too.

The feeling got more intense as the day wore on, and her brain began to feel fuzzy. Normally she'd have something to occupy her, some chore, and if she didn't she could do a bump and be fine. Here, there was nothing to do but roam the ship. The other sailors she saw seemed to politely avoid speaking to her; there was a skittishness and a measure of contrition in their behavior that suggested they'd seen women kidnapped (by Hardson or someone else) before, and they knew better than to approach her.

Even if she wasn't a prisoner, it made sense; better to wait until they were sure she was staying to introduce themselves. She suspected it wouldn't do to accidentally make an impression on the captain's new would-be bride, either. If she fell for another crew member, who knew what chaos would result? As the day wore on, Holly felt sleepy and exhausted, and though it became objectively clear that she was neither a prisoner nor an untouchable prize, her thoughts were no less destructive.

She considered sharing her feelings with Marcus, but instead merely told him what Hardson had said to her about not going to Astoria. Marcus wasn't upset about it in the least, and seemed to be looking forward to a new adventure. She wasn't in the mood to talk to him about that, either.

Holly spent the rest of the day irritated and exhausted. The mood and the sleeplessness that fed it stretched into two days, then three. Hardson was nowhere to be seen, Marcus began making friends among the crew, and Holly just watched the sea move past. Not that there was much to look at.

chapter 32

_Three days before Princess Aiyana's trimester
celebration_

Shiloh's story

"Tell me another story," Shamshoun said. "You're a natural, of course."

Shiloh frowned at him. "I don't tell good stories because I'm a felid and it's some natural ability," she said, letting her offense show. "I lived on the traveling circus with a master storyteller, and I learned from him. That's why I'm good at it."

He grunted and nodded. "Doesn't matter why."

"Saying things like that will make me not want to tell any more stories."

"Going to leave, then?"

She considered. She hadn't gotten up from her squat by the clear plastic wall, so it was obvious that she wasn't going anywhere. "No, I can talk some more."

"Oh, good. Thank you."

"It's not because of your cheerful demeanor, though." Bored of recapping the last two months of their travels, Shiloh fed him more anecdotes about life with Gallamore's, since he seemed to like them so much. She was a bit surprised she had so many. She hadn't been particularly social with the rest of the staff during her four years on the traveling circuit, but she'd picked up so much by osmosis. She told Shamshoun about Tom the storyteller, and his funny top-heavy bookmobile truck. She told him a couple of Tom's stories as well, and though she wasn't anywhere near as good, Shamshoun enjoyed them. He didn't speak to her any less gruffly, but as she spoke he rested his head back against the wall and closed his eyes, as though he were watching her words unfold in his mind.

She stayed with him for as long as she could push her nerve, and wanted to ask him about how he'd ended up on the Excelcis, but she had to get back. The longer she stayed, the more convinced she became that Mahnaz would wake up, find her gone, and come looking. That wouldn't go well.

"I'm going to go now," she told the ursid after spinning him a yarn about a particularly disastrous attempt at hunting rabbits with Swan that left him apparently asleep, with an absent little smile of amusement on his face. It was the first time she'd seen him honestly smile.

"Sleep well, Shiloh Gallamore," he said, not opening his eyes.

Shiloh made her way carefully back through the ship, avoiding the occasional patrolling sailor...then came face to face with Dorim as she rounded the corner. The bodyguard was standing outside Mahnaz' cabin.

She jumped, startled, but he merely nodded at her and stepped aside so she could go in. The passenger cabin, insulated against the ship's noise, seemed muted after the throb of the engines and the susurrus of sound from the prison cells was partially blocked out. For a few seconds, all she could hear was her heart pounding. As she shut the door behind her, she could hear Mahnaz breathing, slow and steady. He hadn't woken up, not that she'd expected him to. It hadn't taken long to figure out that he slept hard.

That was perhaps the only improvement over traveling out in the dirt with Ivy and the others; she had a warm body in the narrow bed with her, so she could sleep better. Never mind that she didn't like him much, it felt nice to have a person there. She curled in next to Mahnaz and was asleep in moments.

In the morning, she came awake as soon as he stirred. The room was a box. The mattress was uncomfortable and the blankets itched. The small porthole let in enough sunlight to brighten the room in spite of the industrial-gray paint on the walls, and she blinked once, waking up. Mahnaz was a bit slower, and she pushed herself up and looked down at him. He didn't get more physically appealing with familiarity, thanks to greasy hair and an unpleasantly round belly with twiggy legs.

He had paralyzingly bad morning breath as well. Shiloh stayed away from his face, and got out of the bed so he'd go brush his teeth before it occurred to him to try and kiss her. He did seem quite smitten with her—more than likely she was the prettiest he'd ever had—and that was a little bit endearing, in a pathetic kind of way.

She might have been able to feel sorry for him, if he weren't so hateful. Later, up on the deck, he asked her about life with the circus. "Anna," he said, "tell me what it was like to work with *shifters*. I hear that the circus has them working alongside humans, in some cases."

Shiloh thought about what Anna Vienna might have said, and about the woman herself. Anna was always distant, even slightly disinterested in talking to Shiloh, and over time she'd figured out that it was less personal and more a product of where she'd come from. The few times that she and Anna had spoken were awkward; Shiloh could tell that Anna was fixated on the novelty of *talking to a felid*, and thus had no idea what to say to her and no desire to figure it out, which made Shiloh feel annoyed and patronized. This had developed into a sort of mutual condescension, which hadn't done either of them any good in terms of developing a friendship. "Hm," she said, buying time. "Mostly I tried not to talk to them." This was partly true, so it had a good honest ring to it. "I never knew what to say."

"You weren't harassed?"

"Never. Even if I had been, Mr. Gallamore would have put a stop to it."

"I heard that Mr. Gallamore died with the traveling show."

"No, that was Mr. Morse, the ringleader. Mr. Gallamore stayed in Strip City."

"Ah yes," Mahnaz said, nodding. "That's right. Did you have to perform with shifters?"

Shiloh wondered if Mahnaz was always this obsessed with shifters, or if it was just because of where they were. "No, my act is a solo performance."

"I'd love to see it some time."

She put on an enigmatic smile. "I'm sure you would."

This made him grin and put a hand at the small of her back. His hands were bigger than it seemed they should be; he seemed to carry all of his bulk in the upper half of his body without being broad-shouldered or athletic. "So. The military men who are here with us. Zhuan and Vitter. They have asked me if they could talk to you."

"About what?"

"About your time in captivity. I understand, lovely Anna, that this could be terribly upsetting for you, and so I want you to know that if you do not feel comfortable talking to them about it, I will tell them no on your behalf."

Shiloh thought that the real Anna Vienna would've been perfectly capable of telling them no, but it seemed safer to continue with the broken-winged bird charade. "Why do they want to talk about that?" she asked.

"You have been through the interior of North America, in the hands of a known group of guerrillas. They think that you must have seen and heard a great many things that will be of use to them. Places they went, people they talked to, their ways of behaving and operating."

Shiloh flashed suddenly on the Inchin caravan they'd followed, and its abrupt end near Little Rock. And the bad men in Horrible Little Shithole. Sino-Indians did seem to get themselves killed quite frequently in North America, and she hadn't considered how this might look from the other side. She made a show of putting on a brave face. "That seems...smart."

He squeezed her shoulder. "Don't force yourself. I can hold off their like easily enough. They can wait to do the interview when we're in Singapore, if I tell them to."

Shiloh didn't look at him. The ocean was featureless, other than the captured pirate ship following them. *Excelsis* dwarfed the *88 Fists*, at over twice her length and several times taller. Were they sailing closer together Shiloh could have looked down on the smaller ship easily. As a prison, the ship made sense; even if a prisoner escaped to jump overboard, she might be badly hurt just from hitting the water, and then where was there to swim to?

She had to find out where the others were. Shamshoun had said that there weren't any other felids aboard, so the concern of another felid outing her was gone, but she wasn't sure how she could reverse her feigned fear of "going near the shifters," in order to get down into the prison section unattended.

The ship was enormous, big enough to remind her of the hotels in Strip City. Of course the Laddin and other places had fifty and sixty stories compared to *Excelsis'* seven, but for a boat it was tremendous. She spent the first day getting a routine down. Marcus had been quiet after his tour of the lower decks, and hadn't met her eye at dinner. Mahnaz, she found, preferred to stay in his cabin as well. She stayed with him for a day, but got restless quickly. Shiloh hadn't been below the third deck, where the cells began. No, wait, it was the fifth; they counted from the bottom up, even though they were accessed from the top down. The deck level was actually the fifth story. The sailors were very particular about the terminology, and Mahnaz was happy to be able to explain it to her, so she let him.

"I need to exercise," she said told him. She guessed that this might be a good way to get away from him for a while. It was unlikely he had any interest in running.

"Will you be okay by yourself?" he asked. There was genuine concern in his voice.

"Yes," she replied, then added, "They're all in cages, right?" It sounded like something he'd expect her to say, and she was right; he smiled and squeezed her arm. The words felt nastier coming out of her mouth than she expected, and it was all she could do not to frown. She wished she hadn't referred to the imprisoned shifters as *them*.

Mahnaz didn't notice, and she escaped him.

At first she did run; the *Excelsis'* deck was long, and she ran along a long flat area near the bow almost all the way to the stern. It was open enough that she had no concerns about running into a sailor, and jogging back and forth was good for working up a bit of a sweat, after a fashion. It wasn't the most entertaining activity, but better than nothing. The rush of endorphins from the exercise emboldened her as well, and on her fifth pass up the deck she made her decision, opened a stairwell door, and headed down.

The transition from bright sun to interior light was a sudden one, and it seemed dim for a moment. Shiloh blinked until her eyes adjusted, then started down the steps.

She descended into the bowels of the *Excelsis*. Barely one staircase down, it felt like she'd stepped out of the world. The fresh sea air disappeared, replaced by a thick, physical stink that was unlike anything she'd ever experienced. It was a miasma of desperation and unwashed bodies and multispecies effluvia, and she understood now why Shamshoun was so sanguine about being sequestered in his own cell topside. Mahnaz and the others had *willingly* toured this? She hadn't even left the stairwell yet, and it felt like she was knocking on the door of some unimaginable hell.

She stopped at the first door she came to, one level down, feeling the misery on the other side radiating through the metal like heat. Would someone try to stop her if she went through? She guessed not; the sailors seemed to treat the prisoners like so much cargo, and she and the Sino-Indian diplomats had run of the ship as long as they stayed out of the way.

Shiloh twisted the latch and pushed the door open. It took a bit of a shove, thanks to the water-tight seal around the edge, and then she was in a much larger space, filled with noise. A cacophony of shouts, yells and howling bounced off of the heavy walls and door behind her, assaulting her ears. The narrow hallway was actually a catwalk, bordered on one side by cells and the other by a railing and open space. Shiloh looked over the railing and saw that it extended to the deck below. The catwalk and cells ran all the way around on both levels, and cells about twice the size of Shamshoun's held four to six people each, sometimes more. She stood at the railing for a moment, trying to take it all in. There were no beds or obvious facilities in the cells; sanitation seemed to consist of a grate-covered trench in the center of each. All of the cells were made of thick clear plastic, like Shamshoun's, and she could see streaks and spatters of blood or worse on many of them. Most of the prisoners were naked, separated by sex, and as she watched, she saw individuals shifting; a canid here, a falconid there, unable to unfurl its wings in the small space. Across the way below her, a cell full of cervids was jumping rapidly between human and deer forms in the midst of some sort of disagreement.

With a chill she realized that one of them was *Kroni*. He was being cornered by five other cervids, and remembered what he'd said about male deer-shifters not getting along. Why had they put so many of them in one cell? Shiloh watched helplessly as the situation in the cell degenerated into a five-on-one brawl, and Kroni quickly disappeared under a storm of fists and kicks. At least two of the cervids shifted, and a body was slammed sideways against the front of the cell, blocking her view. She could hear shouts coming through the small slits in the plastic walls.

The shifters to either side of the cell were watching impassively, as though this happened a lot. Shiloh's hands tightened on the rail as Kroni fought back valiantly, shifting and flipping to kick one of his attackers in the face. It threw one of them back, but the others caught him in the air and held him even as he shifted back to human. He was pulled down to his knees, his face pressed to the floor, held down by three sets of hands, and one of the other cervids positioned himself behind. Even after seeing the erect penis, Shiloh numbly didn't realize what was about to happen until it did, and then she was running again, just tearing blindly along the catwalk, some instinct wanting to find the stairs down or just jump over the edge, she could handle a fifteen-foot drop, and...then what? Open the cell, somehow? Even if it was possible to get it open, how could she help by rushing in? Likely that would just mean a bad ending for both Kroni *and* herself.

So she ran again, surfing a wave of helpless shock and outrage that was fueled by the moans and shouts from the cells that she passed, one after the other, so many of them. *Excelsis* was a long ship, and the cells seemed to go on forever. It was an animal instinct, they were hurting her friend and she had to do *something*, even though there was nothing useful she could do.

Find the others. That's what she could do. Ivy and Swan, and Holly. Knowing where they were was the first step to getting them out. She'd managed to stay out of a cell, and the next step was to *do* something with that advantage. Marcus seemed earnest but useless, and she doubted he was going to do anything unless someone told him to. He reminded her of some of the teamsters with Gallamore's, hard workers if given instructions but not particularly likely to act on their own.

Mindful of her ongoing Anna Vienna performance, she didn't stop running, but changed her pace so she was jogging instead of sprinting madly. The catwalk was a reasonable enough running space, more suitable than the deck in fact if she ignored the shifters in the cells and the miserable emotions of the place, which she imagined Anna Vienna would be able to do. She herself might've been able to do it, a few months ago, before leaving the circus.

Before going to the felid Stronghold.

Shiloh didn't want to admit to herself that seeing the felids' ancestral home had changed her, even though she'd been dragged there against her will. Not to mention nearly raped and murdered. She'd avoided the reality that she was one of them for so long, it felt unnatural to embrace it, even a little bit, and yet there it was. It didn't matter what she considered herself, or that she almost never shifted and hated her cat-form; these people would have her thrown naked into one of these cells if they knew what she was.

As a headliner at the circus, things had been stacked in her favor for much of her life. So why did she feel that, on some level, she liked the world *better* this way, cruel and unfair?

She'd made a circuit of the upper deck of cells, glancing at the prisoners as she passed, but didn't see Swan. She found a staircase and ran down to the lower level, maintaining her casual, just-exercising mien, and began checking the cells below also. She did her best not to look into the cell where Kroni was being raped as she passed it, deliberately unfocusing her eyes and praying that he didn't see her jogging past, not helping him. He and the others probably already thought she'd betrayed them for the promise of a warm bed. As she passed some of the cells, especially the canids', there were reactions as they sniffed her out, could tell what she was, but the hue and cry she expected wasn't raised in her wake. What did they think of her? Did they think she was some sort of turncoat, currying favor with the Inchins by selling out her fellow shifters?

She couldn't think about that right now. Swan wasn't on the first level, either. Maybe they were keeping her separate because she was human? But where? As she reached the last cell on the first floor and started another lap, a door opened above—one of the stairwells—and a sailor stepped onto the catwalk. Shiloh gave him just the barest glance and kept jogging, and he said nothing to her. Of course he wouldn't. She was one of the Important People, and he was just a sailor. Not a shifter. She had to remember that.

But she wished it didn't make her feel so rotten to do so.

There was another doorway at the far end of the lower level, and she tried it, finding a short hallway leading to a room of triple-stacked bunks. A few of them were occupied—this was where the sailors slept. If she continued, she imagined, she'd find their bathrooms and other facilities. She wanted to go down again, but the next watertight door she found was locked.

As she wandered she encountered a few more sailors as well. The first two didn't acknowledge her, but the third asked if she was lost. All of the sailors had accents. Anna Vienna had too, come to think of it. Nobody seemed to have noticed that she didn't, though, and Shiloh thought it prudent not to try and mimic the accent. She wasn't good at impressions.

"I am," she said, giving him a smile but not too much of one. "I'm looking for the way back to the deck. I was running, and took a few turns..."

"Sure," he said. He was young, and fresh-faced, and he had the scrubbed-clean, polite air that a lot of mariners had, that she often found herself unable to resist. Another time...but no, she couldn't fuck around right now. Mahnaz struck her as the possessive type. He was almost certainly enjoying being her savior, and wouldn't take kindly to perceived competition.

Of course, now she was thinking about it, the sailor's scent touching her nose. He smelled nice. Shiloh went ahead of him when he pointed the way to the stairs up, sliding him out of her field of vision. She had to find Swan, Holly and Ivy. Later that evening, maybe she could sneak out and talk to Shamshoun some more, about the prison section.

She reached the deck, fresh air and sunlight, and felt better. She felt stained, like there was something clinging to her that she could never wash off, but better.

Still unchallenged by anyone, she worked her way back toward the bow of the ship, remembering to break into a jog. The metal decks were beginning to hurt her feet, especially in the little sandals they'd given her, so she altered her pace until it was bearable. The blocky set of decks at the front of the ship, where she and the other diplomats had been housed and where the solitary cells were, crossed the ship entirely, and she had to go inside if she wanted to reach the bow itself. Shiloh went up a deck, crossed the big flat area again, and entered the door she thought was closest to Shamshoun's cell.

She'd misjudged though, and found herself in a hallway with similar cells, that she hadn't seen before. How had she missed this one? The ship was logically laid out, but she hadn't thought to search it systematically. She also hadn't noticed before, but the solitary cells like Shamshoun's had solid walls, unlike the group cells below which were transparent. She had to walk down the hall to see into them. She didn't hesitate, continuing forward like she owned the place.

The first cells on either side were empty, but halfway up the row she was rewarded; Ivy was on one side, Holly on the other. Holly was standing, Ivy sitting, and they were both pressed up against the plastic as though trying to get as close to each other as possible. "Keep moving," Holly said, nodding toward the ceiling. "They're watching."

Shiloh cut an eye in the direction Holly indicated, saw a small rounded box on the wall. Of course; a camera, like in Shamshoun's hallway. This one might be working. She didn't stop walking, but glanced down at Ivy as she passed. She was sitting with her knees pulled up to her chest, looking unhappy. Ivy met her eyes. Shiloh gave her a small smile, and got a brief smile in return.

So Ivy didn't hate her, at least. Maybe she understood. At the very least, they knew she was still free and alive and were glad about it. Shiloh felt a bit of the despair lift. She wanted to say something, but stayed in character, remained Anna, and kept moving.

When she opened the door at the other end of the hall, she was in a familiar corridor. The tour had started here; a door similar to the one she'd just exited led to the hallway where Shamshoun's cell was. Shiloh considered going that way, to see if maybe they'd stowed Swan in his hall again, but a hand fell on her shoulder. She flinched away from it, dropping her arm and turning, found herself face to face with the man in white. Zhuan, his name was.

"Miss Vienna," he said with a little nod that was almost a bow. "Are you lost?"

"I was exercising. I was running outside, and came in a different door," she replied.

"I hope you didn't encounter anything...upsetting."

"I saw them," she said, as there was no sense in pretending she somehow hadn't noticed her purported captors in the cells. "I'm not as afraid now."

"That's good. You are quite safe here," Zhuan said. Something about his words didn't quite reach his eyes, and Shiloh felt as if he still had his hand on her shoulder, holding her there. She stiffened her spine a bit and shook the feeling off. Zhuan was the master of this floating charnel house, but he had no power over her unless she gave it to him. "Acrobats are such fascinating people," he said, not taking his eyes from hers. "Such odd mannerisms."

"That's because we are always performing," she said. "It becomes a part of you. Every movement, every step, every gesture is a part of something larger." That didn't sound like something the real Anna Vienna would have said, but he wouldn't know that.

"Hm," he said. A smile touched his lips, but there was something dead about it. "That's an interesting philosophy. I feel as though I'm being challenged to catch one of you when she is revealing her true self."

She angled her head flirtatiously. "However you choose to take it," she said, hiding the cold feeling he gave her.

"Would you like to see where the others are?"

"The others?"

"Your captors," Zhuan said. "We put those two together. It seems to be extremely upsetting for them to be apart. They're twins, you know."

Shiloh nodded.

"It was like separating a mother cat from her kittens. They calmed down considerably when they could see each other. Most interesting. The cervid is down in the general population of shifters, if you feel sufficiently recovered from your ordeal to go down there."

"I already did," she said. If there were cameras in the prison area, and she didn't doubt there were, then they already knew.

Zhuan raised an eyebrow. "Did you, now?"

"I like to challenge myself. Mentally as well as physically." *That* sounded like something Anna Vienna would've said.

"Did you see your...friend?"

"No," she lied. "I..." she considered saying she couldn't tell them apart, but that was a bridge too far. "I wasn't looking," she finished. Better to stay closer to the truth.

"On the lower levels there's additional security. If you'd like to see, though—"

"No," Shiloh said, quickly. She wanted to know, but if she seemed too eager to find them all Zhuan might suspect something.

"In that case, lunch is being served, if you'd like to wash up and join us in the officers' mess. It's good to eat a healthy meal after exercise."

"Thank you, I'd like that."

chapter 33

Sixty days before Princess Aiyana's trimester celebration

Holly didn't sleep.

Without her music box, sleep wouldn't come; she stared at the ceiling, or where she would see the ceiling, if it weren't pitch-black, and felt the time sliding too slowly past. But she remained stubbornly conscious, her mind empty and full at the same time. After an eternity, morning came.

And then the next night, she repeated the process. At night, the day replayed in her head; a few hours spent following Vadim, the engineering officer; some time spent under the warm, humid skylights of Dilly's greenhouse, listening to the rustle of growing vegetable plants and the hiss of irrigation systems; staring out at the sea feeling worthless.

After several days of this, she started to get irritable. Had killing Elden been worth this? She thought of Makkhana telling her she was free, and wanted to shoot back, *And this is better?*

That was what made her snap at Marcus, eventually. He wanted to talk, constantly, and asked endless questions about her life, about the things she'd told Makkhana for his video, about her opinions on things. During the day she avoided him (and he was distracted chattering with the other sailors anyway, always scribbling in his little notepad), but in the evenings, as she lay in her bunk, he liked to ramble while he sketched, the notepad's greyish glow casting a wan light in their room.

She wished she had taken Hardson up on the offer of a private cabin, but didn't want him to know she'd changed her mind about that either. He'd see it as her softening toward him, or find some way to take it as an insight into her character, and she was quite sick of other people deciding what her character was, thank you very much.

She wasn't even sure she knew, herself.

This was a puzzle that Marcus seemed bent of solving. Maybe he sensed her uncertainty, and had some misguided notion that he could help if he drew her out about it. This reminded her of therapy sessions with Dr. Olai, and that didn't improve her mood either. Whatever the reason, he wouldn't stop asking about the day she'd killed Elden and the others, and the days leading up to it. He wanted to know what had been going through her head, what had driven her over the edge, what she thought kept other Myawis from doing the same, if she thought it was a circumstance of her particular situation or if it was something brought on by the rigorousness of Myawi's training, and if it was possible that Myawi girls were all a heartbeat away from snapping.

He wouldn't refrain from keeping on about it, and she couldn't seem to find a subtle way to dissuade him. Redirecting the conversation only worked for a short time; before falling asleep, he was back on the subject of murder again.

And finally, she'd had enough. Marcus asked, "Do you think Elden had any idea that something was amiss? That he knew you were on the verge of turning on him?"

She scowled at the ceiling in the dark. "Very few people know that they're about to be murdered, Marcus," she snapped. "Did you, when they locked you into that descent pod?"

"I beg your pardon?"

"You may not have it. Answer the question, Professor McEvoy. Did you know, when they closed you into that capsule and shot you off of your space station, that you were being murdered?"

"If you mean that figuratively, in that I wasn't—"

"I do not. I mean it literally. Your survival was an *accident,* Marcus. Your pod was supposed to crash into the ocean. Whatever student you had your affair with—whoever's son he was—it seems that all was not forgiven or forgotten with your 'reassignment.' So you can answer your own question, having survived what was supposed to be your very timely death: did you have any idea that something was amiss?"

He was silent for a long moment. When he spoke again, he spoke quietly, and in his lecturing voice. "I don't believe you understand the situation, and you have no way of knowing—"

"Oh, but I do, Marcus. I saw the emails. You were supposed to crash in the ocean. You landed *half a planet away* from where they claimed they were sending you. Yet they can hit an individual airplane with the EPRC, any time they please. You think that was a simple, silly miscalculation?

They were surprised when you turned up and started filing your reports, and they've been ignoring your signals ever since. It wasn't until you made it to Singapore that the Lunar University relented and asked Elden to download and archive copies of your research."

"You can't know that."

"Of course I do. I was essentially Elden's secretary, remember? Question time is over; let me sleep." Holly glared at the ceiling for a moment, then closed her eyes. She heard Marcus moan quietly, take a few tremulous, shaking breaths, and then get out of bed. He left the room.

She was still awake when he returned, but she pretended to be asleep. He smelled faintly of wine, and dropped off into a snoring sleep.

In the morning, she roused herself without waking him. If she'd gotten any sleep, she didn't remember it, and the edges of her consciousness were annoyingly jagged. Breakfast. She needed something to eat. Thankfully, Minnijean kept hours like a domestic. When Holly wandered into the mess hall she had her pick of things to eat. She didn't talk to any of the crewmen there, though she had managed to learn half of their names already just by listening.

About half of the mariners were originally from North America, the rest from Sino-India, Zeeland, Australia, or Tanzania. Marcus hadn't been kidding about there being multiple sailors named Bob, either. There were at least eight, and they were distinguished by nicknames: Holly met Vodka Bob, Jar Bob, Fisher Bob and Doornail Bob, so named because of his stature, during her travels. She also met the Bonefish. The Bonefish was a small man with a bushy gray beard. He appeared to be in his seventies, but was as spry as any of the men a third his age. He smelled like fish, spoke in an odd patois that he seemed to have made up and referred to himself in the third person, all of which Holly found oddly endearing. Razor and Minnijean made frequent appearances as well, checking up on her.

Marcus had also not been wrong about Razor's duck; there was a mallard on board that had imprinted on Razor through unknown circumstances. Razor walked and talked like a shifty, savvy street fighter, but she exhibited an affectionate softening when it came to the duck, whose name was Coriander.

After Hardson, Minnijean seemed to be the authority on the ship, keeping her finger on the pulse of life aboard the *Fists* like a protective aunt. Like a domestic, she also knew most of the gossip. It reminded her of Shmi and Holly found herself drifting toward the galley before mealtimes to hear the latest. She didn't offer to help cook or clean, ignoring little fizzles of guilt at not doing so. It was hard to get used to the idea that she wasn't expected, but once she did it was a pleasant thing. On the other hand, Minnijean was lightly troublesome, because she wanted very much to be friends, and wasn't deterred by polite aloofness or outright hostility. There was little to do but wander the ship. Holly thought that perhaps when they finally did make port, she'd see about getting a book or five to read, if she was staying aboard. It was a passing thought; she hadn't put any thought into if she was staying. It was possible that Hardson had no intention of letting her leave, for that matter. Holly watched the ocean for an hour, thinking about her last conversation with Marcus and feeling some regret at what she'd said, but she wasn't sure if the guilt was genuine, or just Myawi training telling her that she should feel bad. The expanse of gently rolling water was huge, and seemed more than willing to swallow up her thoughts and concerns. The ship was the only man-made object in sight, and it was hard to imagine that there was a world out there anywhere that had the least bit of interest in her or any of the crew.

The problem with having nowhere to go but into her head was that she didn't *want* to be in her head. The ocean absorbed her immediate ruminations, but had no answers.

She stared at the sea and tried to think of ways to escape herself for good. She considered cutting her hair off, shredding her clothes, smearing herself with garbage and refusing to bathe or shave or make herself presentable in any way. She could be the ship's madwoman, answering to no one, unpredictable and enigmatic. The fantasy lasted long enough for her to visit Dilly's garden for some dirt. She intended to smear a heaping handful of mud on her face and chest, letting it grind into her pores and tumble into her shirt, but instead Holly dipped three fingers into the dirt, hesitated, then daubed it on one cheek, experimentally.

She hated the way it felt instantly. She tried rubbing it in, and the gritty, unkempt, uneven feeling got worse.

It's not the only way, she thought. *A Myawi is not covered in dirt.* She tried to take another scoop, *willed* herself to...and didn't. What she wanted right now, even more than she wanted to start her new life as the *88 Fists'* inscrutable mistress of mud, was to wash her face and hands.

Holly returned to the mess hall and went to one of the large sinks in the kitchen to wash up. "Back again," Minnijean said when Holly entered. "You sure like it down here, don't you?"

"It's familiar," Holly said. The wall panels had been salvaged from someplace; warm wooden panels covered up the sterile steel walls. A large section of it consisted of panels that lit up like a window, and plants framed it. Near the door hung a chore board, a calendar and an announcement board. At the working end of the kitchen there were cabinets with rolling metal doors, containing food, a few books (the most interesting of which she'd read in her first few days on the ship) and other communal items.

"Are you homesick, then?"

"Not really. I suppose if I have a home at the moment, it's here."

"If?"

Holly met her eyes. "Don't, please."

Minnijean smiled, "Doesn't hurt to remind you."

"I know I'm welcome here. I'm not thinking about that right now."

"Got a lot of other things to consider, do you?"

"Maybe. For the moment I'm just not thinking."

"Seems like a waste."

Holly thought, *Because my life to date has been so productive,* but didn't say it. "What are you making?" she asked instead.

"This? This'll be a birthday cake, for Vodka Bob," Minnijean said, raising her spoon out of the batter for emphasis. "He asked for a honey cake. Otherwise lunch is sandwiches today. Finishing off the last of the greens before they start wilting. We'll restock next port."

Holly nodded with a slight smile. "And when is that?" It was a long ocean crossing to Zeeland, so they hadn't been to shore since leaving Strip City and Holly wondered if Hardson would confine her to the ship on Mama Lola's orders, or risk her going ashore and not coming back. She wondered if she would even bother escaping onto shore if the opportunity presented itself. This funk of motionlessness was getting tiresome, come to think of it.

"No telling."

The intercom on the wall suddenly gave three short buzzes. A moment later, Holly felt the ship change direction, a distinct shift in the soles of her feet and the pit of her stomach. She was still surprised that after a few days aboard, *88 Fists'* motion was barely noticeable unless something changed dramatically. The shift in direction seemed to presage a shift in urgency as well; she could hear crewmen rousing themselves from the bunks down the hall and a general increase in activity.

"Oh, now you're in for a sight," Minnijean said.

"What is it?"

"What we do, sometimes." She began putting the food away and latching cabinets closed. "Lunch is going to be late, if they spotted fruit. You'd best stay out of the way in here. Embrosia will be along with the rest in a moment."

"Fruit?" Holly asked. She didn't have to ask what "others" Minnijean meant, because the *Fists*' personnel officer arrived moments later, with women, children and Marcus in tow. Holly hadn't met most of the women except in passing; she recognized the one named Kiva, but couldn't recall the name of the one who accompanied the child named Grem. At eight, Deux was the eldest of the eleven children aboard the Fists, all progeny of various crew members. Fry came in with two children, kissed them both, gave Holly a glance, then left them with Minnijean.

"Protecting our treasure, whilst we sample someone else's," Minnijean said by way of explanation. Embrosia and the other women were getting the children settled; they seemed familiar with the drill.

Holly nodded, wondering where Fry was going. She moved toward the door, stepping aside as another woman carrying a toddler came through, then peered out into the hallway. "Where are you going?" Kiva asked.

"Let her go," Minnijean said. "It's her choice."

"But it's not safe!"

"Her choice," Holly heard Minnijean repeat as she stepped out of the galley. She followed a general surge of people toward the deck; most of them were carrying or strapping on pieces of makeshift armor as they went. Outside, much of the crew's attention was focused on another ship. It was larger than the *88 Fists*, and appeared to be a cargo ship of some kind. Holly recognized the logo of a Beijing company, but she couldn't remember its name.

She could see that she'd be in the way if she stayed on the deck, with everyone moving toward the rails, some carrying weapons, so she went forward, to the bow. Along the way she glanced up at the bridge, saw Hardson up there along with his officers, and Marcus was watching from there as well. Hardson glanced at her, but made no indication that he'd seen her.

At the bow, the cover had been removed from the equipment there and she saw that it was a massive cannon, air-driven if the tanks mounted next to it in a heavy-walled cabinet were any indicator. What appeared to be the tip of a spear protruded from the barrel, equally massive; the head was easily four feet across. Dilly was at the controls wearing a large, bulky breastplate that had once been a street sign, and a sailor named Bull, who usually tended to the airplane on its pad, was next to him with binoculars relaying information.

"Hey," Dilly said, noticing her. "You shouldn't be up here. It's dangerous."

"Then why are you up here?" she asked.

"Because I have to...you know. The harp. It's different for you." He seemed to be flustered that she was looking directly into his eyes, so she kept doing it. "You're...you know." He glanced at Bull, who kept his eyes trained on the approaching boat.

"Because I'm fertile?" she said, and Dilly's cheeks flushed over his beard.

"No—well, yeah. I mean, the Cap'n wanted you here—on the ship, I mean, and ..."

"Almost to mark, Dilly," Bull said. "Don't think they've made the harp yet. I see no big guns on deck."

Holly wanted to ask more questions, but she'd be interrupting them if she did, so she made sure she was out of their way, her back against a bulkhead, and watched. Bull called out distances, and Dilly adjusted the harp's vertical and horizontal orientation with a pair of cranks. They drew slowly closer, and then at a signal from Bull, Dilly fired the cannon with an ear-splitting whoosh of escaping gas. A metal harpoon, fifteen feet long and as thick as a tree trunk, leapt across the distance between the ships and buried itself in the side of the cargo ship with a concussive thud. From the deck of the *88 Fists*, a collective cheer went up. Bull and Dilly immediately leapt to securing the cable attached to the harpoon to a large winch and switched it on. There was a rumbling groan that shook the deck beneath her feet and the winch's rusty barrel began to turn slowly, retracting the cable.

"To prevent them from escaping?" Holly asked.

"Gotta reel her in so we can get aboard," Dilly said.

"She tries to run before the head's retracted, the harp'll rip her hull wide open," Bull added with a note of pride.

Holly nodded, watching the crew massing at the railing in anticipation. She counted about thirty all told, most of their faces obscured by armor and helmets, and they were armed with a mixture of swords and blunt weapons. All wore black and green bandannas on their arms or heads. She guessed that they were for identification; if there was a melee, they'd need to recognize their own at a glance.

Such a fight seemed inevitable, as a similar contingent of sailors had appeared on the deck of the ship they were attacking. The distance between the two vessels shrank slowly, the *88 Fists*' prey growing gradually larger and larger. Holly watched it absorb more and more of the horizon, and as it drew within shouting distance the men and women on the deck began yelling back and forth, threats and taunts. The voices on the boat they were attacking were less confident, she noticed (or maybe it was her imagination), the shouters aware that they didn't have as much of a choice in what happened next as their attackers did. By comparison, the crew of the *88 Fists* looked much more ready to fight. There was a fierceness in them that Holly'd only seen hints of previously.

She supposed she ought to have felt pity for the ship they were attacking, but she didn't. She was curious to see how it unfolded, even though the outcome seemed all but certain, and the individual players didn't matter all that much to her. She was a bit surprised that she felt so detached from it all, but not shocked enough to question it.

And then it was happening, the distance between the ships was all but gone, and ladders with hooks on the ends were being thrown across, attaching to the railings of the *Fists'* prey. People immediately began running across the makeshift planks, which were angled upward due to the difference in deck heights.

"Gonna go play?" Bull asked.

"You got the harp?" Dilly asked, and when he got an affirmative the big bearded sailor threw on a helmet, charged down the deck to the nearest ladder and began making his way across. Dilly didn't step nimbly along the ladder's rungs; he attacked them, flinging himself across the dozen or so feet that separated the two ships. Holly followed him without thinking about it. She ran with him to the railing, clambered across the ladder and when Dilly reached the other ship and threw the first man he encountered backward onto the deck, she stepped onto the deck a moment after he did.

Chaos surrounded her. Shouts and screams all around her, bodies clashing and tumbling and unrecognizable. Every voice she heard sounded at once familiar and unfamiliar, and she had no hope of telling who was making what sounds. Someone was shoved into her, and she pushed them roughly away. It felt good, to shove someone. She was struck again from the other side, another body crashing into her, and staggered from the impact. Holly stumbled into someone else, shoving hard, and this time the person fell. His opponent took advantage of the unexpected help and kicked the man as he went down. A primal elation surged through her. Holly didn't notice which ship either man was from, and she didn't care. She only knew that she wanted to knock more people down

Holly was hit, a glancing blow on her shoulder, and she hit back, grabbing the first person who appeared in front of her and throwing herself on him, riding him to the deck. She was reminded of straddling Rehsil, beating his brains out with a shattered coffee mug, but she had no weapon this time. *Don't punch him; you'll break your hand,* she remembered someone telling her once. Was it true? Holly balled up her fist and punched the man in the face, and cried out in pain as her hand erupted in agony.

It didn't seem to have much effect on the man, who rolled over and threw her off. He snatched a knife from his boot and his hand flashed out to her neck. The blade scraped across her collar and her attacker stopped and frowned, either noticing that she was a Myawi or that she was fertile. Which it was didn't matter. Holly grabbed his wrist and twisted the knife away from him with her left hand, the one that was still working, and shoved him away, into the melee. Someone else staggered toward her, knocked away from another fight, and she dropped the knife and stepped into him with a wrist-lock throw like she'd used on Rehsil. The flipping body was a gratifying sight and feeling. Her hurt hand was just an irritation, she could fight with it. She threw somebody else, then kicked a balled-up sailor who was already on the ground.

She was grabbed from behind, her collar grabbed and then she was spun around. "Rabbit of the *moon,* Holly!" Razor shouted in her ear. "You've got no rag, I almost—What are you doing here?"

"Going where I want!" she yelled back.

"Well, you want to follow me, then," Razor said, giving her a friendly shove toward a doorway that was suddenly unguarded. They rushed through without being challenged. "Forward. Stairs up to the left. Follow them."

Holly was slightly disappointed to be out of the melee, but she wasn't sure why. Her hand was starting to hurt again. "Where do they go?" she asked, heading up.

"Bridge. Fight's almost done. We get the captain to stand down, nobody else gets hurt."

"We?"

"What, you came all the way over here to watch? Just follow me, and stay where I can see you. Next time you want to join a harvest party, put on a bandanna," Razor said, bounding up the steps past Holly. "Someone could've split your head open."

Holly didn't get a chance to respond. Razor reached the top of the staircase, and had control of the room by the time she got there. There were three crewmen—officers, Holly guessed—at the controls, and all three had their hands up, their eyes locked on the wicked-looking sword that Razor carried.

"Now, really folks. You really want to lose lives over this? Seems silly to me. We'll be here and gone before you even know it."

"You are not the captain," one of the hostages said, stepping forward. "Let me speak to your captain."

"Shut up," Razor said. She turned quickly and with her off hand, threw a sizeable knife into the console. It struck with enough force to puncture the metal and create an impressive spark, and stood there quivering dramatically. The three officers flinched and cowered. Razor laughed. "That's what I thought. Holly, would you please press that yellow flat-topped button three times?"

She saw the button Razor indicated, and crossed the bridge to it. The well-worn plastic wasn't marked. Holly gave it an experimental push, and the ship's horn blew, making her jump. She blew the horn twice more. From here she could see the deck, and the fighting down there stopped almost immediately. *88 Fists* sailors, one of them Dilly, began to line up their opponents along the railing, facing outward. "What are they going to do?" Holly asked.

"Hands on the railing, while we shop," Razor said with a little chuckle.

"Shop?"

"Of course. This is just a shopping trip. Weapons, ammunition, any special food we want, any special cargo we want. Medicine. Just some necessities. They'll be underway in an hour. Would have been less if some folks haven't tried to be heroes," she added, indicating the defeated captain with an eye roll. "Anything in particular you're looking for?"

"An electrostim rig," she muttered.

"Yeah, the cap'n won't allow that. No drugs either. Same thing, really."

Holly resisted the urge to make a face, but wasn't going to argue with Razor. The adrenaline rush of the fight was receding quickly, and her hand was beginning to throb. She wanted that rush back, and wished she'd stayed down on the deck, to knock more people down. That had felt good.

"You'd better get back over to the *Fists*. Cap's going to be annoyed, he sees you over here."

"I don't care if he's annoyed."

"Course you don't. Just trying to help. Are you hurt?"

Holly was flexing her hand. "No. Not much."

"Hit someone in the face with a closed fist, didn't you?" Razor grinned. "Hold it up."

She frowned, then did so.

"Wiggle your fingers. Looks like you didn't break anything. You want to hit people, let me know and I'll show you how some time."

"I think I may want to hit people," Holly said, feeling an unfamiliar smile curling her face.

"Anger management is a good life skill."

Something in Razor's tone was less than complimentary, and she immediately thought of Yinka. In an instant, the endorphin rush evaporated. Where had that sudden bloodlust come from? She was relieved that she hadn't killed anyone, acting like a maniac.

Down on the deck, the captured ship's crew was being made to stand along the railing in a row, and both crews were operating with the same practiced efficiency. People who'd been knocked down were being helped to their feet, injuries tended to regardless of which side they were on. There were other rules in place here, whether formal or informal, and she wasn't familiar with them. There was no telling what she'd have done if she'd still been carrying a weapon like Hatton's huge pistol.

Holly returned to the deck, squinting at the sun in her eyes. It seemed much, much brighter out on the ocean, compared to on land. She flexed her aching hand. It was going to bruise—bruise *again,* rather, the purple spots from her fight with Rehsil had faded but the deepest of them was still visible—but that was okay. It felt like a badge of honor, somehow, something she'd done to herself. She toyed with the notion of getting a tattoo on her face like Fry's, of carving scars in her flesh, of filing her teeth to points. Something not-Myawi.

None of these things appealed enough for her to seriously consider them.

Hardson was on the deck of the captured ship, surveying the scene while the rest of the crew searched for plunder. He caught Holly's eye and raised an eyebrow, the cheerful gesture and slight head tilt clearly indicating that she should come to him. She stopped and stared at him for a moment, then ambled across the deck to where he stood.

"I must say, I did not expect to encounter you in my workplace."

"I had some curiosity about what it was you did for a living," Holly replied. "Now I know."

He seemed hurt. "This isn't the whole picture, my dear."

"No?"

"Not even slightly." He glanced past her, quickly monitoring the progress of goods across the ladder-bridges linking the ships. "Were you interested in learning the entire process?"

She thought about it, then nodded. "I think I am. Not because I'm thinking about staying, though."

"Mama Lola will be sorry to hear that."

"I am curious about her, too. Will I get to meet her?"

"I'll have to ask her."

Holly made a face. "I'm beginning to think she doesn't exist. She's just a cipher, a false superior upon whom you can blame the unpopular decisions you make."

Hardson grinned. "That could be true also. It's possible the matriarch of the *88 Fists* died years ago, and I've just been coasting along on her imagined authority ever since." He tugged lightly at his beard. "I wonder who's been eating all of her food, in that case?"

"You have, of course."

"Ahh," he said, making a face. "The woman loves coconuts. Anything with coconut in it. I can't stomach the things. Do you know she has Minnijean scramble them into her eggs, sometimes? Repulsive."

"A likely story," Holly said. She was amused, but didn't smile. "So what happens after you're done robbing this ship?"

"Ah. You disapprove."

"I didn't say that. I just asked a question."

"We let them go, of course."

"Let them go?"

"Absolutely. We're cheerful and opportunistic thieves, my dear, not murderers. That's best left to filth like Silverback. And I will admit, it can be quite a challenge to adhere to a strict no-killing policy when your opponents are not so limited, you know?"

Holly scanned the sailors standing at the railing, many of whom had clearly been badly beaten, but saw nothing that looked like a potentially mortal injury. There were a couple of men and a woman nursing obviously broken limbs, but there were no bodies amid the broken gear and debris left after the melee. The chaos of the fight had been like a movie, and some part of her expected it to be littered with corpses afterward, like a battlefield. "Hm," she said. Hardson seemed to respond more verbosely if she acted as though she was losing interest.

"It's better for us that way, you see."

"How so?"

"Well, it pays to be a nuisance to the shipping companies. The returns diminish greatly when they consider you an actual threat. The *Fists* is known for occasionally taking a bit of sport, but they also know we'll let 'em go with all hands afterward. They fight because they're paid to, but certainly not as hard as they would if they were fighting for their lives. And the cargo carriers don't pursue us, because their insurance covers what little we take."

Holly nodded. "Who's Silverback?"

"Not good people."

She waited.

"Another pirate, but one with a much less civilized approach. The opposite of decency, in fact. He sinks ships, takes everything, kills all hands."

"Sounds like a demon."

"So you won't believe in Silverback either, eh?"

"I didn't say that. But I don't consider you trustworthy, so..." she shrugged.

"You'll have no trouble learning about Silverback. His ship has the same name. Ask at any port we go to."

"Oh, you're planning to let me ashore?"

"Why wouldn't I?"

Holly looked at him for a long moment. "That's true. I'm not your wife."

He met her gaze. "Even if you were, I let her go ashore. Why would I make an exception for you?" Hardson laughed. "Oh! The look on your face is too precious. Yes, I have a wife. You've met her—Fry. I'm surprised she didn't say anything. No, I take that back, I'm not surprised at all." He laughed again. "We tend to keep it quiet."

"So...her children are yours?"

"I am a proud *ba*."

She smoothed the frown off of her face and added this new information to what she knew about Hardson. She could tell even from his brief mention that the powerful tattooed woman she'd met meant a lot to him.

Of course they weren't in Singapore any more. In North America and with mariners it wasn't uncommon for men to have more than one wife, or for women to have several husbands. Some large blended families had both. She wasn't going to give him the satisfaction of more of a response than she already had, of course. "Well," she said. "I will leave you to your plundering."

Hardson tipped his hat with a grin.

chapter 34

Fifty-eight days before Princess Aiyana's trimester celebration

There was a disused-looking ladder running up the side of the bridge, and one early morning Holly found herself with a sudden urge to use it. She was slightly disappointed but not surprised to find that she wasn't the first; the graffiti and paint that covered the rest of the *Fists* was evident up there as well.

The view was pleasing though, a panoramic spread of placid ocean stretching to the horizon on all sides. She had the feeling of being in an endless, shallow bowl of water, but the depth of the ocean beneath was still felt in her bones, as though she were at the top of a skyscraper. In the distance she could see clouds, a storm swelling and cottony white as it prepared to dump rain somewhere off in the distance. Close to the water, there was a light haze but the top of the bridge put her above it and she could see miles of...nothing. The air was a just-right temperature, and for a moment she could have been on a leisurely cruise, ready to head back to the house later in the afternoon and get Elden's...

Holly felt the faint smile that had crept onto her face disappear. Why had her thoughts gone there? Of all the people on the ship, even the most abrasive of the mariners, it was still herself who got on her nerves the most.

She stood and watched Bull and the pilot, who called himself Switch5, perform maintenance on the *88 Fists'* seaplane. It seemed like the plane should have a name, same as the ship did. Odd that the crew hadn't named it.

A scrape on the rung made her turn. It was the Bonefish. He only came far enough up the ladder to rest his elbows on the roof, then pointed off to Holly's right. She turned, and saw something flying in the near distance, a plane high over the water.

264

After a few seconds of watching, it became clear that she wasn't looking at a distant airplane but at a large bird, not particularly far off and drawing closer. It continued to grow—without actual landmarks, Holly couldn't tell how close it really was. By the time it spread its wings to land she could guess by its size that it was a falconid. She looked curiously back at the Bonefish, but he was gone.

The falconid landed on the fore deck, near the seaplane. Holly climbed quickly down and headed in that direction. By the time she got there, Fry, The Bonefish and Vodka Bob were there standing in a respectful half-circle.

"Welcome to the *88 Fists*, Nefelibata," Fry said to the shifter, who was quickly donning a lightweight green modesty garment. "You're quite a long way from land. Are you lost?"

"No, ma'am," the falconid said. She was tiny and slender, as many of them were, just under five feet tall and built like a teenager, with skin the color of terracotta and black eyes and hair. Holly realized she recognized her. "I am on my way to Zeeland, and hoped to find a place to rest, if you would do me the kindness? I need no provisions." Her eyes passed over Holly, then came abruptly back. "I've met you," she said, her face friendly.

She remembered. "You came to dinner with one of the students from Singapore, in Strip City," she said. "With Gurrit, yes?"

"Indeed!" Nefelibata broke into a kind smile. "Such a nice boy. And you're Professor Ono's servant."

"Not any more," she replied with a quirked eyebrow that felt like a threat. She remembered Vitter asking her about a falconid.

"No no, of course not. Forgive me. I did not expect to see you here. There has been a lot of speculation as to your whereabouts."

"I'm sure there has."

"Shall I keep your secret?"

"That would be very much appreciated," Fry said. She glanced over her shoulder at some aural cue that Holly didn't hear, and Hardson came out the door she was looking at a heartbeat later. He was dressed in his full captain's finery, complete with coat and hat. Holly imagined he'd had to dress quickly, considering the hour. As far as she'd seen, Hardson was a night owl and was rarely at breakfast, which was from eight until ten.

If he had been roused from sleep, he didn't show it. "Miss Nefelibata," he said. "So nice to see you again." He tapped Vodka Bob on the shoulder, and the sailor nodded and excused himself with a grunt.

It was Fry's turn to raise an eyebrow. "Everyone knows her but me, apparently. You've met?"

"Of course I have! Miss Nefelibata has quite the wide range, and she's a much-beloved fixture and news source. I've never seen you at sea before though, my dear. Are there extenuating circumstances?"

Nefelibata favored him with a little bow that reminded Holly of a diplomat's gesture—which, she was beginning to realize, it was. "There are indeed, Captain. I'm flying to Zeeland."

"Rabbit's mortar, woman! That's a long time to be in the air!"

"It is a relief to find a friendly landing place," she said with a modest shrug.

"Well, I have good news for you. We're on our way to Zeeland as well, and from there a rousing tour of the Australian coast. Mama Lola's got us on a mysterious errand. It appears to be the season for them."

The falconid gave a single nod, cutting her eyes at Holly again. "We may be on the same errand."

Hardson tilted his head back with a sigh. "Oh, Mama," he said to the sky, "what are you getting us into?"

"Sometimes you have to sail through the storm," the Bonefish said. "There ain't no around." He gave Nefelibata a grin, showing cracked teeth. "Ain't the same when you're flying though, is it? Sky's gonna return you to the ocean double-quick."

She seemed unsettled. "I suppose that's why I'm happy to find a safe place to land."

"Mama has a way of steering us toward the storms," Hardson said. "I'm not sure how safe this place will be, if she has her way. But I'd be honored if you'd sail with us to Zeeland., Miss Ambassador. Rest your wings."

She gave him another single nod. "Thank you."

Holly moved away from the group, to the railing, but kept her ear on the conversation. The way Nefelibata looked at her made her nervous. It was the same sort of sharp-eyed look she remembered getting from Vitter. Sometimes it seemed like there was no middle ground any more. People either looked at her and saw only the collar, or they looked directly into her soul. Holly wasn't sure which she preferred.

chapter 35

Three days before Princess Aiyana's trimester celebration

"I've fought shifters, you know," Mahnaz said. Shiloh had accompanied him and Dorim to the mess hall, where they'd fallen into a conversation with two of the *Excelsis'* sailors. "During my mandatory service, of course. I was stationed in Quarshi, and the remote villages there are plagued by shifters."

"Traveling packs," Dorim said, nodding. He spoke very little, seeming to prefer being a piece of mobile furniture exuding directionless malice. When he did, his voice seemed to be coming from very far away. She found it unsettling.

Shiloh saw Mahnaz instantly preen, interpreting approval in his bodyguard's voice. "Yes. They roam the area, canids and cervids. Live in wagons and old beat-up cars, and they travel like North Americans. They'll set up camp near a town and rob people, rape people. But as soon as we learned where they were, they'd pack up and move. When we caught them, we'd put them down. We learned the basics in training, of course, but nothing can prepare you for the first time you come face to face with one, without a wall between you."

"I know exactly what you mean," the bearded sailor said. His shirt indicated that his name was Burdick; the other was Hua. "Even in chains, and with the neck snares, we've had a few close calls."

"It's all about knowing which species you're dealing with, of course," the chancellor said. Shiloh had the feeling that his words were unnecessary advice to the other three. "If you're facing an ursid, you might as well start digging your own grave."

Burdick agreed. "Felids are usually the weakest. Oh, and falconids, but that's because they're so small."

"Once they're in bird form I hear they can snatch you right off the ground."

"That's bullshit," Burdick said. "They can't lift a man. And you don't see them a lot. Anyway, canids are fierce but they'll stop if you're fighting hard enough."

"You just have to show them you're not afraid," Mahnaz agreed.

"Tcha," Dorim said. He had a handful of nuts, and was eating them mechanically.

"Felids would rather run away; they have a nasty bite but as long as you don't let them get at your throat or the back of your neck, you're just in for a lot of knife wounds basically. Ursids always attack with their shoulders leading the way," Burdick said. "I had a cousin in the counter-shifter squad. He said the best defense was to attack forward and down. Duck under the initial strike and then come up. And if they're in bear form, they have a big blind spot to the rear. What did you fight?"

"A canid," Mahnaz said. "Huge. An alpha female, I think."

"Worst kind," Hua agreed with a nod.

"Ever faced one?"

"I've never had to fight a shifter," Hua said. "I'm in Engineering. I'm only topside because most of the experienced crew is over on the pirate ship. But I know that they don't keep alphas on board, not in general pop."

Shiloh wanted to ask why, but staying quiet and listening seemed to be the best course of action while the men compared stories. "It's vital to avoid showing weakness," Mahnaz said. "If you can convince a canid that you're not afraid, they won't attack sometimes. And if that doesn't work, a big knife helps. I put mine right through that female's heart. With her dying breath, she shifted into her wolf form, right in my arms. Most disgusting thing I've ever felt." He patted Shiloh's arm.

"We had a cervid charge two armed men a month ago," Burdick laughed. "They were using cutter rounds, full auto, opened fire just as he jumped at them in deer form. He went human in midair, in about four pieces." The men laughed.

"Wasn't any choice but to shoot it though. Cervids are strong and fast, the women too. If violence starts they will fuck you up. They'll power through enough hurts to kill four men."

They went on like that for a while, Mahnaz talking over and over about the canid he'd killed in such detail that Shiloh began to doubt that it had happened. Burdick had more stories about dealing with the shifters on the ship and how dangerous it was. They were all trying to impress her, since she was the only woman in the room. Shiloh guessed that the sailors were wondering why she had gravitated to Mahnaz, and he was trying to prove that he was manly enough to deserve her. It was stupid, and she was stuck listening to stomach-churning tales about all of the ways they'd cheerfully murdered shifters.

chapter 36

Although she'd read about the place quite a lot, Holly wasn't sure what to expect of Zeeland and Australia. They ported at a town in Zeeland whose name nobody told her, and the *Fists* dropped off cargo and picked up a new assortment of goods. Hardson and Nefelibata left on a pointedly secretive errand, returning with three men. All five disappeared into Mama Lola's quarters. "Rainbow Snakes," Razor explained to Holly, catching her skulking. Coriander was at her heels. "Big doings afoot."

"Why is she here? The falconid."

"I haven't heard for sure," Razor said. "I know she's traveling on the say-so of some falcon council, who are really nervous about the way that Sino-India treats shifters."

"I don't know if I trust her," Holly said. She explained Nefelibata's dalliance with Gurrit. "Her being here...it can't be a coincidence. One of the police officers who held me afterward was asking about a falconid that had been seen in the area. I'm sure it was her."

"Well, that's a new branch of the tree. She's shown zero interest in you since that first day."

"I know."

"She and Marcus have been going on a lot, but not about you. He's mostly lecturing her about the things he's seen. I know that Vadim and Ghosthorse are glad to get a break from him," she added with a laugh.

"Where do we go next?" Holly asked, not comfortable talking about Marcus.

"Cap says Mama Lola plotted out stops in Zeeland and Australia, about a half-dozen of them. We'll be up and down the coast for the next month or so, it sounds like. Lot of little cargo hops. She has people here, wants to see 'em."

Holly nodded absently, looking over the railing. There was something different about the color of the sky in Zeeland, but she couldn't put her finger on what it was, exactly. The port was smaller than Singapore's, with a friendlier feeling to it, but for some reason that just made her feel more exposed. She'd have preferred the towers of boxy containers and brightly-painted cranes that gridlocked Singapore's port.

Razor pointed out some of the different flags to her. "Those two are South African," she said. "The big cargo freighter's Chinese, and the smaller two are both Indian. The boxy ship out in the harbor," she pointed to a smallish, armor-clad ship, "is the *Rattenkonig*. They're privateers like us. And farther out, that row of three ships? Brother Nations military."

"Why are they here?"

"Making a show of force, mostly. *Rattenkonig* is a Rainbow Snakes volunteer. Zeeland doesn't have a standing navy, just a lot of volunteers who come and go at will."

Holly nodded. "Seems disorganized."

"It probably is. I wouldn't know," Razor added. "I prefer to stay out of naval military engagements if I can. A little piracy is one thing, that's good for the soul. But nobody's trying to outright *sink* anyone." She thought about it a moment. "I guess that's kind of ridiculous. But hey, it's a world-view and it's mine."

Coriander quacked and broke into a shuffling run along the deck then leapt, taking flight and soaring away from the ship.

Holly's surprise showed on her face, and Razor grinned. "He'll be back. Probably saw a fish."

Holly smiled in spite of herself. "So why didn't you go ashore?"

"Didn't feel like it. Why didn't you?"

"Afraid of who might see me."

"Me too," Razor said, nodding. It seemed like an opening to ask Razor about her no doubt mysterious past, but Holly couldn't really bring herself to care very much. Razor let the moment pass without apparent offense, then took an object from a deep pocket and handed it to Holly. "This is for you."

She took it; it was an electronic notepad. "What is it?"

"Your roommate's little journal. He came up on deck three, four days back, middle of the night, and tried to throw it overboard."

"How did you get it?"

Razor laughed. "He went up to the bridge and threw it from there.

Landed on the plane deck. I think he might've been a little bit drunk. Anyway, I figured he might want it back some time, and if he did, you might want to be the one to give it to him."

"Are you suggesting it's a good idea for me to make a peace offering?"

"I have no idea why you two fell out. Don't care either, since it doesn't look like anyone's going to murder anybody." She gave Holly a look that made her think about Yinka dying. "It just seemed like a thing to do."

"Thanks," Holly said. She wasn't angry at Marcus any more. The idea that he'd attempted to throw away all of his research was a bit shocking, and she certainly hadn't intended for her angry words to make him give that up. She decided to watch him closely to see if she could determine if he felt better without the perceived responsibility of continuing his chronicle, or if he regretted discarding it. Then she could decide if it was best to return it to him or not.

Marcus got along well with the various visitors, and spent much of his time chatting with them and Nefelibata. Hardson allowed him to sit in on their meetings. He didn't offer Holly the option, and she decided not to be offended by this.

The next day, they were underway again. The rumble of motion was actually comforting, and she felt whatever misgivings she'd had about Zeeland dropping away. They were at a new port by the end of the afternoon, and the process of visitors was repeated. This went on for two weeks, an endless series of ports, cargo swapped on and off, and people going in and out of Mama Lola's cabin. Holly helped out here and there just to have something to do, and eventually retired to the cabin and let the days blur together in a haze of visiting Minnijean in the kitchen, wandering the ship, and staring at the wall trying to sleep.

On the sixth or seventh day of wandering between Zeeland and other ports, there was a tap at the door, and she looked up to see Dilly. The big man looked like he really didn't want to be there. "Holly. Hey. Cap'n says to give you this," he said, holding out a package wrapped in plain paper.

"He didn't want to bring it himself?"

"Well...he's busy. On the bridge. You know."

She smiled at him, and he couldn't meet her eyes any more. "I know. Thank you, Dilly," she said politely, thinking that Hardson had found another music box.

She was already thinking of things to say to him, that it wouldn't work, that she needed the specific Myawi box she'd had and each girl got a different tune, but the parcel wasn't a music box at all. They were books, four hardcover novels from various genres. He might have had a specific reason for buying each, or he might have taken them at random from a store's shelves; it was impossible to know without asking him—which she wasn't particularly interested in doing.

There was a rumble of thunder from outside, and the ship jolted suddenly, the floor dipping first one way and then the other.

"What the shit," Dilly said, heading for the deck as soon as he regained his footing. Holly put the books on her bed and followed him, closing the door to her cabin behind her the way she'd seen the other sailors do in emergencies. On the way up, she passed Embrosia leading the children and mothers down to the galley.

The source of the excitement was visible as soon as Holly stepped out from behind Dilly's broad back: there were two other ships pacing them. Judging by the smoke, one had just fired on them. She heard the humming whisper of a military helicopter, too, but didn't see it when she scanned the horizon.

There was no time to ask someone what was going on, so Holly followed Dilly across the deck to the railing and looked. There was a ship ahead of them and one coming alongside; Holly saw a Chinese flag and the name *Vinko Bogataj* on the side. *Vinko's* guns were aimed at the *Fists*, and there were several smaller boats in the water, little gunships that quickly surrounded them. On the *Fists*, water cannons were manned at intervals around the deck. Holly guessed that they were to repel boarders, and thought it ingenious—they couldn't run out of ammunition, at least.

Looking out over the water as she tried to follow Dilly, Holly tripped and barely caught herself before going down. The shooting started a moment later. For some reason the distant crackle of gunfire and the sound of bullets smacking into the armor and superstructure didn't terrify her, though she knew objectively that it probably should. She could be killed at any moment.

The sound of the *88 Fists'* deck guns returning fire was louder, and added to the chaos. Holly had lost track of Dilly so she kept going forward, to the bow where the harp and chaingun were. The noise was deafening from forty feet away and she plugged her ears but pressed forward.

She recognized the sailor manning the weapon—his name was Nyman, she remembered. When he saw her coming, he grinned and tossed her a pair of earphones similar to the ones he wore. Holly put them on quickly, then stepped behind Nyman so she could watch without being in the way. He was picking his shots carefully, trying to keep the smaller boats back.

Every so often he'd raise the chaingun and send a few shots winging toward the *Vinko* as well.

Holly saw the helicopter then, as it made a pass over them. Nyman shouted and raised the chaingun to snap off a few shots in its direction, warning it away.

Two of the skiffs came suddenly around the front of the ship; Nyman threw himself to the deck and a fusillade of shots clattered around him. He got up, shouted something Holly didn't hear, and jumped right back into it.

Another skiff got in front of the *Fists* and hung there a moment, attempting to block their path until it was clear that the larger ship had every intention of running right over it. As it wheeled away, a man stood up in the back with a rifle and fired two shots. Both found Nyman, who yelped in surprise and took a step away from the gun before falling to the deck. A moment later the ocean in front of them erupted as one of *Vinko's* main guns opened up as further deterrent to their continuing forward. The explosion of water made Holly dive to the deck, and she was hit an instant later by a cascade of water so big it felt like a piece of furniture thrown on her back. She was drenched in an instant, aspirating a bit of salt water with her gasp. Coughing, she struggled to her feet as the *Fists* came up out of the spray and found she'd been washed several feet back. Nyman had gone even farther and fetched up against the railing groin-first, his legs dangling out over the edge of the ship.

The smaller skiffs continued to buzz the ship, coming closer to take potshots at the people manning the water cannons. The helicopter returned and made a low pass over the front of the ship as well, staying away from the chaingun at the stern and spattering the superstructure with high-velocity slugs.

Holly didn't think about it; she adjusted the ear protection, then jumped forward and assumed Nyman's position at the bow chaingun. It seemed easy enough, with curved bolsters for her shoulders and twin hand-grips. She rotated it experimentally, getting a feel for the way it worked, and then pulled the trigger. The gun responded with a powerful crack, and she saw a splash surprisingly far off in the water.

She got the hang of it quickly; it was certainly easier than shooting Hatton's gun, since it absorbed its own recoil. Holly tracked one of the smaller boats, triangulating her shots with the splashes her misses made, and then shredded the smaller craft when it fell properly into her sights. Another bark from the *Vinko's* guns showered the deck with water, but Holly did her best to ignore it, trying to shoot more of the small boats. She wasn't able to hit them, but her shooting kept them wary and that seemed to help.

Another ship came suddenly into view, and she felt a moment of panic before realizing it was the *Rattenkonig*, flying the Rainbow Snakes' flag. The ship was smaller but more heavily armed than the *88 Fists*, and unleashed a devastating volley at the *Vinko*. Holly joined in then, and could practically see the warship think twice about pressing the attack. After a brief exchange, the Sino-Indian navy began to fall back. Soon she had no targets left, as they left the strike force behind. She left the gun for a moment to look back, and saw that the *Rattenkonig* wasn't following, but holding position and keeping the Sino-Indian ships from pursuing.

She looked down at Nyman, who was glassy-eyed with shock but conscious. "Well, that was fun, wasn't it?" she said.

chapter 37

Thirty-two days before Princess Aiyana's trimester celebration

Shiloh's story

We followed a caravan across the plains, and Ivy took us on a hard and fast run to Detroit. I think she learned a few things about travelling from the Benzers, because she drove faster than I'd seen her go before, and it was only a two-day trip from the big river. Swan said it normally took three or four. In Detroit, we picked up cargo bound for Strip City. It turned out people were asking for Ivy specifically, after hearing about her leading the circus home. The Vovo was well-loaded with letters, small packages and other cargo, and Ivy seemed pleased for the first time in weeks. We left Detroit for St. Louis.

St. Louis had been torn up by Sam Ward's Army just over a year before. There were a great many new ruins all around the old ones from the Fall, but the city was still a gathering spot for travelers and nomads and traders because of the river.

There was a little place that Swan hoped hadn't been wrecked, so I went to find it with her and Kroni. At the end of the day, Ivy really liked to be alone for a few hours. We usually made ourselves scarce so she could have her quiet time. I didn't always go with Swan and Kroni, but this time Swan said she wanted me to see this place, if it still existed. She said I'd like it—you can tell when she's being sincere and when she's fucking with you, if you pay attention—and I had spent a happy night with a big burly nomad boy last night, and with his big brother the night before, so I was feeling pretty content.

Miracle of miracles, the place had survived the ravages of war. It was a sturdy, severe-looking building surrounded by the nubs and stubs of taller buildings that had come down during or after the Fall. At one point the road went over a fallen skyscraper, and through another one, and beyond that Swan's place stood. She said it was called Sister Fister's Blistered Biscuit, and the lights streaming through the multi-colored windows made it feel like a place I wanted to be inside of.

Inside, the building was cheerfully crowded. The walls were mosaic tile, with a pattern that crawled onto the windows to create the colors visible from outside. There was an S-shaped bar up the middle, a pattern made out of mirrors on the ceiling, and a jaunty piano player who was absolutely tearing the place apart, as the musicians used to say. I saw people dancing, though the dance floor was too small for me to have any proper fun so I stuck with Swan and Kroni. They found a spot in a high-backed booth and we got a round of drinks and a slice of cake for me. The biggest and most unpleasant difference between traveling with the circus and traveling with Ivy was that there frequently wasn't any food. More than once we'd gone a day or two without anything to eat—after a week or so I figured out why Ivy was always hoarding extra bits of whatever she had to eat when there was a square meal.

"I'm glad this place is still here," she said. Kroni nodded in agreement. "You ever stop in St. Louis, with the circus?"

"No," I told her. I was looking at the ceiling, where numerous items—a cello body, a fancy chair, a bicycle frame with no wheels—were hung from wires. "It was always late in the season by the time we got here. Rushing back to Strip City."

"You missed out," she said. "You sad, not travelling with the circus any more?"

I shrugged. "I quit, didn't I?"

"Yeah, why did you anyway?"

I thought about it a minute. Swan seemed like she was being serious so I gave her a serious answer. "I didn't feel at home there. Not because of the disaster. Even before that. I just...you and Ivy and Kroni made me realize that I didn't feel like I belonged."

"But you grew up there."

I nodded.

"They were your family."

I made a face. "Everyone always says that. But they didn't like me that much."

"That's because you're a huge bitch. Or you were, at least. You're better now. Not all sunshine and chipmunks, don't get me wrong. But you're okay as anyone."

That made me laugh. Kroni gave a little *heh* also. Like Ivy, he could go for hours without saying a word, which I imagine made Swan a little crazy sometimes.

"And anyway, that don't mean anything. Much as people at Gallamore's didn't like you, you were important to them and they'd have stood by you, if it came to it."

"Maybe," I said. I didn't really want to talk about it. "But when I got taken away, it was you guys who came after me. Not them. After everything else happened," I shrugged, "I didn't want to be there any more."

"Still, you could've stayed with the felids at the Stronghold, too."

"No, I couldn't have. Or did you not notice that they were trying to kill me when you guys arrived to rescue me?"

"They weren't trying to kill you, stupid, it was a game. Anyway, you're right, that's a dumb idea, you're probably not welcome there *now*."

I could have pointed out that she had been the one who'd blown up the felids' chicken coops and held a gun to the head of Clarabow, the queen, but there wasn't much point. "Yeah, I burned that bridge myself." I shrugged. The conversation was making me feel out of place in Swan's cool, happy traveler-bar, and I didn't like that. "Most felids treat being exiled from the Stronghold like some kind of death sentence, but I don't really care. For one, my mother was exiled too, before I was born, and for two, I don't *like* felids, and they've never liked me, in case you hadn't noticed."

"I don't know, Kissel was pretty sweet on you. Till you tried to tear his face off anyway."

"Shut up about him. It doesn't matter why I decided to stay with you guys. What matters is what is, and you're stuck with me now. What about you? Where's your ancestral home?"

Swan looked at me over the edge of her drink and her face broke out in a lazy smile. "Dallas," she said, then took a big drink.

"And you left there."

She nodded. "But that was different. I left to go be something else. You're still a circus girl, only without a fancy trailer with your name on it no more."

"She is more than that," Kroni said.

"If you say so. I'm not saying it's a bad thing. I know we've got fed more than a few times thanks to her makin' folks laugh and clap. But who she is, that hasn't changed."

"Then maybe I was never a 'circus girl,'" I said.

Swan gave me another of those over-her-glass looks. "You tell yourself that, you're a liar."

I took a moment to enjoy my cake, which was really good. Like I said, sometimes food was scarce, and if spinning hoops and juggling and doing acrobatic tricks meant that I could get food, then I'd do it. "Do you say that because you're too shy to sing for trade?" I asked her.

"The fuck?"

"You have a beautiful voice. I've heard you sing, more than once, usually when you think no one's listening. You could get plenty of trade."

Her Cradle's mask hid it a bit, but Swan actually seemed to be blushing. "That's not what I do, Miss Kitty."

"Not now. But it could be." Needling Swan too much was a good way to catch a fist in the mouth. I'd seen it happen more than a few times. So I didn't push it.

Kroni did. "I like it when you sing," he said.

"Well, then when it happens, know it's just for you," she said gruffly. "Not for anyone who's willing to toss me a piece of sausage."

"I don't care if you're mad," I said. "It's true, you are a wonderful singer and you should do it more. The world needs more of that. I'm going to get more cake." I slid out of the booth before she could answer and went to the bar.

chapter 38

Holly lay awake, staring at the ceiling. Marcus snored lightly beneath her, a soft, intermittent rumble like a cat's purr. The noise didn't bother her. She'd been awake for long enough to count almost six thousand heartbeats, waiting for sleep that wouldn't come.

She didn't think about anything, just counted heartbeats. It didn't feel bad to exist without existing. No images spun through her head. No stray thoughts flitted about. She had cleared her mind completely, and there wasn't anything there. Yet she still wasn't sleeping.

And then, abruptly, there was. *She was in a wide open lot of some kind, sun beating down from above, and she was walking around a battered, sand-blasted vehicle, looking at its tires and getting it ready for the day. It wasn't terribly hot yet, but it would be soon enough. Holly glanced at the horizon, then at the trees filling what had once been downtown, surrounding the remains of the Great Arch, and a breeze stirred her hacked-short hair, making her aware of the dirt on her face.*

A rapid tap-tap-tap on the door snapped her out of the hallucination, back to her room on the *88 Fists*. Marcus' snoring didn't change; Holly slipped out of the upper bunk and padded to the door.

It was Razor. "That was fast. Can't sleep?"

"I can never sleep," Holly told her.

"Well, stay quiet and come up on deck. There's something you should see."

"What does Hardson want to show me?"

"Not the cap's idea. Stay quiet."

Holly followed. Razor led her toward the front of the ship, up toward the bridge. The night air was cool, the sky black and star-speckled. The ocean reflected it, an endless shimmer in all directions, and it was a moment before Holly realized there was another ship next to them.

Lights off, the derelict craft loomed out of the dark, a solid shape that wasn't dotted with starlight. From what she could see the ship was smaller than the *88 Fists*, but not by much. It hadn't been immediately noticeable because all of the lights were off.

"Is it a ghost ship?" Holly asked Razor.

"More or less," was the reply. "Recent, though." Spotlights played over the boat, which was just a few dozen yards away. "Pirates most likely."

"You mean they were attacked by pirates, or they were pirates?"

"Attacked by. See the bullet holes? And she's sinking, too. She's riding low in the water. Probably be on her way to the bottom by first light."

"We attacked a ship not long ago. Why do you sound so upset?"

"We do things differently. This looks like they met *Silverback*."

"I've heard of him. Them. " They were drawing closer to the dead ship. "And what's the difference between *Silverback* and *88 Fists*?"

"Maybe you should wander over there and see, when they board. No one's going to stop you."

She looked at Razor, who wasn't looking at her. "Maybe I will." There was an urge to resist doing what Razor might want her to do, just on general principle, and then Holly decided not to care. She'd go where she wanted for her own reasons.

After stopping quickly in her room for her boots (Marcus still didn't stir; if he was awake he was staunchly ignoring her as he had been since she'd yelled at him), Holly went to the main deck, where the *Fists'* tender was being prepared to go into the water. She paused long enough to put her boots on, then climbed aboard behind Fry, stepping in front of Ghosthorse to do so. Ghosthorse was the biggest man on the crew, a full head taller than Dilly, and she'd heard his V-shaped physique remarked upon by male and female crew alike. His face was like a cliff from which words rarely tumbled, and he was the first sailor Holly had seen who carried an actual sword.

"Hey," the big man said. She glanced at him, then chose a seat and sat down. She was next to the Bonefish, who slapped her knee lightly with a little chuckle.

"Fry?" Dilly asked. He was at the wheel of the tender, scanning a checklist.

Fry looked at Holly, then shrugged.

He didn't seem to have gotten the answer he wanted. "Is it safe...?"

"No way of knowing," she said. "But she's made her decision." She opened a small case on her hip and took out several bracelets, handing them to Dilly, the Bonefish and Ghosthorse. She paused, then gave one to Holly as well. The others were putting them on, but Holly looked at hers first. "Baby bird," Fry said.

"What does it do?"

"Sends little chirps to tell us where you are, in case you get lost. Monitors your heartbeat so we know you're alive. If you take it off, we'll assume you're dead; don't expect anyone to come looking."

She met Fry's eyes for a moment. It was just an explanation of the device, not an attempt to frighten her. Their insistence upon letting her do whatever she wanted annoyed her. Holly once again pushed away the urge to change her behavior. She wanted to go and see the derelict ship, and they'd let her do so. What they thought of her decision didn't matter. And what was one more device monitoring her whereabouts? She snapped the little plastic band over her wrist; it automatically cinched itself snug, a little reassuring squeeze.

"There might be an ambush," Dilly said. He was talking just past Holly now, no longer addressing Fry but not quite talking to her. She looked at him. When he accidentally met her eyes for an instant, he stammered. "Sometimes, ah, they leave people behind. Attack the ships that come to, ah, salvage." She smiled inwardly.

"Ain't nobody home that ship," the Bonefish said. "She dead."

"Why are we going over there?" Holly asked him.

"The Bonefish is going to get what there is to get."

"Salvage," Ghosthorse added. "See if they left us anything worth taking."

The Bonefish asked, "Why's the Meowy gel going? Couldn't say."

"Leave her be," Fry said. There was a tone in her voice like she expected Holly to regret going. It stopped short of being openly mocking, but she got the sense that if Fry had her way she wouldn't be on the boat right now.

Just as they were getting ready to cast off, Razor joined them, barely glancing at Holly. Fry handed her a baby bird without comment.

The Bonefish was still looking at Holly. "She lookin' for herself," he said, with another little laugh, and nudged her shoulder. "Maybe you find her there."

88 Fists' tender had a lumpy, wobbly ride even though the sea was relatively smooth. They pulled even with the stricken ship quickly, before the rough ride had time to get unpleasant, and a glance from Fry told Holly to stay in her seat while the boat was tied up and secured. A folding ladder had been attached to the railing by the time Holly was given the go-ahead to climb onto the derelict's deck, and she was slightly disappointed to have missed seeing what sort of knot was used to tie it on.

She was the last one onto the deck. But that didn't bother her. It had a much different feel from the ship they'd attacked, and from the Fists; this craft was very much dead, and felt like a dead place. Perhaps it was because her engines were shut down, or the dark, but there was a funereal quality to the stillness of the deck and the way the boat rode the waves.

"Feel that?" Razor asked, tilting a hand back and forth to indicate a rhythmic rumble coming from below the deck somewhere, keeping time with the ship's rocking. "That's water in the lower decks. She's definitely flooding. You want to have your look around, do it fast."

"Razor!" Fry called. "You've got Minnijean's shopping list."

"I do indeed. Time to get to work. Have fun, Holly."

The others had fanned out along the deck, which was empty apart from a few scraps of cloth snagged in gaps in the metal. The remnants of bodies that had washed overboard? She wasn't sure. Either way, it seemed that below-deck would be more interesting, so she found a door and went inside.

From here she caught the scent of dead things, strongly. Sight followed a moment later; there were very dim emergency lights casting a faint blue haze on a hall that smelled of smoke and shit. Without the lights she'd have tripped over the bloating corpse right in front of her, in fact. Holly squinted into the gloom and saw a hall strewn with bodies and broken furniture. There were bullet holes in the walls, and the smell slammed into her nose with a warm, gelatinous feeling, sliding into her stomach and forcing her to suppress a gag. The sound of thumping water was louder here, closer below her feet.

Holly looked into a few of the rooms she passed, saw cabins full of destroyed things, everything smashed to unrecognizable bits. She found the galley, where the bits were more familiar, but still largely reduced to scrap. She swallowed the taste of bile in her throat. She didn't want to, didn't want to think about it, but she'd been counting bodies since she'd come in the door. There were nine so far, and it was possible that not all of the severed limbs belonged to them. Razor's comments about Silverback seemed to be blunt honesty rather than hyperbole. There was a bearded man's severed head in one of the sinks, dead eyes focused on the ceiling. Above her, she heard a voice, maybe Dilly's, call out, and Fry answered him, distantly.

And there was another voice, this one from below, and much smaller. For a moment she didn't quite recognize it as a voice, just a faint cawing sound. She froze until she heard it again. Definitely not a sound produced by the faltering ship. With difficulty, Holly followed it through the galley to a door that was partly ajar due to a severed leg. She pushed it open and found a staircase heading up and down.

"Hello?" she called. Could it be some sort of trap? Was she about to get her head chopped off?

The sound came again, from the bottom of the stairs, resolving into a voice. "...help," it said. The emergency lights left the bottom of the staircase in shadow, but Holly went down anyway, feeling equal parts fearless and apathetic. She wasn't sure she cared if it was a trap. There were two more bodies at the bottom of the steps. The metal railing had been smashed away from the post, as though they'd both been thrown down there. Holly looked closely, and heard the small voice again. "I'm here," it said.

She was looking right at it. There was a large body in some kind of uniform on top of a smaller one in a very dirty lab coat. The hand attached to the lab coat moved slightly, fingers flexing, then waved.

"Here," the voice, female, said, struggling to stay above a whisper laced with enough raw pain and fear to raise gooseflesh on Holly's arms.

Holly went down the steps two at a time, slowly. "I'm coming," she said. The damaged staircase groaned as she came down. She reached the woman and touched the hand first. "I'm here."

The fingers clenched her hand tightly. "Please don't be a dream," the woman said. "Please."

"I'm not. My name is Holly," she said. "I'm going to move this person off of you, okay?"

"Yes." The desperately clutching hand let go. "Yes, yes, get him off of me, please. I can feel him putrefying."

Holly tugged at the body and stopped when the flesh felt like it was going to deglove. She saw that fluids leaking out of the corpse had stained the lab coat. She choked back a gag and tried again, this time rolling the body. It let out a watery groan as it moved, dead air pushing through the dead throat, and the smell got worse.

"Watch my leg!" the woman pinned underneath the body said, her voice going high with pain. "Oh my leg my leg!"

Holly stopped what she was doing and looked closer. The woman's leg was impaled through the thigh on the broken stair railing post. She'd fallen on it and slid down; nearly three feet of metal stuck out of her flesh, pinning her like a display insect. The wound had been roughly and clumsily tied with what looked like a torn section of clothing, the cloth stained brown with dried blood. "I'm sorry," she said. "I can't lift him. I need to get help."

"Help. Others," she gasped. The pain had taken most of the energy out of her.

"Others?"

"Dr. Imerlish. Shell. I think. She's the only one. Survived."

"Where is she? Where are they?"

The woman pointed with her other hand. "Crew quarters. They were alive. When the pirates left. The others went quiet. Before." A shudder ran through her, turning into a tremor.

"Hey, shh, calm down." Holly sat on the floor, heedless of the treacle of gummy body fluids there. She moved so she could see the woman's face, which was half obscured by dried blood. "What's your name?"

"Caroline. Caroline Xiu. Graduate student. Shanghai Ligong."

"The university?"

"Yes. You...Myawi girl?" she asked with a slightly incredulous tone in her weak voice.

"I am. What happened to this ship, Caroline? Quickly, the ship is sinking and I want to go get help for you. We won't hurt you, I came from a ship called the *88 Fists* and we're going to help. They're up top salvaging things."

"Attacked. Pirates. Killing everyone. Captain. My advisor. All of them. I fell. Antonio fell on top of me. Covered me." She shook. "Heard them talking. To Dr. Imerlish. Deal they made. He was trying. To protect the formid."

"Formid?" Holly asked. "A termite shifter?"

Caroline nodded. "Captured one. Dr. Imerlish and Dr. Telwyck and the mercenaries. On our way back home. From South America."

"With a *formid?* That's amazing." There hadn't been a formid in captivity in over a hundred years.

"Yes." Caroline roused herself a bit. "Imerlish begged the pirate to spare them. The pirate captain...challenged him to a fight. Said he couldn't fight and offered a test of wits instead. I think chess. If Dr. Imerlish won two of three they'd spare him. But. But. While they played..." Caroline's face fell, and she had to try a couple of times before she could continue. "The pirates raped the women who weren't killed in the attack. Vera and Dr. Saia, the other scientists. Gwen, one of the sailors. Miki and Shell, the domestics. Dr. Imerlish is Shell's benefactor. They raped them all. I think in the same room. I think they raped the formid, too, after the women started dying. It went on for at least a day. But he won, he won two games. I know I heard Shell after it was all over, but not the others."

"And the pirates left after that?"

Caroline nodded again. Talking was tiring her out, and Holly felt badly for interrogating her. "They did something. To the ship. I could hear the water coming in. I'm so thirsty. Do you have any water?"

"I'll get some. And help. The others are down that hall?"

Caroline nodded.

Holly stood, pausing to wipe her hands on the dead man's coat. There wasn't much point in trying to get the gore off of her pants; it had soaked through and she could feel it on her skin. She looked up the stairs, then went through the door to find the others Caroline had spoken of first. If they were trapped as well and she could let them out, they might be able to help more quickly than the others could. The hallway was dark; the emergency lights had gone out completely. Was the sound of thumping water even louder? It seemed like it was. The floor seemed to move under her feet; if there was a deck below this, it was probably flooded. "Is anyone in there? Dr. Imerlish? Shell?"

"In here," came a male voice.

"Can you move? Are you hurt?"

"I am not injured," Imerlish called, "but we do need help, quickly. She'll be dead soon if we don't get help."

Holly's heart raced. "I can't see. I'm going to get a light, and then I'll be back."

"Yes, thank you," came the curiously calm voice.

She stepped carefully past Caroline on the steps, then rushed up, through the mess hall and back the way she'd come. The dead bodies were just a part of the scenery at this point, the smell an unpleasant memory in her nose that she was ignoring, much as her stomach wanted to unleash its contents. Once up on deck, she looked for Razor or Fry, and found the latter helping Ghosthorse and the Bonefish with a block and tackle as they lowered a haphazardly-packed metal crate into the tender.

"Find anything interesting?" she asked Holly with a smile.

In the moonlight, the gore she'd gotten smeared on herself was obvious. "Survivors," she said. "At least three."

"Anything *interesting?*" Fry repeated. "Don't have use for more mouths to feed."

Holly blinked at her. "What?"

"They may have gotten lucky in the short run, but it's their time. Silverback doesn't leave beating hearts behind him."

"He did this time," Holly said. "They beat him at a game and he spared them."

She looked skeptical. "Did he? This ship's been scuttled and the lifeboats and provisions have all been taken. Not much mercy there."

Holly squared her shoulders, raising her chin to Fry. "Don't you dare leave them here."

"Or what?" Fry asked. "You'll stay here too? Sink with them? I've got my own family to look after, Holly, blood and chosen. Everything's either an asset to that survival, or it's not."

"Bad juju," the Bonefish said. "The Bonefish don't toss back nothin' if the sea chose to spare it. Don't make her mad."

Fry glared at the Bonefish, then back to Holly. She even glanced at Ghosthorse, who shrugged. "I think she's right," he said.

"You think she'll consider you husband-worthy if you agree with her," she snapped. "Fine," she said. "You can explain it to Mama Lola, since she likes you so goddamn much."

"They need help. One of them is trapped and I can't move her. And we'll need a light, possibly first aid."

The groan that came out of Fry's mouth suggested that she was already regretting the decision to help. "Fine," she said again. "Ghosthorse, go with her. I'll find Dilly and we'll be along. Bonefish, radio the captain and tell him what's going on. Where?" Holly gave her directions, then returned with Ghosthorse.

Razor met them in the mess hall. "What have you found?"

"A survivor," Holly said. "This way." Both Razor and Ghosthorse had lights, and in them Caroline looked worse. Her eyes were closed, and her leg was an alarming mess of scabbed blood and angry flesh where the railing punched through it.

"That's not good," Razor said.

"Miss Xiu?" Holly called, and got no response. "Caroline?"

"That girl's dead," Ghosthorse said.

"No, she isn't, I just talked to her." Holly took Ghosthorse's light and started down the steps, her shadow looming large down the narrow stairwell.

Razor said, "Get a grinder. Gonna need to cut that post off. Fry said to bring her home?"

"Yes. And the others."

"Huh. Not much time. Lower decks are flooding fast. Think those stairs will hold you, David?"

The big man tested the first one with his weight, and the whole structure sighed. "Maybe. Aft stairwell clear?"

"Yeah, but you have water coming up. I'd tell Fry and Dilly to go that way too."

Holly let them talk, making her way down to Caroline. "Hey," she said softly, touching the woman's shoulder lightly. "Caroline. Caroline." She let out a sigh of relief as Caroline's eyes cracked slightly open. "I came back," she said. "We came back, we're going to get you out."

"Water," she whispered.

"Soon. We have to get you out first. The ship's sinking. Do you see the light up there? That's Razor coming down to help you."

"Thank you," she croaked.

"I'm going to help the others now, okay? I'll see you on the ship." She expected Caroline to complain, but the exhausted woman merely nodded and closed her eyes again. Holly went through the door again, this time with illumination.

There were more bodies in this hallway, though not as many as upstairs. The room Imerlish was in appeared to be a cargo hold of some sort, with knocked-over boxes and damaged equipment scattered about. What looked at first like tangles of rags amid the debris resolved themselves into two more bodies, and there was a woman sitting against the wall in shredded clothes with her knees tucked into her chest. Holly saw the glint of a domestic's collar as the light passed over it. It was a Shushen collar. Expensive. Not as expensive as Myawi, but close. Holly couldn't tell what the girl looked like because of the way she was curled up, but she wore a single bright yellow shoe. She saw an overturned chess board and some scattered pieces near the center of the room, and finally a man cradling a naked child in his lap.

Holly went immediately closer. "Dr. Imerlish?"

"Yes." His round face was bruised, but he still looked dignified, and fussed with his hair. He glanced at her collar and she saw him notice and seem to dismiss her in that instant.

"I'm here to help."

"Of course you are," he said. Even in his exhaustion, he had an authoritative tone that reminded her of Elden. There was a more desperate edge to his voice, probably from stress. "Use your light. I must find the last box of jelly."

"Jelly?"

"Yes yes, the fiends won't have taken it with them. I couldn't find it in the dark, and she's on the brink of starvation. Of course it's only staving off the inevitable if we don't return to the colony, but we need not discuss that now." His manic rambling made Holly nervous.

"Is it for the child?"

Imerlish chuckled. "Not a child, my friend. Just a worker."

Closer now, Holly could see that the small person on Imerlish's lap was fully grown, a woman no more than four and a half feet tall, with slender, muscular limbs and a spare body that seemed to have not an ounce of fat on it. There was an odd tilt to the woman's flat face, some ethnic marker Holly had never seen before. "She's a shifter," Holly said, understanding.

"Yes, and a very long way from home," Imerlish said impatiently. "Help me find her food." He put the woman gently on the floor, cradling her head, and got up in a crouch, tutting to himself as he forced his back upright. "Ah, been sitting far too long. I didn't want to lose her in the dark."

"We don't have much time," Holly said. "The ship is sinking."

"This will only take a moment. Shell, help me look." Imerlish glanced at the woman sitting against the wall. He didn't seem to see the bodies in the room, and stooped to root through the wreckage on the floor when he got no response from Shell.

Holly went to her. Her face was battered, both eyes swollen almost closed. She was conscious, but stared hollowly. "Shell?" she asked softly. "I'm here to help. Can you hear me?"

Shell's eyes remained in the middle distance, but her head angled in a brief nod.

"I need the light!" Imerlish said impatiently. "Shine the light over here, please!"

Holly turned the light in his direction but kept her eyes on Shell. "Can you get up?" she asked. "Or will you need someone to carry you? We're going to leave this ship before it sinks."

Shell's lips moved, but no sound came out.

"Don't try to speak. I know you've been down here without water for a long time. We have food, and water, and a doctor. Just nod if you think you can make it up on your own."

There was a long pause, and then Shell nodded. Ghosthorse, Dilly and Fry were coming from the other end of the ship now, and their lights splashed into the room as they passed on their way to help Caroline in the stairwell. Fry paused long enough to look into the room and play her lights around. "Dear God," she said.

"There are three," Holly said, realizing as she did so that she should check the other bodies, just in case one of the other victims had survived.

"Silverback needs to *die*," Dilly said.

Holly trained her light in Imerlish's direction so he could see better, and he soon found what he was looking for. "Ah!" he barked in triumph, taking a foil-wrapped package the size of a book from one of the boxes.

"Razor," Fry called down the hall. "Get down here and check this room for scavenge, would you? What is that?" she asked Imerlish.

He had carried the package over to the formid, and was unwrapping one end of it, revealing a reddish, translucent blob of gelatin. "It is royal jelly," he said. "At least that's what I call it. It is what they eat."

"They?"

"The little woman is a formid," Holly said.

"A shifter?" Fry's brows went up, and her rifle seemed to unsling itself. "A *termite-shifter*? Not on my ship. She stays here, I'm sorry, whoever you are. You're not talking me into that, Holly. That thing stays here, and anyone who disagrees can stay with her."

"You're making a big mistake," Imerlish said.

"I don't know you, sir."

"Dr. Enzen Imerlish," he said. "And you should know that there is a reward posted by the Garrity Society for Academic Zoology for a living formid. If we can return her to Shanghai Ligong, she is worth six figures."

"What, is she a child?"

"No, just a worker," Imerlish chuckled.

"So they're all that small?"

"The workers are," he said again. He seemed to enjoy knowing more than Fry. He held the jelly above the formid's face, and suddenly she animated, reaching up with both hands to take the block from him and taking a large bite from the side of it. She ate mechanically and quickly.

"Workers?"

"Yes, the workers. There are workers and soldiers. Much like with most eusocial creatures, ants and termites especially."

Fry sighed. "Listen, sir—"

"Doctor."

"Listen. The ship is sinking. There's not time for a lesson. If you want me to...what's it doing?"

The formid, having consumed the block of jelly in several large, efficient bites, had gotten up and looked at everyone else in the room with apparent disinterest. She walked away from Imerlish, who remained crouched on the floor, and went to the nearest wall. She looked at the wall, touched it with her fingertips as if testing its strength, then rapped on the metal bulkhead with her knuckles. She then began walking along the wall, pausing every few steps to drum on it again, repeating the same rhythmic pattern.

"She is trying to signal to her sisters, her nest mates, that she's lost," Imerlish replied, smiling. "She does not know where she is, and cannot hear the others." The formid continued around the room, stepping blithely over Shell when it reached her. "They communicate over long distances through sound, you see. She'll continue to do that until she grows hungry again, and then she'll stop. If we return to the colony, I can get more food for her—without it, she'll starve in a matter of days—"

"That's not happening," Fry said.

"That is wonderful to hear, thank you. The things we could learn about them from studying her. The money—"

There was an explosion. Holly jolted at the sound and her ears were ringing before she fully comprehended that Fry had raised her rifle and shot the formid through the head. The little shifter's brains had made a fan-shaped pattern on the wall, and she collapsed where she stood. "Don't care." She ignored Imerlish's cry of shock. "Now, are you coming?"

He actually took a step toward her. "You foolish—"

She pointed the gun vaguely in his direction, not actually aiming at him. "Yes, Doctor, I'm sure you don't like me very much right now. But I'm the only one here with a ship that will be above water in the morning. So. Would you like to come aboard? I really don't care either way."

He didn't take his eyes from the dead formid. "Why?"

"One, I don't want a dangerous shifter on my ship."

"She was a *worker!* Harmless! The soldiers are the dangerous ones, and even then only when—"

"*Two*," Fry continued, "you said yourself that you have no food for her left, and I have no intention of sailing to South America so you can get more. So she was fated to starve, and I spared her that. She died with a full belly and that's more than many of us get in this world. Now, we are leaving. Are you coming with?"

He took a deep, resentful breath. Holly thought he looked like a sulking child. "Yes."

"Good. Holly here is bent on saving all of you and I wasn't looking forward to listening to her complain if you chose to stay behind." She tossed a wink that she'd probably learned from her husband at Holly. "Let's go."

On the way out, Holly saw Shell's other yellow shoe in the debris. Out of habit, she grabbed it quickly and stuffed it into a pocket.

chapter 39

Sixteen days before Princess Aiyana's trimester celebration

The *88 Fists* spent several days battened down at a tiny port on an equally tiny island, riding out a vicious storm. Holly read all of the books Hardson brought while she was cooped up in her cabin. Marcus eventually relented enough to be in there at the same time as she was, but he slept, or pretended to sleep, and she wasn't yet sure if he wanted his notepad back or not.

She didn't want to wait for him to talk, either. There had been something half on her mind since Zeeland, but she couldn't focus her thoughts for long enough to remember exactly what it was. There was something that she wanted.

It was in this frustrated state that Fry found her, greeting her in a clear, concise way that might have been mistaken for irritation if Holly didn't know her already. "Holly," she said. "You're off to the main stateroom. Mama Lola wants to talk."

"Why now?" Holly asked.

"Don't know," Fry said, angling her head. "Maybe you made an impression. I doubt you've done anything to make her angry enough to throw you off of the ship, though. I wouldn't get your hopes up."

Holly didn't smile. "And why would I want that?"

She got a furrowed brow and rolled eyes in response. "You don't need to be condescending. You've created quite the headache for Murr—for the captain. Your scientist, Dr. Imerlish, is just full of demands. Entitled little bastard. I don't know when I've ever felt so much like putting a stray back where I found him. Congratulations."

"He's not mine. What's he demanding?"

"Oh, equipment, computers to study the information he brought back.

He seems to think that the university sent us for him. His assistant thinks he's round the bend."

"She's probably right. Professors are like that. What will you do with him?"

"Mama Lola hasn't said. Maybe she wants to talk to you about that." She led Holly around the superstructure, to the stairs that led to the officers' quarters.

"Fry, what am I doing here? I was under the impression that Captain Hardson wanted me for a wife."

"He does."

"But he's got you."

She reached the top of the staircase, met Holly's eye, and nodded with a slight smile. "He does indeed. And my childbearing days are over."

"Hm," Holly said.

"I know," Fry said. "But look." She reached out as if to touch Holly's shoulder, but stopped short, respectfully. "We could have quite the nice little tribe. The *Fists* is a good ship, with good people. We won't force you, but...consider it."

She thought of the contentious relationship between Lakshmi and Professor Naveen's wife. Thinking of Shmi was a little jab of pain in her heart. "And how would you feel about it?"

"I'd rather have a village to raise my children," Fry said, stopping at a closed door. "And I'm very choosy about who joins that village. Unlike some, I don't extend invitations to every unmarked woman who steps aboard my home. But we can talk about that later. I'll leave you here."

Rather than ask why Fry was leaving, Holly looked at the door. Many of the doors on the *88 Fists* had been customized, the original metal doors long since removed and replaced with other materials. This door was wood, and old. It had been trimmed to fit the rounded opening, but retained a rustic look, like the entry to an austere church, or a barn. The latch was hammered metal, and slid into a recess in the wall.

She slid it, and the door eased out toward her. It looked like it should creak, but it didn't.

A soft scent of incense wafted out toward her, utterly unlike the rest of the ship. The room was dark as well. Holly didn't hesitate before stepping inside, and it was like she'd suddenly left the ship and stepped into a comfortable club, or possibly an old opium den. Heavy curtains covered all of the walls, but she could see the glint of daylight through small gaps; Mama Lola could open the curtains and see to port and starboard if she chose.

Holly imagined the windows afforded a reasonable view of the deck as well.

There was a tiny old woman curled up in a chair that looked like a pile of pillows held together by an elaborate wooden railing, looking right back at her. She wore dark glasses, in spite of the dim room, and her hair was artfully dyed henna and curled in a smooth bowl around her head. She was small and frail-looking, but her voice was strong. "Good afternoon, Holly."

"Afternoon," she said and nodded politely. It was a reflex, and she was instantly annoyed with herself for doing it.

"How are you enjoying your time on my ship?" Mama Lola asked. Her voice was high-pitched and firm, curled by an accent that Holly couldn't place.

"It's been an unexpected turn," she replied honestly.

Outside, the wind buffeted the windows, unseen but making its presence known. She scoffed. "*Tssch*. It's a good ship. You should stay here."

"I haven't decided yet."

"You think too much," Mama Lola snipped.

Holly raised one shoulder in a shrug and didn't answer, looking around the room instead. "Captain Hardson said I was free to go if I wished."

"*Tssch*. But you don't *want* to."

"I said I still hadn't decided."

"Maybe we let you off back in Singapore. You'd like that, maybe?" Mama Lola leaned forward in her chair. Her right hand, crabbed by arthritis, moved as though she was walking a coin across her knuckles. "Send you right to execution. You need us."

"Mama Lola," she said carefully, "I know this is your ship, and I will try to be respectful. But if you are going to threaten me, we have nothing to talk about. I am a guest in your home."

Mama Lola laughed. "I do what I want! My ship!"

"As you say. But if you want to talk with me then do so. You don't have to push me. Now, you think that I need you?"

"I think so. You're lost. You don't know how to act unless someone tells you what to do, and you like it that way. You could think for yourself, but you don't want to. You're looking for a home," she said. "And there is one here for you, on the *Fists*. There is no place else for you."

"You think so?" Holly asked again. Outside, a rumble of thunder and a fresh blast of wind gave her words unintended gravity.

"I know so. You will see for yourself. Murrough and Fry are good people and will make a good family for you."

"Why them? Why not one of the other sailors? Maybe I don't want to be part of a triad. Ghosthorse seems interested."

Mama Lola chuckled. "There's not enough of you to be everything to one man. *Tssch.* You're a porcelain doll."

Holly gave her a long look. "I'm leaving."

"Where you going to go?"

"Somewhere else. Even if I loved this ship as much as you do, Mama Lola, I'm a danger to it. They'll find me with my collar."

"Anyone comes for you," she said, waving a hand dismissively, "we fight them for you."

"I don't want you to."

"*Tssch.* Nobody's tracking your collar. Can't be done."

She wondered if Mama Lola was making that derisive noise on purpose, or if it was just a habit. Either way, it was getting on her nerves. "You're mistaken."

"You leave, maybe I throw your friend overboard. Little professor."

"He isn't my friend."

"The Inchin girl then. Your stray. She can't swim so good, I bet, with that hole in her leg."

"I'm leaving your room now. It was nice meeting you, Mama Lola."

She chuckled again. "Liar."

Holly didn't respond, but when she was a few steps away from the door, she muttered under her breath. "It's called being polite," she said to herself but knowing she was audible. "Apparently I know some things that you don't."

She returned to her cabin, and found Hardson standing outside it with a knowing look on his face.

"Were you listening at the door?" she asked.

"I never listen at doors," Hardson said. "She approves of you. You should be pleased."

"I see why she appointed you as her public relations person. I don't need her approval," Holly said.

"Whose do you need, then?" She didn't reply. "Despite what Mama says, I'm not going to force you to stay."

"Ha."

"I know how it sounds." More silence. "Why don't you look at me, when we talk?"

She met his eyes. "If I have another mister, Hardson, it'll be my choice. And if you keep me here, *88 Fists* will be destroyed. If not by the Sino-Indian army, then by me."

"That's quite a serious threat. Don't forget this is my home."

She turned away from him again. "Then don't threaten mine," she said, her voice dropping.

"Do you want me to put you and your friend ashore?"

"Mama Lola just threatened me with the same thing. I honestly don't care right now, Captain. Just...give me...something to do, and pretend I'm not here. Let me cease to exist. Please." She met his eyes again. "Please."

"The world's a poorer place without you, my dear, but as you wish. In that case, we're meeting the *Tobias* as soon as the weather breaks, for a cargo swap. Report to Minnijean. She'll get you with Azzy's cargo crew and you can help them get everything repacked for land travel. And do let me know when you'd like to rejoin the world, assuming it doesn't rejoin you first."

He gave her an expectant look, as though he was waiting for her to ask him what he meant by that. She didn't give him the satisfaction.

The *88 Fists* carried small amounts of cargo for land-bound merchants, and Mama Lola was particular about things arriving undamaged. So, Azzy and a rotating group of crewmen were charged with repacking everything, to ensure that it would survive whatever overland journeys awaited it. Holly spent an afternoon in the *Fists'* cargo hold with chattering crewmen, taking things out of boxes and putting them into smaller boxes. Holly made polite conversation and thought about how far from home some of these items had come, and how prized some everyday goods like toothpaste and ibuprofen were outside of Sino-India.

In the evening, she took a stack of small, unfinished boxes to the dining hall after dinner, joining Shell, Minnijean and Caroline at a table. She couldn't quite get the hang of folding them without ugly creases, so asked for some to practice with, the better to teach her fingers the muscle memory. "Really throwing yourself into it, aren't you?" Minnijean asked with a smile.

"If I'm going to do it, I'd like to do it well," she replied, annoyed. Holly didn't feel as though she'd thrown herself into anything, though. She'd been given a task, and she'd done it. She found herself immediately more concerned about Shell, who seemed to be recovering quickly, but only physically. Shell looked fragile, with narrow, birdlike shoulders and wide hips. Her heart-shaped face had lovely cheekbones under the bruises, and no Cradle's mask.

She was quiet while Minnijean was in the kitchen. When the ship's "mom" left to take a tray of evening snacks down to the children, she opened up to Holly and Caroline about the fear that she'd gotten pregnant during the multiple rapes she'd suffered on the *Silverback*. "I'm late," she said, looking at her bright yellow shoes. "I just know I am. And...I don't know what he'll do." Shell was kneading dough for bread. Caroline, on the other hand, had relaxed quite comfortably into the role of passenger while her leg healed. She wrapped herself in castoff clothes, chopped off most of her hair, and very pointedly and publicly resisted Hardson's attempts to convince her to become the ship's new doctor. Holly liked her for this.

"Dr. Imerlish?" Caroline asked.

She nodded. "His mother sent me to him. She hoped I'd give her a grandchild."

"So tell him it's his."

Shell shook her head. "But he never touches me, not for three years now. Everything is work for him. Everything else is just in the way. The only difference I make is that his home is cleaner."

"There are worse things than carrying a stranger's baby," Caroline said.

"She knows that," Holly said. "It's different for us."

"Why? Because you're domestics?" She frowned, and Holly could almost see her thinking about domestics in a way she'd never considered. Her tone changed, turned more sympathetic. "I suppose it is."

"It depends on what Imerlish thinks is...on what he wants to do. Have you told him?"

Shell shook her head. "He hasn't spoken to me since the other ship."

Caroline looked uncomfortable, and Holly guessed it wasn't because of her healing injuries. "I'm sure he's been busy," she said. "With the data from the formid."

"Aren't you helping him?" Holly asked.

She shook her head. "Even if he asked me to, I don't want to. The man's insane, I want nothing to do with him. I just want to go home. Which, will be an interesting task, since I have no identification or money. The captain says we're bound for Strip City, and I can disembark there. No idea how I'm getting home. Or what the state of my degree is going to be, with my advisor and the rest of the department dead."

Holly thought of the grad students from Hatton's department whom she'd put in a similar situation. "Your family will be glad to know you're alive."

"There is that. Small silver lining, I suppose." Her tone was sour. "I just want to be on dry land again."

Holly was curious about why Dr. Imerlish hadn't spoken to or checked on his domestic, though. The academics she'd worked with could be focused to the point of rudeness, it was true, but she couldn't imagine just ignoring your Shushen girl, especially after what she'd been through and what he must have gone through to save her.

Imerlish had taken over the bunk belonging to Gaptooth Bob, who had died in the fight with the *Vinko*. He spent his days belowdecks mostly, poring over pages and pages of notes and transcribing new ones, trying to get everything entered into his memory pad, whose body had been repaired with tape.

He didn't look up when Holly approached, but said, "Wait a moment," forestalling her from breaking his train of thought. Imerlish wrote for a few more moments, then looked up with a slight frown, as if registering who she was for the first time. "What is it?" he asked.

"You've got a lot to transcribe," she said. "Why isn't Caroline helping you?"

"She's Telwyck's student, not mine," he snapped. "Why would I give valuable research to my chief rival's scion?"

"I apologize, I didn't realize."

"Of course you didn't. I've got quite a lot to do thanks to your captain. I really wish she hadn't shot my specimen and sent her to the bottom of the ocean."

"You don't think she was dangerous?"

"Of course not." Imerlish began writing again. "I told you, there are soldiers and workers, and she was a worker. All she knew how to do was gather supplies and build walls. When those...those filthy, filthy men forced themselves on her, she didn't fight back. The soldiers are larger. The queen's guards...monsters. Fifteen feet long, with jaws large enough to snap a man in half. They're too large to even shift into human form; I'm not sure if there are physical limitations or if they just lack the latent HNE to manage the transformation and survive. I'm the first human in ninety years to see them and live, you know. All they want is to serve the colony. Anything that doesn't threaten the colony is beneath notice. We could learn from them."

"What if they encounter a rival colony?" Holly asked.

"There *is* no rival colony. All of the formids were born of the same queen, the one who mutated and led the revolt in Peru. The formids live in harmony with their world, not that humans are keen to let them go on doing so."

He sounded aggravated, but Holly couldn't quite tell if it was the notion of human xenophobia or something else that was getting him wound up. She attempted to mollify him out of force of habit. "Well, hopefully the knowledge you're bringing back will help people to understand them better, and lead to better treatment."

"They don't want to be understood, that's the conundrum. What they want is to be left alone, but we won't leave them alone until we've been able to learn about them. I understand that now. So many others don't, or won't." He looked up from his tablet and met her eyes. "We are, by nature, an invasive and destructive race. No place, no matter how beautiful and perfect, is safe from us."

"The formids seem to be safe enough." The termite-shifters had held the entire South American continent for a hundred years or more, which Holly didn't need to point out.

Imerlish snorted. "Bah. Ironwood expeditions, lithium hunters, thrill-seekers. I'm sure there's as much traffic on formid shores as there is to any port in Zeeland. The difference is that they fight back. En masse if need be." He shook his head. "You can't fight them face to face. You can't fight them head-on, there are too many of them. There will always be too many of them. The men that Telwyck had with him, mercenaries, they figured this out the hard way. Twenty of them went ashore with us, and the idiots attacked and killed the first worker they saw. We found ourselves facing down two thousand soldiers within minutes. We barely got out with our lives. I believe only four of us made it back to the ship."

"I'm curious now. How did you survive?"

He gave her a grin that showed crooked, neglect-stained teeth. "Camouflage," he said.

Holly found Imerlish's sudden animation interesting; this was the first time he'd visibly focused his attention outside of himself. Of course, he had shifted into teacher mode, just like Elden used to, only he was the condescending sort of professor that she'd always disliked. Imerlish clearly preferred research and his own learning to teaching others. Still, the fact that he was engaging with her made her push back the desire to ask him about Shell for a moment. She raised her eyebrows, encouraging him to continue.

"As I said, the workers are bred to find food for the colony, or to build, or to perform very specific tasks. Anything that doesn't interfere is beneath notice. The formids communicate primarily through percussion, as you saw on the ship." At Holly's nod, he continued. "They also use scent markers somewhat extensively. This is a common eusocial trait. Scent is primarily used to identify colony members from outsiders. From other humans. There was a worker killed during the clash with the mercenaries, and as the others fled, I took the opportunity to retrieve her body. When we returned to the ship, I was able to identify what I believed was her scent gland. I applied the contents to myself and snuck back ashore. I was able to walk right into the colony."

She pictured him smearing a dead formid's innards on himself, and kept the look of disgust off of her face. "And you went in there to study them?"

"Yes, of course," he said. "And to bring back a living specimen. The university was prepared to pay handsomely for a dissectable formid, but considerably more for a survivor. I first set about collecting enough of the workers' food to feed a captive all the way back to Shanghai Ligong. They are socialized only to eat the jelly, you see. Offer a worker anything else and she wouldn't recognize it as food.

"When I had enough, I was then able to learn the habits of the colony and easily capture a worker. If we hadn't been waylaid by the damned pirates, it would have been an easy task to keep her alive all the way home." He smiled again; Holly glanced into his eyes so she wouldn't stare at his teeth. "Telwyck was quite upset that I was going to win the grant, of course. He generously offered to share in my research."

"You declined?"

"What did I need him for? At that moment—and this—there is no one in the world who knows more about the habits and customs of the formid nation than I."

"That's very impressive."

"It is," he agreed. "What I learned would fill volumes."

"Then I'd best let you get back to work," Holly said. "Have you spoken with Professor McEvoy about your experience? His area of expertise is North America but I'm sure he'd be interested."

"I haven't had time to talk to the man," Imerlish said, visibly losing interest.

"What about Shell?"

"Who? Oh, yes, the girl. What about her?"

Holly angled her head. "She was injured during the pirate attack."

"Yes, I know, she suffered a bit of a beating while that man Silverback was trying to distract me from my game so he could gain an advantage." Imerlish's voice didn't change at all. He had started typing again.

"A bit of a beating? She was *raped*. Repeatedly."

"Yes, that too. I'm sure she'll bounce back. She'll be fine. She likes to help out in the kitchen, and makes rather tasty bean cakes—perhaps she could assist you?"

It took an effort to keep the edge out of her voice. She wanted to shout at him, tell him that Shell was pregnant and terrified and that he ought to go and talk to her, but didn't want to violate the girl's confidence. She also wasn't sure what she'd do if he showed the same indifference that he had to everything else. Holly realized that a part of her wanted to hurt him just for being Shell's benefactor. What would Hardson and Fry do if she split Imerlish's skull, or threw him overboard? Would they even care? Holly realized she was clenching her fists, and made a conscious effort to stop, forcing her shoulders to relax, pushing the calmness down to her fingers. "Perhaps," she said finally. "I'll let you get back to work, then. It was interesting talking to you."

He nodded absently, and didn't appear to notice when Holly left.

She closed the door behind her. Up on deck, the sun warmed her face as though she'd been below decks for a year, and she closed her eyes to enjoy it. She heard Razor's boots on the metal grate, so she wasn't startled.

"Did that go as you expected?"

"I don't know what I was expecting," Holly said honestly. Razor's mouth quirked up in a half-smile. "He *saw* everything that happened to her, and it just...didn't register. He's as much a sociopath as that man Silverback."

"He might've shut it out," Razor said. "Certain level of shock and brutality, the brain shuts down just to cope with it. Knowing that if he lost, they'd all die; that might've been just what he had to do."

"Maybe," Holly said. Her eyes were on the sea. "He's still not forgiven. What's going to happen to him?"

"Most likely we'll put him ashore in Strip City. All three of them. Unless the others want to stay. The grad student, Caroline, doesn't seem like she'll stick around. I don't think she's caught the allure of the sea," she added with an amused look. "The housegirl? Who knows?"

"She's not a housegirl, she's a Shushen."

"Sorry," Razor said with an apologetic nod. "Been at sea too long, I don't talk to many domestics. I forget it makes a difference to you guys. Not you specifically, if you don't consider yourself a Myawi any more. You know what I mean."

"I know what you mean. And thank you for noticing."

"Higher training, higher price. I'd want people to recognize that too. There's something regal and respectable about it, you know."

"About what?"

"About being made for something better, but still willing to muck it out in the trenches if necessary. You still have that bearing. That's why Dilly's afraid of you," Razor added with a little laugh.

"Is he?" Holly said, even though she'd noticed.

"'Course he is. You look like you should be standing next to royalty, not on our grubby ship. He's just a farmboy from somewhere in North America, I don't even remember where. He and Ghosthorse go back and forth about you all the time. Dilly's seen the Deshmus on video and it's like he's seeing spirits come to life, I've never seen a sailor so enraptured by them. And you've got that consort-of-royalty look, being a Myawi—former or current."

"After all this time, eh? I suppose I'll have to dirty myself up even worse to fit in, then."

"Good luck with that," Razor said.

Holly watched her go.

When she returned to the room, Marcus was in bed with the blanket pulled up over his head. He didn't react when she said his name softly, but she suspected he wasn't sleeping. "Marcus," she said again. "I revealed some unpleasant truths to you, and I did it in a hurtful way. That wasn't very kind of me. But you should know that, whatever the reasons behind what you're doing, I think it's a good and worthwhile thing." She took his notepad out of her bag, and set it on the pillow near his swaddled head. "Your former colleagues may not be listening to you, but there are plenty of others who would like to hear what you have to say. You shouldn't stop."

He still didn't answer. She returned to the deck, closing the door behind her.

chapter 40

Thirty days before Princess Aiyana's trimester celebration

Shiloh's story

Ivy waited until we reached Nashville to go through the gear we had collected from the crashed Inchin rigs, then traded most of it for supplies while we were there. She didn't seem interested in pursuing that particular mystery any more, and had a weirdness about looking at it at all. I got the feeling when she finally did look at it that she really wanted to be rid of it and forget the whole business.

There were an awful lot of Sam Wards in Nashville. Swan and Kroni were a bit edgy, but Ivy asked around and the vine said they hadn't been causing any trouble or trying to forcibly take any gear, so she settled.

There was a rig that got her interest, though. We traded for some fresh fish (that was my idea) and Swan fried it for us, and we ate near the rig because Ivy said she'd had issues with gleaners last time she was in Nashville. There were four or five other scav rigs parked around the fire near the trade depot, and she just stared at one of them. "That's a Gallamore's rig," she said finally.

That got my attention right away. "What?"

"It was, anyway. There's a cargo box built on the back of it now and the front end's gone, but it used to be the rig that hauled the Caterpillar. I wonder who's rolling it?"

"Are you sure?" I looked at the rig, but it didn't look anything like the big kenny that had hauled one of the traveling show's rides.

"I am," she said. "You can still see the Gallamore's colors on the other door."

I felt myself frowning, and a weird sense of outrage, like whatever scav had rescued the truck after the disaster had stolen something from me.

It made me think of my trailer. I had wondered a few times what might have happened to it. I hadn't been there when it happened, but I saw it afterward, and it was full of blood—somebody got killed inside the thing. When I think about it I miss my trailer, though. It was pretty, and comfortable, and I liked all of my pillows and fluffy things.

That was another life, though, before the horribleness. And the Gallamore rig wasn't a Gallamore rig any more, it belonged to the person who'd found it after it was abandoned. I did wonder who it was, and while we ate I watched it for a bit, until the scav who was driving it came past. He was tall and thin, with long white hair that trailed behind his head like a flag as he walked. He had a beard too, but it was trimmed closer to his face. He climbed up into the rig, then came out again and headed for one of the bars on the square. "Do you know him?" I asked Ivy.

She watched him. "I've seen him before. Don't know his name, though. He's from the southwest, somewhere in the desert, I think."

"Do you think he found the rig, or got it from someone else?" For some reason I was still weirdly offended by the fact that he had it.

"No way of telling," Ivy said incuriously.

"Not our business anyway," Swan said.

I gave her an eye roll. "I know that. I'm just talking. You want to go over to the bar?"

She gave me that half-smile she uses when she's amused. "Going to try and meet him?"

"I don't know, maybe."

"I'm sure if you tumble with him he'll be happy to tell you all about his new rig and how he got it."

"Don't be crass," Ivy said without looking up.

"I don't care that much," I said. "But I do want to see if they have anything fun to eat at the bar. The fish was really good."

"Chess pie," Ivy said.

"What's that?"

"Go find out," she said.

"Yeah, let's go visiting," Swan said. It was never hard to convince her to go out for a drink.

I checked my outfit; it was good, I felt cute enough. I wasn't planning to find a playmate, but you never knew. Swan said, "Come on, Shiloh, your costume's fine," and acted bored.

"You're a terrible stage manager," I told her, and walked past her. She fell into step beside me as we walked away from Ivy's fire. It was a nice night, with no clouds and lots of stars visible. The woods surrounding Nashville were noisy with cicadas, and the town smelled of horses. So many horses—more than rigs or bicycles, by a significant margin.

"I've been to this bar before, it's a decent place," she said. "Good roast beef, if they have any. Usually there's some fellows singing a song or two." I nodded, and she tilted her head at me as we went inside. "You okay?"

"Okay how?" Inside, the bar was pleasantly active without being rowdy, and it smelled of tobacco and unwashed bodies like most of them do.

"After seeing that rig. Might've had bad memories."

"No worse than yours," I said. "You were there when it happened."

She got to the bar before I did and got us a beer each. She knew I didn't like beer but always got me one anyway. "Eh, that wasn't any kind of thing. Bit of noise, a lot of shooting, and rescuing lots of screaming circus girls, the usual accidental heroics in the service of trying to get myself killed. You went back the next day, though. Must've been ugly."

I didn't really want to talk about it with her. Swan could be a good person to talk to every once in a while. She was actually rather insightful when she wanted to be. Trouble was, she almost never wanted to be, and she wouldn't have any problem amusing herself at my expense if that was what she felt like doing. "It was," I said simply.

She was about to say something else, but then she turned away from the bar and bumped into a tallish, red-haired guy with a pair of crooked glasses and a prominent Adam's apple. She started to excuse herself (or insult him), but then looked into his face and stopped dead.

He looked back at her, his magnified eyes blinking, and his voice was barely a whisper as he said, "Vanya?"

Swan put her drink on the bar, then smashed her forearm across his neck and punched him in the solar plexus as he recoiled backward. He doubled over with a strangled, whooping gasp of surprise, and then she hit him behind the ear. He went to the floor in a sprawl, and his glasses fell off. She stomped on them, shattering the lenses. "We have to go now," she said to me.

The man appeared to be unconscious, and everyone was staring at us now.

"Wait," I said. "What did you do?"

"Shut the fuck up," Swan said. She grabbed my upper arm, hard, and pulled me toward the door. I followed so she didn't pull me over.

"Who was that?"

"Which word didn't you understand, Miss Kitty?" she asked as we reached the door. "Shut? Or the fuck up?"

That was the end of bar time for the night. I never did find out the name of the scav with the Gallamore's rig.

chapter 41

Seven days before Princess Aiyana's trimester celebration

Holly was edging sideways to fit through the kitchen door with a serving platter on each hand while Yuying passed her going the other way. This practiced maneuver was only intimidating if she thought about it. The dining room was full to capacity with the entire department. Elden, Dr. Rehsil, Professors Jenoretzke, Aidanab and Hatton, and the rest sat on the left side of the table, where they could see out Elden's panoramic windows. Marcus, Vitter, Dr. Olai from Myawi, and Professor Imerlish were there also, sitting with the staff. The grad students had their backs to the skyline, and Caroline was with them too. Holly had given the guest of honor seats to Marcus and Vitter, so there was plenty of access to the professors.

She served the food quickly and went back for the next plates. Even with herself and six other domestics serving, it was still a task to get everything to the table. She had it under control, though, and was proud of herself.

In the kitchen, Yinka was moving pots from the stove to the counter, dumping the contents down the sink and grabbing fresh ones from the cabinet. "What are you doing?" Holly cried.

"It's not right," she said. "You're doing it wrong, and I'm going to fix it."

"Yinka, we need to serve that food. There's no time to prepare more!"

"I'll do it. Go and tell them that we have to start over," she said implacably.

"This is my kitchen." Holly grabbed a tray of vegetable dumplings from Yinka's hands. "Serve the rest of the course!" Shell squeezed between them to get a platter, then out again without a word.

Yinka ignored Holly and poured out another bowl of soup. Holly grabbed her by the hair and rammed her face into the side of the refrigerator.

Her head cracked open like an egg, blood fountaining garishly, but Holly did it several times more, until gore soaked the ceiling and countertop.

When she let the now-headless body drop, she saw that the food had all been taken out in the meantime and was glad the other domestics hadn't gotten distracted by the drama and violence. They were good at their jobs. Elden called her from the dining room.

When she answered the summons, she saw that they had stripped all of the other housegirls naked and plugged wires into them. Cords ran into their heads, bodies and arms like needles, disappearing into the skin. It looked painful, but Holly knew they didn't hurt. Machines that were like bone-knitters, but for their brains, replaced some of the food on the table. Holly called out to Shmi, trying to warn her to unplug it before they turned it on, but her friend didn't respond. She could hear Vitter and Dineen having a discussion about which program was the best. Vitter was insisting to Dineen that he should be allowed to use his program on Shmi because his housegirl was dead, and sure enough Nielle was there on the floor. The automatic vacuum cleaner was trying to suck up her hair.

"Here's your seat, Holly," Elden said, beckoning her. He had two chairs and two plugs and she heard him say, "I am saving one for Ivy."

Holly protested, but her voice was gone. She spoke, but her words were coming out of the television speakers in the next room, and were easily ignored. She resisted anyway, trying to explain to Elden that she didn't want this. Fingers were pulling at her clothes, peeling her formal outfit off. No, it wasn't someone else doing it, she was doing it herself.

Nielle suddenly whispered in her ear. *"We are what we've done,"* she said, the words burbling in her broken throat, almost cut off completely by her collar which was several sizes too small.

With that, Holly's hands were on Elden's shoulders, and when she squeezed her fingers sank effortlessly into his flesh. She pulled, and he came apart like a paper bag full of innards. Holly went around the room, pulling the cords out of the domestics' bodies and tearing their benefactors to pieces along the way. She barely noticed who they were, and slaughtered the grad students and Marcus as well. The orgy of violence left her covered in blood and torn chunks of flesh. Her clothes were heavy with it, clinging to her body.

Holly stood on the table in the silent dining room. "You're free now," she said to the other housegirls. As the words left her lips she realized they were dead also, crumpled naked and unscathed next to the savaged corpses of their benefactors.

She wasn't sure what she had done wrong, and her friends had never realized she was trying to help them. She didn't have time to think about that though, because the house was a mess and she had to get it ready for Ivy's arrival, which was in less than an hour. Holly climbed down from the table, slipped in the gore and fell into a puddle of pulped flesh on the floor.

She came awake with something like relief, realizing it was a dream. A moment later she was shaking, and she couldn't stop, her hands gripping the metal rails of the bed as if she were being shocked by her collar.

Stop it, she thought. *It was a dream. Stop it. Stop it. Stop it.* She repeated the mantra until the shakes subsided, forcing her breathing back to normal, pushing down the images of her dead friends and ripped-apart benefactors. Before they went away, her mind's eye replaced them with bodies she had actually seen, in Strip City, and on the *Silverback*.

A little roil of nausea took her by surprise; she pushed it down with the remainder of the anxiety attack, reminding herself of where she was. They were four days out of Zeeland. The *Fists* had just arrived in Strip City. They were back in North America. Holly pushed herself out of bed. She supposed, grumpily, that she ought to be grateful she was beginning to relearn how to sleep without her music box.

As the images faded from her brain, she realized that underneath everything else about the dream was a feeling of longing. These parties, the long hours, the gropes and leers and being no more important than any appliance—some part of her *missed* that.

She decided not to think about that any more.

It had been months since she'd escaped Strip City, but Holly asked Razor to drain her collar's battery nevertheless, just in case Vitter or Myawi was still looking. She entrusted the controller to Razor as well, and made a mental note of the time as well, so they could repeat the ugly process every seven hours.

The last week or so of the voyage back to North America from Zeeland had been surprisingly eventful. Nefelibata had flown away before they were in sight of land, saying they were headed farther north than she planned to go. Upon hearing that Shell was indeed pregnant, Dr. Imerlish seemed to lose what little interest he had in her, and announced that he'd return her to the Shushen school and use the trade value to book passage home. The girl had wailed in horror, and Holly actually started forward at the sound of her cry. She wasn't sure what she'd do if she reached Imerlish, but Fry stopped her with a firm, calm hand nevertheless.

"We'll take her off of your hands, Doctor," Hardson said. Before he could protest, he added, "There is the matter of payment for rescue and passage, after all."

Imerlish seemed relieved to have the matter settled. "Yes, yes, of course," he said, and the matter was closed. When they docked he hustled off of the ship, his research bound up in satchels.

"Get his key," Holly reminded Fry. "So you can remove Shell's collar."

"Right, good point. Doctor," she called, and started forward, with a squeeze on Holly's shoulder that told her she should stay right where she was.

She didn't want to look at him any more anyway, and turned to go back to her room. She didn't even want to see what direction he went in. It was all too easy to imagine slipping off of the ship later that night, finding Imerlish's lodging, and plunging something into his throat.

Really, though, going ashore in Strip City might be a sketchy proposition. Not only was it possible that someone would recognize her face, but she might run into someone like Bazell, or even one of the grad students, if they were still in town. Holly assumed that the rest of the department would have gone home after the murders, but it wasn't unthinkable that Vitter had kept them there.

Holly stayed in her bed until that evening, when Fry and Dilly came down to invite her to dine with them. "It'll be safe," Fry said, seeming to read Holly's concerns in her expression. "We're going to the Half Cold Cat. Safe place."

"I don't feel like going into town," she said. "I've been enough times."

"We're just going out to dinner," Fry said. "Just like the first time we met."

Holly gave her a friendly nod, remembering, but the smile didn't quite make it to her face. "You didn't seem to think much of me then."

"I've had plenty of cause to change my mind."

She considered that. "Okay, I'll come."

In addition to Hardson and Fry, dinner was attended by Dilly, the Bonefish, Minnijean, Vadim and Razor. The Half Cold Cat's lopsided walls seemed completely different this time, as though they'd remodeled it completely (they hadn't) and Holly found it cozy. It was the first time she'd been in a place she might call familiar for several months, and she wondered what had changed. She decided that it must be herself; the Holly Aniram that had visited this little restaurant previously was a very different person from the one who saw it now.

And the Holly Aniram of right now still wasn't much interested in self-analysis. "Why doesn't Mama Lola come ashore?" she asked, to turn her mind to something else.

"She doesn't leave the ship," Hardson said simply. His tone discouraged elaboration. He lightened the mood immediately. "She's not the only one though. We come to this place because it's the farthest we can get the Bonefish from the ocean." There was laughter this time, and Holly smiled as well. The hostess brought drinks, and Hardson raised a glass. As he did so, it occurred to Holly that they had invited her, but not Marcus. "We've made it across once again," he said. "Luck and skill, as usual. And there's no crew I'd rather sail with. For what it's worth, you make me proud." Murmurs of agreement went around the table. Holly watched Fry smile at her husband, and it gave her a warm feeling. It wasn't a feeling of belonging, but she liked seeing it.

Fry's eyes came to her. "I never talked to you about what I heard, that you jumped in on the chaingun, back in Zeeland," she said. "After Nyman went down."

She responded with a shrug, not interested in confirming or denying. Fry had had weeks to ask her about that, so she was choosing to mention it now for some other reason.

"I saw her up there. Holly wants to try her hand at every job," Razor said with a grin.

"You could have stayed below."

"Should have," Minnijean admonished.

Holly rested her hands on the table, looked at her fingers. "It seemed like the thing to do," she said.

"How so?"

"Without Nyman at the gun, we could have been boarded," she said. "It was a gap in the ship's defenses."

"That it was," Hardson said. "And I thank you for closing it so skillfully."

Holly downplayed any notions of heroism with a tilt of her head. "Shell and Minnijean tried to stop me from going above deck. I suppose I should have let them. At first I was just thinking to pull Nyman to safety but by the time I got there, he was already dragging himself to shelter," she said, giving the sailor a bit more agency than he'd actually shown.

"Who showed you how to use the chaingun?" Dilly asked.

"Nobody did. It seemed pretty self-explanatory. And there are simple instructions on the side telling you how to reload the belt." She added, "I've had to replace the delivery nozzle of a Sun Dragon printer. After that, this was easy." The others laughed, except for Dilly who frowned as though he wasn't sure if she was making fun of him. "To be fair, Dilly, nobody's shooting at you when you're replacing a printer nozzle. Hopefully. Things can get hectic around finals time, though."

"Finals time?" he asked, even more lost.

She gave him a smile and launched into a brief explanation of life at the university. Almost without thinking about it, Holly fell into entertainment mode, holding the floor just long enough with amusing anecdotes to get the others talking, then retreated to the outskirts of the conversation with only an occasional interjection to keep things spinning. Now that she'd lived with them on the ship, she knew the things that would amuse them, the observations that would keep dinner lively. She hadn't even realized she was picking those things up; it was second nature. The food wasn't bad either. She found herself relaxing.

It wasn't until she realized that she was doing it, she was acting like a fucking Myawi girl at a dinner party, that her mood faltered. Holly didn't let it show on her face or in her mannerisms, but she suddenly wanted to fall silent, to push her chair out and go back to the ship. She wasn't unhappy per se, but she had painted herself into a role that she wasn't sure she wanted to play. Of course, abruptly abandoning it was not only anathema to her entertainers' instincts, but would draw unwanted attention her way as well. So she just stayed on the social ride, letting the conversation flow and letting Hardson and the others feel like they were getting to know her. She got Dilly to blush almost every time she talked to him, she charmed Minnijean, she stopped short of openly flirting with Hardson, but didn't bristle at his gentle come-ons. And when it was over she felt energized and drained at the same time

The group returned to the ship late, but there was a command from Mama Lola awaiting: she wanted them to leave port tonight, to move away from the docks and get out toward open sea. There they'd drop anchor, and then steam north at first light. This didn't seem to surprise the crew; Mama Lola could be mercurial. Hardson made the preparations and *88 Fists* slid out of her berth.

Holly still slept fitfully at best, so she stayed up, walking the deck for a while and listening to the world turn. Now that they were close to Strip City, she could read the news, so she went to the little console in the mess hall to do that as well.

Everything she read seemed to be something Elden would have asked her about, or something she'd have laughed over with Shmi, but she pushed through the bittersweet feelings, trying to get a sense of what the world had done without her in it. It seemed to be more or less the same. It had been some time, so she found pages and pages of reactions to her Ivory Sisters interview floating around. The fallout (other than serious financial troubles for Myawi) was still being determined. Interestingly, there were a number of pundits who, while they stopped short of condoning the massacre (that was what they were calling it, the "Strip City Massacre," and, like Vitter, they were saying that she'd killed six people instead of four: Shmi's name was on the list of dead, as was Marcus'), appeared to understand why she might have done it, based on her interview. There was no mention of the Ivory Sisters. The Myawi school had released several statements, of course. The school's fortunes had taken a hit, but not as serious as had been initially speculated. Having the favor of Sino-India's stars had its advantages, of course, and the most vociferous of Myawi's critics had never been the sort of people who could afford one anyway. There was evidence that new domestic contracts were down slightly across the industry, but it was too soon to tell if the trend was waxing or waning.

Of course people wanted to know her whereabouts, too. The speculation appeared to be that she'd vanished into North America after escaping from her pursuers, intent on finding her sister. Some were convinced that she was dead; others insisted she'd last been seen on a ship headed for Zeeland. There were a few open calls from magazines hoping to talk to her, not sent to any of her or Elden's existing accounts, which would be watched of course, but in the form of tags left on the news articles themselves. Makkhana's interview had only whetted the appetite of the media, and they wanted more of the high-dollar domestic who had risked it all and committed murder to find her sister.

She shut the terminal off. She'd never had much patience for breathless speculation about the latest celebrity or star or war criminal or whoever, and now she herself was turning into one.

Walking away from the electronic words and imagined voices felt good. Once she'd have felt compelled to read it all, if only to keep up with the chatter that the others would be going on about and be able to make informed comments. Now it didn't matter. She touched her collar as she ascended to the deck. She had a few more hours before it went live again. She mused that she was starting to get used to the nerve-frying agony. It felt like...penance.

The deck was deserted, the ship unusually quiet even for a late evening. They were anchored with lights, out of the channel but close enough to it that Holly could easily see another boat sliding slowly past, a sleek, modern hydrofoil. With a bump of surprise, she recognized it from several months back: it was the *Mermaid's Parasol*. The ship Nielle had died on. The pleasure liner was moving slowly, the sound of some sort of on-deck party lilting across the water to her. She could see lights on in some of the cabins, and festive multicolored lights winking all around the rear deck.

Her lips curled in a wistful smile at the sounds of genteel merriment, but she was thinking of Nielle, choking and turning purple as her collar strangled her. Vitter must have known she was associating with the Ivory Sisters and killed her. Perhaps he meant to ferret out her connection, but he'd obviously failed to find Makkhana.

The *Mermaid's Parasol* was slightly smaller than *88 Fists*, and much more delicate-looking. As it drifted slowly past, Holly walked the deck in the same direction, her eyes on the boat, her thoughts moving in a dozen different directions at once. When she ran out of deck, she found herself up on the harpoon pedestal, at the front of the ship.

The smaller boat bobbed neatly through the waves, moving slowly on her hull rather than the hydrofoils, and the sound of conversation from the rear deck echoed to her over the waves. They were so close she imagined she could smell the hors d'ouvres. Bacon-wrapped scallops, or some sort of curry sushi. She thought of the sailors dumping Nielle's body overboard, and imagined a bird sitting outside of its cage, looking in. Then, in a motion so smooth it seemed practiced, she pulled the cover off of the harp and fired it.

The massive harpoon coughed, visible as a white blur in the dark as the cable uncoiled behind it. She had misjudged her aim, and the spear struck the *Mermaid's Parasol* barely two feet above the waterline. Designed to penetrate thick steel, the spear disappeared all the way into the composite hull. A flash of light through the hole suggested that she'd put it into one of the cabins. The music and conversation on the deck faltered, and Holly heard the harsh clack of the harp's head springing open. She turned on the winch to start retracting the harp and saw the *Mermaid's Parasol* immediately lurch sideways as the line tugged her around. The noises of the party on deck were suddenly punctuated by cries of alarm as the boat yawed. Holly ran down the deck to the forward chain gun.

She was aware of what she was doing, and moved quickly and methodically. *Why* she was doing it didn't seem to matter in the moment; it was something she could think about later. Yinka popped into her mind—*just hold her down*—and Holly brutally pushed the thought away.

She reached the gun, put the earphones on, checked to see that the battery was connected and then leaned into the shoulder braces, swinging the muzzle around to bear on the luxury cruiser. She thought of Makkhana saying that Vitter had probably poisoned Nielle himself, and of the crew members aboard the ship who'd treated her death like an inconvenience to the other well-heeled passengers. The doctor who had known it wasn't an allergic reaction. Down on the *Mermaid's Parasol's* deck, crew members were looking over the railing at the damage the harpoon had done, and pointing back at the *Fists*. There was a flash, followed by the faint pop of a pistol.

You want inconvenience? Holly thought, and squeezed the trigger. The report was like an impact, even with the ear protection, and a brilliant orange flare lit up the water between the two ships. Holly couldn't see what damage had been done, or if she'd even hit the boat (though at such short range, how could she have missed?), but the people on the deck were running around like ants now. *I'm sure this is very inconvenient for you,* she thought, and fired again, and again, each shot quicker than the last. The muzzle flashes came closer and closer, creating a strobing view of the *Parasol*, and she could see what was happening now, massive holes exploding in the ship with each new flash. The ship looked like a cake that was being poked repeatedly by a massive chopstick. Fires broke out on the lower decks in at least two places.

There were more muzzle flashes from the smaller craft as the crew took up arms and returned fire. She began to come around, in an effort to keep the retracting harpoon from tearing out her hull. Bullets began thwacking into the deck and bulkhead around Holly, more felt than seen or heard. From the *Parasol's* bow, a larger weapon was brought to bear, and some sort of rocket flashed between the two ships before impacting hard at the harpoon deck, blasting the winch and sending the cable flying free.

With the hot wash of the explosion, she sensed rather than saw the *Fists* coming to life behind her, everyone spilling out from below deck, and she imagined the engineering crew getting the lower bulkheads sealed off. That was their task, to seal the lower decks within two minutes of an emergency beginning. Had it been two minutes yet?

She kept shooting, walking her fire to where the rocket had launched from. The *Mermaid's Parasol's* smooth hull was shredded, and the revelers had fled the upper decks. A second rocket was launched, this one striking the *Fists* just above the water line, and then Holly concentrated her fire on the huddled figures that it had originated from.

There was shouting behind her. She heard Fry yell, "Just *hit* her, Dilly!" followed by a snarl of frustration. Someone grabbed her shoulder—she spun as she came away from the chaingun and got a glimpse of Fry before the woman all but threw her into Dilly's arms, a shove with astounding strength behind it. He caught her roughly and muttered an apology, but his massive arms wrapped around her. Holly didn't struggle against him, and let him hustle her below deck.

He took her back to her room. With the chaingun fallen silent, things were already quieting down outside. The ship had heeled slightly to one side and the engines were grumbling hard; they were on the move and changing direction.

Marcus was up, and pacing, and he stopped when Dilly nudged Holly into the room. "Sorry if I hurt you," he said softly, though he hadn't, and ducked right back out again. He started to close the door, but Fry ducked in first.

"What's going on?" Marcus asked. "Were we attacked?"

"I was going to ask the same question," Fry said. They were both looking at Holly now. "Because I'm not sure I have the whole picture, but when I got on deck, it looked like you were firing our chaingun at a private luxury liner."

"I harpooned it first."

The ship's XO glowered, the flames on her cheeks seeming to dance. "Care to tell us what it did to offend you?"

"I was aboard it once," she replied. Holly had a sense that Fry was dangerously angry, yet she wasn't particularly afraid. Fry would be calm, if she was planning to shoot someone.

"And you wanted to *destroy* it?" Marcus' voice was breathless, like he was conducting an interview.

"Professor, hush!" Fry said, struggling to rein her voice down from a shout. "Holly, listen to me. Whatever your grudges, whatever your feelings toward that ship? *We don't do things like this.* Filth like Silverback does. We don't. We're not like him."

"Maybe I am."

Fry shook her head slightly. "We choose our targets more wisely," she said. "What have we gained, for the ammunition wasted, and the damage we took?"

"Closure," Holly said. Why did she sound so insane?

"Not very nutritious."

Silence fell, and settled in. About ten minutes later, the door opened again, and Hardson came in. His hat was off, and he looked tired.

"What's the verdict?" Holly asked. "Am I being thrown overboard?" The flippancy came unbidden; she was fairly certain they wouldn't kill her, even for this. At worst she'd be put ashore, which was what she had wanted in the first place.

"What did Mama Lola say?" Fry asked.

Hardson shook his head. "She thinks it's hysterical, of course."

She touched the bridge of her nose and closed her eyes. "Once a pirate, always a pirate."

"That's about the size of it. Holly, congratulations. The old woman thinks quite highly of you now."

"That's nice to hear—"

"I'm not sure it's a compliment. I do spend much of my time talking her out of getting us killed, you know."

"I didn't think the *Mermaid's Parasol* posed any threat to us."

"Come on, Holly, you're smarter than that. Think beyond the ship. You're right, there's not much a little ship like that could do if you decided to chew up her passenger cabins with a chaingun—though, I will say, those hand-fired rockets didn't do the *Fists* any favors. She's a very old ship, you know, and I'm sure it'll turn out to be worse than it seems. But that's neither here nor there. What you seem to fail to realize, hot-headed Holly, is that whatever you did to the *Parasol* and the rich folks aboard who couldn't stop you doesn't matter as much as *who might be pissed off about it.* What powerful ship owner have you enraged? What Beijing star lost his nephew or step-cousin on that ship, and who will he pull a favor from to ensure that the navy comes after those who did it? They let us live only so long as we don't force them to deal with us, understand?"

She thought about it for a moment, then nodded. "I understand," Holly said. She still couldn't bring herself to say she was sorry. "Was anyone aboard the *Fists* hurt?"

"No."

"Good," she nodded.

"I doubt we can say the same for the other ship. You knew her name?"

"The *Mermaid's Parasol*. Good."

Fry, Hardson and Marcus all reacted to the anger and bitterness in her voice. "Was it that bad, what they did to you?" Fry asked softly.

"Yes," Holly said. "I have been thinking about that a lot, and it was. Are you putting me off the ship?" She saw Marcus start to speak, and guessed that he was going to ask if he'd have to leave with her, if she did.

"Do you want to leave?" Hardson asked.

The question made her feel lost inside. She wasn't sure if she hid the feeling or not. "I don't know."

"We're not putting you off," Fry said. Hardson coughed and cleared his throat as though he didn't entirely agree, but didn't contradict his wife.

"I don't think I'm going to marry you two, or have babies for you."

Fry reached out slowly and squeezed Holly's shoulder. "Not a condition of staying," she said.

"I'm not going to apologize, either."

"Also not a condition of staying. But please don't do it again. As the captain says, we have a reputation we'd like to uphold." She was smiling with a genuineness that Holly couldn't help but return.

"By Grandpa Rabbit, she smiled!" Hardson laughed, his aggravation seeming to recede in an instant. "If I had known that was what it would take, I'd have found a boat for her to shoot up two months ago!"

chapter 42

Six days before Princess Aiyana's trimester celebration

>> Haichen Qui cheerfully confirmed that he won't be singing at Princess Aiyana's trimester celebration next week. "My wife loves to see me perform, of course," he said in an interview, laughing, "but I think my place will be next to her, on this special night." The Brother Nations' favorite vocalist did appear at a surprise performance in Shanghai. Qui made an unscheduled stop at the Citadel performance venue and took to the stage, delighting hundreds of fans...

—Tinzee's Tea Room

Hardson collected Holly the next morning and took her up to the damaged harpoon deck. Razor was there as well, with Coriander in tow; Holly expected the captain to ask for privacy, but he didn't.

In fact, Razor spoke first. "Bad juju, Cap."

"How bad?"

"*Mermaid's Parasol* was a luxury cruiser. Chariot of rich folks and attendants to stars, mainly. Not the shining ones, but not inconsequential either."

"What's the toll?"

"She sank this morning. The harp tore her wide open, and the chaingun did the rest. We're close enough to Strip City's port that there was a decent rescue effort. Looks like between fifteen and twenty-five souls lost all told, out of seventy-four. And before you ask, yes, they're looking. Not for us specifically, but the crew got a good enough look for a reasonable description."

"Chances of pursuit?"

"Depends on who was aboard. Still hasn't been released. If we were closer to Sino-India, they'd be on us for sure." Razor looked at Holly. "Thank you for not doing this closer to Sino-India. I don't fancy getting blown out of the water by a Silver Dragon rocket."

"Nor do I," Hardson said sternly, looking at Holly as well. "My children live aboard this boat, you know."

"I've already watched you sail deliberately into danger, Hardson. That argument's weaker than you think," she said. "But your point is taken. I will behave myself."

"I hope so."

"I'm doing as well as I can, Captain. I haven't had a good night's sleep in two months, you know."

He met her eyes, gave her a sad smile, and turned away, walking back down the steps to the main deck.

"I think he wants to throw me off the ship," Holly said, turning to face the ocean, "but Fry won't let him."

"More than likely. If it was my ship, I'd have pitched you overboard as soon as that went down." At Holly's surprised look, she raised an eyebrow and grinned. "Of course, I would've been paying enough attention to you that it wouldn't have happened in the first place. I read up on the Myawi music boxes. Cap shouldn't have tossed that. Anyway." Razor stepped lightly up onto the railing and sat there, balanced on the edge. "I lied a little."

"About what?"

"The *Mermaid's Parasol's* passenger manifest. No one particularly important aboard. Though it looks like Professor Imerlish won't be returning to Shanghai Ligong after all." This time Holly's look of surprise got a wink in response. "Good news for you though. Last thing you need is Myawi knowing what ship you're on. They're acting like it's all blown over, but I don't doubt they'd snatch you in a heartbeat if they had the chance."

"Professor Imerlish had been at sea since before the murder," Holly said slowly. "He wouldn't have known who I was anyway."

"I think he'd have figured it out when he got back and talked about his experiences. Which he would have. How'd you find him?"

She decided not to tell Razor it had been a fortuitous coincidence, and tilted her head enigmatically as a response. "What about Caroline...?"

"Still in Strip City. Couldn't afford passage, especially not on a fancy little hydrofoil like the former *Mermaid's Parasol*. I'm sure someone will give her a loan for a ticket, but it'll take a few days."

"We should have taken her home," Holly said.

"Tell that to Mama Lola. She won't be going anywhere near the eastern coast of the Brother Nations if she can help it. Think she's actually pushing

Hardson to head south to Zeeland again, and it's practically a war zone right now. We got out just in time."

"Is Mama Lola really happy about what I did?"

"Wouldn't surprise me. She started out as a pirate, you know."

"I didn't know. Tell me."

A gusty breeze caught Razor's short hair, tousling it. "Thought she'd have told you the whole story when you interviewed with her."

"We didn't really get along. It was a short conversation."

"Eh, better than most get. I told this story to Marcus already, but the short version is that this ship was a military vessel before the Colony Conflict, and continued to be so afterward. Her name was *Barry* back then. She was involved in quelling an uprising in the island region that used to be called Micronesia, which they've been fighting over, island-to-island, for years now. Mama Lola was in one of the cities that the ship was sent to pacify. They rounded up and executed the revolutionaries, and she was there. Said they raised their fists in defiance even as they were shot."

"There were eighty-eight of them, weren't there?" Holly asked.

Razor nodded. "Didn't go as planned. Mama Lola led a counterattack that took the ship, renamed her, and then used her in the short war that followed. It was only about a year before the Indian navy backed off. After that, she kept the ship, and...there you go. It's always been a toss-up whether the *Fists* is a pirate boat or a nautical trade vessel. We go back and forth depending on opportunity."

"So Mama Lola thinks the former, and Hardson the latter."

"That's the equilibrium we live under. It's not bad as it sounds, though."

"So I've noticed. Do you know where we're headed?"

"North," Razor said. "Beyond that, not sure. Cap will want to get away from Strip City, in case there are military ships about."

She allowed herself a rueful look. "They'd come after us for this, wouldn't they?"

"Like a shark scenting blood. Good news for you is that there aren't any."

"How do you know?"

"I have my ways. Cap doesn't always agree with them, or believe me, but the coast should be clear."

"Razor, are you with the Ivory Sisters?"

"The *Fists* is my home, not Sino-India," Razor said. "We don't have domestics here. As you may have noticed. I like to think it's a more stable arrangement."

"It's a nice home," she replied. Her question had been dodged, which was less than a confirmation but more than a denial. Holly filed the information away.

She went below for a while. The mood of the ship was normal; Hardson had made it sound like the crew would be angry with her for putting the ship in danger, but nothing had changed. Minnijean greeted her cheerfully when she went down for a snack, and Holly spent some time in the playroom with the children without anyone questioning her about the night before.

Sometime around the fourth or fifth game of Horses and Chariots, Hardson came to find her. "Tomorrow morning, we're going ashore," he said.

"That's an interesting tone. Should that concern me?"

"You've got nothing to fear. We'll bring Marcus along as well."

She nodded. "What time would you like us?"

chapter 43

Five days before Princess Aiyana's trimester celebration

Marcus was carrying his notepad when he met Holly and Hardson on the deck, and he walked them to the seaplane. She smiled to see him using it, and he returned her smile. "Good morning," he said to the captain.

Holly looked at the plane, and Switch5 inside at the controls. Hardson bade her board first, and she thanked him and climbed inside. "I was beginning to wonder if you ever used this thing," she said, teasing him.

"It's for special occasions. Buckle in, and try not to move around too much while we're on the crane." Once everyone was inside, the crane on the *88 Fists'* deck raised the plane, turned it, and began to lower it into the water. "How are things looking, Switch?"

The pilot nodded.

"Is this a special occasion?" Holly asked.

"It is. I've decided to shoot both of you and throw you in the ocean."

"Captain!" Marcus cried.

Holly just raised an eyebrow, and Hardson and Switch5 both burst out laughing. "I kid, I kid. Oh, Professor, I'm sorry, I couldn't resist. No, I'm taking you to see your sister, Holly."

It was her turn to be utterly gobsmacked. "...what?"

"I did say that I'd assist you in your search to find her," he said. "And I did say that I know plenty of people. Ask the right questions, you get the right answers."

Holly made a noise that didn't qualify as a word. The seaplane thumped into the water with a little splash, and began rocking with the waves. Switch5 started the engine, and she raised her voice to say, "I hope you're not just saying this to see the look on my face."

Hardson nodded somberly. "That, I would not do. I really found her."

She turned to look out the window as the plane began to move. Her eyes threatened to fill with tears, and she willed them back. She watched the surface of the ocean skate beneath them, then drop away, and allowed herself a pleased smile at the feeling of upward and forward acceleration. The *Fists* swung briefly into view as the plane banked.

"Aren't we too close to North America to be flying?" Holly asked, thinking of the EPRC.

"We're in a bit of a hurry. Switch knows to stay low."

Indeed he did. The little plane didn't get much more than fifty feet above the waves before dropping back down, sometimes skimming the tops of the highest waves. Holly had flown before, traveling in the Brother Nations with Elden, but the seaplane had a different, bouncy gait as it fought through the air. It felt as though it was suspended from a string, swinging back and forth, rather than surging confidently through the air. She looked at Hardson, who was looking out his window at the water with a pleased smile, and at Marcus, who looked less happy. He had a sling bag in his lap, and his notepad in his hands. She remembered him saying that he'd gotten in the habit of carrying everything important with him at all times, because he'd lost so many things unexpectedly.

She unbuckled and changed seats to sit next to him. "You look nervous."

"Yes, well. Perhaps I am, slightly. I must admit that your sister and I did not part on the best of terms, let's say."

"What happened?"

"At the time that we met, I felt it expedient to, ah, conceal the nature of my proper origin and the circumstances by which I found myself in North America. Given the widespread lack of knowledge of the colonies, you see, I did not want to find myself attempting to explain to a disbelieving populace that—"

He was winding up to lecture for several minutes, so she interrupted him. "So you lied about being from the colonies."

"Yes. And it seems that scavs place a rather high value on honesty, such that when it did come out that I was not from Norleans as I had allowed Ivy and others to believe, she reacted very poorly. I was ordered, ah, out of her sight without a chance to explain myself. Such as it were."

"I have noticed that you get along with nineteen of twenty people," Holly said, "but that twentieth one, you really know how to upset."

"Quite astute."

"I'll do my best to keep her from killing you."

"I'm sure she wouldn't—"

"You're afraid she will. Even now, talking about it, you've got the same look on your face that you had when you thought I might kill you."

He seemed embarrassed. "Well, you must admit that I had good reason to think that. I meant no insult, of course."

"I'm not insulted. It was a reasonable concern. And a valid one."

Marcus shifted. "Yes, well. In regards to Ivy, I might be a little concerned, yes. It is true that she was under quite a bit of stress at the time, but—"

"Shh. I said it's okay. Leave it."

Marcus nodded. His hand tapped the edge of his notepad. He gave her a look as though he was going to say something about the notepad, but said nothing else for the rest of the short flight.

They landed in a small cove and taxied to a small dock where a rowboat was tied up to the other side. Hardson got out and tied the plane up, then waved in the general direction of a tiny cabin that was almost completely hidden in the woods on shore. Holly followed the direction of the captain's gaze, saw the cabin, and caught a glimpse of a hand in the window, waving back.

The person in the cabin—a fisher, perhaps?—didn't come out as Hardson untied the rowboat and motioned for Holly and Marcus to hop in. He took the oars and they rowed another mile or so up the coast. Hardson sang a jolly-sounding but sad song along the way. It was in Mandarin, about a young woman kidnapped by soldiers and forced to serve in a brothel. Hardson sung with enough of an accent that Holly suspected he had learned the words to sing the song and carry the tune, but not what they meant. She didn't tell him.

The wooded shore gave way quickly to sprawling, sandy beach. Hardson brought them in and pulled the boat ashore, taking care that only he got his feet wet. "Are you ready?" he asked Holly. She nodded, and the three of them set off walking up a long, hilly beach. Holly looked at her feet, her Wing boots digging into the sand, occasionally coming down on a tuft of beach grass or a hank of dead seaweed. Her heart was pounding, and she didn't want to look up, or look around. A part of her told herself that Hardson had to be mistaken. Surely if Ivy was alive, and nearby, she'd *know* somehow—

And then Holly looked up and saw her. It was like a bump of simultaneous déjà vu and unreality. She realized that until this moment, looking up the beach at a slightly distorted mirror version of herself and a few other figures in the background blurring into inconsequentiality, she hadn't really *believed* Ivy existed, hadn't really considered the reality that her sister was alive.

And yet, there she was. Ivy broke into a shambling run toward her, favoring her left leg, and Holly matched the speed, leaving Hardson and Marcus behind. She ran, covering the distance in what felt like an eternity and a heartbeat all at the same time, and then she stopped.

Ivy was thin, her face hollow and smudged with dirt. Her hair was chopped short, pushed up at awkward angles by the goggles on her forehead, and bleached by the sun. And she had dots drawn high on her cheeks. Holly remembered—their mother had put them there, on the left for Holly and the right for Ivy, so that the other members of their caravan would know which twin was which. But Ivy was wearing one on each side.

Without even thinking about it, without a moment to wonder what she was going to say, Holly licked her thumb and wiped the dot off of Ivy's left cheek, leaving a clean spot. "That's mine," she said.

What happened next was something like a hug and something like a collision and it felt like being immersed in a perfectly warm tub after a long, difficult day. They had their arms around each other and for a moment Holly wasn't sure where she ended and Ivy began. Ivy smelled of oil and metal and mechanical things underlaid by dust and a tang of ground-in sweat, and Holly felt a staggering wave of love pouring off of her that she wasn't sure she deserved and hoped she could reciprocate. It was the most wonderful, overwhelming feeling, and they knelt in the sand and enjoyed it, even when the soldiers surrounded them with guns and ordered them to their feet.

Holly snapped back to reality in an instant. Where had they come from? There was little time to question; as they stood, heavy gloved hands seized them and pulled them apart. This caused Ivy to erupt like a badger in a snare. She twisted against the clutching hands, pulled toward Holly and dragged both of her captors several steps across the beach. Holly turned against the grip and broke free of one of them, reaching for Ivy's hands, but a fierce yank snatched her backward. The soldier twisted her arm into a wrist lock and slammed her down, driving her face into the sand. Holly aspirated a mouthful and coughed, spluttering to clear her face. When she opened her eyes Ivy had broken free of her captors and was charging toward them with a spike-ended hammer in one hand. Before she could smash it into the side of someone's skull, a fourth soldier tackled her from the side, hard enough that both of them were smashed right out of Holly's field of vision. The hammer flew out of Ivy's hand, spinning wildly in the air before thumping impotently to the sand.

A voice was screaming, "Don't hurt her! Please no don't hurt her!" in English and in Mandarin. It was her. Holly realized she was screaming, and a Myawi *never* screamed, but she still didn't stop.

chapter 44

Holly leaned against the clear plastic wall of the cell, pressing her cheek as close as she could to Ivy, who was doing the same. Her sister was shaking slightly, no doubt from the unfamiliar surroundings as well as the shock of their reunion and sudden capture. Holly's heart pounded as well. They were in a bad place. A very bad place. She was nervous, but Ivy looked like she was hiding feelings of being downright terrified, and Holly didn't think this impression was just because she was so thin, a gaunt, skittish-looking version of herself. It wasn't hard to imagine that she'd never been in a cell like this, or imagined a place like this, having spent her entire life out in the dirt. The textures would be wrong. The smells would be wrong, and the sounds as well. It was a miracle perhaps that she wasn't incoherent and pounding at the walls screaming.

"Ivy," she whispered.

That got an immediate smile.

"What I've gotten you into...I'm sorry."

"You haven't gotten me into anything," Ivy said. "I've had so many run-ins with the Sam Wards this past year...and the Inchin soldiers, we fought them too. I didn't realize they were working together, or that things weren't scaled with them."

"Scaled...you had trouble with them before?" They were talking quietly, but Holly noticed that Hardson was watching them, standing as close as he could to the wall of his own cell.

Ivy nodded. "A lot of travelers ran into trouble with Sam Wards, since we're the ones out there most. I've had at least five. I suppose they've started remembering who I am."

Holly shook her head. "Not this time. They were chasing me. The man

who led them, I know him. He's been chasing me since...I killed my benefactor. It happened a few months ago."

"I know."

"You know?"

Ivy smiled. "I dreamt about you. I was there."

"You...were there?"

She nodded and smiled. "You choked him with your hair."

Holly's eyes filled with tears. "I think I dreamed about you too, Ivy.
But I didn't know."

"Didn't know?"

"Didn't know it was you. I..." She couldn't tell Ivy that she'd forgotten
her, or that she'd assumed she was dead. The words wouldn't come out.
"You were driving once...in the rain. Trying to pull another truck with a
rope, but it broke."

"That was the day Mr. Morse died," Ivy said. "Not the best day to
share. Sorry about that."

She sounded rueful but amused at the same time; Holly guessed that
she was just happy to be close, no matter the circumstances. She'd spent
her whole life searching. Holly was joyous as well, but the feeling wouldn't
come to the surface. There was frustration in that: for years she'd had no
problem slipping into a social and welcoming mode for people she didn't
care that much about, and now Ivy was here and she could barely muster a
genuine smile. It was better to change the subject. She wanted to ask about
the other people traveling with Ivy, but the cameras at either end of the
hall might be wired for sound, so giving anything away could be a bad idea.
There was a way to find out, though. She met Ivy's eye, glanced meaning-
fully at the camera, and said, "I'm so glad you got my message."

Ivy nodded, but when she said, "Yes. Meet at Mother's favorite place,
you said," she wasn't at all convincing. It was good enough, though. Holly
had a feeling that she'd be talking to Vitter later, and if he mentioned contact between herself and Ivy, then they were hearing the things they said.
Having made her statement for the benefit of the cameras, Ivy looked at
Holly with a tiny, mischievous grin. "You talk funny, you know."

"This is a strange ship," Hardson said, raising his voice to be heard
across the hallway.

"How so?"

"I've never seen or heard of it, for starters. And it looks like a hospital
ship, apart from the color and flags."

"Could it be a floating hospital?" Ivy asked.

"I doubt it. T'would be better marked if it were. And that doesn't explain the sailors. They were awfully well-armed for naval nurses."

"Hm." Even in this situation, Holly found herself getting irritated with Hardson quickly. It seemed that she had less and less patience for him with every interaction.

When he spoke again, she realized instantly that he wasn't addressing her, by his tone. "My manners fail me. You are, I presume, heavenly Holly's twin? I am Murrough Hardson, captain of the *88 Fists*."

"Yes, sir. Ivy Aniram."

"Forgive me. I'd kiss your hand if circumstances permitted," he said, indicating the walls that separated them.

"That would be a ridiculous thing to do. You don't know where my hands have been," Ivy said.

He laughed; Holly watched Ivy's face, her eyes drawn to the scar on her sister's temple. She wondered how it had gotten there, what had marked her. "You land travelers aren't as dirty as you're reputed to be," Hardson said with a purring laugh. "Your sister has been our honored guest and crew since the incident in Strip City, and I'm glad to meet you."

"I'm not on your crew," Holly said.

"As you seem to delight in reminding me."

"Thank you for keeping her safe."

He bowed. "I've done my best...at some cost."

"You are *not* negotiating a finder's fee," Holly said, her voice taking an edge.

"It's okay," Ivy told her, meeting her eyes then looking back to Hardson. She pushed herself to her feet with some difficulty, her knee brace binding up a bit, then faced Hardson, whose cell was directly across the hall from hers. "You talked to Jonathan Connally, I presume?"

"I did. He told me of your search."

"And how long it was?"

Hardson merely nodded.

"Then we're in your debt. What do you require?"

"Ivy, don't." Holly realized with a jolt what hadn't occurred to her til just now—they were both fertile. The idea of both her and Ivy being married to Hardson and Fry raced through her head. Elden had wanted the same thing, or something similar. Interestingly, with Ivy here, it seemed like less of a nightmare.

"It's okay," she said again, patiently. "Captain?"

"There was a great deal of damage done to the *Fists*," Hardson said.

He gave Holly a look, and she felt simultaneously uncharitable for assuming that he'd put the marriage idea back on the table as soon as the chance arose, and disappointed that he wasn't so smitten with her that it was the first thing he thought of. "It happened as a direct result of her actions, and it's significant."

Ivy glanced down at Holly, who was still sitting on the floor. "I have some repair skills. Never worked on a ship before."

"We have our own mechanics," he said. His smile was gentle, the same one he used when talking to his children. "I suspect, though, that the ship's too far gone this time. We need a dry-dock, certainly to fix the hull damage, but we also need things we can't acquire. She's an old ship, and her heart is going."

"So...what do you need from us?"

Hardson was silent for a long moment. "I honestly don't know. But now you know the situation I'm facing. Perhaps you'll think of something. I have seventy-three souls looking to me to keep their home functional and safe, and..." he trailed off. "That may not be possible."

"I'm sorry," Holly said. She was looking at her feet.

"It's not on you. Recent events haven't helped, to be sure, but this was in motion long before you came to us. Her turbines are beyond old, and new parts?" He shrugged. "I doubt Sino-India would sell them to us, given the *Fists'* history. And in her current condition, I don't even know if she could make it there. She needs to be beached for repairs, and for a ship like the Fists, that sort of a temporary drydocking is often...permanent."

"I'll think of something anyway," Holly said. The thought of the crew having to disperse, living and working aboard other ships, was terribly sad, and she didn't want to see that happen.

"Perhaps it's karma, for tossing your music box overboard," he said. She thought at first he was being facetious, but the look on Hardson's face suggested he was serious.

"We'll scale it," Ivy said softly, speaking more to Holly than Hardson.

"Hard to do when we don't even know where we're going," she replied. "No place good, I'm sure."

As if on cue, Vitter appeared at the end of the hallway. He walked with casual purpose, almost an amiable stroll, the confidence of a man who had never been disagreed with. The two sailors behind him looked considerably more on edge, hands on their guns, and they remained several paces behind him. When Vitter reached Holly's cell, he touched a thumb-sized key card to it and the door sighed open. "Walk with me, Holly," he said. "Talk with me."

"Not without my sister."

"She can join us in a moment."

Holly didn't move.

"Or, if you'd like, I could have her thrown overboard. Or the cervid. Or their exceedingly unpleasant friend. It's quite a long way to shore." He addressed Ivy. "How well can you swim with that knee brace?"

"Don't," Holly said. She stopped herself from saying *please*. "Don't threaten her. I'll come." She started toward the door. Ivy got to her feet and put a hand on her own cell wall, but said nothing. Holly pressed her hand to the same spot. "I'll be chattier if she's there, though."

Vitter looked at both of them carefully. "Noted," he said, then smiled suddenly, a wolfish grin that made no pretense of being friendly, and stepped aside in an "after you" gesture. Holly went.

The first sailor led her down a couple of decks to a small room that appeared to have been converted from a small medical examination room. She noticed that he stayed well out of arm's reach, which she found amusing. The room was windowless, the walls featureless metal. An examination table was bolted to the wall, and three chairs lined neatly up next to it. Vitter paused long enough to hand his sidearm to one of the sailors, pulled a chair out for her, then sat on the exam table, regarding her with that same quirked smile. He nodded to the men behind her, and the door closed behind the sailors as they left the room.

He was keeping out of arm's reach as well. "I'm not in any danger from you, am I?"

"Not as long as Ivy remains safe." There was no use in pretending that he couldn't use her sister to get to her; best to make it an up-front thing.

"Hurting her is the farthest thing from my mind," Vitter said. "I find conversation preferable to torture or coercion."

"Tell that to Shmi."

"I can't very well do that, since she drank all of that toilet water, now can I?" His expression softened, and he shook his head. "That morning did not go the way I hoped. That Myawi Protector Anshul...he's an ape. He reminds me of all the reasons the military prefers not to use HNE-enhanced soldiers. Sadistic and uncreative when provoked."

"You didn't stop him, either."

"I don't believe that you know what happened at all; you were running away at the time, and witnessed nothing. Now, please don't interrupt. I'm quite surprised to see you, you know."

"Are you?"

"I am. I'd really like to know what's going on. Why the assassination attempt? Why have you returned? Tell me about your friends."

"I have friends?"

"Oh yes," he said. "You are *quite* popular. Why did you come back? Who directed you to attack that ship, and where did you get military hardware? Please don't answer my question with another question."

"It was a spur of the moment decision," Holly replied, guessing that Vitter would assume she was still being flippant.

She was correct. He shook his head slowly in irritation. "Who was your target?" Holly said nothing this time. "I can tell you didn't expect this," he said. "Such a rapid response. Do you know where you are?"

"The ocean, I'd imagine."

"Be respectful, and please don't underestimate me. You won't trick me as easily as you did your benefactor."

"I suppose I won't," she replied. Ignoring the impulse to apologize was getting easier.

"The captain of course has his own agenda, and I'm sure he'll have his own questions. You can talk to him as you see fit, I suppose, but I'd prefer that our conversations remain amiable and honest."

"That seems reasonable. We didn't have a chance to talk much that night I made dinner. What would you like to talk about?"

"My interests are quite simple, actually. I need to know what your goal is, and who's sending you toward it."

"That is so much more complicated than you know."

He smiled that wolf's grin again. "Is it?"

"I think I'd like to have my sister with me now."

"In a few minutes."

"No. Now." Holly closed her eyes and sat still, imagining herself turning into a ceramic doll. Vitter could do what he liked to her. She wondered if he knew that she'd been tortured before, that sadist Rehsil hurting her for sport. She hadn't cried out for him and she wouldn't scream for Vitter either.

He was silent, and she tried to imagine what he was doing, to hear his motion. He shifted on the bench, then sighed. After a moment he said, "Very well," and went to the door to speak with the sailors.

chapter 45

Chancellor Mahnaz was agitated and peevish. A clumsy and failed attempt at morning sex, after which Shiloh tried and failed to downplay her disappointment, probably didn't help matters. Once dressed, he paced the room. Shiloh was in a bit of a funk too. She wasn't attracted to him and hadn't particularly wanted sex until he'd pawed at her, but he'd been unable to get it up and now sex was all she could think about.

"Anna, this is unacceptable." He waved a hand immediately in her direction. He spoke with the same clipped accent as Vitter and the others, now heightened by annoyance. "Tchaa, I know it's not your fault. We would have been late even if we hadn't stopped to rescue you. But I should have been in Singapore two days ago. This delay is not good."

"You'll arrive in time for the trimester celebration, though?"

"I will, with a day to spare. But Princess Nipa...she's already in Singapore. I'm her chokidar. It is my job to keep an eye on her—she can be a rash child—and I am not there. Obviously the reasons for my delay are understood, but..." he paced. "She will be intolerable. Her father will confine her to the house if she has no one to watch her."

"He can't watch her himself?" Shiloh asked. She put her hands between her knees and squeezed them together, flexing her feet and trying to keep her mind on the moment. There wasn't going to be morning sexy, not even bad morning sexy, and that was how it was. She could accept this, but it was angry-making.

Mahnaz didn't stop pacing, but gave her a patronizing smile. "Of course not. Pravit has too many other matters to tend to on such an occasion. Nipa is sixteen, she's no child of course, but she still need supervision." He pounded a fist into his hand. "Rabbit's mortar, this is my *duty!* The girl will be incorrigible!" It seemed like a bad idea to ask him why someone else couldn't do it for him, but he answered the question anyway. "I have been Nipa's chokidar since she was eight. There is no one else for this job."

"I understand. We'll be there soon, though. And when we get there, I can help."

"You're right, of course," he said with a smile. His eyes lit up. "She might like meeting you. The princess loved the circus when she was a child. Loved the performers. She wanted to be a horse-rider once." Mahnaz pushed his glasses up his nose and ran a hand over his greasy face, his expression shifting from one of frustration to satisfaction like he'd pulled a blind. "Let's go talk to the captain and get an update on our arrival. Soon we should be getting into radio range, and I can let them know I'm close."

He opened the door and stepped out into the hall, and Shiloh followed. She absorbed a touch of the chancellor's puffed-up, self-important air. The sailors sneered at them behind their backs, but she was playing the part of his girl-toy. She made eye contact with at least one of them, sensing more than seeing the cut of his shoulders under his uniform, and the sexy thoughts started to creep in again. She did her best to push them down.

Captain Yang was on the bridge, as was Vitter, and Shiloh was surprised to see Captain Hardson there as well. He was shackled at the wrists, and Vitter held a phone to his ear. Hardson was chatting with the person on the other end, Vitter watching him very carefully as if dissecting every one of his words.

"Captain—" Mahnaz began, and Yang cut him off with an impatient wave. The chancellor huffled and looked at each of the other sailors on the bridge in turn, saw no allies, and shut his mouth.

After a moment, Vitter said, "I think that's enough," and took the phone away from Hardson. The *88 Fists'* captain didn't protest, and stopped talking immediately.

"Thank you, good sir," he told Vitter. "I think you'll find my crew much better behaved now that they know I'm alive and healthy. My first mate, Dilly, will cooperate fully with your men."

"Remarkably chipper for a man who's most likely bound for prison."

"I see no reason to be unpleasant," Hardson replied. "I shall save that for those who deserve it. You're just a man doing his job. Isn't that what we all strive to be?"

"I hope your good will is sustainable," Vitter said.

Mahnaz was sick of waiting. "Captain Yang, can you *please* tell me approximately what time we can expect to arrive in Singapore?"

Shiloh saw a look of intense annoyance shoot across Vitter's face. Mahnaz didn't, but she wasn't here to keep the man from embarrassing himself so she said nothing. Vitter clapped Hardson on the shoulder, nudging him toward two sailors who took him off of the bridge. Once they had left, he turned to Mahnaz. "Now, Chancellor, that you are *not* about to reveal details of our destination to enemies of the Brother Nations, what can I do for you, rather than disturbing the crew of this ship?"

"I can't imagine you'd be particularly concerned about what a man bound for the death penalty might overhear."

"And it's not your job to be concerned about that; it's mine."

Mahnaz puffed himself up a bit. "You're correct, that is not my job. What *is* my job, is to see to the needs and safety of Princess Nipa Deshmu, who is at this moment waiting in Singapore for me. I would like to know when we are likely to arrive."

"About twenty-four hours, I am told by our captain," Vitter said, not bothering to hide his impatience. "Right on schedule in fact. Aerial transport will be dispatched to transport you and your entourage as soon as we reach the harbor. And we do apologize for the inconvenience of saving you. I am fully aware of your importance; the *Excelsis* is not a ship that's diverted to rescue duty lightly."

The sarcasm went right over Mahnaz' head. "I am grateful. I will be glad when this ordeal is over. And what I've been through is nothing compared to Anna's experience."

Vitter shifted his attention to Shiloh. "Will you be accompanying Chancellor Mahnaz in Singapore, then?"

She made herself sound as miserable as she could. "My family was the circus. They're gone now." There was a lot of real feeling in her words.

"Mr. Vitter!" Mahnaz snapped. "Of course I'll be hosting her. It's not necessary to be cruel."

"I apologize. You must understand, Miss Vienna, that I wasn't hired for my interpersonal skills," he added.

Shiloh thought that he most certainly had been, only not in the way people might expect; she nodded and murmured that it was okay. "I need to exercise," she told Mahnaz.

"Of course. It's very bad for athletes to be cooped up on a ship like this," he told Vitter. "She must train almost constantly." It was an effort not to snort laughter, thinking of all the time she and the other performers had spent in Gallamore's trailers, traveling from city to city. Being cooped up was a part of traveling circus life. She didn't contradict him, though, and took her leave.

Shiloh lay low for the day, splitting her time between jogs (she passed down the hallway where they were keeping Hardson, Holly and Ivy twice; the first time all three of them were in their cells, the second it was just Hardson and he was asleep) and napping in Mahnaz' bed. She really wanted to practice one of her own routines, though she didn't have a hoop handy, but worried that if someone had heard of Anna Vienna's act, they might realize she was doing something entirely different. She skipped dinner, citing exhaustion and ennui, and dozed until Mahnaz returned, failed a second time to fuck her and fell asleep.

She lay awake, staring at the ceiling. His heavy arm lay across her belly, his thigh pressed against hers, and the sensation of skin on skin was at once maddening, because she wanted to be touched, and repulsive, because of who he was. Slowly, carefully she wriggled out from underneath him and went into the bathroom. Shiloh slid the door closed behind her, sat on the floor of the tiny shower stall, propped her feet against the wall and masturbated angrily.

It took the urgency out of her desire, but wasn't enough to make her sleepy, so she went to visit Shamshoun. There was a new occupant in one of the cells: a badly-beaten Kroni. He lay curled up on the floor with his back to the hall, and didn't move when she came in.

"Still fighting with the others," Shamshoun said by way of explanation. "The cervids don't get along."

"I know," she replied. "I know him."

The ursid gave a slow nod.

"It's good they took him out. The others were killing him."

"This upsets you."

"There's some reason it shouldn't?"

"Apologies," he said, bowing his head slightly. "It should. There is more than that though. It feels as though the song is about to change."

"Maybe it is. We're not far from Singapore now."

"I will miss your stories."

"I have to do something before then," she said.

"And what will you do?"

Shiloh slid down the clear wall to sit on the floor. "I don't know. My moment hasn't come yet."

"Perhaps you should make one."

"I'll know when it's time," she said, shaking her head.

"Yes. You will."

"I won't last long there, will I? In Singapore. Mahnaz says there's a big event going on. The trimester party. He's frantic about it. But...there will be security, and they'll know. About me."

"Almost certainly," Shamshoun said. "The Sisters won't want to get involved, but they may be willing to tell you how to get underground. There are ways to hide."

"What do I do? Who are the Sisters?"

"The Ivory Sisters. They help domestics, and sometimes shifters. Until you find them, don't shift. The government can track the energy, can see it flare. Try to get braces."

"Braces?"

"Sharp eyes will know what you are by the way you move. There are those trained to see. The braces change that."

"Where do I get them?"

"From the Sisters," Shamshoun said.

Shiloh wanted to complain that this wasn't as helpful as she'd hoped for, but it was the best Shamshoun could do. "Thank you. What would you like to hear about tonight?"

"Not a good night for stories. The watchman's been making extra passes."

"Has he?"

He nodded. "Getting close to home now. Running a tighter ship. And they're nervous."

"Why?"

"No telling. Perhaps it's the party. The air has been pulled tight."

Shiloh nodded. She hadn't felt anything out of the ordinary in the mood of the ship other than Mahnaz' stress. "I'd better go."

"Yes, you'd better. Farewell, friend." He shifted, and touched his nose to the clear plastic. She was struck by an urge to return the favor, to let him see her cat form, and that was utterly out of character for her but somehow seemed right. Instead, she kissed her fingertips and touched the door next to his nose, then padded back into the main hall.

One turn later, she almost ran into the sailor on duty for the night; another thirty seconds and he'd have caught her talking to Shamshoun.

He startled backward, and she mirrored him. "Forgive me, miss," he said, and bowed.

She found the gesture charming, and smiled at him. "It's okay. I couldn't sleep, so I was walking..."

He nodded. She saw his eyes drop down to her chest, almost reflexively, then back to her face, then back down again. "It's...it does get quiet on the ship at night."

Shiloh looked into his eyes, maintaining the smile. "We could be the only ones awake," she said.

"Just about," he replied. "Skeleton crew, with most of the guards over on the captured ship."

"So you've been working extra?"

He nodded.

"That's...that's awful. What's your name?"

"Tomas, miss."

"I'm Anna, Tomas."

He was looking at her tits again, and she let him, raising her chest slightly. "I...I know."

Capitalizing on someone else's fame was curiously annoying, but she did her best to look flattered. "Can I walk with you?"

He stammered again, then nodded.

It wasn't difficult after that. Shiloh walked with Tomas for a circuit of the ship, chatting aimlessly and stroking his ego, and partway through the second round she pulled him into the empty mess hall and shoved her hand into his pants. He responded without hesitation (and with much less clumsiness than Mahnaz) and she did him standing up, just inside the doorway. After he came it was equally easy to lift his keycard from his belt. Shiloh realized she could do it, then did it and told herself it was what she'd intended to do all along, though really she'd mostly been wondering if she could get away with a quickie now that they were close enough to shore that word probably wouldn't get too far. He kissed her forehead and thanked her, cupping the back of her neck with his free hand, and she relaxed into the contact, humming with pleasure. When they disengaged, the moment dissolved and his awkwardness returned; he was grateful when she excused herself for bed, and didn't notice that he'd lost his passkey. With luck it would go unnoticed for a while.

She slept wonderfully.

Shiloh waited for much of the next day, waiting until Vitter sent a sailor to tell Mahnaz that their transport was on the way. He was one of the ones who'd been sitting with them at lunch—Burdick, that was his name.

The chancellor looked out the porthole and saw only sea. "We're not to shore yet."

"No, sir, we'll be about twenty miles out when the copter meets us."

"Are we not docking? Why so far away?"

"It is bad enough that we have brought the *Excelsis* this close to the city with so many important people here," Burdick said archly. "Do you have any idea what would happen if they knew how many shifters were aboard?"

"Ridiculous. They're locked up securely."

Burdick rolled his eyes; now that the trip was almost over, the hostility no longer needed veiling. "This ship isn't even supposed to *exist*. You'll need to be ready to leave as soon as the copter lands," he snapped, and stepped briskly out of the room.

Mahnaz looked after Burdick for a moment, as though he realized he'd missed something and couldn't figure out what it was, then took an ornately carved bright wooden box from his luggage. He set it on the table and opened it, revealing a glowing screen inside. He brightened when it chimed at him.

"Excellent, I am tied into the grid again." He started tapping at the screen as though trying to remove something that was stuck to it. Shiloh saw that he was reading.

After a minute of silence, she said, "I'm going to go run then," just to get his attention.

Mahnaz nodded absently. "You go along, I'll meet you later. If you see Dorim, would you let him know I need him?"

She gave him a little pout, but being left alone was exactly what she wanted. She made her usual circuit, and found Shamshoun and Kroni where they'd been the day before. Holly and Ivy were missing from their cells again, but Hardson was there. He gave her a jaunty salute as she came down the hallway. She stopped in front of his cell and met his eyes.

"They're with the smart man again," he said. "I believe he takes them to lunch almost every day. Hard to say whether he's interrogating them or trying to date them."

Shiloh nodded. Her heart pounded. This was the point of no return, the first step out onto the stage. Time to push back uncertainty and stage-fright; the show was happening now. She took Tomas' key out of her pocket and waved it in front of the cell door, where the latch was. A light gave a little green flash and the door popped open a fraction.

Hardson raised an eyebrow. "So Ivy was right."

Shiloh nodded. "We're close. They're sending someone to pick up Mahnaz and me. I have to find the others," she said.

"But of course you do. Shall I accompany you?"

"I think I'll be safer by myself. If they see you..." she let the thought hang. "But maybe I'll see you after?'

"Perhaps," he said, grinning.

Shiloh left him then, her heart pounding. She needed to find Swan, and guessed that she might be in one of the deep cells. After that she could come back up and free Kroni and Shamshoun, and maybe Holly and Ivy would be back in their cells as well.

She was passing through the shifters' general-population area when she realized that Hardson might create some sort of chaos, and she wouldn't be able to get back up to the cells easily. Of course, if he did that, he might free the others himself. Would he release Kroni and Shamshoun, though? He didn't know them, only Holly.

She pushed the thoughts out of her head. She couldn't worry about anyone's part but her own. She was through the shifter hell quickly, but this time instead of turning to go through the crew's quarters, she stopped before the locked door. Shiloh hesitated. If they caught her beyond it, she could tell them she'd found it open. They might believe her.

She swiped the key, and the door popped open just as easily as Hardson's cell had. The hallway beyond was painted the same featureless grey as the rest of the ship, but it seemed heavier, as if the very metal were thicker. The lights were a different, colder hue, and the shift in mood seemed intentional. The doors had mechanical deadbolt locks and heavy metal doors, and it smelled more overtly of fear and blood. The rooms on either side of the hall were larger than the individual cells, and several had operating tables in them. In the second one she passed, a dead and dissected man lay on the metal table. In the third, there was a large dead dolphin. Shiloh looked away and kept moving forward. There appeared to be eight rooms, and the doors were closed at four of them. The last, at the far end of the hall, was open and Shiloh froze as she realized there were voices coming from within. She debated whether she should duck into one of the empty rooms, risking being trapped if someone should close the door, or if she should go back, get out of the hall entirely. Before she could decide, there was a shout and a thump from the open door at the end of the hall, and Shiloh recognized Swan's voice.

She rushed forward without thinking, was halfway through the doorway before realizing she was being an idiot.

Of course by then it was too late. There were four men in the room with Swan; three sailors including Burdick and Captain Yang, and all of them looked up when she rushed in. "Oh, joy, it's *you*," Swan said. Two of the men were holding her arms. Her left hand and right foot were ruined masses of pulped flesh. The injuries were scabbed, not all of them fresh.

The captain glanced at Shiloh with a raised eyebrow. "The door was open..." she said softly.

"Of course it was." It was impossible to tell if he believed her or not. "Have you come to watch?"

"Gonna fuckin' drown me," Swan said. Her voice was husky and rough and she sounded like she was completely out of her mind. She wrenched her uninjured arm free and grabbed Burdick's beard, pulling him off-balance and then cuffing him hard on the side of the head with her mashed hand. "Go out and close the door, Miss Fluffy. I ain't leaving."

"Silence! Miss Vienna, if you could please—"

Swan laughed. "You idiot! That ain't Anna Vienna, that's—"

The third sailor swung a truncheon and caught Swan right across the mouth. Shiloh heard teeth break with an awful, wet grinding sound. The sailors released her arms, and Swan folded to her knees, semi-conscious.

Yang shrugged, adjusting his coat with his shoulders. He glanced at Shiloh, dismissing her with his eyes, and walked over to where Swan knelt. "I told you to be silent," he said.

Swan snapped her head up so fast that runnels of blood flew out of her mouth. She snarled something unintelligible, then spat blood and fragments of shattered teeth into Captain Yang's eyes. She lunged forward and tackled him, grinding her forearm across his face, and the captain screamed a shrill cry of pain.

The sailor who'd hit her stepped forward, and Swan smacked the club out of his hands. A kick to the knee sent the other stumbling, while the third rushed to the captain's aid.

Swan looked at Shiloh, her face a bleeding, jagged-toothed rictus. "You," she said, "leave." Though the captain was screaming that he was blind, Shiloh could hear Swan's low growl perfectly.

"I came to find you."

"Don' give a shit. Na leaving thish room. Na going inna wadder." Her torn lips slurred her words. One of the sailors was up and Swan moved around behind the table, putting it between the two of them. "Go reshue Shroni," she said.

"No—"

"Shiloh, if you're still in thish room after I shill these fishfushers, I'monna *shill you too!*" She ducked under a punch, grabbed Burdick by his ears and slammed his face into the metal table, her eyes wild. "Fush your fashe, Bird Dick!" she yelled.

Shiloh scrambled for the door, and pulled it shut behind her. Inside, the table let out several toneless gongs as Swan smashed the sailor's face against it. The deadbolt clacked automatically into place.

She had locked the captain of the ship in with Swan. It didn't matter who won the fight; the captain was still trapped. The violence had unsettled her, though, and Shiloh found herself moving back toward the upper decks, intent on following Swan's instructions.

When she passed back through the general-population area, she considered releasing all of the shifters trapped there. It would certainly create chaos, and maybe they could help her. She actually stopped in front of a cell and took the key out, holding it near the lock but not swiping it, when she realized that if she set off a general alarm, they might lock down the cells where Kroni and Shamshoun were before she could get there. Holly and Ivy would be lost to her as well. Okay, the high-security cells first, then. The shifters inside the cell she stood in front of looked at here, seeming to be a mass of pleading eyes, and one of them whined as she turned away, pocketing the key.

An alarm sounded suddenly, an insistent, chattering tone that sounded like the aural equivalent of a strobe light. Shiloh froze, wondering what she'd tripped. A door slammed open at the far end of the shifter ward, and three sailors raced in. They ran up the steps with barely a glance at her, though, heading for the upper decks. Was this part of the normal docking procedure, or was something else amiss? Maybe Hardson had left his cell and done something.

As if to confirm this, the ship jolted violently, a physical crash. Shiloh lost her footing and fell against the wall with an undignified squeak of surprise.

What could they have hit that was big enough to make the massive *Excelsis* shake? A moment later there were distant thumps. Gunfire? No matter; she broke into a run, pounding up the steps to the upper decks as well. The urgency of the moment was in the air now, the world on the cusp of being very hard to keep up with.

When she came out onto the main deck, there were too many people. She saw with a shock that the *88 Fists* had come alongside *Excelsis*, the ship's upper decks so close it looked like one could jump across, and sailors wearing makeshift armor and green and black bandannas were clambering over the railings, running across ramps that were now linking the smaller ship to the larger. The sailors of *Excelsis* seemed to have been taken completely by surprise, and were mostly in the process of retreating. It was like stumbling into an open-air bar fight.

The Sino-Indian sailors were being beaten down left and right, their superior training no match for what appeared to be a great deal of rage on behalf of the mariners. Orders were being shouted, not all of them in English, and more than one voice called out Captain Yang's name. Shiloh ducked and bobbed her way through the melee, trying to stay below notice. She got some distance, then took a staggering punch to the side of the head that might or might not have been intended for her on the way to the second deck. She reeled sideways into the bulkhead but kept going, barely staying on her feet. *I'm fine*, she thought reflexively. Not hurt bad, keep moving. As long as she could move, continuing was the most important thing.

She raced into the high-security hallway with the card key held in front of her like a weapon. Shamshoun was on his feet. "Alarms," he said. "You?"

"No, the other ship, they're attacking somehow. Fighting everywhere. We're not close to shore. If I let you out, they might shoot you…"

He put a hand on the clear plastic. "If you open the door, Shiloh, any songs I choose to play beyond that are mine, not yours." The massive ursid was standing directly in front of the door now, watching her, his eyes dark.

She glanced at Kroni's cell.

"He is alive," Shamshoun said, "but not talkative."

Shiloh unlocked the cell door and stepped back.

"Thank you, Shiloh Gallamore," he said, and the rumble of his voice made her heart pound and her spine tingle. She nodded, the thrill washing through her, and then unlocked Kroni's cell as well.

He didn't respond when the door popped open, but when she crossed to where he was curled up on the floor, she saw that his eyes were open, looking up at her. "Kroni," she said softly. "We're almost in Sino-India. The other ship…there's fighting everywhere. We can escape but I need your help."

He blinked, but didn't move.

"Something's happening. I didn't do it. I let the captain of the other ship out; he must have signaled his sailors to attack. And I found Swan, but she wouldn't come with me. She's locked in a cell with the captain of this ship. She might've killed them all by now but they hurt her real bad…"

Kroni took a long, deep breath and stretched his legs, sitting up.

She saw Shamshoun move toward the end of the hall. "They are coming," he said, then disappeared through the door.

Shiloh kept talking to Kroni. "I know they hurt you too. I saw but I couldn't do anything, I'm sorry. I'm so so sorry. I don't know where Ivy is, or her sister. We have to go."

He stood up. "Swan. Where?" he asked.

"Deep below. Past the shifter cells. She said not to save her."

Kroni nodded. He flexed his hands, then stepped out of the cell, turned on his heel, and locked Shiloh in.

Her eyes went wide. "*Kroni!*" she shouted, slapping her palms against the thick plastic.

He wasn't even looking at her, his eyes focused on the far end of the hall. Two sailors rushed into the hall, then pulled up short, eyes going wide as they saw that Shamshoun's cell was open and Kroni was out in the hall facing them. One of the sailors shouted over his shoulder in Chinese, and they were joined by four more. They looked tired and battered; Shiloh guessed that they'd been fleeing the fighting on deck.

Kroni stared them down. "Get back in your cell!" one of the sailors yelled, with predictably negligible results.

And then Shiloh realized that he hadn't locked her in the cell as a betrayal; he'd done it to keep her out of the way. He put his head down and charged the sailors. Kroni roared as he did so, the sound echoing off of the walls, and he hit the first two sailors like a rockslide, throwing one into the wall and slamming the other backward into his fellows. It was like watching men try to dance with a tornado. Kroni ran right over the falling men until he was in the midst of them. He kicked one face-first into the wall, stomped one of the men on the floor, deflected a punch with his forearm and hit the sailor who'd delivered it in the throat, and then shifted. Kroni ducked his head, gored a man, and spun, lashing out with his hooves. Flecks of blood hit the clear walls, followed immediately by splatters. He shifted again, did a flip over the man in front of him then shifted back to deer form and kicked the hapless sailor halfway down the hall. In seconds all six sailors were down. The clear cell walls were painted with ghastly splotches of red, and Kroni was holding two truncheons. He paused long enough to deliver skull-cracking blows to three of the downed men, then snatched a key card off of one sailor's belt and let Shiloh out.

He looked like he expected her to say something, but she didn't. There was a hollowness in his eyes that she'd never seen before. She remembered him talking about Sino-India, talking about escaping it, and she knew this was the last place that he wanted to be.

"Swan," he said.

"I'll show you. We have to go back below, to the shifter cells." She led the way back out onto the deck.

The fighting had shifted from unfocused melee to siege as the *Excelsis'* crew organized a defense. Shiloh saw green and black-outfitted sailors at both of *Excelsis'* deck guns, and another wave fighting farther up. The focus of the sailors' attention seemed to be keeping the attackers off of the bridge and away from the pad, but the door to the shifter cells wasn't unattended. There were sailors and a small skirmish between them and the doors leading below. Shiloh stopped, putting her back to the wall around the corner before they could see her. Kroni stopped with her. "Where?"

"Inside. Past the cells, there's a door. The key will open it." She quickly explained where Swan was. She didn't say that she was afraid Swan was already dead; it was unlikely to help Kroni's state of mind. "If we can get in there, I can open the shifters' cells. Let them all out."

He shook his head. "Find Ivy."

"But we should let them out."

"No, we should not. If there is a general escape, they will sink this ship."

"They're dead anyway if we don't," Shiloh said. The plaintive, desperate whine of the shifters who'd seen the key card echoed in her ears.

"Possibly," he replied, "and I'd rather not go with them." She hesitated, and he said, "Alive and free, we can come back for them."

Shiloh thought for a moment that he was just saying it to placate her, but he met her eyes, and she decided that he meant it.

He didn't wait for her to respond, and sprinted around the corner. She waited to hear shots, screams, some terrible sound of mayhem, but none came. When Shiloh poked her head around the corner, the door was open, two bodies on the ground, a third being wrestled to the ground by two *88 Fists* sailors, and Kroni was gone.

To find Ivy, then. Shiloh started back inside, but was distracted by a loud thumping that vibrated the air. At first it seemed like gunfire, but then she saw the source. It looked like an enormous mechanical insect, painted gray and white, drifting in a lazy dragonfly hover toward *Excelsis*. It appeared to be—no, it really was—*flying*.

She stared at it, blinking in confusion and disbelief. It was making its way *toward* the pad, which was the perfect size for it and, she realized, probably where it was meant to land. It brought wind as well, a gale whipping across the deck. It was amazing and terrifying and beautiful all at once.

Someone grabbed her arm. Shiloh spun, expecting a sailor, but it was Mahnaz. His eyes were round and frightened. Dorim was behind him, eyes on the deck. "They've escaped! The shifters are loose!" he cried. "We've got to get off the ship, Anna, this way!" He pointed at the huge, magnificent dragonfly-machine.

Without even thinking about it Shiloh fell back into her Anna Vienna role and followed him. Looking appropriately concerned was easy, since she wasn't sure she wanted to go with him and they were running toward the pad rather than away from the flying thing. Dorim led the way, literally tossing aside anyone who got in his way. He burst through the fighting men on the deck like a scrunge blocker and easily cleared a path for Mahnaz and Shiloh.

When they reached the pad, two of the mariners from the Fists had gotten there first, a man and a woman. Dorim let the man approach, absorbed a punch and then collected him as easily as if he were fighting a child. He took a forearm in each hand and then *pulled*; Shiloh heard the sailor's arms dislocate over the cry of anguish. The woman feinted to one side, a knife flashing in her hand, and she came in low and fast but Dorim blocked her thrust with a quick swivel of his hips. He held the injured man with one hand and lashed out with the other, a swing that looked wild but connected neatly with the side of her head. Dorim was easily twice her size, and the cuff knocked her right off of her feet. Once she was dispatched, the bodyguard took the injured, barely-conscious sailor's head in both hands and squeezed it. As the man's skull crunched under his fingers, Dorim got a look of vicious amusement on his face. It was the first expression Shiloh had seen him make, and it did not make her feel better about being near him.

Mahnaz pulled her forward. The side of the dragonfly-machine was open, revealing a couch-equipped interior. Vitter was there, already scrambling aboard with the assistance of two Sino-Indian sailors.

She looked for Marcus, but didn't see him. "Wait," she said, but it was lost in the chaos of the moment, and the noise of the machine, the arms on hers helping her into the flying thing, the shouting of men all around. Before she could think of a way to seriously resist, Dorim climbed in, wiping his hands on his pants, and closed the door, cutting off the deafening noise from outside, and the craft gave a lurching leap upward. Outside the windows, *Excelsis'* deck dropped rapidly away from them. The world tilted, and Shiloh swooned for a moment. She was familiar with the brief weightless sensation from aerial silks, but never from an entire *vehicle*.

They were speeding away from the ship. In the air. Over the water. Away from Ivy and Shamshoun and the others. It seemed like they should be falling, but the dragonfly pulled them up and up and up.

"Rabbit's mortar, that was close," Mahnaz said. "Are you hurt?"

She shook her head, thinking, *Now what?*

chapter 46

Holding Ivy's hand was the most wonderful feeling in the world. Holly could let it overwhelm everything else, the feeling of her sister's warm, rough-fingered hand in hers as they sat together.

The days on the ship slipped quickly into a pattern, thanks no doubt to the military command. Each day, Vitter would collect them both some time in the early afternoon, take them to the little conference room, and just talk with them. A couple of times there had been snacks and water. He was clinical rather than friendly, and sometimes there were veiled threats, but he remained mostly civil as he asked them endlessly about conspiracies and plans that didn't exist. Holly had made her terms clear and as long as Ivy was there with her, she'd talk freely. Vitter seemed to know about the Ivory Sisters' involvement in her escape in Strip City—with the interview all over the web, there was no way he couldn't have—so the only thing she held back was Makkhana's name, claiming she'd never known it. Her willingness to describe the operation there seemed to placate Vitter, and kept him from becoming belligerent. She did mention that she'd been to Makkhana's shop on an earlier visit to Strip City, with Nielle, and Vitter's lack of surprise confirmed that he'd known of his domestic's involvement.

She found it easy to lie to him when it suited her, and it only once flickered through her head that this wasn't the Myawi way.

Sometimes Vitter asked about other things; her life with Elden, her life in North America, and where she'd been for the past few months. Holly played it closer to the vest with the last; she knew Vitter was interrogating Hardson as well, and didn't want to accidentally implicate the *Fists* in any wrongdoing. When he questioned Ivy, she took Holly's cue and was generally honest, seeming bemused about why Vitter would want to know about the wanderings of a scav—but Holly noticed that she didn't mention "Anna" the circus performer other than to say, "You'll have to ask Swan and Kroni about her." Ivy was a terrible liar, and Holly was glad Vitter didn't press her on the matter. He didn't seem particularly interested in Swan and Kroni.

After the interviews with Vitter, they were taken back to their cells for a time, and then Zhuan took a turn. He was less friendly; Holly was not sure if this was by design, so that they were more likely to open up to Vitter, or if his was just a more aggressive interrogation style. She guessed it was a mixture of both. In any case, they weren't allowed to hold hands when Zhuan was with them.

Zhuan's questions were more direct. He was flustered when Holly didn't deny that she had killed Elden, but still insisted that she hadn't been ordered by anyone to do so. Zhuan would slap her until her cheek felt like it was bleeding, which she tolerated silently. Ivy had to be restrained by two sailors when this happened. Zhuan reversed the tactic as well, slapping Ivy around when he wasn't satisfied with her answers. Holly was better at concealing her rage, and didn't struggle against the men who held her.

He got less information from them than Vitter did, a fact of which he was aware and which seemed to make him more and more frustrated the closer they got to Sino-India.

On the day that Hardson said would probably be the last day of travel, Holly asked Vitter about this directly. "Mr. Zhuan is getting impatient with us, isn't he?" she asked.

"He has his own agenda," Vitter replied. "I could not say if it was going to schedule or not."

"And what about you?"

"Me?"

"Your schedule. Are things going according to it?"

He smiled that joyless politician's smile. "I think things are going quite well, thank you very much. Our time together is coming to an end."

She nodded, but didn't reply. Ivy squeezed her hand.

Vitter didn't speak for a moment, looking at their intertwined fingers. "What would you say, if you were to be brought before the gods?"

"I don't know that I'd say anything," Holly replied, as though this sudden swerve into the philosophical was the most natural thing in the world. "There would be too much at stake. What do you say to a power that could change you, unmake you, unmake everything with a word? What would I say to an entity that could redefine or completely erase my entire existence with a simple thought? I think I would wait to see what the gods said first."

He angled his head with a nod of respect. "Very eloquent. Good-bye for now," he said. Without a glance back, Vitter rose and left the room. The door locked behind him.

Usually they were ushered back to their cells, leaving their interviewer in the room behind.

"What's happening, do you think?" Ivy asked. The change in routine hadn't been lost on her.

"We're getting close to Sino-India, I'd imagine. I suspect that they haven't gotten what they wanted from us, but will have to hand us over to someone else once we're there. Vitter was hoping to learn our secrets for himself first."

"But we don't have any."

Holly smiled. "Not as many as he thinks. He still wanted to get them first."

"Why?"

"Politics. Men like him work for a department, and have rivals in other departments, and if he were to break us first, the others would give him face for that." Ivy frowned, and Holly explained, "More respect. Vitter and Zhuan only have a few minutes to get whatever they can from us, which thus far hasn't been enough."

"I have nothing to tell."

"And with you here, I have a reason not to," Holly replied, squeezing her sister's hand.

"What do you mean? What are you not telling them?"

Holly leaned close to Ivy's ear, in case Vitter had left some sort of recording device in the room. "*That there's nothing to tell,*" she whispered.

"Why does he think there is?"

"I don't know," she said. "There—"

She was interrupted by the door crashing open, and Zhuan burst in. He pulled the two of them apart by dragging Holly's chair away from Ivy's. "*Separate!*" he shouted. "You're going to talk, right now. You're out of time. I will have no more games."

"Am I the one who is out of time?" Holly asked him, her voice mild. She hoped that Ivy would note her calm lead and follow it.

"Oh, yes. You'll both be dead by morning."

"Then I don't have any reason to tell you anything, do I?"

Zhuan narrowed his eyes. "Your final hours can be made to last a lifetime if you will not show me respect." He attempted some of Vitter's casual demeanor, but it didn't suit him at all. "Do you hate me so much, that you would allow your sister to suffer for it?"

"I don't hate you. I find you boring."

"Boring?"

"Yes."

"I bore you?" He seemed honestly taken aback.

Holly decided not to hold back. "You're filled with a banal sort of malice, but at heart you're too concerned with being respected to be honestly evil. So in the end you're just unpleasant and uninteresting."

Zhuan took a deep, slow breath. "You would do well to fear me. I am a killer."

Holly sighed to cover her racing heart. "So you have said many times these past few days. You kill. You were the best in your academy at killing. You do one thing well, like a hammer. But even a hammer blessed by the gods is still just a tool." She met his eyes. "I don't fear tools, Mr. Zhuan. I appreciate them and the things they can do when properly wielded. But fear? Hate? Respect?" She shook her head. "You don't respect a tool for doing the only thing it knows how to do."

His face darkened toward purple, and he ground his teeth together audibly. "You may as well tell me," he said. "I know everything already."

The opening was so clear Holly almost wondered if it was a trick. Thinking back, quickly, though, Zhuan had consistently been easier to lead than Vitter was. She gave him a nudge, just to see. "I'm sure you know much less than you think."

Zhuan scoffed and stood upright, folding his arms. "I know that enemies of the Sino-Indian state have turned you rogue, and you have murdered several important members of a peaceful information-gathering team whose goal was only to aid the Brother Nations in securing peaceful political connections with the city-states of North America. You narrowly escaped custody before we could find out who you are working for then." Holly prompted him with her body language, looking at turns defensive and concerned. It wasn't difficult. In fact it was shockingly easy and she marveled that it hadn't occurred to her to consciously do it sooner. "I know that you disappeared into the wilds of North America, presumably to be reunited with your sister, where you worked against our ambassadors to North America, raiding and killing them. Then you resurfaced working with pirates to attack a diplomatic ship in an effort to assassinate the chancellor, who is the guardian of the youngest Deshmu princess, and that such an attack would certainly disrupt the upcoming trimester celebration in

Singapore. Considering the number of politicians who will be in the city for that event, you're clearly planning to take advantage of this situation." He gave her a condescending smile. "The first part of your plan is already thwarted. How do you expect to carry out the rest?"

Holly smiled at him. "Myawi do not break confidences," she said.

Before he could speak, an alarm went off, a low, chattering tone that seemed to come from everywhere at once. They hadn't heard anything like it the entire trip, and apparently neither had Zhuan.

When the alarm started blaring, Zhuan moved in a blur, stepping past Holly, drawing his sidearm with one hand and shoving Ivy's face into the table with the other. He put his weight on her back, pressed the gun into the base of her skull hard enough to make her cry out in discomfort. He locked eyes with Holly. "Tell me what is happening, right now! What have you set in motion?"

"No!" Holly shrieked, composure lost, seeing only the pistol digging into her sister's hair. Zhuan's question barely registered at first. A moment later *Excelsis* shuddered, a vibration that ran through her superstructure as though the ship had collided with something. The lights flickered, and Holly's chair slid several inches away from the table. Zhuan lost his balance but regained it before Ivy could struggle away.

"There's going to be one less of you if I don't get some answers!"

"What do you want to know?"

"Where are you getting your orders? Why was Professor Ono eliminated?"

"Just don't hurt her," she said, stalling for time, her hands up and out, supplicating. Zhuan refused to believe that she'd killed Elden in a fit of rage. But what could she say that he'd believe? The threat of losing Ivy was too large, it wiped out the story-telling part of her mind. She knew she could spin a convincing tale for Zhuan, she could tell him exactly what he wanted to hear if he'd just let Ivy go for a moment.

"Now!" He bore down, and Ivy snarled in pain, her cheek crushed against the cold metal. She was grasping at her leg brace, trying to steady herself. The alarm went on.

"You already *know!*" Holly shouted, trying to draw his attention to her, to take it away from how badly he wanted to hurt both of them. His finger was on the trigger. There was no way for her to reach him before he pulled it, nothing she could even throw to knock his hand away.

"The one they call Huasheng is your controller, isn't he, Myawi?"

He would have accepted it if she'd just said yes, but she couldn't help herself. "I have no controller, you *imbecile*," she said. The truth in the statement put an edge in her voice that made Zhuan move slightly, his body coming more upright. He was subconsciously acknowledging her as a threat. Holly took a step toward him. They weren't chained up this time, and Zhuan seemed to realize this.

As soon as the pressure on Ivy's back relaxed slightly, she struck. She flexed the hand holding her knee brace and tore the side off of it, ripping the leather straps apart and breaking the hinge. Ivy threw herself against the arm holding her down and stabbed upward with the jagged metal spike, and before Zhuan could react it was buried in his face. It was a glancing blow that cut up the side of his jaw then ripped into his cheek. Ivy rolled her head out from under the gun as he recoiled and pulled the trigger, sending a bullet punching into the table. She brought her hand back again, adjusted her grip, and stabbed him in the neck. Her mouth was open and she might have been shouting, but Holly's ears were ringing from the gunshot and she couldn't be certain.

She heard Zhuan scream though, blood bursting bright against his white uniform and beginning to pour out of his face. He clawed at Ivy's improvised knife; she went for the gun.

Holly saw her moment and was taking it before she realized, rushing forward and grabbing Zhuan's hand on Ivy's. She got his wrist and turned it, trying to pull him the rest of the way off of her sister, but the angle was bad and she didn't have her center, so she all but fell into him.

It was enough of a distraction for Ivy to wrest the gun out of his hand. She let him take the broken brace hinge away from her, and dug her fingers into his maimed face, pushing him away. Zhuan stumbled backward, out of Holly's grip. Ivy pressed her attack, driving him back into the wall. Holly got a glimpse of a terrible, terrifying look of animal violence on her sister's face as she stuck Zhuan's gun under his chin and blew the top of his head off. She let him go and he crumpled to the floor.

The sound of the second gunshot died away, and after a moment they could hear the alarm again. The twins froze, both of them breathing heavily. There were shouts in the hallway, but nobody tried the door.

"Just now," Holly said, "you looked exactly the way I feel."

"Hold on to that feeling. I think we're going to need it."

"Can you walk without your brace?"

"Yes. Not quickly. Where are we going?"

"I don't know."

There was a brief commotion outside, and something slammed into the door, then the wall next to the door, then slid down the wall. Holly and Ivy shared a look, and Ivy angled her head as she raised the gun, indicating to Holly that she should get out of the potential line of fire. She moved until she was standing behind her sister.

The latch clicked, and the door swung slowly open. "Do not shoot," a deep voice said. "I am a friend." Ivy glanced at Holly as Shamshoun stepped quickly into the room and closed the door behind him. He bowed to the twins. "We meet again, kind one," he said. "Do you remember me, from the vineyard?"

Ivy looked at Holly, who frowned a moment and then nodded in recognition. The fact that he was naked helped. "You're...the ursid we saw outside Strip City."

"We are sung together again," he said. "I am Shamshoun."

"Ivy Aniram," Ivy said reflexively.

Holly introduced herself also, enjoying the feel of her surname on her tongue, and in Ivy's voice as well.

Ivy rolled her eyes a little. "Your *accent*," she said with a little smile, then became serious again. The gun was down at her side now.

"How..." there were too many questions to ask Shamshoun at once. "You came to find me?"

He nodded quickly. "I spoke at length with your friend. Shiloh. She freed me, and the cervid as well." Ivy said nothing, but Holly saw a thrill of relief go through her. "The other ship has attacked."

"Hardson," Holly said, thinking of the crew of the *88 Fists*, storming this ship to rescue their captain. "Shiloh must have let him out when she was looking for us. I wonder how she got a key?"

"I think I know," Ivy said. "Did you see Swan?"

"No. They will kill the shifters in the cells. We must go," Shamshoun said. He looked at them, briefly down at Zhuan, and then opened the door. "I will clear a path. Follow."

Holly gave Ivy her shoulder for support, and the two of them followed Shamshoun. When they entered the hall, the ursid shifted. Whatever else was going on, whatever chaos the *Fists* was causing, the sailors weren't prepared for a bear charging down the hall and out onto the deck. The few men they saw threw themselves out of the way before he had to raise a paw, and Ivy didn't need the gun.

They went down a hall that appeared to be officers' quarters, and Marcus called out suddenly. "Holly?"

"Follow us!" Ivy called to him, and he did, mercifully without asking any questions, his eyes on Shamshoun. The ursid opened the door to the deck, and they were assailed by noise and wind. Holly saw the *Fists'* crew busily clearing the decks, clashing with the *Excelsis'* crew who were rapidly falling back to the bridge. There was a helicopter leaving the pad.

Holly felt Ivy stiffen, then pull back. "What...what is *that?*" she gasped.

"Helicopter," she said, urging Ivy forward. Marcus stumbled into the back of them, bumping all three out into the open.

"She's never seen one before," Marcus said. "It's a flying machine," he explained to Ivy.

Ivy's face was pale, though the copter was rapidly speeding away from the deck. Holly assumed it was heading for the mainland. She could see the shadow of Singapore on the horizon. The helicopter passed over a small boat headed toward *Excelsis*, some sort of military skiff. In the scrum on the deck, she saw Dilly hammering away at a sailor's face, and Ghosthorse pulling an attacker off of Vodka Bob, throwing the man bodily over the side of the ship. And Hardson was coming toward them now. Fry, Vadim and the Bonefish were close at hand, keeping the fighting at a safe distance.

"Angelic Anirams!" the captain called. He was ebullient in the chaos, and wielding two obviously pilfered pistols. "Fear not, for we are liberated. The esteemed Mr. Vitter has fled already, and there's no sign of *Excelsis'* captain. The bridge will no doubt fall momentarily, and then we're bound for home before the navy arrives."

Shamshoun shifted and turned to Holly and Ivy. "The man took Shiloh," he said, pointing to the vanishing copter.

"Took her?"

"Yes."

"We need to get her," Ivy said. She was interrupted as Kroni found them. He was carrying Swan.

"Oh, no, Swan's hurt," Marcus said needlessly. Ivy's response was more visceral, a sob that Holly felt in her shoulder. As she was folded over Kroni's shoulder, Holly could only see blood in Swan's white hair. Kroni was significantly battered himself, and lowered her to the deck with visible effort.

She looked grim; her face was a misshapen ruin of bruises and blood, scarlet sheeting down one side from a scalp wound and staining her hair. Both the knees of her pants were torn out and the flesh below scraped. Where her shirt had pulled up at her side, the hip was purple with bruises. Her right arm was slicked with blood to the elbow, the fingers scraped and battered, but that looked more like injuries she'd inflicted rather than those she'd taken. Her left arm...was gone, halfway up her forearm. A bandage had been hastily wrapped around it; Holly recognized it and the tourniquet as having been torn from a sailor's uniform. She was forcing, ragged, wet, snoring breaths through her shattered mouth, but was nowhere near consciousness.

Shamshoun squatted at her side, carefully avoiding Kroni, who appeared to be prepared to attack anyone who tried to take her from him. He looked the injured woman over, bent close to listen to her breath, and nodded. He pushed himself up. "What is her name?" he asked, and Kroni told him in a barely audible mutter. "She needs space," he said, moving his large body away.

"Kroni, they've taken Shiloh," Ivy said. "Where are we, Captain?" she asked Hardson.

"Just outside rocket distance of Singapore, I'd imagine," he said. "We won't be here long."

Ivy immediately protested. "But they'll kill her!"

"Better her than us," Hardson replied. Marcus immediately chimed in as well, and the conflicting calls for action merged into babble.

Holly looked at the last skirmish on the deck, where Razor appeared to be directing efforts to batter down the door to the bridge. She thought of the look on Ivy's face when she'd shot Zhuan, and tried to conjure the gleeful, berserker rage she'd felt the last time she'd joined the crew of the *Fists* on a shipboard battle, but nothing came. She was tired. She was worn out, and she was back in Singapore, which was at once home and the last place on earth that she'd be safe. They could track her collar here, easily, and her desire to fight everyone until her last breath had fled. All Holly wanted was...what?

Right now she wanted what Ivy wanted, and Ivy wanted to get Shiloh back, if they could. So they had to live long enough for that to happen. Holly's eyes focused on the little boat that was still approaching *Excelsis*. Had it been dispatched to collect Vitter's prisoners? The fighting on the tall ship's deck wasn't visible to whoever was approaching, so they had no idea of the situation.

Get Ivy into the city to get Shiloh back. Keep her safe. Get out of Singapore again.

Holly spoke, and it sounded like her voice was coming from someone else. "Don't sail away," she said, loudly enough for the others to hear her. Hardson looked at her like she was insane, but she didn't let him interrupt. "The trimester celebration. The city's full of celebrities and tourists. If you sail back out to sea, they'll sink you with a big rocket. If you enter the harbor, they can't."

"We've got Dragon's Tongues of our own now," Fry said. "*Excelsis* carries two of them."

"Then sail them both into the harbor. Vadim and his crew can take parts off of *Excelsis* to repair the *Fists*. Not to mention her stores and weapons."

"And how long do you propose we camp out?"

"Not long," Ivy said. "We'll find Shiloh and come back."

"I don't see much advantage to this," Hardson said. "What am I getting for my crew's time and risk? He looked theatrically out at the sea. "Not to sound smug, but you haven't got any trade."

"We do have trade. This ship."

He looked amused. "How's that?" Holly got the distinct sense he was actually teasing Ivy.

Fry seemed to agree. "There's not time for this, Murrough."

"You wouldn't have taken it without us," Ivy said. "Shiloh let you out. Holly and I killed Zhuan."

Kroni interjected, "Swan killed the captain," his voice a dangerous rumble.

"You'd rather be a merchant than a pirate," Holly said.

"That is true. Still, I'm not encouraged, considering you're playing with our lives."

Holly shrugged. "If that's the case then we were all dead the moment I shot up that ship. No less my fault, but a foregone conclusion anyway. Trust that I'm trying to fix it."

"You've shown a talent for it thus far."

"I know," Holly said. "I was acting without thinking."

"And now?"

"That's changed."

He nodded. "You look different. You have since we collected your sister. So, we sit tight in the mouth of the dragon and trust that we won't be eaten. I think I am going to have a hard time convincing Mama Lola that this is the right course. She's never put much stock in fairy tales."

"With as much spit as this puts in the Brother Nation's face, I think you'll be able to talk her into it. Heal the *Fists'* damage, maybe."

"We could do that," Hardson said. He looked thoughtful.

Fry's face was a soldier's squint of speculation. "You are absolutely full of surprises, aren't you?" she said.

"If I'm going to do a thing, I do it well," she said with a casual shrug.

"For better or worse. This isn't the trade you think it is," she added. "We're not offering you the ship as compensation for the trouble I've caused—we're offering you the time to do your repairs and loot what you will from it. Vitter's going to be focused on me, and if he thinks that doing that requires keeping you unmolested, he'll do so."

"I'm sure there will be scores of covert attempts on our lives," Hardson said, "but you are making me feel better about this scheme, I will admit."

"It's just like chess," Holly said, realizing as she did so that she was thinking out loud. "Except that there are five players, with shifting alliances, the board's not square, and I only have seven pieces." She sighed. "Easy, right?" She was suddenly weary. She'd been eating poorly for days.

"We don't have time for philosophy," Fry said again. "We've taken the bridge, by the way."

"I'll see what I can do to convince Mama Lola," Hardson said.

Holly nodded, looking at Ivy. "We need to borrow that," she said, drawing their attention to the little boat that was almost within hailing distance. "To get to shore."

"Meowy gel's thinking ahead," the Bonefish said.

Fry looked from him to Holly to Hardson. "Fast decision time. I'll go," she said. "Murrough, your children miss you. Bonefish, I need Dilly and Ghosthorse with me, fetch them."

Shamshoun stood up with a grunt that unmistakably said he intended to come along.

Ivy shifted her weight, leaning on Holly's shoulder. "Kroni...?"

"I will come."

"You don't have to."

"I never have."

"I think I should stay on the *88 Fists*," Marcus said, though nobody had asked him. "I will be able to keep an eye on Swan as well," he said. "I'm sure she'll recover, and it would probably do to have a familiar face there when she wakes. That said, I, ah, perhaps this will help you." He dug briefly in his bag, then came up with the Myawi Protector's controller.

"You had that with you?" Holly asked, her face brightening.

"What is that?" Hardson and Ivy asked at the same time.

"Razor returned it to me after he borrowed it from you. I, ah, though that we might be put off of the *Fists*, when we went to meet Ivy. So I brought my belongings with me. Once we were aboard the *Excelsis*, I felt as though it should remain...our secret."

"Thank you, Marcus." To Hardson, she said, "We wouldn't get far in

Singapore with my collar live."

"What do you mean by that?" Ivy asked.

"My collar," she said, touching it. "It sends out a signal, to tell Myawi where I am. So I couldn't be stolen," she added, her lips curling in disgust.

There was a moment during which no one seemed to know what to say, which stretched long enough that it started to annoy Holly. Finally, Kroni looked at Marcus, then at Ivy, and touched Swan's uninjured shoulder gently. "You will take her," he said to Hardson.

Hardson frowned. "That woman is dead," he said. Holly twitched, remembering Ghosthorse saying the same thing about Caroline.

"She is *not*. And even if she is, you will take her to your ship. She will not stay here."

"I'm sorry, my friend."

"Whatever it takes," Kroni said. "Whatever your price. I will not bury her on this land. Nor at sea. She must go home." Swan let out a labored, snuffling breath. Marcus knelt next to her, taking her hand.

Hardson looked at him for a moment, then glanced at Fry, who nodded. He reached out and stopped just short of touching Kroni's shoulder. "I understand. You have my word, good sir."

"Let's go steal a tender," Fry said. She sounded ten years younger.

Holly helped Ivy move across the now-cleared deck. At the edges of her vision, she saw Azzy and Zenzen corralling captured sailors from *Excelsis*, and wondered what would become of them. She felt pulled along by the moment, but still separate from it. Even though she'd set it in motion, it seemed to be a thing apart from her. It ought not to have been a surprise. Of the people moving quickly across the deck toward the winch that raised the tender out of the water, she had the least experience with any of this.

That didn't seem to matter to the others. Razor met them at the hoist, and she and Dilly lowered the winches that pulled the smaller boat up to deck level. Holly and Ivy reached the railing in time to see sailors below attaching the cables, moving with a boredom spawned by routine.

This changed in an instant when Ghosthorse and Fry threw lines over the top of the hoist and belayed themselves rapidly down in graceful, controlled falls. The tender was an enclosed box, tapered at both ends, and they landed on its roof before their victims could mount any reasonable response. Ghosthorse yanked the hatch open, pulled a man out and tossed him into the water. Fry snaked lithely past him, entering the cabin. As this was happening, Razor tossed a second line down, and Ghosthorse secured it. There was a small slider to step on; she explained it with quick hand motions and Kroni made the next rapid descent to the deck. Shamshoun followed, then Dilly.

By the time Holly and Ivy reached the deck of the tender, all four of the sailors crewing it had been flung overboard. "The others will collect them," Fry said.

"Or you could leave them," Kroni muttered.

"We're not at war."

"Squirrels say," he replied. Before Fry could respond there was a light thump on the roof, and Razor dropped into the cabin, which was already at its capacity with seven people crammed inside.

"What are you doing?"

"Supervising," she joked with a grin. "Your husband suddenly remembered the last time you and Dilly piloted a tender, and suggested I come along."

Fry laughed, apparently in spite of herself, and Razor slid into the pilot's seat of the little boat. They throttled quickly away from *Excelsis*. Holly felt relief at being away from the ship, and trepidation at what they were going toward; the two feelings cancelled each other out. She replayed the Bonefish's comment in her head, and realized that he'd been wrong, she wasn't thinking ahead. At least not far enough.

Ivy stepped away to sit in one of the tender's forward-facing chairs, but kept Holly's hand in hers. Holly caught Dilly looking at them. He looked away when he saw that she was looking back and she could see a blush under his beard.

"There are prisoners on this boat," Shamshoun said. He was looking aft, at the bulkhead.

Razor tapped one of the displays, bringing up a new screen. "So there are," she said.

"Prisoners?" Kroni asked.

"They weren't just planning to pick you up. They were dropping off as well. Got five out of six cells full."

"We must release them."

"Why don't we find out who they are first, big guy," Fry said. The ursid nodded at her.

"The cells open to the outside," Razor said. "I can release the doors from here, one at a time.

"I will go," Shamshoun said. Fry nodded at him and they both moved toward the door.

Holly gave Ivy's hand a little tug, but she said, "No, I'll stay here." She was fixated on Razor's hand on the tender's controls, as though she were trying to puzzle out how the little boat worked. "You go and see."

Holly squeezed her sister's hand. "Come with. Please."

Ivy smiled and stood, waiting to be helped out.

There was a railing and a surprisingly wide walkway—the better for potentially wrestling with prisoners, she guessed—leading down each side of the tender. The cells' walls were angled inward, like hoppers. Holly and Ivy held back while Fry and Shamshoun opened each one and brought the occupants out. At the back of the tender there was an open deck that looked like a truck could be driven aboard, and they took the prisoners there. Holly looked out past the trail of churned water behind the tender, saw *Excelsis* and *88 Fists* quite some distance away. They were separated and starting to turn to follow the tender. Ivy scanned the ocean around them, her eyes reflecting fascination.

Holly turned back to the liberated prisoners. Closest to her were a dark-skinned, stocky couple wearing prisoners' togs. The man had been beaten badly, and lay slumped on the deck; they'd had to carry him out. His face, shoulders and chest were heavily tattooed with intricate tribal patterns, and his uninjured companion had similar ink on her shoulders, lower lip and chin. The other three, judging by their clothing, were canids, a wiry man with stringy black hair and crisscrossed scars on his arms and legs, a slightly overweight teenager with the same hair and a similar face, and a muscular, nearly hairless man. All were shackled neck to ankle with shifter snares.

Without speaking to Fry, Shamshoun began removing the snares and quietly introducing himself. The couple said nothing to him, but the stringy-haired canid said, "Sizza Wexsun Kuroi and Marf Wool. Pup's Koon Kuroi," he added, indicating the teen. "What happener outdere?"

Holly hadn't talked to a canid in so long that his accent and speech were impossible to follow. Shamshoun answered for her. "You're not going to the prison ship any more, Wexsun Kuroi," he said.

Wexsun gave him a broad grin, showing dirty teeth. "Escaped hell den."

"That's right," Fry said.

"I'm Narooma," the tattooed woman said, looking from Shamshoun to Fry to Holly. "Thank you." She favored each of them with a gesture that was somewhere between a nod and a bow, then bent over her companion and ripped the flimsy coverall he wore off of his body with a savage yank. "What—" Fry started to say, and then Narooma grabbed her man and rolled him overboard. Moving faster than any of them, she dove out of the boat as well. She leapt expertly in the direction they were going in, arrowed neatly into the water and disappeared with barely a splash.

"What?" Ivy asked nonsensically, looking at Holly. "Why?"

There was a splash twenty feet to starboard, and a dolphin leapt out of the water. Narooma's prison coverall surfaced briefly. The dolphin jumped over it, and was joined a moment later by a second, slightly larger one.

"Ah," Shamshoun said, grinning.

Fry was equally sanguine. "Delphids."

"So it would appear."

"Murrough would be disappointed. He's quite enamored."

"What?" Ivy asked again, completely lost.

"Dolphin-shifters," Holly explained. "I assumed they were shifters, it just didn't occur to me to wonder what kind."

"I've never heard of dolphin-shifters," Ivy said.

"They keep to themselves," Fry said.

"She's right. I've been at sea for almost five months and I've never seen one."

"I suppose you haven't. If you're dealing with delphids things are usually either very, very good or very, very bad."

Ivy watched the spot where the delphids had last breached with an expression of rapt amazement, but they didn't appear again. She saw Holly looking at her, and gave her a little smile.

"We're not safe yet," Holly said.

"I know. And we have to find Shiloh."

"They haven't heard her true voice yet," Shamshoun said. "When they do there will be no time."

"Tell me what's happening next," Fry said to Holly.

She was watching Singapore rise up on the horizon, drawing closer much more quickly than she expected. Shamshoun reached down and trailed a finger in the water, as though he were seeking a bit of momentary pleasure even in this tense moment. There were hundreds of pleasure craft anchored, even a mile out from the harbor; rich tourists in town for the trimester celebration. Holly had a sense of things moving very rapidly, and the entire moment was unsettled in a dangerous way. She pondered Fry's question, and didn't want to say she wasn't sure what was next. Ivy saved her, by asking, "How easy will it be to find Shiloh in that city?"

Razor threaded the tender among the boats, most of whom were settled in quite happily, camping on the water. "It won't."

"The man she is with is named Mahnaz," Shamshoun said. "He is some sort of chancellor."

"I can look him up when we get to shore," Holly said, her mind racing. She needed to drain her collar, and it had just occurred to her that she didn't want to ask Ivy to do that.

Her thoughts were interrupted by Ghosthorse. "Fry," the big man said. "We're being stalked."

Following his pointing finger, she saw a dark gray craft moving through the field of anchored pleasure boats. It was heavy-looking and ungraceful, clearly a military craft, and there was purpose in its path. A moment later, she saw a second one, this one circling far to starboard in an effort to get in front of them.

"Oh, that's not good," Fry said. "Those are gunboats. Inside, everyone who's not going to be shooting." Wexsun didn't need to be asked twice; he clicked his tongue and the other two canids followed him immediately. Shamshoun followed them, and Holly helped Ivy toward the cabin.

Ghosthorse had filled Razor in, and she looked pensive. "Can we outrun them?" Holly asked.

"Doubt it. But for you, I'll try."

The glib response didn't soften the hard truth. The little boat bounded over the waves. The sea was fortunately calm; large waves would have slowed their progress considerably.

"Can everyone swim?" Razor asked.

"Swim?" Koon asked nervously.

"If they start shooting at this boat with heavy weapons, the best chance of survival is going overboard," he said. "If I tell you all to bail out, no questions. Am I clear?"

Holly took a breath and squeezed Ivy's hand. She leaned out of the cabin to look back at the pursuing boats, which had drawn within a couple hundred yards, then ever closer. Razor kept going, churning in a straight line away from the boats, which were now close enough to make out the Sino-Indian naval flags and serial numbers. Holly could see at least one mounted gun on the bow of each. They were open boats, almost twice the size of the tender, with a large wheelhouse.

"We're not going to get to shore this way," Razor said, spinning the wheel quickly. The tender ducked to starboard and began running parallel to the shore. "They'll be on top of us the minute we dock. And with so many civvie craft around, we can't shoot at them."

"They can't shoot us, either," Holly observed.

"Unless one of them lobs a Scorpion drone on board."

She wasn't sure what that was, but Razor sounded certain so she decided to trust her. "How will getting out of the crowd help?"

Razor made a face. "I'm not sure. If we can lead them around long enough, the *Fists* might be able to reach us. Chaingun will shred those little GF boats."

The cabin was too cramped, and Holly didn't like only being able to see forward. Maybe she'd gotten too used to being on the open ocean. "I'm going back out," she said.

This time, Ivy didn't argue about staying inside, and followed.

Now that they were in clear water, away from the partiers, Fry and Ghosthorse had their long guns readied, though they weren't aiming. Holly approached. The pursuing boats had both fallen in behind them, and even as Holly watched they drew visibly closer.

"Razor says she's going to circle back toward the *Fists*," she said.

Fry nodded. "Not sure we'll make it."

"She said that too."

"Kroni's a good shot," Ivy said, "if there's another rifle."

"Maybe," Fry said. "Wait—"

As she spoke, the water in front of the first boat seemed to boil, and its bow dove abruptly beneath the waves, as if it had sailed improbably into a ditch. The engine roared as it self-righted, and then a dozen delphids jumped out of the water on either side of it and into the boat, shifting into human form in midair. They swarmed the men at the guns and in the back, beating them to the deck or simply grabbing them and jumping overboard. At least two severed heads flew into the air over the sudden melee, macabre and jaunty. The chase boat was overwhelmed in seconds. The second boat suffered the same fate a heartbeat later. As a final indignity, the first boat veered violently into the second's path, and they collided as the delphids dove back overboard, returning to the water as quickly as they'd come out of it.

The wrecks dropped quickly behind them.

"What...what just happened?" Ivy asked, her voice rising toward shrillness.

"I think...the delphids said thank you," Holly replied. She felt almost as shocked as Ivy seemed, but kept it out of her voice. There was a growing realization that Ivy was now very far from everything she knew, and possibly more than a little bit confused and frightened no matter how glad she was to be reunited. If nothing else, coming from the barren openness of North America on a prison ship and promptly having to navigate a crowded harbor was bound to be something of a strain. Adding a delphid attack of toe-curling viciousness to the mix didn't help matters. She took Ivy's hand. "It's okay." Ivy's eyes were a little wild, her face pale, making the scar on her temple stand out, but she nodded.

"Ghosthorse, tell Razor to take us in to shore before they send more backup," Fry said. "And fuck etiquette."

Razor clearly got the message; the tender rotated abruptly back toward shore and the engines roared as the throttles opened wide. This time they pounded through the cloud of pleasure craft, kicking up a wake that drew shouted complaints as it set the boats around them to bobbing and tossing.

There was a whining sound, and Holly looked; it had come from Koon. "Wheregoin?" Wexsun asked. All three canids were looking nervously at the rapidly approaching shore as Razor looked for a place to put in.

"To get on the closest train," Holly said. "Just to keep moving." She realized, judging by the way they were dressed, that the canids probably hadn't come from a large city. They wouldn't have, in Sino-India, it was ridiculous to think so. She tried to imagine what Singapore must look like to them; a threatening maw of human civilization. "We have another shifter to bring home," she said. "We'll keep you safe."

"Ey, cap. You pulled us out of hell, we run with you," he said confidently. His eyes still darted nervously.

The boat paused abruptly, then reversed quickly into a space between two others, leaving barely a foot or two to each side. Razor yelled, "All off! No point in tying up, we're not keeping it." Fry jumped quickly ashore, Ghosthorse following, and they helped the others quickly off. Razor came last; she shut the tender's engine off and stepped onto the dock just as the boat began to drift back away from the shore, thumping roughly against the craft on either side of it.

Holly got her bearings; they were less than a block from a train station. She wondered if Razor had known this also. There was no need to speak, so she led the way, helping Ivy along. There was no conversation until they reached the station. Holly realized she'd forgotten to think of how to actually pay for it, but Razor had a pass and scanned them all through.

"You've been to Singapore?" she asked her.

"Once or twice," Razor said, raising her voice to be heard as a commuter train hissed into the station. The rush of air smelled like home. "We're rescuing a friend like them?" she asked, nodding toward the canids. Shamshoun and the canids all looked nervous and uncomfortable, and their scruffy clothes were already drawing attention. Ivy looked equally out of place, and seemed at once fascinated and disoriented by the train. As the train pulled out of the station, she noticed other passengers openly staring at them. Fry and Dilly didn't blend all that well either, she had to admit. There were about ten other passengers on the car they were on, and many of them looked as though they wished they were somewhere else.

They weren't going to get far like this. She nodded to address Razor's question, and quickly recapped what she knew of Shiloh's activities on *Excelsis* in hushed tones. People generally minded their own business on the trains, but there were exceptions.

"She was convincing enough to be taken into the *city?*" Razor said with a grimace. "Right before the trimester party? She won't pull it off for long. What is she?"

"She is a felid," Shamshoun said.

Razor grimaced again. "Gods. The only thing less subtle than a felid is a deer-shifter." Holly glanced at Kroni, who didn't react. "And they've got HNE detection in the city on a regular day, let alone now."

"HNE? Detection?" Ivy asked

"Shifters create a burst of HNE when they shift. Hyper-natural energy, sorry. There are machines that can collect it, read it and track it."

"Like your necklace."

Holly kept the pained expression off of her face. "Not exactly."

"She almost never shifts," Ivy said, looking out the window as the city began to slide by. She didn't seem comfortable with the motion. "I think she'll be safe."

"But will *you?*" Razor continued. "Have you seen the web? To say that Myawi and the government don't like you very much would be a laughable understatement. Even if the kids and revolutionaries think you're wonderful, there are all manner of convenient accidents just waiting to happen to you."

"I can't think about that right now."

The train began slowing suddenly, braking harder than it would if they were coming into a station...which it wasn't. The line had just turned away from the shore and started to parallel the freeway.

"That's not good," Fry began, and as the train came to a complete stop, an object the size of a cantaloupe smashed the window across from them. It was black and yellow metal, and shaped like a rounded pyramid. When it landed, hooks sprang out of each face and slapped the floor, digging in, and lights flashed on it surface.

"*Sneezer!*" Razor shouted, eliciting an immediate response from the other crew members.

Fry screamed, "*Down!*" and threw herself into Holly and Ivy, driving them to the floor. Dilly landed on them a moment later. Holly had an impression of frenzied motion, chaos. Razor took two steps toward the little pyramid and kicked it, hard. It didn't move. The impact smashed one face off of it, and Razor staggered. Ghosthorse appeared to be moving to do the same to his side when the other two faces spat smoke and fire with a sound like a harsh mechanical sneeze, and the rest of the train car's windows on that side shattered. Ghosthorse's clothes and exposed skin were shredded; he staggered backward, fell, and began to bleed from numerous wounds. The people caught in the smoke twitched and jerked in their seats, slumping to the floor or leaning back as if asleep. Spatters of blood on the walls and seats suggested that this was not the case.

Razor had destroyed the face plate pointed in their direction, so whatever the drone had fired hadn't come their way. Shamshoun and the rest, behind Ivy and Holly, were unscathed.

"What—" Ivy said from underneath Holly.

"Sneezer. It's a breaching drone," Fry hissed. "Stay down." She pushed herself up, squashing Holly and Ivy painfully, and rushed toward the door. Dilly followed her. Razor went toward the door at the other end of the car, drawing her knives. Kroni, Shamshoun and the canids seemed to catch on quickly and split their attention similarly.

The doors at either end of the car were thrown open, and Holly saw bodies in riot gear forcing their way in at both sides. She was shocked to get a glimpse of Vitter, and then pandemonium erupted. The breach squad was clearly surprised not only to find survivors, but aggressive ones, and paused for just a heartbeat.

Shamshoun, Kroni and Wexsun didn't hesitate at all, and Marf was right behind his alpha. Whatever Vitter had been prepared for, it wasn't a wave of animal-form shifters falling onto him and his men. Shamshoun struck to his left, Kroni to the right, and Razor crashed right into the middle. She saw Kroni shift from human to deer mid-fight, and a body went down when he did. Holly glanced to the other end; Wexsun and Marf hit in a brief storm of teeth, ripping out throats while Fry and Dilly disarmed the remaining men, the former with slightly more grace.

It was over before Holly had a chance to look back and forth. The two riot cops fighting Shamshoun hadn't stood a chance. Wexsun was knocked violently to the ground but the soldier who struck him got Marf's teeth in his neck instead. Razor dispatched a riot cop with a knife stuck up under his chest armor. Fry snatched up one of the dropped rifles and trained it on Vitter. Kroni shifted and did the same.

He looked surprised, to say the least. After a moment, an expression of respect slowly spread over his face, and he raised his hands. "This was unexpected. I feel as though I may have played right into your hands."

"Don't," Holly said, extricating herself from Ivy who was watching the entire scene dumbstruck and motionless. "We're not going to kill you."

"We're not?" Dilly asked.

"No, we're not. Mr. Vitter doesn't have any power any more, now that we're on the mainland. I'm someone else's problem now, aren't I?"

"Why do you say that?" Vitter asked, his voice guarded.

"It doesn't matter why. It's true, is what matters. This was your last chance to seize us before someone else took over." She was sure that was why he'd been willing to sacrifice the civilians. Holly's thoughts went briefly to Ghosthorse, and she pushed them away. She needed her stoic, unruffled Myawi face right now. "That said, I could be plenty of trouble, couldn't I? This close to the trimester celebration? With so many stars and important men in Singapore? And you brought me here just in time for it!" She smiled, suspecting that it made her look more unhinged than cheerful.

He narrowed his eyes. "What do you plan to do?"

"And *why* would I tell you that?"

"Perhaps I could help."

"I have no reason to think that you'd have any interest in helping me," Holly said. "Or any of us," she added, indicating Ivy and the shifters.

"Let's talk then. I'll give you one."

Holly considered letting him say his piece. She considered asking him what his men had been doing side-by-side with Sam Wards' Army, a fact which seemed to have caused Ivy some distress. She considered taking Vitter hostage. All of these options seemed like they'd end with him finding some advantage over her, though. Her greatest strength at the moment was that he had no idea what she wanted or what she was capable of. Neither did she—but Vitter was convinced that he did. So she shook her head, slowly. "There's nothing to talk about, and nothing you can help me with, Mr. Vitter. I have things to do."

"You have to realize that there's no way the navy is going to let your friends run back to Zeeland or Australia with the *Excelsis*."

She resisted the urge to smile, and heard Fry chuckle behind her. Holly kept her face neutral. "Your hands are tied; that's not your decision."

"And why do you say that my hands are tied?"

"Because," Holly said, "they aren't running anywhere. They're going to drop anchor right where they are. I don't believe you can afford to blow up two ships within a mile of the trimester celebration. Not a day before the biggest party in the Brother Nations."

Vitter's eyes narrowed slightly. "You think that I won't, do you?"

He had tried to mask the reaction, but she caught it. "I know that you won't. There will be an awful lot of people asking questions. Not to mention dozens—maybe hundreds—of dead shifters in the water. And who knows how many will escape ashore, right into the arms of your glitterati? I think you're smart enough to avoid that."

"I suppose if you're wrong, you'll be blown up with them."

"Oh, I'm not going to be aboard. I'm going to Semangat Terang with my sister. To visit my mother's final resting place, such as it is."

He actually laughed. "You think—"

Holly raised her voice slightly. "I beg your pardon, but I wasn't asking your permission. We'll be quiet; you don't have to issue a press release or anything, though I imagine it would improve your standing in the public eye, and the Myawi school's as well if you did. But you're going to let me do this. And yes, once it's done, we'll return to the *Fists*, return your death ship, and sail out of your life forever."

"I don't believe that I trust your pirates to sit tight and behave themselves."

The pirate next to her took a breath to speak. Holly put a hand on Fry's forearm before she could. "I do. If I had hostages, I might demand a big vid so that they could watch the celebration, but we'll make do. I think I'm asking enough of you."

Vitter folded his arms.

Now Holly smiled at him with genuine cheer. "It's a huge mess, I know. But we'll work together to make the best of it, won't we? I mean, a secret prison full of shifters, stolen right outside of Singapore with a rogue domestic at the helm? That would be terrible news for Beijing and Mumbai to have to deal with right now, wouldn't it? And I can't imagine how the stock market would react. I suppose you had no choice but to bring us directly here, though." She sighed dramatically. She had to stop toying with him; they longer they dallied, the closer reinforcements got. An exploding commuter train was not going to go unnoticed. "If only we hadn't killed Zhuan and gotten out. On the bright side, maybe now you'll be promoted, since his position must be open."

"I will have you killed when this is over," Vitter said.

Holly nodded. "I know." She looked around at her companions. "We should go," she said.

Kroni held out a hand to Vitter and snapped his fingers, impatiently. Vitter scowled at him, then reached slowly into his jacket and withdrew a sidearm, handing it over. Kroni snapped again. "Link," he said. Vitter handed over his phone.

"We'll need a rig," said Ivy.

A third snap of the fingers, and Vitter barked, "Do you think I was driving? *That* fool had the key," he said, pointing. Shamshoun went through the pockets of the riot cop whose throat Marf had shredded, found the keys, another gun, a knife and a wallet. Wexsun shifted back to human and began riffling through the other dead men's pockets and equipment pouches. He motioned for Koon to join him with a snap of his head, and the younger canid moved from where he'd been crouched to help carry things.

"Why don't you sit here for a while?" Holly said to Vitter, who scowled at her. Fry stepped up behind him and cinched one of the shifter snares she'd taken off of the canids around his wrists, then pushed him gently to a seated position on the floor.

Then she kicked him in the ribs. "For William," she snarled.

Holly looked and saw that Dilly had taken a moment after the fight to cover Ghosthorse's face. "I'm sorry," she said.

"You didn't do it," Fry replied, not taking her eyes off of Vitter. "Let's go. Keep moving, capitalize on his fuckup."

Once they were outside, Razor moved ahead of them, toward the large police vehicle at the curb. Passersby were staring now, confused, but there was no way for them to avoid drawing attention at this point. Sized to carry twelve riot cops in full gear, the squat, burly truck looked as ungainly as an armadillo but held the ten of them easily.

"I can drive," Ivy offered, but Razor was already behind the wheel. Holly didn't argue; though earnest, Ivy sounded shellshocked and exhausted as well. The truck grumbled to life with a shudder and a diesel-powered clatter.

Razor looked at the console, then flicked several switches. "Cameras and sound are off," she said. "We're free to talk." Once everyone was aboard, she pulled out into traffic and shut off the flashing lights. "So where are we going?"

"To get Shiloh," Holly said.

"How do you plan to do that?"

"I need to slow down a moment. To think."

"That man," Fry said, presumably meaning Vitter, "is not likely to give you that luxury. Nor, from the sound of it, will your former domestic school."

"That's why I'm with her," Ivy said suddenly.

"Well, that and possibly a bit of separation anxiety," Razor added with a wry grin, then looked disappointed when nobody reacted.

"Right now, head north," Holly said.

"We're on the coastal highway. Still thinking about Semangat Terang, like you told the man?"

Holly just nodded, though she hadn't realized this was that road. Serendipity, she supposed. Semangat Terang was about a three-hour drive from Singapore.

"Heyza, alpha," Wexsun asked her, bobbing his head. "You want Kuroi pack taggy?"

"Yes, please, if you are willing," she said, assuming that Wexsun was offering to come with them. She wasn't sure what the three canids could do, but under the circumstances it seemed wise to accept all the assistance that presented itself. "What I want, more than anything," she said to Ivy, "is a hot bath. I wonder if I could talk my way into a hotel?"

chapter 47

One day before Princess Aiyana's trimester celebration

>> Inside the Trimester Celebration Amphitheater! With the official twenty-four hour celebration of Princess Aiyana Deshmu's third trimester just hours away, we've got an exclusive look at the converted stadium that will house the event. The former Koralyi Stadium in Singapore has been completely revamped over the past three months with two performance stages, a five-star restaurant that will host Silver Dragon chefs, special skybox seating for the many stars and politicians who will be in attendance, and even a six-story waterfall in the atrium. Designer Ressi Carroll says that...

—Shairpie Shrivastva's Den

It occurred to Shiloh that she could have pulled away from Mahnaz, run the other direction, even run back to Ivy, and that would have been the end of it. Unfortunately, the utterly unfamiliar sensation of the helicopter jumping into the air and the world unspooling suddenly beneath them distracted her, and soon it was far too late.

They crossed the harbor quickly, a handsome rock garden of boats and docks passing below and then the city rose up around them, buildings reaching up for them like living mountains. The speed and roil of motion outside and the strange, crisp smell of the air inside the copter were disorienting. All she knew was that she was getting farther and farther away from Ivy and the others, and being carried farther into a place that was indescribably dangerous for shifters according to Kroni and Shamshoun.

It felt like falling down a well too deep to jump out of.

She retreated into her head, watching and waiting. The helicopter landed at a wide field with other similar craft, and Dorim exited first, ushering both of them out. Shiloh didn't hear what Vitter said to Mahnaz as they departed because Dorim collected her and whisked her off to a bright red car that was waiting for them. At the wheel was a man so similar in dress and build to Dorim that he could have been his twin brother. The men shared a fraternal nod as Dorim deposited Shiloh in the car and waited for Mahnaz to arrive. Mahnaz introduced the second man as Weeshu. Both of the big men with purple sigils rode up front, behind a glass partition, leaving Shiloh and Mahnaz alone in the back.

The car was eerily silent compared to anything else she'd ever ridden in, and that also bothered her. How did it move without making any noise? At a glance, Singapore looked similar in makeup to Strip City, but the closer she looked the more different everything was. Why wasn't there any dirt?

Mahnaz seemed to pick up on her panic, but of course misinterpreted it. "It's okay, Anna," he said, taking her hand. "We're safe now. The fighting will be contained on the ship. There are only a few of them, against two companies of trained soldiers. If they're not back in chains by now, they're dead. And either way, they can't get to you. Please stop shaking," he said, stroking her hand with his thumb. It was rough, and his rubbing the same spot on the back of her hand quickly became irritating. She turned her hand slightly, so he was rubbing her palm.

"Where are we going?" she asked.

"My lodgings in Singapore. Once we're there, we can get you some new clothes, and something to eat. We haven't much time before the trimester celebration, and I've got so much to catch up on, plus whatever trouble the princess has likely gotten herself into by now. But soon, you will have plenty of time to relax after your disastrous travels, I promise."

It occurred to Shiloh that she wasn't sure where Anna Vienna was from, in Sino-India. Was she from Singapore? Was Mahnaz going to expect her to know her way around the town? The city's name wasn't familiar to her, so she hoped that meant it had never come up, and Anna Vienna was from someplace else. Fortunately Mahnaz got into an animated conversation on his phone while at the same time tapping away at his screen in the little jeweled box; he mostly ignored her for the whole drive.

She didn't listen to Mahnaz' phone calls beyond hearing him repeatedly apologizing for his lateness and giving abbreviated versions of the reason for his delay. They drove into the heart of the city. The buildings soared, dwarfing Strip City's towers, and they were just as heavily decorated, if less garish. The road narrowed but the volume of vehicles seemed to double. For a while she tried to keep track of where they were going, but this quickly proved to be an exercise in futility. The buildings turned the streets into a haphazard array of man-made canyons, sometimes in a predictable grid layout, other times chaotic. Shiloh's sense of direction was average at best, and with the horizon and landmarks blocked by buildings she was hopelessly lost.

The car arrived in front of a building with a glass atrium and a dark green marble floor that contrasted with white walls. Mahnaz stepped out and helped Shiloh out. "Welcome...home," he said, bowing and smiling grandly.

Shiloh looked up at the building. She couldn't even tell how many stories it had; it went up and up and everything blurred together after fifteen or so. "Thank you," she whispered. She was getting lightheaded, too much sensory overload and it was hard to keep up with everything going on around her. The feeling was familiar; she'd fought it on stage enough times, when she was playing justin for another performer and didn't know the act as well as she'd like.

"It's grand, isn't it?" Mahnaz led her in; the car pulled quietly away behind them. He chattered at her, talking about the building's history (it was currently owned by the Deshmus, of course), about the special engineering that had gone into the elevator, about the various other suites on different floors. Dorim shadowed them protectively; it was like being followed by a bipedal truck. The Deshmus used the top four floors exclusively, and that was also where Mahnaz lived when he wasn't chaperoning Princess Nipa. The elevator was the size of a large dressing room and it thrust upward silently, pushing them into the sky.

Shiloh closed her eyes and felt the ground sinking away from her. She was hungry. The problem with this situation was that, unlike a performance, it wasn't going to be over in a few minutes. Shiloh could tell herself to hold on, but there was no telling how long she had to hold on for. It could be a few minutes, or it could be days before she had a moment alone.

She wasn't completely lost, though. She knew elevators; they had them at the Laddin, where she had lived in Strip City in the off-season before leaving the circus. She knew Mahnaz, and all of his awful smells and annoying mannerisms. And when the doors opened, she'd no doubt know other things as well. Shiloh could knit a web of familiarity out of the little things, and that would buoy her through the rest.

"I'm sure the princess is as patient as a monkey looking at grapes, wanting to go out," he was saying. "She can be like a restless puppy sometimes, and it gets more extreme as she grows older. I think she'll be excited to meet you, though."

Shiloh pulled herself together, put on her Anna-face. She didn't ask why; Anna was conceited enough that *of course* a perfect stranger would want to meet her. *You used to be like that yourself,* Shiloh thought. "I should have a shower first," she said instead.

"Of course, of course." The elevator ride ended, and Mahnaz bowed, letting her step out first. "And a proper meal."

Rather than a hallway, they were in another grand entryway, with an arched ceiling soaring three stories above them and decorated with an artistic pattern woven in lights. There was a spiral staircase going up all three levels, and the open terraces were lined with plants. The far wall was tinted glass, and the city and Singapore harbor spread out before them. Shiloh was genuinely impressed; she didn't remember it being so majestic when they were driving through. "Fuck," she gasped.

"Staying here does make up for having to deal with her, sometimes," Mahnaz said, smiling. "Such a *kanak-kanak masalah.* Just between you and I." He motioned toward the spiral staircase. "This way, please. The girl knows she is a problem child, of course," he continued in a low voice. "Jealous of the attention her sister receives, no doubt. Like any teenager would be."

Dorim stood near the door, and had been joined by Weeshu. Now there were two trucks. They didn't follow as Mahnaz took her to the second level, where he led Shiloh to a massive bedroom. "This is my suite," Mahnaz said. "You'll stay here with me," he said, puffing himself up a bit. "Why don't you get out of those filthy clothes and get cleaned up? I've got some things to attend to. Yu-Hwa will bring you something new."

"You-hwhat?"

"The domestic," he said. "Don't worry, they're all Shushen girls and boys, nothing like that rogue Myawi you were with. Mother Deshmu had one Myawi, and they got rid of her immediately after that scandal broke, just as a precaution."

Shiloh had no idea what he was talking about, but smiled and nodded. The prospect of new clothes was appealing. One tiny upside to all of the stress and fear of this unfamiliar city.

The bathroom attached to Mahnaz' suite was astonishing, all by itself almost as large as her sizeable travel trailer had been. Shiloh undressed and spent twenty minutes wandering around the bathroom, trying the tub on for size and capering about in a multi-directional shower stall big enough for five people. Finally, she decided to shower, and that was the moment she needed, to decompress and let some of the fear and confusion go. Shamshoun had escaped, as well as Ivy and Holly, and she could hope that Kroni had made it out as well. Shiloh wondered how she was going to find them again.

She emerged from the shower feeling much better about things, more stable. A small stack of neatly folded clothes had appeared on the counter, though she hadn't heard anyone enter to put them there. Shiloh slipped into a soft, yellow silk dress that was unflatteringly tight across her hips and belly, brushed her hair, and went back out to Mahnaz' suite.

He wasn't in there, but she could hear him talking loudly. He was on his phone again, sitting in a comfortable-looking sunken couch a floor below her. At the railing, Shiloh could look right down on him. He saw her and waved.

She made her way down the spiral steps in a leisurely fashion, looking around as she did. There was a mosaic of a bird—a peacock, maybe—on the wall near the ceiling whose tail draped down all three levels, parts of the mosaic covering the walkway railings and doors that it passed over. There was a reassuring solidity to the floor and stairs, as though everything had been designed for the purpose of being pleasing to the touch, and Shiloh was happy to be barefoot again (though a pair of pants would have been nice).

It seemed like it might be rude to wander more, so she joined Mahnaz on the couch, sitting far enough away from him to keep from disturbing his call but close enough that it wouldn't seem like she was avoiding him. He sounded like he was in his element at least, issuing orders and discussing seating arrangements and travel times with the person on the other end of the phone. "I know it's a 24-hour event," he said, "but Princess Nipa has her own schedule to attend to as well. They've cancelled her tutoring for the day but she still has responsibilities. Yes, yes, I know, I've got the times for the entrance walk and closeups, she'll be there. The delay is over, Neya, I'm back in control now." He tossed a glance at Shiloh, acknowledging her. A serving girl, whom Shiloh assumed was Yu-Hwa, appeared with a tray of sushi and placed it on the low table in front of them, next to the pitcher of water. Mahnaz motioned with a hand that Shiloh should serve herself.

Shiloh sampled the sushi, and barely held back a groan of soul-deep satisfaction.

He didn't notice her pleasure, and continued yammering. Finally, he said, "I've got to go, I'll be in touch. Yes, at six-thirty." Mahnaz put the tiny phone away. "Better?" he asked her. She'd eaten half of the platter.

"Yes, very much."

"Would you like to meet the princess now?"

"Of course."

Back upstairs they went. Mahnaz tapped wall panels here and there along the way. Some of the switches illuminated lights, others didn't do anything as far as Shiloh could tell. On the third floor, they entered a room whose massive skylight and bay windows put Mahnaz' palatial suite to shame. A young woman wearing a media headset with a clear visor sat on the bed with her back to the window, facing the door. "Chokidar!" she chirped. "Took you long enough."

"Princess," he replied with a bow. Shiloh started to do the same, but stopped halfway through; it felt silly. The princess didn't notice. "You heard about the attack, I assume?"

"Yes," she said. "And I've been stuck in this stupid apartment for two days now. *Two days!* I'm missing everything!"

"We'll make up for it, I'm sure," he said patiently, ignoring her outburst. "I met a North American performer," he said, indicating Shiloh. "Anna Vienna, it is my pleasure to present Nipa Deshmu."

Nipa swiped her headset off and dropped it on the chair as she stood to greet Shiloh. She was a pretty girl, long-limbed and graceful, her skin beautifully mahogany-colored, with a corona of perfectly-tended black hair and mischievous eyes. She gave Shiloh a quirked half-smile. "Nice to meet you. Were you in the attack too?"

"A different one," she replied.

"Did Chokidar give you those clothes?"

Shiloh couldn't help but make a face, and nodded.

"Ugh! Men! Why would you put her in that, Chokidar? Come with me, Anna, we'll get you some proper clothes. You have such a cute face! Do you want to come dancing with me this evening?"

"Dancing?" Shiloh asked, feeling herself brighten genuinely. She hadn't been to a decent dance in months, and the idea had immense appeal.

Mahnaz took on a waspish tone. "Princess, you're expected to stay in tonight—"

"Oh, piss on that. I want her to meet my friends and I'm not staying in this apartment one more night." Her tone was petulant, but also the words of a girl used to having her way. Mahnaz put on a bold front, but Shiloh could tell it was cracking even as Nipa ushered him out. "Go go go! We're going to find better clothes for Anna and you can't be in here if we're trying on clothes. You too, Gull," she said to a massive man Shiloh hadn't even seen, who stood up against one of the garishly decorated walls like he was part of the frieze. He was six and a half feet tall and bearded, wore a professionally tailored suit, sunglasses that masked his eyes and expression, and a turban. He was larger than either Dorim or Weeshu, but had the same spooky mien. He didn't have the same strange tattoo though. Gull nodded in acknowledgement of Nipa, and strode out of the room. With his bulk in motion the room seemed to change shape.

"Princess—" Mahnaz tried again, but she had all but pushed him out the door already, and then closed it behind him and turned to Shiloh.

"Now it's just us girls!" she laughed. "Tell me all about the attack. Are you really a performer?"

"Yes," Shiloh said. "Bandits attacked the traveling circus I was a part of, and killed almost everyone." She wondered if she should add the lie about being Holly and Swan's prisoner, decided not to.

Nipa didn't seem to care that the story was open-ended. "That's amazing!" she gushed. "Did you see people die? Did you have to fight? What's your favorite color?" she asked, changing the subject instantly and bounding to a wall panel. At her touch, part of the frieze separated from the wall, revealing a massive wardrobe. Shiloh had never seen so many clothes—not even in Gallamore's costume department where the outfits for the entire traveling show were stored.

"Yes to the first two," Shiloh said. "And I like that blue."

"It's indigo. Oh, it'll look wonderful on you, do you want to see?" Nipa was pulling the outfit Shiloh had indicated out. "What do you do in the circus?"

"Several acts. Aerial silks, balance beam, acrobatics...hoop," she added, out of pride. Anna Vienna was actually terrible at the hoops but Shiloh figured she was dead, she could have a bit of a promotion.

"You do all of those things?" Nipa sounded genuinely impressed.

"I do."

"I don't believe you."

Shiloh shrugged.

"You really do all those things?"

"And more," Shiloh said.

"That's amazing. I can't wait to introduce you to everyone." She considered the clothes she'd pulled out. "You're shorter than me so this may have to be hemmed down. I'll call Yu-Hwa once we choose something. Are you staying here with Chokidar Mahnaz? How did he come to bring you here?"

Shiloh told an abbreviated version of the rescued-by-*Excelsis* story, which was good enough for Nipa. At the princess' direction she ducked into a little dressing room to try on the indigo outfit. It consisted of form-fitting pants that clung quite pleasurably to her legs and were shot through with sparkles, like a night sky. There were flared black panels from the knees down that covered her feet, and a half-sleeved top with a deeply scooped collar and exposed midriff. She couldn't tell what the material was, but it felt like it was caressing her skin. Shiloh was instantly in love with it. Nipa could apparently tell, and mirrored her glee when she came out of the dressing room.

"That's so much better! Oh, you chose so well! You need a belt though, and some shoes. Oh, you are so *cute!* We're going to be *beautiful* tonight! You should show me how to do my hair like a circus girl. Can you do that?"

For the first time in several days, Shiloh felt comfortable. Even in the middle of this city where she'd be killed if found out, she felt like herself. Her belly was full, and she was going to go dancing. "I can do that," she said with a smile.

chapter 48

*One day before Princess Aiyana's trimester
celebration*

>> Three months after a sensational mass murder in Strip City committed by one of its elite housegirls, the Myawi domestic school continues to struggle with a tarnished public image. After the deaths of three University of Singapore professors and two domestics on an explosive morning in late July, the domestic known as Holly eluded capture and disappeared into the wilds of North America. She has not resurfaced, and though the school would like to presume that she is dead, the court of public opinion seems to think otherwise.

Myawi's exclusive domestics are rare and prized among the wealthy. The school graduates less than 25 girls annually, and has long been considered the gold standard of the industry thanks to extensive training in a dizzying array of disciplines, a strict appearance policy and elaborate amenities packages for the stewards of Myawi girls.

An interview with Holly distributed by the Ivory Sisters two days after the murders cast further aspersions on the Myawi school. In it, Holly details the sometimes cruel tactics used by the school to train and mold young women in the school's image. The combination of public safety concerns and the exposure of its training program's dark underbelly had an immediate impact on Myawi's bottom line, with placements plummeting over 70% in the months following the incident. The domestic industry as a whole saw a 24% dip in placements during this same time period, but seems to be recovering where Myawi has not. Myawi responded by offering additional training and psychological evaluations for all of the 363 Myawi girls who are currently active, as well as voluntary recalls and refunds for benefactors whose charges were deemed to be marginal. In spite of this, the school has unattached, available domestics for the first time in almost three decades. Myawi defends its refusal to cut prices in response to the public-relations hit by pointing out that...

—Listening Woman Syndicate

Fry took the wheel. Holly instructed her to get back on the road and drive to the next town. "We need to get rid of this truck as soon as we can. Vitter will be able to find it."

Ivy smiled a secretive grin.

"What?"

"I can't believe I forgot how *pushy* you are," she said, the smile broadening.

Holly made a face at her. "You need a shower," she chided. "Are you feeling better?"

"A bit. I can drive, if you want."

Holly patted her shoulder. Since they were already on the road and rolling, the belated question suggested that Ivy might still be in shock. "No, it's fine, Fry's got it. I need to find a public terminal so I can check the news."

"May I offer an alternative?" Razor asked, producing a Taerom travel terminal in a disc-shaped green and silver lacquered box. "Battery's charged. It's an old piece of garbage."

"Good thinking," Fry said.

"I always get junk portables when I'm in the Brother Nations. Easier than finding a café, and I can toss them if I need to."

Dilly gave Razor's shoulder a proud thump. "I love land-work with this always-prepped little shit."

"What is that?" Ivy asked as Holly opened the lid of Razor's battered flatscreen and powered it on. It was an old model, but it would do.

"Our best friend and worst enemy," she replied.

"Ident has already been burned out of it," Razor said.

Holly nodded absently, tapping the screen to get a search window up. "What was the name that she was using, Shamshoun?"

"Anna Vienna, she called herself."

"That was one of the performers with Gallamore's," Ivy said. "She died. But we don't have those terminal things in North America, so they wouldn't know that here, would they?"

"They might. It's an electronic vine, basically."

Ivy nodded uncertainly. Holly typed Anna Vienna's name and that of Gallamore's, and half a dozen windows popped up with pictures of Anna Vienna. "That's the first thing that Vitter's going to see when he looks her up. So he knows she's not Anna Vienna. The next thing he's going to do is try to figure out if she was even with Gallamore's. He'll call up a cast picture." Holly did this as she explained, tapping and stroking the screen with her finger. A new bouquet of photos sprang open, replacing the first set. "And what pops up *next* is a whole lot of photos to choose from." She tapped a photo of a small group of performers standing on a stage and it expanded in size. "And there she is. And who's she got her arm around?"

Ivy looked stunned, seeing herself. "That was after we got the survivors back to Strip City," she said. "They made us all go up on stage in front of the home show audience."

Holly nodded. Another tap caused several similar photos to spring up. "Is she...*kissing you?*"

"She bit my ear!"

"Now I'm more confused."

"They didn't tell us that we were going on stage, we just went through a door and suddenly there we were. I was scared. I stood there for as long as I could, but Mr. Gallamore just kept talking, and calling out names, and everyone was waving and screaming, and then he called my name, and...I think I was going to faint. My heart was beating so fast, Holly, I thought I was dying. And then Shiloh bit me, to keep me awake. She made it look like a kiss so nobody would know."

Holly smiled. Razor chuckled and said, "Adorable story, but Holly's right. The minute Vitter sees that picture, it's big trouble."

"But he won't know she's a—" Ivy began, and Holly tapped two more photos and got a picture of Shiloh in her stage costume with her hoops, with the caption *Felid Superstar Shiloh!* She held the screen up so Ivy could see. "Well, shit," she finished.

"Exactly."

"How long before that happens, do you think?"

"No telling."

Shamshoun growled. "Find out where she is, and I will go to her. Protect her."

"I don't see that happening, big fellow," Razor said. "Doesn't seem like 'subtle' is your strong suit."

"Just so," the ursid replied.

Holly continued tapping at the screen with one ear on their interplay. There were no news items about the altercation at the docks, nor about *88 Fists* and *Excelsis*, which was odd but not surprising. She found what she was looking for nevertheless, under a short social-news item entitled *Princess Nipa's Chokidar Survives Strip City Ordeal*. She found a photo of the "ratty little man" (as Shamshoun had called him) that Shiloh had been with, as well as his name and an address. She showed both to Shamshoun.

"Found her," she said.

"I will find her."

"I'll go with you," Razor said. Holly noticed that Razor didn't ask Fry's permission, as usual. Both Fry and Hardson seemed content to let her do as she pleased.

Fry seemed to agree anyway. "Good plan. I know Holly needs extra hands and hearts, but we've got too large a group to move quietly at this point. We'll get picked up for being illegal pilgrims."

Holly considered. "Semangat Terang's three hundred miles north, and Singapore is seventy miles south. Can you and Shamshoun get there, and find Shiloh?"

"Like falling into a pit," Razor said. "Shamshoun, you and I are going to go and find a car."

She nodded. Holly thought it a futile gesture; as easily as she'd found out that Shiloh was a shifter, Vitter would as well. She'd be dead before any rescue could arrive. She chose not to say this in front of Ivy. "Before you go," Holly said, holding up a hand, "I need to get in touch with the Ivory Sisters. I want to let them know that I'm home, and I'm hoping they'll be able to help us get to Semangat Terang."

"Is that wise?" Fry asked. "I can't imagine that any communications to them won't be immediately flagged and tracked. Same with the ship, if this man after you is as persistent as I'm told he is."

"I think he is," Holly replied. "And you're right, if I contact the Sisters openly he'll be even more wound up. I am hoping that he will, in fact. He wants to hide the fact that I'm here."

"Why?"

"Like Razor said, there are a lot of people who saw my story and agree with it, at least in part. That it was wrong. That I was justified. As long as I'm quiet, it become old news, gets replaced by other things. If I'm here, and moving around, and making noise, people don't forget about me. They know what Vitter's up to. The more questions people are asking, the more they want to find out what I'm up to, the less power he has."

"Huh," Dilly said. "That's smart."

"Exposing the Sisters isn't," Razor said. "They may avoid you precisely because things have gotten so political. And they don't touch shifter politics."

"Not openly," Shamshoun said. Holly saw Kroni look at him with interest, then sink back into his thousand-yard stare. All of those who had been held prisoner were exhausted, she knew. They wouldn't be able to do much without a night's sleep, and she herself was thinking about where she might be able to get an electrostim rig. Hardson might not allow it on the ship, but a bump or two over the next few days would be helpful. It occurred to her that she didn't know what Ivy would think of that, though. Ivy might not even know what a stim rig was. Surely it was no worse than drinking to get drunk or taking the occasional drug (though it was more useful than either of those things) but she wasn't sure how Ivy felt about those vices either.

The feeling that she was getting to know her twin sister as if they had only recently been introduced was unsettling, and unpleasant. Holly pushed it away.

"I think we're getting close to the next town," Ivy said. The rough jungle that framed the road was dotted with houses, then abruptly gave way to paved roads and buildings. "Never mind, we're here. That was sudden."

"A lot of the towns along the highway to Singapore have grown over the past fifty years," Holly explained. "What used to be tiny villages have been settled by the Colony Conflict refugees from Europe."

"Both China and India pushed 'em out," Razor said. "Something about a history of oppression and bad feelings. Too many cultures to try and assimilate all at once. So they went where there wasn't anybody. Well, where there were less people to complain, anyway."

"At home it's the opposite," Ivy replied. "After the fall the woods closed in, swallowed up the smaller towns."

Razor nodded, then glanced at Holly. "Where should I go?"

"Anywhere off the main road," she said.

"Find a cheap vehicle to carry the rest of us, and I'll buy it," Fry offered.

"No go inta woods?" Wexsun asked.

"I don't know yet," Holly said. "I think the first thing we should do is find a place to sleep for a few hours, and eat some proper food. Half of us have been in cages for the better part of a week."

"Waste of time," Kroni grumbled.

"I'm with him," Fry said.

"Well, I'm not. I need to think, and I can't think if I'm rushing and uncomfortable. And I'm not interested in getting my friends and family killed. I have a lot of things to do and I suspect it's only going to get more hectic the farther things go. So, with that in mind, I would like to rest, and freshen up. That way, when Vitter sees us all again, he'll wonder why we are so calm and composed, and it'll frighten him."

"You really are quite extraordinary, Holly Aniram," Fry said.

There was no further argument; they found a motel that was recently built but decorated in a garish pre-Fall European-villa style. Dilly and Razor registered for rooms; theirs were the least distinctive faces (and least likely to already be on the news), and by checking in separately Holly hoped the proprietor wouldn't remember them as a single large group, should Vitter show up to search. She delegated rooms—herself, Ivy, and Fry in one, and Dilly and Kroni in the other. Wexsun and the other canids eyed the room suspiciously and announced they'd be sleeping elsewhere; she didn't ask where they might go and asked them to return at dawn. After Razor and Shamshoun went their separate way, headed for Singapore, Fry suggested that Kroni and Ivy leave to get rid of the truck they'd stolen from Vitter.

While Ivy was gone, Holly explained to Fry the problem of her collar. This was met with yet another enigmatic arched eyebrow, but she used the remote to drain the battery without complaint. Holly was grateful; she'd have to tell Ivy eventually, but didn't think that her sister was ready to electrocute her, or even to watch it happen. On the bright side, Holly was getting used to it, and while she couldn't move, she also endured the agony in silence. "Another few weeks of this," she said to Fry afterward, "and I'll be able to do it in a crowded room without anyone noticing."

Spoken aloud, it wasn't as funny as she thought it would be.

Ivy and Kroni were gone for a worryingly long time, but when they returned Ivy explained that they'd driven it several miles farther north before ditching the truck, to throw Vitter as far off of their trail as possible. The long ride and walk back had been an opportunity for Kroni to talk to Ivy as well, but it seemed as though not much had been said. "He's upset about Swan," Ivy said simply when they were back in the room. There was a very small kitchenette, and Holly found herself looking longingly at the oven. At some point she had quietly vowed she'd never cook for anyone ever again, but there was a flicker of a desire to do it now, for Ivy. She wanted to balance some of the terribleness that Ivy had been through since they had been together.

Besides, she thought, *it's who I am*. Thus far, since reuniting with Ivy, she'd done nothing but ruin her sister's life. Making her food was at least a way to balance that. A small, possibly pathetic offering, but it was what she had for the moment.

Unfortunately, she couldn't shop. If someone recognized her, they'd be on the run again. She was determined to get this one night, if they could. So she sent Dilly. Fry handed over a credit tab without complaint, and Holly sent the big pirate off with a long and very specific list of things to bring back. She'd make enough to feed everyone, naturally. It wasn't just Ivy who'd extended herself and suffered on Holly's behalf, after all.

She was a bit surprised at how much she missed the process of selecting just the right ingredients for a meal, though. The bustle and controlled chaos of the market, the pleasing moment of finding just the right dragonfruit.

"You're going to need new clothes," Fry said, interrupting her thoughts. "Minnijean pulled out some of your stuff and gave it to me to bring. I brought changes for Marcus and Murrough too, so your friend the cervid might find something he can use." She opened her gear bag and pulled out a smaller sack, handing it to Ivy. "For your sis and the canids we're going to have to get new stuff, though. Seems quicker than finding a laundry."

She nodded. "Can you go?"

"Looks like I'm the only one who can."

"We will need a vehicle as well," Holly said. "Something big enough to carry all of us. I'm not risking the train again."

Fry said, "Seems like a good plan. I'll see what I can find. Murrough's going to laugh at us, coming ashore to do all this shopping. Usually I'm the one telling him to reel in the spending on clothes."

Holly made a mental list, a task that would have been easier with a bump. She wanted to keep the shifters out of sight, as some people could spot them at a glance. She wanted to get in touch with the Ivory Sisters, and get her face back on the news if possible. And she wanted to get to Semangat Terang, then get her friends back to the *Fists* and get them away from town after the trimester celebration, while Vitter was hopefully caught up in whatever political intrigues would inevitably arrive due to Zhuan's death. With luck, Vitter would be too busy fighting for his job to pursue the *Fists*, or to risk the public relations nightmare that would result from direct confrontation with so many stars in town. She was counting on that.

She took a deep breath, closed her eyes.

"You need to sleep," Ivy said.

"So do you. I'm used to being up late. Besides, I have to cook."

"No, you don't."

"I want to. It will make me feel better."

Ivy frowned, but the stern look didn't stick. "Okay, fine. But after dinner, bed."

"Promise." She opened the folds of clothes Fry had brought, and laughed. "Oh, Minnijean."

"What is it? Who's Minnijean?"

"She's the crew's mother. She's quartermaster and usually the cook, and she meddles in everyone's business," Holly said. "And she gave Fry my makeup kit to bring to me."

"You need a makeup kit?"

Holly blushed a bit. "It'll make me feel better. Also, it'll make us look less alike, which will help us if people are on the lookout for twins."

"Our hair's different."

"It's a start. I don't know if it's enough." She reached over and touched Ivy's arm, squeezed her hand. "How are you doing?" she asked.

"Tired."

"Well, rest. We'll be on the move before long."

"No time to rest," Ivy said. "We have work to do."

"I can take care of it."

She frowned. "You don't have to treat me like a broken bird, Holly. I can help."

"I know my way around a kitchen, thank you." Her words came out more tersely than she intended.

"I'm sure you do. But that's not what I'm talking about. You're being bossy. You're not going to let me do *anything* if you can help it."

"Ivy, don't—"

"You'd put me in a bed if you could. You won't let me drive, and you're going to try to keep me out of it when we get to the place where Mother died too."

Ivy's petulant tone annoyed Holly. "If you whine about things that haven't happened yet, you're just going to make them come true."

"Shush, you. I'm actually good at breaking stuff. Comes with having the ability to fix it."

"This is a little bit different, I think."

"How is it different? That's why we're going to the place. We both want to tear it apart. Finish what Mother started, right? If we're going to break stuff, I can help."

Holly gave Ivy a look. "And how many factories have you destroyed?"

"How many have *you*? You're giving everyone else jobs, and I, I, I can't help but notice that you haven't given me one yet! Stop, stop protecting me!" Now it was Holly's turn to smile and get an eye roll from her sister in return. "What?"

"You still stutter when you get upset."

Ivy took a breath and closed her eyes. "I've been stuttering for sixteen years."

The amusement faded. "I hadn't noticed until now."

"That's because it stopped...till just now." She let that sink in. Holly caught her meaning immediately, and it was like a slap. Ivy stood up. "You're my family. I'm here with you, I'm here for you, and that makes me happy no matter what else is going on. I'm taking you seriously, everything you do. I, I, I wish you'd do the same for me." Ivy turned and limped toward the door.

Holly jumped up. "I am taking you seriously! I'm sorry!" Ivy didn't stop. "Ivy don't you give me no-face!" she snapped, the annoyance spilling out. So much for Myawi stoicism, she thought immediately. No-face had been intolerable and ridiculous when they were children and it was the same now, if not worse. "You can't leave! Where are you going?"

"To the other room," Ivy said, and shut the door behind her.

Fry watched her go. "Saw that coming. At least I didn't have to send you two to your rooms."

"Apparently you're more perceptive than me."

"Not really. Just used to watching the kids argue."

Holly refrained from giving her a sour look. "I'm just worried about her. She can hardly walk."

"Fair way to be. Just don't treat her like a baby."

"She already told me that."

"When you were kids, you were the assertive one, weren't you? The one who spoke for you both, if you both had to be spoken for?"

"Mother treated us like individuals," Holly said. "She painted dots on our cheeks, so that the others could tell us apart and do the same." She thought about it, letting the pleasant memory roll around in her head a moment. "But you're right, it was usually up to me to choose what game we played, or what chore to do first. Which is strange, because she was always the smart one."

"Well it's no wonder she's annoyed you're sidelining her, then."

"Not you, too. Let this be between me and Ivy, please."

"Well, you'd best sort yourselves out quickly, then. We've got a world happening." Fry slipped out to run the requested errands. Holly waited a few minutes after she left, then went into the bathroom with the portable. She fussed in the mirror for a while, washing her face and cleaning herself up. After ten minutes, the face in the mirror was her familiar Myawi face again. It wasn't an unpleasant sight. She touched her collar, then turned on the portable's camera.

She looked into the camera and put on her best hostess smile. It was surprisingly easy, and even more surprisingly comfortable. "Hello, Brother

Nations. It's Holly Aniram, and I'm still alive. I've been to quite a few new places and seen things I'd never imagined, and it's given me time to think. I've found my sister, and my friends from Strip City will be glad to hear that I'm in a much better place than when we last spoke." That was a close enough reference to Makkhana; she was careful not to say his name, even though it was almost certainly a pseudonym and even more likely that Vitter already knew it. "I've got some things to do here at home, so you might be seeing me around. I miss so many of you. I hope you enjoy the trimester celebration, though I don't think that I'm going to make it to that. I...want to get some closure. We're going to go see my mother, or at least, to see the place where she died. I've thought about this trip for a while, and I need to go.

"I know we talked about this in Strip City, but I couldn't really articulate what I was feeling at the time. But it's this: one of the things I always loved most when reading books, or watching dramas, or especially in hearing other people's stories about their children, were the moments. It's contrived in fiction, but I've been assured by people who have children that it happens for real as well, especially when they get older and begin to transition from children into adults. They get their own personalities, you know, and as a parent, you begin to meet them. And as a child, you meet your parents as well. Sometimes this is hard to do, sometimes it's easy. Sometimes it's disappointing. But every so often, there's a moment, in the wake of some difficult time, where both child and parent are reminded of their bond, and the love they share, and they're proud to be a part of the other's life. I really love seeing those moments. I always imagined what it would be like to have my own, with my mother. And right now, I'm angry and grieving because it's never going to happen. I'm never going to have a moment of my own with my mother, and neither will Ivy. That chance is lost forever. And if I can put faces on those responsible for taking that from us, Heaven help whoever they're attached to."

She stopped the recording and hesitated before sending it. Makkhana would understand, if he saw it. Vitter would hear it as a threat. Did she really want to provoke him that way? Was it a wise move?

Holly decided that yes, she wanted to threaten him a little bit, and posted the message to a newsline that was frequented by domestics. If the Ivory Sisters didn't find it there, someone would certainly forward it to them. Vitter would almost certainly see it. Anything to make his bottomless fountain of condescension falter, just for a moment.

A knock at the door twenty minutes later was Dilly, returning with groceries. Ivy was also back in their room; apparently she'd returned while Holly was making her video. "Perfect timing," she told him. "Dinner will be at six-thirty sharp," she said.

"Should...should we come to your room?"

"Yes, please." Holly went immediately to the kitchenette after Dilly departed. "He can't take his eyes off of you," she said to Ivy.

"What?"

"You heard me. Dilly's positively captivated by you."

"What?" Ivy said again.

"You're like me, but more familiar, I think. Ever since I boarded the Fists he's been shambling around the edges, mumbling whenever he has to talk to me, never making eye contact. I think I don't make any sense to him; he's not used to dealing with domestics. Razor told me he's star-struck, too, because I'm a Myawi. He looks at me like I'm some kind of empress or angel dropped into his midst. Awe, but also something like fear."

Ivy leaned on the small refrigerator as Holly started hulling beans. "Some men are afraid of fertile women. They do just fine if you've had the Cradle, but if you haven't, they don't know what to do."

"That's part of it. But...I imagine they never had a high-end domestic on the ship before. I'm too false, I've had too much practice in saying the right thing...oh, that sounds terribly conceited. Here," she said, finding a small jar of peanut butter, "I promised you this. Open that and take the first swipe with your finger."

She took the jar with a raised eyebrow. "You don't sound conceited. You're saying he knows how to talk to scavs, but not empresses or angels."

"Or women who look like that to him, anyway."

"Dilly seems nice, but I'm not really interested in finding a husband."

Holly shrugged. "It was just an observation."

"Some day, you have to tell me what a meowy is and why it makes people afraid of you."

"Myawi," Holly corrected with a smile. "Eat your peanut butter."

She did as she was told. "It's *delicious!* It's so *soft!*" Ivy was on her third double-finger-full of peanut butter in seconds.

"I told you. Hey, don't eat the whole jar, you'll spoil your appetite."

"Always pushy," Ivy said, her words slurred by peanut butter. "Always acting like the little mommy."

Holly reached over and took the jar away from her. "Go take a shower. When Fry gets back you're going to change clothes."

"I like these clothes."

"Well they smell, and you need new things."

Ivy gave a little shrug that suggested agreement without admitting it explicitly, and headed for the bathroom. A moment later the shower started, and there was a chirp of surprise from Ivy, muffled by the bathroom door. Holly wondered what she'd discovered that had surprised her.

Once dinner was underway, she powered the portable up again. Her video message had already been viewed over three thousand times. There were comments, which she skimmed. Most were complimentary messages of encouragement, though there were a few death threats blended into the mix. Mostly there was nothing there that she hadn't had said to her face by domestic-haters at one time or another, but one voice in particular outlined a detailed plan to capture them both, torture them and cut Ivy's throat before delivering Holly to Myawi to get what she deserved. The threat to her sister made her blood run cold and hot at the same time.

She decided to take her own advice to Ivy, and held on to the feeling. She'd need it later.

chapter 49

Dilly Henderson's story, as told to Marcus McEvoy (part 3 of 5)
Sorry, I get longwinded about the garden pretty easily, but I can see from your eyes that your mind's going a-wandering. We can talk about my lemon trees later.

I actually ended up on the *88 Fists* because I got in a fight with Vadim, you know. I was working a big farm outside Astoria. Steady work, but not much to do. They had more hands than land. I did okay there, since a lot of those fellows were there more to look for wives than to work, if you know what I mean. I didn't mind. I like working the earth, growing things. I had a little garden plot outside the workers' cabin, not much good for anything, but it was a hobby. Sometimes I'd go into town with the others, drink, get in fights, the usual stuff. So one of those times, the *Fists* was in port, and there got to be some talk. I was pretty drunk that night, don't remember exactly what was discussed, but their big man, that was Vadim, ended up squaring off against our big man, which was me. Now, Vadim's big, but he's not really a fighter. I don't even rightfully know why he got into it. I laid him out, collected my bets, and then helped them drag him back to the ship. When I got there I passed out. Woke up in the morning to Razor and Fry telling me I ought to leave, unless I wanted to head out to sea. As they were walking me off the ship, I saw the kids playing, and the decorations on the walls and thought it looked like a pretty nice home. And then I saw that garden, which the captain really wanted to have but they only had Fisher Bob to tend to it and that man's never worked the earth in his life. It was a sorry mess, and I said so. So Fry says if I think I can do better, she might have a place for me on the ship, and we all had some breakfast and talked it over. And I've been here ever since, what, probably five years now. They call me the garden officer now.

All the time I've been aboard, good times, rough stuff? Nothing ever happened like when the Inchins from *Excelsis* stormed us. Happened so fast we weren't even sure why they were there. We didn't have a chance to get the little ones to safety. Fry got everyone to stand down so nobody got hurt. Sometimes it's too late before you even realize what's going on or figure out why everyone's shouting. Usually it's us doing that to cargo ships though, not the other way around.

Razor speaks enough Inchin to get by, so I asked him later what they were saying, and he got a cagey, nervous look on his face. "They know we were in Zeeland," he said. "The skirmish with *Vinko Bogataj*? They know that was us, which means it looks like we're with the Rainbow Snakes and causing mischief."

"That's bad."

"That's an understatement. S'also a mixed blessing, because I'm thinking if they didn't want to go through the *Fists* down to the last rivet, they'd have just sunk us with all hands."

It sounded like shit news either way to me, but being alive's always a start. Truth be I was already set to kill the bastards because of what they'd done to my tomatoes. They released us from quarters to perform necessary duties, but sent a bunch of us back, me included, since our workings weren't immediately ship-related. I got a look before they frogmarched me back though—two of the bastards, stomping around in the plants to get at the tomatoes, just picking them like they were ripe! I might have raised my voice, which would account for them being rough taking me out of there.

It's a bad time, being outgunned and locked up in your own home. Even with ship-invasion plans in place, it's a tense thing. Razor and Fry and the others can take refuge in their own trickster natures. They relax in the face of invaders because they know there's a backup plan. They've got their tripwires laid and they're just waiting for the right moment. Minnijean and Azzy are more the kill 'em with kindness type. It took the Inchins a day to decide that Minnijean and Shell weren't aiming to poison anyone, and started making them cook. And some of the guys just focus on their work. Vodka Bob's like that. Switch5 was glad for not having anything to do. The Bonefish, he's just crazy, there was no telling what he was thinking. He kept wandering out of quarters even, I'd glance into his room across the hall and he just wasn't there, and I know the Inchins hadn't let him out to do any work. No idea where he'd gone.

Me, I didn't have any of that to fall back on. It was a pretty stressful time. I couldn't relax and wait for the plan; I just wanted to punch the shit out of these disrespectful men who'd come into our home, pawed through all our things like it was nothing, wrecked my tomatoes. We go on board ships, we don't make it personal. We don't tear up their stuff. They were lecherous to Shell and Anju, too. I stood up and stared one of them down when he laid hands on Shell the second morning. He pointed his gun in my direction. I didn't flinch. Heard Ghosthorse stand up behind me, and Vadim, too. The Inchin spat on the floor, and then he slung his gun back down and went back to his position guarding the hall, keeping us in.

I had a thought that if Holly had been on board and he'd tried that with her, I'd have had to take that gun away and shove it up his ass, no matter what the plan was.

So the boarding plan is this; you figure the captain's going to be locked up tight, and the invaders are going to look to the first mate to take over his duties. They also know that if they take both the cap and the first mate, the crew's going to be a little more chaotic. So, if the *Fists* is boarded—I say if because before the thing with *Excelsis*, it never happened, least not in the five years I had been aboard—then Sessil, the ops officer, steps up as first mate. Fry doesn't let invaders know that she's first mate, or that she's the captain's lady, otherwise they'd try to use her against him. Shuriken Bob and Maian step up too, so that Razor and Vadim can pretend to be regular ship rats. And then we wait. When they took the captain and Holly over to *Excelsis*, Fry let us know she was waiting for word from him. We didn't get it before reaching Sino-India, we'd act anyway, but she didn't want to put him in danger.

The Inchins made a mess in the two days before we heard from the captain. Forced everyone into quarters at once, so we were crammed in there like too many sheep in a fold. Even dragged Mama Lola out of her room and put her with everyone else. That didn't sit well with anyone. We made up a pallet for her, made her as comfortable as we could, but it was wrong and disrespectful. The *Fists* has a way, and these Inchins had no care for it. Mama Lola's earned her quarters, and that's how it is. Once they got Shell cooking, they made her roast up the chickens Minnijean brought for eggs, too, every last one of them.

So I was twisted tighter than a Geowa sniper's braid. It was a long couple of days. Spent a lot of it getting food put down my face by Zibby. She's picking up Minnijean's way of knowing the crew, and she's figured out that stuffing my face keeps me mellow I guess. It worked, any way.

That's no way for a body to live, trapped in your own home.

Second day out we got word from Sessil that the captain was alive, and that was Fry and Razor's signal to do their thing. The Inchins thought if we got up to mischief it'd be at night, so we did the thing just after breakfast. I only knew my part, which was to bust the head of one of the men guarding quarters. Turned out to be the one who'd pointed his gun at me too, so that was satisfying. I didn't have any trouble. Some of the others did. There was some shooting in Engineering, Pee Bob and ZenZen ended up taking bullets. They got to the infirmary too late for Jar Bob to help. The rest of the down-below crew cleared their zone. All told it took about sixteen minutes to retake the ship. I know because Razor timed it, and told me. I imagine if the Inchins knew they'd have felt pretty stupid, thinking they could hold the *Fists* with just twenty men. You don't corner a badger in its nest.

Mama Lola died the next morning. Nothing happened to her. She was even happy the night before. We took her back to her quarters once the ship was clear, and she shared her good rum with everyone. And in the morning she just didn't wake up. That was a kick. We all stood down and had our moment for her, and then we started making ready to get our captain and Holly back.

There were some who weren't sure about Holly. We took a lot of damage in Strip City, when she shot up that little hydrofoil, and there wasn't any reason or profit in her doing that. Vadim and Sessil said she was unstable, and didn't want to give that kind of crazy a chance to happen again. Razor and Minnijean defended her, talked about how mixed up she was after all the things that have happened to her. "She's good at heart," Minnijean said, and just her saying that was good enough for a lot of us. Minnijean knows people. The folks who've lived in Sino-India and know about domestics like Maian and Jannik agreed, and so did Shell.

Minnijean kept looking at me, the way she does when she's not going to let you get away without saying anything, so I cleared my throat and said, "I don't see what there is to argue about. We're going over to get the captain anyway, might as well bring her home too." It's hard to talk with so many eyes on me, so I may have stammered a bit. Suspect I did, since Razor tried not to laugh. The discussion ended there, though, and we set to preparing the *Fists* for the next thing.

I spent the next day cleaning up the damage those damn commandos did to the garden. Sonsabitches tore down several of the hanging plant trellises, busted up the corn and beans trampling on them, but about half of 'em survived.

Next day we were getting in sight of Sino-India. Singapore, they said. Maian pulled down the news reports and told us what was going on locally, even though we weren't going ashore like usual. Razor was nervous about trying to get the captain and Holly back from *Excelsis*, because that ship carries a pair of Dragon's Tongue rockets. Wouldn't matter if the kids were in their hardboxes, because the *Fists* would be in pieces after a direct hit from one of those. Vadim had concerns too. We were still nursing damage from Strip City, and the Inchins forcing us to sail hot across the Pacific hadn't helped our old heart any. Fry wanted to have the captain home and be out of the area before Sino-Indian navy showed up, which wouldn't be long with the trimester celebration going on. And even then nobody was sure we'd be able to outrun them.

I decided not to think about any of that. We needed to get the captain and Holly back, and that was all I was going to think about. The rest of it was details, and I'd bang through 'em as they came.

When we first went over the railing onto *Excelsis*, I saw the captain right away, and then we pushed the Inchins back fast. They're better organized than the average cargo ship crew, and didn't break and run. It was obvious that their best fighters were the ones we'd already cut down and tossed overboard a couple days before, though, because the fight was more chasing than actual fighting. I stuck by Razor and we took the first Dragon's Tongue easy. The other one went just as quick. They never even got them powered up.

That part went smooth. The rest of it was a little harder. I think we surprised 'em, but Sino-Indian navy are trained well. They fell back and rallied, got their men armed and even if they weren't the trained men, they still held the bridge and a few positions for a good long time. We got through thanks to having more people, but we lost Anami, French Bob and Harts before it was all over. Took plenty of scrapes, too, but that was just fighting stuff. Losing friends is harder. Harts, she and I had dallied a few times, and she was good to talk to. So we did our thing, but losing people, that made it bittersweet. You know?

I was glad to see the captain, and Holly, and her sister was there too. Holly talked about looking for her sister a few times. I'm not sure how she got on *Excelsis*, and seeing them together struck me. They're twins. Even though the other one—her name's Ivy—has short hair and different clothes, they look just alike. Like twins are supposed to, I guess. Anyway, I was struck by her. Same way I was by Holly, I guess. But different. Everybody was struck by Holly. Me and Ghosthorse went back and forth about Holly, but really if it came down to it I wouldn't have pushed past him for her, if he wanted her. Ivy was like...if she had a shadow, maybe. I don't know. But her, I wanted to follow. Reminded me of my Da, talking about staying with Ma.

I knew I wanted to stay close to Ivy. To both of them. When they said they were going into Singapore to snatch up a shifter friend of theirs who got taken, I raised my hand to go.

Razor gave me a look. He knows I don't mind a fight now and then but I like it best with my garden. Following Holly and Ivy into Singapore had a pretty high chance of mayhem and death. So when I stepped up, he gave me another one of those looks, and stepped up too. Razor's good people. I like him. Sometimes I pretend I don't know when he's taking jabs at me, because it gives him such a charge.

As far as I was concerned, there wasn't any way we *weren't* going to help out Holly and Ivy, because it was the right thing to do. You know how you just know a thing's right, somewhere inside, like your grandmama whispering to you from the beyond? It was like that. The Bonefish has a word for it, but I can't remember what it is now.

chapter 50

Eighteen hours before Princess Aiyana's trimester celebration

>> Aiyana Deshmu arrived in Singapore this morning. Her yacht *Calypsa* docked at the Deshmu's private marina, and a crowd of almost two thousand was on hand to cheer the Brother Nations' favorite princess...

–Heart of Singapore News

The nervousness Shiloh felt about being in Sino-India rapidly evaporated over the course of the evening. She and Nipa spent three hours choosing clothes, jewelry and makeup. One of the domestics brought another tray of sushi and snacks. Shiloh sensed that Mahnaz was glad to have his charge distracted; she periodically heard him on the phone or intent on some other business, but he never attempted to separate the two of them.

When night fell, Nipa and Shiloh took the elevator down to a garage two levels below the spectacular atrium. Mahnaz and Gull accompanied them. In the garage, Nipa led the way to a massive automobile, a long and low sculpture of muscular yet delicate shapes that reminded Shiloh of a bird in flight. It was painted a rich, dark red that seemed to shift colors as they walked toward it. Gull folded himself into a small seating area at the very rear, while Nipa ushered Shiloh into the larger passenger cabin in the center. Mahnaz got behind the wheel.

The upholstery was white, velvety leather and warmed from within. It was like sitting on something alive, an impression that was furthered when the car's electric motor came to life with a soft hum. Lights raced around the interior, outlining screens and dials whose purpose was a mystery. Shiloh smiled at the light show.

Singapore by night was like nothing she had ever seen. It was hard to pretend to be familiar with it. Row after row of skyscrapers soared into the sky, an endless parade of lighted columns ascending into the heavens above them. With each block the car traversed there was a new sculpture of light arching above. Nipa touched a button and the car's roof turned transparent. Shiloh's face stretched into an involuntary grin at the sight of the buildings passing overhead and the skybridges connecting them. Most had colors slicing through the structure to surround windows or disguise them. The road curved to accommodate the shape of a series of towers shaped like a waveform. Another's façade was covered from the tenth to the twentieth floors in a matrix of tiny points of light that worked together to show detailed animation on the side of the building, no doubt advertisements for the company that owned the skyscraper.

"Do you want to do a stim bump?" Nipa asked.

"Princess..." Mahnaz complained from the front seat.

"Oh, don't whine, Chokidar, I can't have a drink and it's not kokina, so let me have a little fun. It's not illegal." She put a little crown on her head, then plugged it in to a jack in the console. The crown lit up with pretty green and white lights, and Nipa sighed pleasantly, rolling her head against the headrest. After about half a minute she passed the crown to Shiloh. "So nice," she said. "Your turn."

She put the crown on, not sure of what to expect. It had small metal fingers that pushed through her hair to her scalp, like a comb. Once in place, her whole head seemed to tingle, as though it were vibrating very quickly. She didn't feel anything other than the physical sensation at first, and then the world seemed to...open up. The colors got richer, the sounds more nuanced. Shiloh could hear small noises from the car's drivetrain that she hadn't noticed before, and the contrast between light and dark outside seemed more pronounced.

It was even more beautiful than it had been during the day. Shiloh could feel the city alive around her in a way that wasn't present in the walled cities in North America, a thrumming symphony of the multitudes of people on the sidewalks, the electricity flowing through the buildings and the sheer weight of the history of the place, a city that had seen so many things happen in the past century. Shiloh found herself keenly aware that she wasn't even nine years old, in the face of so much accumulated life. A human born at the same time she was wouldn't even be an adult yet, and here she was, riding in a car with Nipa, who was almost twice her age and just over half her maturity level, and Shiloh was pretending to be a woman who'd been young by human standards yet older than her mother had been when she died. It made no sense and too much sense all at the same time.

She was aware of herself as well, her feet wrapped in tiny moccasin-like shoes that matched the wonderful outfit Nipa had helped her build. There was a familiar rubbing pressure at her neck from a close-fitting necklace, the powdery touch of makeup on her face, the spangle of earclips and a little hair piece. Nipa had been surprised to find that Shiloh had no piercings, and had suggested a clip-on nose piece that had later been discarded (and a good thing too; it was uncomfortable). The pants hugged her thighs and dipped under the little pouch of her belly in a way that made Shiloh feel aware of the muscle and the curves that sheathed it, two kinds of power wrapped into a single entity. She felt cute. She felt gorgeous, and predatory, and otherworldly.

Nipa was more at home in the environment, but she looked equally otherworldly. Shiloh had helped her to select a costume that evoked the circus, instantly enamored as she was of Shiloh's profession. Ironically, the outfit Nipa had ended up with, a cheerful embroidered dress with a strappy top and high boots, was very similar to the one Anna Vienna had worn in her first year on the traveling show. She'd done a unicycle act, balancing bowls on her head and tossing them with her feet. Shiloh had actually partnered with her until one of the unicycles broke after the Dallas show, then the spare followed suit a week later and they couldn't get either of the chains repaired. Anna Vienna was a solo act from that point forward; thankfully the third unicycle had survived the rest of the tour. Shiloh hadn't missed that act; it had been easy enough to learn, but the unicycle's seat chafed terribly, which added fatigue to doing her own act. Still, if she had one now, she could prove to Nipa and Mahnaz that she was really a performer. The ability to catch just about anything Nipa tossed at her was good for laughs, but not really impressive.

"I love the city at night," Nipa said.

"It's like a dream. So where are we going?"

Nipa said something in a language Shiloh didn't recognize: "*Longda chowsay.*" She leaned forward and waved her hand, and a map of the city lit up in the back of the front seat. Nipa tapped the map in a few places, then drew a line with her finger. "Watch this," she said, grinning.

Ahead of the car, a translucent red dragon suddenly materialized, swimming in the air about eight feet above the road, several car lengths in front of them. It did a little circle in the air and then darted away from them, following the road. The car accelerated gently in pursuit. The dragon floated gracefully, its long body curving around the corners, and the car turned when it did. When they were slowed by traffic, the dragon spun in lazy circles in the air ahead of them until they were able to move again.

"What...?"

"Projected on the inside of the car," Nipa said, laughing. "They can't really see it outside, it's just for us. Isn't it fantastic? I can choose different animals, too," she said, tapping the screen. The dragon changed colors, then turned into a brilliantly colored flock of birds, then a tiger, running stealthily along several feet above the ground, then a griffin, its wings flapping gently as it allowed the car to keep pace. "There are others as well, but those are my favorites."

"That's amazing," Shiloh said. She wondered what Ivy would think of this rig. "So he just follows the dragon to where you're going?" she asked, indicating Mahnaz.

"Chokidar? Oh, he's not driving. The car drives itself. I tell it where to go."

"I've been in North America a long time," Shiloh said.

"It's brand new," Nipa said, sounding as though she was reciting from memory. "Royce's autodrive is the best in the industry. So much better than having a domestic driver."

The dragon led them to a circular drive in front of a building that looked like one of Strip City's casinos. Carved wooden dragons were lit by inlaid scarlet and gold light strips, and the entryway appeared to be made of a carpet of golden coins spilling forth from the doors. The coins were molded into the shape of steps and formed a mosaic that crept up the walls, giving the impression that they were climbing a massive pile of gold to get in the door. There was a lounge-like waiting area outside serving drinks that also seemed to be part of the line to get inside. A dozen or so strange flying creatures that looked like massive insects, some as large as rabbits, hovered above the crowd. Shiloh frowned. Were they projected on the windows as well? "Are those...birds?" she asked, even though she could tell they weren't.

"What? You mean the fairies?" Nipa laughed. "Don't they have fairies in North America? They're just cameras. Taking video for the newsfeeds. Some of them are police, but mostly not. They're going to swarm around me like baby birds when we get there, watch."

Almost before the car stopped, Gull was out of the back and opening the door for Nipa, who stepped out to a chorus of cheers and shrieks from the crowd. Just as she'd predicted, most of the fairies dove toward Nipa, circling around her head like enormous gnats. Shiloh recognized the starstruck adulation, an order of magnitude more excited than what she'd gotten at Gallamore's, and it was odd that not being the object of it didn't bother her. A year ago it would have. Perhaps it was enough that they all idolized Nipa, and Nipa seemed to idolize her in turn.

An intoxicating rhythmic bass thrum rolled out of the intertwined dragons around the club's entrance. Shiloh really couldn't wait to get inside. Her mind was still fizzing pleasantly from the bump, and every nuance and detail of the world around her seemed to be standing out. She was having an easier time assimilating. Earlier she'd felt bewildered and overwhelmed by the city, but now things seemed to make sense, the cacophony of cars and people shouting and music playing from the videos on the buildings made sense. She could tell that they were going to walk right past the waiting area, Nipa, herself, Gull and Mahnaz, and that Mahnaz was the only one who looked ill at ease. Gull was scanning the crowd constantly, and once he stepped quickly forward and put his hand on a man's chest, shoving him casually back into the crowd before he could collide with Nipa. The princess seemed unaware of the intervention.

And then they were inside. Shiloh's heart soared at the sight of the dance floor. The focal point of the domed room, it was lit from within, a round floor with concentric rings of colors divided into equal segments. The music was delightfully deafening, and the dance floor was the lowest point of the room, allowing everyone else to look down onto it.

Nipa led the way with the ease of a regular; they went immediately into a small hall and ascended a narrow, curving staircase that brought them out high up the side of the dome, onto a small private balcony with couches and tables. There was a small bed in the corner, and a collared domestic stood by what appeared to be a snack and drink cart. "Welcome, Princess," she said, her voice clear enough to be heard over the music. Nipa nodded to her, plucked a drink off of the cart and sat on the couch nearest the edge of the balcony. Gull took up a position near the wall; Shiloh figured out that from there he could see into the club and still watch the doorway to their balcony. Mahnaz sat on the bed and she got the sense he was positioning himself there so nobody would be able to use it for sex. Mahnaz' agitation was clear from the way he'd given angry-eye to every boy who'd looked at Nipa as she passed through the club, and in the way he relaxed a bit now that they were in a private space.

Shiloh joined Nipa on the couch, looking down into the club. "This is wonderful," she said.

"I come here every time I'm in Singapore," she said. "It's my favorite. The dancing is the best. And the people too. And they don't allow fairies, so Chokidar doesn't have to worry about embarrassing photos," she added with a wry grin. "You worry anyway, don't you?" she called over her shoulder.

As they watched, Shiloh saw that the rings on the dance floor periodically rotated slowly in opposite directions. The dancers were regularly spaced, one person in each segment of the ring, so when the floor rotated they were paired up with a new person. It was different from the dancing at the Gallamore's after-parties, with very little physical contact, but a greater sense of spiritual intimacy. Or maybe she was imagining that. Nevertheless, every dancer seemed enthusiastic to move with their new partner, regardless of gender, and that made Shiloh smile.

Around the dance floor were more couches, less ornate than the ones in Nipa's booth, and concessions around the edges. Shiloh saw a few gaming tables, more modern than the ones in Strip City, and farther away from the edge of the dance floor another roped-off area that looked to be a small restaurant.

"Can we go dance?" Shiloh asked. The music was intoxicating, rhythmic and complicated, and she could feel her hips and feet practically begging to move to it.

"You like to dance?" Nipa said excitedly. "Yes, let's! Chokidar doesn't like to dance," she said, shooting him a pout, "and he doesn't trust boys to watch over me properly, so I usually don't get to. Chokidar, can Anna take me to dance?"

"Princess, it's very chaotic."

"Gull will watch over me. And I have Anna," she whined.

He gave a long-suffering sigh and looked at Shiloh as if he expected her to empathize, as if he hadn't just heard that she wanted to dance as much as the princess did, if not more. Then he smiled magnanimously. "Enjoy yourselves," he said.

They bounced down the steps. Along the way Nipa said, "That's our booth for the night. Gull won't let anyone but us in there, and Chokidar will want me to check in every half hour. Usually he says his ears hurt and makes me leave by one, but with you here we shall be able to stay out later. Do you mind if we stay when he leaves?"

"I want to dance all night," Shiloh said.

Nipa shouted, "Me, too!" as they reached the main floor and raced gleefully to the dance floor. They quickly found empty segments next to each other on the second ring in, and Shiloh let the music take her. She closed her eyes and moved her body, the motion a miracle of happiness.

She had to remind herself to stay within the confines of her spot on the circle, which wasn't hard, and she could feel people looking at her, which felt wonderful. It had been too long since she'd performed. She thought of her hoops, and wondered what had become of them. They had probably abandoned Ivy's rig after kidnapping everyone. If gleaners had found it, which was likely, everything would be long gone. There was a pang of sadness as Shiloh realized they might be lost, along with her bicycle, and she worked a melancholy thread into her dance, letting the emotion find a release in the downbeat.

The dance floor rotated every other song, moving slowly enough that it took an entire song to change squares. Shiloh watched and saw that it was common to switch into an empty square when one came by, so she did. Other dancers crowded close, all vying for space on one of the squares close to Nipa. Shiloh at first regretted moving, stepping out of the princess' aura, but she collected her own band of admirers instead, much smaller but equally gratifying. Most were too hyper or too obviously drunk to be interesting, but there were a couple of exceedingly attractive faces in the crowd as well. One fellow switched squares three times to keep dancing with her, then gave her a little bow, handed her a card, and departed without looking back.

Shiloh looked at the card, which read, "My name is Tapia Bartussek. I like you." Below it were unfamiliar letters and characters in languages Shiloh couldn't read. She presumed it was the same message repeated. It was an unusual come-on, bold and shy at the same time, and it made her smile.

Nipa was on the far side of the dance floor now, but Shiloh didn't mind. She felt at home here; the club had a comfortable feel to it, rewarding of a willingness to jump in with both feet. A boy she'd danced with twice offered to get her a drink, and she declined politely. Shiloh didn't like to get drunk while dancing; it made her clumsy. The offer was pleasing, though, so she gave him a hug and let him have a squeeze.

That might've been a mistake; the physical contact just made her want more. She extricated herself from the boy before things could get too heavy and skipped off of the dance floor to find her own drink.

She immediately noticed a girl moving through the crowd directly toward her. She stood out, partly because of her milk-pale skin and curly black hair, but mostly in the way that she moved. Her pale blue eyes were on Shiloh and she was smiling and making odd little rolling motions with her fingers. She recognized them immediately, shit shit *shit*, the girl was a felid, and trying to talk to her in felid-speak, right out in the open. Would anyone see and know what it was?

Shiloh didn't wait to find out. She caught the girl halfway, grabbing both of her hands to stop the eager signing.

"Pretty girl!" the felid said with a big smile. "Pretty girl will dance with Bee?"

"Hush," Shiloh said, not releasing Bee's hands. "Follow me," she said, leading her to one of the tables, hoping that the noise would cover their conversation, hoping that nobody had noticed the hand-speech. Shiloh sat Bee down, held a hand up cautioning her to stay, then got halfway to the bar intending to get water before realizing she had no way to pay for it. Could she just say she was with Princess Nipa? That didn't seem like it would go over well. She scanned the area, saw Tapia Bartussek lounging in a chair, looking content. He'd do. "Hey," she said. "Do you want to do something nice for me?"

"Depends on what it is."

"Buy some juice for me and my friend," she said.

Tapia smiled, a lazy, sexy smile. Dammit. "With pleasure," he said, and accompanied her to the bar.

Thankfully, he didn't insist on returning to the table with her, but resumed his slow, grinning prowl of the club. Shiloh watched for a moment to see if he gave his card to anyone else, but he didn't.

Bee was still at the little table when she returned, and smiled a bright smile. She was young, barely an adult, a couple of inches shorter than Shiloh. Up close and out of the lights, Shiloh could see very faint tabby stripes on her face, partly hidden by makeup. Her forearms were striped as well, just lightly enough to go unnoticed if someone wasn't looking, pale bands of color. "Bee—"

"No, don't. Talk like a human." In this at least the danger was convenient; felid-speak grated on Shiloh's nerves. "My name's Shiloh."

"Honeybee," the girl replied. "Bee. It...this club is not friendly? To felids?"

"Are you kidding? This *city* isn't friendly. This whole *place* isn't—Bee, what are you *doing* here? How did you get here?"

Her smile faltered. "Sailed from Astoria. Bee and...we, we wanted to see. Mariners talked about the pretty city, and so we decided to come and see it."

"How long have you been here?"

"Six days?"

"Oh, fuck me. I think you're lucky to be alive. Where are your friends?"

Bee's expression went from uncertain to stricken, and her lower lip trembled. "Bee doesn't know," she said. "They went off into city. Having fun."

"How many others?"

"Shiloh?"

"How *many*?"

"Five? Bee...I saw Salina yesterday, at foodshack. She was fine! She said she was here, at Dragon's Den Club, the night before, and said I should come meet her here too."

"Is she here?"

Bee looked around, her eyes starting to fill with tears. "No..." Her lip trembled again, and her happy mien unraveled with startling speed. "Jelly and Marnie don't come back to hotel. Grant either. Where are they, Shiloh? They're just out playing, right?"

"I don't know if they are, sweetie." *Sweetie?* The word just fell out, and made no sense; Shiloh didn't like felids, especially young ones, and any other time she'd have felt nothing but a desire to punch Bee in the face. So what was with *sweetie*? Maybe Bee's vulnerability was making her maternal. Oh, fuck it. It didn't matter why. What mattered was that this kitten had gotten herself into a horrible place, and she needed help. "Where's your hotel?" she asked.

Bee was getting more upset, starting to cry openly. "Down by curvy towers," she said. "Down by water."

"Okay," Shiloh said. "We need to go there, and get your things, okay? I'm going to help you get home."

"Bee's sorry. I'm sorry. We didn't know. Why didn't anyone say? We didn't know."

"It's okay," Shiloh said. The despair in Bee's voice reminded her of the canids on *Excelsis*, whining as she and Kroni had left them in their cell. She had a sudden image of Bee in one of those cells, crying and confused, and tasted bile in her throat. That was it. That was why she wasn't punching this girl. "Stay here a minute, okay?" She returned to the dance floor, looking for Nipa. The princess wasn't on the dance floor, so Shiloh looked up at the private balcony to see if she could follow Gull's gaze. This worked; Nipa was near a raised platform where paid dancers gyrated professionally, talking to a husky-faced boy who was sharing his drink with her. Nipa was poised like a courtesan, wrapping a lock of hair around her finger and tonguing her lip after every sentence. "Hey," Shiloh said, cutting into their conversation, "I need to leave for a minute. There's a girl whose friends left her behind, and she's feeling sick, so I'm going to walk with her back to her hotel."

Nipa looked appropriately concerned. "This is a bad place for a girl walking alone. The college boys around here run amok some nights. Does she need money for a cab?"

"No, I'm going to walk with her."

"Oh, she's afraid she'll get sick in the car, I bet. Okay. But hurry back, so Chokidar doesn't make me go home."

Shiloh smiled and nodded toward Nipa's drink. "Gull's watching you, you know."

"He doesn't care. He won't tell Chokidar. And I *know* when he's looking." She raised both her eyebrows and took a big drink, which made the boy she was talking to laugh. Nipa rolled her eyes as the alcohol hit her, and leaned against him with a laugh. "Come back and saaave me, Anna..." she giggled.

Shiloh returned to the table where she'd left Bee, who was thankfully still there. She had regained her composure and dried her eyes, but the happy carefree smile was gone. "Okay, let's go." They skirted the dance floor on their way out. Shiloh watched the room to see if anyone was taking special interest in them, but the cheerful chaos of the club seemed to be working to their advantage.

They cleared the crowd and line of people waiting to get in, and Bee pointed the way. "Is not far," she said, starting to tug at her belt. "Shiloh and Bee can run."

"Wait, no," she said, realizing what Bee meant. "Keep your clothes on, stupid. Don't shift here. That's how they find you, when you shift."

"Oh." Bee put her belt back on awkwardly with a somber nod. "Talk human too," she said. "Forgot."

"Don't forget. This is a bad place."

"It's...it's a pretty place, though?"

"It is."

"Whyfor's—ah. Why is Shiloh, why are you here?"

"I took a very wrong turn," she replied.

"You really think the others are gone?"

"Yes." The streets were lit almost as brightly as daylight; only the quality of the light, muted by the dark sky, was different. Fortunately a festive atmosphere permeated the city, presumably because of the trimester celebration, so the two girls in club attire didn't stand out. The sidewalks were surprisingly full, once they got away from the club and started moving into the shopping and restaurant districts. Evening markets were in full swing.

Bee led them right through a large one that had marketfronts soaring up three stories and an awning with colorful patterns projected onto it.

Shiloh kept looking over her shoulder, remembering the things she'd learned from Ivy and Swan about being a scav (especially a fertile-looking one) in unfamiliar dweller territory, though many of the lessons for surviving in the dirt didn't apply in a bustling city. They did their best to join the crowd.

They made it most of the way to the hotel before Shiloh caught a man looking curiously at the two of them as they waited to cross a street. She met his eye and he bowed politely at her. When the light changed, he followed, and on the far side of the street he took three quick steps forward and grabbed Bee's upper arm, barking at her in a language she didn't understand. Shiloh grabbed his wrist and put herself between him and Bee, trying to pry the hand off, and he switched to English. "What are you?"

Shiloh shoved him back with both hands. He wasn't a very big man, fortunately, and the forceful push surprised him enough that he let go.

"Demon!" he yelled. Now others were looking. "Demons here!"

"You're crazy!" she shouted back. "Don't you dare touch my sister, frog-face!" She was reminded of conflicts with town-dwellers while with the traveling show. The performers were strictly forbidden against fighting with locals, and the best response to harassment was to get away, ideally without being followed back to the performer's village. Shiloh hoped that onlookers would assume she and Bee were fertile and take their side against a shouting man, especially if she hinted that he was a pervert. Humans would assume Bee was a teenager, and the light was poor enough that her tabby stripes looked like part of her club outfit. "Run," she said to Bee, nudging her into motion away from the fellow. "Run run run."

And they did, they burst through the crowd and fled the scene. No one made an effort to grab them, but as they turned to run down a less crowded street Shiloh heard a whir above and behind them, a hissing buzz like a hummingbird but far too loud to be that. One of the fairies was following them.

"Don't look back," she said. They slowed from a run to a more reasonable quick walk. Running would attract too much attention. "Keep going."

The street ahead was much more crowded, and people in the crowd held signs and lanterns with slogans emblazoned on them. One had Ivy's face drawn on it—no, wait, it had longer hair and a collar, it was Holly, her sister. What was going on? They burst out into the crowd, which was agitated but not unruly. The sidewalks were lined with cops wearing body armor, standing like a fence made of statues. The people in the street were a mix of young and old, mostly younger, and they were singing and chanting. Shiloh couldn't make out the words.

Bee pulled her close. "One block that way." Her voice was filled with a mixture of excitement and terror.

The crowd gathered in the streets around Bee's hotel worked to their advantage; they escaped into the cool air inside the lobby without further incident. The noise of people drowned out whatever craft had been following them, but once they were inside Shiloh glanced out the window and saw half a dozen little lights winking above the crowd. There were fairies hovering over several of the larger collections of chanters. She guessed that one had been following them as well.

No matter. Either they'd lost it, or it was waiting outside the front door for them.

"Quickly, Bee," she said. "Your things." Could they go out a different door, in case it was waiting for them? Who was watching them?

They took the stairs instead of the elevator. As with Mahnaz' penthouse, Shiloh marveled at the similar style to the buildings in Strip City, but with different materials and a stronger sense of newness to it, as though it had been built this morning.

When they reached her room, Bee swiped her key, opened the door and immediately flew backward out of it, hitting the opposite wall. For a moment Shiloh thought she'd been thrown, but then she reached it and saw what was in the room. Bee had recoiled under her own power.

From the doorway, she could see overturned furniture and part of a feline body, lit by a fallen lamp. The felid's head had been cut off. Blood had sprayed the wall and floor. To the left, the bathroom light was on, and there was blood on the floor in there but if there was another body, Shiloh didn't see it.

Bee let out a deafening, drilling wail of anguish that sounded not at all human. Shiloh turned and slapped her hand over the girl's mouth to shut her up. "It's too late," she said. "We have to go."

She didn't need to tell Bee twice. As they moved back toward the stairs, a door to one of the rooms at the far end of the hall opened and two men in body armor stepped out. They pointed and shouted, drawing weapons. She guessed that had been waiting for more felids to come back, if they'd known there were several staying in the same room.

Shiloh and Bee ran at the same time, slamming through the stairwell door as a huge wad of something wet splattered the wall behind them.

"Down fast," Bee said. She jumped over the railing and and across the open air, catching the rail on the opposite side a level down, then turned and leapt back, dropping to the next lower floor. Shiloh followed suit. They descended five stories that way, bounding down the air shaft, and when it ended at the second floor they heard the men up there just entering the stairwell. They pulled themselves up against the walls so they couldn't be seen.

There were no shouts from above, but she heard the distinct sound of a pistol being cocked.

Shiloh and Bee moved silently, out into the halls. They made it out of the hotel, and exited through a different door. The protest was behind them now, the chanting being led on by someone using a megaphone.

"What now, where now?" Bee asked.

Shiloh honestly hadn't thought this far ahead. "Pedicab," she said finally. It would get them off of the street and away from the area as quickly as possible. They boarded a rickety gold bicycle rickshaw and took cover under its garish awning. "Where to?" the driver asked.

Again a reminder that she hadn't thought this through. She wished Ivy were here.

"The harbor," Bee said. At Shiloh's look, she said, "That's where we find a ship home, right?"

She nodded, glancing out the back window to make sure they weren't being followed by any more fliers. The coast seemed clear.

At the harbor, there were more late-night partiers, though not as many and with a different flavor of rowdiness. These were people affluent enough to own boats, after all, not college students. There was at least one lewd comment directed their way, but Shiloh quickly found a little inn with private rooms, and got money from Bee to pay for one. The proprietor smiled knowingly and passed Shiloh a key.

The room was a silent escape, an oasis in the chaos of the city. Bee went directly to the sink and was noisily sick. Shiloh sat on the bed and gripped the blanket with both hands, empathizing but not moved to nausea. She rolled her shoulders, forcing herself to relax, and trying to think of what to do next.

Bee rinsed her mouth and spat. She drifted out of the bathroom like a ghost, then sat on the bed with her back against the wall and her knees to her chest, just breathing. Her shoulders heaved, shaking the mattress. In the harsh light from the cheap ceiling fixture Shiloh could see the tabby stripes on the young felid's arms, legs and face much more clearly. It was a wonder she'd lived six days. "That...that was Marnie," Bee said. "Why'd they do that to her?" she whined.

Shiloh didn't have an answer for her, so she said nothing. Nothing would help anyway. She'd seen the bodies of dead friends before, and no words made that better. Moving on autopilot, she sat on the bed next to Bee and wrapped an arm around the smaller woman's shoulders.

Bee uncoiled just enough to mold herself into Shiloh's lap, putting her face in her belly and wrapping arms and knees around Shiloh's legs. She caressed Bee's back gently, willing the heaving breaths to slow down. Her mother had held her like this, she remembered suddenly, when things were frightening. An unexpected encounter with a pheasant, rock-throwing boys... Bee seemed to welcome the contact.

"Whatfor others?" Bee asked, lapsing farther into her felid dialect. "Shiloh must help Bee find Salina and Jelly and Grant before Inchins do."

She wanted to complain that she wasn't the one to turn to, she wasn't that much older than Bee and her friends and there was no point to her being in charge, but she didn't. Bee just went on looking at her, expectantly, like a child, and Shiloh nodded. "I'll try." *They're dead, you little idiot*, she wanted to say. *You're all idiots and they're all dead and you should be too.* But Bee wasn't dead, and Shiloh was determined not to let that change.

"Salina would go to club. Salina told Bee to meet at club."

She nodded again. "I'll go back. You stay here."

"If Salina is there—"

"I will see her. Keep speaking human, okay? At least until we find a ship and are away from this place."

Bee nodded. "And no shifting."

"Right, no shifting. Stay in this room until I come back for you. Are you hungry?"

The younger felid looked at her, tears in her eyes again, shaking her head. "Bee doesn't want to be alone," she said in a small voice.

"You'll be safe here. I will come back in the morning, whether I've found them or not."

"And then Sh—then we can go?"

"And then we can go."

"Okay." Bee crawled off of the bed and down into the narrow gap between it and the back wall of the room. She pulled the blankets and pillows down behind her, disappearing into a pile of linen. Bee was acting a lot like Shiloh had, as a kitten. It wasn't helping her objectivity.

That seemed to be goodbye enough. Shiloh put her hand on the hump in the blankets that was Bee's head, then left, taking the key with her.

A second pedicab got her back to the club, after some back-and-forth because she didn't know its name. The description of the door was sufficient in the end, and Shiloh was back at the club in ten minutes.

Which left two ticklish questions: first, how to pay the pedicab driver, and second, how to get back into the club without Nipa or any money?

The first was addressed when the cab was immediately mobbed by a group yelling that they wanted to go downtown, almost before she disembarked. Shiloh slipped away in the confusion, then settled for striding purposefully toward the club's door, looking like she knew where she was going as she bypassed the line (which was even longer now; judging by some snatches of conversation she heard as she went past, word had gotten out that Nipa was there). The bouncer with the square hair met her eye with a nod of recognition, and stepped aside, opening the door for her. So he remembered seeing her with Nipa previously. Good man. Shiloh gave him a curtain-call smile as she went past.

The pounding music wrapped itself around her again, vibrating pleasantly behind her sternum, and the safe-space feeling returned. She found Nipa quickly, now dancing near the center of the rotating floor. Shiloh moved in that direction, casting her eyes about for another felid, something of a hopeless task in the midst of the sensory overload. Shiloh found a square to dance in. The feeling of playing the role of Anna Vienna was stronger now; she was getting up on stage literally and figuratively, and thoughts of the dead felid in Bee's hotel room, worries that the men in body armor were right now finding her and chopping her to bits, fears that she'd suffer the same fate before dawn, all of those things were stuffed up inside because what mattered right now was the dance, the performance. Anna didn't usually dance at the afterparties, so the dancing was actually all Shiloh, but nobody would know that and she indulged because it was part of the performance. It wouldn't do for Nipa or Mahnaz to wonder why she'd left and returned distraught, after all.

The dance floor carried her around to Nipa eventually, and the girl saw her and smiled. They enjoyed an entertaining pair of dances together, and then Nipa grabbed her hand and pulled her off of the floor. Shiloh felt a ripple of interest go through the crowd as they passed through, people wondering who the girl with Princess Nipa was.

"I'm having so much fun!" Nipa laughed as they ran up the steps. Something about her tone made Shiloh smile back.

They returned to the private balcony. Mahnaz was on his feet the moment they arrived. "Princess, I really should get back..."

"Yes, you should," she said. "I have Gull and Anna with me, we'll be fine."

To his credit, Mahnaz hesitated. Shiloh could see why; Nipa was clearly waiting for the opportunity to slip her leash. "It'll be okay," Shiloh said to Mahnaz. "Tell me what the rules are, I'll enforce them."

"Yes, Anna can be in charge," the princess agreed.

"Very well. Just this once," Mahnaz said, "because it's Aiyana's celebration. No boys," he said to Shiloh, "no drink, no drugs, and no pictures. Gull will help keep the photographers away." He handed Shiloh a rod of sculpted silver slightly smaller than a pencil. "Transmitter for the car," he said. "It will come to you when you need it."

"I have mine!" Nipa said, sounding put out.

"And now you each have one, my dear." He looked at both of them, then smiled. "Enjoy the rest of your evening. And Anna, thank you. I look forward to seeing you tomorrow." With that, he turned and headed down the stairs with a grateful bounce in his step.

"No drink!" she cackled. "I'm already drunk. Do I look drunk?"

Shiloh grinned in solidarity. "No. But no boys, I'm enforcing that rule." Since it was unlikely that she was going to find a playmate (or have time to play even if she did find one), there was no point in letting Nipa have one after all. It seemed unlikely that Gull would allow them to have any strangers on the balcony in any case. Shiloh had a brief fantasy of being fucked over the railing, overlooking the dance floor. It seemed even less likely that Gull would fuck her there, not that she'd let him. Still, there was a twitch of disappointment that it wouldn't happen. Missed opportunity.

Nipa pouted, then burst into giggles again. "There's nobody cute here anyway," she said. "Let's just go dance some more.

"I don't know, I met a guy," Shiloh said, taking out the card and showing it to her. "Tapia Bartussek."

The princess studied the card briefly. "Don't know him," she said. "Is he cute? Point him out to me, let's go!"

"Hold," Shiloh said, stopping at the snack tray long enough to grab a double handful of grapes, cheese and edamame. With all the running and stress, her appetite was huge. They bounced back down the steps.

It was actually a relief to have their chaperone out of the building, just the two of them out to play now. Even though she was playing a role, Shiloh's Anna mask was at its thinnest here and she imagined that if Nipa had been around the Gallamore's travelling show they'd have gotten along quite well, so long as the girl didn't know what she was. For a moment, she felt at home.

Tapia was still at the bar, and Shiloh pointed him out. "I want to meet him," Nipa said, so they found a spot near him. This led to an instant crowd at the bar, with women shouting Nipa's name and shrieking gleefully if she smiled and nodded in their direction, and men attempting to get her attention, which she assiduously refused to do. There was a respectful circle of elbow room kept around them, but the ring of people outside created a clamoring chorus that threatened to drown out the music. Everyone was taller, which made it a bit claustrophobic. She thought of Gull, watching over them—well, over Nipa, but perhaps she'd benefit some from that attention—and felt better.

In the eye of this storm, Tapia seemed surprised to be caught with Shiloh and Nipa. "Well, hello again," he said, addressing Shiloh after bowing to the princess. "Have you returned to tell me that she's your date tonight?"

Nipa giggled. "Anna said you were cute," she said, "and I said I wanted to meet you."

"Oh my," he said, feigning concern. "Can I have a moment to make sure I'm properly presentable? This is a very important moment."

"You're fine," she said. "Where are you from?" The conversation was hard to follow, so Shiloh backed up a few steps. Tapia was still interested in her more than the princess, so she faded back lest Nipa find a nugget of jealousy. The fact that he hadn't completely shifted his attention was a point in his favor though; he probably wasn't one of the photographers that Mahnaz was worried about.

Someone touched her elbow, and she turned to see who it was. She didn't recognize the slender man with the girlish face and short-cut black hair, but he smiled at her. "Shamshoun," he said.

Shiloh did her best to mask the surge of emotion that went through her. "Excuse me?" she said, touching her ear. "You know Shamshoun?"

"I'm here with him."

"Let's dance," Shiloh said, grabbing his hand. "I'm going to dance," Shiloh called to Nipa over her shoulder. The princess laughed.

Shiloh found two squares next to each other, and dragged the man with her. He was wearing black clothes that had faded to dark gray, newish boots, and a wide belt that looked like it normally had things attached to it. "Who are you?" she asked, now that the music would mask the conversation from those around them. She moved her feet and arms in a gentle dance, enough that she could lean over and speak to him while she moved.

"My name's Razor," he said, doing the same. He moved like he wasn't used to dancing, but faked it reasonably well, considering. "Shamshoun's not here, he's outside. Ivy and Holly sent us to get you out of Singapore before things go bad. And they will."

"I know," she said. "He made it off the ship?"

"He did. They all did."

Shiloh allowed herself a sigh of relief. It occurred to her that this might also be a trap, but how would he have known she was on the prison ship, let alone talking to Shamshoun? Razor seemed safe. "Who are you?"

"I sail under Captain Hardson, on the *88 Fists*."

Ah, the other ship. She decided to trust him. "Where's Shamshoun?"

"Staying out of sight of the security staff here. He's a big guy, people notice him."

"He shouldn't be in the city. It's too dangerous."

Razor flicked an eyebrow in a way that suggested he was quite familiar with Sino-India's shifter policies. "Tell me about it."

Shiloh wanted to see him, but ducking out of the club again felt like it might be a bad idea; Anna's role was to keep an eye on Nipa, and Mahnaz might react badly if she disappeared and something happened.

There was nobody to stop her from just leaving, of course, if Razor was really here to take her away. What was Mahnaz going to do, fire her? Shiloh put on a club dancer's silly smile and did a slow little spin, glancing across the club at Nipa as she did so. The princess was still talking to Tapia, and now there was another boy chatting her up as well. The newcomer offered her a drink, which she declined with a smile. The second time he offered it, however, she gave him an embarrassed eye roll and took it.

She wasn't responsible for this girl, who had a bodyguard and the adoration of an entire club wrapped around her. She and Bee and Shamshoun were in real danger; she could just...ah, fuck it, she *couldn't*.

"I can't leave yet."

"Chaperoning the princess?" Razor asked with a grin.

"Something like that. I need help, too."

"Ah, complications."

"There's another shifter."

"From the ship?"

"No." She explained briefly about meeting Bee.

"They picked the worst possible time to come to Singapore," Razor said with a slight headshake. "Where's Bee now?"

Shiloh reached into her waistband and handed him the hotel key. "I can meet you there tomorrow?"

"Or we could go now."

"I think...this is going to sound stupid, but I think I'll be angry at myself if I do."

"That does sound stupid," Razor said, "but I don't know you so I'm sure there's a bigger picture. Be safe. Ivy is really worried about you."

"I'm worried about them, too."

"I left them in good hands." The dance floor was turning, moving him slowly away from her. "See you tomorrow, then." Razor kept dancing for a short while longer, then sidled off of the dance floor.

Shiloh continued to dance and fell into her own head for a while, starting to second-guess herself, wondering if she should have gone with Razor. But no, just a bit longer, to shed the stress of what she'd seen with Bee. She'd be better able to deal with it all tomorrow.

Anyway, it was too late. She'd made her decision.

There was a change in the air around her, something she felt in the mood of the other dancers, and she saw that Nipa had joined her, moving into the square next to her. The princess grinned devilishly, and she returned the expression. In that moment there was motion in the corner of her vision. Without a thought, Shiloh stuck her hand out and caught the bottle that was flying toward Nipa. The princess gasped in shock; a moment later and it would've hit her in the side of the head. Several others saw, and eyes widened. Someone pointed back in the direction it had come from, and there was a man standing with his hands upraised with an unmistakable "I didn't do it!" look on his face.

Gull slammed into him a half-second later. Shiloh hadn't even seen how he'd gotten from the balcony to the ground floor so quickly. Had he jumped? Was that even possible? He'd have broken both his legs, jumping down three stories. However he'd done it, Gull had the alleged bottle-thrower on the ground and in a painful-looking arm lock. His suit jacket had split up both arms, revealing that he had a strange tattoo sigil similar to Dorim's. The bodyguard's eyes were on the rest of the room, scanning for secondary attackers. It seemed like a good time to move off the dance floor, so Shiloh took Nipa's hand and led her away, back toward the stairs.

"Did he throw that?" Nipa asked, looking astonished and flushed with excitement. "Did he throw that at me?"

"I didn't see," Shiloh said. She put the bottle on a convenient table. "Let's go upstairs for a moment." The club staff was beginning to swarm, taking over for Gull, who wordlessly accompanied them back upstairs. A man whose shimmering silver suit suggested that he was the manager or club owner followed them up as well, asking Princess Nipa to forgive the incident, that it appeared to have been an accident and a misunderstanding, not an attack of any kind as the agitators in the city had been kept out of the club, naturally. Nipa didn't appear to be listening to his apologetic patter; Shiloh only paid half-attention to it, and when they got to the top of the steps Gull wouldn't let him onto the balcony.

Nipa flopped onto the lounge. "That was exciting, wasn't it? Oh, my goodness!" She fluttered a hand over her chest. "Sometimes even the best clubs aren't safe, you know?"

"Most places in North America aren't safe. You always have to be careful."

"That was amazing! You're so amazing. This has been the most wonderful night. Thank you for saving me."

She'd saved two girls in the same night, lovely. The thought lent itself well to a wry smile.

"Come here and sit with me." Shiloh did, and Nipa stroked her hand. "Kiss me," she said. Shiloh did that too, tasting alcohol on the princess' lips. When she pulled back, Nipa followed.

"Gull?" she asked.

"He's here to watch everyone else, not me. Besides, Chokidar said no *boys*."

Shiloh suppressed a laugh. "He should have known better."

"He wouldn't have known. I've never kissed a girl before." There were waves of happy lust coming off of Nipa, and it was giving Shiloh a warm feeling. Maybe she'd get to play after all. She leaned closer, her dark eyes flitting all around Shiloh's face. "You're soft. You feel nice." The princess slipped an arm around Shiloh's waist and tumbled half onto her.

Shiloh laid back with it and caught her, and they both giggled some more. She started to say something and the girl kissed her again, more wanton this time. "I can do more than feel nice," she said.

"Are you Chokidar's girlfriend?"

"Not exactly. He just thinks he rescued me." As she spoke she realized she'd let her Anna mask slip, but Nipa didn't seem to notice.

"That's too bad," she said. "If you were, then I could steal you from him." Shiloh had to admit, as their lips came together again, that Nipa was probably a better kisser than Mahnaz. The thought sparked a naughty little giggle against Nipa's mouth, and that made the princess laugh back.

"You're drunk," Shiloh said.

"I am. I shouldn't be out in public. I'll make a fool of myself, and embarrass the Deshmu family name," she said, making a face. "It's late. Let's go home, and I'll sober up, and then we can both crawl into bed together. There are other things I've never done with a girl, and I want to try them with you."

She slipped her hand up Nipa's dress and squeezed her warm thigh. "Okay."

chapter 51

Ten hours before Princess Aiyana's trimester celebration

>> Singapore police are strongly denying rumors that a felid was shot in the city on Wednesday evening. First reported online, the reports of a police shooting near the downtown Akitara steakhouse quickly escalated to blurry online photos of what appeared to be a special-weapons team cleaning up the corpse of a large feline. Eyewitnesses said the animal was seen to shift before it was killed. Police took statements from more than twenty people on the scene, but dismissed any speculation that the shooting victim was a shapeshifter and explained that the animal was an exotic pet that escaped from a shipping container.

"The confusion is understandable," said police spokesperson Ren He Laixheng, "especially on the eve of the trimester celebration. But we have been working to ensure that there are no incidents…"

—Kalypso News Syndicate

The evening couldn't have gone better, all things considered: Fry found a vehicle, a burgundy Chengdu ten-seat van that wouldn't catch anyone's eye. Dinner was a success, and Holly was quite cheered by the fact that Ivy had three helpings and finished with a happy, proud gleam in her eye, and she slept wonderfully for the first time in weeks, listening to her sister breathing next to her. Their argument of the evening before seemed to have been forgotten.

In the morning things went smoothly, and after Kroni, the canids and Ivy changed into their new clothes they left the hotel. "Can I drive?" Ivy asked. Holly nodded.

Ivy pulled up short as they approached the van; there was a woman dressed in ill-fitting clothes leaning on the hood. She was barefoot and carried an oblong object about three feet long wrapped in what appeared to be a ripped bedsheet. Her wrap dress appeared to have come from the same bedroom set. When she raised her head and her shaggy black hair fell away from her face, Holly saw her chin tattoo and realized it was Narooma, the delphid.

Narooma saw her and a smile of recognition broke across her face. "Hi," she said. "I'm going with you. Hope that's okay."

"And what if it isn't?" Fry said.

"Then I'll follow you around, duh," she replied. "Might be kind of hard to keep up, though." She indicated the van. "This is your bug, right?"

"It is," Holly replied. Narooma stepped away from the van, and Ivy got into the driver's seat while the others climbed in back. Holly stayed outside to talk to the delphid. "Why are you back? I was quite surprised when you left us. I had never met a delphid before, so it didn't occur to me that was what you were."

She laughed. "Silly. I came back because I chose to. Gavinder gave me a choice, he said I could stay with him like he wanted or I could come back and help pay our debt. He still can't believe that I don't want to be with him."

"And who is Gavinder?"

"Gavinder's the prince of the Zaal territory," she said with a hint of condescension, as though it was obvious. "He wants me to calve for him but I don't want to, so he's trying to convince me. Which is nice of him really, nobody'd stop him if he tried to do it by gangbang, but then he chased me so damn far and was yelling and fooling around so much that we got caught. So he can say I'm paying our debt all he wants, even though it's his fault. I don't really care, he's got something else to think about now. And you need warriors, I can tell."

Holly took a moment to process all of this. "You'd better climb in and come with us," she said.

"Oh, good. I was hoping I'd get to sit down. How do you put up with having feet all the time? They hurt so much!"

That outburst made Fry smile; she introduced Narooma to everyone while Holly gave Ivy brief instructions on how to start the car. The van lurched a couple of times on the way out of the lot as she got used to the electric motor's response but she had the hang of it within a mile or so. "These rigs are so quiet," she said, mostly to herself. She was mellow and businesslike, Holly noticed, imagining her sister feeling most at home when behind the wheel. The town quickly fell behind them, and the four-lane road was soon a narrow portal through jungle again.

"You'll have to teach me to drive some day," Holly said.

"Of course."

"I tried, in Strip City, but it didn't go well. Narooma, how did you find us? And thank you for stopping the boats that were after us," she added.

"Eh, that was nothing, those warriors were out looking for me and Gavinder anyway. They knew the dirtyfeet took us, but couldn't get us back. You guys made it easy. All that extra killin' energy had to go somewhere. I found you 'cuz we went to your ship and asked where you were headed. Found the cap'n, and he told us where you were going, all the ways up to Semangat Terang."

"You're the only one who came?"

"Nobody likes coming up on the dirt this far. Besides, all you need is me. Too many big crunchy warriors," she waved a hand, "we'd take over the whole island by accident. All sorts of trouble then," she laughed. "Hey, are those crackers? Can I have some?"

Fry reached into the bag of leftover groceries and handed them to Narooma, who received them eagerly.

"I love these. So crunchy and dry! Almost as good as crustybread," she said.

"What's in the wrap?" Fry asked her.

"My axe. Be silly to go into a fight without it, wouldn't it?"

"You're expecting a fight?" Holly asked.

"You're not?" Narooma replied, raising her eyebrows.

She smiled in spite of herself. "I didn't say that. I haven't yet decided what I'm doing."

"We are being followed," Kroni said. He was looking out the rear window.

"Where?"

"There is a blue car, some distance back."

"Are you sure?" Holly asked.

"There are a lot of cars," Ivy said. "All going the same direction. "It could be a coincidence."

"I think it is not," he said, not taking his eyes from the rear window.

Holly turned around and looked out the back, scanning the cars. Fry did the same. Traffic was sparse—in the back of Holly's head it occurred to her that anything more than five cars was probably "a lot" to Ivy—and she spotted it quickly. "It's not a coincidence," she said, recognizing the vehicle. It was a Myawi Protector. She'd forgotten to discharge her collar.

"Then we should speed up and outrun them."

"I don't think we'll be able to. If we run, they'll chase."

"Then we fight," Kroni said.

Narooma grinned. "Toldja you needed warriors."

Holly remembered the Myawi Protector—Kalida, that was his name—cutting down the college boys like saplings. She wondered how many Protectors were in the car, and what they were going to do. Would they take her away from the others if they didn't resist? Kill her on sight? The burly blue car drew closer, unmistakably intent on them now. "It's Myawi," she said.

"Your domestic school?" Fry said. Based on the tone of her voice, she'd seen enough of the Ivory Sisters interview to know how bad a development this might be. "That can't be good. Are we stopping, or making them force us?"

Before Holly had a chance to answer (or even decide), the Protector had come alongside them, then pulled slightly ahead. The tired electric van wasn't a match for the big blue car. Ivy jerked the wheel toward it as it passed, but the van barely swerved. "It's stopping me from hitting him," she said. When the car was ahead of them, she accelerated, only for the van to reduce speed again when they drew within a few inches of the back of it. "Why's it stopping me?" she yelled.

"Anti-collision," Holly said. "Don't let him stop in front of you, or we'll stop too."

Ivy cut into the left lane. As soon as their nose came out from behind, the Protector stuck a hand out the window and fired a slickgun pistol at the road in front of them. The goo hit the road and sprayed outward in a fan shaped pattern, splattering the van's windshield as well. All four tires were coated in an instant. The Chengdu yawed sideways. This time, when Ivy attempted to correct, the steering wheel obeyed but there was little response from the tires.

"He's slicked us up," Holly said. "We've got to stop!"

"It's easier to drive without people shouting." The van's slide continued, and it looped drunkenly on the pavement as though it was made of ice. Ivy groaned in the back of her throat as she steered fruitlessly, trying to bring it back under control. "This is going to be bad," she said in a strained voice. She barely got the words out before the van hurtled into the gravel bed by the side of the road, then hit the embankment separating road from jungle. There was a tailbone-jarring bang from underneath, and they were launched into the air, where the rear corner bounced off of a tree. The impact turned the rear windows into opaque spiderwebs of cracks with a whipcrack of exploding airbags and threw the van into a drunken, two-wheeled spin, around once, twice, seeming for a moment that it was going to stay on its wheels and then tumbling over onto its right side and sliding with an ugly scrape of metal against concrete.

Holly had fastened her seatbelt out of habit. She was the only one. Ivy fell onto her when the van flipped, and Holly instinctively threw her arms wide, catching her and holding on as tight as she could. The impact knocked her wind out. In the back of the van, she heard Kroni and Narooma tumbling with yelps and grunts as the van slid to a stop. The air was filled with smoke and powder.

"Out," Kroni said immediately. He ripped the deflated airbag down with a savage jerk, then put his hands on the floor and kicked up into a handstand, knocking out the left-side passenger window (now facing the sky) with both feet. Fry and Narooma were in motion at the same time. Narooma grabbed her axe and vaulted out of the van; Fry touched Holly's shoulder and met her eyes. Ivy was disoriented again, and accepted Fry's hand. Dilly kicked out the back window, and Wexsun followed him out that way.

Holly struggled with her seatbelt. Through the windshield, she could see the Protector's car had stopped right next to them. The Protector was out of the car. Another passerby slowed, and he pointed at it. "Keep driving!" he shouted, his commanding tone seeming to vibrate the window. As he yelled, he brandished the slickgun pistol casually, and the gawker accelerated away.

She got the seatbelt off and scrabbled for her bag. Fry had helped Ivy out of the van, and leaned to one side so Wexsun could scramble out. Marf and Koon followed, staying in their wolf-forms. "Out, out, out," she was saying, her voice like a low, insistent alarm.

"I'm coming," Holly said. "I can make it." Fry pulled herself out. Holly looked through the windshield again. Kroni had jumped down and was standing between the overturned van and the Protector. "No!" she yelled. Did he know what the Protectors could do? Ivy's friend was about to get himself killed. Holly lunged for the broken window. She didn't know what she was going to do—give herself up?—but she was moving without thinking.

She heard the slickgun's distinctive coughing blast as Ivy helped her up onto the top of the van. The shot caught Kroni low, across the legs and feet, and he went down immediately, his charge turning into an ungainly sprawl. He stopped almost at the Protector's feet. Holly saw the sigil on his chest flare as he brought his fist down as though driving a nail into the ground. There was an audible crack when he hit Kroni's chest.

"We can't fight him," Holly said, "we can't, he'll—" she stopped as Koon and Marf raced at the Protector, blindingly fast. He didn't try to shoot them. He kicked the pudgy juvenile canid aside almost casually, then rotated and presented Marf with his forearm, jamming it into the canid's mouth before he could go for his throat. He clubbed Marf on the top of the head with the gun, apparently ambivalent to the bite.

Fry was moving then. She jumped over the downed Kroni, sidestepping the frictionless sludge on the ground, and seized the Protector's gun hand, twisting the barrel upward. The Protector lifted his arm and quickly reversed the grip, grabbing her instead. In the same motion he swept her legs. As she went down the Protector rotated with her fall, swinging Marf bodily up and over his head. Holly felt her mouth drop open as he hit Fry with the canid, using him as a furry, living club.

And then Narooma cut his head off.

She had unwrapped her axe, which was a battered-looking length of iron with one end hammered into a heavy open crescent like a stylized letter P. She moved with deadly purpose, almost as quickly as Marf, stayed in the Protector's blind spot, and came from behind him. The axe didn't look sharp, but it struck the side of his neck and cleaved straight through; his head popped off like a snipped flower, followed by a shocking gush of crimson.

A car that was passing as this happened veered out of its lane, then steadied and kept going.

"Oh, no," Holly said. She jumped down from the van and helped Ivy down. Ivy paused, looking at the underside of the van, which was pointed toward the road. Thick, white smoke poured out of a gash in the belly pan, so dense that much of it was dropping to the ground like a stream of viscous liquid.

"What?" Ivy asked.

"The battery's damaged," she replied. Of course, Holly realized, the cars in North America were combustion-powered, not electric. Ivy had probably never seen a battery fire before. "It's going to burn. We have to get away from it." The obvious fire also made it more likely that someone would actually radio for emergency services soon. Of course, once someone saw the headless body in the road...

The Protector's body had fallen between the cars, and wasn't visible until the cars went past, but the rapidly spreading pool of crimson pumping from his neck would change that quickly.

Ivy took a step to follow and immediately fell against the side of the van with a snarl of discomfort, favoring her knee. She composed herself for a moment then started limping toward where Kroni lay on the ground. Holly followed, supporting her. Kroni was conscious, his teeth gritted in pain. "I'm fine," he gasped.

"Don't lie. You're worse than me," Ivy said. "I heard something break. Can you move your legs?" He pressed his lips together and nodded. She released a sigh of relief. "Rest a minute."

"Don't touch him," Holly said. "It's frictionless gel. It'll cling to everything it touches."

"She is right," he said ruefully, looking at his slimed-up legs.

"What, you done this before?" Narooma asked.

He made a face that wasn't quite a smile. "Something like it. Ivy, I have at least one broken rib. I cannot shift."

Holly had a moment of confusion. The canids chose that moment to reunite around them, sniffing each other to ascertain there was no damage. The motion made her blink, slowly, trying to take stock of what was happening. Everyone was alive. The Protector was dead, but they weren't out of danger.

"Why'd you let him grab you?" Narooma asked Fry as she pulled her to her feet. "That one's got the magic in him, you can't ever let them grab you."

The HNE sigil on the Protector's chest had gone dark when he died. "You've fought enhanced people before?" Holly asked.

"I've fought just about every kind of people," Narooma responded.

Ivy looked back at the overturned van. The smoke was getting worse, and the vehicle was almost completely shrouded in white smoke now. "Should we take his car?" she asked. Fry was already quickly searching the body for additional weapons. She looked at the Protector's weighted gloves and pulled them off as well. It was lightly appalling, but pragmatic.

"We can't, it'll be traced easily. And we won't all fit."

"What, then?" She watched another car go by.

Holly thought quickly. By now someone would have reported the crash, even if the fight hadn't been seen, and an emergency vehicle would be on the way as soon as a traffic camera confirmed what had happened. There might be other Protectors on the way as well, with her collar live.

A little Volvo camper pulled up on the far side of the accident. "Holly!" an unfamiliar voice called.

She turned, frowning, saw a man she'd never seen leaning out of the side door, beckoning her.

When she hesitated, looking to Fry, he said, "It's okay, we came to help. To get you to Semangat Terang." He was joined in the door by a woman wearing an Axtellia's collar.

"If they're spiders," Ivy said quietly, "we can take their rig." Her tone implied that she didn't think this was the case, and Holly decided to go with her sister's instinct. They started toward the camper. "Oh no, the food," Ivy said, looking back at the wrecked van. The smoke was turning from white to black; the damaged battery cells weren't flaming yet, but would be soon.

"We'll get more later."

Ivy looked pained; Holly could see she was upset by the loss of a bag of edibles. She leaned more heavily on Holly's shoulder than before, putting as little weight as possible on her leg.

Fry jogged to the camper, carrying the Protector's gear. Yet another car went by without slowing. They were fortunate that this far out from the city many people were using autodrive, and didn't care to stop and see what was happening, if they were even looking out the windows. Holly helped Ivy limp to the camper, and Wexsun hopped aboard as well, trailed by his companions. If the young people inside were upset by the canids—who were too large to be normal dogs—they said nothing.

"I'm Durloo," the young man who'd called to her said. He was in his early twenties, with round spectacles and a clean-shaven, shiny face. His black hair was cropped short, with patterns shaved into it, turning his dark brown scalp into a canvas. "This is Alice, and that's Amran, at the wheel. We came to help," he said again.

"You arrived at a good time. Why did you think I needed help?"

"Minute you hit the mainland, anyone could see Myawi's thugs were going to be all over you," he said, nodding to the body of the Protector on the ground. "After the train, they've offered private rewards to citizens and the news said there were bonuses for their own people too. Even other Myawi girls. For finding you."

"You here for the reward?" Fry asked.

Durloo shook his head. "We don't support slavery," he said simply.

"Thank you," Holly said. She looked back outside, where Kroni crouched near the side of the road. He was on his knees, but the slickgel made even that four-point stance difficult; his knees kept trying to creep out from under him.

"Ivy..."

"Don't you dare say you're sorry," Ivy said. "You're the one who told us not to come here in the first place, remember?" They shared a look that seemed amused, but neither of them smiled.

"We gotta get that gack off," Narooma said.

"That would be helpful."

Narooma retrieved the cloth she'd had her axe wrapped in, covered the blade again, and used the weapon to push Kroni across the ground toward the camper. He slid across the rough pavement as though he was on ice.

"He's been gelled," Durloo said. "Alice, we need a blanket." They wrapped Kroni's legs in the blanket to keep the slickgel off of the interior of the RV, then helped him into the bathroom. "It'll take a long soak to get it off," he said.

Holly nodded. She'd read about the stuff. She helped Ivy up the steps and into the camper. Inside, it was fitted out for luxury travel, and she wondered where a group of college-age kids had gotten it.

Narooma shook the gel-slick cloth off of her axe, flinging it into the woods. "Okay, let's leave."

"What about the Protector?"

She picked up the severed head, put the Protector's sunglasses back on it, and put it in the front seat of his car. "All fixed," she said. "Send 'em a message."

"I...don't know if that's the message I want to send." Holly started back to the camper. They'd been here too long already.

"Too late to take it back," Narooma said with a grin. "Make 'em sorry they ever fucked with you."

"I suppose he's sorry, at least."

chapter 52

Nine hours before Princess Aiyana's trimester celebration

>> The unexpected return of the rogue Myawi Holly to Singapore barely twenty-four hours before the Deshmu trimester celebration has tongues abuzz throughout the city. Does Holly have a statement to make, after months of silence? Where has she been? It's been speculated that the Ivory Sisters had her in hiding, but now that she's resurfaced—claiming to have her twin sister in tow, no less—the obvious question is: why now?

Her return has had a galvanizing effect on the disenfranchised. Protests against the domestic industry and the treatment of immigrants seem to have tripled in size overnight, and Singapore police have allotted extra officers to ensure that the peace is kept. "As long as things stay peaceful and demonstrators comply with the law, there will be no problems," said…

—Diāo Girl

"So, that was bad news," Fry said as they pulled away.

Holly nodded.

"What did that man shoot Kroni with?"

"Frictionless gel. The police use it. It won't hurt him, it's just hard to get off, and he won't be able to fight, run, or walk very well till he gets it off."

Ivy mirrored Holly's nod. "That's why the van went sideways, wasn't it? It was like trying to drive in mud. I'm sorry."

"For what?"

"For crashing."

Holly smiled. "I wouldn't fault you for that, Ivy. I can't drive at all. We'd be stranded if not for you."

"We were stranded anyway. I need to learn to drive the rigs here."

"Don't fret," she said, squeezing Ivy's shoulder. "I think there will be plenty enough terribleness ahead. I'm going to go and talk to our rescuers now." Holly had a sudden flash back to childhood; they'd been talking in low voices, perfectly audible to one another but unintelligible to anyone else. She'd never wondered how they'd done it, they just put their heads together and talked, and whatever was said was their secret.

It was nice to have that back. She wanted to tell Ivy, but there were extra lines in her sister's face, a touch of strain in her eyes and the set of her jaw. She was still angry with herself about the crash. Nostalgia wouldn't make her feel better right now.

She took out the portable instead, and called up some pages about Semangat Terang, and the things she'd researched after talking to Marcus. "You need to know what happened to our mother," she said. "It's not good."

Ivy met her eyes, nodded, and bent to reading. Curious, Fry slipped into the seat as Holly vacated it and looked over her shoulder.

The camper was spacious enough for Holly to stand and walk forward; it reminded her of being in a very small train, seeing the landscape speeding past through the windows as she walked. Durloo and Alice rode in the front passenger seat and jumpseat, both of which were swiveled to face the rear, and perked up as Holly approached. Narooma sat on the other side. She'd borrowed a cloth to wipe her blade clean, and Alice and Durloo seemed grateful to have something else to get their attention. When she sat down, Amran glanced at her, perked up, and set the Volvo's autodrive, turning the driver's seat partway around so he could join the circle as well.

"It's wonderful to meet you," Alice said. She had shoulder-length black hair with the tips frosted white, and was dressed entirely in purple with matching eye shadow, lipstick and henna; the picture of a liberal college student, other than her collar. Holly guessed she was probably dressed that way as her benefactor's fetish toy, which would also explain how she had the free time to run off to accompany Durloo. Unless he was her benefactor, but that seemed so utterly hypocritical that Holly didn't want to consider it. "I've been reading about you since you escaped."

"Thank you," Holly said. "I'm nobody special, though."

"Don't say that," Durloo chided. "You broke through a lifetime of indoctrination to free yourself."

"And you found your sister," Alice said, glancing at Ivy. "It's so amazing."

She couldn't help but smile.

"What's she reading?"

"About our mother."

"Oh."

"So what are you here to do for me, Durloo?"

He straightened a bit in the seat. "Alice saw your post on the boards. Her benefactor is my manager, and he's gone to Beijing for a meeting—he is so angry to be missing the trimester party. Anyway, we had talked about you a lot, and she said she wanted to do something to help, and we guessed that you had come in somewhere north of us and were headed to Semangat Terang."

"You're from Singapore?"

"Johor Bahru," Alice said. "Just outside. Amran lives in the city. He's an actor."

Holly smiled and nodded.

"We were hoping to help make sure you made it to Semangat Terang. And then afterward, maybe you could attend one of the rallies."

"Rallies?"

"The Sisters are organizing rallies and protests all over the city, during the trimester party. There is so much media coverage, it's a good time to let our voices be heard."

"Against the domestic industry?"

Durloo nodded. "People would love to see you. Be inspired."

Holly raised an eyebrow. "And how many other escaped domestics do you expect to see there?"

Alice and Amran looked at each other. "We want to inspire people to cut their collars," she said. "Right in front of the cameras."

This wasn't a new means of protest, but tended to result in a lot of arrests and recaptures, or worse. Holly knew it wasn't uncommon for domestics who publicly cut their collars to be attacked by counter-protesters on the spot, making the act equal parts radical and foolish. She didn't point this out. "And what stands between me and Semangat Terang?"

"A lot of bad people."

"Like the one whose head just got snatched?" Narooma asked.

Alice paled a bit. "Worse than that. Vigilantes. Slave supporters think you're a murderer."

Holly decided that she preferred Narooma's approach to dealing with the activist kids. "I *am* a murderer," she said.

"But...it's not the same thing," Alice said.

Holly didn't answer that, just tilted her head in acknowledgement.

"There are people talking about the bounties. About shooting you with rifles as soon as they see you."

"A girl got killed this morning in Little India. She wasn't even a domestic. Someone just shot her from a car because she had long hair like yours."

"They don't know if that was the reason," Amran said. He glanced at the camper's controls.

"It was. It's not safe for you out there. There are people who want you dead. Myawi wants you dead."

Holly didn't see the point of arguing about that; whether the Protector's intent had been lethal or not didn't matter. She glanced back at Ivy, who was still reading, her frown deeper than before.

"It's another three or four hours to Semangat Terang," Alice said. "Are you hungry?" Holly shook her head.

"I am," Narooma said.

"There's food in the mini-fridge," she replied. "I love your tattoo."

"Tā moko," she replied with a polite smile. "Not just a tattoo."

"It indicates social rank, is that correct?"

"Something like that," Narooma said.

"Doesn't that make it the same thing as her collar then?" Durloo challenged, indicating Holly's neck.

The delphid stared levelly at him while crunching on a rice crisp. "Okay, you're just stupid."

"It might be dangerous, helping me," Holly said.

"Already knew that," Narooma said.

"I apologize, I wasn't trying to condescend. I just want to make sure you've thought this through."

"We want to help," Alice said. "What other choice do we have?"

"You could let us take the camper, and get off at the next town. If you're worried about being shot at, I wouldn't fault you for that. I...I know some of the people I've enraged," she said.

"Not all of them," Durloo persisted. "We can help you. I'm staying."

"Me, too," Amran said. He met Holly's eyes for a moment, blushed, and looked at the floor.

"And me," Alice replied.

Holly nodded and thanked them again, mentally adding more pieces to her board. To pass some of the time, she explained to Narooma why she was going to Semangat Terang. It was a chance for the activists to hear that part of the story in greater detail as well.

The camper was a convenient way to travel, with snacks and a restroom aboard. Ivy seemed much more familiar with it; it wasn't that different from their nomadic travels as children, other than the road being much nicer and the camper being air-conditioned. Holly watched Ivy, who seemed calm and comfortable with the forest speeding past. Fry put her head back and went to sleep; Narooma chatted with Ivy as they shared a box of rice crisps.

About an hour later, Durloo's phone rang. He looked at it, frowned, and answered in a low voice. "There's a phone call for you," he said to Holly a moment later.

She mirrored his confusion. "Who is it? The Sisters?" He shook his head, and handed it to her.

"Hello, Holly," Vitter said.

With the phone's vid switched off it was easy to mask her surprise. "I didn't expect to hear from you so soon."

"Yes, well, I've got a bit of a typhoon brewing here. It seemed expedient to take advantage of a few resources I have available. We have files on all of the local activists with certain, ah, sympathies, and I assumed some of them would reach out to you. I hope you realize the sacrifice I am making, alerting Mr. Durloo and his little cabal to our surveillance."

"And what's driven you to take such a drastic measure?" Holly asked, letting her sarcasm show.

"Drastic circumstances, of course. By the way, the police are putting up a roadblock about a mile ahead of you." As if Vitter had willed it, the Volvo's autodrive chattered an alert to get Amran's attention as traffic began to slow. Holly looked forward and saw flashing lights on either side of the road, a row of police vehicles. Amran turned and resumed control of the vehicle. Vitter spoke again. "Seems that there was a Myawi Protector killed earlier today, and the suspicion is that you may have been involved."

"Shit." Holly slipped away from the front seats, toward the back of the rig. "Narooma," she said, beckoning her to move as well. Durloo reached up and pulled a curtain that separated the front of the camper from the living area in back, then closed the curtain of the window near Ivy as well. Fry roused herself and looked around as well. She didn't ask what was going on, but came to a martial alertness, apparently assessing for herself.

"I'm sure if you weren't guilty, they'd let you right through," he said. She could almost hear him smiling. "I joke, of course. But please, don't despair. Tell young master Amran to obey the rules and refrain from doing anything rash, and they should wave him through without searching his camper. Nothing wrong with a young man and his domestic out for a holiday after all, right?"

"What are you doing, Vitter?"

"I'm helping you, of course. And I'm hoping that you'll find it in your heart to help me in return. I don't expect you to trust me, but perhaps I can get your attention with an act of service?"

"Helping me out of a situation that you put me in is not—"

"I beg your pardon. I dare say you put yourself into this situation, after relieving poor Hashan of his head. I'm afraid I don't have much control over the police when it comes to domestic actions. I do have some influence with Myawi—not as much as I'd like of course, considering the circumstances—but I believe I can be of assistance nevertheless."

"You're right, I am skeptical."

"It is so strange to talk to you like this," he said. "Compared to the way you were when I first met you, that is. The transformation is remarkable. I wonder, did your training and dedication really crumble so easily, or did it never truly take hold in the first place?" He paused, but didn't seem to expect an answer.

"He says we should just drive," she told Durloo quietly. "The police won't stop us."

"I suppose the answer to that isn't important. If you ever feel like discussing it, though, I am honestly curious."

"Stalling isn't going to make me trust your motives any more, Vitter."

"Of course it won't. My dilemma is this: your presence has stirred up a great many nests, so to speak. Both for and against your cause. With so many political and social groups gathered in Singapore, I'm sure you can understand that it's something of a social powder keg at the moment. I would rather that it not explode, but you my dear, are quite the lit match. Now, perhaps you're thinking that a bit of unrest will help your cause. I'm sure your friends with the Ivory Sisters think so." Holly said nothing. The camper had slowed almost to a stop, caught in traffic. "I assure you that it would not go as they are hoping. There a great many itchy trigger fingers at all levels, on both sides, and it wouldn't take much for a peaceful protest to turn into a bloodbath. They have a history of doing that, you know?"

"They certainly do."

"I don't want to see a horde of students and well-meaning activists cut down in the streets. Not because I'm afraid of creating martyrs, mind you. I am concerned about the collateral damage to citizens and to our political process. These young, active minds who aren't afraid to speak out are the future of the Brother Nations, Holly. I believe that snuffing them out would be a great disservice to the intellectual health of China and India."

"So tell your soldiers to hold their fire," Holly said sourly.

"I would if I were in charge, my dear. But I am not. The truce between the Brother Nations is strong on the surface but tumultuous within. There are those who would have China and India at one another's throats. You can imagine what that would do to the global stability and prosperity we've worked so hard to rebuild. And, as I said, given the scope of this event things go far beyond Sino-India. There are foreign elements at play."

"You mean the Rainbow Snakes."

"Among others. There are destabilizing elements from Egypt and even from your homeland involved in this as well. And, I suspect, at the moment all eyes are on you."

"On me?"

"As I said, Holly, you're the lit match in the midst of all these fireworks. You seem smart enough to understand that there are those who'd like to see terrible things happen, for their own ends, but who might not want to claim such perfidy as their own doing."

"Like yourself."

"No. I believe we are living in a golden age, and I would see that preserved. I do not hunger for violence and war."

"Lakshmi would disagree."

"Do you mean the goddess, or your friend? I accept responsibility for that mistake. Anshul, exalted Myawi Protector he may be, is a cruel thug and I regret that his approach seemed to be a reasonable one at the time. But please know that I don't want such brutality to become a signature of our interactions, you and I. Anshul took Lakshmi, and you have taken Zhuan and Hashan. Perhaps we could call a truce?"

Holly was silent. She locked eyes with Ivy and held her sister's gaze until one of them—she honestly wasn't sure which—raised an eyebrow and the other followed suit. The feeling of looking into a slightly distorted mirror made her smile.

"If we were speaking face to face, I'd know if you were considering my suggestion, or seething with rage," Vitter said. "As it stands, however, I am at a loss."

She let him stew a moment longer. "What do you propose?"

"Help me to keep things calm. Whether this means staying away from the center of things, or positioning yourself as a calming element, I don't know. The situation is still developing. But I do not think you should underestimate your influence, and your ability to save lives."

"And if what I really want is to see the city burn?"

"I don't believe that you do. And to prove this, I'm willing to see you and your sister safely back to North America, if we can get through this complicated event without undue bloodshed."

"What about the *Fists*?"

"Captain Hardson and his crew would also be free to go. No prosecutions, no warrants, no port restrictions. And if you don't trust me enough to accept passage back to your homeland, then stay in Sino-India. If things stay calm, I believe I can get you pardoned. Your voice could be heard. I agree with you that there are changes that need to be made in the laws governing domestics, and you could be instrumental in changing them, while you've got the public's sympathies." He paused. "That won't happen if Singapore burns. It certainly won't happen if a Myawi Protector or some extremist murders you and your sister in the middle of a street battle."

"You're offering me quite a lot to stay out of your way," she said.

"Or to stand by my side," Vitter said. She noticed that his condescending tone was gone. Holly wondered if he was doing it consciously, or if it was an honest indicator of his state of mind. "I honestly do not know what the situation will entail at this point; things seem to change by the hour. But whatever it will take to keep the protesters calm, to keep things from boiling over. Make your pilgrimage. Cast about it if you'd like. All I ask is that you be willing to consider staying quiet until the celebration is past, or attend as an ambassador."

She laughed. "You'd put me in the same room as Sino-India's stars? With the Deshmus, and the Prime Minister?"

"Of course I would. I'm sure you remember all of your Myawi social graces. And I trust you not to strap a bomb to yourself, for what little that would ultimately accomplish. You have worked very hard to escape your situation. To retreat into death now, taking everyone you love with you, would be patently ridiculous. Though I do admire that you're willing to threaten such madness, it's not necessary."

"What's he saying?" Durloo asked. Holly shook her head at him slightly. She peered out the closed curtains; pulsing strobes in the daylight outside told her that they'd reached the roadblock. The camper stopped, moved forward, stopped again, crept forward, and then accelerated.

"He waved us through," Alice said. They continued speeding up, back to freeway speed. Holly breathed a sigh of relief, and Alice swept the curtain open again, providing them with a view of clear road ahead.

"Rabbit of the moon," Durloo gasped. "What they'd have done, with a fugitive domestic and a shifter aboard..."

"Two fugitive domestics," Alice added. "Mister Nibbor doesn't know

I'm here, remember?"

"Hush, you two," Holly said. "Vitter, I still don't trust you."

"That's understandable. Does that preclude cooperation?"

She thought about her answer. "No, it doesn't," she said finally.

"I'm glad to hear that."

"I'm not your puppet," she said. "If you want something from me, you can ask. I'll decide what I'm going to do."

"Of course. All I ask is that you listen, and consider."

"Good luck keeping the peace, Mr. Vitter," she said, and hung up. With the call disconnected, she let out a long breath and handed the phone back to Durloo.

"Who was that?"

"Aldo Vitter."

He clearly recognized the name. "*What?* How did he get my phone? Why would he call *you* on it?"

"He's been tracking you," Holly said. "And your friends."

"He knows we're *here?*" Alice said, her voice going high with fear.

"All three of you. And me and Ivy, of course. He knew we were in your camper and I think he was responsible for letting us through that roadblock." She thought about it. "I assume that he knows Wexsun and the canids are here, since he saw us on the train, and they were with us when we left. He may not know about you, Fry, or about Narooma."

If any of this concerned Fry she didn't let it show. "What about the other shifters? Kroni, and the bear?"

"He saw them as well, so he'll know of them. He didn't say anything about them. Or about Razor—she might be in trouble."

"Razor's a slippery thing. I wouldn't worry."

"Should I get rid of my phone?" Durloo asked.

Holly shook her head. "He'll just track us by the camper, or..." she trailed off. Fry gave her a look.

"Or by your collar," she said.

"He can track you with that?" Ivy asked.

"Yes. That's how the Protector found us."

"Then we should take it off of you," she said fiercely.

"We can't." *Idiot!* Why hadn't she thought to search the dead protector for his key? The shock of the violence and confusion of the moment had thrust the thought completely out of her head.

"Myawi collars are impossible to remove," Alice said, sounding regretful. "Not without killing the girl, anyway. Unless you have the key."

"Who has your key?" Ivy asked.

"Professor Ono—Elden, he had it. But his things are long gone."

"What did Vitter want?" Durloo asked.

Holly recounted the conversation for them quickly, including his offer to send her home or make her a domestic advocate.

"He didn't say anything about us," Amran said. "We're going to prison, aren't we?"

"If he's telling the truth, I wouldn't let him do that," Holly said.

"You ask him to take that thing off your neck, if he wants you to be on his side," Narooma suggested.

"It's okay for now," she said. "I can turn it off, and I don't think he knows that."

Fry put her arms up on the seatback, stretching her shoulders. "So what do we do next?"

"Keep driving. Go to Semangat Terang. Maybe wait the trimester celebration out."

"Another hotel?"

"I don't know. My instinct is to stay off of the grid, but if Vitter knows where we are and isn't trying to kill us, that might not matter."

"I need to stop to charge the fuel cell soon," Amran said. "Will it be safe?"

"I think so. Are we coming to a large town?"

"No, small place."

"Good."

"Yes, good," Fry said. "I could use some air."

Holly returned to Ivy's side. Things suddenly seemed to be happening very quickly, and it felt better to be in physical contact with her. Ivy returned the lean gratefully. "I never wondered why you did what you did," she said. Her voice quavered. "But now I wonder how you made yourself stop. There's no way to scale this. All the things you've been through, and what they did to our mother. They should be begging us to just walk quietly away."

"I think maybe they are," Holly replied with a little laugh.

"Are we going to?"

"It might be too late for that."

"Good," Ivy said.

Fry was sitting close enough to hear them. "Careful," she said. "Don't lose your heads, in spirit or in truth."

"How do you mean?"

"I'm not an expert by any means, but I know enough to recognize the feeling of going into the dragon's mouth. That's definitely where we're headed. I'm not afraid of that. But when everything's against you, sometimes keeping your head clear is the best advantage you can possibly have. And you, Holly my friend, have a hard time doing that, from what I've seen."

"I'm calm."

"For now. But I also know these folks hurt you. A lot. And you want to hurt them back. You'll do it any chance you get. Ivy, we've only just met, but it wouldn't surprise me if you took after your sister. And when the chance comes to hit back, you're going to want to do just that. I won't stop you, but I'm going to tell you now to keep looking forward, all the time. Past the moment, past whatever you want to do to hurt these people. Remember what you really want. You keep saying you want to destroy everything, but I don't think that's true."

"Maybe not, but it certainly makes me feel better."

Fry nodded. "You're speaking to my heart. I had quite a temper, when I was younger," she said with a smile. "Best to know when to bottle it, though."

"I've been doing that my whole life, Fry. I think the bottle is full. Too full."

"So what are you going to do? Block the doors of the Myawi school and burn everyone inside? That won't change anything; it'll just get you killed. You're better than suicide by grand gesture."

Holly retreated behind her Myawi mask. "People keep talking as though they know quite a lot about my worth. Vitter said almost the same thing. Whose side are you on, Fry?"

She didn't look away. "The side of the mother who isn't interested in becoming a martyr for her own children to read about twenty years from now, assuming they live so long. I am happy to help you, but I'm doing so with the assumption that your planned path leads us all back to the *Fists* to be reunited with our families." Fry leaned forward, her tattooed biceps straining the sleeves of her shirt as she put her elbows on the table. "Like I said, I appreciate and understand your anger. Both of you. And everyone else's as well. I imagine the canids and Narooma suffered at the hands of Vitter's men. Shamshoun's entire family was murdered by these people. They might kill Ivy and Kroni's friend in Singapore. They might have done that already. Me and Dilly just lost a good friend this morning. These kids who picked us up...I don't even know. What all of that means is that when things go sideways, everyone is going to look to you, Holly, to follow your lead. And if you're not stable, then no one will be."

"What about you?" Ivy asked.

"I'm here to help you and Holly," she replied. "Same as Dilly and Razor. But this isn't my ship. You're the captain here. Are you a captain I can trust?"

Holly looked around at the others. "I don't know," she said honestly. "But I promise to try to be. I'll remember what you said."

"I will too," Ivy said. "I know what she went through. I saw it, in dreams, like it was happening to me."

"Did you?" Fry asked. "I never really believed in the idea of twin-dreams."

"It's true," Holly said. "She described my room in Singapore. I was even able to tell when she had seen it, by the color of the drapes and bedspread." She frowned suddenly. "Ivy, how much have you seen? When I was with Elden. You said you were there when he died, does that mean—?"

"Yes."

"Was that the only—"

"No."

Holly put a hand over her mouth, mortified. "I am...so sorry."

"I still like your accent," Ivy said.

"You—eh? Don't change the subject!"

The camper slowed suddenly as Amran took an off-ramp and pulled into a charging station. She could have sworn Ivy shot her a look of filial triumph as Fry and the others disembarked for a leg stretch. Charging the camper's fuel cell would take about fifteen minutes, so a stretch break was in order. Holly saw with a touch of relief that Narooma had left her axe inside the camper.

Irrationally, she was getting annoyed that Ivy wouldn't let go of her hand. Maybe she wanted to talk. "Are...you okay?"

She took a deep breath. "I've been better," she said.

"I'm so sorry. I thought she was alive until Marcus told me. The letters they sent..."

Ivy nodded.

"This is...this is getting out of control. Has gotten out of control." Why couldn't she find the right words? Such a simple thing, yet she couldn't seem to speak to her own sister.

"What is?"

"Everything. Going to Semangat Terang. The ships. These kids." She looked at Ivy. "It's not going to end well."

"Then they shouldn't have brought us here, should they?"

"Hush, don't talk like that."

"Like what?"

"Like none of it matters to you. Like all of this is just another truck to pull out of the mud."

"Why do you think it isn't?"

Holly pulled her hand free of Ivy's. "You don't understand," she said. "I grew up here. There's so much more going on than you could understand."

"So? Explain it to me."

"How can I explain it to you? You want to avenge our mother, but you're not fighting a person. It's...it's a company, an industry. There isn't any one person responsible, and even if there was, he's long moved on to something else. You want to find who put our mother there? Are you going to go after YYI? The pirates who took her? Or the person whose factory it is? That's the Bright Spirit company. But there's not one man who did it. There's a personnel manager—who might be a domestic too—and a supervisor, and a dozen other people. Most of the people who you'll find may not have even been there seventeen years ago. You can't scale this. You don't understand, you're not fighting a man, it's an army, it's laws and soldiers and traditions and social institutions."

"I can understand those things just fine."

"How? By stabbing them in the neck?"

Ivy glared at her. "You of all people have no right to take that tone with me."

"That's what you want to do, though."

"So do you!"

"But I *know* better!" Holly was surprised to find herself yelling. "You're ready to charge out and murder everyone in that factory, and then what? You can't walk—you're half-dead as it is and most of our technology *scares* you. What are you going to do when they send in a tactical team and helicopters to kill us all?"

"I don't know, what will *you* do? Serve them tea?" Ivy's shouted response was just as startling, if not more so.

"You aren't healthy enough to fight a war, Ivy. Especially one you don't understand!"

"Stop calling me ignorant!"

"I'm *not!* You're just in a very unfamiliar place! You don't know what anything is, or how anything works. You can't *drive*—the stability control got the better of you, remember?" The naked insults and scorn felt alien on Holly's tongue; it was as though her eight year-old self was surfacing and turning a lifetime of learned subtlety into brutal frankness. "I'm sure you're used to smashing your way out of difficult situations but that isn't going to work this time."

"What are you going to do then?" Ivy asked again. Her voice was lower, but still furious. "Tell stories and make food?"

"That's not all I can do."

"Good. I think I like Shiloh's stories better."

Holly made a face. "Well, of course you do. They're about you."

"*What?*"

"You don't like this situation because it's about more than just you. There are more people involved, more lives at stake, and you'd rather it just be you. You don't know how to deal with that."

"I still don't hear you offering any ideas. There are a lot of things I thought you might be when I found you, Holly, but I never imagined that one of them would be *useless*." She pushed herself up out of the chair with difficulty.

"Ivy—"

"Don't. I don't need help. And you should look to your words because I think you're talking about yourself, not me." She made her way to the door and stepped outside.

Holly took a long, slow breath and let it out. Then she realized that Koon was still in the camper, still in his wolf-form, lying as quietly as he could on the bed at the back. He'd heard the whole thing. Wonderful. Koon started to slink out the door, but Holly called to him. "Koon. It's okay," she said. She resisted the urge to speak softly, as though the canid would be frightened by the yelling. Koon was close enough to being an adult, he knew what was happening as well as anyone.

He shifted, stretched, then flopped into a chair next to the door, out of sight of the window lest some passerby wonder why there was a naked teenager sitting in the camper. "Bad times makes for snappins," he said with a shrug.

"How did you and the others end up captured?"

He shrugged again. Holly was struck at how much he was just like any teenager. "Kuroi pack runnin' free, intza woods dark and deep. Got squishy with the concrete, couldn't hunt regular. Broke up a hot-shop looking for tasty, went farther downa doghole than the popps like. Bad luck. Girls ran, mama-alpha's gone. Wexsun said hold and the fire came down, they kill you if you try to take them with so we hyena'd." He looked sad. "No good for the backside. Wex says it's hearts and smiles but I don't know. Sniffs bad weird, yip?"

Holly didn't speak nearly enough canid to follow exactly what might have happened, but Koon seemed relieved to have said it out loud. Ivy came back to the camper and tapped on the open door, before Holly could ask Koon to elaborate. "Hey, there's someone here who says he knows you."

"Moon rabbit...so much for slipping into Semangat Terang unnoticed." Holly stepped out of the camper and saw Makkhana. She smiled and embraced him, quickly introducing him to Ivy and the others. Fry and Narooma were obviously suspicious, but warmed up quickly.

"Even after all of this, you are still impeccably comported," Makkhana said. "As though you'd come from a photo shoot. I saw your message."

"I hoped you would. I didn't know where you were, or if you were even alive."

"If there is one thing I am, it's resourceful," he said. "As are you, I see. May I join you in your camper? We have things to discuss, I am certain. Where is the professor?"

"Marcus? He's gone back to the ship. He's not happy in the line of fire." Ivy made a slightly disparaging sound of agreement.

"Glad to hear he's safe. And you will have to tell me all about your adventures, if you would like."

"Possibly," she said. "No videos this time, though. I'm going to need your help, as much as you can offer."

Makkhana patted his bag, which Holly guessed contained a much more advanced portable than the one Razor had loaned them. "I come bearing gifts. Now, first let's have a look at this camper, and try to shed any little ears we might already have."

Holly smiled at Makkhana. "It's a genuine pleasure to see you," she said.

"You as well," he replied, angling his head. "We have advanced to the next phase, it would seem. And you're talking like a Myawi, which makes me assume that you require something of me."

"A great many things," she said. "Does it show so much?"

"It does when I've heard you speak as yourself."

"I apologize if I was tactless."

"Not at all. It's just an observation. No offense is taken. Quite the opposite: I want very much to help you."

chapter 53

Seven hours before Princess Aiyana's trimester celebration

>> A waste-collection truck caught fire and exploded today in a rural region of Tamil Nadu near Chennai. There were no injuries and minimal damage to property. The vehicle caught fire during routine trash collection, burned briefly, and then exploded violently. Investigators have determined that the blast originated inside the truck's waste-containment unit, and suspect that it may have picked up bomb-making materials discarded by an unknown and unidentified separatist group.

—Owl News Syndicate

Shiloh awoke to warm sun on her face and soft flesh pressed gently against her backside. She hadn't slept so well in days. Was it because she was off the ship, or was it satisfying sex? Perhaps a combination of both. She lay still, feeling Nipa's long, lean body in the places it was touching her: calves, ass, an arm draped across her shoulders and a breast against her back.

The sun was coming in through the skylight of Nipa's room, and they were curled up on silk. There was a surprising temperature differential; her toes were in shadow and uncovered, and they were cold. It served only to regulate the temperature so the sun on her and Nipa's warmth didn't become uncomfortable, though.

She flitted through memories of the night before: riding home with the car on autodrive, pawing at each other in the back seat, slipping into the house quietly and with much muffled giggling, intent on not waking Mahnaz or being seen by the domestics, and then they'd tumbled into bed and there had been an hour of talking followed by forty minutes of sex, and then another half-hour of talking and giggling. They'd proceeded to repeat the pattern until shortly before dawn.

She stretched and sighed pleasantly. It had been a good night. Nipa rolled over and murmured, but didn't wake.

Though Mahnaz hadn't technically prohibited Nipa from bedding another woman, Shiloh guessed that he wouldn't be pleased in any case. Whether a result of jealousy or outrage for Nipa's virginity (based on their conversation, a long-outdated myth that he still believed in), he wouldn't respond well. It was too late in the morning to creep into bed with him and pretend she'd been there all night, but she could at least take pains to not be caught naked in bed with the princess. There was a chance it would prove to be a hazard to her slipping out to meet Razor and get the fuck out of this city.

The clothes she'd worn to the club were scattered around the bedroom. She put them back on, forgoing the jewelry. Once dressed, she rearranged the blankets so Nipa was decent, then let herself out.

Shiloh smelled food immediately, and as she reached the bottom of the steps a girl with an elaborate collar—Yu-Hwa, that was her name—greeted her. "Good morning, Miss Vienna," she said. "There is brunch in the sun room." She pointed the way.

The sun room was another glass-topped room—half of the ceilings in the penthouse were glass. Mahnaz was there, looking at the computer monitor he never seemed to be far from. "It went well last night?" he asked.

Shiloh nodded.

"I heard about the assault," he said. "Bystanders said you performed admirably. Snatched a missile right out of the air, they said." He was grinning proudly, and in the bright morning light Shiloh thought his smile made him indescribably ugly.

She shrugged. "I'm glad I saw it in time."

"Well I am very much in your debt. Can you imagine, the princess going to the trimester celebration with a bandage on her head? Or worse, not being able to go because her skull was shattered?"

The table was set with several plates of fruit and pastries; Shiloh helped herself to some.

"By all means, my dear," he said, nudging the platter closer. "I believe that Pravit Deshmu will want to thank you personally."

She guessed that was Nipa's father, but didn't dare ask. Anna Vienna would know, of course. "Will I meet him?" she asked.

"You will. We should have a brief audience before tonight's celebration begins. He is expected to stop by to say hello to Nipa. We'll have to find you some more appropriate clothes before then," he added with a chuckle and his eyes all over her. "I'm so glad you were willing to humor the girl."

"You don't like it?"

"It's...quite garish."

"Hm." Well, he didn't *need* to like it. She wasn't dressing for him, anyway. In fact, if a man like Mahnaz was turned off by this outfit, so much the better. Shiloh did notice that it hadn't stopped him from looking at her bare belly every chance he got.

"I must say, I was looking forward to getting you out of it. It's a shame you had to tend to Princess Nipa. Did she drink?"

Shiloh debated, then told the truth. "Yes. Some boys gave her drinks."

Mahnaz sighed and rubbed his temple. "I thought they might. Thank you for keeping her out of trouble."

"I am happy to help. You've done a lot for me, after all." Shiloh focused her attention on a plate full of pineapple and several sweet rolls. A domestic, not Yu-Hwa, came in to ask if she wanted any tea or juice. How many domestics were there in the house? Shiloh turned her mind to the question of how to get out. She needed to get back to Bee, and there was a wiggle of regret for not going back to her last night.

The twitch grew deeper when she asked herself how she'd feel if she learned that Bee had died while she was getting fucked.

She could ask Mahnaz if she could go someplace. But where? She had no idea what there was to see. She tried to think of an errand that couldn't be accomplished by a servant, or that he'd want to accompany her on. "When does the party begin?" she asked instead.

"The traditional twenty-four hour celebration begins at four," he said absently, his attention taken up by the computer again.

"Do you think that I could get my hair done?" she asked. "I don't want to take up anyone's time, but..." she ran her fingers through it, lifted it, let it drop. "It would look much better with a trim, don't you think?"

"You are right about that," he said. "I'll have a stylist come up."

Shiloh turned her face away so he wouldn't see the brief grimace of frustration. She might just have to walk out.

Mahnaz was true to his word, though, and twenty minutes later a nimble-fingered young man arrived with a full hair kit. He was slight, wore a domestic's collar and was barely an inch taller than Shiloh, but seemed to have the energy of a much larger man packed into him. She impatiently tuned out his cheerful patter as he washed and touched up her hair. The talk seemed to be more for Mahnaz' benefit than hers anyway. She didn't even remember his name, after he'd left.

He did improve the look of her hair, at least. It was longer than she liked, but it was well-done. While he had been working on it, Nipa had risen and departed for points unknown; Shiloh didn't ask where she was off to, and she didn't change clothes either. Mahnaz was busy making what seemed like an endless stream of phone calls, but he drifted through the house every few minutes to touch her shoulder or her hair. At first she thought he was checking up on her, but after a while she got the sense that he was genuinely wishing he could spend the time with her instead of working. It would have been charming if she didn't find him so unpleasant.

Unsure of what to do and restless, she found a large enough open space in the great room to stretch and exercise. Moving felt good, and she turned her wrists and hips, dancing without her hoops. She did a handstand, and held it, balancing, piking her legs back, then forth. The exertion worked off some of the mild aches from dancing the night before.

She became aware of Mahnaz watching her, but kept doing her mini-routine. It was rotten form to stop just because someone was looking, after all. Much more dignified to pretend he wasn't there, after a quick glance to let him know that she knew he was.

When she was done, he stood behind the sofa, and smiled at her. It was a different expression than the one she'd gotten used to. "I exchanged messages with the Gallamore's circus people," he said. "Mr. Gallamore himself, in fact. I thought they'd be happy to know that you had survived. And he was very, very happy. He hoped you would return for next season's show, with a substantial pay raise, and even sent over a mockup of a new show poster for you."

Shiloh felt her stomach drop, knowing what was coming.

"Funny thing, though, it doesn't resemble you at all. So I asked for the whole cast lineup, from last year, just as a souvenir, and I looked at all of the performers. There's a photograph of Anna Vienna there too, of course...and you don't look anything like her."

She wondered if it was possible to edge toward the door without looking like she was doing so.

Mahnaz's voice took on an edge. "I *did* find a picture of you, though. And I wondered why a performer would want to pretend she was someone else. It couldn't just be professional jealousy. So I looked this other girl up as well. I know why you deceived me...*Shiloh*." He spat her name out like it was a bad taste in his mouth.

"I have to go now," she said needlessly, and bolted for the door.

He was slower than she was, but quick enough to shove a chair into her path. Shiloh stepped up on it, ran right over the top of it and barely caught her balance as it tumbled sideways. She hit the floor running, tweaking her ankle but running anyway, eyes on the door. She was ahead of him easily, but then something hit the small of her back, painfully, and her feet went sideways.

She let out an involuntary shout of pain and hit the floor rolling. Mahnaz was on top of her in that instant, yelling at her and hammering away with his fists, screaming for help. Shiloh rolled into a protective ball, shrieking in response, and kicked back. Her feet jabbed at air, twice, and then slammed into flesh. Mahnaz tumbled off of her, and she scrambled back up.

The front door opened, and Mahnaz' trucklike bodyguards lumbered in, carrying large cups of tea and laughing about something.

"Dorim! Weeshu! Shifter!" Mahnaz yelled, pointing. "She's a demon!"

The response was immediate; Dorim and Weeshu released their cups and dropped into combat stances; one of them drew a curved knife that was barely larger than his hand. Which was immaterial—he had big hands. Shiloh didn't wait for them to come toward her. She turned and ran. Mahnaz tried to grab her, snarling, and she ducked under his hand and ran into the kitchen, then the dining room. The security men were close behind her, too close, there was nowhere to go but the big window and oh so many stories of empty air to the ground.

There was only one exit from the dining room, it was a dead end. Foolish! She kept moving, running around the room in a circle, getting the massive table between her and the guards. When Dorim and Weeshu split to come around either side, Shiloh sprang onto it and ran down the center of the table. She jumped and rolled, clearing one set of grabbing arms, narrowly sliding under the other. They changed direction with her, running back and flanking her as she traversed the length of the table. Mahnaz stopped in the doorway ahead of them. He'd grabbed a large kitchen knife, and pointed it at her. "Kill her!"

She thought of Dorim on *Excelsis*, talking with the sailors about how to kill shifters. Would he know what kind she was just from looking? She hoped not; if he knew she was a felid he'd be bold, but if he thought she might be an ursid or a cervid, maybe he'd be less eager to fight. Shiloh slackened her pace slightly, thinking of Kroni and trying to mimic the way he moved when fighting. The two bodyguards slowed with her; in a moment she'd have to start dancing to avoid getting grabbed. They were big enough to tear her limb from limb. Shiloh let out a very un-Kroni like snarl, and jumped toward Dorim, kicking her legs up into a flip like she'd seen Kroni do before he shifted in midair. She didn't shift, though; the leap carried her onto Dorim's shoulders. He put up a hand to block the kick he thought she was throwing and she landed on him instead. She slapped her hands over his eyes and he staggered forward, unable to catch her weight so high on his shoulders.

Shiloh flapped her hands all around his face, keeping him disoriented. His head was so large and hard it felt like a helmet; she was sure she'd break her hand if she tried to hit him. Dorim's hands came up, and instead of grabbing her he tried to keep her fingers out of his eyes and nose. He stumbled forward into Mahnaz. Both men fell, and Shiloh was ready for it, running again when everyone hit the floor. Up, up, up, she had to make it to the door this time. Weeshu was out of the dining room and right behind her. She sprinted but could tell he was faster, and that knife was ready to slash as soon as he was in range.

He was going to reach her before she made it to the door. Shiloh threw herself to the right, dodging abruptly toward the curly staircase to the second level instead of continuing into the foyer. The unexpected move gained her a bit of space, enough for her to jump the railing and vault, and she clambered up the outside, then jumped to the upstairs railing and somersaulted easily over. Weeshu leapt up also. He managed to grab the railing, but was much clumsier and slower getting himself over. Shiloh didn't wait for him, of course, and ran for Mahnaz' room. She surprised Yu-Hwa, coming out of the room to see what was happening. "Move!" she snapped, thrusting the girl aside and slamming the door behind her.

Mahnaz' attached bathroom led through to another guest room, so she wouldn't be trapped in here. She could hear Dorim and Mahnaz coming up the steps. For a moment she entertained the wild idea of breaking a window and trying to get down the outside of the building. Maybe she could hold on...?

No, that was idiotic. The door was her way out. Around them, downstairs, and to the door. Dorim and Weeshu were too big to fight with, and Mahnaz was still shouting incoherently and probably waving the knife around. He was probably replaying every time he'd fucked her in his head, being disgusted and repulsed and it served him right, if he hated shifters so much. If she'd made the hateful little shit think he'd found himself a cute fertile girl and he was wracked with disappointment and horror? Good. She was still the best he'd ever have, and they both knew it.

She looked around the room for something. The pillows were useless, the blankets equally so. Shiloh considered throwing the bedside lamp, the clock, something, but then the door exploded off of its hinges with a wall-shaking bang. Dorim had hit it hard enough to rip it out of the wall. They *were* like trucks. She fled into the bathroom, cutting quickly through and into the guest bedroom, back out into the hall. She closed doors behind her reflexively, even though they wouldn't do any good.

"She's out here!" Mahnaz yelled. He was too late, and too far away to grab her. She jumped over the railing without hesitation. The fifteen-foot drop made her knees and elbows protest painfully as she hit the floor and rolled, but now there was nothing between her and the door. Shiloh was out in the hallway and into the elevator before Dorim and Weeshu got out of the suite in pursuit.

The elevator was maddeningly slow. She hit the button for the garage, and the panel lit up cheerfully, but it dropped so slowly, down through the glass atrium. Another elevator passed on its way up, and seemed to be moving much faster. The people at the main desk seemed to be unaware of anything unusual going on, which was a relief. Nobody rushed the elevator, or attempted to stop it.

And then she was in the garage. Shiloh rushed out of the elevator, squeezing through the doors as soon as they were open, and ran into the parking garage, looking wildly about for a way out. If she could get to the street, she could find a pedicab, head for the hotel where she'd left Bee.

Headlights washed across her. Shiloh turned, and Nipa's Royce pulled up short, starlights winking beneath the paint. The car gave a little click and a sigh, and Nipa stepped out. "Anna?" she asked, confused. On the other side of the car, Gull emerged, eyes invisible behind his sunglasses.

"I have to leave," she gasped. "I'm sorry. He's going to kill me, I have to go."

Nipa grabbed her arm. "Who is?"

She didn't have to answer; the elevator doors opened and Mahnaz came through, flanked by Dorim and Weeshu. "Get away from the princess!" he yelled. Dorim had a gun now, and raised it.

Nipa stepped into the line of fire. "Stop it!" she shouted. "I'm sick of this! You can't do this!"

"Princess, please—"

"No, *you* shut up, Chokidar! You tell my father that I'm not a baby any more! I'm old enough to make my own decisions and he doesn't get to act like I'm something I'm not. I am going to do what I want and go to bed with whoever I want, and he can't stop me! He has Aiyana and her baby to parade around, he doesn't even need me anyway! We had a good time, and she didn't rape me, I *chose* it! Tell Father to internalize *that!*" Mahnaz's mouth dropped open, and his face drained. Shiloh actually found it slightly comical. Nipa all but pushed Shiloh into her car. "Gull, don't let them follow me," she said, then jumped in after Shiloh. She got behind the wheel this time, and the car accelerated away backwards. "Did they hurt you?" she asked Shiloh.

"No, I'm okay. Just tired from running."

"I'm so sorry they're being like this." The car shot out of the parking garage like a bullet. The royalty prioritization stopped oncoming traffic automatically, and they were blocks away from the scene in moments. Nipa laughed. "I could tell from the look on his face that he didn't know for sure about you and me. I probably made it worse, didn't I?"

Shiloh nodded. "Maybe just a little," she said.

chapter 54

*Seven hours before Princess Aiyana's trimester
celebration*

The group climbed back into the camper, now joined by Makkhana, who took the front seat from Durloo. "A necessary detour," he said, and gave directions to Amran. The camper was silent as they pulled away; probably, Holly mused, because they'd heard her and Ivy screaming at each other. On top of that, they couldn't help but notice that Ivy was now sitting very deliberately apart from her and looking out the window, her jaw set.

They drove away from the freeway and into Kuala Rompin. Like the town they'd slept in the night before, it had the air of a place that had been completely rebuilt within the last thirty years. Multi-family housing and businesses rested uncertainly among scattered trees, and the land bore fresh scars of development.

Their destination was a fancy-looking doctor's office in a new building that had been designed to look older. Ivy looked at Holly with an arched brow, but didn't ask.

"Everything's arranged," Makkhana said. "We'll see you in an hour or so."

Holly rose and nudged Ivy, motioning toward the door. The rest of the group watched silently as they departed.

The heat pressed down on them, then retreated in a wash of air conditioning as they went inside. The receptionist gave them a respectful bow. "Sisters Aniram," she said, addressing them both. "We're honored to have you here."

Holly felt herself slipping into her Myawi-face, and didn't fight it. She'd need it for what was coming. She returned the greeting, then accompanied Ivy into an examination room and motioned to her to lie on the table.

"What is this?" Ivy asked.

"They're going to look at your knee," she said. "I'm hoping they can fit you with a new brace. You'll need to undress—"

"I've been to doctor's offices before."

"I'm sorry."

Ivy shook her head in annoyance and climbed up onto the table, unbuckling her overalls. Holly watched her without hovering, ready to offer a hand, but Ivy didn't need it. She couldn't help but quietly catalog the marks that time had left on her sister—the scar on her temple, another one on her right shoulder, the bracer of vaccination tattoos around her upper left arm, her sun-beaten skin and dry hair. Her knee had swollen nastily after the beating it had taken yesterday and this morning, the skin darkening in an unpleasant bruise. Her fingers were rough, and seemed to be permanently dirty under the nails. Ivy had angles where she herself had curves, a subtle hollowness to her cheeks, a shadow at her clavicle, visible ribs, and yet her body was still so incredibly familiar Holly wanted to touch her to see if she was real. As she watched Ivy, she began to see the muscle as well. Thinking of her as emaciated was wrong—she was wiry and strong, in spite of the story of bare survival her body told. Because of it, even.

Holly felt badly for underestimating her, but also wished she could spend a few months feeding Ivy, washing her hair so it shone as much as hers did, doing her best to make Ivy's strength and beauty come through. With some polishing she'd look...like a Myawi.

It wasn't hard to see how wrong that thought was. "I'm sorry," Holly whispered.

Ivy didn't turn her head. The corner of her sister's eye darkened in a glance, but there was no acknowledgement other than that. Ivy dutifully pulled herself onto the table and lay down, her eyes on the ceiling. Holly draped a towel over her for modesty—apparently that was something they didn't do in North America.

The door chirped, announcing the arrival of the doctor and an attendant guiding the bone-knitter on a quiet air-cushion caster. It was a smaller, less fancy device than the one at the Myawi school. Ivy looked at it with a mixture of curiosity and apprehension. "What's that?" she asked.

"It's to diagnose the damage," Holly said with a glance at the doctor.

He had been told that Ivy might react badly if she knew the device's true purpose, and nodded in agreement. "It will sting somewhat," he said as the attendant positioned the knitter over her knee, adjusting the arms. "It will work below the skin to assess the damage. It will feel like a tattoo."

Ivy didn't protest, just nodded and resumed looking at the ceiling. The attendant taped monitoring strips to Ivy's arm and chest, and a thin sedative feed to her upper lip.

She snuffed at it, frowning. "It smells strange."

"Like rotten fruit?" the attendant said with a knowing smile.

"Something like that. Something."

Holly realized that Ivy had probably never had a sedative before. The gas intended to calm her down would make her incredibly quiescent. It was a good time to depart. "I have to go," she said.

Ivy looked at her and nodded again, closing her eyes with a little frown. She was being stubborn, Holly realized, she was a bit frightened and didn't want to be left alone, but she was also still angry at Holly so she wasn't going to admit this. Well, she could be like that if she wanted to. They were both stubborn. In a few minutes Ivy'd be too high to care.

She went back out to the RV, where the others waited. The heat hit her in a wave as she exited the clinic with a feeling like a daydream being torn away, the real world pressing back in.

Conversation in the camper died when she opened the door. "She's in," she told Makkhana. "I'm going to go now."

He nodded knowingly, but Fry asked, "You're leaving?"

"I have to."

"This about the screaming we heard?"

"Indirectly." She didn't want to get bogged down in a long explanation. "They're going to keep coming after me. I'm going to accept Vitter's invitation and go talk to him."

"Self-sacrifice doesn't become you," Makkhana said.

"Save the platitudes," she replied. "Self-sacrifice is all I've ever done. And with my collar, I'm not safe to be around. And...there's no argument. I can help better this way."

Fry nodded. The look on her face said, *You're the captain of this ship*, and made her uncomfortable. "What should we do, then?"

"Get Ivy home. I'll find a way for you to sail. Just...get all of them home."

Dilly was the first to respond, which made Holly smile. "Swear to it."

"Thank you."

"We'll wait for you," Fry said.

"Don't." Holly stepped back out of the camper, but Fry followed, and began strolling next to her as she headed down the sidewalk. Holly didn't stop; she would feel better when she was out of sight of the doctor's office.

"You're really leaving your sister behind? She's going to be angry," Fry said. "And heartbroken."

"Not as much as you might think. We're each...not who the other expected her to be. And I'm not arguing about this. Just keep her safe, please?"

"Tell me what this really is, first."

"What this really is? Okay, Fry. I look in the mirror and understand, all the way down to the center of myself, that nobody could possibly love me. Which is fine, I'm perfectly willing to accept that. I'm not on a quest to achieve love for myself. I don't always have a sense of what I am doing, but I know I'm not going anywhere and this is the self I'm stuck with. But it also means, if I don't want to be alone, that I've got to be beautiful or useful or interesting, or ideally all three."

"Ivy loves you."

"Ivy loves the *idea* of me. She hasn't *known* me for almost twenty years. She'll figure this out sooner or later." Holly quickened her pace. "Are you going to offer me more examples? You and Hardson like me because I'm potentially useful," she said, slapping her belly with one hand. "Makkhana sees me as a political tool. Minnijean likes having me around to help in the kitchen, and I'm interesting to her. Same with Razor, and Marcus—who really doesn't care about me; he finds me interesting but he's also afraid of me. Like Dilly is. I've built and molded myself into something beautiful and useless, and then turned around and wrecked that as well. I don't have anything left but to make sure that she and the rest of you get home. And the way to do that is what I'm doing now."

"I think...that there are a lot of things wrong with what you're saying."

"I don't suppose it matters either way, does it? I've done everything I can for her. Anything else I do is just going to make her life worse."

Fry stopped. "I don't agree, but I don't think you're going to stand still and let me convince you, either."

Holly shook her head and kept walking.

"Fair enough. I'll see you."

Holly kept walking. It bothered her that she couldn't relate. She had pondered it on the drive up, and her mind kept going back to it, like reflexively touching a paper cut, but she wasn't particularly worried about any of the others. She liked Fry, and Razor, and Hardson as well (well...no, he was charming, in his grating way), but she felt no worry or tension about their well-being, even though they were certainly in varying levels of danger. She had been sailing with them for several months, living with them. The *Fists*, like many ships with full-time crews, prided itself on being like a large extended family, and they'd gone to great lengths to make her feel like she was a part of it, she had to admit. And yet...she just didn't care. She knew she was putting them in harm's way, or they'd put themselves in harm's way to help her, and she couldn't seem to make herself worry that they'd die. When Holly contemplated things going wrong and Razor not returning from Singapore, or Shiloh not making it...she didn't feel anything. She felt like she was moving people around like pieces on a mental chessboard, and their deaths meant nothing more than that they were no longer available to her.

And that made her dangerous to them. Only Ivy mattered. Holly was aware that this wasn't the right way to feel, that it wasn't a good thing—or, at least, it wasn't what she wanted for herself. It wasn't who she wanted to be. But for the moment it was all she had, and the way to ensure that Ivy was safe wasn't to go to Semangat Terang. The way to get them out was to do as Vitter asked, to align herself with him as he'd asked, and let the *Fists* sail while the eyes of the Brother Nations were still on them, while they could pat themselves on the back for using Holly to make things better for all domestics, the same way that her mother had, indirectly. That way, at least Ivy would get out of this place. And maybe...maybe she could find a new place for herself. There was a fantasy that Vitter could make things okay for her if she did as he asked, he could waive rules, get Myawi to call off the death sentence. Even if she was never allowed to appear in public again, it might still be worth it.

Holly found herself walking toward a Rotiharian truck without even thinking about it. Perhaps she'd watched too many movies, but here she was, thinking that she might hitch a ride with a truck that just happened to be going her way.

The big truck was parked on an induction pad, the only sound a quiet ticking that indicated it was recharging. The driver was standing in front, cleaning the windshield. As she approached, Holly saw that he wore a collar. It wasn't uncommon for trucking companies to use domestic drivers, and obviously Rotiharian was no exception.

The driver saw her coming, and turned slightly away as she approached. "I know you," he said, looking over his shoulder at her and not stopping his task. "You'll want to stay to one side; the collar has a camera."

"No sound?"

"Not while I'm on break," he said somewhat ruefully. "I heard you were back. Surprised you're here though."

Holly stopped a few feet behind and to the side of him. "Are you going to Singapore?"

He chuckled and nodded. "Is that where you're going?"

"It is."

"Be honored to have the most famous Myawi in my truck. Even if I can't tell anyone," he added.

"Infamous, I suppose."

"Either way. There's a jumpseat behind my seat you can squeeze into. Once we're on the road don't talk until I say it's okay."

"Thank you. What's your name?"

"Gao," he said. "Nice to meet you, Holly Aniram."

"You seem like you've done this before, Gao." More than one escaped domestic had tried to put some distance between herself and searchers by hitching a ride on a truck out of town. She'd never thought about it before, but Elden's little car with its programmed autodrive was as much a part of her former cage as it was a convenience.

He turned his head again, so she could see his smile. "No. But I've thought about it."

Holly nodded and went to the driver's side of the truck, opening the door and climbing in. Gao's response made sense. The girls who rode out of town on trucks rarely got far—the trackers in their collars made them easy to find. And in the case of domestic drivers, they were just as likely to get into trouble for helping if they were found to be aware of their illegal passengers. Industrial domestics had little enough as it was, and there wasn't much point in risking that. Holly wondered if Gao wasn't being cautious in claiming that he'd never done it before. Then again, she wasn't going out, she was going in. Ferrying her closer to her captors certainly wouldn't be seen as a punishable offense. And if it looked like he was going to be in trouble, she'd claim to have threatened him.

She sat on the floor so she wasn't visible through the windows, even though the windows were tinted. Holly also stayed out of sight of the windshield, thinking that there was a chance Rotiharian had installed a camera on the dash to watch the driver, though Gao hadn't warned her of one. Sitting on the floor, hidden by the driver's seat, she felt comfortable.

A few minutes later Gao climbed up and in, switched the truck on, and drove back toward the freeway. The hum of the electric motor beneath them was comforting, and Holly dozed without realizing it. Gao never spoke except to sing along with the radio; he didn't tune in to any news stations for the two-hour drive.

chapter 55

Six hours before Princess Aiyana's trimester celebration

Shamshoun expected to feel much angrier about being back in Sino-India than he was. He had resigned himself to a swift death upon the *Excelsis'* arrival, and Shiloh's stories had helped with the passing of the trip. But now, things hadn't gone as expected, and he was alive and moving around free once again. This time Shiloh was the prisoner, and he the hopeful rescuer.

He and Razor had found her quickly. Razor had determined what Mahnaz' job was, once Shamshoun identified the little rat-faced man, and they had only to watch the house where Mahnaz lived for less than an hour before Shiloh came out, in the company of Mahnaz and Princess Nipa. Shiloh's masquerade seemed to be stable, and after Razor spoke with her at the Dragon's Den club a new course of action was decided upon.

Shamshoun didn't like it. Razor had said that Shiloh wanted to stay just a bit longer, but every hour that slid past increased the chances that she'd be caught. The night had been a tense one, spent largely in the back of the car Razor had rented. Shamshoun was unfortunately memorable even in human form, though he'd shaved his beard and head in an effort to blend in better. There were no obvious tells that he was a shifter, but his bearded face was known to Vitter. It wasn't unthinkable that someone would recognize him without it. It was harder to hear the rhythm of the world in Singapore; like Strip City, it tended to be drowned out by the ever-present bustle and noise.

Their car was currently staged at a little public park near the edge of downtown, almost ten miles from the water, where the city began to give up its grip on the earth and returned to rainforest. Razor hadn't needed to be asked if they could sleep outside of the grip of concrete fingers, she had just done it, and this made Shamshoun like her quite a bit. The park was relatively quiet as well, save a few well-attended children playing in the grass.

"Rush hour should be over," Razor said, drumming her hands on the steering wheel. "You want to get a bit of sun before we go?"

A stretch would be nice. Shamshoun reached over to open the back door and pushed himself up and out of the car. They had pulled the rear seat cushion partly out so Shamshoun could lie down comfortably, out of sight of the windows. It was better than hunching over in the rear seat, but he was still grateful to stretch his shoulders in the open air.

The atmosphere was warm and calm, but with a tense undercurrent, like the faintest hint of a storm far off, a cloud that could spawn lightning with the slightest provocation. It was more than just the trimester party that had the city poised to burst into storm; there were other factors moving in the air as well. Shamshoun guessed that they themselves were one of those factors. The night before, they'd been able to see the *88 Fists* and *Excelsis* in the harbor, lights glinting over the dark water just beyond the harbor, larger than the assorted pleasure craft that filled the space. That the ships were both still there suggested that Holly's truce was holding for the moment. Shamshoun looked in the direction of the ocean for a while, feeling the slow drumbeat of the world, then returned to the car.

He didn't ask Razor if she was certain about the other shifter Shiloh had said they needed to find. He trusted Shiloh, had seen her and heard her after the things she'd seen on *Excelsis*, and if she said there was a shifter they needed to help then that was the truth of it. Shamshoun thought about what she had said about his song not being finished yet, and smiled. "Let us," he said, and Razor started the car. It was a cheap gasoline-burner, contributing its own noise to the city.

Razor was inclined to prattle a bit, talking about the things they were passing and commenting about the news on the radio. The moment-to-moment news channels were busy, between keeping track of the many celebrities and politicians in town, and waxing lightly hysterical about the possibility of an attack by the Rainbow Snakes or some other terrorist group on the event. Shamshoun preferred to listen; he wasn't paying attention to individual stories so much as he was listening to the picture that it all made. He heard nothing on the news to support the feeling of a storm about to break. This didn't make the feeling go away, of course.

The long drive back into the city was slow, thanks in part to rush hour and Razor's inability to get into the autodrive-cars lanes. It took them just over an hour to make it to the docks, and another half hour to find a place to park the car. Once it was stowed, Razor made a face and touched her nose in a gesture of irritation. "Why did I do that? It's not like we're going to need it again. Should've just abandoned it."

"Today? It would have been collected under suspicion of being a bomb. Might have drawn attention."

"Good point, good point." They bypassed the front desk and went directly to the room Shiloh had given them the key to.

There was a teenager sitting in the hollow between one of the beds and the wall, watching television, and she scrambled to her feet when they let themselves in. The tabby stripes on her lower arms and calves marked her as a felid instantly. "You are Honeybee?" Shamshoun asked.

The girl looked like she would leap through the ceiling if either of them shouted "boo." Her nostrils flared visibly, and her hands fluttered at her sides. "Yes." She glanced at Razor but her eyes were on Shamshoun. She made a visible effort to relax. "You can call me Bee."

"We are friends of Shiloh's," he said.

Bee closed her eyes and swooned in relief, dropping back into her little nest next to the bed. "We're going to the boat? Where's Shiloh?"

"Guess we'd better wait for her," Razor said, introducing herself and Shamshoun. "Don't worry, nobody's going to hurt you with us around. Have you slept?" The girl looked haggard, and Shamshoun wasn't surprised when she shook her head no. "I'm going to close the curtains so you can get some sleep, then. Is that okay?"

"They...they killed my friends," Bee said. "Even Salina. Shiloh would have found her by now, they should be back." A tear ran down her cheek. "They should be back."

"Shiloh is strong," Shamshoun said. "And smart. She will be back."

"I'm wrong, we can't wait." Razor was at the window. "Annnnd we might not be here then," she said. "Containment truck just pulled up out front." Bee sat up with a little squeak of fear. "Don't worry," she said, "we're fluffy."

Shamshoun went to the window, looking down at the narrow street three stories below. He saw the flashing lights first, drawing attention to a heavy, boxy truck like the one they'd stolen from Vitter at the trains. There was a police car in front of it, also lit up. Curious onlookers were beginning to mill on the sidewalks.

"Bee, put your shoes on," Razor said calmly. "And take my jacket." She shrugged out of her thick-shouldered black coat. She wore a loose-fitting sleeveless shirt, a hooded cowl underneath, and a pair of holsters strapped around her narrow shoulders, the handles of two knives visible under each arm. Razor adjusted her gloves. "Do you know about snares? Bee, listen." She snapped her fingers to get the felid's attention. "Breathe slow. Stay calm, I told you we're fluffy. Do you know about snares?"

She shook her head. "Bee doesn't know what snares are!"

"They look like little rings when the police have them in their hands. They will try to toss them around your neck, and then your ankle, like a lasso. You understand?"

"Bee avoids snares."

"Good. This is important; if you do get snared, neck and ankle, *do not shift*."

"Shiloh said no shifting," Bee replied dutifully.

"Yes. But especially if you get snared. It'll break your leg, or your neck. Clear?"

"No shifting."

"Good."

"Bee can't run so fast on two legs."

"That's okay, neither can I," Razor added with a smile. Bee tried to return it but it was clear that she wanted to crawl back into her little nest.

Shamshoun listened to them and watched the police in the street. They were taking steps to move the crowd back, isolating the hotel. The sight of the men in the armor, of the police cars, was making him tense with anger. Was this the last thing that Pepper had seen, crouched afraid and waiting for a contact to take her to a ship, realizing that it wasn't going to happen? He glanced at Bee on the bed. The girl was shivering, her shoulders curling inward, her posture crying out for something to make this not be happening.

"Close that window, Shamhoun, the police will have fairies up."

He nodded. "Bee," he said, "you will be safe."

"Shamshoun and Razor have done this before?"

"She has."

"I have. But don't tell anyone. I'll get in a lot of trouble," Razor said with a wink. "They're going to secure the stairwells and exits, then find out what room we're in and come straight up here. We need to be out of here before that."

"Over the roof?" Shamshoun asked. The hotel was the corner building, so they had two attached buildings to leap to.

"No, they'll be up there too. Straight out the front is best. If we're really lucky, they are looking for her and not expecting you." She beckoned to

Bee. "Hey, little one, look at this." She cracked the curtain just enough to see out and pointed out over the buildings. "You see those two ships close together out there? Past the big one that's coming in. The smaller one, that sexy-looking heap? That's my ship. That's how we're gonna get you home. We just need to get there. That's pretty close, isn't it?"

"Bee can swim that far," she said determinedly.

"It's a little farther than it looks," Razor said gently. "But if you had to, I bet you could. I was thinking we'll get a boat to take us out there. We can do that, right?"

"Razor doesn't need to condescend."

"Sorry. Shall we go, then?"

Shamshoun stripped, tossing the ill-fitting clothes they'd bought him onto the bed. The hallway was deserted, oddly silent; even the piped-in music that permeated cheap hotels like this had been silenced. He led the way to the elevators, then stood between them, listening and waiting, focused on the doors. He could feel the building's tune now, the rustle and hum of the ventilation and of the elevators moving. A slight wash of air from the closed doors heralded the car's arrival even before the chime, and he stood directly in front of the doors.

When the elevator opened, he saw five armored-up policemen waiting inside. As they took in the fact of a huge naked man in front of them and realized what it meant, Shamshoun shifted and lunged into the elevator with them. He spun, throwing himself against them and swatting indiscriminately in the tiny space. Bodies were crushed against the walls and mashed under his feet. Bulletproof vests were opened up by his claws, and blood sprayed against the walls as at least one claw found at least one major artery. One of the cops pulled the pin on a pepper grenade and the elevator filled with choking, stinging mist. Shamshoun shut his eyes and mouth tight and flailed with front paws, turning, feeling helmets peeled off and bones breaking under his attacks. After a moment he was trampling on bodies, and could no longer feel anyone standing. He leaned against the side of the elevator, trying not to breathe.

"Coming in," Razor said. "It's me, they're all down." He heard her taking something from one of the downed cops. "You couldn't have left me one helmet intact? Just kidding."

The gas burned, in spite of Shamshoun's closed eyes. He snorted, trying to blow it out, which didn't help much.

"Yeah, I know." Razor's voice was muffled; she had taken one of the police masks and put it on. Shamshoun guessed that the next few sounds were her doing the same for Bee, giving her a mask. A gun cocked. "Slick-guns," she said, "but live sidearms."

"Razor doesn't take guns?" Bee asked, her voice also canned now.

"Lethals won't work with the wrong fingerprints. Shamshoun, are you okay if I close this door? We're better off going straight to the lobby before they figure out what happened."

He snorted again. The sooner they went down, the quicker he would be out of this box. The air burned, and he continued holding his breath. Mucus was running out of his nose like blood, and his eyes were weeping, in spite of being closed. The insides of his ears burned slightly as well.

The elevator chimed, and they began moving slowly downward. Shamshoun waited. He let the elevator's hum work its way through his body, weaving it into his blood's song. Waiting and watching, the unseen mother earth moving closer to him, welcoming him slowly back. And...stopped.

Shamshoun growled. The inside of his mouth was starting to burn, and he opened his jaws to let irritated saliva flow, drooling on the floor. The air in the elevator was unbearable; he trod on the broken cops, restless.

"I know, you can't see," Razor said. "I'm going to make lots of noise for you. Follow it as best you can?"

The door's chime again, and then the slickgun's distinctive cough repeated four times, followed by shouts of surprise and moist splats as the rounds found targets. Shamshoun heard Bee and Razor running forward and followed, bounding immediately to one side so he didn't run over them and trying to open his eyes.

The hotel lobby swam into watery focus. Judging by the people on the ground, Razor had slicked up the floor on either side of the door, as well as several police and bystanders. She and Bee were out the door in an instant, so Shamshoun barreled forward after them, trailing drool and shaking his head in a desperate attempt to clear his eyes. One of the blurs from the side-lines rushed forward, and he swatted it, throwing the cop out of his way. Shots were fired, but he wasn't struck and there were immediate shouts, Shamshoun guessed at the shooter, to hold fire.

And then he was outside. Bee and Razor had pulled up short, possibly unsure of where to go next, so Shamshoun decided for them. Just as he had on *Excelsis*, he charged straight into the crowd. They parted ahead of the charging, slavering bear, with considerably more panic than the sailors on *Excelsis* had. Shamshoun kept his head; he didn't attack any civilians, just charged forward roaring and slavering, to create a hole through the crowd for Razor and Bee.

The crowd dissolved into a panicked mob as people ran in all directions, trying to escape the ursid that appeared to be rabid. He heard shots fired behind him and hoped the police were shooting over the crowd rather than into it. The mob fled outward in an ever-dispersing pattern, and Shamshoun turned toward the water, intending to lead Razor and Bee that direction. Starting down the narrow street, he encountered a surprised pedicab driver, struggling to turn around amid a flood of fleeing pedestrians. The cab tipped over when Shamshoun slammed bodily into it, tumbling over on its side with a discordant jangling of bells, the rider shouting as he was flung to the pavement.

The chaos was total, the interweaving sounds and rhythms a perfect cacophony of madness. Shamshoun roared with it.

Something exploded in his head, and he was suddenly on his back, then on his side. It felt like the back of his head was missing, though it couldn't be otherwise he'd be dead. Was he dead? No, he was not. There were still people running and screaming, seemingly in all directions around him. Shamshoun shook his head, the feeling coalescing from shocked nothingness into blinding pain. Someone running past. He wasn't sure where Razor or Bee was, and only became aware of this uncertainty in a roundabout way. Blood, he could taste it in his mouth. Shamshoun focused his eyes, and saw a handsome young man, shirtless, wearing bright orange striped pants and a helmet, a road worker perhaps. The young man had a sledgehammer poised above his head. Blood on the sledgehammer.

Shamshoun understood. He took a swipe at the man, who danced backward and then brought the hammer down on Shamshoun's paw. He bellowed in agony and stood up, towering over the young man but almost immediately losing his balance, his head throbbing and seeming to be unwilling to tell the truth about where he was, about which feet were on the ground. His right paw hurt so much, as much as his head.

And the young man, with his hammer raised again. Shamshoun's jaw was on the ground, his hurt paw curled underneath him. He knew he wasn't thinking straight, knew he'd just fallen down, but that was all right. The young man was handsome, and his face was full of determination. He was bold, and strong, his song in tune with mother earth even if he was unaware of this. Shamshoun saw this, and decided that yes, this was as it should be. This would do.

The hammer descended.

chapter 56

Four hours before Princess Aiyana's trimester
celebration

Holly was roused when Gao said, abruptly, "I smell smoke." Holly sniffed, but didn't smell anything. The truck bounced gently as he pulled off the road and stopped. He opened his door, then reached around the door and tapped Holly's shoulder before jumping out, leaving the door open. She heard the noise of the city outside and caught on quickly: he had fabricated an excuse to stop that wouldn't tip off his benefactor company that something was out of the ordinary. She glanced out, then slipped out of the truck. When her feet hit the ground, she saw Gao, turned away from her again and hunched over one of the rear wheels. He didn't look her way, but raised a hand in her direction and waved before walking around the back of the truck.

She resisted the urge to call out her thanks to him, and started walking. She was able to orient herself with the skyline; they were in the city, south of the Woodlands Crossing bridge linking the island city to the mainland. She had to get to the auditorium, where the media fairies were thick on the ground. Getting downtown, to the Koralyi Stadium, where Vitter probably was, would be easy—though somewhat easier if she had a bicycle. Holly briefly considered hijacking a car, like she had in Strip City, then discarded that notion as foolish. If the police caught her before Vitter did, they were likely to shoot her on sight. Stealing a bike presented similar problems, as well as the hurdle of not having the faintest idea how to steal a bike. She thought ruefully that Ivy would probably know how.

Nevertheless, this was her city, and she wasn't out of options. Holly ran through a list of places she knew to be nearby and finally happened upon one—the Crystal Turtle, the domestics' bar. It was barely four in the afternoon, but someone might be there. Considering the odd hours that so

465

many housegirls and industrial domestics had to keep, it was possible that they had a lunch and suppertime staff. With luck she could find a friendly face to loan her a bicycle. And of course Shmi had always wanted her to go there. Well, it was time.

She was in luck; the little basement club was actually rather busy, in contrast to the bar upstairs. Holly wondered if it was because a lot of people were headed down to the trimester celebration, if they weren't there already, leaving their domestics with a light workload or even free time.

The little club was laid out in such a way that it provided cozy private spaces as well as open communal space. Curtains hung from the ceiling, separating tables and groups of small couches or sitting pillows from one another, and a small stage and dance floor comprised the largest open area. She saw a mix of decoration styles, representing several different nations, and smiled to notice that there was no bar or serving counter; this was a place where the domestics could sit and be waited on instead.

A video screen above the stage was tuned to trimester celebration coverage, with shots of celebrities and politicians arriving for the big event. There was a small group gathered to watch that, and others scattered about the tables.

All of these observations distracted her slightly, and it took a moment to realize that all activity had come to a halt when she'd walked in, and all eyes were on her. For a moment, she thought of Shmi saying she could be the first Myawi ever to show up at the Crystal Turtle, and hadn't realized it would be such a big event.

Of course that wasn't it at all. An older woman with a heavy Cradle's mask, wearing a necklace that indicated she was a retired Lotus Flower girl, came toward her with a whisk broom upraised, like she was going to strike her. "Out!" the woman yelled. "Out out out! You're not welcome here!"

Holly froze in confusion, her hand going to her collar. Everyone else in the bar was collared, and Shmi had said that it was a domestic club. "But—"

"Out!" the shout came again. The woman didn't stop, advancing with the whisk and actually swinging it at her. "I have already called Myawi! Protectors and police are on the way! You're not welcome here!"

She turned and ran out the door, leaving the Crystal Turtle behind. Her vision blurred and she realized she was crying. She ran a block, then turned down the first alley she saw to get off of the street. Was she running from the threat of police, or because she was embarrassed? *You're not welcome here.* Of *course* she wasn't! The Crystal Turtle would have been one of the *first* places someone looking for a rogue domestic would look.

The shout echoed in her head. She told herself to stop running, and came to a staggering stop in the alley, one hand on the wall, trying to catch her breath.

Holly's gasps threatened to turn to sob, tears of frustration and self-annoyance just beneath the surface. She was angry with herself for her fractured composure and scatterbrained behavior—but those were Myawi traits she was trying to maintain. "Who are you?" she asked herself, and fought her emotions, wiped the tears from her eyes, willed herself not to sniffle. She knew she was crying for Shmi and Yinka, and for leaving Ivy behind, crying at the idea of Ivy leaving her forever. That wasn't her path, though. She'd chosen this, and she'd let nostalgia get the better of her. She needed to keep her ears alert for sirens; if the Crystal Turtle's proprietor had called the police, they'd surely be on their way in moments.

There were no sounds beyond the noise of the city. The Crystal Turtle was outside of the area where foot traffic was heavy, ceding the more profitable spaces to higher-profile businesses. She wasn't alone in the alley, though. Holly saw a figure at the mouth of the alley, looking her way. The woman met her eyes, then approached confidently. She was dressed casually, but Holly recognized Dr. Olai even before she'd drawn close enough that the acid scars were visible. "Holly," Dr. Olai said.

She couldn't help but smile and bow slightly, at the sight of a familiar and friendly face. "Were you at the Crystal Turtle?"

"I was."

Holly managed a wry smile, wondering if the doctor had seen her tears. She'd lost control of her face for a moment, there was no telling what her expression had said. "I didn't quite expect that reaction."

"Boko didn't really call the police, but she had to send you away," Dr. Olai said. "She can't have runaways there. Especially not so notorious as you. She is constantly under surveillance. The Ivory Sisters are constantly trying to recruit her. They don't realize that they are endangering the Crystal Turtle with their very presence."

"If the police had a reason to shut it down, they would," Holly said. "I realized that after I left. I should have thought of that."

Dr. Olai angled her head, agreeing but not saying as much. "Are you well?"

"As well as can be expected, I suppose," Holly replied.

"That's good to hear."

She wondered if Dr. Olai had a car. Perhaps she could get a ride after all. "Doctor, do you think—" she got out, then barely dodged as Olai lunged forward, grabbing for her arm. Holly pulled back, barely faster than the doctor, and narrowly missed being caught by the electric stun-gun that had appeared in her hand. She backpedaled, getting out of reach, and Dr. Olai advanced.

"You shouldn't have come back, Holly," she said. "The Founder is very disappointed in you. You've embarrassed Myawi...immeasurably."

"Doctor..."

"Please, just come in with me. Stop this selfishness."

"Selfish? They're going to kill me, Dr. Olai."

The doctor nodded. "Yes, they will. But it will be done with honor and love, if I bring you in...I don't want to see you shot down in the street. It will be worse for Myawi than everything else so far." Dr. Olai swung the stun gun again. When Holly jumped back the doctor stepped quickly forward and swept her near leg, sending her to the ground. She buried the stun gun in Holly's belly with a stabbing motion and triggered it. The now-familiar pain and paralysis surged through her body; she gasped instead of screaming. The hand-held stunner was noticeably less powerful than her collar, more discomfort than agony really.

She rode it out. Dr. Olai held the stunner on her for as long as she deemed necessary. The moment that it stopped, Holly was ready, and kicked her in the face.

It was a clumsy kick, to be sure, but it took the doctor completely by surprise, and Holly's Wing boot had more heft than a Myawi slipper. She stumbled backwards and sat down hard on the pavement, and Holly jumped to her feet, knocking the stun gun away. "Holly, please— " she began, and Holly stomped on her chest, turning the plea into an airless shriek. Another stomp curled her up, and then Holly snatched up the stun gun and gave the doctor a sizeable jolt.

Holly squatted and began feeling Dr. Olai's pockets. "I'm sorry," she said. "You were always nice to me, and I liked coming in for checkups with you. I am giving myself up, but I can't do it your way." She found the doctor's ID card and some cash, then the remote for her car. It was a Bright Spirit remote, but similar enough to Elden's car that she figured it out easily enough, and called the car to her.

It took the car two minutes to arrive; a handsome blue and white Bright Spirit Pangolin. By that time, Dr. Olai was sitting up. She watched Holly with an expression that was simultaneously baleful and pitying.

"I'm going to take your car now," she told the doctor. "I won't damage it, and I'll leave it on a charger when I get where I'm going. Do I need to take you with me to keep you from calling the police?"

"I won't call the police," she said, looking at the ground next to her feet. There was a tone in her voice; Holly took it to mean that Dr. Olai didn't intend to call the police, but would call the Myawi Protectors. She'd have to live with that; the alternative was finding a way to incapacitate the doctor, which was just as likely to result in killing her, and she had neither the time nor the desire to risk that. Best just to go, and hope that she got there before Dr. Olai was able to reveal her location. She felt her anger rising again, thinking about Dr. Olai's loyalty to Myawi. Holly fought down the urge to give her a punitive shock just for being a part of the system. She took the stunner with her, got into the car, and programmed the Koralyi Stadium into it, setting the autodrive.

As the little car pulled away from the curb, she looked around the interior. Dr. Olai had left a shawl in the back seat, and Holly put it on, coiling it into a makeshift hijab. Eventually someone was going to see her face and recognize her, but putting that off seemed worthwhile.

chapter 57

Five hours before Princess Aiyana's trimester celebration

>> I'm down with the crowds near the auditorium, watching the stars and celebrities slowly gathering for the party to celebrate the princess' ongoing pregnancy, and under the celebratory surface of the crowd there's a strange tension. It feels like the entire city is primed to explode in one way or another, and every person is awaiting the right cue from the person next to him or her. Will it be a party to end all parties, or a city-destroying riot?

What is truly strange and unsettling to me, is the feeling that a large percentage of the assembled people would be happy to go either way. I am honestly torn between wanting to stay, just in case I can get a glimpse of Noah Bosel, and going the hell home to hide under the covers until this is all over. For now, I guess I'll keep my camera ready.

—Shairpie Shrivastva's Den

It was fascinating, Ivy thought, to lie on the table and watch Holly lie to her.

She wasn't sure what her sister was lying about, but she was definitely lying. Holly was good at lying—always had been come to think of it—and Ivy recognized the little fidgets she had, the barely-noticeable distraction, the shorter flashes of eye contact that meant there was something she wasn't saying. Ivy was still angry with her, so she didn't ask. If Holly felt like there was something she didn't want to speak aloud, so be it.

It was a reasonable guess that the doctor was going to do more than examine her knee. Ivy decided to trust Holly's judgment. She didn't like doctors she didn't know, but it was unavoidable in this case. She didn't even understand the language the doctor was speaking when he talked to his assistant. She took a deep breath and tried to find the warm comfort she should have been getting from her sister's hand on her forearm.

And then Holly left.

When that happened, Ivy knew for certain that the doctor was going to go ahead and work on her knee, without asking her first. Holly had arranged something, no doubt intending to "fix" her broken sister. Ivy felt a stab of annoyance at that. Her sister's fixations on the differences between them, everything that showed that Holly had grown up a comfortable, coddled dweller and Ivy was just a scav, probed at places that were perpetually emotionally raw. She wanted to shout at Holly to stop looking at her like she was an abused dog she was trying to care for. This wasn't necessary—she just needed another knee brace and she'd be fine. The Inchin doctors, who were now talking back and forth across her while someone washed her bad leg as though it was a dirty drinking glass, weren't necessary. They glanced at her like she was just a scav, too. In fact, if Holly hadn't been there, they probably wouldn't have been willing to work on her at all.

Ivy took a deep breath of the strange-smelling air, and this time she felt a sideslip. Her center of gravity seemed to drop down into the table, as though she was falling asleep. She opened her eyes, seeing the smooth ceiling and gently glowing light panels that reminded her of a cloudy day, but the wobbly feeling didn't change. "I don't feel right," she said.

"Just relax," the doctor said, and moved the machine they'd brought in over her leg. There was a pinch just above her knee, and he lowered it into place. Ivy tried to raise her head to see what was happening, and found that her neck didn't want to move.

There was a warm feeling spreading down from her head, down into her shoulders and torso, something not quite like the prickles of a sleeping limb, but similar enough that Ivy flexed her hands to make it go away. She took another deep breath, intending to sit up, and the room took a much bigger sideslip. The colors of the walls seemed to run together for a moment. It *felt* as though she'd sat up, though her vision told her she hadn't moved, and then a roil of imagined motion followed, like a wave striking the far side of a tub and coming back, then sloshing away again.

Ivy was aware of a sharp jolt of pain in her knee. It didn't hurt; she was just aware that something painful had happened. It had come while the wave was rolling away from her. In her mind's eye she could see it, a white-hot point of sensation bobbing away from her, bouncing off the far wall and coming back, and when it came back—

Her breath hissed through clenched teeth. "That hurts!" she said.

The doctor said something to his assistant, who moved to Ivy's side, floating into her point of view and responded in their language. Ivy tried again to sit up, and still couldn't move. She tried to move her hands again, but wasn't sure if they moved either. The machine over the table began to vibrate, loudly. As it did, another pinch of pain dropped into the wave, then another and another, and she was helpless to avoid them as they rolled into her one after the other. Her heart began to pound. She couldn't feel her leg from the knee down. Had they cut it off? Were they cutting her leg off?

"What's happening?" she cried. "It hurts! Stop! Please!"

The assistant said something to the doctor, and both of them were suddenly in her field of vision, staring down at her.

"No!" Ivy snarled. "Stop! Stop it! Holly!" Holly was probably in the next room. Did she know they were cutting her leg off? Dweller doctors wouldn't waste time on a scav, they were just "fixing" it the easy way. Did Holly know? "Holly!" Ivy screamed again. "Please! Make them stop, they're cutting my leg off, *make them stop!*"

Unable to turn her head, she rolled her eyes over as far as she could, watching the door. It didn't open. The table seemed to slip sideways, and the little jolts of pain from her knee bled together into a constant buzz of pain. It was like getting a tattoo, as Holly had said, only much more intense, pain lancing down into her bones, and Ivy could feel the buzzing tool slowly sawing through her leg, cutting off the nerves. She struggled against the paralysis, and thought she felt her arms move. Her good leg might have kicked. The assistant looming over her got a concerned look on her face and bore down on Ivy's shoulders. Maybe she could struggle free.

The assistant said something to the doctor, and both of them were suddenly in her field of vision, staring down at her. The doctor said, "Relax now," and shined a light in her eyes. She heard the assistant press a button that chimed gently somewhere out of sight. The beeping sound went on, drawing out into a long tone, and the painful cutting feeling from her knee went on and on. Ivy wondered why they hadn't just used an axe; it would have been quicker.

She fought to get up again, and this time she definitely felt herself move, it wasn't her imagination. The assistant put all of her weight on Ivy's chest and made urgent noises at the doctor. She took a deep breath, arching her back, and the table folded underneath her, the head and foot bending toward the floor, the center rising up tentlike as Ivy pushed both ends down with all of her might. She was hanging upside down now, shaking the assistant off of her, or perhaps she just fell. They shouted, and they were all falling. Ivy could see the room motionless above her but at the same time her vision had gone completely white, and she was falling backwards off of the table, with the doctor and the buzzing machine and the walls all coming down around her and more surges of pain in the waves coming toward her and—

There was no sensation of waking up, she was just suddenly aware again. She was still naked, sitting up on a warm chaise with a blanket over her. The room was different but the same; the colors were the same, the background noises the same, but the machine was gone and the walls were subtly different enough to tell Ivy she was in a new room.

She still couldn't feel her leg from the knee down, but the blanket revealed the bumps of two legs and two feet, just as there should be. Ivy threw the blanket back and her leg was still there, with a bandage around the knee and bruises radiating out from underneath. She poked it and felt no sensation. It may as well have been made of wood. She hit it, harder. Still nothing.

Looking around, there was an echoey, hollow feeling in her head, almost as though she was dreaming. "Holly?" she called tentatively.

The door opened, but it wasn't Holly. Fry came in. Dilly was with her. They looked out of place in the neat room, too rough around the edges for the neat, even paint and understated decor.

Ivy was immediately concerned. "Where's Holly?"

"Easier for us to help you than her," Fry said. Dilly looked at her, and both of them stepped forward to help her up. Fry had her clothes, neatly folded, and Dilly turned his back while she dressed. It was more complicated than she expected; her leg was completely uncooperative. She practically had to move it by hand.

"They deadened it," Fry said. "So you wouldn't feel pain. Strange feeling, isn't it?"

Ivy just grunted, thumping at her leg with an impatient fist. Holly was sure to laugh at her.

"It will come back. It takes a couple of hours."

"I feel dizzy."

"They probably gave you something to keep you calm."

She stood, balancing on her good leg. "It didn't work." Fry and Dilly helped her outside. The clinic seemed to be deserted as they left; Ivy heard voices behind walls and inside doorways, but saw no one. As soon as they climbed back into the camper, Durloo keyed the motor and put them in motion. Ivy stumbled, her numb leg refusing to behave, and all but fell into a seat next to Narooma.

She shook her head, trying to clear the wobbly feeling. Holly was missing. "Where?" she asked.

Everyone looked at Fry, who looked at Makkhana, who looked back at her before turning to Ivy. "She's gone," he said. The diplomatic tone in his voice raised Ivy's hackles instantly. "To Singapore, to meet with Aldo Vitter."

"The man who's trying to kill us."

"She is trying to end this without violence."

"She *left me.*"

Makkhana faltered slightly, in a way that reminded Ivy of Marcus and instantly annoyed her. "She was thinking to protect you. Us. Myawi can track her using her collar—"

"She left me!" Ivy's mind spun. Just like that, her beautiful, glamorous sister had left her. Holly had left her in that terrible clinic, let them do awful things to her, and then *left?* Did she think she was helping, or had that torment been a parting shot, a statement of how little Ivy really mattered to her? She didn't want to believe that Holly would do that, but here they were. And of course they looked at her to decide what to do next. No one was asking, but she could feel all of them, waiting for some cue. Why did they always decide that she was the "travelmaster?" In the moment, she just didn't care.

Makkhana stopped trying to speak when Ivy yelled. Fry attempted to fill the silence. "We'll go back to the *Fists*," she said. "Razor will find your other friends, and probably Holly as well—she's a resourceful one." Amran was listening to the conversation, and lifted off the throttle preparatory to turning the camper around. "There won't be any attention on us, so it shouldn't be hard."

"No," Ivy said.

"Pardon?"

"I said no. We keep going. To the place where my mother died." She balled a fist and hit her numb leg.

"Semangat Terang."

"Yes."

Fry looked concerned, as did Durloo. "I don't think that's a good idea," Durloo said.

"I am inclined to agree," Makkhana said. "We're a target. Even without Holly aboard, we're bound to be recognized sooner or later, especially with the canids aboard."

Ivy frowned and shook her head. There were too many people and they were doing too much talking. Shaking her head only made it harder to think. Swan and Shiloh were all gone, Kroni was hurt and now Holly had left her too, and she didn't care what any of these people wanted and she was angry and weary of being pushed around and before she really thought about it she turned to Dilly and said, "Give me your gun."

He raised an eyebrow and handed her a big, heavy pistol, and Ivy pointed it in the general direction of Amran and Makkhana in the front seats. "Keep going," she said.

"Fucking hell, Ivy!" Fry exclaimed. Ivy imagined Swan would yell at her for brandishing a weapon inside a rig, but she didn't care. Swan wasn't here.

"Keep going," she said again. "Take me to the place where my mother died."

"Gonna bust that leg up you keep punchin' it like that," Marf said.

"Okay, we're going." Fry nodded to Makkhana, and they accelerated back onto the road. "You don't need to threaten us, Ivy."

She lowered the gun, but held on to it.

"Dilly," Fry said, "you and I are going to have a talk about handing weapons to people who aren't in their right minds."

One side of Ivy's mouth quirked up in a humorless smirk. She wasn't in her right mind, not at all. But she knew what she wanted. They had killed her mother and turned her sister into an idiot and this was not something they were going to forget that they'd done.

She slouched in the seat, resting her head against the window. The gentle vibration made the world spin more slowly. She was going to scale this, and avenge their mother. It seemed right somehow. Holly had insisted that this couldn't be scaled, but that was because she was meant for better things than the ugly business of vengeance. Ivy could do this for both of them.

That was her duty, because she was the dirty one. She wasn't sure if she was envious of Holly for being better than this, or ashamed after having seen herself in comparison to Holly. Shiloh might've understood, but she wasn't here to talk to. She sat and stared at nothing and tried to pretend that she wasn't confused and hurt and enraged by what Holly had done to her. She never wanted to see her sister again, and she didn't want to go on without her.

The others talked a little bit, but Ivy tuned them out. She closed her eyes, and gradually became aware that sensation was returning to her leg. That was a mixed blessing, because it hurt. The pain started as an ache, then settled in deep. By the time the forest around them began to give way to human construction an unknown amount of time later, even the gentle vibration of the suspension against the smooth road was sending bright jolts of discomfort up her leg and into her hip.

"Well?" Makkhana asked. "Is it everything you expected?"

Ivy opened her eyes. Durloo had driven them directly to the center of Semangat Terang. There wasn't much to see. It was a manufacturing city that had been literally carved out of the forest over the course of the past sixty-five years or so. Unlike other factory towns, very little effort had been made to integrate the industry into the landscape, or to make it friendly to look at. Squat, quickly-built housing units formed an outer ring of architecture.

"They're built close together to form a sort of wall," Alice said. "The outer ring is regular staff. Inside of that are the shops and other facilities for the residents, and inside that the domestic housing. The factories are at the center."

"So it's harder for the factory domestics to escape," Makkhana said sourly. He glanced at Ivy. She thought about her mother, escaping from this place twice only to be brought back. The domestic housing consisted of three fifty-story buildings. Each was curved to match the others, as though they had once been a part of a column, but that seemed to be the only concession to architectural design of any kind. Everything was otherwise drab, smoke-stained metal or concrete. Semangat Terang seemed to exist in shades of gray-blue. Most of the vehicles were white or gray; the bicycles and uniforms were shades of blue, none of them bright. The sky was the bluest thing there.

"What do they make here?" Ivy asked. She touched her leg with her free hand, and felt her fingers on her calf. So she hadn't lost sensation permanently. That realization, along with the dull ache that had begun radiating from her knee, improved her spirits somewhat.

"Cars, and batteries for them," Makkhana replied.

"Garbage world," Wexsun muttered.

"What a mess," Narooma agreed, looking around. They had slowed. The freeway didn't go around Semangat Terang, but right through it, slowing down to a more urban thoroughfare. Trucks rumbled past them, intent on the various loading docks. "People come here?"

"Only to work," Durloo said. "I doubt there's a monument or anything for your mother."

Ivy twitched her lips in an expression acknowledging his words. "I, I,

I'm sure they'd rather forget about the whole thing."

"A lot of it was rebuilt afterward. And they had to redesign parts of it to comply with the new regulations that came after. More housing, for more workers."

She nodded. "Are they all..." she paused a moment, forgetting the word, "domestics?"

Makkhana said, "There are citizen employees as well. They're effectively indentured servants. They earn just enough to eke out a living in the dirty factory town and not much more."

"What about their families?"

This time Alice answered. "Semangat Terang is almost all unmarried men and infertile women. There aren't any schools, no places for children. Families with children live and work in other cities."

"Why would people come here?" Narooma asked again.

"They don't have a choice," Alice said. They passed through a private sector, rolling by row upon row of small shops, bars and the occasional temple. "They're slaves."

"Ehhh, not exactly," Durloo said. "Industrial domestics—in the years since what happened to your mother, anyway—are almost always domestics by choice."

"Who would *choose* this?"

"You have to understand," he said with a slightly condescending tone, "depending on where you come from in the Brother Nations, there are forty or fifty men for every fertile woman. And that number goes down as women age and more of them succumb to ORDS. For a man to come to terms with the fact that he's not going to have children, not going to pass on his name? It is a very difficult thing. For many men, it's easier to become industrial domestics. Guaranteed employment, and everything provided for you."

"It's attractive to some artists as well," Makkhana added. Ivy just sniffed and went back to looking out the window. Makkhana directed Amran to drive to the factory, an angular building that was just as cheerless as the rest of the city.

"Who's that?" Narooma asked, pointing out the window. A lone man was walking toward the camper. He wore a neat, clean navy blue suit with asymmetrical white piping and a flower in his lapel, and he was so cleanshaven his face shined.

"I don't know," Ivy said. "Maybe we should talk to him."

"You think that's safe, with half the country gunning for you and your sister, according to these three?"

"Yeah, that's a little dumb," Durloo said.

"I don't care." She met Fry's eyes. "It's not as, as, as though we don't already stand out, and Holly *told* them we were coming here." The man had stopped a respectful distance from the camper's door, but remained intent on it. The sidewalks were otherwise sparsely populated; some of the shops were even closed. Ivy wondered if it was because everyone was working.

"We'll keep you safe," Dilly said.

Ivy had a sudden, vivid flash of the camper being shredded by bullets in some sort of ambush. Given what she'd seen, Holly's enemies were better armed than Sam Ward's army, and not afraid to use that firepower. With that in mind, they were actually in less danger outside of the camper than in it; at least they wouldn't be vulnerable to a concentrated hail of gunfire. "Will they try to shoot us all?" she asked.

"Only one way to find out," Fry said.

Ivy sighed and handed Dilly's gun back to him. "I'm going out, then." As she stepped down from the camper, her knee didn't buckle under her, but the pain nearly sent her to her knees. There were hands at each of her shoulders in an instant; Dilly and Fry, who helped her up. She took a tentative step, then another. She was leaning on Fry, but could tell that her knee was different. Once it stopped hurting, it might really be better. Her surprise that it was working properly was tempered by a fresh wave of annoyance with Holly. If nothing else, her idiot sister could have been honest about what the visit to the clinic was for. It wasn't as though Ivy would've refused treatment. Did Holly think she was too dumb to understand?

The man bowed as soon as she appeared. "Greetings, Miss Ivy. My name is Phosen. It is my honor to welcome you and your party to Semangat Terang, the factory headquarters of the Bright Spirit Corporation." There was a low hum; a little flying craft, no more than six inches across, hovered about fifteen feet above Phosen.

"I don't imagine you have a lot of visitors here," she said. Her tone was level but cold; in North America, dwellers would know to take that as a sign that she wasn't interested in any kind of foolishness but Ivy doubted Phosen picked up on it.

"The city is designed for efficient operation at all levels," Phosen said with another slight bow. "I am happy to answer any questions that you might have. We welcome the opportunity to meet with you and discuss the things that have changed here at Bright Spirit and in the entire industry since the unfortunate incident involving your mother. If you'd like to follow me, we've got some refreshments available. You've come quite a long way."

Ivy could hear the others disembarking from the camper behind her. Fry, Narooma and Dilly all moved immediately away from it, enabling her to relax. "Why would you welcome me here?"

"Bright Spirit is aware of the difficult time that your mother had here, and acknowledges its part in allowing that to happen. It is our hope that you would be willing to see the policy changes that we have made in the intervening years to ensure that such a tragedy never happens again." He spoke like an unusually animated robot, playing a prerecorded message. "Has your sister come as well?"

"She has not," Ivy said. She could hear the irritation in her voice, and Phosen's eyebrow twitched. He didn't ask her any questions, though.

"Are you...offering us a tour?" Durloo asked with an incredulous look on his face.

"We are. We have prepared tours of the auto factory, the battery manufacturing facility, the domestic dormitories and the entertainment district. If you would like to hear about our employee enrichment programs and refugee naturalization center—"

"I want to see the factory," Ivy interrupted, her voice almost a whisper. "That's where she worked, right?"

Phosen smiled at her. "Your mother did work in the automotive facility, but in an older building that no longer stands. The current facility is just five years old, and state-of-the-art. It's just one example of the efforts that Bright Spirit has made to put this unfortunate incident behind us. In addition, we are prepared to make appropriate reparations to you and your family."

Makkhana cleared his throat. "What about the families of ten thousand other domestics employed by Bright Spirit? What percentage of them were also stolen from their families? Will you be making restitution to them as well?"

"I believe that's something we can discuss today," Phosen replied without missing a beat or showing any emotion. "We are here to consult with the twins about what can be done to improve the industry, and right past wrongs."

"This...is awkward," Fry said. She had a hand on the butt of her rifle, but kept it aimed at the sky.

Ivy looked up at the flier above Phosen again. She wondered if his performance was being judged by it, somehow. The idea of being welcomed after their mother had caused so much trouble—and they themselves had made rather a mess as well—was obviously suspect. But if they were sincere it could make things even worse to reject the peace offering. With a factory this big, the company must have quite a bit of power. Perhaps Bright Spirit could scale things, perhaps they could send her and Holly and Shiloh and everyone else home without violence. Perhaps they could use their terrifying medical machines on Swan. On the other hand...Ivy had a hard time trusting unfamiliar dwellers. Aware that she was in a foul temper and probably less inclined to be civil because of it, Ivy decided to accept the offer. "Okay," she said. "I think that I would like to meet with you."

"Don't do anything stupid," Narooma said. For a moment Ivy thought the delphid was talking to her, but her eyes were on Phosen. "You want to make nicey, that's smart. You want to use your mouth for spreading shit, you'll get a fist in it."

Ivy thought Phosen's smile faltered slightly. "Of course. If you'll follow me," he said, turning to head down the sidewalk.

"I'll stay here," Makkhana said, "with the wounded."

"So will I," Durloo added, and spat on the ground. He was glaring at Phosen for some reason. "I don't trust these people."

Ivy looked at Phosen. Her good leg was getting tired, since she was balancing most of her weight on it. "Can I trust you?" she asked.

"Of course. Bright Spirit is happy for the opportunity—"

"You already said that. Here," Narooma said, suddenly holding out a fist. In it, she clutched a bit of fabric that looked like it had been torn from whatever she'd wrapped around herself for modesty. She took a step toward Phosen, extended the fist, and dropped the cloth. Returning to Ivy's side, she unsheathed her axe, spun it deftly in one hand, then pointed the blade at Phosen, keeping it raised.

"I don't—" he began.

"Shut up," Narooma said. "Don't look at me. Don't look at her. Pick it up." She spun the axe again, so quickly this time that the blade hissed audibly through the air.

Ivy glanced from Narooma to Phosen, then back again. Phosen took two steps forward, bowed at the waist and picked up the cloth, without looking up at either of them. Narooma kept her eyes on him the entire time, glaring at him so fiercely Ivy was tensed to stop her from beheading the man when he got in range. Narooma didn't move, though, and when Phosen straightened with the cloth in his hands, she visibly relaxed, and smiled.

"He's okay," she said.

"Good. I think I am definitely interested in some food," Ivy said.

"Me, too."

"She needs to eat," Dilly said to Phosen. "It's been a day."

"If something goes bad," Ivy said to Makkhana and Durloo, "leave."

"Welcome to Semangat Terang," Phosen said again, sketching a quick, mechanical bow. He turned to lead the way toward the nearest concrete building. Narooma and Dilly took up positions on either side of Ivy, with Fry, Alice and Amran close behind.

A truck thundered past on the road, kicking up a cloud of gray dust. Ivy would have felt more comfortable with Kroni and Swan at her side, but...she had who she had. She reserved another spit of annoyance for Holly, who'd left her all alone in this hateful place.

To distract herself, she asked Narooma about the cloth and her performance with the axe. "Trust display," the delphid said simply. "Tells me if they've sent a warrior when they should have sent a talker. A warrior wouldn't take his eyes off me. A talker trusts me not to chop him down. Means I can trust him."

The doors into the building were blue glass, etched with the company's logo. Phosen raised a card and they opened; he ushered everyone inside. She caught Fry watching the doors hiss shut as they cut off their view of the camper, of outside.

The inside of the building reminded Ivy of the *Excelsis* thanks to its overwhelming squareness and lightness, though it was softer and friendlier, with smooth flooring material and walls that seemed to be lit from within. The decor was white and blue, with an occasional yellow or purple detail, and the building hummed with unfamiliar noises and scents. Ivy counted doorways and turns as they moved into the building, so she could find her way out without help if she needed to. It kept her mind off of her leg which, although supportive, was not happy with the walking. They climbed a curving staircase and entered a meeting room that reminded her of the one they'd killed Zhuan in. The memory rose unbidden, and Ivy blinked hard. A moment later she decided they really weren't that similar at all. The walls were painted with whorls of cream, blue and purple that masked the corners and made the room look kidney-shaped, matching the curve of the large table in the middle. A large window on one wall was completely silver, and Ivy realized it was a screen like the little one she'd been reading, not a portal to outside. There were a dozen chairs and Phosen encouraged them to sit. A smaller, square table at one wall was piled high with food; small sandwiches, fruit, little cakes and other items.

"What would you like to eat?" Phosen asked Ivy. "Sit, I'll prepare you a plate." He touched a button on the wall, and the screen glowed, then showed a Bright Spirit logo. Soft music played from hidden speakers.

She was grateful in spite of herself, that he'd noticed she was uncomfortable walking, then charmed a moment later when Dilly took the dish from him and said, "I'll get it," protectively.

Phosen waited while they prepared snacks for themselves. Ivy tried again to sort her head out. She watched Dilly carefully select fruit and vegetables for her, then add three small meat and cheese sandwiches that together were smaller than a single proper sandwich would be. Amran and Narooma decimated the cakes, while Fry and Alice had nothing.

While they served themselves, the screen played a video that talked about the new factory's various automated systems and efficient energy usage, as well as outlining the jobs of the men and women who worked there. Ivy learned that the assembly line produced about five hundred cars a day, and twice that number of batteries. Five hundred! They could build a new rig for every scav in North America in a week or so. The vehicles were built in a variety of body styles, and a few were trucked to another factory where internal combustion engines were installed for the applications that required them. As images of the rigs scrolled past interspersed with film footage of happy, clean workers at their jobs and enjoying leisure time, a disembodied voice talked about the work shifts, the battery factory, and Bright Spirit's vehicle lineup, with emphasis on the four model lines that were produced in Semangat Terang. Glancing at her companions, Ivy saw that Amran and Alice looked interested, Dilly seemed to be mostly watching her, and Narooma looked bored.

At the conclusion of the presentation, Phosen asked her, "Would you like to see the factory?"

Ivy laughed. "Are you so certain I won't try to wreck it?" she asked.

He smiled diplomatically. "I am sure that you won't. As you can see, our latest facility has little to do with the old. We believe, and I'm sure you'll agree, that the industry has moved on with new understanding. Additionally, a tour would help us. If you see something that gives you cause for concern, you are in a unique position to let us know about it, and we can continue to improve the lives of our employees and domestics." Phosen's expression suggested that this part of his script had been intended more for Holly than Ivy, and he seemed embarrassed that he'd said it.

"I can think of one way to improve their lives," Ivy said.

Phosen smiled, and Ivy got the sense he was genuinely proud of the video and the factory. Her appreciation of this was tempered by the shade of condescension. He talked to her like a dweller; it was obvious that she, Narooma, Fry and Dilly weren't from Singapore, and as a result he was talking to them like he didn't think they'd ever seen electric lights before. He gave her a surprisingly unctuous grin, casting aside his android mien for a moment, and said, "Would you like to see the factory?"

She did, and nodded, feeling a touch of irritation at his look of superior satisfaction. It felt too much like she was playing into his narrative, and that just reminded her of how Holly had written a wrongheaded story for her and acted on it without asking first.

Some of that anger threatened to spill onto Phosen, and she was too tired and hurting too badly to completely restrain herself. He saw the look cross her face, as did Dilly; she ignored his questioning look.

"I've had enough to eat," she said. "We can go now."

"Would you like a mobility chair?"

"No," she said, interrupting Dilly's affirmative. To his credit, rather than contradicting her, the big sailor stood and offered her his hand.

To get to the factory, they didn't even have to go outside. Phosen led them out of the room and the opposite direction down the hall they'd come. Heavy doors and carpet muted the noise, so it was slightly jarring when he pushed open a heavy door at the end of the hall and a wave of hissing and clattering mechanical sounds rushed over them. The factory sounds blended quickly into a steady hum of ventilation fans and machines hissing back and forth, and carried the echo of a large indoor space. The size of the space was confirmed as they all stepped out onto a platform overlooking the main factory floor.

No, Ivy corrected herself, it was *part* of the factory floor. The building extended in either direction, the bulk hidden by white and yellow-painted machinery and conveyors hanging from the ceiling. They descended the staircase, which was made of a blue-tinted version of the same hard material that the cells on *Excelsis* had been made of, to the main floor. Ivy had a sense of being on a trail through dense woods, except instead of trees she was surrounded by machinery. Coverall-wearing workers moved with unconscious efficiency among the machines, and as they began to walk and Phosen pointed out what was happening, Ivy began to make sense of it. The new rigs started as raw bits at one end and rode a rail in the floor, being assembled piece by piece the whole way. More of the workers wore domestic collars than not, and though they noticed Phosen and his charges, none paid much attention to them.

The Bright Spirit representative talked a lot about the cars, giving them meaningless horsepower and efficiency numbers and showing them various features. Fry asked sarcastically about the strength of the batteries, which sent Phosen off on a long tangent about the specially-designed security cell that protected all of Bright Spirit's battery packs, and how it was the best in the industry. Ivy half-listened to Phosen's narrative, and tried to imagine her mother working here. It was clean, nothing like the hell on earth that factories like Detroit's steel mill were rumored to be, but there was something unsettling about it, being in a place that seemed more machine than nature. Ivy was comfortable with her rig, but the people here seemed like they were all parts of that vast machine, stripped of their humanity. If what Durloo had said was true, some of them were here by choice, but there was no way to tell volunteers from conscripts.

Lost in thought, she fell slightly behind. Amran and Alice stayed with Phosen, while the rest fell back with her, forcing their guide to slow his pace and let them catch up.

"Moving as fast as I can," Ivy said brusquely, not apologetic.

"He doesn't come down here a lot," Fry said. "That's why he's walking so fast."

"Why do you say?"

"His shoes are too nice, for one. Also, he knows what everything does, but doesn't use it himself, so he doesn't want to get hung up answering questions if he can help it. You notice that, Dilly?"

Dilly nodded. "Workers don't know him, either."

"Neither do I," Ivy replied. She didn't want to think about Phosen. There were too many things to look at in the factory. The new rigs were painted bright colors—red, silver, blue and mauve—and she wanted to run her fingers over their glossy shapes. It was a neat concept: piles of stuff went in one end, and rigs came out the other. As they neared the end of the line, the image was more apt. The cars on the sliding rail were almost complete, and when they reached the final assembly area where workers fussed over the nearly-completed cars looking for flaws and attaching the last few pieces, Phosen led them outside into a lot with hundreds of rigs. Ivy couldn't keep a gobsmacked look off of her face, and he bowed with another condescending little smile.

"As you can see, Bright Spirit's efficient manufacturing system produces results."

"And you have this many people coming to get them here?" Ivy asked.

"Oh, no. Once final assembly is complete, the cars are charged inductively. At full capacity, they'll either wait here until sold or be transferred to overflow lots using the autodrive systems. Bright Spirit also offers a home delivery program that will deliver your new car directly to your door."

"My folks got that, with the last Nissan they bought," Amran said.

Ivy squinted up at the sky; the sun had come out, and it seemed like they'd been in the factory for much longer than they had.

The little flier was back, also, she noticed. She heard the whisper of its propulsion system first, then saw it, taking up its previous position just out of Phosen's line of sight.

Narooma followed her gaze, then suddenly grabbed the back of her shirt, hard, and hauled Ivy backward. There was a chattering noise from the drone. Phosen made a bleating sound like a faraway goat and tumbled to the ground. Dilly threw himself into Ivy, knocking both her and Narooma to the ground.

Prone on the ground, Ivy saw Amran reel backward, clutching at his face. Alice took a step toward him with a startled cry, then clapped a hand to her ear and fell as well. Fry had her gun out and squeezed off four shots in rapid succession, shooting into the air. At least one of them struck the little flying thing. It rocked violently to one side, seemed about to right itself, then veered abruptly and spiraled into the ground.

"Why are they sending killer fairies?" Fry hissed.

"Because a big fat reward!" Narooma yelled. She had her axe at the ready, but stayed near Ivy. Dilly eased away from Ivy, hand on his gun and eyes on the rest of the lot full of cars. Fry whistled to him and tossed the shot fairy in his direction; he plucked it skillfully out of the air, then bent it in half. "Whoever's flying the buzzer is a bad shot," Narooma said to Ivy. Phosen was on the ground flat on his back, unmoving. "Bullet for you hit him instead." Ivy looked from the dead Bright Spirit representative to the delphid, slowly catching up to what had just happened.

"They tried to kill me," she said.

"If any of the rest of you assholes were thinking about claiming the bounty on the twinsies, let me know right now so I can get rid of you," Narooma said, glaring at Fry and the others.

"Not me," Dilly said immediately.

"What about *you?*" Fry asked, challenging Narooma.

She seemed to swell up in indignation, the whites of her eyes showing for a moment. "What am I gonna do with a pile of human money, tubachick?" Narooma shouted. "Even if they gave it to me in cakes, I'd have to eat them all at once and that would ruin it!"

"Did...did you just call me a *whale?*"

Ivy held up a hand to stop the argument. "I'm convinced," she said.

"Are you okay?" Fry asked her.

"They tried to kill me. I'm, I'm, I'm...really angry."

"Me, too. I want to know who was flying that thing, but they could be miles away. Can we—" Fry started to speak, but was interrupted by another gunshot. An impact shattered the side window of a car next to her, showering her with glass. Everyone ducked. A second blast hit the side of the building, darkening the air with dust. "Inside!" Fry shouted, and gave Ivy a shove toward the open door where the cars were coming out. She couldn't tell where the shooting was coming from, but a third shot hit several feet to her left, slamming into open parking lot and gouging a sizeable crater. The others moved quickly, rushing through the doors and inside. One of the collared domestics working on the new cars looked up and asked a question in a language Ivy didn't recognize. She waved him back, motioning him away from the doors.

"Who's shooting?"

"Can't see," Dilly replied. "Sounds like it's coming from high up, maybe the top of one of the buildings. Close, though, not a sniper."

"Oh, no, no, no it isn't," Fry said, peeking out the big door. Visibility was hampered by the sides of the building, which formed a loading dock around the new-car exit. "Shit, shit, shit. It's a helicopter, running silent. He's passed beyond the building, far side. He'll be back."

"A what?" Ivy asked.

"Flying thing."

Her eyes widened. "Like the one that took Shiloh?"

Fry nodded. "Means the military have found us."

"So?" Narooma asked, twirling her axe in one hand. "What do we do now?"

Ivy took a deep breath. "If they want to scale it this way, then I will. We get the workers out of this factory. Destroy it. Get on the train to Singapore, find my stupid sister. Return to the *Fists*. Go home." Ivy caught her eye. "It's, it's a plan for tomorrow and beyond," she said, remembering what Fry had said to Holly. "Do you trust me?"

Fry smiled. "I'm with you. We need to get out of the open, though," she said with a meaningful glance at the parking lot, where there were now three bodies on the ground. They were just far enough from the doors that none of the factory workers had seen them, but it was only a matter of time before someone did.

"Back to the place where we came in?"

"Yes. And not the slow way," she said, pointing at a small vehicle that was basically a platform with two seats, six wheels and a big flatbed on the back. Fry got behind the wheel and the rest climbed on. The little cart hummed as it pulled away from the wall. Ivy saw some of the workers glance up at them as they went past, but as they'd seen the group with Phosen on their way down nobody seemed to care.

Getting back to the main entrance took no time at all. Rather than go back upstairs to the meeting room, Ivy moved toward the lobby.

"Don't let it close," Fry said. "Door will lock you out."

"I just need to know if Kroni got away. Durloo was supposed to drive away if anything happened—"

As she spoke a shadow darkened the door. Ivy flung herself backward, and a moment later Amran's camper crashed through the doors, tearing away part of the wall as it thundered halfway into the building, opening a massive hole in the outside wall. The floor shook with the impact.

Durloo leapt out of the driver's seat. "Where are they?" he cried. "Amran and Alice?"

"Are you insane?" Fry screamed at him.

"Why are you still here?" Ivy said. "Why did you crash the rig?"

"They killed them! We saw on the security feeds!"

"They did, foolish boy, and now they can kill you too!" Fry snapped. "Stop shouting!"

Makkhana climbed down from the RV. He looked a bit shaken, possibly from the trauma of smashing the vehicle into the building. Ivy thought he looked unused to physical activity. Behind him, Koon and Marf helped Kroni down. The discomfort in his normally stoic face made Ivy wince in sympathy.

Makkhana looked around with a sad smile, then met Ivy's eyes. "I'm as disappointed as you no doubt are," he said. "We didn't see them massing until it was too late."

"Police?"

"Military and Myawi Protectors," Makkhana replied. "Much worse. The factory's surrounded on four sides, and I suspect they'll be coming in here after us soon enough.

"Let them come. I am going to wreck this factory and I want you to help," Ivy said. Makkhana made a pained face. "What?"

"I don't know if that's the best course of action. We like to keep our political actions out of the realm of property destruction where possible. It dilutes our message."

"This isn't a political action," Ivy said.

"I beg to differ."

"Why did they kill them?" Durloo shouted. He ran to the shattered door. "Fuck you! Swine!" A massive gunshot hit just outside the door, throwing dirt into the lobby. Durloo staggered back, coughing at the dust. Another shot hit the back of the camper, and it rocked visibly.

"Helicopter's back," Dilly said nonchalantly, clearly amused by Durloo's near miss. Narooma laughed; Ivy made a shy, reflexive smile that lasted for an eyeblink. Everything had gone sideways so suddenly. She'd trusted Phosen, and forgotten that he was a dweller, and dwellers lied when it mattered. Even so, she couldn't shake the feeling that he hadn't known about the forces surrounding them. He'd been so proud of the factory; certainly he wouldn't have approved of its being attacked.

The door leading into the factory opened, and a man in a navy blue coverall with white stripes on the legs looked out. "Grandpa Rabbit's balls! What's happening out here?"

Wexsun was the quickest. He grabbed the man, and gave a yank, pulling him into the lobby. The man stumbled, almost fell, then gasped in surprise as Narooma caught him and hauled him up without much apparent effort though she was shorter than he was.

Fry got his attention. "Where's your public-address system? This is an emergency." The man looked around at them all, clearly confused, and pointed inside the door. "You should leave now," Fry said, giving him a nudge toward the front doors. She quickly found the communication panel on the wall, studied it for a moment, and tapped a few buttons.

"Would you like to make an announcement?" she asked Ivy.

Ivy bit her lip. Holly would have been better at this. She took the handset and imagined her sister's voice. "Attention Bright Spirit Company," she said. Her voice, cheerfully neutral, echoed back at them from the halls, startling her. It sounded more like Holly than herself, even without an Inchin accent. "I am Ivy Aniram, and this factory belongs to me now. I'd like everyone to leave in an orderly fashion and go home, so I don't have to hurt any of you. Thank you."

"Well, *that's* not going to work," Narooma said, looking at the ceiling.

"It might," Fry said. "Factory domestics and town employees aren't going to stand and fight for this place. They have no reason to."

"Most of them probably know who you are by now, too," Durloo said. "They know what's coming."

Two men in coveralls identical to the first man's came around the corner, saw the intruders standing there, and charged them, shouting. A rising rush of voices indicated that more were coming.

Dilly stopped both of them, clotheslining the first and throwing the second bodily into the wall. When the man tried to get up, he punched him back down again. That seemed to be enough to convince the rest of the Bright Spirit employees to just keep moving.

"The hellacotter thing?" Ivy asked.

"They're after us, they won't shoot the workers." They stood aside and let the workers file past. Ivy looked at the domestics' collars, cheap unadorned units with obvious GPS trackers bulging from the sides and chrome logos on the front contrasting with the dull sheen of the collars themselves. They were much less ornate than Holly's.

"You know what's coming, don't you?" Durloo shouted at them as they walked past. "You know what's coming!"

"Durloo, stop it," Ivy muttered.

"Don't tell me to stop! My friends are dead. We did nothing, and they killed them, just like your mother."

Ivy kept her voice low. "At least they were here by choice."

He stopped and took a deep breath. "I am sorry. It's just...I am very angry."

"I understand. And I'm, I'm angry for you. I'm sorry that happened."

"They're trying to stop our protests."

"I know. Help Kroni out of the lobby, please. Find him somewhere to lie down, or he's going to try to help." Durloo nodded, but didn't move. Ivy considered the queue of Bright Spirit workers filing past, the domestics and the regular citizens mingled together. She hit the PA again, and repeated her message.

"Perhaps we should not have told them we were coming here," Makkhana said to Ivy without reproach.

"We had our reasons," she said.

"What happens next, assuming I can't talk you out of destroying the place?"

"You can't. I'm going to Singapore, to find Holly."

"Are you?"

She frowned at him. "Of course I am."

"And what then?"

Ivy shrugged. "I haven't decided. Maybe I'll slap her to death."

"If I may," Makkhana said. "I am going to assume that you'll want to make a statement of some sort. With special forces already on the ground, I imagine we've got ten minutes or less before they compromise or cut off the feeds to this building. Whatever you need to say, time is running short to say it."

"I don't have anything to say," Ivy said.

"Well, I certainly do. I'll find the security office; there will be a terminal there," he said. As he passed one of the men Dilly had knocked down, he reached down and took the worker's ID card.

"Go with him," Fry said. "We'll make sure there's nobody hiding here to surprise us. Dilly," she called. "Narooma? You ever secured a perimeter?"

Narooma grinned. "Way easier with walls," she said.

"Good. Let's go. We need to block access and sweep up stragglers."

"What do you want me to do?" Durloo asked.

"You sit down a minute," Fry said, even though he was speaking to Ivy, "and calm down."

"Calm *down?*"

"Yes, exactly. Took me half the day to get her sister mellowed out," she said, "and I don't need you spitting the dummy as well."

"They murdered my friends!"

"I know, I was there. But screaming and yelling about it won't avenge them, kid. Take that anger and turn it productive."

"This is *productive?*" Durloo's voice went up again. "You say Holly has turned herself in, and we are almost three hundred miles from Singapore? How is this *productive?*"

Narooma put her hand on his shoulder. Though they were the same height, she had a much larger physical presence and seemed to tower over him. "Hey. Listen," she said, her voice surprisingly soft. "I want to tell you a story. Imagine there are two men, okay, two men who say they are on your side, they are there for you and they want things to be better. And then things don't get better. Someone comes along and splits your head open, because things are bad. You're dead.

"And after that one of the men says, 'See, this system has to change, it's bad, and we have to work to make it better but we can't make it worse, we have to talk about it and make it so this didn't happen for nothing.' He gets his people and they make signs with your face on them and yell your name, and say you are why things have to change. And maybe people listen, or maybe they don't.

"The other man doesn't say anything. He does his funeral song over your body and then he gets *his* people, and he goes out and finds the someone who split your head open and he splits their head open. He pulls their house down with his bare hands. He grinds them and everyone like them into bloody dust in the street. He burns your name into the walls of the ruined city. Maybe the system changes and maybe it doesn't, maybe people understand and maybe they don't, but either way the city is gone and everything is gone and that's the way it is now.

"Now. You're alive again, it's before things got worse, and you can choose. Which one of these men do you want to follow? I'm not saying who's right or wrong, I just want to know who you consider to be truly *your people*. Is it me? Of course it isn't. See, that's what you don't understand. You're all sparkle-eyed and you want to help, but you can't help me. You don't even know who I am, and you didn't ask. You don't know who my people are, and you didn't ask. You don't know anything outside your little coconut head. You can't help her if you don't know who she is, either."

Durloo blinked at her. "You're insane," he said.

"Wrong. I'm a shark-killing, temple-burning, queen-slaying *warrior*. That makes me someone you don't talk to that way." She was holding her axe in one hand, and casually let the head slide toward the floor.

Fry seemed to see the trouble brewing. "Dilly. Narooma. We're going, Ivy. Back soon."

Narooma showed the whites of her eyes and smacked her lips, taunting Durloo, and followed Fry.

Wexsun silently led Ivy to a foreman's office where Makkhana had commandeered a computer. The other canids were already there, and Durloo arrived a moment later, Kroni leaning heavily on his shoulder. "No outside windows," Makkhana said. "View of the work floor. This is a good room. I can try to find your sister, if you'd like. For what it's worth, she did choose the best possible time. With the trimester celebration beginning this evening, he can't quite afford to shoot her down in the street."

"He, he, he tried to shoot us right *outside*," she pointed out. Holly wasn't safe. She expected Vitter to treat her respectfully and reasonably, and he wasn't going to. "How do I get to Singapore from here?"

Makkhana smiled again. "She did say you were quite the schemer."

"Who?"

"Holly. She talked about the two of you, when you were children."

"And she called *me* the schemer?"

His fingers continued to move on the little keyboard as he talked to her. "Was that not true?"

"Everything was always her idea," Ivy said. Because Makkhana's attention was split, hers was as well. She looked at the walls, which shared the curvy blue swirls of the meeting room, and tried to calm her racing heart. She wasn't afraid, just angry. She tried to imagine what her mother had felt, being in this place. What the other workers felt, if any of them thought constantly of children they'd lost. Of her own, broken sister.

"Good news for you; I'm a bit of a schemer myself. There's an express train, to Singapore, that takes about an hour."

She looked doubtful. "We didn't have much luck on the last train."

"You didn't have the Ivory Sisters' help last time."

Ivy cocked her head at him. "People you work for?"

"Good people. There's an unorthodox solution in the works. I suspect the only thing the folks outside are waiting for is a headcount of employees," Makkhana said. "Once they determine there aren't any hostages, they'll come in after us. The presence of the Myawi Protectors concerns me. They can track Holly's collar, and must know that she's not here. This suggests that they're operating as mercenaries. Not good for us. But, as I say, I think there is a good chance of getting everyone out."

"How long will the head count take?"

"Once your sailor friends have finished shooing the last stragglers out? No more than an hour."

"That's enough time. I, I, I am planning for the factory be on fire by then," Ivy said.

"On...fire?"

"Family tradition," Ivy deadpanned with a nod.

"This is not a good idea," he said. "I said it before, and I'll say it again. This isn't North America, Ivy. You'll only cause more trouble this way. This isn't even Bright Spirit's largest factory!"

"I don't care." He started to protest, and she shut him down. "I'm not asking you for permission. And I know you helped her trick me into that doctor's office. I'm going to go, and when I come back I'll need help moving Kroni."

chapter 58

Three hours before Princess Aiyana's trimester celebration

>> Many of your younger viewers might not be familiar with the origins of the celebrity rush. The fun tradition of having celebrities run through inclement weather and other, more creative obstacles before entering a formal venue dates back over thirty years. As a prank on the cast of "Great Storm New Orleans," director Hay Mazily worked with his special effects department and HNE experts to create a pocket thunderstorm that rained only on the traditional red carpet. Carefully directed wind gusts destroyed even the most expensive umbrellas, and the starring cast was soaked to the skin in their finery. The movie won every major award that year, and the crowd-pleasing run through the rain was seen as good luck. Ever since, event planners have competed to come up with complex ways to harry the arriving celebrities.

Princess Nipa's reported to have chosen a snowstorm for her trimester celebration's red carpet rush, to commemorate the skiing trip on which she and Haichen Qui first met. The Jue-Ichi HNE Laboratory supervised setup of what's expected to be one of the most impressive displays ever...

—Interview with director Gan Phee from *Do You Believe This Shit?* by Rosso Patek

Dr. Olai's car took twenty-five minutes to get to the auditorium, automatically rerouting around the heaviest of the traffic. Eventually the roadblocks got the better of the autodrive and it reported that closed roads wouldn't let it get any closer. Holly stopped the car, programmed it to return to approximately where she'd left Dr. Olai. Just before she closed the door, she tossed the stunner on the passenger seat.

Sending the car away felt like severing a lifeline. The feeling was there for a moment, then gone, and she joined the crowds on the sidewalk, feeling exposed and anonymous at the same time. The throng had a general motion toward Koralyi Stadium. Many of the pedestrians carried blankets and snacks.

There was an open-air park named after some minor figure who'd had a part in resolving the Colony Conflict a few blocks from the stadium. As she passed it, Holly saw a large simulcast screen set up. Other people watched the road, looking for fancy vehicles that might indicate the presence of famous faces, and of course there were street vendors selling portable food and tacky souvenirs. There were protesters too, carrying folded signs as they made their way along the crowded streets to where the television fairies would be gathered. Holly saw a few police fairies hovering above the crowd, and made sure not to give any of them a full view of her face.

Moving through the crowd was easy enough; she had plenty of experience at being unobtrusive. With her collar covered, no one gave her a second glance, and she made it to the edge of the throng on the red carpet without trouble. Of course, people were piled twenty deep around the red carpet even though the brightest stars weren't scheduled to begin arriving for another three hours. The street in front of the doors had been blocked off for the traditional celebrity rush. The red carpet stretched from the doors of the auditorium all the way across the street, a ten-foot wide path through the crowd. Four HNE stations had been set up on pedestals with people in place to control the arcane energies; when the time came, a pocket blizzard would be created that the stars and politicians would be forced to run through to reach the doors. Ridiculous as it was, Holly was impressed; a snowstorm in Singapore on a warm summer evening would be quite the thing to see.

She backed away from the tightest of the throng, considering, then had an idea.

There were so many fairies hovering above the crowd it was almost a flock. Anti-collision software kept them from running into each other, but the air was thick with them, a mixture of police, security, media and private fliers, all taking pictures and shooting video for those who couldn't be at the trimester celebration. Holly watched them for a while; most hovered a few feet above the heads of the crowd, the better to get tight-angle shots without other fairies blocking their view. Holly moved to the back of the crowd, at the edge of the road where she had room, and took off Olai's shawl. As she tied the ends of it together, she heard someone behind her say, "Hey, is that a Myawi girl?" She turned and winked at the person, eliciting a gasp, then swung the shawl over her head and jumped, catching a fairy in her makeshift net. It buzzed madly, trying to get free of the cloth, and she grabbed the sides firmly, mindful of its turbofans. She didn't want her fingers shredded.

Holly unwrapped it, turned it over, and looked into the tri-ocular camera's beady glass eyes. The markings on its dorsal side indicated that it belonged to Kalypso Free Broadcasting, a minor news feed. "Hi," she said with a smile. "I'm here." With that, she threw the fairy upward; it automatically corrected its flight and began hovering again, but also followed her when she walked away from it. She had been recognized.

Holly kept walking, skirting the crowd at the entrance to Koralyi Stadium. It wasn't long before a second fairy joined the KFB drone, and then two more. She could imagine her image going out on the wire, and hundreds of drone operators trying to figure out where she was. When she had ten or fifteen of them following her, she stopped walking, spread her hands to show she wasn't carrying anything, and waited.

Vitter took less than two minutes. He gave her a smile for the cameras, but it wasn't reflected in his eyes. "Thank you for coming," he said. Holly saw no obvious escort, but guessed that he had men among the crowd in case something happened.

"Thank you for the invitation."

"I didn't expect you so early."

"My travel plans were flexible," she said, "and I had some extra time in the city. I've seen the sights, so I thought it best to just come down."

Vitter smiled again, and Holly returned it. He stepped aside, indicating that she should follow him to the front doors of the stadium, and as she fell into step beside him some cheers went up from the crowd. "Forgive me if I don't offer you my arm. I've never understood the public's fascination with murderers," he said, his words audible to her but not to the fairies above them or the noisy spectators.

They walked up the red carpet together. Holly kept her face a neutral but pleasant Myawi mask, and decided not to let it drop once they were through the doors and inside. It was easier if she didn't think about it.

The atrium of the Koralyi Stadium was colossal, and had been remodeled for the trimester celebration. A massive reception was in the works; buffet tables and food stations were being set up, as well as some smaller performance podiums, yet another viewing screen so the events inside the stadium would be visible, and a booth where attendees could send Aiyana and Haichen personalized greetings and congratulations. An army of domestics and caterers was hard at work putting the final touches on the party.

"This way, please," Vitter said. "I'm going to have to have you searched and scanned, of course."

"Of course," she said.

"Would you prefer having a female? I wouldn't want you to become upset and injure one of my security people."

"I don't have a preference," she said, to be agreeable.

She regretted it a moment later when Vitter handed her off...to Anshul. "Please make sure she's not carrying anything dangerous," he said. Vitter's face remained neutral as well; if he was taking any pleasure from having her searched by the man who'd killed Shmi, he didn't let it show.

Anshul, on the other hand, thought it was quite amusing indeed, and gave her a facetious bow. "Right this way," he said, leading her to a small room and closing the door behind them. It was a meeting room of some kind, just a few feet square with two chairs and a desk that was partially molded into the wall. Anshul sat at the desk and kicked his feet up, plucking a pencil out of the holder that was part of the desk and playing with it. "You know how this works," he said. "Open your mouth." She did, and as she leaned toward him, she could see burn scars on his face from when Shmi had sprayed him in Strip City. She glanced at the glowing sigil that was most likely part of the reason he still had a face. He nodded upon seeing she didn't have a Spitting Cobra or anything similar. "Off with it. Everything. Put your clothes on the table here."

He stayed a safe distance from her, presumably in case she'd secreted some weapon that she might lash out with, and stripped to her underwear. As she placed items in front of him, he ran his hands over and through them, looking in all of the pockets.

"I said everything," he said. "I want you standing there in your collar and nothing else."

Holly complied, suddenly struggling to keep the emotion off of her face. She had no reason to feel upset, she told herself. She'd stood naked before well over a hundred men and boys, during her time with Elden. This was no different.

She told herself that, at least. But it was. Anshul wasn't the dedicated Protector who'd joined Kalida to protect her after the college boys' attack. He was the cold-blooded beast who'd drowned Shmi, a woman a third his size who posed no threat to him. She met his eyes as they crawled over her. Anshul's manner was of indifference and a hint of lust tempered by...guilt? Because he wanted her? She doubted he felt badly for the things he had done, as a Protector. Holly imagined he might have already forgotten about

Shmi; that wasn't it. He was trying to reduce her to a similar status though, that of a worthless piece of meat that he could abuse, and it didn't seem to be working. "I don't know why more benefactors don't just keep you girls like this," he said, raising an eyebrow at her. "Don't you agree?" There was a forced sincerity in his voice; he was trying to upset her, and it wasn't convincing. Holly didn't give him the satisfaction of an answer. He fondled her underwear, then stood up. "Turn around," he said. He passed an electronic scanner over her back—checking that she hadn't actually inserted a weapon or explosive into her body—then needlessly ran his hands from her shoulders to her thighs. He'd taken off his gloves, and the unexpected skin-to-skin contact made her twitch.

It doesn't matter, she thought. Oh but it did, and the anger she'd only just pushed down and gotten under control was rising again. When he ordered her to turn and face him again, it must have shown on her face, because he ducked his head slightly to look into her eyes.

"What, you don't like this?" Anshul asked. "You think because you disgraced yourself, that makes you an ordinary woman?" He laughed. His hesitancy was fading now that she was reacting. She should've kept her Myawi mask on, that was what was intimidating him. Now it had slipped, and she couldn't seem to get it back. "You'd have been better off coming in here with a bomb. That would certainly wreck my day, wouldn't it?" He scanned her front, then ran his free hand over her body, gently at first, then more roughly. "Can't be too careful," he said.

She almost hit him. She got so close as to tense her arm to strike. Holly remembered the way Razor had shown her, fist and knuckle right in the soft side of his neck. Even if the stiff collar of his jacket caught most of the blow, it would be enough to rock his head satisfyingly, leave him with a stunning headache.

And then what? He'd hit her back, and he was much stronger. This man had shattered Shmi's face with a single punch. At best, it'd hurt a lot. At worst, he might beat her to death and tell Vitter she'd had a weapon. So she held herself back, she endured it and concentrated on keeping her face still, not meeting his eyes lest he see the desire for mayhem there. She imagined the feral, murderous look she'd seen on Ivy's face after her sister had killed Zhuan, imagined her own features contorted thus. But no, not now. She wasn't here for herself, she was here for Ivy. She'd see her sister and her friends safely over the horizon, and then one day when Anshul had forgotten about this, she'd bury something sharp in his throat.

"I can see your nose flaring," he said. "You're thinking about hurting me, aren't you?" He stepped around behind her again, twined his fingers in her hair, doubled it around his hand and pulled her head back. "I'd beat the flesh off of your back for what you've done to us," he said into her ear, his voice a low and angry growl, "but our government man wants you looking happy and healthy for your tea with the Chancellor. I'll find some other way to hurt you. How quickly do you think you can compose yourself?" He grabbed her hip and pulled her tight against him, the armor on his chest digging into her back.

There was a tap at the door, and it opened a crack. Kalida looked in. Anshul released Holly and immediately triggered her collar. The jolt of electricity took Holly by surprise, and she fell flat on her back as her knees locked and her back arched. She managed not to make a sound, which seemed to disappoint Anshul, and he held the shocker on for longer than was necessary. He stopped it before draining the collar, and left her gasping on the floor.

"There was a sound," Kalida said.

"She had a foolish idea," Anshul replied with a grin. "I talked her out of it."

Kalida nodded. "Mr. Vitter needs her now." He closed the door.

Anshul grabbed her clothes before she could, and handed them back to her one item at a time, waiting for her to put on each thing before giving her the next. He handed her clothes out of order, and it wasn't hard to imagine he was doing it on purpose. He'd know the routine that Myawi taught, and would know it'd put her off-balance to be unable to follow it. She concentrated on working the shakes out of her hands, telling herself that it didn't matter any more, but a decade-old habit was difficult to ignore.

It took a ridiculously long time to get dressed, of course. Vitter didn't seem annoyed, and she was led to another hallway in the back of Koralyi Stadium, containing a series of larger meeting rooms. The smell of catered food followed them, as did Anshul, though he had reverted to security-guard mode. When Vitter took Holly into one of the meeting rooms, he joined them, standing in a corner like a statue.

"Myawi has insisted on having a representative present," he said. "I hope you don't find that too upsetting. My hands are tied in the matter. Legally, of course, the school is responsible for you."

Vitter was arrogant and his insincerity annoyed her tremendously. She resolved that the best way forward was to refrain from letting him bait her, though, and nodded pleasantly. "Who will we be meeting with?" she asked.

"Chancellor Shay appears to be your biggest proponent. There will also be Anmarie, from the Lotus Flower school, and the cultural minister from China, Mister, ah what is his name? Gao-Shay. And possibly Prime Minister Hudri. I believe that representatives from two of the major networks have also requested to attend. With your permission, of course." Vitter relaxed in his chair. "If you'd be more comfortable without the media, of course..."

"It's quite fine, thank you."

"It'll be a short while before they join us, traffic being what it is. Can we chat a bit first?"

"What about? We covered so much on the *Excelsis*."

"Oh, you're far too complex for me to have gotten to the core of you that quickly. My people skills aren't that good."

She almost told him that was obvious, considering the way he'd treated her thus far today, but held her tongue. Either he was being honestly self-effacing, or it was a weak attempt to make her underestimate him. Vitter seemed to have a knack for tripping her conversation reflexes, making her give honest answers to keep things moving. She didn't want him knowing what she was thinking, either by her own words or by omission, if she responded insincerely to him. If he was making her uncomfortable on purpose, then she didn't want him to know it was working, and if it wasn't intentional, then she knew one of his weaknesses. Best to smile and nod politely. Still, the feeling that he'd found a button to push made her second-guess herself.

"I do hope we can accomplish some policy changes," he said. "You're providing us with a unique opportunity."

"I think it was always available to you. I just called attention to it."

"You think so many domestics are unhappy? It would seem that your situation is a bit atypical."

"I agree."

"You do?"

"Absolutely. I do keep telling you that I'm not a part of any greater movement, and you refuse to believe me."

Vitter smiled, a bit reptilian. "You'll forgive me if I find that hard to accept."

"You don't need my forgiveness," she replied. "But it's true."

"So what would you have me believe? That your extensive training suddenly fell away, all at once, because you learned the tragic truth about your mother? That you then proceeded—you, a...plaything trained to serve and please—proceeded to *kill* the top three members of a highly sensitive think-tank with your bare hands, before spiriting a fourth key member into hiding with you and turning him to your cause?" He shook his head and put his elbows on the table. "No, Holly, you've had quite a *lot* of help. But that doesn't matter, at this point. We're past all of that foolishness, and the next step is to sit down and determine what comes next."

"I am wondering what that is, exactly. How long until the meeting begins?"

"Any moment now," Vitter said, without looking at the time.

"I don't believe you," Holly said, opting for bald-faced honesty. In the corner, Anshul chuckled.

"And why is that?"

"Because you haven't offered me a drink. And perhaps that's just because you're being deliberately rude to me, but if there were chancellors on the way you'd have drinks and snacks in here as well. You might have even picked a windowed room, in case one of the gentlemen wanted to smoke. So you've pulled me out of sight on purpose and I think you'll keep me here, if you can."

Vitter stood. "What do you want, Holly?"

"I want my sister and the *88 Fists* to sail safely, and to work with whatever committee is formed to improve domestic legislation. I think you were quite clear in your offer, and I accepted it."

"That's very honorable," he said. Anshul sniffed again, as if he was holding back laughter. "Have you considered that I might not share your sense of fair play, though?"

"Of course I have," she said. "But there are people who expect to see me. I know they've seen my video, and I've seen their responses. I came here peacefully and into your custody. How much face will you lose if I turn up dead before Chancellor Shay has a chance to shake my hand?" She tilted her head at him. "I understand if the proper meeting etiquette didn't occur to you—it was my focus for many years, after all, and I'm bound to notice things you wouldn't. I would even be willing to serve the tea, if you don't have a domestic to spare at the moment." She couldn't resist throwing in the last, and it brought the barest hint of a flush to Vitter's cheeks. He still might opt to kill her on the spot, but hopefully she'd given him pause.

"This is not going to go the way you hope it will," he said.

"What do you want from me, Mr. Vitter?"

He clasped his hands behind his back. "You've given me a bit to think about, of course. I admit that it had crossed my mind to make you disappear from this room, but you're right, that's not something I can do. And

I would hate to disappoint Chancellor Shay, since he's so fond of philanthropic gestures, and the idea of being a big brother to the world, as you know.

"So, congratulations! You'll be attending the trimester celebration as my guest! And you'll be the perfect Myawi for the cameras, do you understand? I'm sure you don't care the least about yourself, but if you think you've got me at a disadvantage because I can't destroy *Excelsis* and *88 Fists*, I would remind you that sarin gas doesn't cause attention-getting explosions." Holly tried not to let the shock of that realization reach her face; she wasn't sure she succeeded, because Vitter smiled. "So let's not forget that I have life-and-death power over this situation. What do you say? Do you want to walk behind me, or do you prefer European style?"

She took a calming breath, trying to release tension from her shoulders. "Whatever you prefer of course, Mr. Vitter."

He extended his elbow, and she rose and took it. "Much better. Now, let's go and make another video, to let your adoring fans know what you're up to."

chapter 59

Four hours before Princess Aiyana's trimester celebration

"Where are we going?" Shiloh asked as Nipa's Royce sped through town. She'd left the priority mode on, so other self-driving cars moved out of their way, and it routed itself around the few that were human-driven. The system actually tweaked the timing of the traffic lights, so they cruised through the city without stopping, threading effortlessly through traffic.

"I don't know," she replied. "Where should we go?" She turned the television on, then groaned. "Nothing but news," she said. "Everywhere I look, all the feeds, all the stations, everything's about Aiyana and Haichen and their stupid baby and the stupid party," she grumbled. "I can't wait until all of this is over. We should just hide, and not go."

"Won't they track you down?"

"What, with the car's scanner? Father could, but Chokidar would have to tell him first. And he's not going to tell Father that he doesn't know where I am. Not today of all days."

"You sound like you've done this before."

Nipa grinned. "Maybe. Just for a couple of hours. We should stay gone longer this time, though."

"I think that he'll come looking for you this time," Shiloh said.

"Why, because there are so many stars in the city? It's totally safe, and he knows it."

"No, Nipa, because of me." She tilted her head back, looking at the car's tinted glass roof and the patterns that swirled in it. Above them, the tall buildings loomed. She couldn't bring herself to say it, though. "He's going to be angry and afraid for you, because of me."

Nipa slid closer to Shiloh, wrapping an arm around her. "You wouldn't hurt me," she said, and kissed her.

"Of course I wouldn't! But I lied to him about who I am. My name's not Anna. It's...it's Shiloh."

She tensed a bit, waiting for Nipa to make the connection, or to look her up. The girl did neither. She just smiled. "That's a beautiful name! So North American! Shiloh. That's so much prettier than Anna!"

Shiloh couldn't help but smile, and it was nice to be called by her real name. "Nipa, I lied about my name because...of who I was traveling with. In North America. The military captured my friends and I, my friend Ivy, and others, and I lied about who I was so they wouldn't take me too. Because I had to help them." The princess was frowning slightly. "To help Ivy, and her sister Holly," Shiloh said.

Nipa's mouth dropped open. "Holly the Myawi? You know Holly the Myawi? You...you came *back* with her?"

"And Ivy, yes."

"Are you *joking*? You traveled with Holly?"

"I'm not joking, Nipa."

"Wait, and her sister, too? She found her sister?"

"She did. I was there."

Nipa was bouncing with excitement. "I can't *believe* this! You are so amazing!" She threw her arms around Shiloh in a hug, tumbling half on top of her, and then kissed her again. "Oh, oh, I know where we can go, we just have to go over to the university. I know some people over there who are putting together a protest, they're all about domestic rights and abolishing that system. It's basically the same thing as slavery, you know. It's not the right thing to do, especially if we consider ourselves the world's big brother. Oh, we have to catch them before they head out, they're going to *love* you!" Nipa tapped the screen, sliding the news feed off to one side so she could make a video call. Shiloh couldn't quite see the screen, though she was curious. "Hi Wan, it's me," she said when the line was picked up. "I'm going to come over before you leave."

"Daddy let you out for a while, Princess?" the voice on the other end said. Male and young. Not a surprise.

"No, I took off. Chokidar's being ridiculous about my new friend. You have to meet her. She's from North America, and she traveled over here with Holly the Myawi."

"That's bullshit. All of her friends are with her in Semangat Terang."

"Don't call me a liar, Wan Niguel. It's true! I'll prove it to you, we're coming over."

Wan chuckled patiently. "All right, see you in a few minutes then."

Nipa clicked off and the news feed came back up, showing men who looked like soldiers milling around the outside of an ugly concrete building that looked like a factory. A headline in the corner of the screen read, *Bright Spirit Standoff.* "Wan is a nice guy, you'll like him," Nipa said. "He's a graduate student, and really politically active. Father would be so angry if he knew I was spending time with radicals. But you, you're more radical than *any* of them!"

"I'm just me," Shiloh said, trying to think of a way to get Nipa to drive her to the hotel where she'd left Bee...but then how would she explain Bee? "How far is it to the college?"

"About fifteen minutes. That's enough time for you to make Chokidar really mad, and fuck me again."

Oh but she had to get to Bee...dammit. There was a feeling like her body was acting on its own, and she grinned. "It is, isn't it?"

For better or worse, sex in a moving car took Shiloh's mind off of the ocean of worries and fears that were following her around, and though Nipa didn't quite get her off, it was enough of a rush to improve her mood and put a glint of optimism into her thoughts. She'd find Bee.

Nipa's car looked ridiculously out of place on the campus which, while clearly affluent, was not the sort of place that the owners of otherworldly luxury cars would necessarily frequent. Shiloh caught many eyes on the rig. They wouldn't be traveling incognito any time soon.

Wan Niguel proved to be a sharp-eyed young man in a red and gray suit. He looked Shiloh pleasantly up and down and smiled at her, and she smiled back as they entered his apartment. There were several other students there, all dressed similarly, and Shiloh realized it was a uniform of some sort. The group was sharing a tray of food and watching a news feed similar to the one that had been playing in the car. At the moment it was showing the same factory that had been on-screen before, but now there was smoke coming out of some of the windows.

"What's happening?" Nipa asked.

"They're saying Holly the Myawi killed some more people, and might have set a fire in the factory. She also killed a Myawi Protector out on the freeway. You traveled over with her?" Wan asked Shiloh, who nodded. "Pretty exciting."

"Shiloh was there when Holly found her sister," Nipa volunteered.

"On the beach in North America?"

Shiloh nodded again. The news feed moved on to a new report, this time in Singapore. Without warning, an image of a dead bear in a city street burst onto the screen. It had been tied to a lamppost, and its jaws hung open at an awful, crooked angle. Blood matted its dark fur and two of its paws appeared to be missing. "RABIES SCARE—URSID KILLED IN DOWNTOWN SINGAPORE," the feed read.

Shiloh recognized a corner shop in the background by its distinctive all-green awning and front wall; it wasn't far from the hotel she'd left Bee in. The fact that she was looking at Shamshoun's body hit her like a punch in the stomach. She forced herself to listen, in case they had news about Bee or Razor, but there was no more, just a report that an ursid had appeared unexpectedly in town and begun attacking people. Some had questioned whether this might be related to Holly the Myawi, but the bear had already been identified as a Sino-Indian citizen, an escaped convict in fact.

The report went on and on, with more and more lurid footage of Shamshoun's body. Some of the damage to his face and paws had apparently been caused by souvenir seekers cutting and ripping pieces of his body off.

Shiloh got up, quickly, and looked around for the restroom. She found it, retreated inside, and locked the door. She snatched a towel off of the warmer mounted on the wall and pressed her face into soft, welcoming fabric, allowing herself to cry for her friend. The newsfeed was turned up loudly enough to cover any sounds she might have made as she sobbed into the towel. Shamshoun was dead. His song was over, as he would have said. But Bee was safe. She had to be.

When she came out of the bathroom, Wan looked at her, concerned. "You okay?"

"Not feeling well," Shiloh said. "And those images made me sick."

"We have a daybed in the back room, if you want to lie down for a few minutes. How long are you guys staying, Nipa?"

"I don't know. I switched off the chaperone so Chokidar can't recall the car, though."

"Still hasn't changed the code?"

She laughed. "Of course not."

Wan nodded, handing her a beer. "Well, for as long as you need it, it's there," he said, nodding toward the room where the bed was. "We're going to leave for the protest in a couple of hours."

Shiloh glanced at the newsfeed. It had switched again, to coverage of a group of shouting youths that Wan and the others seemed to know, because they started laughing and cheering. "I think I will lie down," she said. Nipa looked at her, took her hand and squeezed it in a gesture of empathy.

The room was dim, had a drape instead of a door, and smelled heavily of some kind of spice she couldn't identify. The bed was clean enough, if a little stiff thanks to a cheap cushion. It was what she needed though; a moment to close her eyes.

chapter 60

Three hours before Princess Aiyana's trimester celebration

>> Amateur skywatchers take note: the Luna Colony will be visible in the skies over much of the Brother Nations this week. In honor of Princess Aiyana's trimester celebration, Luna promises a spectacular lightshow. Be sure to check out our map of the best viewing times!

—Tinzee's Tea Room

Ivy returned to the factory floor, steadying herself against the wall. The rush of adrenaline had pushed the pain in her leg back, and now it was just a dull roar that was making her sullen. The more she used her knee the stronger it seemed to get, though. It didn't feel ready to be out of the big brace they'd put on it, but she planned to take it off as soon as she felt able.

The factory was quiet now, the machines on the line gone still. There were a few devices beeping, as if calling for their operators. From somewhere farther up the line there was a crash of metal, a slamming door. The noise reminded her that she didn't have much time.

The electric cart was where Fry had left it. It took Ivy a moment to figure out how to make it go, and then she turned it around and headed toward the beginning of the vehicle-building line. Wexsun and Marf followed her, bounding alongside in wolf form and then jumping on the back of the cart. "Do you know how to work any of these machines?" she asked them. The canids chuckled in response. She couldn't tell if that meant yes or no. Ivy wasn't in the mood to play canid games, so she asked instead, "Let me know if anyone had is coming," and got affirmative whuffs in response.

At the first assembly station they came to, Ivy stopped the cart. It was early in the process, and the vehicle being assembled was little more than a blue-painted cage, the outlines of a vehicle sketched in metal. It didn't even have doors yet. The battery was barely visible under the floor, wrapped up in its safety shield, and Ivy considered it, thinking about their van burning in the road.

There was a large rolling toolbox at the station as well, filled with a mind-boggling assortment of perfect, shiny, slightly green-tinted wrenches, screwdrivers and more arcane tools. "Find me a bag to put these in," she told Wexsun and Marf, and the smaller canid loped off to look around. Ivy selected a large hammer and a flat-headed screwdriver while she waited. She looked at the car's battery "security cell," and couldn't see a way to get at it. There wasn't a gap in the floor big enough to even get the screwdriver into. She needed to go to the battery factory itself, which Phosen hadn't taken them to, but had pointed out the robotic arms that brought the batteries. Ivy drove slowly, tracking the battery-carrying robots and occasionally stopping while Marf and Wexsun loaded scavenge into the little crate they'd found for her and put on the back of the electric cart. When they reached a cafeteria of some sort, with tables and chairs and a group of machines along one wall with fancy packaged food inside, Ivy used the hammer to break the glass, and the canids collected the edibles as well.

Farther down the line, in the battery facility, she saw what she wanted; hundreds of battery packs, lined up on spidery metal carriers and waiting to be carried off for installation in vehicles. Without a word to either of the canids, she got out of the cart and limped purposefully to the nearest battery with the hammer and screwdriver. She pounded the screwdriver through the battery's shell like a spike. It was a satisfying, solid sound, like driving a stake into the ground. Ivy pulled it out and repeated the process. The third and fourth holes she made sparked, and a wisp of smoke began to issue from them. With a grim smile, Ivy moved on to the next.

"Help help?" Wexsun asked. He and Marf had watched , and now each carried a hammer and screwdriver. Ivy nodded. The canids took to it with delight, laughing as they drove their own spikes into the batteries and left holes in them. They were like children with new toys. Together they punched holes in thirty or forty batteries, until Ivy called them back. The first battery she'd damaged was drooling acrid, viscous white smoke; it was probably time to be away from them.

On the drive back through the factory, Ivy stopped a few more times to add more scavenge to the cart. Marf and Wexsun jumped eagerly out of the cart whenever she stopped and pounded holes in the batteries of the unfinished vehicles on the production line, finding the gaps in the protective casings that she hadn't had the time to look for.

Motion caught her eye: Makkhana, at the window of the foreman's office, waving down at her. She stopped the cart and went upstairs. Her leg felt more and more swollen as she kept using it, but she ignored the discomfort. When she got to the office, Kroni was standing, leaning against the wall, and Makkhana looked proud of himself. "I hope the floor down there isn't a battlefield," he said. "I've a plan to put into motion—with your permission."

"What is it?"

"An escape," Kroni said. He sounded exhausted, but pleased.

Ivy didn't like the gray pallor in his face, though. "You're hurt worse than you thought," she said.

He nodded. "Those men are...unnaturally strong."

"If you can help him downstairs, I'll be finished in a moment." Koon, the third canid, hopped off the desk he was sitting on and moved to help Ivy with Kroni.

"You've set off the fire suppression system, by the way," Makkhana said without looking up from his work. "It put out the first three fires you set, before it ran out of retardant; there are still at least ten batteries burning in the battery plant alone, and I couldn't see how many more you damaged. I think you are going to get your wish."

There was a reproachful tone in his voice, which she ignored. "Good," she said.

"Go to the other end of the factory, where the finished cars are. As soon as that smoke starts breaching the roof and they know the extinguishers have failed, the corporate folks are going to begin moving the cars, using the self-driving mode. Minimizing losses," he added. "I'll reprogram several to take us past the staging lot, and we'll hide in them."

Ivy didn't follow all of it, but Makkhana sounded confident and that was enough for now. She headed downstairs with Kroni. Once they were on the steps, she asked him, "Am, am I doing the right thing?"

"You are doing what I would do," he said.

The air tore at their noses as they opened the door to the factory floor; the smell of burning batteries. The air was clear, but the cough-inducing chemical smell suggested that it wouldn't be for long. Koon hacked in immediate discomfort. She didn't see the other canids, and told Koon, "Go find your family, and meet us at the far end," she pointed toward the end of the assembly line.

Kroni settled onto the cart. He glanced at the crate on the back, now overflowing with tools, food, coveralls and several first aid kits, and found the energy to favor Ivy with a knowing smile.

There was a thump and a crash of falling metal from the direction of the battery plant. It was well over three hundred meters to the door, but through the forest of assembly stations and machinery a haze of black smoke was creeping in their direction. It looked like some of the lights had gone out. Looking more closely, Ivy saw some of the partially assembled vehicles on the line beginning to drool heavy smoke as well.

Makkhana opened the door. He was carrying his terminal, and had grabbed a helmet as well. "I appreciate you waiting," he said. "I made some statements on your behalf before the gateway went down, as well. At this point I assume the powers that be took us offline, but it very well may have been you," he added, looking back toward the battery plant.

Ivy didn't respond, and got the cart in motion. Some distance down the line they found Fry, training her gun on a door barred with metal gates. Ivy guessed from the signage and scanners that it was an employee entrance. The door rattled and rocked in its frame, being struck repeatedly from the outside.

Fry glanced up when she saw Ivy, gave a quick nod. "Team of six. I locked them out, but they'll be through that door as soon as they get a battering ram, or just blow it off the hinges."

"How long?" Ivy asked.

"No idea. Five minutes?"

"Then let's not be here then."

She didn't need to be told twice, and joined them.

They found Narooma next, coming from the opposite side. "Some sillies tried to come in the loading dock," she said, "so I broke their heads. If that's okay with you."

Fry smiled. "If it wasn't, it's not like you can do it any differently."

"Good point. Well, they started it. I was just defending myself. And my door."

"Did you block it?"

"No, they knocked it down. But I threw them back out so the others know not to do that again." She spun her axe around her hand and made a threatening sneer. "Is something on fire?"

"Yes," Ivy said.

"Is it on purpose?"

"Yes."

"Oh, good."

Fry gave Ivy a wry half-smile that crinkled the tattoos on her cheeks.

"You and your sister are like cyclones. It's starting to smell like we shouldn't be here any more. Let's corral Dilly and get moving. Dilly!" she shouted without warning at ship's-deck volume. Ivy flinched in surprise.

The summons worked, though; DIlly came at a run, from the finishing end of the plant. He moved fast for his size, and Ivy mused that he had a similar look of delighted dishevelment to Swan's after she'd been in a fight. Narooma and Fry hopped on the cart and Ivy set off again, meeting Dilly halfway. She was surprised that the cart didn't seem to be working any harder with five people aboard.

"Having fun?" Narooma asked him as they drew even with him.

"Yeah, huge laughs," he replied, slowing to jog alongside the cart, then hopping on. Ivy accelerated again when he was aboard. From the area of the battery plant, far behind them, something exploded with a *crumpf* sound that sent a tremor through the building. "We have a plan to get out?"

"Assuming Ivy doesn't bring the building down on all of us first," Makkhana deadpanned. They had reached the end of the line; the open bay doors at the end of final assembly looked out on the parking lot full of new Bright Spirit vehicles of all sizes.

"I'd stay inside," Fry said, pointing toward the killzone where Phosen, Alice and Amran still lay, about forty feet outside.

"Yes, do," Makkhana said. "There are enough cars inside for us to do what we need to. Keep an eye out for fairies, please; we don't need them seeing what we're up to." He opened his terminal and went to the first car, began typing.

Marf suddenly raced past them, ducking Fry as she helped Kroni up, and went after a man who'd appeared near the doors, backlit by the sunlight. There was a shout of pain and Durloo yelled, "It's me, it's me, get off!" The canid continued snarling, and Durloo fell.

Koon and Wexsun were right behind, in human form. Wexsun smacked Marf on the head. "Friend!" he yelled. Marf yelped and growled briefly, but let him go.

Durloo had been bitten on the arm, and cradled the bloody wound. "He didn't recognize me?" he gasped.

"What, what were you doing out there?" Ivy asked.

"Sending a message to my friends in Singapore," he said, his voice harsh with pain. "They're going to regret trying to kill us. All of them are going to regret this!"

Ominous black smoke continued to gather at the far end of the factory. Closer to this end, a few of the nearly-completed cars were issuing battery smoke from beneath. A big explosion from the battery plant jolted the floor and shattered interior windows. Ivy saw a rush of orange flames through the black smoke, far far down the line. They could hear the fire now, a dull roaring that seemed to vibrate the air.

"No more time for debate," Makkhana said. "Time to select your rides, everyone. I've collected the vehicle numbers."

"What's happening?" Durloo asked. Makkhana explained quickly.

"We can't all go to Singapore," Ivy said. "I'm going to find Shiloh, and my idiot sister. But Kroni needs to get back to the ship. And Durloo, you've lost too much." She didn't add that she thought he was unstable.

"We shouldn't split up," Durloo said. "We're stronger together. Especially the wounded," he added.

"I disagree," Ivy said. "Too large a group is easier to target." She tried not to snap at him. She was feeling overwhelmed with so many people to keep track of, and concern about getting Kroni to safety, plus Makkhana's reluctance to go along with the things she was doing, were added pressures on top of everything else.

"We don't have to go in the same directions," Makkhana said. He typed as he talked. "The staging lot is about ten miles from here, safely away from the fire. The cars will follow the factory vehicles for a few miles, and can then go anywhere after that. I can send them back to the coast to meet the ship, or to the train station. I think that trying to drive all the way to Singapore might be stretching credibility, as well as the initial battery charge. The train is faster anyway." He swiped at his screen, and the trunk of a small aqua-blue sedan popped open. "That one's bound for the coast."

"That one's for you, Kroni," Ivy said. He looked for a moment like he might argue, then nodded wearily.

"It'll stop a few times," Makkhana explained. "There's an emergency handle in the trunk. When it reaches the destination, it'll honk its horn once and then shut down. That's your cue to come out."

"Hopefully there will not be guns in my face," he said.

"I've done this before," Makkhana said with a smile. "You'd be surprised at how well it works."

Kroni nodded again. "Shall I take your treasures?" he asked Ivy.

The scavenge! She'd almost forgotten. "Yes, please," she said. Dilly, listening in, quickly figured out what was going on, and loaded some of the items from the crate into the trunk once Kroni was in.

"This is foolish," Durloo said again.

"I didn't ask you," Ivy said, this time letting her voice take an edge.

"Ain't going Singy," Wexsun said. "No Kurois, not there." Ivy nodded, feeling slightly relieved. The canids had felt hard to control, and she couldn't help but think it would be an awful irony if they'd escaped the *Excelsis* only to die trying to repay her.

"I assume you prefer to ride together. If you're willing to trust me," Makkhana said to Wexsun, opening the liftgate of a large red car with his terminal, "the car will take you wherever you'd like. The coast? Farther north?"

"North," the canid said with a curt nod.

"Done," he said, and the canids went their way.

"I'm taking the train back to Singapore with you," Makkhana said to Ivy.

She nodded, then glanced over her shoulder as another rumbling explosion shook the floor. It was closer this time, and the blast was punctuated by the sound of pieces of machines being thrown around. "Fry, do you mind returning to the ship?"

"Don't have to ask me twice," she said. "Dilly's going with you though. I still have a sailor ashore in Singapore and I don't trust Razor to keep herself out of trouble."

"I'm going with her," Narooma said, pointing to Ivy. "That's where the exploits are."

Fry gave Ivy a look of amusement. "We'll wait for you," she said to Ivy. "Don't die." With that, Fry headed for her own car. Dilly moved like a valet, stowing the rest of Ivy's scavenge in the other coast-bound vehicle.

Out in the parking lot, smoke was beginning to drift past in the sky, blown from the burning end of the factory. Ivy saw that the vehicles closest to the gate had begun moving, out in the lot. Makkhana didn't look up, but said, "Time's short. Your turn, Ivy. Durloo, decide where you're going, or stay here." His voice was surprisingly hard.

"Will you even fit in one of these trunks?" Durloo snapped.

"I'll do what I can."

Ivy decided not to get involved; they could fight it out amongst themselves. Makkhana directed her to a little rig in a pleasing shade of blue, and she got inside. Just before he closed the trunk, Dilly handed her a sandwich from one of the machines, a bottle of water, a packet of sliced carrots and the slickgun they'd taken from the Myawi Protector. "Just in case," he said.

She smiled at him. "Thank you. See you soon."

The trunk closed.

Ivy surprised herself by dozing off after a few minutes. She roused briefly when the car hummed to life and began moving, but was in a hazy, in-between wakeful space so she wasn't certain how long the drive was. The car stopped a few times, and she heard voices around it, close then fading away. She had a muddy half-dream of being extremely young and riding in a rig with Holly, tucked side-by-side into a large basket, her mother at the wheel.

The car eventually stopped and the horn chirped, and that roused her. Time to get out. She pulled the safety knob Dilly had pointed out and the trunk sprang open. She was in a parking lot, one of a row of five Bright Spirit cars that had come from the factory, and Ivy assumed that the featureless building adjacent was the train station. The sky was half sunny, half black with smoke, and she could hear the fire roaring but couldn't see it.

Makkhana was pulling himself out of the last car in the line. Narooma, Dilly and Durloo were already out. She had a strange feeling, realizing now that Kroni was gone, she was alone here, in a way.

As she looked toward the factory, there was a louder, deeper boom accompanied by a ball of orange that wafted merrily up into the smoke.

"Well," she said. "That's interesting."

"It will get worse," Makkhana said.

"Everyone keeps saying that. You're sure?"

"They are making no effort to put it out. It will burn as it finds more fuel, and there is much more." Another explosion sent another mushroom up next to the first. "We should board, before they stop the trains," he said.

Ivy expected a crowd of people trying to get out of Semangat Terang, but the platform was almost empty.

Durloo explained. "They'll have cancelled any shifts tonight, and will be holding people to make a proper count of casualties. Anyone who'd normally be taking this train back to Singapore is probably stuck in whatever building they're keeping the staff in."

"Good for us," Narooma said.

As they boarded the express train, there was another, louder explosion, this one accompanied by a wild spray of sparks like fireworks that shot a hundred feet into the air and the sound of shattering windows. Immediately after that was a flash so large that it momentarily eclipsed the sunlight. The blast that followed rocked the train, shook the ground and cracked several of the train's windows. Dilly and Durloo cried out in surprise, and Ivy ducked and put her hands over her ears instinctively, an action which did nothing to prevent them from ringing for a moment. The black cloud had mushroomed swiftly outward from the factory, and was beginning to block out the sunlight over the train station.

The conductor shouted once for any stragglers to get on the train, and the doors were closing in that moment. The train began to move with a silent urgency, scrolling the blackening sky and orange flames away for a view of Semangat Terang's buildings, then of surgically cleared jungle as the factory town dropped farther and farther behind them.

The car they were in had varied seating, and was empty apart from another couple sitting at the far end. As they chose a C-shaped set of six seats that faced one another, the two got up and exited the car.

"For what it's worth, Ivy, I suppose you've avenged your mother," Makkhana said.

"It's scaled when it's scaled," she replied reflexively.

"And who decides that?"

She looked at him, letting the question hang, then turned to Narooma. "You didn't flinch at all. Have, have you seen something like that before?"

Narooma nodded. "Inchins got rockets. A Demon's Tongue missile can blow a ship the size of this train into nuggets," she said. "Nothing left bigger than your hand. That boomer was almost that big."

Makkhana interrupted them; he was looking at his terminal. "You're quite the news sensation, Ivy. Live feed from Semangat Terang. They've already rewrapped it in dragon skin, of course," he said, turning the screen around so they could see.

A serious-looking man stood in front of a desk, staring back at them so intensely that Ivy had to remind herself he couldn't actually see them. He said, "We have been in communication with the Myawi, who spoke of wanting to make a pilgrimage to Semangat Terang to honor her mother's memory. She was in discussion with members of the domestic industry and of our own social services to do this, and then she would turn herself in. The Prime Minister even made the controversial offer of a partial pardon, followed by a consulting position on a committee to improve the lives and training of domestics throughout the brother nations."

"It doesn't look like that's happened," another voice off-screen said.

"No, John, I'm afraid not. Upon reaching Semangat Terang, she and a gang of violent extremists and shifters murdered a Bright Spirit repre-sentative in the street, then barricaded themselves inside the plant and set several fires." An image of the factory burning replaced the intense man's face. The fire was much smaller in the photo—it had been taken at least an hour ago. "We're told that those fires have gotten out of control, and there are still Bright Spirit employees held inside the plant."

"They're making you look quite dangerous," Makkhana said.

"Am I a 'violent extremist?'" Narooma asked with amusement.

"None of that is true!" Ivy complained. "Holly isn't even *here!*"

"It's possible that they know that," Makkhana replied. "Vitter doesn't need to shoot you if the public decides that their celebrity cause of the moment is too distasteful to follow. Unfortunately for them, we can get a message from you sent right back out. They think you're still in the factory. Maybe they're hoping you've made some sort of suicide pact."

Ivy's mind raced. Trying to consider what a faceless mob of dwellers with no connection to what was going on would think was exhausting. "I don't know what to do," she said. "Should we tell them that I made sure not to hurt anybody?"

"Don't show weakness!" Durloo snapped. "I've contacted my people in Singapore. They're going to avenge our fallen friends," he said, rubbing at the bandage on his arm. "This is war now."

"Elaborate, please," Makkhana said.

"I have friends who got work assignments at the trimester celebration," he said. "Food service, security, that sort of thing. They can get weapons in there. The stars will think they're safe, but they aren't. And at hour twenty, they'll find this out."

"Wait, what?" Dilly asked.

Ivy and Makkhana stared at Durloo. "You're going to do an assassination?"

"Yes. We weren't going to, but now they've gone too far. Killing Alice? Amran? They don't care about us. They think we're disposable. We'll show them who's truly disposable."

"Who?" Makkhana asked. He seemed surprised as well.

"The Prime Minister. That bastard Vitter. The Deshmus. All of them, anyone who's close to them. If the whole celebration exploded like that factory back there? That would be fine with me. Incinerate them all, in your name."

"*My* name?"

"Yes! All of the wrongs they've done to you. Ivy, there are thousands of us, all here for you. You and your sister," he added.

"No," Ivy said. "If you're going to incinerate people in my name, I'd prefer you asked if that's what I wanted first."

"It's too late," Durloo said. "It's already going to happen. I've set it in motion." He smiled, with more than a hint of madness, then looked at

Narooma. "Now you see what kind of a man I am," he said proudly.

"Tubachick," she spat derisively.

"Durloo, I don't want this."

"But the people do! Look at the feeds! Haven't you seen the people in the streets calling your name? Students are marching on the Myawi school! Women are rising up and taking their lives back! Just like your ancestors did, in Astoria."

Ivy clenched her hands. She wanted to say something, but no words came. Makkhana spoke instead, his words slow and patient as if he were talking to a child. "We appreciate the support, Durloo. But not like this. This...this isn't a way to correct what's wrong. This is just mass murder."

"By taking out the figureheads, we gain control of the dialogue."

Narooma scoffed. "No, we don't. I'm all for knocking off heads that're too fat, but don't pretend it makes anyone listen to you."

"Just leave," Ivy said.

Durloo looked stunned. "What?"

She pointed to the far end of the car. "Leave. Go. You're, you're, you're not doing these things for me, you're doing them for, for yourself. Admit that. Get out of this car."

"Ivy, this is the best way—" He was interrupted by the heel of Narooma's hand, which thumped hard into his chest and twisted to wrap his shirt around her fist. She dragged him out of the seat with one hand and and sent him tumbling to the floor without getting up. He gasped in pain, then withdrew his phone from his vest pocket with an incredulous look on his face. "You've smashed my phone! Look at it!"

"You weren't using it for anything good anyway," Narooma said with a shrug. He glared at her, and she jutted out her tattooed chin, widening her eyes in a mocking rictus.

"You are going to buy me a new phone."

"Make me. Listen to the words." She pointed at the far end of the car. "Go back to your own school. Anywhere but here."

Durloo got to his feet, his face dark with anger. Ivy deliberately didn't look at him, and only caught his glare in her peripheral vision. He looked from Ivy to Narooma to Dilly, then stomped down to the far end of the train car. The door whispered open and he went through to the next. Ivy watched him go, as fascinated by the doors as she was confused by this latest turn.

"So," Narooma said once Durloo were out of earshot. "That one lost his head and lit a big fuse. Your enemies are telling lies about you, and if that one's plan works out, it's going to make them look like they were telling the truth all along."

"Succinctly put," Makkhana said.

"Turns out I'm not stupid," she replied. "So what next?"

"What I want hasn't changed," Ivy said. "Holly. Shiloh. Home."

Makkhana said, "I wouldn't have much confidence in our chances of actually sailing away if Durloo's friends attack the stars at the trimester celebration and blame you. No one's going to object to Vitter sending the Fists and *Excelsis* to the bottom of the harbor after something like that."

"If someone shoots a princess, I wouldn't get on that boat," Narooma agreed. She had one of her feet in her lap, and was rubbing it. "'Member those Demon's Tongue rockets I was talking about? They can't use 'em in the harbor, but once you're over the horizon? Pouf."

"I would rather that didn't happen," Ivy said softly.

"It might not," Makkhana said. "There are other pieces in play."

"Tell me what that means."

"I'm not sure I can explain in a way that makes sense."

Dilly looked around the empty train car. "I've got time," he said with a shrug. Narooma laughed.

"The Ivory Sisters avoid certain types of political action, as I said. But that doesn't mean we are unaware of other...factions."

"Like the Rainbow Snakes," Narooma said. "They been sneakin' north for two weeks."

"You know of this?"

"The way you dirtyfeets think you can foop around in our ocean without us knowing is cute. Stupid, but cute. They're staying away from the Inchins, but yeah, we saw 'em out there."

"Mama Lola was talking to the Rainbow Snakes, when we were in Zeeland," Dilly added. "Couple of 'em sailed with us for a while, before we headed back to Strip City."

Makkhana nodded. "As I said. Other factions."

"So does one hand work well with its brother?" Ivy asked.

"Are you kidding? There are so many appendages flailing about...I'm not even sure if they're all hands. Between encouraging the sane actions and trying to discourage pocket madmen like our friend Durloo, I'm astounded the Sisters have had time to organize anything at all."

chapter 61

Two hours before Princess Aiyana's trimester celebration

Shiloh's nap stretched out, and turned into a brief half-dream in which she was back on the *Excelsis*, trying to figure out which cell had the felids in it so she could let them out. It just wouldn't come to her, because she had to ask Mr. Morse, the ringmaster, for permission to remember.

That thought made no sense at all, and pushed her back into a consciousness she didn't remember leaving. Dim room. Cheap bed. Smell of spicy food and too many boys crammed into a smallish space. The voices from out in the main room went up suddenly, everyone cheering as if a point had been scored in a game. Shiloh shook her head and rubbed her eyes. She stretched both legs, her shoulders, her arms, before deciding that she was putting off returning to the world, and went back out into the main room.

The newsfeed showed the factory again, but the fire was much larger. Black smoke turned the day to night, and angry orange fireballs rolled through the structure, which was well on its way to being completely ruined. She had a moment to wish the scrolling feed on the bottom was in a language she recognized, and then a searing white fireball erupted, momentarily overwhelming the camera's auto-focus and blanking the video feed. When it came back the camera was panning rapidly back, showing an orange pillar rising several hundred feet into the black smoke. The image was accompanied by another set of cheers.

Nipa saw her first. "Look, she did it!"

"Did what?"

"It's the Bright Spirit car factory, the one where Holly the Myawi's mother was killed! She went back there. She said she was going to honor her mother's memory, and she did! By *destroying* it!"

"Fuckin' amazing," Wan said. He looked at Shiloh. "You were telling the truth," he said. "She did find her sister. They're both here."

"I knew that, obviously," Shiloh said, feeling that odd gap between human age and maturity versus her own again.

"Sorry. Lots of people have made lots of wild claims the past few months. Everyone saying they knew her before the murders, when they can't even tell one Myawi from another."

"I don't know anything about Holly. I was traveling with Ivy. Where are they now?"

"Still in the factory," the tall skinny boy said.

Shiloh's fingers and toes went cold. "In *there?*" What she was seeing on the screen wasn't survivable. If Bee and Razor were dead too, she'd be alone in Sino-India...

Nipa caught the look on her face first. "I'm sorry, Shiloh."

She'd brought her fingers to her mouth, nails pushing between her lips. *Don't panic*, she thought.

"Teach 'em all a lesson if she burned herself up," the skinny boy said. "They can't hurt her any more." He raised his drink to the newsfeed.

"They're not in there," Wan said. He wasn't watching the feed, but hunched over a portable on the cluttered table. "Look." He held the screen up so Shiloh and Nipa could see Holly sitting in an interview chair of some sort. "This is live. The factory video's on a ten-minute delay."

Behind Holly, a dark green velvet drape was partly open, showing a hallway bustling with activity behind her: wait-staff pushing chromed trays, security men with radios, a tumult of formalwear. Wherever she was, it wasn't Semangat Terang.

"That looks like the back of Koralyi," the skinny boy said. "She's backstage at the trimester."

"Shush," Nipa said. "Can't hear." They turned the sound on the newsfeed down and the portable up.

Holly was smiling. "Hi," she said. "It's me again. Soon I'm going to introduce you to my sister Ivy." She grinned. "I found her. I didn't get a chance to tell you that before. I've been out of the loop until the past day or two, so I am only just getting all of the messages of support. And the hate mail. Some of you *really* don't like me," she added. "And that's fine. I'm not doing this to be liked. This...this didn't start out as politics at all, I'm just living my life. Life being what it is, though, people are trying to create movements and tell me what I should be saying. What I'm saying is this: I wouldn't let Myawi speak for me, in the end, and I don't intend to let anyone else speak for me, either.

"You probably heard that we just destroyed a factory. And we did." Holly went on to refute the claims that her sister had wantonly murdered hundreds of workers at the factory, and speculated that she'd done what she could to make sure people were safe before lighting the fires. She talked for a while about the people trying to kill her as well. "We received an invitation to come and talk to some important people," she said finally. "We're going to accept that, Ivy and I. She's on her way to Singapore, to have a chat about what's gone on and what we can do to make things better, and then Ivy and I are going to go home. That's it. I've got no ulterior motives. I would like to accept the Brother Nations' invitation to sit down to tea, while Prime Minister Hudri and Chancellor Shay from New Delhi and Mr. Gao from Beijing are all in town for Princess Aiyana's trimester celebration, and then I promise to get out of your faces and off of your feeds. Sorry, Shairpie," she added, flashing another dazzling smile, "but I'm going to decline the extremely kind offer to host your variety show." Holly made a mischievous smile that wasn't quite a wink, and the video ended.

"If anyone's coming down from Semangat Terang," Wan said, "then they're on the express train." He had pulled up some other information on the other side of the screen. "It arrives in forty minutes."

"They're gonna kill 'em," the skinny boy said.

"No, they won't. Not after she said she's coming to talk."

"Holly the Myawi's already here," he said, pointing to one of the many images on the big screen. Shiloh was surprised to see Holly, smiling and talking to a man in a suit. "So that must be her sister on the train."

"The wild twin? On a train? How would she even know to get on a train? Bet she's killed everyone aboard." Shiloh slapped the boy's arm, hard.

"David's listening to his scanner, he just messaged. They're getting ready to take her out before she gets here. No way are they going to let her near Singapore. Not after she already blew up one city today."

"The police wouldn't do that, would they?" Nipa asked. "Betray her after saying they'd talk to her and her sister?"

"They absolutely would. We should go down there. Call some other people. Why aren't they stopping the train?"

"Sounds like they already tried," the skinny boy replied. "Communication to the train is down. They can't shut it down remotely, and the express trains are full autodrive so there's no driver."

"We should go down there," Wan said again. "We have to. Let them know we know what they're going to do and they can't get away with it."

"Station's going to be packed. Full of cops too."

"We could go," Shiloh said. She nudged Nipa. "They wouldn't shoot you, would they?"

The princess looked at her and smiled a slow, lazy smile. It grew into an irrepressibly wicked grin.

chapter 62

*Three hours before Princess Aiyana's trimester
celebration*

>> Fires Rage in Semangat Terang as Holly the Myawi Heads for Singapore: The
Bright Spirit factory town lies in ruins after a surprise sabotage attack by the rogue
Myawi domestic Holly and an unknown number of accomplices. Fires in the city are
completely out of control at the time of this report, and the entire town is reportedly being evacuated. In a video released immediately afterward, Holly can be
seen on what appears to be an express commuter train, and she announces her
intent to come to Singapore. The chatlines are abuzz with speculation that she's
already on her way. She claims to want to meet with leaders of the Brother Nations,
and Chancellor Shay has already stated that he is willing to speak with her. But
should she be allowed anywhere in the city with so many important political figures
attending the Deshmu trimester celebration? It's clear that the results of another
act of mayhem would be catastrophic.

                                              —Heart of Singapore News

Makkhana had his eyes on his portable. "Your sister's message from last
night is being seen. Widely. Two newsfeeds have mentioned it, but no one
has shown it yet."

"Well, that's no good," Narooma said.

"Actually, it's better than you'd think. If they're not playing it, that
may be because the government is asking them not to. This censorship is an
indication that they see you as a serious threat, otherwise they wouldn't be
concerned as to whether or not it aired."

"But it's no good if nobody hears her message."

"This is where they always make their mistake. Just because they won't
let it on the major feeds doesn't keep the message from getting out. And if
they don't dragon-skin it for themselves, it gets out without any dragon-

skin. Views are already over four thousand, and people are already starting to gather at the station in Singapore to see you when you arrive."

"We got an audience?" Narooma asked.

"I don't know if it's time to celebrate just yet," Makkhana said. At the far end of the car, there was a chime as the door slid open. Durloo had returned, and four men in uniforms came with him. They looked like policemen, and judging from Makkhana's reaction Ivy guessed that was what they were.

Durloo had a vicious grin on his face, and looked at them from under hooded eyes. "Now, it begins."

Ivy got to her feet, her leg less steady than she would have liked. "What begins?" she asked.

Durloo drew a long knife and advanced slowly on Ivy. She took a step back. The police spread out behind him, but didn't seem intent on stopping him. "The revolution, of course," he said, still smiling. "The time has come for the Ivory Sisters to strike. The flames of martyrdom await."

"You are not of the Ivory Sisters—" Makkhana began. Without looking away from her, Durloo lunged past Ivy and stabbed him through the throat. His words became a choked gurgle of surprise.

She let out a formless shout of horror. In the same moment, the police rushed forward. Two of them drew their guns and fired at the group. Makkhana saved Narooma by throwing himself into the aisle, his bulk absorbing at least five shots as he fell.

Narooma let out a piercing battle-cry and charged the gunmen, swinging her axe. She dove at the last moment and attacked wide and low, chopping across their legs. One limb actually sailed into the air and hit the wall. Dilly was moving at the same time, charging the shooters with equal boldness. He used his bulk and plowed over the first man, grabbing the second and throwing him into the wall.

Ivy tumbled to the floor, losing sight of both of them, and pulled Durloo down with her. When he hit the floor, she rolled him onto the arm that held the knife, trapping it, then threw herself on top of him, banging his head against the hard floor until he went slack and dazed.

She looked to her right. Makkhana lay in the aisle, his eyes open, a steady stream of blood pumping out of his neck. Ivy thought he was dead already for a moment, but then he pushed his portable toward her with unfocused eyes, just his thick-fingered hand moving, shoving the little computer toward her.

On the screen, she saw herself, looking stunned. It was recording her, presumably the same way Holly had recorded herself. Did she really look that angry?

But she got it.

Ivy's confusion dropped away in that moment as she watched the pitched battle. Narooma jumped lithely over Dilly and another policeman writhing on the floor, ducking a three-shot burst that spalled the window behind her along the way. The delphid threw her axe and knocked the gun out of one man's hands, then grabbed the next nearest one and tossed him to the floor.

Either Durloo had decided to help the police, or they'd been there waiting for him and he'd been working with them all along, Ivy concluded. It was like Makkhana had said; even if they weren't repeating Holly's message, it had been received. Vitter couldn't afford to let her get to Singapore Not because she might miraculously find some way to assassinate everybody, but because she and her idiot sister might do just the opposite and charm the Prime Minister and chancellors the same way Holly had already charmed a significant chunk of the populace, apparently. And now Makkhana had the portable recording of what was really happening, so they couldn't change the story this time.

Ivy pressed Durloo's face into the floor, her entire weight on his head. He grunted and snarled, struggling uselessly. Narooma grappled with one of the police, then threw him into the cracked window; it shattered under the impact and the man vanished with a cut-off shriek. An eardrum-battering buffeting of wind immediately filled the train car. Ivy stayed on top of Durloo and pulled Makkhana's portable toward her, turning it so the camera saw her face up close, then toward the end of the car to film as Narooma kneed one of the police in the stomach and then hammered her axe into the back of his head as he doubled over. Dilly had rolled over on top of the last man, sitting on his head, groin pressed into the man's face, shouting something Ivy couldn't hear over the wind rushing through the broken window.

All three of the remaining police were down, one of them clutching the stump where his leg had been and groaning. Narooma ignored him, grabbed Durloo by the throat and dragged him away from Ivy. Weakly, he waved his knife at her and she slapped it away.

Dilly got up and manhandled the man he had been sitting on through the broken window, then stepped up to help Narooma wrestle with Durloo. The young man spit in Dilly's face; the sailor responded by punching him five times in the ribs. Durloo shouted and writhed in pain, struggling to get free. Narooma gave Dilly an irritated glare as Durloo kicked her in the shin, and angled her head toward the open window.

Ivy had just a moment to turn the camera away as without hesitation, Narooma and Dilly lifted Durloo between them and threw him off of the train. The young man disappeared through the window with a Dopplered cry. Narooma watched for a moment, then hunkered down next to Ivy and Dilly.

"That was fun," Dilly said.

"Brutal exploits," Narooma agreed.

"You think he had more friends?"

"I hope that was all of them," Ivy said.

"You look tired."

"I am. I don't want to have another fight."

"Eh, I'm all right," Narooma said.

"We're here for you," Dilly agreed.

chapter 63

Shiloh managed to get Wan to give her a sandwich out of the refrigerator, and ten minutes later she and Nipa were back in the Royce, speeding across town yet again. Nipa programmed the car to meet the train from Semangat Terang, and it set off immediately for the station. The commuter trains stopped on the outskirts of the city, where riders transferred to smaller local trains that went into the city. It was a half-hour drive through traffic, but with the Deshmus' priority mode on, they got there in twenty. The sandwich was nasty, but she ate it anyway.

Nipa's car pulled past the police cordons up to the curb. An officer in riot gear held out his hand when it stopped, coming to the window. Shiloh was in the back, Nipa behind the wheel. The officer was visibly surprised when she rolled the window down. "Princess," he gasped. "I beg forgiveness, but you will have to wait here. There is a dangerous situation."

"Shut up," Nipa said, closing the window and turning the autodrive off. She turned the wheel and the Royce climbed up onto the curb. The sidewalk wasn't blocked to traffic, and Nipa guided the massive car along it until they reached the main entrance. The train station featured a large open arcade with shops down each side. The vendors had been shut down by the police, so the space was wide open, and Nipa drove straight through, knocking down a couple of stalls along the way, until they reached the back of a veritable wall of cops in riot gear.

They could see the train entering the station, slowing to a halt.

"Perfect timing!" Nipa shouted. She nudged the gas, then nudged at the line of cops with the car's massive bumper. The policemen instinctively parted for the car, most of them visibly confused when they recognized it. Nipa steered clumsily onto the platform, scraping a wall as she did so. The car veered and for a moment Shiloh was afraid they were going to drive right onto the tracks, but Nipa straightened it out and then pulled up to the stopped train, between the doors and the wall of armed police.

"Don't get out," Nipa said.

Ivy looked out of the train almost immediately, her eyes confused and wary. Shiloh hit the button that opened the rear doors then, so Ivy could see her. "Hi! We need to go," she shouted. Ivy rushed forward, with a woman and a big man in blue coveralls right behind her. As they piled into the car Shiloh realized the coveralls were spattered with blood, though neither of them appeared to be badly injured.

Nipa hit the button to close the door behind them. She spun the wheel and the car rotated almost in its own length on the train platform, the rear end catching a trash can and sending it flying in the process. They accelerated back the way they came. Shiloh watched the cops, who were uncertain, caught between orders to shoot Ivy and Holly, and orders not to shoot the youngest Deshmu princess. They did attempt to close ranks and stop the car, but Nipa punched a button on the console and a massive cloud of steam shot out from behind the Royce's front grille as they reached the wall of cops. The men shouted and dove out of the way. The car sped through, only thumping a few of them before it reached the street again and accelerated away. Nipa turned the autodrive back on and hit three switches before turning around to talk to her new passengers.

"Hi, Ivy um, Holly the Myawi's sister," she said cheerfully. "I'm Princess Nipa Deshmu, and it's wonderful to meet you." She made an elaborate little formal bow in spite of her seated position. "Shiloh told me a lot about you, and I read about you and I think that what you're doing is amazing. Who are your friends?"

Ivy gave Shiloh a look; she had caught Nipa's use of her real name, and the fact that she knew it seemed to be a big item in Nipa's favor. "It's nice to meet you, Nipa," she said. "I'm Ivy Aniram, and this is Narooma and Dilly. Thank you for picking us up."

"It was going to be a bloodbath if we didn't," she replied.

"Yes," Ivy said, "I, I think it might have been. Are they following?"

"Nope," Nipa said. "Anti-abduction measures. Autodrives attempting to lock on to us are being fried. And they can't drive manually fast enough to keep up." Ivy frowned in mild confusion at the terminology but didn't ask any questions. Shiloh did notice, now that Nipa had pointed it out, that the Royce was going much faster than it had previously.

"Where are we going?"

"Back to the house," she said. "Everyone will be at the trimester celebration."

Shiloh frowned. "What if they're not? What if Mahnaz is still there?"

"Trust me," Nipa said. "He won't be."

Shiloh felt herself relaxing a bit for the first time all day; Ivy was here. She smelled of smoke, but she and her companions were here, if a little roughed up. "You're not limping."

"Holly got my leg fixed," Ivy said. "It still hurts." There was a tone in her voice that suggested she didn't want to talk about that.

"Are the others okay?"

"Kroni's hurt," she said. "Not bad. They're on their way to the ship."

"What about Swan? Did he find her?"

Ivy nodded. "She's, she's on the ship too. She was alive when I saw her but not doing well."

"Is that your friend who was hurt?" Dilly asked.

"Good friend."

"She'll be okay on the *Fists*," he said. "Jar Bob will take good care of her."

When they arrived, Nipa took them directly up from the garage so they didn't pass Dorim and Weeshu in the lobby, assuming they were still there. True to her word, the huge apartment was empty. Shiloh all but threw herself into the couch. "I'm so glad you're here," she said to Ivy.

Ivy didn't respond for a moment. She was looking around the huge room, and out the windows to the city far below. The expression on her face suggested that she was afraid to touch anything. "You look like you've done well," she said finally. Her voice was barely a whisper.

"I made good friends," Shiloh said.

Narooma bowed to Nipa, her manner surprisingly formal. "Princess! Seen you in pictures. It's wonderful to meet you and I thank you for your hospitality."

"You're welcome," she said. "Would you like something to eat? I'll get Yu-Hwa."

Ivy was looking up at the ceiling, and out the massive windows at the city laid out below. The sky quickened toward dusk. "I always wished I could have shown you my rooms at the Laddin, in Strip City," Shiloh said, joining her at the window. "But this is even better."

"Do you want me to show her around?" Nipa asked Shiloh.

"We don't have time," Ivy replied. "We need to get to the trimester celebration."

"She needs to get Holly out of there," Shiloh said, remembering the conversation at Wan's house.

"You know where she is?" Shiloh nodded, and explained what they'd seen on the news.

"I can take you," Nipa said.

"Is that...a good idea?" Shiloh asked, thinking again of Mahnaz.

"We need to get Holly, and then get back to the ship," Ivy said with a sigh. "That's all."

The idea of going home was the best thing she'd heard all day, and Shiloh nodded. Nipa ushered them into the kitchen, where a domestic was already quickly putting together snacks. The rich girl looked out of place, and Shiloh got the impression that she was rarely in there. "You guys look tired. Anybody want to do a bump? I'll go get my kit." A glance at Shiloh betrayed a teenage desire to please, and then Nipa bounced upstairs.

Nipa's domestic laid out a small spread quickly, then vanished as silently as she'd arrived. Narooma started munching on the crackers even as Yu-Hwa put them down, and was clearly intent on eating all of them. Nobody challenged her. Dilly sniffed suspiciously at a wrap with vegetables and cold fish before popping it in his mouth. "Princess seems pretty infatuated with you," Narooma said to Shiloh, glancing to the doorway to make sure Nipa was gone.

"Shiloh, did you...?" Ivy began.

She rolled her eyes at her. "What d'you think? She doesn't know about me, though. Pretty sure she'd be afraid of...you know."

"Oh, Shiloh."

"It's...I'll tell you later."

The conversation ended as Nipa returned with the stim rig, did a bump and then grabbed one of the little sandwiches. She stuffed half of it into her mouth without ceremony and passed the stim to Shiloh, who remembered how to use it from the last time. Even so, she couldn't help but smile when the rush hit her. So much nicer than alcohol.

She passed it to Dilly, who showed a puzzled Ivy how to put the crown on her head. She flinched away at first, like a suspicious cat. He apologized and tried again, explaining what he was doing. Shiloh asked Nipa, "Will you help me get my friends to safety?" She assumed the answer would be yes, but it seemed polite to ask.

Nipa nodded earnestly. "Of course! Nobody will hurt them. What they're trying to do to you is bullshit. We'll talk to my father."

"That seems—" Ivy began, and then Dilly activated the stim rig and she frowned. "What is this?" she asked, reaching up to touch the crown. "What did you do?"

"Perk you up a little," Dilly said with an indulgent smile.

Ivy took the crown off and looked at it curiously. There was a another question forming on her face, but anything she might have said was erased when the front door was thrown open, thrust into the wall and held there. Several pairs of footsteps rushed in, heavy boots, big people. They couldn't see the door from the kitchen, but Shiloh jumped to her feet.

"Princess! Where are you?" Mahnaz shouted.

"Shit," Shiloh hissed.

"Yes, Princess, come out," a second voice called. She recognized it as the boy from the club the night before, Tapia. "The police are here, and it's for your own protection."

"Go fuck yourself, Chokidar!" Nipa yelled. She jumped up from her chair and rushed out into the foyer. "I told you to leave us alone!"

"*Fuuuuck*, not again," Shiloh groaned. She'd gotten lucky getting out of the penthouse the last time. She risked a glance out into the great room. It was definitely Tapia. Dorim and Weeshu were also there, followed by a brace of uniformed cops.

"Back stair," a voice said quietly. It was Yu-Hwa, the domestic, appearing again as suddenly as she'd gone away. "Before they search the first floor." She tapped the wall on the far side of the stove, then pushed a section of it aside, revealing a staircase going up. She gave Ivy a meaningful look, which seemed to be understood and reciprocated.

Ivy snatched up the cloth that the rest of the sandwiches were on, wrapping it into a little bundle and moved quickly for the door, nodding to Narooma and Dilly.

"What is that?" Narooma asked, peering up.

"Servants' staircase. For the domestics," Dilly said, nudging her out of the way so Ivy could go first. Shiloh followed. Dilly closed the door quietly behind him and came up the stairs as well.

"Should we use it to go back down again?" Ivy asked.

He shook his head. "They'll search it eventually."

"Do you think they're after me, or you?" Shiloh said. "Mahnaz found me out. And *then* he found out about me and Nipa."

Narooma snickered laughter. "Oh, dear," Ivy said.

They came out onto the second floor, emerging into an unobtrusive nook in the hallway, and were greeted by a grinding, scraping sound. Nipa had run up the front stairs, pushed a large bureau out of her room and was trying to use it to block the top of spiral staircase steps. Mahnaz was halfway up the stairs, alternately shouting at her and trying to placate her, having success with neither.

"Stop right there, or I'll crush you!" she yelled. "Help me crush him!" she shouted when she saw Shiloh and the others.

"That's not a good idea," Ivy said. Shiloh rushed forward and reached Nipa first. The girl didn't protest when her arm was grabbed.

Tapia drew his gun and took a quick shot at Shiloh. This elicited a flailing attack from Mahnaz, who threw himself on the officer, screaming, "Imbecile! You'll hit the princess!"

"Assholes!" Nipa screamed down the steps. "I'll shit in your eyes! I'll shit in your mother's eyes!"

Dilly grabbed the edge of the bureau, but rather than pull it back, he pushed it over the railing. The men at the bottom scrambled to get out of the way; Mahnaz and Tapia dove to either side and it hit the floor between them with a dull cracking crash. Narooma followed it, screaming, "Hee-yaaaah!" as she hip-slid down the circular railing with shocking speed. At the bottom, she palmed Mahnaz' face and shoved him into Tapia. The nearest police officer dodged the tumbling bodies only to receive her axe in the side of his head.

That gave Dilly time to get down the stairs as well, and he threw himself into the fray with apparent glee. Shiloh gaped in amazement and horror; she'd seen plenty of fights but rarely had a balcony-height view of one. The big sailor charged through two police officers, tossed them aside, and ran into Weeshu. The men collided, grappled, then crashed to the floor. Narooma was driven into the living room by Dorim, backing away but making strange faces and sticking her tongue out at the bodyguard, tossing her weapon from hand to hand.

Tapia got to his feet, tapped Mahnaz on the shoulder and started up the steps. "Shit," Ivy said, moving to the top of the staircase. She took the slickgun Dilly had given her out of her pocket and aimed it at the two men on the steps. Tapia's eyes widened, and he started to reverse direction, but not before Ivy shot him. A cloud of thick, clear goo splattered over both Tapia and Mahnaz with an undignified splat. The chancellor immediately lost his footing and fell, whacking his face hard on the stairs; Tapia cursed and grabbed the bannister, losing his footing as well and sliding slowly back down.

"We need to get out of here," Shiloh said to the princess, guiding her quickly away from the top of the stairs, "and we can't fight all those cops."

She wasn't entirely certain about that, though; it looked like Dilly and Narooma had already killed at least two of the policemen. Mahnaz' big bodyguards were another matter entirely, though.

"There's the well."

"Well?"

"It's an emergency exit. In case of, I don't know, in case something happens," Nipa said, her eyes watching the battle below in fascination. "Straight to the ground floor. It's in my room, I'll show you."

"Go, I'll follow," Shiloh said. Ivy followed Nipa, but Shiloh hesitated at the railing. She didn't want to look away. The violence turned her stomach, but Ivy's friends seemed nice and she was worried about them. As she watched, Dilly dispatched a third police officer with little apparent effort, and then Weeshu grabbed him from behind in a chokehold. Dilly snatched fruitlessly at the arm locked around his throat and went to his knees.

Behind him, Narooma gave an ululating, exultant cry and swung her axe in a figure-eight in front of Dorim, driving him a step backward. She shouted again, eyes wide and went after him with an overhead attack that he easily sidestepped. Unfortunately, he wasn't her target. Narooma lunged forward with the attack, and her axe split Weeshu's head almost in half. The stricken man grunted loudly and seemed to struggle trying to maintain his grip on Dilly, then fell forward onto him.

Dorim let out a baritone howl of anguish. His curved knife was in his hand, and he went after Narooma with a flurry of rage-driven attacks that drove her back toward the windows.

"Dilly!" Shiloh called, seeing him extricating himself from Weeshu's corpse. Tapia was on the floor at the bottom of the steps, apparently unable to move, but he was on his radio; there would no doubt be more police coming before long. Dilly looked up at her, then to Narooma to see if she needed help. She was holding her own. Dorim got in close to her, slicing his blade up across her ribs, and she pulled him into a hug with the weapon braced out to one side, preventing him from using it. She headbutted him in the face, and he returned the favor. The blood that spattered from her mouth made Shiloh think of Swan being struck on the *Excelsis*, her flying, shattered teeth, and she made a sound in the back of her throat.

It got worse. Narooma looked dazed, but she swung her axe behind her with intent. It hit the window, spalling the glass. Dorim grabbed her hair with his free hand, pulling her head back. It looked like he intended to bite her throat out. Narooma kept her grip on him and dropped her weight, pulling him off-balance and spinning him around. They both went into the cracked window—which bowed outward alarmingly under the impact of Dorim's massive shoulder, then popped out entirely. Dorim and Narooma disappeared through the sudden opening. Shiloh could have sworn the woman was laughing when she went.

Dilly gaped at it for a moment, then scrambled quickly to his feet. Mahnaz reached clumsily for his ankle, and he pulled his foot away. "Watch out for the goo on the stairs," Shiloh called, and he stepped around the mess as best he could. Dilly and Shiloh followed Nipa into her room.

The princess had opened a door next to her closet door, revealing a small room that looked like an elevator. "Where's Narooma?" Ivy asked.

"She kilt the other big guy and jumped out the window," Dilly replied.

"Out the *window?* We're *fifteen stories up!* What's she doing?"

"Going splat in the street in a few seconds, I guess."

"Christfuck," Ivy hissed.

"She bought us space to move, let's don't waste it."

It was a squeeze, but all four of them fit inside, and Nipa slapped the single red button on the wall. The door slammed shut, there was a clank from within the walls, and the room *fell.* Shiloh gasped in surprise; Ivy threw her hand against the wall and made a noise in the back of her throat. They fell for several seconds, and then a knee-bending deceleration kicked in hard enough to make everyone stagger and bring spots to their eyes.

When the doors opened, they were in the garage.

Shiloh couldn't help but smile. "Neat," she said. Ivy was gasping in shock, and Dilly helped her out of the well.

"We should go," Nipa said. She gestured to her car, and it came to life, easing quietly out of its parking spot.

"No," Ivy said. "We need to separate. Take Shiloh to the docks, and I'll go get Holly. Can I take one of these cars?" she asked, looking down the row of antiques.

"You're going to take one of Father's cars?" she said with a frown, then shrugged and grinned with a powerful appreciation for mischief. "Neat, go ahead. He keeps the keys inside them."

"How do I get to...what are they calling it? The trimester event?"

"Easy," Nipa said. "Turn right out of here and then left at the first big road. Follow all the cars. Koralyi Stadium is covered in red and gold lights."

Ivy nodded. "Shiloh, if you get to the docks you can find the others. Fry and Kroni should be there."

She wanted to ask if Ivy had heard anything about Razor, or Bee, but there wasn't time so she just nodded and climbed into the car with Nipa.

"Let's go," she said.

"Where?"

"Toward the docks." She tried to remember what the hotel she'd left Bee at was called, but couldn't.

Nipa was behind the wheel, but her fingers danced over the screen that controlled the car's navigation system. "Why?"

"We have to help some friends."

She nodded. "I'll help," she said, giving Shiloh a moment to wonder what she'd have done if the princess had balked at helping. The car surged forward, ascending the ramp to the street.

chapter 64

*One hour before Princess Aiyana's trimester
celebration*

Holly wished she had Ivy at her side.

She didn't need filial support or comfort. She knew she was in her element, moving among the stars and politicals as Vitter paraded her about. The Myawi mask didn't seem to fit any more, though. Holly was aware of putting it on, of subsuming something of herself. She could see it, in her unwillingness to tolerate Anshul touching her, in her open defiance of Vitter. A year ago, she'd have borne it all without a second thought, might have even joked about it with Elden under the right circumstances. It was as though she'd outgrown her old life without even realizing; maintaining the façade in the face of everything else in her mind was actually difficult, and all she could think about was Ivy. She wished her sister could be there just to sample the food. The trimester celebration's buffet reception was in full swing, less than an hour until the first performers now, and a dozen servers flew past every few minutes with a new round of delicacies to sample. This was the sort of place she'd hoped to show Ivy, rather than the chaos of the past week or so. This party would be easier if they were together, if she could just be her sister's guide.

Holly felt sick and sad about abandoning Ivy. This was the best strategy, but pragmatism had blinded her to the fact that it no longer felt natural to be Myawi. She didn't like the feeling of moving backward. This wasn't who she was any more. She didn't want to be around these people, and didn't want to think about Ivy sailing back to North America without her, even though it was the very thing she was carefully trying to orchestrate. What mattered was getting Ivy and her friends—her new family—to safety. Nothing else.

Holly concentrated on charming the people whose hands Vitter had her shake. The tricky part was doing this without visible irritation at reverting to her submissive-Myawi self. No one was pulling her strings, and it was hard to act like a Myawi while still communicating this fact. When a minor movie star named Kisi made the mistake of speaking to Vitter instead of her during their conversation, she joked, "Now this is an interesting change. Instead of worrying that men are staring at my chest instead of my face, I need to be concerned that they're looking for a nonexistent benefactor!" She didn't think it was particularly funny or eloquent, but it got a laugh out of the five or six people in the circle, including Kisi. Anshul, who had made a point of staying in her line of sight at all times, continued to glower.

"My apologies," Kisi said, bowing to her. "I will look beyond your collar. Do you plan to keep it?"

She touched it, dragging her thoughts away from Ivy and to the conversation at hand. "I hadn't really thought about it. To be honest, I am somewhat attached to it."

"And it to you," he replied, triggering another round of mirth.

A portly, well-spoken and presumably extremely rich man named Byabel spoke up at Holly's elbow. "Many domestics do find a measure of personal security in the ornamentation of their profession," he said. "Like a badge of honor." He turned half away to accept a glass of wine from a server. Unlike the many smaller events she'd been to, the staff at the trimester weren't domestics. Naturally the Deshmus would have hired a company ready to go above and beyond, if the servers' costumes were any indication.

"It is that," Holly said. "And yet, they're used to track us as well."

"To protect the domestic's well-being."

"And the benefactor's investment."

Byabel nodded, conceding the point. "Still, I don't think these things are mutually exclusive."

"No, they just make the issue murkier. And if domestics were able to remove their collars, it would completely defeat the purpose. So maybe there's a fundamental problem with the system."

"Is that what you're proposing?" Kisi asked, sounding eager. For what, Holly wasn't sure.

"I am not proposing anything at all," Holly said. "I can't pretend to know what every other domestic wants. I only know my situation, and I'm hoping that a closer look will be taken at the system in place."

"Because it needs work." This came from a Kalypso Media reporter whose name Holly hadn't caught. Since she'd grabbed their fairy and given them the first look, the little network had been all over her. Someone had mentioned offhandedly that Kalypso had been one of the first to break her interview with Makkhana, too.

"I think that's obvious."

"And what about the good that the system does?" Byabel asked. "I'm going to speak frankly, from both a social and a political perspective, and point out that in addition to thousands of people employed by the domestic industry, there is a significant social and political benefit to having it as an option, both for young women who've suffered ORDS and have no prospects, and for recent immigrants to the Brother Nations. It's been posited that it keeps many young men out of trouble as well." He paused to accept a piece of sushi from a passing server. "I think there are a large number of benefits."

Holly nodded. "It still needs work." She felt like she was stuck at everyone's center of attention; the spotlight never drifted away from her naturally as most conversations tended to. Every time one person was finished with their curiosity about her, another would arrive. In this moment, she was the star, and she had to use that to her advantage. She accepted a piece of sushi as well, giving the server a smile and thinking about Semangat Terang on fire. Ivy had used her destructive streak quite effectively; she could certainly play to her own strengths.

"Do you care to give an example?" the Kalypso reporter asked.

"Other than the obvious," Vitter said, "since no one here is advocating that domestics rise up against their benefactors."

Holly cut her eyes at him. "Of course not," she said. She took a moment to lift her sushi roll theatrically, making eye contact with all of the people currently in the conversation circle, then ate it, savoring the taste. "Delicious," she said. "The food really is wonderful." As she spoke, Holly flicked a wad of wasabi that she'd surreptitiously scooped out of the roll into Anshul's eye.

The Protector flinched, then gasped in pain. "Ssshit!" he hissed. "You foul—!" She'd gotten him good, and as the paste went to work on the surface of his eye his anger turned to genuine distress. His HNE enhancement made him stronger and faster, but pain perception hadn't changed. He tried to wipe it away, which only succeeded in smearing the green stuff around, and stumbled backward into another group of people. Several people rushed to help. He went down to his knees and had to be helped away.

"Now," Holly said without raising her voice while the drama unfolded, "when I first arrived here, I had to be searched. Which, under the circumstances, was perfectly reasonable. That man chose to go above and beyond the call of duty. He molested me and threatened to rape me. And he could have. Assaulting a domestic isn't treated the same way as assaulting a citizen.

"As a domestic, if I did what I just did, my benefactor would be liable. Same if I had attempted to defend myself when he touched me. And there would be no charges pressed against him. So, what should I have done, if I were in the same situation and still Myawi? Reporting a Myawi Protector to the school or my benefactor would have less than no effect. Defending myself would do nothing. So," she said, "the recourse would appear to be to smile and take it. I grant that there are some upsides to the domestic industry in terms of keeping the peace among people who've lost hope, Mr. Byabel, but how would you feel about your daughter having to make that choice?"

"Would you say that abuse is a common thing for domestics to endure?" a new voice asked. Holly met the questioner's eye; it was another media person she didn't know.

"I think it's impossible to say, because a lot of bad things have been normalized to the point that housegirls don't think of them as abuse anymore," Holly replied.

There was a moment of silence among the group, as they absorbed this, and then a fanfare from the auditorium announced the first act of the evening. Exuberant music burst through the open doors, and many of the guests in the atrium began moving toward the entrances.

Vitter touched Holly's shoulder, indicating that she should remain. He waved at the last few fairies that hovered above, and they moved off to give them privacy. "We've got more time, and I'm sure there are more people who'd like to speak with you."

She nodded; she didn't much care for Blackberry and Raspberry anyway; they were a fairly stale pop band who had been favorites of Aiyana's when she was a preteen, and had existed largely on her support in the years since.

"You could have told me that Anshul mistreated you," he said.

"Why would I have done that? For all I know, you told him to do it."

"Yes, well. I didn't, and you made your point nicely."

"I hope that I did. The next time someone else touches me without permission, I'll hit back."

Vitter nodded. "As is your right. By the way, we'll be sitting down to tea with the prime minister and the others tomorrow."

She nodded.

He leaned closer, speaking sotto voce. "I expect you've gotten your hopes up rather far, as to how this is going to end."

Holly gave him a head tilt. Seeing a fairy tracking them from a short distance off, she smiled as well. "Why do you say that?"

"You've underestimated the strength of the castle you're attacking, if I may speak metaphorically. Even though you've made a calculated effort to make everyone think you're just a poor deranged domestic who's lost her way, I know who's behind you, and I know what they are—and aren't—capable of. It's not going to be enough."

Holly thought about it a moment. "This is the truth of the matter," she said calmly, dropping her smile. "Any castle can be torn down. It doesn't matter how big it is. Somewhere, there's a bomb big enough to destroy the whole thing. And if there isn't, if I don't have that bomb, then I just start worrying away at the problem. I started with nothing. You had all the pieces on the board. And I was patient, taking one piece at a time. And now? Elden's dead, Rehsil's dead, Zhuan's dead, and I have a stolen ship, as well as my very stubborn sister who, I'm sure you noticed, has blown up a factory. Your castle's not as big as it was when I started, is it?"

He looked at her for a long time. "Your sister's on her way to the city, you know."

"Good. Forgive me if I'm not contrite about Semangat Terang. What Ivy did will certainly make them think twice about killing her mother in the future."

"Don't be glib. They're planning to kill her."

She stiffened. "Who is?"

"City Defense, of course. She's not exactly sneaking in; they know when the train will arrive. She'll be taken into custody at the station, and if they encounter the least resistance..." He shrugged.

"Well, then stop them."

"Why would I do that, when I went to such great lengths to ensure that this would happen? Quite an afternoon's work, if you ask me. After that fire was set, your sister and her cohorts boarded the train here. I had a man with them the whole time. If any of them are still alive when the train arrives, then I imagine things will get quite interesting."

Holly frowned for just a moment before focusing on her expression, on keeping her face neutral. She hadn't finished taking in all of this new information when Vitter put her hand on his elbow again.

"Let's go emjoy the show, shall we?"

She refrained from commenting as they entered the arena, which had been converted into a massive stage. She followed Vitter to the VIP section where he was seated. They were a short distance from the Deshmus' viewing box, but still quite close to the action. Aiyana and Haichen had prime seating within hailing distance of the stage, which extended halfway across the arena to accommodate the many performers and stars who'd be speaking over the next twenty-four hours.

Holly was momentarily grateful to be out of the spotlight for a few minutes. Blackberry and Raspberry gave a raucous show and she was quietly grateful when the lights came up and it was over. After that, the actor Shairpie spoke for an embarrassingly long time, mostly about how proud she was to see Haichen and Aiyana so happy and successful. Holly realized that she didn't need to listen to the speech because she wouldn't need to discuss it with the other housegirls later, and it was a curiously freeing moment.

She savored it, and the next performer she only gave half of her attention to. It was just as well, because Vitter abruptly rose in the middle of it, beckoned Holly to follow, and made for the doors.

Vitter had a phone to his ear as soon as they got out the doors, and he led her back to the meeting rooms. He closed the door behind them, his expression distracted as he listened to the phone. Vitter sat down made a sound of bald-faced surprise. "Bartussek, did you say there's a *delphid* in the city?" He turned to Holly. "What have you done?"

So Ivy was accompanied by Narooma at the very least. Out of habit she tried to suppress her smile, then decided she didn't want to—or couldn't. "I can assure you, I have no idea," Holly said. "I'm not responsible for my sister's actions. Did they not ride the train as you expected?"

His expression clouded. "It doesn't matter," he said. He addressed his phone again. "Do what you can to clean it up and keep me posted," he said to the man on the phone.

chapter 65

*Twenty minutes after the start of Princess Aiyana's
trimester celebration*

>> "The Brother Nations' air superiority is the chief deterrent to open warfare,"
according to analyst Seth Kang. "That's why the Colonies' no-fly zone is so rigidly
enforced, and why air travel is so strictly regulated. The day that the Rainbow Snakes
field a viable air force…will be the start of a very interesting period in history."

—Owl News Syndicate

Ivy walked down the row of Deshmu cars, trailing her fingers across the
shiny metal. All of them gleamed as if they were made of colored ice. She
felt like her feet were barely touching the floor; whatever it was that the
"bump kit" or whatever Nipa called it had done to her, it was pleasant.
Everything seemed very simple; find Holly, get back to the ship with everyone, go home. Whatever came up, she could handle it.

Her fingers touched a rig that felt right, and she chose it. It was blood
red with a black hood, a mechanical sculpture from many years before the
Fall. It had a long hood and a predatory look, yet was smaller than many of
the others lined up in the garage, a bit smaller even than her Vovo. There
was a sigil on the front fender that she guessed represented Nipa's family,
since each car had one, and below it block letters that read "Mach I." Ivy
walked to the driver's door, enjoying the feel of the slick paint under her
fingertips, and got in. The low roof and narrow back window made it seem
even smaller inside; there was no space for cargo, just four seats. She pulled
the door shut. It was surprisingly heavy, and shut behind her with a thump
and clatter like a wall dropping into place, separating her from the world.
"I'm taking this," she said.

"This one? Why this one?" Dilly asked.

A smile jumped to her lips unbidden. She felt confident and loopy and cheerful. "Because it's the right one." She touched the shifter experimentally, put her feet on the pedals. It felt familiar. She found the key dangling from the ignition, and the car woofled to life with a seismic rumble and throb that echoed through the garage and seemed to shake the ground. She smiled. "And it sounds right. Are you coming?"

"Are you sure you can drive it?" Dilly opened his door.

As answer, Ivy had the car rolling almost immediately, headed for the exit. "We don't have time." She had to raise her voice to be heard over the sound of the engine. The rig was monstrously powerful, lurching and bucking underneath them as they rolled out of the underground garage. Where Nipa and Shiloh had turned left, Ivy turned right, saw the road relatively clear ahead of her, and accelerated briskly.

Actually that was putting it mildly; the rig created a cloud of thunderous noise and smoke then launched itself out of it, throwing both of them back in their seats. It took Ivy by surprise but she gathered it up easily; once she might've been terrified but this felt like the most natural thing in the world, simple directions and cargo—Holly—to pick up. Next to her, Dilly made a sound that was somewhere between a laugh and a groan of discomfort. The other cars on the road seemed to be moving backward. Ivy was getting used to driving with so many other vehicles moving about. They were certainly easier to dodge than bicycles and handcarts in Detroit. The roads were wider, too. Many of the cars seemed to move out of her way, and she remembered Holly saying that they had little electric brains that didn't like getting too close to other rigs. Her "Mach I" didn't have any such qualms, as old as it was, and as an experiment Ivy tried driving between two slow-moving vehicles.

They both eased aside, letting her through.

She laughed, and sped up. The back wheels lost traction for a moment, barking on the pavement, and Dilly's corresponding bark was definitely discomfort this time. "Don't worry," she said.

"I'm not," he replied without conviction.

The large intersection that Nipa had indicated came up quickly. Ivy was going faster than she intended when they reached it, but turned anyway. The car's tires gripped the pavement steadily, Dilly had to grab hold of the dash to hold himself in place, and they made the turn without much effort. "This is wonderful!" Ivy exclaimed. She wondered if there'd be a way to get this rig on the boat as well. She had no idea what she'd trade for it, but perhaps it could be considered a part of scaling her mother's being murdered and Holly's being enslaved. That seemed more than reasonable.

On the wider road, traffic was heavier, except for an empty center lane, so Ivy drove down that one. At one point she clipped a bicyclist who shot out in front of her without warning, just a glancing blow that sent the bike and rider tumbling but didn't harm her rig at all. There was no time to stop, so she kept going, the lights of the evening stretching out ahead of them.

Nipa had been correct about the stadium being obvious; the whole building was outlined and sheathed in red and gold lighting, and more lights sparkled and crackled above it like continuous fireworks. Ivy identified it from half a mile away without trouble. Traffic thinned, then got heavy again as they breached an outer ring of taxis and hired cars carrying people the final few blocks to the stadium. The empty middle lane disappeared, and the sidewalks filled up with pedestrians, the dark night punctuated by flashing lights. Ivy weaved between the newer vehicles with no heed whatsoever for lanes or traffic rules, and the car's roaring engine drowned out most of the shouts of outrage that spread in her wake.

"Always forward," she said as the outward-curving edge of the massive auditorium peeked out from between buildings. Closer, they could see patterns in the multicolored lights that swirled happily over its surface. They formed shapes and good-luck wishes before breaking up into randomness again. The sidewalks were full, the streets lined with parked limousines. The road had been blocked off by temporary bollards. Ivy cut deftly around them with two wheels on the curb, eliciting more shouts. They sped toward the crowd near the entrance, where dazzling lights lined a section of sidewalk ahead of the doors and the air was full of swirling smoke. The snarling, roaring car was moving quickly enough that no security personnel were foolish enough to step in front of it.

The noise caught the crowd's attention easily; cameras and eyes swerved to meet them, and a swarm of little hovering fairies streamed toward the car as well, micro-spots peppering it with light.

Ivy shut the car off and pulled the key out of the ignition. She realized as she did so that she'd done it out of habit, the same way she'd pull the dead man's handle from a rig. So she was already thinking of this one as hers. The thought made her laugh. Dilly frowned slightly.

"I don't want to go through that mess," she said, "but I suppose I have to."

"Where do you need me?" Dilly asked.

Ivy considered. Outside the car, she could see some of the people on the sidewalk pointing to the car, to her. There was that crawling feeling of being the center of attention. Shiloh wouldn't be there to bite her ear this time, but she had to walk through that to get to Holly. And out again. "I can do this," she said. "I need you to find Fry, Razor, whoever else. Shiloh and Nipa will be down here somewhere, too."

"Chaos is what we do best," he said jauntily, and opened the door. "When you get to the water, look for an orange and white flashing light. Orange, white, orange, white. That's our sign."

She nodded. "Thank you." Dilly squared his shoulders and walked straight into the crowd, which parted around him. The little hovering fliers followed him with their lights for a moment; one peeled off and tracked him, but the rest stayed on the car until Ivy got out.

When she did, someone in the crowd applauded, and shouted in a language she didn't recognize. The applause spread, and there were lights on her then. The cheers were shot through with angry screams, and Ivy heard scuffles as they were forcibly cut off. She focused on moving forward. The crowd parted ahead of her, and she moved into the lights and smoke.

The attention remained focused on her. Soon she reached the brighter lights, and the crowd opened completely; she was at the start of a wide, red-carpeted cordon that led to the doors. It was cold; the air had turned impossibly, ridiculously cold, and a breeze had sprung up from nowhere. And the swirling she'd seen wasn't smoke, it was...snow? Ivy stood, dumbstruck for a moment at having stepped into a snowstorm. But she had; it was snowing, and snowing hard. Ivy squinted, raising a hand to keep it out of her face. The red carpet beneath her feet was soggy with two inches of half-melted slush. There were cheers, and an amplified announcement in a language she didn't know, and two people went splashing past her in the snow, arms raised to keep the snow off, laughing. They were neatly dressed, and both carrying their shoes which clearly weren't suited for snow.

Nonplussed, Ivy turned and started for the door, walking rather than running. Someone shouted her name, and a question—"Ivy! Are you working with Pravit Deshmu?" This was followed by a question in that Inchin language she didn't know, and then a dozen shouted questions, instantly overlapping into unintelligibility.

The back of Ivy's neck seemed to tingle, and her shoulders were tensed, waiting for the sting of a bullet, the snap that would tell her she'd been wrong about this and end her life in the same instant. The voices overlapped until they became background noise, and although it was no more than a hundred feet, the walk seemed to be miles long.

It ended in a pair of tall, carved, red and gold-painted doors that opened for her as if by magic, admitting a rush of snow into the building before cutting off the cold air immediately. When the doors closed, sound returned, the joyous noise of a thousand people enjoying a party in a massive atrium. At the back of the hall, four enormous video screens showed the larger-than-life face of a man who appeared to be a comedian of some kind. At least two of the flying drones came through the doors with her, whirling around and dropping to chin level to get shots of her face as she took in the gigantic space. The ceiling was at least a hundred feet high, and from it hung naga sculpted in a dozen different styles, intertwined and swaying gently.

Ivy stared openly at the mythical snakes for a few moments, completely overwhelmed. Unlike the crowd outside, the stars and politicians in the atrium crowded in on her, extending hands and offering pats on the back. As she watched, the screens with the performer on them suddenly changed, showing a sea of faces in blurry motion and then, suddenly, Holly's face. Her sister looked startled, and the look of naked shock made Ivy smile. The background of the images wasn't the atrium she was in, though. Where was Holly? She moved forward, shouldering her way past people trying to shake her hand where necessary. She could smell food, and the exotic scent made her mouth water, but she had to find Holly first.

Identical doors lined the back of the atrium, all but two closed, and a pair of uniformed people stood watch at these. That must be the way in to the performance area; that was where Holly would be. She pushed forward with renewed purpose. Someone Ivy didn't see spat in her face as she went past, even as another loud voice from the opposite side cheered her on. The crowd's mood shifted, alternately supportive and dangerous. She couldn't dawdle out here, lest she end up stabbed in the gut by an unseen attacker.

The crowd pressed in, and Ivy continued forward against the tide. When a second person spat on her, she whirled and punched the offender in the eye. The fancily-dressed woman staggered backward and fell, taken completely by surprise. Ivy didn't pause, continuing on her way until she reached the open door. One of the ushers looked as though he was about to demand a ticket, but the other opened the door for her.

Ivy's first impression was of gold and green pillars covered in paintings of some sort of furry, raccoon-like animal. Representations of the animals decorated the soaring ceiling and the many pillars going up to it, and there appeared to be a massive pile of toy stuffed animals at one side of the stage as well. That was a bit unfortunate for the audience on that side, since the show was being performed in the round.

Sections of the walls were animated, showing close-up views of what happened on stage and sometimes cutting to the audience. She hadn't taken two steps into the arena when the spotlight hit her. Ivy was facing a screen, and suddenly she was looking back at herself, magnified impossibly. She actually stopped walking—her own look of surprise reflected back at her. She scanned the room, squinting against the light but unable to see very far, and then Holly came out of the glare and took her hand. The audience immediately erupted into applause.

Holly smiled, put her hand around the back of Ivy's head and pulled her close so their foreheads touched. "You're not right in the head," she said, her words drowned out by the crowd and music as the band struck up a spontaneous tune. "I'm glad you're here."

Ivy pulled away from the embrace and slapped Holly in the face as hard as she could. The audience gasped collectively, a sound like a wave crashing. Her sister staggered, taken completely by surprise. As she recovered, a thunderstruck look on her face, Ivy slapped her again. She took Holly by the back of the head, mirroring the first greeting, and pulled her fiercely into the head-to-head embrace. "What's the matter with you?" she hissed through tears. "You *left* me! They *hurt* me! I was scared and you were *gone!*"

Her words shattered Holly's party-girl mask more thoroughly than the scarlet handprint on her cheek had. Holly looked abashed and nauseous, suddenly regressed to her eight year-old self. "I...I only wanted to help."

"Shut up. This is an awful place and I'm angry you made me come here," Ivy said. She let her hand relax, and caressed Holly's hair.

"I can see that. I'm sorry."

"We stay together from now on. I'm here for you. No matter what."

Holly touched her slapped cheek. "I'm so sorry," she said again. Her voice shook.

"It's scaled," Ivy replied gently. "We need to leave."

"Soon. Welcome to my world," she replied. "Look now, up at the politicals in their boxes." Holly urged Ivy subtly forward, moving slowly. Ivy looked at her, watching Holly consciously rebuilding her social armor, changing back to the face she'd used on the video, smiling as though the place where she'd been slapped—which was almost certainly going to bruise—didn't hurt. Ivy was envious of the skill. Holly gestured without pointing. "See the young woman in the tiara scowling down at us? That's Aiyana Deshmu, whose party this is, and I'm sure she's upset because we're stealing her spotlight. Don't take it personally. Her husband Haichen is the intrigued-looking fellow next to her, and that quirky smile is what's made him a movie star. The older man on the other side of Aiyana is her father, Pravit."

"I borrowed one of his rigs," Ivy said. "Oh, and I'm pretty sure Shiloh had sex with his other daughter." Haichen beckoned to the two of them to join them, and the audience began to applaud. The applause spread, and after a moment even Aiyana joined in, putting on a smile as the camera picked her up again.

"So...you're not going to be one of his favorite people, then," Holly said with amusement in her voice. "The man standing up and smiling, in front of them, is Chancellor Shay. He wants to talk with us. Vitter almost stopped him—"

Ivy saw the man before Holly did, a gunman in street clothes and a white headscarf. He was directly below the politicals' box, and he quickly brought up a stubby gun and unleashed a burst in their direction. She felt Holly jerk suddenly and violently to the side, and turned as her sister fell to her knees. There were other gunshots, followed by screaming—Ivy got a glimpse of more white-scarved men in the audience, shooting—and she dropped to her knees to help Holly, and then—thunder.

There was a deafening roll of thunder outside, startling and loud and ongoing and Ivy suddenly realized she wasn't touching the floor, and as she did, the floor came back up to meet her feet, Holly tumbled into her side, and they both fell to the floor. A second peal of thunder, even louder, was accompanied by a thin scattering of debris cascading down from the ceiling and a chorus of screams from the audience.

Not thunder, Ivy realized, sluggish to catch up. She wasn't sure what it was, something happening outside, but it wasn't the weather.

The next roar came from inside the auditorium, as the security measures on the VIP boxes were triggered. Aiyana, the Deshmus, and all of the politicals vanished in dark blurs as their raised seating platforms closed around them like reversed flowers and fell into the floor. Ivy thought she saw Shay knocked off of his feet by the blast cover as it deployed, but it happened too quickly for her to be sure. A rush of dust forced her to close her eyes, and then they were getting jostled by the rest of the audience, who was bolting for the exits. There was a brief crackle of gunfire.

Ivy half-pulled, half-dragged Holly toward the stage, making a high-pitched noise in the back of her throat, terror that she was just dragging her sister's dead body. Holly had wrapped her arms around her neck but didn't seem able to get to her feet.

When they reached the stage, out of the rush of panicked people, Ivy squatted down with her, cradled her. "Show me where it hurts," she said, and Holly indicated the side of her neck.

"Can't breathe," she gasped. She looked stricken and panicked.

Ivy made a soothing sound—she actually sounded like their mother, she realized. She stayed calm. Holly was making noise, so she was getting air. "It's okay. The bullet hit your collar," she said. "Bounced off."

"Is it damaged?" she asked. Her voice was barely a whisper.

"Tiny dent," Ivy said, running her fingers over the shallow crease the bullet had left. Without the collar's interference, the shot would have gone right through Holly's larynx. "Strong stuff. Fuck, if it hadn't been there..."

Holly tried to clear her throat. "Lucky me," she croaked.

"What happened?" she asked Holly. "Where did they all go? All the people?"

"Security system. They'll be in vaults in the basement now, until it's safe."

"Seems safe. Whatever happened is outside."

"And we have to go out there with it," Holly said. She pointed: Vitter was coming down the now-blank aisle where the politicals' boxes had been. He was flanked by ten severe-looking men who were dressed in various kinds of formal wear, but all moving like soldiers.

"There are more." Ivy pointed toward three more men arrowing through the crowd to join Vitter's group. These were dressed differently, wearing uniforms like the men on the train had.

Holly frowned, tracking their path backward to one of the standard boxes, where another group of politicals in suits lay slumped. "Oh, no, checkmate," she said.

"What?"

Vitter's group pushed forward, moving at an angle to them. Ivy guessed that he was moving toward where he'd last seen them. "We have to get out of here," Holly said. "Outside, now."

"The chancellor—?"

"Locked in a safe-box. They won't come out for hours, and if Vitter finds us we'll be dead by then. He's taken over, he's killed the ministry's standbys and put himself in charge."

Ivy met Holly's eye and nodded. The doors were a chaotic press of bodies and struggling as the crowd fled for the exits. A white-bearded man in a European-style tuxedo, his collar askew, saw Holly pushing forward and grabbed her. "What have you done?" he screamed hysterically in her face. "Traitorous whore, what have you done?" Holly turned away, breaking his grip, and Ivy punched him hard in the throat with an audible snarl. He staggered backward, making a comical croaking noise, and Holly shoved him into the first row of chairs.

Ivy could feel her emotions trying to get sucked into the miasma of panic that surged through the room in invisible waves, and took a breath to detach herself from it. Holly seemed to be trying to do the same. "Through the stage?" she asked, nodding in that direction.

"Yes, yes. Follow Russian Gecko."

"Who?"

"The comedian who was up there. This way." Holly mounted the stage without hesitation and pulled Ivy up after her. They became instant targets on the raised platform; she heard a shout and then a pop of gunfire that did nothing to calm the mood in the room. Ahead of them, the closed stage curtain twitched as a bullet went through it.

Holly put her head down and ran, and Ivy did the same. She heard more gunshots, then a grunt as someone climbed the stage to pursue them and a gasp and thud as the person went down, taking a bullet that might've been meant for her. Ahead of them, a security guard stepped out from behind the curtain. Holly pulled up short; Ivy ran around her and into the man, palming his face and throwing her full weight into him. He tried to catch her but the impact plowed him off his feet and they fell together. She felt the back of his head hit the hard floor, leaving him dazed.

"Tell me again what's happening?" she asked Holly as she scrambled to her feet.

"Vitter's going to blame all of this on me and bring the whole city down on us." Backstage was abandoned, with scattered water bottles, set lists and other detritus all over the floor. Holly moved toward the first door she saw and Ivy followed. They entered a wide, cluttered hallway lined with doors leading to dressing rooms. Lighting equipment and rolling carts full of props and instruments were pushed against the walls, some of them pulled askew as the celebration's performing and rigging staff had fled the gunfire. Ivy turned and closed the door leading to the backstage area behind them, then wedged a piece of metal in at the base. Holly saw what she was doing and nodded toward a large rolling shelf with heavy-looking lights on it. Together, they rolled it in front of the door and set the brake. "Fire exit," Holly said.

"I have a rig, if we can get out."

"You *have* been busy," Holly said. The building shook again, the floor shuddering beneath their feet.

"Someone's setting off bombs," Ivy said.

"Could be. This way." Holly pointed and they ran down the hall. As they passed one of the dressing rooms they could hear sobbing coming from behind the partially-open door and shared a look, but didn't stop to investigate.

An exit door was just two corners away. Ivy tried to get her bearings, to figure out which side of the building they were on so she could take them back to the rig. It wasn't hard; she'd explored enough windowless pre-Fall hulks to have a reliable internal compass, and she was reasonably certain she knew the way out.

A man stepped out in front of them, emerging from an enclosed stairwell just next to the windowless fire doors leading outside. Ivy recognized the helmet and armor he wore; it was another of the Myawi men. Holly gasped and pulled up short. "Oh no, she said. "It's Kalida."

chapter 66

Nipa called Wan, and breathlessly told him what was happening. "Where
are you headed?" he asked. "Are they chasing you? They're chasing the
twins. News says they kidnapped you."

"We're not even with them," Nipa said. "We're in my car, going down
to the—"

She was interrupted by a massive impact that threw the car off course
and slammed both of them against the seats. A truck had hit the side of
the Royce, hard. A warning chime from the dashboard sounded belatedly.

Shiloh looked through the side window and saw a large, angry-looking
truck alongside them. Heavy armored plates gave it a distinctively crab-like
look, and flashing lights dazzled her eyes. With a snarl of roaring exhaust,
the truck surged forward and cut over, nudging the Royce a second time,
across the center line of the road.

The car continued stubbornly on its path, weaving back and forth as its
anti-collision system interacted with the other vehicles. Nipa cried out and
covered her eyes, but Shiloh couldn't look away. The police truck hit them
again, to the tune of more urgent chimes from the dash.

"We have to turn," she said to Nipa, wishing that Ivy—or anyone who
could drive—was here. "Can't we go a different way?"

"I don't know!" the princess cried, burying her head in Shiloh's chest.
The truck swerved in front of them again and car veered sharply right,
clouting a pair of bicyclists as it narrowly avoided a bus. Whoever was driving the truck was using the Royce's anti-collision system against it, herding
it like a sheepdog. The big black vehicle closed on them again, nudging the
left front fender to urge them toward the curb. Shiloh disentangled herself from Nipa and grabbed for the wheel. She'd seen Ivy drive frequently

enough, the steering wheel made sense.

All she did was make it worse. She yanked on the wheel, there was a chime and a light lit up on the dash. The car jumped onto the curb with a violent bang, went briefly airborne and then plowed into a building in a shower of wreckage. The windshield and side windows turned into opaque spiderwebs and the interior of the car seemed to collapse in toward them. The Royce stopped with a fierce impact; Shiloh found herself upside down between two of the seats.

It took her a moment to orient herself, but she wasn't hurt. The car was tilted at an angle that seemed to be getting worse, or maybe her head was spinning. Wan was still on the line as well, shouting Nipa's name.

The princess was screaming endlessly, her hands over her head. Shiloh scrambled over the seat to her, trying to get her attention. "Where does it hurt?"

"My leg! Fuck! My head! Fuck! What happened? Did we crash? Fuck!"

"We did, now shut up." Nipa wasn't bleeding, and didn't appear to have any serious injuries. "Let me see your head. I think you're okay."

"Fuck!"

"It's okay."

"Fuck! Shit! I hit my arm, Shiloh, my arm! And my *knee!*"

"Shut up if you're not hurt!" she snapped, realizing as she did that part of the reason Nipa's self-centered melodrama annoyed her was because it reminded her of herself a year ago. "We're fine, stop screaming."

"Are you guys okay?" Wan called. His voice was slightly distorted; the speaker had been damaged in the crash.

"Yes," Shiloh said. "We hit a building. A big truck hit us and made us crash."

"Was it the police? Where are you?"

Nipa whimpered and curled closer to Shiloh. "I don't know."

"We can't stay here," Shiloh said. "We're trying to get down to the water, Wan."

"Why?"

"None of your business," she said curtly.

"I don't know where we are, Wan. Fuck!"

"Calm down, Nipa. If you trigger your beacon, I can tell you where you are."

Without pulling away from Shiloh, Nipa opened the console and pressed a button, which flashed three times then lit up red.

"Got it. Wow, you guys are way downtown, close to the auditorium.

I'm on my way."

There was a thump at the window. Shiloh looked, squinting through the spalled glass, and saw a helmeted police officer, or soldier, she wasn't sure which. It was Shiloh's turn to swear.

"We're surrounded by police, Wan," Nipa said.

"They'll trackback this," he said. "Breaking." The video went black.

She gave Nipa a hard nudge. "Hey. I think they want us to get out," she said.

"Chokidar?"

"I don't see him."

"Fuck them," Nipa snapped. She pushed several buttons on the dash. One triggered jets of steam, as it had at the train station. This time they came from the front, both sides and the rear of the car, judging by the hissing from beneath and the startled and pained shouts from outside.

"Should we go?" Shiloh asked. The driver's side door wouldn't open, but the other did, creaking open and knocking something over as it did so. They were in some kind of shop, but with the lights out and the wares mostly scattered and shattered by the car's intrusion, it was difficult to tell what kind. The blasts of steam had thrown dust into the air, and she could only see a few feet. The air smelled of smoke and tea leaves.

"I can't walk," Nipa said when Shiloh was halfway out of the car. "I can't feel my legs."

Shiloh looked at her, saw her moving her knees, and pulled her out of the car, setting the princess on her feet. "How about now?" she asked.

"I'm afraid, Shiloh." There was real, naked terror in Nipa's voice.

"I know," she said. "But we can't stay here, we have to keep moving or something terrible will happen."

"If you keep moving in the wrong direction," Tapia called from beyond the slowly dissipating steam, "I suspect something even more terrible will happen. Depending, of course, on how terrible you consider being burned alive when that car's battery ignites. Terrible accident."

Nipa let out a little cry of fear and started to dive back into the car. Shiloh stopped her.

"Forward, you two. Slowly."

Shiloh helped Nipa pick her way across the glass- and wreckage-strewn floor. She glanced around but saw no bodies—hopefully the shop hadn't been occupied.

Tapia was on the street with his back to the big truck that had forced them to crash. Traffic was slowing, but a second, smaller police vehicle had arrived and there were two natty uniformed men directing cars around the scene. Five of the helmeted and heavily-armed men flanked Tapia, who shared their gear but was bare-headed and wearing a barely-visible headset. "You really are a spoiled brat," he said to Nipa. "Anti-kidnapping measures? Really? Who do you think *designed* them? We could have made it so you died in that crash," he added in a lower voice. "Sit down," he barked.

Nipa looked at the sidewalk, which was littered with debris. "*Here?*"

"Sit!" one of the riot cops shouted, and pushed Shiloh down.

The princess stepped forward and slapped him, her hand making a hollow thud on his helmet. "Don't you touch her!"

Shiloh grabbed Nipa's hand and pulled her gently down to sit next to her.

"I can't believe you're making us sit in the gutter, like animals. My father's going to have every one of you fired and banished from the city. He'll kick your children out of school—"

Tapia squatted in front of them, his head tilted and an enigmatic smile on his face. He interrupted Nipa by taking her hand in his. "Little girl," he said, "dearest princess. Shut the fuck up." He dropped her hand and stood up. The pleasant expression on his face didn't change as he kicked Shiloh hard in the stomach. Nipa screamed, starting to wind up more invective, and he interrupted her again without raising his voice. "I may not be able to touch you, but I can stomp your darling girlfriend to death in front of you. Your father...will thank me," he added. "I think you should stop talking."

Shiloh tried to tell Nipa that she agreed with Tapia, but could only gasp in pain. She gritted her teeth, trying not to vomit as the sandwich she'd just eaten came up in her throat.

Nipa threw herself on top of Shiloh, trying to shield her from more kicks. "Get out of the way," Tapia said calmly. He looked up as a second armored truck pulled up behind the first, disgorging more heavily armed men and Mahnaz.

Mahnaz marched forward, looking from the scene on the sidewalk to the destroyed store, in which Nipa's car was barely visible. There was a deep look of concern on his face that relaxed when he saw Nipa sitting on the sidewalk. For a moment it was warm, relieved, and Shiloh could see that he honestly cared about the girl. Then his eyes found Shiloh and hardened again. "What happened, Captain?" he asked Tapia.

"Tried to get her to stop, and she lost control of the car," he replied. "No civilian casualties, thank goodness." He angled his head, clearly speaking into the headset. "Sir. We've stopped them, she's in custody. The chancellor is here as well. Understood." He turned back to Mahnaz. "The twins are at the trimester celebration. I'm taking this one in, and you can get the princess to the show as well—"

"I'm not going!" Nipa shouted. Tapia looked down at her, moving his foot casually, just enough to touch Shiloh, and she stopped.

Mahnaz glared at Shiloh. "Promise me you'll kill it," he said.

"I believe Vitter would like to chat with her first."

"Ten thousand," he said in a low voice, so the other police wouldn't hear. "I'll give you ten thousand to kill it, right now."

"Chokidar!"

Tapia smiled indulgently. "Chancellor Mahnaz, that's hardly—"

"Twenty thousand. Thirty, if you let me do it. Right here. Tell Vitter the filth tried to run. Thirty thousand."

That got a raised eyebrow. Tapia's expression didn't change, but he tapped his holster thoughtfully, then pulled the pistol, clicked a switch on the side and handed it to Mahnaz. Nipa screamed. Shiloh tensed, looking past the men, picking a direction to run in. Traffic had been diverted off the street, so it was clear. She might be able to jump to the top of one of the trucks, use the grab rail to vault up. Mahnaz couldn't possibly be a good shot, though the police might shoot her as well—

The world suddenly ended. The concrete beneath her trembled, and everything else was drowned out by a rush of noise. It was so loud that Shiloh couldn't even *see* for a moment. There was a sense of something large passing overhead, a sudden rush of wind, and a ground-shaking blast of sound. Shiloh tumbled over onto her side, feeling Nipa falling with her, and opened her eyes to a world opaque with dust.

She didn't hesitate to seize the moment. She grabbed Nipa's hand, but the girl was still half on top of her so Shiloh just stood up and ran, half-carrying Nipa for several steps through the gray dust cloud. There were thumps and crashes—heavy things, she realized, debris falling into the street—so she moved closer to the storefronts, out of the open area. Nipa started struggling against her, and Shiloh let her down. She kept moving and held Nipa's hand, so that when the princess' feet touched the ground she was forced to run.

The dust began to thin, and there was another rolling peal of thunder ahead, moving from right to left this time, across their path. It was followed by rumbling explosions, an orange flash in the darkening sky and a cacophony of noises beginning to rise from across the city: building alarms, sirens, crashing glass and other, unidentifiable noises coming from all directions.

They just had to make the end of the block before the dust cleared. Shiloh urged Nipa faster, and they finally made it, around the corner, hopefully out of sight of Tapia and the rest.

"Bombs!" Nipa gasped, coughing. "Those were planes! Dropping bombs! What's happening?"

Shiloh had no answer, so she didn't offer one. She'd lost track of which direction was toward the water. Something was on fire, judging by the rising orange glow in the sky, but she couldn't tell how far away it was. They moved under cover of darkness and dust. No pursuit materialized as Shiloh made another turn. "I don't know which way to go," she told Nipa.

"I need to sit down," the princess said. "I'm so tired." She let out a little shriek and cringed against Shiloh as another plane shot overhead, accompanied by a series of crackling explosions that sounded like they were just a block over. "What are they *doing?*"

An ambulance screamed past, siren wailing, and quickly rounded the corner behind them. It was followed by a fire engine, and as Shiloh turned to watch it go past she saw the truck Tapia had been in. It drove through the intersection they'd just crossed, but they were on the move as well, no doubt searching. Shiloh froze for several seconds, fighting the awful fear that the truck would reverse back into sight and rumble toward them, but it didn't.

"I know where we are," Nipa said. "The mall is that way. The nice one," she added, pointing farther up the block.

"How far?"

"Close. Maybe three blocks." Another plane passed overhead with a roar. Were they going in circles?

"Good. Let's go there." She started looking into the storefronts they were passing. Most had closed their doors and turned off the lights (that, or the power was out) but she saw people inside, looking back at them.

As they passed a little boutique with frilly, spangly clothes displayed in the windows, the door clicked open. The proprietor stepped out with a puzzled and awestruck look on her face. "Princess Nip—" she began, and then the glass door behind her shattered and her throat erupted. Her neck burst in a splattering of gore and her head flopped suddenly onto her shoulder, connected only by a thick flap of muscle on one side.

Shiloh and Nipa were lightly sprayed with blood, and screamed in unison. Through the shattered door Shiloh saw the second police truck. Tapia was on the back of it, manning a huge mounted gun, and seeing that Shiloh realized what had happened, what was still—she pushed the shrieking princess to the ground and threw herself on top of her, and the truck fired again. There was an audible clang somewhere beyond them as the bullet embedded itself in a storefront. Was he shooting just at her, or at both of them?

Running down the street was suicide. Shiloh grabbed Nipa by the arms and dragged her into the boutique. The princess' foot struck the dead shopkeeper, which made her scream anew, but they got inside before any more shots were fired.

"Why are they trying to kill me?" Nipa screamed.

Shiloh pulled the girl to her feet again, hustling her through the shop to the back, hoping there was a rear exit. There was a back door; they banged through it, setting off a fire alarm whose clatter was lost in the chaos already engulfing the city, and ran up the alley, turning down the next gap between buildings. It smelled of sewage and smoke, and Shiloh could hear the fire now, see the heavy orange glow in the sky. "Keep moving."

Nipa stumbled; she was trying to run and inspect her scraped elbows at the same time. She seemed fascinated and bemused by the injuries; Shiloh imagined that the girl had never actually fallen without someone to catch her before. At least she wasn't complaining. "Are...they're trying to kill you and all of the North Americans, aren't they? And Holly the Myawi?"

"That would appear to be what's happening," Shiloh said.

"But they can't do that! They said they wanted to pardon her! To make things better for the domestics!"

They pulled up short at the end of the alley so Shiloh could look up and down the street. This road was smaller, but choked with cars, all of them jammed up and trying to go different directions in a panic. It looked like a slow-moving river, going in both directions. A scooter raced by on the sidewalk, trying to beat the jam, and they had to duck back to avoid it. "I'm not going to go back and try to remind them of that, if that's okay with you."

"But why would they shoot at *me?*"

Shiloh thought about it. "To make it look like I killed you, maybe. Because I'm Ivy's friend, it would look very bad."

Nipa stopped walking and looked fiercely at her. "You would never do that."

"No, I wouldn't. Which way is the mall?"

"We're closer. You can see it, at the end of the street." Nipa pointed, and Shiloh saw a bright blue-green glow of decorative lights on the side of a building.

"Good. Go there. I think...I think you might be safer without me."

"What?"

"They won't try to hurt you if you're not with me."

"I'm coming with you," the princess said, reaching out and taking Shiloh's hand. "They can't do this."

The earnestness in her voice made Shiloh smile. "I have to go," she said.

"So let's go," Nipa replied.

"That's a bad idea. You need to go to the mall." A half dozen reasons flew through her head, and she knew not one of them was going to convince this willful, stone-headed girl that going to the mall and getting to safety was what she wanted, so she didn't even try. There was only one way to do this. "I really enjoyed spending time with you," Shiloh said sincerely. "Thank you for...everything." She didn't want to, but she peeled off the lovely indigo top that Nipa had loaned her, and skinned out of the pants and moccasins as well. The night air was cool on her skin.

Nipa was looking at her, utterly confused.

She could feel eyes on her from the cars stuck in traffic. On some level she was terrified beyond description, but Shiloh paid it no mind; this was an important moment and she and Nipa had center stage. She took the girl's face gently in her hands and kissed her. "I'm sorry for getting you into so much trouble," she said. "Go to the mall. You'll be safe."

"Shiloh, wait."

She didn't. Heart pounding with fear (and maybe a touch of shame?) she turned, took two steps, and shifted, breaking into a sprint as she did so. The world seemed to change shape as her vantage point dropped, as the colors changed and the sounds and smells amplified. She could hear the fire, smell it. A high-pitched hum assaulted her ears from all directions, and she identified it as the motors of all the cars on the road, normally too high-pitched for her to hear. There was a noise behind her that might have been Nipa screaming, and shouts of surprise from the cars on the road. It actually felt good to run—coil and spring, coil and spring, faster faster faster—and Shiloh streaked down the block so quickly that Nipa couldn't have kept up even if she'd tried running after.

At the end of the block she turned, leaping up onto the cars choking the street, and ran across the tops of them, leaping from one to the next. Another plane howled past overhead, trailing explosions and faraway destruction, and the noise and fright spurred her even faster. For a few minutes Shiloh wasn't sure she could have shifted back if she wanted to; it was as natural as flexing a muscle, but she was in her cat-form so rarely that she had to concentrate to get back. A bit of panic made it even more difficult.

That was a concern for later, though. Another turn, and she was farther from the mall. Was there a touch of sea-scent on the air? She could hear car doors opening as she passed, more people shouting. Would a mob form and come after her? She could outrun any people who gave chase.

It didn't matter. Shiloh rounded a corner and saw blinding lights, a hulking mass in front of her. It was the military truck, with Tapia at the wheel.

chapter 67

One hour after the start of Princess Aiyana's trimester celebration

Holly grabbed Ivy's elbow and pulled her to a stop; her sister seemed to be intent on running right through Kalida to get to the exit door if she had to, and that wasn't going to go well for her. "Stop," she said. "We can't."

Kalida didn't slow his careful, measured stride, his eyes on her. "Holly," he said. "I am just here for you."

"You want her, you get us both," Ivy said, stepping between them.

Holly touched her elbow again. Ivy had to understand, she'd seen what had happened when they had tried to fight the other Protector. They should go back the other way, back to the door they'd blocked. With Ivy's knee fixed, they could certainly outrun him. She had time for these thoughts, and then there was a blur of motion, and Kalida had Ivy by the neck.

"No, *don't!*" she cried.

Kalida just held her. "Come here," he said, beckoning with his free hand. He held Ivy off the ground with little apparent effort. She struggled, trying to kick him, but the blows bounced off of his chest armor with no effect.

She didn't have a choice. She wouldn't let him snap Ivy's neck. Holly could hear sounds behind her now; someone was definitely working to get the door to backstage open. Vitter would be sending people to flank the building as well.

She slipped back into her Myawi porcelain mask. If nothing else, she wouldn't let him see that she was afraid for her sister. Perhaps if she could get close, she could—

"Turn around," he said.

Holly did. She heard and felt Kalida approach, felt Ivy coming closer as well, heard her struggling to breathe. They were both warm behind her.

"I swore to protect Myawi's children," Kalida said. "I protected you, when it was necessary. It was my duty." He paused to take a slow breath through his nose, as though he was unused to speaking so much. "They talked about you, in the news feed. I saw your story. I heard it from your lips. I saw the hurt that it did to Myawi. Men and women have resigned. They have wondered how this could have happened. They have wondered what went wrong with you. And now they have sent me here to kill you. It is not my duty to take you home. It is my duty to kill you."

She heard Ivy struggle fiercely. Kalida's hand rested on the back of Holly's neck suddenly, his fingers brushing her braid aside to touch her just above the collar. She closed her eyes, tried and failed to speak, and swallowed to clear her aching throat. She had to beg him to let Ivy go, after she was dead. If only he would grant that mercy—

"I reject this duty," Kalida said. He moved his hand, and her collar shuddered suddenly, then opened and slid off of her neck. She was too surprised to catch it, and it hit the floor with a broken, toneless clatter. "I cannot be a Protector, and allow a Myawi to die. I cannot be a Protector, and kill the Myawi they have ordered me to kill. I cannot be a Protector, and refuse their command. Do you understand?"

Holly turned slowly around. He was looking down at her. He released Ivy, who took several steps back, then grabbed Holly's hand and pulled her out of his reach. She considered his question. "You can't be what they made you into any more, so you don't know what you are."

"I think that it is better, if you are not Myawi," he said, tilting his head slightly. His foot snapped out and kicked the collar away. "All that you are should be yours."

"And you as well," Ivy said. "Maybe it's better if you're not a Protector?"

Kalida reached up to his shoulder and touched a button there; a small green light on the shoulder piece went out. "I think that I am not that, any more," he said.

"You could come with us," Holly offered.

"No," Kalida said. He didn't elaborate, just turned around and walked back into the stairwell. His boots echoed on the steps as he climbed.

Holly looked at her collar on the floor. She could feel the air on her neck, and her exposed skin felt cold. She started to reach up to touch it, but didn't want to feel the collar's absence. She looked at Ivy's neck instead, imagining that hers looked much the same. There was a desire to grab her collar, maybe even to put it back on. It *belonged* there. It made her Myawi.

In the same moment it was very easy to imagine Ivy slapping it out of her hands if she picked it up. No, the collar was staying here. At least she wouldn't have to endure another electrocution to deactivate it. And if she didn't feel comfortable without it, she'd just have to live with it. That decision had been taken out of her hands.

Ivy was looking at her, and suddenly pulled her into a hug. The pounding on the backstage door was getting louder. "Let's go," she said.

Thankfully there were no people outside the fire exit, but there was a fairy buzzing about. Holly picked up the nearest hard object to come to hand, a fist-sized rock, and threw it at the drone, striking a glancing blow that knocked it wildly off-course. It spun in circles, bounced off the wall, then faltered upward, trying to get out of range. "They know we're here now," Holly said.

"That's okay." Ivy led the way. They hugged the building, moving quickly past loading docks to the street.

Things had changed a great deal. The red carpet and elaborately orchestrated snowstorm at the main entrance, formerly lined with well-wishers and star-spotters, had vanished, replaced by running crowds, smoke, debris and fire. The ground was still thick with slush and mud.

It took a moment to take in the scope of the riot. The entrance and street were a chaos of running, fighting people. In one place, three police officers beat a downed man; a few feet away, two college boys were wrestling a slickgun away from another riot cop. Holly saw a limousine on fire, she saw a man and woman with a pair of bolt cutters removing a laughing Axtellia girl's collar, she saw a man she recognized as a news anchorman running with a fairy buzzing along behind him, staying high enough to be out of reach of stick-swinging rioters.

As she took all of that in, a plane shot past in the dark, so low that the thunder of its passing shook the ground. Behind it, less than a quarter mile away, a building exploded at the tenth floor, vomiting flaming masonry onto the streets below. Ivy gaped at it. "Flying things again!" she shouted, the edge of panic in her voice raising gooseflesh on Holly's arms.

"Keep moving, that way, that way," Holly said, urging Ivy toward the street where she had parked the car. "I don't think this is part of Vitter's plan," Holly said. "Still not good. Someone else is attacking the city." She was trying to stay calm, the better to be prepared if Ivy panicked, but it was hard. The air smelled of smoke and the greasy stink of slickgun gel, and there was a palpable air of charged emotion.

"Attacking the city? With planes?"

"They carry big bombs."

"They still *make* bombs like that? We read about them when we were little, but..." Ivy trailed off as they both nearly tripped over a prone body in the dark. The erratic light flashed over her, revealing that it was a domestic. Someone had shoved a metal bar into the back of her collar and twisted it until the girl strangled.

"Oh, no..."

It was Ivy's turn to pull Holly. "Keep moving," she said, returning her sister's words to her.

"It's Holly the Myawi!" someone yelled. They both looked, saw a man pointing, and a small crowd of students around him roared in approval. People rushed toward them, waving signs. In the erratic light, Holly couldn't read them, but it seemed to be a supportive crowd. Still, there was safety in anonymity.

A heartbeat later, the man who'd called out was struck by a slickgun round, and a crackling volley of bullets erupted over the heads of the crowd, sending them into a collective crouch. Holly turned toward the source of the noise and saw Vitter, leading his men out the doors. He shouted to the beleaguered riot police and pointed, and a hasty cordon quickly formed in front of them. Vitter shouted into a radio, tapped one of the men at his side and pointed toward the docks, and several policemen peeled off in that direction. Having an authoritative voice to rally to, the cops quickly massed up. Riot shields were being distributed. "We have to go," Holly said to Ivy, taking her sister's hand again. They couldn't move with the crowd behind them, though.

Vitter was handed a megaphone. "Attention! My name is Aldo Vitter, and I am in temporary command of the Domestic Security Council," he said. Holly got a sinking feeling in her stomach, losing the last tiny shred of hope that maybe she was wrong. But of course he'd exploit the loophole he'd found. He'd only be in command for a night, but there was plenty he could do in that time, and she and Ivy were unlikely to survive to see it. "Detain those women, any rioters, and clear this street." The police started to move forward, but hesitated as a small barrage of thrown items came from behind Holly and Ivy as the crowd stood up again. There were several slickguns and net guns at the ready, but nobody fired. Vitter looked angry, but didn't back down. Another jet howled past overhead, the background rumble peaking and drowning out all else, and this time a helicopter raced past in its wake, climbing high above the city. Holly saw light streaking from its guns but couldn't hear it. Vitter spoke quickly into his radio again, then walked out in front of the crowd. "Is this what you want?" he asked.

Holly opened her mouth and was surprised when nothing came out. Ivy spoke instead. "Is this about what we want?" she replied.

"It won't be for long," Vitter said.

"You're the one who invited us here."

"I suspect that was a mistake." The police seemed to take this as some sort of a signal, and began moving forward. The crowd behind them surged forward then, around them, rushing the police, and chaos descended again. Slickgun rounds were fired, and then the wave of rushing protesters broke against the police wall. The line held, but it was enough for Ivy and Holly to move backward, against the tide. The rearmost ranks of rioters broke as well, running down the street. Rocks were thrown. They passed a fire engine that had blocked the road, and Holly pulled Ivy around behind it, getting them out of Vitter's sight. She wanted to see Ivy's face.

Her sister was wild-eyed but still with her, it appeared. "The fliers scare me," she said. "I'm okay." Her eyes went from Holly, to the road, to the ground, and then she turned and looked at the fire engine behind her, running her fingers over the smooth metal. The action seemed to center her.

"Can you drive?"

"Of course," Ivy said distractedly. She looked at the cargo boxes on the side of the rig, opened it experimentally, then began peeking in all of them. She reached into one that was already open and took out a three foot long tool that combined a crowbar, hammer and axe. "I've never seen a fubar this big," she said. She carried it and they went another half-block past the fire engine, to where a beautifully restored antique car was parked. Except for a share of the dust that everything else on the street wore, it was undamaged, though the screaming jets and bombs threatened to change that at any moment. When Holly saw Pravit Deshmu's seal on the front fender, she realized in an instant why it hadn't been vandalized in the chaos. Somehow, seeing that Ivy hadn't been joking about stealing a car belonging to the wealthiest family in the Brother Nations was like a glass of cold water tossed in her face. She hadn't believed it at her core, because things like that just didn't *happen*. And yet her sister had done it. In fact, a rather long string of things that *just didn't happen* had been going on all around her for days, maybe weeks, and Ivy had been at the center of the storm.

Well, Ivy and herself. Why had it taken her so long to start believing in them?

Once in the car's passenger seat, the weight of the past few minutes hit her like a rock dropped from outer space. "I don't know what's happening, Ivy," she said. "I don't know what to do."

"What do you mean?" The car woofed to life, and Ivy seemed comfortable to be behind the wheel of a vehicle. She whipped it around in a tight circle and drove up the street, leaving the riot behind.

"I mean Vitter's in control of the police, the military, *everything!* Not permanently, but certainly while all of the politicals are locked in their safe-boxes! And no matter what he does, whatever measures he takes to protect the city, they'll thank him for it tomorrow. He's free to kill us both, destroy the *Fists*, anything. Anyone he wants. Any mess he makes, he can clean up. He sent helicopters out to drop sarin gas on the ship. They're all going to die, everyone on the Fists, on *Excelsis*. They're all going to *fucking* die and it's my fault." She took a deep breath. "I thought I could do this his way and keep you safe, but he tricked me."

"Those men, the ones who were with him in the auditorium. They were there even before he knew you were coming. Durloo worked for him also."

Holly looked at Ivy in disbelief. "What happened?"

"Narooma and Dilly killed him. But he killed Makkhana."

"Oh, Grandpa Rabbit..."

As they moved into the city, the roads were choked with cars, some abandoned in the chaos, others still trying to fight through. Ivy found their car's headlight switch and began forcing her way through the mess as quickly as she could. Her apparent complete disregard for traffic rules served her well in this task. "The planes?"

She tried to consider it. "I don't think so. I think..." She considered the horizon, the glow of fires. Was one of them near the airbase? It was impossible to tell for certain. Much as she wanted to explain to Ivy, to have an answer for her, there wasn't anything to say. "It'll be impossible to get past the bridges," she said. "They'll be full of cars."

"We have to stop soon. There's not much fuel in this rig."

"Then what are you doing?"

"Getting us away from Vitter. We get out of sight of him, we hide, we move again when it's safe."

"Move where?"

"To the harbor. To the *Fists*. Meet the others."

"Ivy, that's—"

"That's what?"

"I don't know," she sighed.

"This is where you lived, right? Show me where you used to live," Ivy said. Holly looked over at her, saw her sister grinning. "I'm not kidding. Tell me which way to go."

Holly sighed. "Turn left up ahead, where that bus is stopped."

"I think I'm getting used to driving with so many other rigs on the road." She joined traffic and accelerated, the car surging forward like a living thing.

"Be careful," Holly said.

"If there's one thing you don't have to tell me how to do..." Ivy said, getting a warning tone in her voice. The fact that she was talking more loudly to be heard over the car's roar made her sound even angrier.

"I'm just trying to keep you safe."

"I can do that myself," Ivy said.

"As you keep telling me."

The car's roar became throatier and deeper as she downshifted and sped up, cutting past a bus as though it was standing still. It almost seemed to Holly like the car was making a noise of aggressive agitation for its driver. "You can't do this alone," she said. "You, you, you're already on the edge of falling down. Let us help you!"

"Am I not?"

"No, you're not! You're treating me like a broken bird. But I'm tough, as tough as you. At least."

"You could barely walk, Ivy! Who's on the edge of falling down? You're malnourished, beaten up and covered in scars, and—"

"And filthy. I know." She swerved again. "There's a car with flashing lights back there, what does it mean?"

"Is it following us?"

The car cut sharply to the right, diving down a side street, the rear end fishtailing wide. Ivy's hands on the wheel twitched and she gathered it up, then accelerated again, roaring past a three-wheeled electric cart that appeared to be loaded down with an apartment's worth of possessions. Ivy looked in the mirror for a moment. "It is," she said.

"That will be the police. Or the military police. Doesn't matter. They're all after us. I'm...I'm sorry for calling you dirty."

Ivy made a face. "I don't care about that. I'm a scav, I've been called 'dirty' so many times I barely hear it," she said in a lower voice.

"But I'm your fucking *sister*."

"And you've called me worse. You can't hurt me with words, Holly. I'm hurt because you don't trust me." The narrow streets tore past at a dizzying rate. Holly was surprised that she wasn't frightened, even knowing how foolish it was to drive in the city at these speeds, especially with people and cars erratically fleeing from the chaos. Deep down, on some reptile-brain level, she trusted Ivy's driving, trusted her not to kill them both. She knew she was in good hands. So why couldn't she do it at the surface? Ivy made another turn, then another, a rapid series of sliding left-rights that put the flashing lights behind them out of sight. "They can't keep up with us," she said.

Holly could tell they were near the big farmer's market, and tried to get her bearings. They were headed away from downtown. When they hit a larger boulevard, she recognized it. "Go left," she said. Ivy complied immediately; it was almost like sending a voice command to the autodrive. Another police car appeared almost immediately. Of course they'd be converging, Holly realized. And still, she didn't feel worried that Ivy wouldn't be able to handle it. This wasn't the numbness she'd been feeling about almost everything else, this was really just a genuine lack of belief that Ivy could fail. She was happy at the wheel of Pravit Deshmu's pre-Fall toy; she seemed to belong there. And what she'd clearly fought through to even get the car...she'd been wrong to think Ivy was the weak link.

Ivy spoke suddenly. "You don't trust me."

"I do trust you. I think I trust you more than anyone."

"You're terrible at showing it."

"I'm *afraid*, Ivy. I'm so afraid that something will happen to you! I'm afraid that you'll realize—that you'll just...leave. And I'm afraid of going with you."

Ivy actually looked at her for a moment, her eyes wide. "Why would I leave?"

"Because your friends...Ivy, they're so much better than me. They've come so far to help you, they care so much about you—I want to, but I don't know if I'm capable of it. I'm nothing without my collar, Ivy. I even forgot about you, I thought you were dead and never thought about you, all that time. I don't deserve you, I'm no good to you and I don't want to see the look in your eyes when you realize that."

Ivy stomped on the brakes so hard the tires screamed against the pavement. For a moment Holly thought it was because of what she'd said, but a truck loaded down with hastily-stacked furniture and boxes cut across in front of them. It would have hit them if Ivy hadn't slammed the car almost to a stop. The police vehicle pursuing them braked hard, swerved around them, and the slid into the back of the truck with a crunch of shattering plastic. She shifted, floored it again immediately, and the car surged forward again. There was another car ahead of them now, a big Nissan, and it sped up to stay ahead as more approached from behind, trying to keep its advantage on the anarchic streets as it made its escape. Ivy stayed directly behind it and pushed the car ahead of them to go faster and faster, and the boulevard stretched on what seemed like forever. Ivy's eyes were locked on the road ahead of her, her mouth slightly open in concentration as they weaved in and out of traffic, spending as much time off the road as on it. The car in front of them was struggling to stay ahead, then finally hit a curb hard enough to break some part of its suspension. Their ancient car seemed to be much more forgiving of large bumps; Ivy bounced over the same curb and kept going, around the stricken Nissan. When she hit the throttle again, the car seemed to be channeling anger from her.

"Ivy, please say something," Holly said.

"It's, it's, it's not a good time to talk," she said through gritted teeth.

"I don't care! The way things have been going there may *never* be a good time. Tell me what you're thinking."

Ivy threw the wheel to the right, downshifting and letting the car's rear end slide wide again. "I wish you'd quit trying to think for me, and just, just think for yourself."

Holly stared at Ivy, feeling like she'd been punched in the heart. Ivy didn't look back at her. "I...I don't think I know how. I'm sorry," she said.

"I said you're not allowed to apologize to me any more. Tell me why you're afraid to come with me."

"Because I don't want you to leave me."

"That's, that's, that's stupid! You're afraid to come with because you don't want to be left?"

"In North *America!* I don't want to go to North America, Ivy."

"Why not?"

"Why not? Look at this city! I love it here! I'm somebody important here, even if I'm just a domestic, I have a place..." she faltered, realizing that none of these things were true anymore. "I'm afraid of having to shoot biters and keep watch for gleaners and people from Little Rock trying to steal me," she said finally. "I'm afraid of not having electricity and television and fresh mangos. I'm afraid of being trapped out in the dirt during snowstorms and thunderstorms. I'm afraid because I don't know what to do or how to help, I'll just be a useless ornament like I am now and you'll eventually see that and leave me behind. I don't think I can live the horrible way we did when we were children, Ivy. Not anymore."

"I like my life," Ivy said, sounding hurt.

"I know you do. But I don't want it." She put her chin in her hand and looked out miserably the window. "How did you know to turn there?"

"Was that the way? I just did. I think I saw that little shop with the pink awning in one of my dreams, and you rode your bike this way. And I think you might be stuck with my life. If we stay here they'll kill us."

"I know," Holly said. "I know I have to go with you. And I'm glad to be with you. I'm just...this is not how I pictured it happening."

She saw a smile cross her sister's face. "Me, either."

"I wanted to bring you here, though. Once I remembered...I always wanted you with me. Elden was...well...I wanted you to live here with me. We had such a nice place." Holly sighed. She couldn't tell if the weariness was lifting as they talked, or getting heavier. Ivy took a turn that led them away from the place she'd used to live, but she didn't correct her; keeping ahead of the police net was more important now. "I suppose it's just as well. If you've really been seeing my life through dreams, seeing everything, I imagine you'd have killed Elden even if I hadn't."

"You'd have been really angry with me when I did."

"Maybe," Holly replied. "I think...I think I need you now. I'm exhausted, Ivy." She felt tears, and didn't try to wipe them away. "I'm so tired. After I killed him, after I knew I couldn't be Myawi any more, I didn't have anything, I didn't want to go on. I couldn't sleep without my music box and I had no chores to do and nobody to do anything for and that should have felt like freedom but it didn't feel like anything. I felt like I was waiting to die, Ivy, but every morning the sun would come up and I was still here. And I didn't even care enough to do anything about that."

"What about now?"

"I want to care. But I can't tell if I do. I don't want to die, if that's what you're worried about. I'm not going to kill myself. But I don't feel like I care if I live either." She sighed. "It should have been you. If they had taken you and Mother instead, you wouldn't have broken. Not like I did. Myawi made me a broken thing."

She expected Ivy to tell her she was being ridiculous, to disagree. "How can I help?" Ivy asked. Her eyes and attention were on the road, but she sounded utterly focused on their conversation at the same time, in a way Holly had never felt before. She felt like if Ivy turned and looked at her, her sister would see right to the core of her and there'd be no need for words any more.

She didn't know what she was going to say until it came out. "I'm not used to not having someone need me!"

"So you've been trying to make it so everyone needs you," Ivy said matter-of-factly. Had she understood that all along? And if she had, Holly thought, it was unfair that *she* didn't have any piercing insights into *Ivy's* mind at the same time. It was just another layer of useless-feeling. "But you don't need to do that. We already need you. I need you."

"Except that you don't, Ivy."

"I have spent my entire life looking for you—"

"I know. And you've had a life this whole time. You *want* me with you. But you don't *need* me."

"I, I don't feel whole without you, Holly. I think that qualifies as a need. And I can't believe you don't feel the same way."

"I don't. I don't feel like anything. Not even an incomplete whole. I don't exist."

Ivy made a face. "Well, I'm going to keep you around until you do, then. You, you say you don't know who you are any more, but if we die today, you'll never find out either." She made another sharp turn, the car leaning so far on its chassis that it felt like it might turn over. It didn't, of course, but the engine stumbled. "We have to stop soon."

"It's okay, we're almost there." They were farther away from the aerial battle now, and the smoke only obscured part of the sky, lit by the glow of fires on the other side of the city. Still, it was surreal, returning to what had been home for so long with the streets in utter chaos, moving far too fast in a stolen antique car with Ivy at the wheel. Holly couldn't even process it all. She realized she was touching her neck, but her collar wasn't there.

How were they even going to get in?

No matter, the garage was coming up. The gate was open, and bent outward; someone had probably knocked it down trying to leave after the power had gone out. She pointed, and Ivy drove right in. The interior of the garage was dark, and the walls blocked out the sounds from the city.

Ivy quickly pulled the car into an empty slot away from the entrance, out of sight of the road. They seemed to have made it without any pursuit. Holly instinctively touched her pocket, checking for her keys, then clacked her teeth in frustration. How were they going to get in?

chapter 68

Narooma

Alright, listen listen listen, I'm gonna tell you about my weekend in Singapore. I went up and got my feet dirty and had exploits, the most crunchy brutal exploits. You want to know the warrior way, this is how it's done. Listen! Listen and know and go.

It started when I was dallying with Gavinder, or he was trying to dally with me, at least. Prince of Zaal or not, he's a bore and I'm not nearly as impressed with him as he is with himself. Course he can't suck that into his mind, and so he's constantly chasing and teasing, and he was playing the game a little too focused and that's how we got snapped up by Inchins, just a stupid regular patrol boat that put a screamer in the water and before we could figure out which way to run we were all netted up.

Gavinder tried to fight them, went human and did for one, but there were too many and they got us both up in hooks. Spent six days in a dry dry box, fettled up and next to no food, just shouting. They were taking us to the bad ship, the death ship, they were just waiting for it to come to take us aboard and cut us into pieces. And there was nothing we could do, both of us chained to the wall, chained to the floor in the dark. Poor Gavinder doesn't know when it's time to stop boasting, and they punch-stomped him good. For a while I thought he was dead, but he's as tough as he is pompous and he pulled through.

And then we got a rescue! A bunch of humans and shifters they had aboard slapped their way out, and they busted loose and stole the box they were carrying me and Gavinder in! Stole the box, then let everyone out and says they're from the *88 Fists*, you've seen it. That's right that's right, these were Mama Lola's people. I know, I know! So many exploits.

Soon as we got out on the water, I gave Gavinder a flip over the side and then I followed him, we slipped our feet and got back to clear water. Zaal people came quick as they could, and then when some Inchins came after

Mama Lola's people there were twenty of us waiting for them, crunchy warriors who pulled their silly lily pads out from under them, put 'em all under the water. Mama Lola's people, they didn't go back to the ship, though, and stayed ashore.

Gavinder said we owed a debt to Mama Lola's people. Said I could either canoodle with him, or go get my feet dirty and pay that debt, make whatever they needed right. He thought I was gonna be too scaredy to go ashore for him? I think he was a little miffy that I picked feet instead of him. Ha!

So I got my axe and floated out to the *Fists* and told them I'm there to help, what do they want me to do? They told me where the folks were ashore. Took me a little while to find them, sneakin' through trees and forests inland, but I did. They had a little bus ready to drive north. Mama Lola's people were helping out a pair of twinsies and some shifters. They knew Inchin was a bad place for 'em, they were trying to get 'em out, trying to get peace for the twinsies' mother's spirit, bunch of different noble missions. What they needed was warriors to help make it happen.

Well, they got me, that was more than enough. They had a tough cervid named Kroni, Mama Lola's firstie named Fry and a crunchy sealion named Dilly, three little canid wolfies, some others along for the ride. I met some Ivory Sisters too, nice folks. Course we didn't get very far in that little bus before a crunchy tough warrior showed up to stop 'em, crashed the bus and stood down the others. He was a scribble-man, all muscle and mean. Went through Mama Lola's people like it was nothing. Kroni got all slicked up, Fry and the wolfies got thrown. I came in from the blind side and hakkapalled that warrior with one swipe, right through the neck! Slapped his thinkball right off, magic or not, he never even saw me coming. I put his head where his friends would find it. After that the twinsies had a big fight and the pretty one left out on her own.

The scruffy one, Ivy, was mad and sad but she said we should keep going, and we went on to one of those big Inchin smoke factories. Dismal, miserable concrete town where everything's stained with burnoff from building junk nobody needs, and nobody ever smiles. They gave us something to munch on and took us for a lookaround. I was getting sick of that by then. Had been in feet all day, and that makes me crawky. The factory there's where the twinsies' momma died, and Ivy said she was going to break it down, to let momma's spirit rest. What she had to do was keep the brutals from coming in long enough to set it alight. Them factories burn good if you get 'em going, you know that.

Ivy put me at the back door, and sure enough, there's six brutes angling to come through. I blocked off the door, told 'em to go home. They tried to come through anyway, broke the door, so I gave one of them a boost into the wall, throatsmacked another, shoved them all back and gave them a roar. That made 'em stop a second. Then I told 'em their mothers would cry when they saw what I'd done to them. Whether or not they believed me, I showed 'em soon enough..

Three of 'em made like they needed to help their friends. The boldest one stepped forward, probably thought the box he was wearing on his chest was gonna help him, and I spatchcocked him open from the bellybutton up. He went down screamin', and the next one I busted across the eyes and threw him down in the first one's mess. Didn't give them a chance to pull any shooters, I cracked their heads open and axed the arm off of the first one, the one who went into the wall. Three four five, I hacked off arms and heads and feet and threw them around. Not a one of 'em got a chance to run away. Drew the marks that said it was my door now. Nobody else tried to come through after that, ha.

Ivy set her fire, and it was a good one. Big black burn, lit up the sky, explosions shook the ground. That whole city burned to the ground, nothing left but concrete. After that, Fry and Kroni went back to the Fists and the rest of us got on a train, bound for Singapore. Ivy said she had more to do and she wasn't leaving her friend or her sister in Singapore and she was going even if we didn't come. So I went. This was working out to be a good exploit and I wasn't done yet either.

The train? Fastest thing I ever rode on, locked inside a tube and streaking along without stopping, three hundred miles in an hour, can you believe? There was some sit-time before we got to the city, so we rested, I had some crustybread the Ivory Sister was carrying. Good stuff. Then one of the Ivory Sisters turned out to be a traitorboy! I thought he was a bit eely to begin with, and he wasn't a good mate, he went his own way and made more trouble. Ivy threw him out of the pod and he turned on us just like that! He came back with some thumpers with him, they jumped one of Mama Lola's boys and cut the Sister's throat.

I say they were sneaky, but they didn't know who they were fucking with. Ivy tackled the traitorboy, so after that it was four of them and two of us. I did a hard axe throw to the left and jumped the one on the right, peeled the one off of Dilly to get him back in the fight, and then quick knocked one of them right through the window, spash and he was gone. Gave another one a new face in the back of his head with my axe. They thought they had crust? They didn't last but a few seconds against us. Barely warriors, that blep.

Ivy already busted up the eely traitorboy pretty good, so he wasn't putting up much of a fight, and me and Dilly had no trouble putting him out the window. This time I watched and saw what happened, he flipped out far enough to hit a tree and spocko! Train was going so fast he just came apart, like he got tail-slapped by a spermachick. Three more kills for me, though every one of 'em should've known better.

After that we put ourselves in disguises, so we could blend in with the other workers on the train. I didn't mind, I can fight just as well in human clothes. Didn't have to though. Got to Singapore just when it was getting dark.

There was an army waiting for us at the train station, guns and shields and swords, but then Ivy's shifter friend showed up in a big purple car and took us out of there right past everyone. Apparently she made friends with one of the Deshmu princesses. When I saw she was a kitshifter, I got that. Kitshifters are good at making friends, I've known a few. The princess took us back to her place and had her girl make me and Ivy and Dilly some food, bread sandwiches and wonderful crackers, dry and crispy. The house was nice, high up in one of the towers, right next to the canal and looking down on the city.

Then the police chased us there and knocked the door down. Even though she was a princess she was young, couldn't tell them what to do. Me and Dilly laid the police out, except for the cagey one and another eely fellow who stayed out of the punching. They had a couple of big brutes with them, scribbled warriors who weren't brothers but dressed like they wanted to be. Finest challenge I'd had all day, and I whacked 'em to a standstill while the others fell back. Princess said there was a way out upstairs but they needed time, so I kept the brutes busy. Gave 'em face, split 'em up. Dilly helped. They wanted to be brothers but didn't fight like brothers, went one on one, so I did a side-bob and put my axe in the one fighting Dilly. Damnfool had his back to me and I split his thinkball right down the middle, just like Koodle taught. You fight everybody, not just the tubachick in front of you. Anyway I got that kill and the other one let out a howl like nobody's business. He got mad but he got stupid at the same time, came at me with a little blade, put some beauty marks on my belly. I laughed at him, right in his *face*. He wasn't going to take me down, scrawls or not, he was too mushy. I wrapped him up and took us both out the window.

You ever wonder what-for we warriors do cliff dives, higher and higher, this is what for! You test your bravery regular, it's there for you when things get brutal, isn't it? I did a big death-drop, down down down, face down and then shifted just in time to enter. Bet my axe made a bigger splash than I did!

Good dive or not, it was still a pretty good whack to the melon, so I had to roll around a bit to shake it off. Wasn't going to be able to hearsee for shit for a while! I dead-reckoned it through the river back out to the sea. Had to dive deep a few times, when the Inchins started shining lights around, looking for me. Made it out easy. The *Fists* was anchored a ways out, a quarter mile outside the bay or so, close enough to see but too far to swim. The deathship was parked right next to it. Works out, Mama Lola's sailors stole it! And the Inchins, they were watching those boats like orcas, little patrollies bouncing all around it, helichoppers in the air too. And then while I was watching, one of the helichoppers headed out over the *Fists* and the death ship. And it started dropping cans, one after the other. I could just barely see them in the light, floof, floof as they went down. The Inchins were dropping poison gas on the ships, hoping to smoke down everyone on board for an easier kill.

I swam out there just in time to catch Inchin water spiders climbing up the sides, all guns and knives and gas masks. Mama Lola's people were dealing with the water spiders on the ratlines. I stayed in the water and did for the ones still on their boats. They were in little rubber bobbers. Good for sneakin' quiet, but not so good for staying afloat. I popped at least four of them with my axe, flipped two more over. We were far enough out that I could've shouted for Zaal warriors to come help me, but my melon was still ringing a little. Besides, what did I need help for? The water-spiders who were swimming good, I grabbed them and took them down deep, a hundred feet, and left them there. The ones who weren't got tail-slapped and axed, and it wasn't long before the sharks came out. I put eleven more warriors in the ocean in that fight.

By the time I was done with that, I got up to the deck. I missed the fight up there, but there were only eight warriors on the ground after that one, and all of Mama Lola's sailors were healthy. They were taking shots at the helicopter with the gas, trying to make it go away, and that's when the Rainbow Snakes flew in with those loud, ugly, brutal flyers they stole from the Inchins after that little thing in Zeeland a couple of years back. Three of those flyers came in, and they unleashed hellfire and thunder right on Singapore! Right on the city!

That sure as swash got the helichoppers to forget about their poison.

The *Fists* was all ready to ocean off, too, but then there was another rubber bobber full of water spiders that came over the side and we had to spatch them. This batch was tough, I got a nasty scratch from mine before I got his arms round behind him and dropped him on the deck, broke his shoulders and back.

Fry started asking the new captain, "What about the twinsies and Razor?" I guess they still had people ashore, not just the twinsies and their friends. He grumbled a lot about it being dangerous to wait, they didn't have much time before the Rainbow Snakes pulled out and they still had to load gear from the death ship.

And then suddenly The Bonefish steps up and says he'll go back to shore and get them. And I was like wah! I didn't know The Bonefish was sailing with Mama Lola, I'm in for that, everyone knows you always go along if The Bonefish has a plan because he doesn't do *anything* without a reason, so while the new captain was saying there wasn't a boat to spare I said, "We don't need one!" and went over the side, and The Bonefish went with me. I shifted, let him grab my fin and carry my axe, and we swam back into shore, past all the Singapore folks trying to flee into the ocean on their little party boats. It looked like whoever wasn't trying to run away was fighting with the police, there were soldiers and goo-guns and things on fire everyplace. When Inchins decide to ruckus, they ruck everything. The planes were doing big eights over the city, one ratterchatterchatterkaboom attack after the other.

We sneaked up on shore, jumped the dock by a little park, and The Bonefish said, "You gonna stand out a little, 'Rooma,'" and I laughed because he was right, I lost my pants. We went up and down the shore, and found the other one of Mama Lola's sailors, a girl named Razor who had another kitshifter with her, rescued from the Inchins. The Bonefish went and stole a boat for them, and then he told me to go hunting big fish while he looked for the twinsies, which was fine by me. There were plenty of warriors running about, lots of big boys and girls who liked shooting cry-gas and slime at people who were running away. They were surprised to see me! The first three just froze, holding up their little shields like they didn't know what to do when a proud crunchy naked warrior's coming down on them screaming. One of them shouted at me to stop but of course I didn't, I jumped up over the middle one's shield and hootspa! Right in the face with my metal! The one next to him was a speckle-faced girl; I rolled and took her leg off at the knee and she went down screaming for her god. The third one threw down his gear and ran away pissing himself, and I let him go. I can fight with a little shield, so I took it.

After that I just went hunting, like The Bonefish said. I followed the path, and let the normies go, but cracked heads if I saw someone wearing warrior's garb. There were a bunch of different kinds I'd seen, but I knew which ones were the fighters. I came upon a big, big frenzy as I got close to the place where the party was. One of the Rainbow Snakes' planes stitched the ground up pretty good near the crowd, right where I had been running a few seconds before in fact, and that was pretty exciting but it got everyone to punching everyone else and pushing up against a wall of warrior police that was slowly pushing them back. They were at the top of a big corner staircase like a ziggurat stage. I was down the stairs from them so I went up the side where there weren't as many. Maybe the shield helped and they thought I was one of theirs, in the dark, but I was able to pick two off the edge, bashed one down with the shield and put my fingers in the other one's throat when he looked to see what was going on, and then I was behind their line. I looked for the biggest fish around and found him, a white-hair with a fancy suit on and a battle jacket over that, talking into a radio and looking at a little screen in his hand. I could tell he was a big fish by the way he didn't look at the wall of battle right in front of him, but kept looking at the sky and out toward the water. He was directing the game, not playing in it.

Least that's what he thought! All the noise, he didn't hear me coming, yapping on his radio. There was a warrior behind him who tried to get in my way but I ran right over him, he thought I'd stop and fight him and I didn't. The big fish turned at the last second but I was already swinging one handed, up from the feet into the face. Split him from chin to crown. He stumbled back a couple of steps, looking at me cuz he didn't even know what just happened, a big red crack running down the middle of his face and teeth falling out. I danced around him, did a little tailspin on my feet and hoicked my axe into his stupid neck, opened that up so nobody'd be putting him back together again, and then gave 'em all a war shout so they'd know who did it.

When you bust up the leader, one of two things happens: a good gang of fighters will make sure you regret it. A bad gang will scatter. This one fell apart when I hakkapalled the one at the top. One or two of them came at me at first, and I put them on the ground next to him, and then the line of shields just fell apart and there were people running everywhere, taking the goo guns away and turning them back on the police, or on each other. The police backed up inside the big auditorium and blocked the doors and stayed there. Every time the Rainbow Snakes made another close pass, a bunch of people would run up and try to get inside, and they got shot or beat down.

The whole square and staircase emptied out pretty fast, except for small tangles of fighters still going at it. From here it looked like the whole city was on fire, but I remembered from the water that it wasn't as bad as it looked. I started off to go check on The Bonefish before hunting some more, and got tagged from the side by a big scrawled warrior. Felt like a tubachick had just run right into me. I turned with it and gave him a whack as I fell, but he was all boxed up and my axe skipped off of his chest armor. I went down the stairs, rolling rolling rolling on hard ground, and came up ready for him. He walked down the steps with a big grin on his face. I recognized his armor, he was dressed like the one whose head I knocked off in the street the day before. Must've been a blood brother, because I could tell he wanted me.

"You ought to put some clothes on," he said to me.

I said to him, "You ought to learn to feel the wind on your skin." He kept walking toward me, and when he was three steps above me, I brought my axe out to the side, stomped the ground, gave him some monster-face. He actually stopped and laughed. He got serious when I feinted like I was going to take his head too, but I switched it up on him and hacked straight down, got the side of his leg instead. I know that stings like you wouldn't believe. He caught my axe on the upswing and hit me in the chest, high and hard. Felt like he had rocks in his glove—maybe he did—and that knocked me back. I laughed at him anyway, slapped the same spot to show him it didn't hurt. Next punch I ducked, came up under it, went for the throat with a straight axe-thrust and he grabbed me round the waist, dodged the blade, jumped backward and rolled in midair, fell on me.

The ground hurts, you know that? Some crunchy warriors jump up on rocks just to get used to that full-body smacking feeling, and you probably laughed at them when you were a little one, but it's important. Takes you by surprise. Plus it was the second slam I'd had, counting the jump out the window. My melon hurt for *days* after that. I had my arms free when we landed so I let go of my axe and put his eyes out with my fingers. You want to be a warrior up on the dirt, you have to learn to fight with everything, even fingers! That started him howling, and he reared up, flipped back. I went up with him. He reached out and started grabbing for me, and I spun around and got on his back but kept my finger hooked in one of his eyes, yanked his helmet off with the other. Let go of his face and grabbed the back of his head, swept the arm and splap, smacked his face into the ground hard as I could. I did it twice more. Figured he'd be dead but he suddenly breached and threw me off, then got up and started walking away from me, waving his hands in front of him, yelling at me to wait, he was blind. I have no idea why that would make me wait, it was me that made him blind, but before I had a chance to say or do anything else a truck came screaming up the sidewalk, police truck with the lights all flashing, and ran him down! Blew him in half, not five feet in front of me! I'm not making it bigger, his bottom half went forward and his top half went up and you could hear bits of him hitting the ground for a full minute after, sounded like rain on palm fronds. I'd have been mad that truck stole my kill if it hadn't looked so funny.

chapter 69

Shiloh tensed to run again, but froze when she heard the distinctive clack-clack of a large gun being readied and heard Tapia say, calmly as ever, "Don't do that, please." Past the glare of the truck's headlights, she saw a mounted gun on the back of it, and a figure at the ready. Tapia hopped down from the driver's seat. "Thank you," he said.

From the other side of the truck, Mahnaz jumped down and ran toward her. She started to turn to face him, but he moved with surprising swiftness and kicked her in the side. It was a poor kick, but still took her by surprise and shocked the air out of her lungs. She crouched low, protecting her belly, and looked up at him, feeling her ears flattened, tail lashing back and forth. Shiloh didn't give him the satisfaction of a sound, but opened her mouth in a silent hiss. The sight of her canines seemed to give him pause, but he maintained enough of his rage to spit at her.

"That's enough, Chancellor," Tapia called, sounding amused.

Apparently he'd lost the gun the policeman had handed him, because he turned back to the truck, squinting into the lights. "Let me kill it," he muttered. "Let me kill it now."

"Can't do that. Anna—excuse me. *Shiloh*, would you mind shifting back into human form? The city's in a bit of a panic. The last thing I need is a mob ripping my prisoner to pieces. And I'd rather not have to put a snare on you."

He had a reasonable point. Shiloh shifted back. Mahnaz made a sound of disgust, though he still stared at her naked body.

Beyond the glare of the truck's lights, Tapia clearly was, too. "I can see why you were so...charmed, Chancellor."

"Shut up. You'd have done the same, don't you shame me."

"It was me, I wouldn't be ashamed. Step forward, young lady." She did, moving past the glare of the lights. Tapia was smiling indulgently, and she kind of wanted to go for his eyes, but there was still a man riding in the back of the truck, helming the mounted gun. One of the truck's back doors was open, and he gestured to it. "If you would be so kind?"

She wanted to tell him that she didn't want to die, but it wouldn't have done any good. The cheerful boy she'd met at the club was still visible in Tapia's face, but there was a malicious hardness there as well. This was someone who'd taken his position because it would enable him to hurt people once in a while. Shiloh climbed up into the truck, and he shut the door behind her. He hit a switch, and she heard both doors lock. Tapia climbed back in behind the wheel and barked impatiently for Mahnaz, who struggled up into the passenger seat.

"What have you done with the princess, monster?" he yelled at her.

"See?" Tapia said. "We need her after all. Wouldn't you have felt foolish if you'd shot her on sight? That said, you'll get farther with sweetness. Shiloh, where has Princess Nipa gotten to?" he asked.

His condescending tone was perfectly pitched to enrage. "I ate her," she said.

"Liar!" Mahnaz barked. "She was with you ten minutes ago!"

"Oh, I'm sorry, I was talking about last night," she said, not breaking eye contact with him. His face reddened. For a moment she thought he might come across the seat after her. "She went in another direction. I didn't see where she was going."

"If the princess is hurt, I will enjoy watching you die."

"You were going to enjoy that anyway," Shiloh replied, rolling her eyes. Even with murder clearly in his eyes, it was entirely too hard to take him seriously, knowing what he looked like naked.

"*Enough*," Tapia said. "Do you need to disembark to find your charge, Chancellor?"

Mahnaz looked out the windows. The night sky was orange and black, and the sound of the jets seemed to shake the air before subsiding to a background rumble and then peaking again as another one flew past. "I think I'm safer with you," he said.

"Then please stifle yourself so I can follow the radio chatter." Tapia started the truck, which growled to life with a diesel clatter rather than the electric whirr of most of the vehicles in Singapore.

"Where are we going?"

"To make ourselves useful as ground support. Besides, it's a good idea to get away from here. I'm sure some of those kind civilians over there are looking for this one, after they saw her running through traffic." Shiloh looked out the front windshield, in the direction he nodded in, saw a small group of people standing on the corner very obviously looking around. He saw her looking. "Yes, my dear, I think you slipped aboard at just the right time. Lucky for you, we're on our way out of here anyway, so you don't have to talk to them. You're going to behave yourself, right?" He met her eyes with a look that confirmed that his jovial tone was a ruse. Shiloh nodded. He put the big truck in gear.

"Where are we going?" Mahnaz asked.

"Anti-aircraft defense," he said. "The airstrip and naval base have been severely damaged. There are concerns that they'll turn their guns on the city next."

"Who's doing this?" Mahnaz asked.

"The Rainbow Snakes, most likely. Am I right?" Tapia asked Shiloh.

"How would I know?"

His response was a knowing grin that suggested he thought he knew more about her than he actually did. Shiloh sat back in the seat and looked out the window.

"We need to put some clothes on it," Mahnaz said.

Tapia didn't look away from the road. "What for?"

"I can't stand the sight of it."

"So don't look. And if you can't do that, give her your jacket. I think it's obvious that we don't have time for a shopping trip." The truck bullied its way through traffic. Tapia actually hit a few cars, pushing past them between lanes, before finding a clear stretch and flooring it. They drove several blocks before reaching an open square, a small park. Shiloh saw a fence and some sort of fountain before Tapia drove over the fence and got as close to the center of the open area as he could. They waited.

When one of the jets streaked into view, the gunner in the back of the truck opened up immediately, sending a noisy chain of bullets arcing off into the night. The noise startled Shiloh and she ducked and covered her ears. Shell casings tumbled across the roof like rain. The plane was there and gone in an instant, and Tapia's gunner stopped immediately. She heard the gun swivel back to wait for the next attack run.

chapter 70

"Why would people live so high up in these towers?" Ivy asked, exasperated. She was using the fubar she'd just picked up as a walking stick. "How far are we going?"

"Elden and I lived on the twenty-third floor," Holly said. She was half a flight behind, pacing herself while her sister rushed. "We don't have to go all the way up. I told you we can't get in." Ivy ignored this, as she had been since they'd left the car. The building shook slightly as something else exploded out in the city. "Besides, when the power is on, there's an elevator."

"That would make a difference," Ivy panted. She gratefully pushed open the door at the twenty-third floor. "You lived…to the left," she said.

Holly shook her head. "So strange that you dreamt my life."

"Not all of it," Ivy said. "Just the embarrassing parts."

She knew Ivy was poking at her to keep her in the moment. Some part of Holly's brain resisted the attempts to manipulate her, but at the same time, it felt like it was working. She took the lead and showed Ivy which door it was. "As I said, I don't have a key—"

"I do." Ivy planted the crowbar end of the fubar against the door close to the latch, forcing it into the gap. She threw her body against it, ramming it farther in, then leaned backward and the latch all but exploded, breaking noisily and flinging broken bits of itself across the hall. The force of Ivy's pull thrust the door violently open.

It was dark, lit only by the light from outside, but Holly could tell instantly that it was someone else's home now. The mirror on the wall, Elden's favorite Kamisaka Sekka reproduction, the end table were all gone, replaced by different things. The tile on the floor was the same, but where the wood floor should have begun was now covered with tacky bamboo-mat flooring.

"Hello?" a female voice called down the hall. Ivy raised her giant fubar, but Holly stayed her hand, recognizing the voice.

"Yuying?"

A candle appeared at the end of the entry hall, a face floating above it in the dim light. "Holly?"

"What are you doing here?"

"Professor Aidanab bought the house, after...you know. He always liked Professor Ono's—your—place. Ah...is this your sister? Would you like something to drink? The professor is out, but I can fix you something."

Holly shook her head. "Don't be ridiculous, Yuying, we just broke into *your* house. I just...we just need to rest for a moment."

"Something to drink would be nice," Ivy said. "And it's nice to meet you. I'm Ivy Aniram."

Yuying bowed formally. "It's very nice to meet you as well. Please, make yourselves at home." She smiled at Ivy. The expression turned uncertain as her eyes went to Holly, and then she turned and went into the kitchen.

Holly led Ivy into the living room, then opened the door and showed her out onto the balcony. Inside it was too awkward, the wrong furniture in the wrong places, the walls the wrong color. The balcony hadn't changed, though. "I remember this view," Ivy said. "I always thought it was Dallas, or Strip City. But I couldn't figure out what part. Stop squeezing your neck," she added.

"I feel naked without it," Holly said, taking her hand away from her throat. "It feels cold."

"Well, stop rubbing it. Your skin's chafing, I can see it."

"I'll get used to it."

"Didn't it bother you?"

"No," Holly said. "It was fitted. And I wore it since I was first made a Myawi. I hardly noticed it." Ivy caught her hand and pushed it back down; Holly hadn't even noticed that she was trying to touch her neck again. She smiled. "It was a part of me."

"I can tell you're not sure if you should be happy or sad," Ivy said.

"Both, maybe."

Yuying joined them with a tray of quick snacks, cut fruit and tea. "I'm, ah. That is, I am glad to see you," she said to Holly. "Both of you."

"I'm glad to see you too, Yuying. I missed you."

"You, ah. You look strange. Without your collar."

Holly smiled. "I'm still getting used to it. You seem nervous. Where's Professor Aidanab?"

"Gone."

"Gone?" Ivy asked.

"When the bombing started, he took the car and left. To get across the bridges, before they filled with traffic."

Ivy's voice took on an immediate edge. "And he *left you here?*"

"His car only seats four," Yuying said, "and he had to pick up some of the grad students."

"But he *left* you," Holly said. "With the city on fire, he left you."

"I'm sure it will be safe."

"Probably. And still."

There were tears in Yuying's eyes, and she sniffed. Holly could see that she was hiding genuine fear for her life, burying it deep. She knew the tricks they'd all been taught to do that. The city below them rumbled with the sounds of breaking glass, sirens, screaming and distressingly frequent gunfire and other percussive bangs. The helicopters were now engaging the planes that had strafed the city, and the noise of that combat came and went irregularly.

"You should be gone when he comes back," Ivy said, all but voicing the thought Holly was too tired to articulate. "Would you like to come with us? Back to North America? Don't give me that look," she said to Holly, "we *are* getting back to the *Fists* somehow."

"Thank you, but I couldn't," Yuying said. "My mother...I couldn't leave her."

"You could always go home," Holly said. "We could take your collar off. It only hurts a little," she added with a wan smile.

Yuying looked nervously at her again. "May I ask you a question?"

"Of course."

"Did you...did you kill Shmi?"

Holly crushed her eyes shut. Her voice shook with emotion, a rippling fabric of unshed tears. "I did *not*. The others...that was me, but Shmi was murdered by a Myawi Protector. She helped me escape, and the Ivory Sisters cut her collar, and then she was murdered."

Yuying nodded, and a tear escaped onto her cheek. "I prayed that was a lie. I'm sorry she died. Yinka too."

Holly picked up on the acknowledgement of her tacit confession. "So am I. About both of them. I didn't want to hurt Yinka. Things got...bad."

She nodded, let the moment pass, then smiled gently. "You're so different. We never felt like we knew you very well, but even so. I can tell you've changed."

Holly wanted to ask how Yuying thought she'd changed, but didn't. For a few surreal minutes, the three of them sipped tea and watched part of

Singapore burn. From what Holly could see the damage was bad, especially in the direction of the airbase, but the city wasn't in peril, assuming the populace didn't panic and make things worse. The helicopters and jets continued to play cat and mouse over the city, and she thought she saw return fire from the ground as well.

There was a knock at the door; a creak and thump suggested that the broken latch had given way at the knock and allowed it to swing open. Yuying got up dutifully and went to greet the newcomers.

For a wild, paranoid moment, Holly thought that Yuying could have quietly called the police, or Vitter. Surely he'd have assumed she might come here, this was a mistake—

But that was ridiculous. The police wouldn't have knocked, not after the events of this evening. The way things were going, Vitter might just as soon fire a rocket through the window as send somebody up. Yuying returned from the door with two people: a scruffy college boy she didn't recognize and Princess Nipa. She put her candle on the side table and said, "This might be the strangest day I've ever had. Holly, the princess says she's here to find you."

Nipa looked distraught and confused. She had a small bundle of cloth in her hands. "It's you," she said, looking at the twins. "It's both of you. Is she here?" she asked. "Is Shiloh here?"

"She's not," Ivy said. "Did you get separated?"

"The car crashed. They made it crash. I didn't know," Nipa said, the words coming out in a rush. "I'm sorry I didn't know. Chokidar was going to kill *her*! He had a *gun*! And then the explosions came, and she said I had to go away from her to be safe, and she..." The princess started crying. "I didn't know she was a shifter! How could I have *known*?"

Ivy took her shoulders. "It's okay."

"But they kill shifters. She must think I hate her, that I want her killed. That's why she ran away, isn't it? Is she coming here?"

Ivy shook her head. "I don't think she'd even know to come here."

"How did you find us?" Holly asked. Both she and Yuying eyed Nipa's companion warily, though politely.

"My friend Wan," she said, indicating the scruffy college boy. She wiped immodestly at the tears on her face. "He said you might go to where you used to live, and looked up the address."

"Rabbit of the moon," Holly gasped. "Vitter will have thought of that too—"

"I floated a rumor that you were headed to the Myawi school next,"

Wan said. "Said you'd already been spotted passing the Woodlands Crossing. Got friends who backed it up," he added proudly, "so most of the military's headed in that direction."

"So we can get to the ship, then," Ivy said. "If we had a car."

"You can take mine."

"No," Holly said. "I think you should get the princess to safety, and maybe take my friend out of here also, once she decides if she wants us to cut her collar."

"Holly..." Yuying began, then trailed off.

"Now is the right time. In the chaos, nobody's going to notice the alarm. And housegirls are cutting their collars all over the city."

"It's true," Wan added. "We cut fifty of them at the train station."

"But what would I do?"

"I can't help you there," Holly said with a wry shrug.

"We should go," Ivy said.

Nipa clutched at Holly's arm. "I want to see her again."

"I don't think you can," she replied gently. "The rest of your family is in the safebox at the stadium. We saw them go in. They weren't hurt. But they might not be out until tomorrow. You and Wan should get somewhere safe. There are bad people about tonight."

She expected the princess to stomp her feet and insist, but her only response was a somber nod. "I understand," she said. "Please...give this to her for me? It's the outfit I loaned her. She took it off, when she...when... anyway, I want her to have it. She liked it, and she looked so beautiful in it. And tell her I'm sorry." Holly accepted the bundle of neatly folded clothes Nipa gave her. "And...and tell her I love her. I won't let them hurt her, if she comes back. My father won't let them hurt her."

"I'm more worried about your father hurting *me*," Wan muttered.

Holly didn't react to the aside. "I'll tell her," she said. "But go now. Find someplace safe, and stay there, until you hear that your father has come out of the safe-box. Understand?" Despite the misdirection, Holly was sure that if Nipa had found them, Vitter would too. He wouldn't send all of his troops in one direction if there was an alternative.

From the still-open balcony door, the sound of one of the helicopters defending the city grew deafening as the craft came close. It hovered just out of sight of the windows, the rotor wash buffeting the building and kicking the curtains around. The sound of the attacking planes was almost familiar at this point—a barely audible hiss followed by a burst of noise— and as it happened yet again, they could hear the helicopter returning fire.

"It might be a bad time to leave," Wan said.

"You're probably right," Ivy said. "We have to go though, Holly. If we're going to make it."

To the *Fists*, Holly realized. The last thing she wanted was to be back on that ship, but the alternative was even less acceptable. And Ivy was right; there wasn't much time. She hadn't told Fry to wait for her; it was possible that they'd already pulled anchor and were headed out to sea, under cover of the unexpected aerial attack. She shared a look with Ivy, and they moved toward the door. She stopped to give Yuying one last hug on the way out. "Please be gone when he comes back," she told her.

"Don't worry," Yuying replied.

chapter 71

Mahnaz glowered at Shiloh. She glared right back at him. "Deceiver," he spat.

"You saw what you wanted to see," she replied.

"You *used* me! I believed I was helping you!"

"You did help me. And I helped you, too. Not my fault you think you're better than me." He spat at her again. She tried to think of a pithy response, but nothing came this time.

"If you're done, Chancellor," Tapia said, "we need to move. The other two have been spotted and we're close. Are you riding along, or staying here to look for your charge?"

Mahnaz didn't hesitate. "I'm coming," he said.

"Then make yourself useful and restrain her." He handed him a pair of cuffs, a collar and a chain. "Wrists and neck," he said. "Then attach the chain to the ring in the floor."

"You don't need to put those on me," Shiloh said.

Tapia keyed a mic, presumably signaling their roof gunner, then started the truck. "I don't recall asking your permission, my dear," he replied. "Chancellor, some shifters get sensitive about being chained up, so be careful."

"I can handle her," he said, crabbing clumsily over the seat. "It's not the first shifter I've killed with my bare hands. Isn't that right?" he said to Shiloh. As Tapia accelerated, he lost his balance and flopped heavily into the back.

Shiloh pushed herself up against the door, eyes on the chains, remembering Mahnaz' boasting on the *Excelsis*. She also remembered that she'd thought he was a liar at the time, and she thought he was a liar now. Shiloh adjusted her feet deliberately, digging her heels in but also giving him a good look up between her spread legs. Predictably, he hesitated. She had no illusions that he'd relent, but remembering that she was the best he'd ever have and could never have again gave him pause.

"We're in a hurry," Tapia called from the front seat. The truck roared, the city speeding past. "You have about four minutes till we're on-scene. Put the cuffs on her, Chancellor."

Shiloh glared. "Don't *touch* me, fuckface."

"What are you waiting for, Chancellor?" At Tapia's urging, Mahnaz moved forward.

"I said don't touch me, fuckface."

"Make yourself useful, man!"

Shiloh was shouting, "don't touch me!" a third time as she shifted, and her words became an earsplitting, screeching yowl. She kicked and clawed at Mahnaz with all four legs, hissing and spitting. He fell back, screaming and trying to cover his face, and she went after him, battering his head and shoulders. She felt her claws tear through his clothes and find skin.

Tapia didn't stop the truck, but shouted encouragement. "Don't curl up! They can't scratch through bone, they aren't *strong* enough! Stop panicking!" The chancellor swung blindly. He didn't connect, but his arm pushed her face aside, and she bit it. "That's it! Push back! Push back!" Mahnaz did, forcing his forearm farther into her mouth and her head back. She kept clawing at him, but he levered his greater bulk up and rolled over on top of her. Tapia screamed more orders, telling him to hold her down, to keep his weight on her so she couldn't twist free. The truck swerved back and forth with their struggle.

"Give me a gun!" Mahnaz screamed. His face was bleeding now, from multiple rakes.

"You don't need it! Watch the hind legs! Hold her head down against the seat just like you are, your weight on her. *Hold her head!* Grab her lower jaw with your free hand. Your shoulders will keep her from clawing your face, trust me. Grab her lower jaw and pull it straight down, hard as you can. Break it."

To her horror, Tapia was right; when Mahnaz leaned forward, she could only claw ineffectually at his shoulders, and as he bore down she couldn't turn her head or chest. Her jaw was forced painfully downward but she couldn't open it far enough to release him and free herself. She tried biting harder, but couldn't get more purchase than the bloody puncture wounds she'd already made and the taste of his blood was nauseating.

Shiloh struggled, got her rear legs under him, and kicked at his stomach instead. Her claws found purchase in flesh through already-torn silk, and she thrust with all her might, kicking and raking, up and out. Mahnaz cried out in pain. She did it several more times and there was a feeling like tearing through the wall of a tent, a horrid wet *rip*, and his cry of pain turned into a roar of agony. Shiloh felt her claws hook in his belt and pelvic bone, reared back, and kicked some more. Mahnaz let her go and his hands flying to his belly, where a frightful mess of innards spilled through his clutching fingers. Shiloh snapped her head free and squirmed out from under him, then shifted and threw herself to the opposite side of the truck so she could kick him repeatedly, driving her heels hard into his shoulders and the back of his neck. His howling didn't stop. She was reminded of an unpleasant incident near Savannah, when one of the big circus rigs had run over a dog, half-crushing but not killing the animal. Mahnaz' tortured, braying screams reminded her of that dog.

She still kicked him again. Then she grabbed the chain that he'd been trying to put on her, and hooked the snap-link into the ring on the floor. Tapia hissed in aggravation, shouting Mahnaz' name as he wrestled the truck around another corner. The chancellor wasn't hearing him, he wasn't doing anything but screaming and trying to hold his guts in. Tapia drew his gun; Shiloh slid directly behind his seat and threw the collar around his neck. There was some sort of self-ratcheting-device on it, and it immediately tightened.

"Shit," Tapia hissed, barely audible under the wounded chancellor's bellowing. He dropped the gun on the floor, where he could reach it but she couldn't. Shiloh scrambled over into the front passenger seat. She braced herself against the door, and then kicked Tapia in the face as he turned to see what she was doing. The blow caught him square in the cheek and broke his glasses into three pieces. He recoiled from the impact and the truck immediately swerved to the right, sideswiped a parked car with a grinding bang, then struck the next and launched briefly into the air. Shiloh saw the night sky through the windshield, then city again, and then stars as the truck hit the ground and she hit the seat an instant later.

The landing disoriented her, but she kicked Tapia in the head again as soon as her vision cleared. He grunted, rocking back in the seat. He blocked her third kick, but the impact still bounced his head off of the window.

Shiloh rolled over, opened the door and jumped out. Her bare feet crunched unpleasantly on cubed glass and debris, an immediate reminder that she was conspicuously naked. Mahnaz' screams echoed out of the open door. She opened the back door and dragged him out, eliciting further howls from him. He tumbled into the street, and she saw that his guts were coming out. He curled into a fetal position, trying to hold himself together.

She pulled his sherwani off anyway, ignoring his renewed braying. She held it up; it had come open during the fight and thus escaped significant damage. There wasn't much gore on it, so she put it on. It slumped on her shoulders, and was long enough to almost reach her knees. Pulled tight, it looked like a terrible-fitting dress, but at least she was less obviously naked. Looking around, she saw a body in the street some distance in front of the truck. It was wearing the same gear that Tapia's men had—it was the man who'd been in the gunner's chair. She guessed that he'd been flung there when the truck crashed, and he wasn't moving.

There was a pop from inside the truck. Tapia had recovered enough to retrieve his gun from the floor. Shiloh broke into a run, away from the truck and up the block, but a second pop came from inside the vehicle and she guessed that he was trying to shoot the chain around his neck, not her. He clearly hadn't succeeded yet.

It was a good time to get moving, then. Where were all the people? The aerial attack on the city had caused a short burst of panicked people fleeing in cars and on foot, but now the streets were deserted, and even the crash and gunfire hadn't drawn anyone out, that she could see. Shiloh felt eyes on her, just like she was on stage, but couldn't tell where they were when she scanned the blank windows all up and down the street. She also had no idea where she was, or which way the harbor was. Maybe if she could find another car like Nipa's, she could use the map it had, assuming she could figure that out.

A wave of fear and despair tried to overtake her, and she forced it down. Shiloh rushed down the street until she was around the corner, to at least get out of Tapia's sights and avoid a bullet in the back. As she turned the corner, the gun popped again.

The new street was narrower, and deserted except for swirling dust. Shiloh couldn't tell if it was just her imagination, but the city seemed to have fallen suddenly quiet, hushed enough that she could hear herself breathing. The battling helicopters and jets had moved off, and with them no longer overhead she could hear herself making little scared gasps like she was a lost child. Shiloh tried to turn the noises into a coherent sound, something useful, a word, just to get the jitters out, and she meant to tell herself to stop it but what came out was, "Ivy," and she sounded even more scared and alone than she felt.

Being lost and alone was particularly terrifying, and she was already full of adrenaline and fear. She wanted to hide, to wait for someone to come get her, but that wasn't how things worked of course, hadn't been for a long, long time.

Pick a direction and go in it, she thought. *That's all there is to do.* It might be right, it might be wrong, but with Tapia no doubt about to get free or call for reinforcements, any motion was good. Shiloh listened to the suddenly quiet night, the city that was no longer alive and bustling, and made a decision.

She crossed the silent street, then went down a narrow alley that smelled unpleasantly of cats. The smaller space was comforting, in a way, and there were places to hide among the trash cans, though she hoped she wouldn't have to.

Two people passed the alley's exit ahead of her—and one of them was almost certainly Ivy. Shiloh recognized her friend's ambling gait in an instant, and inferred that Holly was with her as well. Were they going to the ship? She broke into a sprint. Wherever they were going was better than here. Anywhere with them was better than alone.

chapter 72

Ivy heard the approaching footsteps first, bare feet slapping the pavement. Holly felt her tense up, noticed the shift in her sister's body language before she heard the sound.

It was Shiloh. Ivy laughed quietly and hugged her. "You lost your clothes," she said.

She made a face, looking down at the jacket she was wearing, which had probably been in much better condition recently. "I...things went wrong," she said. "I had to shift."

Ivy urged Shiloh and Holly into motion, continuing in the direction they'd been going in. "We know," she said, and explained how they'd run into Nipa. "Sorry there's no time for you to get dressed again. We have a long way to go."

"At least half an hour walking," Holly said. She was doubtful that the *Fists* would still be there when they arrived, either because Hardson had fled in the confusion or because it was in pieces. She hoped the latter wouldn't be the case, and there hadn't been any massive explosions from the direction of the water that would suggest it...yet.

"Wait," Shiloh said. "There's a rig."

"Can we start it? Where?"

"Two blocks." She pointed. "There might be a really angry police officer in it." Holly raised an eyebrow. "It would take too long to explain."

"No need," Ivy replied. Holly thought she detected a knowing tone in her voice.

The truck was still there, as Shiloh had said, a police special-tactics unit truck with a machine gun mounted in the back. Mahnaz lay on the sidewalk next to it, curled into a fetal position on the passenger side. Both right-side doors were open, and they could see a man in the driver's seat. At a nudge from Ivy, Shiloh and Holly walked down the middle of the street to draw the driver's attention, while she took a more circumspect route. Holly didn't doubt that Ivy would make good use of the fireman's tool she'd liberated.

When they drew close, Mahnaz moaned, "Please help me," almost unintelligibly, then fell silent again. He didn't look up. Tapia was waiting for them, gun at the ready when Holly opened the door, standing to the side in case he decided to shoot. "I can only assume you've returned with friends," he said, "since my people would have identified themselves by now."

"That's right," Shiloh said.

"You have me at a disadvantage, dear. I must confess that I can hardly see you." He waved the gun back and forth. "At this range I'll surely hit one of you, but not the other."

"So you're down to one bullet," Holly said.

"Oh, it's the Myawi! Ah, I fear that I've given myself away. Pain's so damn distracting. I think your felid broke my cheek."

"She doesn't belong to me. But I have good news for you, then. We're just here to take your truck."

"And what are you going to do with my truck, dear?"

"Will you need to know for your report?"

"It would help. Quite a number of forms to sign to get them to let me take it, you know."

Holly shrugged. "I don't have the time, to be honest. Would you mind getting down from there?"

"That's the thing. I can't." He indicated the collar around his neck. "Someone in present company has chained me to the floor—" He was interrupted by Ivy pulling herself up into the cab of the truck from the passenger side. Tapia turned immediately, tracking the gun around toward her, but she blocked his arm with hers and thrust the hammer end of her new fubar into his face. He twisted his head so it was a glancing blow.

Holly jumped forward and grabbed Tapia's feet, pulling them out of the truck. He slipped off the seat and fell; the short chain on the collar snatched him up before his feet hit the ground, leaving him dangling by his neck. He clutched at the collar with a look of alarm, then flailed for a hand-hold to pull himself up. Holly tried to keep a grip on his feet, but he kicked her off, scrambling back up into the truck to get some slack in the collar.

By this time, Ivy had his gun. She put it to the top of his head, and he went very still. "Do we need him?" she asked Holly.

"We don't."

"Wait! Stop!" Tapia said quickly, holding his hands up. "Listen. I'm almost blind without my glasses. I'm unarmed, and you have my only means of communicating with anyone." As he spoke he reached up and pulled out his earpiece, tossing it into the street. "There's no need to kill me. And someone should tend to the chancellor, since it sounds like he's still alive. And leniency...you have my word that I'll make sure your mercy is considered, should you be caught." He looked frantically from Holly to Shiloh.

"Arrogant prick," Shiloh said.

"Do you trust him?" Holly asked.

She looked at Ivy. "It's scaled," she said. Ivy took the gun away, and Tapia relaxed visibly.

"Looks like it's not your day," Holly told him. Shiloh climbed up into the back seat and unhooked the chain; Ivy shoved him out of the truck. "Lie on your face," Holly said. "Stay there until we're gone. If you get up before we're out of sight, Ivy will come right back and run you over. Understand?" He complied.

Ivy slid into the driver's seat. Once all three of them were in, the truck woofed to life. "Which way?" Ivy asked. Holly directed her. "The truck's going to have a transponder," she added. "They'll know where we are as soon as he calls in that it's been stolen."

"How long will it take us to get there?"

"If you trust me," Holly said, thinking quickly, "less than five minutes." With the city in disarray, they could use footpaths and ignore one-way signs. Cutting across a few pedestrian-only zones would give them a much more direct route. It wasn't as though they were going to get pulled over and ticketed.

"Of course I trust you," Ivy said, and the truck rocketed forward.

Holly looked in the mirror as they pulled away; Tapia was still prone on the ground. "I feel like I'm going to regret not killing him," she said.

"If you wish you had killed someone that you didn't, you can fix that," Ivy said. "Not so much the other way around."

"That's true." She wanted to talk about it more, but this wasn't the time. "Go past the next intersection and there will be a little park on the left. Drive through it." She expected Ivy to protest, or ask if she'd heard properly, but the truck veered immediately in the direction she indicated. The truck vaulted easily over the curb, threaded the gap between the gates and tore down the footpath. The front bucket seats held them easily in place; behind them Shiloh slid back and forth a bit, and braced herself but didn't complain.

They chased the truck's headlights through the dark city. Many of the street lights had gone out, but the intermittent glow from the fires reflected in the sky cast an eerie orange-brown pall. Cutting through the park took them past four blocks and saved several turns, giving them a straighter path to the water. Holly directed Ivy down another street. This one was blocked by rubble where the top half of a building had collapsed into the street. Rescue workers were hard at work, using flashlights to dig into the wreckage. She took a breath to tell Ivy to turn around and go back, but there was no time. The truck's roaring engine didn't let up, and Ivy steered toward the shallowest section of rubble.

"Rabbit's mortar, don't hit them," Holly whispered, but Ivy was already set on her path. The yellow-clad figures in front of her scrambled out of the way and the truck hit the leading edge of the piled metal and concrete with enough speed to take flight. The road dropped out from underneath them and the engine revved wildly for an instant as the wheels left the ground. The truck nosed down almost immediately, returned to earth with a violent crash that flung Holly partly out of her seat, and they were still moving, sliding to one side as Ivy dodged a parked car on the other side of the obstruction in the road. The tires chattered on the pavement until the truck straightened out, and it seemed like they were going faster than ever.

"Where did you learn to do that?" Holly asked.

"Right back there," Ivy said.

"I'm sorry I asked."

"This is a really nice rig. It'll take good care of us."

"Keep going straight," Holly said. "There's an angled road coming up, you'll want to follow that to the left." Ivy complied; they passed a group of people running across the street, possibly rioters fleeing the chaos. There was no way to avoid the arena; they were going to pass within a block of it. "There may be more people in the road as we get closer," she said.

"Just let me know which ones to hit," Ivy deadpanned. She didn't take her eyes off the road, making minor steering corrections as they powered down the wide street. The big road crested a hill and the water came into view, the lights of boats twinkling on the water. Holly looked, and thought she saw the *Fists* out there still—yes, that was it, and she could see the bulkier *Excelsis* still next to it.

"They're still here," she told Ivy.

"Dilly told me they'd shine a light. Orange and white."

"I'll watch for it." The plaza in front of the auditorium whipped into view, and she directed Ivy to turn. "Go across it, and down the steps at the far end. There's a promenade along the water."

"This is where we were before."

"Yes." Holly was surprised to see that the red carpet area was more empty than they'd left it. The police line appeared to have broken, and there were several bodies scattered about, police and civilian. There were a couple of scattered fights still going on, but the participants seemed just as intent on avoiding the truck as Ivy did them. A few protesters were spry enough to throw rocks and bottles at the police vehicle as it went past, but the armor made any damage negligible.

Rather than jumping, Ivy slowed down to drive down the steps, the truck's tires thumping rhythmically. "Left or right?" she asked, then went left at Holly's instruction.

"Straight along here and we'll be at the marina. Almost there. Bear left, if you get too far to the right we'll end up in the water. I see it! There's an orange and white light down there!"

A Myawi Protector stumbled out into the walkway ahead of them. Holly recognized Anshul, and he was injured. The Protector's helmet was gone and there was blood streaming from both eye sockets.

She didn't care why. "You can hit that one," Holly said.

Ivy accelerated. The truck's front bumper struck Anshul and launched him up into the windshield. He hit it right at the top, spread-eagled, just below his armored chest plate, and the leading edge of the roof split him in half. His upper torso tumbled over the roof and landed in the road behind them; the rest of him punched a twelve-inch hole in the thick glass windshield and admitted a foul jet of innards, blood and flesh pulverized into pudding. Most of it sprayed between the front seats, soaking Ivy and Holly's shoulders, and the back windows were instantly rendered opaque scarlet.

"Fuck!" Ivy yelled, barely keeping the rig from swerving off the walkway. The windshield had mostly held but was now spalled all the way across. Blood and cracked glass made the view of the road ahead tricky. "Is Shiloh okay?" she asked Holly.

"*No she's not!*" Shiloh screamed. She'd been sitting in the middle of the back seat, directly in the path of Anshul's remains, and she was indistinguishable from the rest of the mess on the seats, windows and ceiling. "She's not ever going to be okay again—" This outburst was cut off by a froggy belch and then Shiloh vomited explosively.

"Oh, dear," Holly said.

"I can't see," Ivy reported, lifting off the gas. "We can't go much farther."

"We're close enough," Holly said. "And that needed to happen." From the back, Shiloh gagged again and let out a little wail of misery.

Ivy brought the truck to a stop and shut it down. They helped the extraordinarily befouled Shiloh out of the back, and again Ivy was the first to realize they weren't alone. "Narooma?" she said, confused.

"Who else would it be?" the delphid replied.

"You jumped out of a building."

"Just like a cliffdive," she said proudly.

"You found yourself!" The Bonefish laughed, addressing Holly. The orange and white lights were on a small collapsible post, and he took it quickly down, folding it up. "We waited right here, and you walked right to us."

"Fry had you wait for us?"

"The Bonefish said we should. Fry and the cap'n are going to be chewing the straps by now, we should go."

Narooma grinned. "That one was mine," she said, pointing to the front of the truck and the horrid smear that had been Anshul. "He ran off before we could finish."

"He killed my friend," Holly told her.

"Well, he won't do that again, will he?"

"We have to get back to the ship, quickly. Vitter's in charge of everything right now. The government's in lockboxes. He could authorize them to sink the *Fists*."

"Not to worry," she replied. "Bonefish, where's that boat you borrowed?"

chapter 73

Shiloh stood very still. She was covered head to toe in guts, and the effluvia was turning gelid as it dried on her skin. She held her arms out from her body; she didn't even want to feel herself, and paradoxically worried about smearing it around. There wasn't any convenient cloth to wipe off with, other than the clothes Holly had brought, and she didn't want to ruin the lovely outfit Nipa had gifted her.

So that was a silver lining; at least she hadn't been wearing it.

Still, dressed in a dead man's blood and guts was not an ideal end to the evening. She spat, trying with little success to get the taste of it out of her mouth, and watched as the grizzled man they were calling The Bonefish putted a sleek little open boat up to the dock.

Narooma nudged her, heedless of the gore. "You look like you want to clean off," she said. Shiloh nodded. The delphid tossed her axe into the boat, then jumped off of the dock into the water. She came up a moment later in her dolphin form and spat water directly into Shiloh's face.

"Hey! No! *Asshole!*" she shouted, blocking the stream with her hands.

Narooma reared back in the water, making a chattering sound that was unmistakably laughter. She shifted back. "Get you all clean if you swim with me. I'll take you out to the boat. T'other little kitshifter's out there already."

It took her a moment to parse what Narooma had said, and she was almost afraid to hazard a guess. "Bee's safe?"

"As can be," The Bonefish said.

"Jump in, hold on to me," Narooma said, then shifted back.

Shiloh looked at Holly and Ivy. The decision didn't take much deliberation. "I'll see you out there," she said, and jumped into the water. It was bracingly chilly and salty, but it wasn't the remains of a dead man, which made it infinitely preferable. She felt Narooma's long, smooth body come up beneath her, and grabbed the delphid warrior's dorsal fin. In an instant she was streaking forward, water slicing over her body and taking the remnants of the gore off. Narooma swam fast, staying close to the surface so Shiloh could keep her head above water, and in seconds they were a hundred feet from shore. At that point Narooma paused, swam in a slow circle, and submerged gently, giving Shiloh fair warning. She held on to the delphid's fin as Narooma dove, keeping her eyes shut.

And then they were moving forward again, some distance under the water. It felt like they were going even faster; the speed threatened to peel her fingers loose, but Shiloh held on. Her lungs started to burn, and as if reading her mind Narooma surfaced briefly. The clatter of helicopters and far off gunfire reached her ears. They swam on the surface long enough for Shiloh to breathe, and then Narooma slowed down and repeated the submerging process. Shiloh squeezed Narooma's fin lightly to let her know that she got the pattern, and they ducked under again. The water got colder the farther out they went. Shiloh kept her eyes closed, because it was easier, but nevertheless became aware of the yawning depth of water beneath them as they entered the shipping channel, a feeling like the bottom falling out of the world. Narooma ducked under regularly, presumably avoiding patrol boats; they reached the *Fists* in a few minutes.

The air smelled of smoke, but it was quieter than in the city; the most prevalent noise was water lapping against the hulls of the big boats they were now between. Narooma shifted and tread water next to Shiloh. "I can toss you up there," she said. "Ivy said you did circus?"

"I did."

"I'll push your feet, you jump the rest of the way. Easy, right?"

She considered the distance to the deck. Worst-case, she'd fall back into the water. "Okay."

"I have to take you under a bit. Tuck your legs, feet flat, face pointed up, arms at your sides. You'll know when to jump. I can tell you don't swim so great but I'll keep you safe, okay?"

"Do it," Shiloh said. She thought she was a reasonably good swimmer, but didn't argue. The water was cold, and now that she'd been washed off, she wanted to get warm and dry again.

Narooma shifted, bumped Shiloh's arm, and when she took hold of the delphid's fin again, they submerged, going down ten feet, maybe more. The water pressed in on her eardrums. Shiloh had a brief moment of fear when Narooma left her in the dark, but remembered her instructions and put her feet together, arms down. Her body drifted for a few seconds that felt like minutes in the silent dark, and then something touched her feet. It was Narooma's snout.

The pressure increased, and they were moving up, up, up, water racing past Shiloh's face. They rocketed into open air; Shiloh opened her eyes and saw the ship's hull moving rapidly downward past her. As the urge from below began to ease, she pushed off, eyes on the railing. She actually cleared it by a reasonable margin, had time to get ready for the catch as she began to fall back down again, planting her feet on the edge of the deck. The main lights were off, but low orange lights illuminated the decks.

Her arrival took several people on the deck by surprise. She recognized Captain Hardson, but not anyone else. It was hard to be certain if he was grinning because he recognized her or if it was because she was naked.

"Hi," Shiloh said. Before anyone else could answer, Narooma grabbed the railing next to her and pulled herself over.

"Well, *hello*," Hardson said. "It's been a noisy night, but if it's raining beautiful women it can't be all bad."

Fry gave his shoulder a playful swat. "Hello, Narooma," she said. "And you must be Shiloh. I'm Fry."

"The others are on their way," Narooma said. "The twinsies and The Bonefish are in a boat."

"And not a moment too soon," Hardson said. "There are fliers incoming. The gas grenades were quite amusing, but the next act will be high explosives and rockets. It is our time to leave the party."

"You can't outrun those things," Narooma said.

"That is true. But we have friends close at hand. *Rattenkonig* and *Vergissmeinnicht* have sailed dangerously far into Sino-Indian waters to accompany their own fliers, and they've got better defenses than we do. If we join them when they scarper there's a decent chance we won't all end up seasoning the waters tonight."

The Bonefish arrived then, with Holly and Ivy in his stolen cruiser. A ladder was lowered for them, and when the twins came aboard, they were clearly relieved to see Holly and Narooma safe.

"Thank you for joining us, Bonefish," Hardson said. "Also, if you ever do that again, I'll throw you into the deepest trench I can find."

"What did he do?" Holly asked.

"Went back for you," the captain said good-naturedly. "We had emergencies enough on board, but he and that one," a nod toward Narooma, "decided to go looking for you instead. I have no control over the delphid, but The Bonefish has responsibilities, as my crewman." Shiloh grinned at his cheerful tone. Her eyes were adjusting to the light, and she saw other familiar faces on the deck now; Razor, an exhausted-looking Kroni, and Bee, who rushed over and hugged Shiloh tightly when she saw her.

"Had to be done," The Bonefish said. He never seemed to stop grinning.

"Well, we appreciated it," Holly said.

"Happy to be back on the *Fists*, are you? Never thought I'd see the day."

"It's been a strange day," she said wearily.

"That it has. Get below, and we'll throw off the lines to that derelict and put some distance between ourselves and the shore."

Shiloh had followed the conversation, and realized they were talking about *Excelsis*. "You're leaving the other ship behind?"

"We've no crew to sail her, my lovely," Hardson said, "and she wouldn't go far even if we did. Vadim and his team outdid themselves gleaning last night and today. Best to leave her here as a target for the incoming fliers—"

"What about the prisoners?"

"That'll be a mess for the politicals to clean up. Not literally, of course."

"You're going to leave them in there?"

Hardson drew himself up, though he was clearly uncomfortable being the target of Shiloh's ire. "It is somewhat kinder than flinging them into the ocean," he said. "Those that don't drown would come ashore to find torches and clubs waiting for them. And before you start a speech about dying free, I'd ask you to imagine just how unpleasant it is to be tortured to death by a mob." Shiloh made a little noise, and shivered.

"Then we should bring them with us," Ivy said.

"The *Fists* can't support that many—"

"We'll make it work," Holly said.

He fixed her with a dark look. "You still seem mistaken as to the chain of command on this ship."

"I'm not on your crew," Holly said. "Neither is Shiloh. I understand the *Fists* is your home, but you need to open it. Right now." She was much more aggressive than Shiloh would have been, but Holly and Hardson seemed to have history, and she stayed out of it.

Fry touched Hardson's arm before he could make what appeared to be a rather bombastic response. "I need all hands at their stations to prepare us for a full blow to catch up to the Rainbow Snakes," she said to Holly. "We lost seven people in the gas attack, and the boarding attack on *Excelsis* killed four more."

"I can help her," Razor said.

"No, you can't," Fry replied. "I need you here."

"I'll go," Holly said. "Ivy, Shiloh and I can open a lot of cell doors."

"Me, too," Narooma said. Shiloh met Kroni's eye, and he nodded. She smiled; he'd remembered his promise. In the moment that took, Holly had convinced Fry to allow Shell, Minnijean and a couple of the older children to help out as well.

Bee looked up at Shiloh. "What happens?"

"We've got to rescue the shifters from the death ship," she said. "Can you help?"

"Bee can open doors," she replied confidently.

Hardson looked angry, but Shiloh got the feeling it was more for show than anything else. "You have eight minutes," he said, addressing her and Holly, "before I drop those crossing ladders. No more. If you're walking across at eight minutes and five seconds, I'll drop the ladder with you on it and you can swim back to shore. Understood?"

Shiloh nodded; Hardson handed her a stack of the keycards that opened the cells. She passed one to Ivy, took two for Bee and herself, and Holly took the rest, distributing them to the others. Kroni was suddenly at her shoulder, and handed her a lumpy jumpsuit. "You look cold," he said.

"I am, thank you. How's Swan?"

"Alive," he said. From his tone, he had no interest in elaborating.

Holly sorted out a quick strategy; Minnijean on the *Excelsis'* deck, directing people across the ladders, someone else halfway there to point escapees in the right direction, while the rest would focus on opening the cells in the main area.

Unsurprisingly, things had changed since Shiloh had left the ship. The hallways were strewn with debris and in many places panels had been removed from the walls. Captain Hardson's crew had taken the lightbulbs out of half the fixtures, and the fixtures themselves in some cases, leaving wires hanging. Doors were propped open, and as Shiloh saw no bodies she presumed that the *Fists'* crew had removed them.

Shiloh led the way. There were more missing pieces of the ship visible as they went, but the large under-deck area ringed with cells full of shifters appeared unchanged. She imagined that the salvage crew had bypassed this area entirely. It smelled much worse than before, the air stale and nearly unbreathable. Apart from Kroni, the others were seeing it for the first time, and Shiloh understood the mingled expressions of shock and revulsion on their faces. Bee in particular looked distressed, so Shiloh was glad when Holly staged her at the main door, to guide the freed prisoners to Minnijean, bucket-brigade style.

"If these scumfucks have one delfie in here," Narooma said, "just *one* of our folk, there's gonna be a war."

"That might be out of our hands," Holly said.

"The door down there leads to the other solitary cells," Shiloh said, pointing. "I don't remember if anyone was in them. There were a lot of them."

"I'll go," Narooma said. "If I take too long, I can catch up," she added with a grin, then spun her axe confidently and went down the nearest staircase.

Holly, Ivy and Shell started upstairs, while Shiloh and Kroni went down. She saw Holly start first; she opened the first cell she came to, told the shifters inside, "Go. That way," pointed, and moved on to the next without answering any questions. It was quick, and Shiloh did the same; she and Kroni started on opposite sides and moved toward meeting at the far end. The first cell she opened, the two prisoners inside burst out and immediately shifted. They were falconids, and their massive wingbeats kicked up dust. They returned to human, then stood side by side and bowed to Shiloh. "We are in your debt, friend," one began. "I am Anouhya, and my companion is Talaria—"

"Talk later," Shiloh said. "In four minutes we're trapped on this ship when it burns."

Anouhya followed Shiloh to the next cell. The canids within rushed out and followed Shiloh's pointing finger up the steps. On the catwalk above she could hear a growing number of footsteps heading up and out. "I understand. Is there some assistance we can offer?"

"Stop talking and *go*," Shiloh said, moving on to the next cell without looking at them. Each cell seemed like it took longer to open than the last. When she had to wave the card twice at a few of them, she almost screamed in frustration. Canids, falconids, an ursid—Shiloh opened the doors and let them out. They fled in human and animal forms. A few tried to hug her and she shrugged them off, struggling to move forward to the next cell. She focused on her own row, wondering in the back of her head if Holly was ahead of her, if she was the last. She was almost certainly going much slower than the others, and the stress was making her fumble-fingered. She almost dropped the keycard once.

She and Kroni met at the far end. He was standing in front of the cervids' cell. All five of the cervids inside stood looking back at him. When Shiloh tried to unlock it, he stopped her.

"Kroni?"

"We can't let them out."

"Are you insane?" It sounded like Holly and Shell were mostly finished with the top section. A pair of freed prisoners came out of the high security section as well. One limped, and helped the other.

"We can't," he said implacably, not taking his eyes from them. "Leave them."

"Why not?"

"Because they'll attack me."

"They wouldn't!"

He nodded. "They would. Right here. We don't have time for it."

"That's fucking stupid. Hey!" Shiloh banged on the cell wall. Two of the cervids in the back looked at her, but the biggest one didn't take his eyes from Kroni. "We need to let you out, and we don't have time for stupidity. Are you going to cause trouble?"

The biggest one stepped closer to the wall, his breath fogging the plastic between him and Kroni. "It won't take any time to kill this spotted *shit*," he said. "I took you once," he said. "You come back for more?"

Kroni sighed. "You see?"

"You're going to die if we don't let you out!"

"I don't need you to let me out. I'll get out of here myself." He still didn't even look at Shiloh.

"What if we just leave the key for them? Push it under the door?"

Kroni shook his head. "If they come out, we're going to fight. It can't be any other way. He won't let me humiliate him like that."

"If I come out," the cervid said, "you're going to *die*. And then I'll taste your little girl. She'd like that."

Shiloh looked at him. "You can't be serious. Are you serious?" She looked back at Kroni, who was still staring at the cervid. Rather than anger, his face held an expression of disappointment and sadness. "Is this because you're still angry at them?"

"No," he said, shaking his head slowly. "I'm not angry. They can't help what they are."

"Then why—"

He gave a half shrug, and looked away, then down at her. "I can't help what I am either. Leave them. Please."

The cervids in the cell watched Kroni turn and walk away. They made no entreaties.

"Kroni, we can't!" she called after him. When she turned back to the cell, the cervids were sitting back down again, in their various corners. They'd lost interest in her completely.

From the high-security area, two more people rushed out, with Narooma behind them. "All clear," she said. "Gotta go, gotta go."

Shiloh let herself be swept along with Narooma, and didn't look back at the cervids. There wasn't time to argue with Kroni, and if he was right, the stupid cervids would get them all killed.

Holly was the last one out, staying until everyone was past. When she crossed the ladder bridge, Ivy was waiting for her. The deck seemed to be full of people, and Minnijean was wrangling them as best she could, sitting people down so she could get a head count. The ladders were disengaged, and the *88 Fists* turned away from the shore, the thrum of engines deepening.

Shiloh stood at the railing as they slid away from the larger ship. She unzipped the coverall, which stank of the *Excelsis* after just eight minutes in the hold, and threw it overboard. "I'm sorry I couldn't rescue you," she whispered, thinking of Shamshoun.

Kroni was looking at her. "It's hard," he said. "Saying goodbye."

"Shut up," Shiloh replied. "Just shut the fuck up." The Fists powered out toward the open ocean. Shiloh sat down and hunched her shoulders as the wind picked up, thinking of the fact that the rest of her clothes were in North America.

Bee squeezed up next to her, running a hand across her chilled shoulder. "Be warmer if Shiloh shifts," she said.

"I don't want to."

The younger felid pressed closer, sharing body heat, for which Shiloh was grateful.

chapter 74

*Six days before Princess Aiyana's trimester
celebration (rescheduled due to the Rainbow
Snakes attack on Singapore)*

Holly awoke from a murky fog of exhaustion and ground-in shock. She knew that it was morning, she knew she was on the *88 Fists*, and that was about it. She suspected that she'd slept, but couldn't recall for how long or at what point she'd bedded down. It was as though her mind had just wandered off for a while, and now it was back.

It seemed like it had been months since she'd been in her bed on the Fists. She stared at the ceiling, hearing Marcus' familiar breathing on the lower bunk. There was a swirl of half-formed thoughts in her head; she was so tired she could sleep forever, but she could feel the sunrise in her bones and her body howled at her to get out of bed. She had the old familiar feeling of needing to make breakfast and prepare the house for the day, nattering in the back of her head like a childhood anxiety dream even though that life was long gone.

Long gone and now she had Ivy back. Where was Ivy? Holly rolled to her side and sat up. She avoided knocking her head on the ceiling with a practiced shoulder hunch. Ivy obviously wasn't on the narrow bed with her. She tried to remember what had happened the evening before, but it was lost to exhaustion. Holly didn't remember even coming to bed, let alone where Ivy might have chosen to bed down if not with her.

The awful thought that the past week or so might have been an unusually vivid dream stoked the boiler urging her to move.

She climbed slowly, deliberately down, mindful of aches and pains from the past few days' activities and a metallic taste in her mouth that was probably residue from the smoke and trace amounts of tear gas she'd inhaled during the attack on the city. She could smell fire and dust in her hair. When she ran her fingers through it, sandy debris sifted to the floor in the dark. Her stomach gave a little jab of discomfort to remind her that she was hungry, too. All the more reason to make breakfast.

Holly swept her hair up into a loose braid as she left the room, her hands moving unconsciously thanks to years of habit. The main lights in the hallway were off for the night, but the dim evening light showed that the floor was crowded with sleeping bodies, curled up against the walls and on each other, some human, some animal. Animal-form falconids perched on the backs of sleeping canids.

The refugees from the *Excelsis*. So she hadn't imagined everything. So where was Ivy? Holly went to the mess hall out of habit, stepping gingerly and silently over sleepers the whole way. The ship was quiet, with a familiar vibration telling her they were underway, not docked. The mess hall was half-lit and also crammed to bursting with sleeping bodies in chairs and on the floor. A few of the refugees were awake, and glanced her way. Holly heard voices in the kitchen and crossed the room in that direction. She recognized Minnijean and Shell before she got there and found them in the process of starting food: an army's ration of rice and vegetables, from the look of it. "But what about the dog-shifters?" Shell asked Minnijean.

"They'll be fine," was the amused reply. "Good morning, Holly," she said with a smile. "Tea?"

"Yes, please." Something in her belly would be nice. She accepted a mug gratefully. "Have you seen Ivy?"

"Last I saw the rest of your people, they were in medical," Minnijean said. "The fellow with the busted rib won't leave his woman's side, since he got back." Holly noticed a subtle change in Minnijean's tone when she said *your people*. There was a nudge there, an acknowledgement that the *Fists'* mama-bear didn't expect Holly to be staying aboard as part of the family. She didn't hear any judgment in the tone.

"Do you need help? I can come back, after I find my sister."

For a moment, she thought Minnijean was going to tease her for offering her exclusive Myawi culinary skills in the kitchen, and tensed for the sarcasm. It didn't come. "Would be appreciated. We're not short of food yet, but we will be short of hands when these folks start waking up. If you see Deux up and about, send him down as well."

Holly nodded. "I'll be back." She returned to the hall and went to the medical bay. The small cabin was dominated by two examining tables and a wall-to-wall cabinet. One of the beds was occupied by Swan, and an injured sailor she recognized as Azzy was on the other.

Kroni was asleep in the doctor's chair and didn't rouse when the door opened, but Swan was awake. The flesh around her eyes was purple-black and so swollen it seemed impossible that she could see, and her mouth was twisted up in an asymmetrical curl that looked like a psychotic smile. Her blood-matted hair had been shaved, and she had enough bandages that she needed no modesty garment.

"Hello," Holly said. "You're Swan, right? I'm sorry we were never properly introduced." She avoided looking at the swaddled stump of Swan's arm.

"S'meechu," she lisped. "Sorry s'nod...more chu meet," she added, huffing an ironic laugh.

"I was looking for Ivy. Don't talk if it's uncomfortable."

"S'fine." Swan rolled her head a little, trying to focus, and flexed her cut and bruised fingers. "Nushing hursh."

Holly nodded. Of course Swan was on powerful painkillers. "I'm glad you're still with us. That I'll have a chance to get to know you. Ivy thinks very highly of you."

She huffed again, and mumbled something Holly didn't quite catch, possibly about living to regret her words. Then Swan drew herself up and took a deep breath. "I. Hate. D'ocean," she said. "An' we're shill on it."

"Is she complaining about being on a ship again?" Razor asked from the doorway. Holly started slightly and turned, seeing the weapons officer's smirk. "Seems like most of the buttons you push, that's the recording she plays."

"Ey, fuck you," Swan said.

"I know," Razor replied, nodding. "And before you ask, it'll be a few days yet. We're bound for Zeeland."

"Zeeland?" Holly asked.

"Safer for the moment. *Rattenkonig* and *Vergissmeinnicht* are sailing with us, just in case the Brother Nations decide to launch a long-range Dragon's Tongue after all. I think we're in the clear, though. Depending on how Beijing decides to feel about the strafing of Singapore, that is. Looks like the rain of blame is falling largely on the Rainbow Snakes, and on you."

"Me?"

Razor nodded. "It's a good thing people like you so much. Not many politicians are willing to step forward and denounce you yet. They're waiting for more evidence. We'll have to see what Chancellor Shay says once they decide it's safe to bring them out of the lockbox, probably later today. Long story short, I think we got away with it. But if it turns out we didn't, Zeeland's safer than North America. They can fix her teeth when we get there, too." She turned to Swan. "Soon as we get to land, we'll get you eight brand-new teeth knitted. You'll be begging to come back on the water in no time."

"Pshuh," Swan said. "Whaddma do with yarn teef." Holly said nothing. Razor was right; she'd heard that dental bone-knitting, though a fairly common practice, was notably more unpleasant than internal knits.

"Razor, where's Ivy?"

Razor pointed in the general direction of the stern. "Slept on deck with the felids. She didn't want to come below. I thought Dilly was going to ask her if she wanted to bunk with him, but he's being a gentleman about it. Which is kind of unlike him."

Holly frowned. Had she been so tired she'd left her sister behind?

"Felids," Swan said. "Y'mean Shiloh."

"Yes, and the other one."

"Ain' no other one. Shiloh hates felids."

Razor smiled patiently. "I suppose she decided to make an exception."

"Maybe you godda wrong Shiloh," Swan muttered, then laughed, then coughed. "Hey. Holly. Shiloh saved us? Fromma...cells?"

"She did."

"Huh." She nodded, started to say something else, then didn't. Holly couldn't tell if Swan's eyes were open or closed any more, and she said nothing else.

"Is she asleep?"

"Probably. Jar Bob barely had enough painkillers left over for Azzy by the time he finished loading her up."

"No," Swan said abruptly. "Holly."

"Yes?"

"Few weeks ago, I saw my brother. Firs' dime in...six years. He misses me. I...was scared. So I...smashed his face. I wish...ah. So don' do Ivy that way. 'Kay?"

"I'll try not to. I should go."

A moment later, Holly was climbing the stairs to the outside deck, stepping over and around the sleeping refugee shifters who filled every available corner that wasn't exposed to the elements. The sun was coming up, and she was reeling with the reality of the day and what had happened and what was still happening, and she was still feeling too active and wound up to sleep, and here she was.

"Heroic Holly," a familiar voice called. She turned and saw Hardson standing at the railing of the bridge, looking down at her. Shiloh was next to him, standing flirtatiously close.

"Have you seen—" Hardson chuckled and pointed toward the stern before she even finished.

She nodded in gratitude and headed astern. Ivy was sitting near the broken harpoon launcher with her back to the water, knees pulled up and her arms wrapped around them, looking back up at the *Fists'* superstructure. Ivy's eyes shifted from the ship to her, and her face seemed to tighten slightly. Just like that, everything was awkward. Whatever Holly had thought she might say to her sister was going to be the wrong thing. Without the framework of disaster, was there anything holding them together? She considered turning around and going back downstairs. The look on Ivy's face suggested that she wished the same.

Just as suddenly, Holly decided that it wasn't going to be that way. She crossed the deck to where Ivy sat, walked a short distance past her, and then sat down facing the ocean, pressing her back into Ivy's. She was a bit surprised to find that the aggressive, dismissive feeling melted away almost immediately. This was where she belonged. Assuming Ivy would have her.

"I'm afraid," Holly said. "Just a little bit."

Ivy pressed backward into her gently. "But you know it'll be okay."

"I know you'll *try* to make it okay."

"I will. Will you help?"

"Of course." The words came without hesitation. She shifted slightly, so her head was resting on Ivy's shoulder instead of directly behind her. She could feel Ivy leaning into her as well; their weight supported each other.

"Are you going to scold me for coming to get you?"

"No. Mom would have."

Ivy shrugged. "She'd have been mad at you for running off in the first place."

"I was trying to *help.*"

"So was I."

Holly smiled, leaning her head back farther so she was looking at the pink and blue sky. "Then I suppose we're even. That part, Mom would be happy for."

Ivy didn't say anything for a long moment. "I hardly ever thought about her," she said, her voice heavy with guilt. "Only you."

"That's okay. I did the opposite. I'm so sorry."

"It's okay. I'm sorry I broke your city, Holly. I know you liked it."

That made Holly laugh. "I don't think that was entirely your fault. Semangat Terang was, but I would have helped you do that, if I was there."

"You did help."

"Did I?" She felt Ivy nod. "How?"

"By pissing me off."

"I'll keep that in mind the next time I need a city destroyed," she said, and they both stifled giggles. "I'm sorry you didn't get to keep Pravit Deshmu's Mustang."

"The rig?" Holly nodded in answer. Ivy sighed pleasantly. "It was pretty fantastic, wasn't it?"

"You looked so happy driving it. Even with everything going on, you looked happy."

"I was happy. I think I was a little bit loopy. Shiloh and Nipa did something to me, with a little crown...anyway, it's okay. That rig was too small. I'll need to find us a new one when we get back. Maybe a bigger rig, something for all of us."

The matter-of-fact way Ivy included her made Holly warm. "All of us?"

"You and me. Shiloh. Kroni and Swan." Ivy shrugged. "Whoever else wants to come, I suppose."

Holly considered the sky. The pink and orange clouds were fading to white, the sky itself turning paler blue. "Where are we going?"

"I don't know yet. I never...I never thought much about what I'd do when I found you. I suppose it'll be obvious when we get there." She had tilted her head back to match Holly's, except she was looking at the underside of the harpoon launcher. "This spool is broken," she said, staring into the cannon's guts.

"Not surprised. I think I broke it."

"I can't take you *anywhere*," Ivy said with a huff of amusement.

"I'm afraid of disappointing you, you know."

"I know, but you probably won't. I haven't even met you, remember?"

That made Holly laugh. "Hi. I'm Holly Aniram. It's nice to meet you."

"Ivy Aniram," her sister replied, matching her mirth. "I've never seen hair as long as yours. How do you keep it from getting tangled?"

"I brush it every night," Holly replied.

"That sounds troublesome. You don't ever think about cutting it?"

"No."

"But what if—"

"I said no."

"Well, good," Ivy said. "I like it. Nobody's touching my sister's hair, because it's beautiful."

"You think so?"

"I do. I still think it'll be less useful than a squirrel in a canoe, but it's a part of you. Till you say it isn't any more. Are you still sad about your collar?"

Holly sighed. She saw a gull wheeling far above the ship, and followed it with her eyes. "Not really. Part of me thinks I am, but I'm not."

"I think that's good."

Emmy Jackson

Made in the USA
Middletown, DE
26 August 2023